Francis Foster Barham

A rhymed harmony of the Gospels

Francis Foster Barham

A rhymed harmony of the Gospels

ISBN/EAN: 9783337259808

Printed in Europe, USA, Canada, Australia, Japan

Cover: Foto ©Andreas Hilbeck / pixelio.de

More available books at **www.hansebooks.com**

A

RHYMED HARMONY

OF THE

GOSPELS.

BY FRANCIS BARHAM & ISAAC PITMAN.

Printed both in Phonetic and in the customary spelling, as a Transition Book from Phonetic Reading to the reading of books as now commonly printed.

LONDON:
FRED. PITMAN, PHONETIC DEPOT, 20 PATERNOSTER ROW, *E.C.*
BATH:
ISAAC PITMAN, PHONETIC INSTITUTE, PARSONAGE LANE.
JAMES DAVIES, 5 ABBEY CHURCHYARD.

1870.

THE PHONETIC ALPHABET.

The phonetic letters in the first column are pronounced like the italic letters in the words that follow. The last column contains the names *of the letters.*

CONSONANTS.

Mutes.

P p...ro*p*e, *p*ost........pɩ
B b...ro*b*e, *b*oast.......bɩ
T t...fa*t*e, *t*ip...........tɩ
D d...fa*d*e, *d*ip..........dɩ
Ç ç...*ch*eap, fe*tch*......çɛ
J j...*j*ump, bri*dg*e......jɛ
K k...lee*k*, *c*ane.......kɛ
G g...lea*gu*e, *g*ain.....gɛ

Continuants.

F f...sa*f*e, *f*at...........ef
V v...sa*v*e, *v*at..........vɩ
Ŧ ŧ...wrea*th*, *th*igh....iŧ
Ꝺ đ...wrea*the*, *th*y.....đɩ
S s...hi*ss*, *s*eal.........es
Z z...hi*s*, *z*eal..........zɩ
Σ ʃ...vi*ci*ous, *sh*e ....iʃ
Ʒ ʒ...vi*s*ion, plea*s*ure...ʒɩ

Nasals.

M m...see*m*, *m*et.......em
N n...see*n*, *n*et.........en
Ŋ ŋ...si*ng*, lo*ng*........iŋ

Liquids.

L l...fa*ll*, *l*ight......el
R r...mo*r*e, *r*ight...ar

Coalescents.

W w...*w*et, q*u*it.......wɛ
Y y...*y*et, *y*oung......yɛ

Aspirate.

H h...*h*ay, *h*ouse.....eç

VOWELS.

Guttural.

A a...*a*m, f*a*st, f*a*r...at
Ɑ ɑ...*a*lms, f*a*ther....ɑ
E e...*e*ll, *a*ny, h*e*r...et
Ɛ ɛ...*a*le, f*ai*r, b*ea*r...ɛ
I i...*i*ll, pit*y*, f*i*l*i*al..it
Ɩ ɩ...*ee*l, *ea*t, m*e*re...ɩ

Labial.

O o...*o*n, n*o*t, n*o*r...ot
Ω ω...*a*ll, l*aw*, *ough*t...ω
Ʊ ɒ...*u*p, s*o*n, c*u*r...ɒt
Ơ ơ...*o*pe, c*oa*t, p*ou*r..ơ
U u...f*u*ll, f*oo*t.......ut
Ɯ ɯ...d*o*, f*oo*d, t*ou*r..ɯ

DIPHTHONGS: Ɨ ɨ, Ȣ ȣ, Ʉ ʉ.
as heard in b*y*, n*ow*, n*ew*.

⁎ See the Note on Reading Poetry in the Appendix, page 261.

PREFACE.

The superiority of the Bible over all other books has been fully proved. Its transcendent merits are acknowledged by all fair judges. This being premised, we proceed to the purpose of the present work.

It is generally agreed among scholars, that the original Old and New Testaments were composed, partly in prose, and partly in poetry or verse. Kennicott, Louth, Jebb, Boothroyd, Boys, and other authors, have established this fact. So curiously are these two forms of composition blended and intermingled in the Hebrew, Syriac, and Greek Bibles, that it is sometimes difficult to discover to which class certain sticks or lines (in which they were first written,) most properly belong. Even the translators of the Scriptures in ancient or modern languages, retain so much of the parallelism, or correspondence of clauses, which distinguished Oriental poetry, that the reader continually feels that they still savor of poetic composition, especially in those passages where the grandeur of the images and the beauty of the sentiments are peculiarly conspicuous.

The great majority of the translations of the Bible are very properly prose translations, which attempt to give the sense of the original literally word for word, and sometimes partially observe the correspondency of clauses. But beside these, many poetical or versicle renderings have been given of certain books of the Bible, in different ages and nations. Among these, we may notice several poetical versions, or paraphrases of Scripture, by the Oriental, Greek, and Latin Fathers, as Ephraim, Gregory, Nonnius, Cyprian, Hilary, Juvencus, and the pious poets of the mediæval ages.

At present we must confine our attention to the productions of this nature in our own land and language. Poetical versions of the Scripture were early favorites with the British and Anglo-Saxon races. Not to mention attempts of this kind among our Keltic and Saxon ancestors, on which a curious essay might be written, we may cite some of the poetic versions of more recent periods. In Queen Elizabeth's days, good old Hunnis translated *Genesis* into verse. Others attempted other books.

For instance, *Job*, *Psalms*, *Ecclesiastes*, *Canticles*, *Isaiah*, the *Lamentations*, and the *Acts of the Apostles*, have all been versified by Sandys, Sternhold, Hopkins, Tye, Blackmore, Merrick, Tate, Scott, Young, Butt, and others; while Fellowes, Samuel Wesley (the father of John Wesley), and Boys, have given poetical versions of other parts of the Old and New Testaments.

As far as I am aware, the Gospels, though the most interesting and important parts of the Bible, have not yet appeared in English verse, and I therefore set myself to supply a poetical rendering of them. In so doing, I followed throughout Townsend's Harmony of the Gospels, contained in his admirable edition of the Bible in chronological and historical arrangements. This mainly agrees with all the best Harmonies of the Gospels, and enables us to read the sacred record of our Lord's life, words, and actions, in regular unbroken order, satisfying to the intelligence.

If I am not mistaken, the Gospel record not only abounds in the Divinest Wisdom, but the most exquisite poetry; and furnishes an inexhaustible store of the purest sentiments and images.

In order to render the Gospel history more attractive, I have composed this poetic paraphrase of it in that antique ballad verse, which seems most pleasing to the majority of the English. It is in this that most of the Psalms of David have been already rendered, from Sternhold downwards. Into this verse Chapman translated the Epical ballads of Homer, with brilliant success. It appears to be less formal and wearisome than many other kinds of English verse. It possesses a certain sprightliness and vivacity of spirit, and a venerable quaintness of style, which make it a general favorite, especially with those who are fond of mediæval ballad poetry, and ancestorial chant and song.

I have therefore purposely and studiously emulated the antique style of Sternhold, Chapman, and other old national balladists; because I see that the Bible, as an ancient Oriental book, can be best presented to the sympathies of the people in that sort of venerable verse in which they have been accustomed to sing their national Psalms and Hymns. I believe that if they can relish much of the Old Testament in this verse, they will still more relish much of the New Testament therein, being more interesting and important. It is now first presented in the same attire, not only sanctioned but sanctified by long usage. Many of the attempts to render Scripture in what is called classical verse, have been very unsatisfactory, as Merrick and others have proved. I have therefore steadfastly abstained from all those classical elegancies and refinements, which appear to me incongruous with the Hebrew, Syrian, and Hellenistic phraseology, and which I have been accustomed to develope in other poems, wherein Grecian and Roman learning might be more properly exhibited.

Whatever the fate of this devotional exercise may be, I do not despair that a period may arrive when certain varieties of evangelic poetry (which in its very nature is holiest and best,) will once more become popular. True religion is so much akin to refined sentiment and natural imagery, that they ought to be conjoined in many forms of poetical composition, such as the general community can relish.

This rhymed paraphrase of the Gospels is very complete. I believe it includes almost every text in the Gospel Harmony, in the order of the Harmony, with the exception of the genealogies, and certain minute particulars that could not appropriately be introduced in verse.

In forming this poetic paraphrase, I have consulted, during several years, the best editions of the original New Testament, the best translations of it in ancient and modern languages, as well as its principal critics and commentators; and I trust it will be found a faithful and lucid interpretation of the sacred text, throwing light on many of its obscurities, and removing some of its difficulties.

This work may therefore be considered a new experiment in biblica literature. It forms a Gospel Epic, in our old national ballad verse, so prized by the English for its quaint simplicity, pathos, and power. My principal aim is to impress the Divine truths of the Gospel on the minds of the lovers of poetry, and make its leading doctrines and facts familiar as household words, by the aid of rhythm and rhyme. I would do the same service to the Gospel of Christ that so many have already done to the Psalms of David. Though the Gospels are, thank God, so generally known to the people, I do not despair of interesting many hearts by this novel and poetic mode of illustrating their beauties.

The supereminent merit of the Gospel, as respects its theology, morality, history, etc., has been frequently noted. But it has not hitherto been sufficiently honored for its poetical excellences. Yet, when truly and impartially investigated, it appears to deserve no limited admiration from the lovers of poetry. A Harmony of the Gospels is the grandest Epic in the world. What Epic has ever treated of so magnificent a theme as the manifestation of God in the form of man, to redeem mankind? In tracing the history of the Messiah through its succesive stages, the Gospel epic exhibits the noblest unity of design, and the noblest variety of wonderful incidents. It is indeed the Epic of epics. Its very fragments have given birth to the finest poems, which have distinguished the names of Milton, Klopstock, and other religious bards.

This poetical paraphrase may prove serviceable by supplying teachers and learners with a rhymed version of all the passages they wish to impress on the memory. It likewise furnishes a great many hymns for singing, as the ballad measure suits many of our best hymn tunes.

Though my work lays claim to fidelity rather than to brilliancy, it has cost me more prolonged labor than some will readily imagine. I trust this humble tribute to the Redeemer of Mankind will not prove vain and worthless. I have striven to make it faithful, without being pedantic; animated, without being extravagant; simple, without being puerile; and quaint, without being fantastic. May it kindle and increase the sympathy of youth and age for the Holy Scriptures! May it interest the solitary student, and the social circle, in the glorious themes of Revelation; and so enrich the memory with the Divine oracles, that the Christian life may be more manifest among us!

In order to assimilate to the Epic form this poetical paraphrase of the Gospel Harmony, it is divided into twelve books.

With one word on the orthographic dress in which it appears, I conclude, and commend the reader to the gracious words that depict the life of the Incarnate God.

I am gratified to know that my fellow-citizen Mr Isaac Pitman, who has labored more than a quarter of a century for the reformation of our *accidental* style of spelling, and in the dissemination of an admirable system of Phonetic Shorthand, has undertaken to present this work to the world, both in the old spelling and in the new, so that children who learn to read in either style may, from this book, gain a knowledge of the other. As to the merits of the two styles of spelling, I agree entirely with what that great scholar the Bishop of St David's says of the common orthography:—"I look upon the established system, if an accidental custom may be so called, as a mass of anomalies, the growth of ignorance and chance, equally repugnant to good taste and to common sense. But I am aware that the public clings to these anomalies with a tenacity proportioned to their absurdity, and is jealous of all encroachment on ground consecrated by prescription to the free play of blind caprice." As the constant dropping of water wears away stones, so, I trust, will the constant dropping of the waters of truth, as developed in phonetic and orthographic science, wear away this stone of stumbling and rock of offence that bars the way to the temple of knowledge.

P.S.—I was much assisted in preparing this work for the press by my very pious and amiable wife Gertrude Foster Barham, recently deceased, whom I hope to meet in heaven. I have also to acknowledge the kind and careful revision of the work, and the improvement of numerous lines, by my friend Mr Isaac Pitman. F. B.

Bath, 23rd December, 1869.

RHYMED HARMONY OF THE GOSPELS.

BOOK I.

The history of Jesus Christ,
Our blessed, only Lord,
His Gospel, or Glad Tidings, here
We from the first record.

SECTION 1.

General Preface.—Luke 1. 1-4.

As many men have heretofore
  Endeavored to relate
The wondrous mysteries of our faith
  In Christ, the Lord, most great;
Delivered to eye-witnesses,
  And ministers of Him
Who is the very Word of God,
  Worshiped by cherubim;
It seemèd good to me, also
  In these things well informed,
To write them down in order, thus,
  That many hearts be warmed
With clearer knowledge of these truths,
  Divinest, purest, best,
Of all that man on earth can learn
  And cherish in his breast.

SECTION 2.

The divinity, humanity, and office of Christ.
—John 1. 1-18.

In the beginning was the Word,
  The *Logos*, Truth divine,
That was with God, and that was God,
  And all good did enshrine;
And all things by this Word were
      made,
  Without Him nought could be,
For He possessed the power and might
  Of sovereign Deity.

BUK I.

Đe histori ov Jizɒs Kr̨ist,
ɜr blesed, ɷnli Lord,
Hiz Gospel, or Glad T̨idiŋz, hir
wi from đe ferst rekord.

SEKΣON 1.

Jeneral Prefɛs.—Lɯk 1. 1-4.

Az meni men hav hirtufɷr
  endevord tu relɛt
đe wɒndrɒs misteriz ov ɜr fɛŧ
  in Kr̨ist, đe Lord, mɷst grɛt;
deliverd tu į-witnesez,
  and ministerz ov Him
hɯ iz đe veri Wɒrd ov God,
  wɒrʃipt bį çerubim;
it simed gud tu mi, ɷlsɷ
  in điz ŧiŋz wel informd,
tu r̨it đem dɜn in order, đɒs,
  đat meni harts bi wormd
wiđ klirer nolej ov điz trɯŧz,
  div̨inest, pųrest, best,
ov ɷl đat man on erŧ kan lern
  and çeriʃ in hiz brest.

SEKΣON 2.

Đe diviniti, hųmaniti, and ofis ov Kr̨ist.
—Jon 1. 1-18.

In đe beginiŋ woz đe Wɒrd,
  đe *Logos*, Trɯŧ div̨in,
đat woz wiđ God, and đat woz God,
  and ɷl gud did enʃr̨in;
and ɷl ŧiŋz bį đis Wɒrd wer
      mɛd,
  wiđɜt Him nɷt kud bi,
for Hi pozest đe pɜer and m̨it
  ov sovren Diiti.

In Him was that eternal life
Which is the light of men,
Without which light dim reason gropes
In error's darksome den.
And this great light then shone abroad
To illume the sons of earth;
But Ah! too few acknowledged it,
And sought celestial worth.

John's Testimony.

There was a man sent forth from God,
Predicted from of old,
And John the Baptist he was called,
A prophet true and bold.
He was the faithful messenger
And witness of the Word,
That men might recognise its light,
And worship Christ the Lord.
He, though a prophet, was mere man,
And not that Light divine;
But he was sent to tell mankind
That Light was now to shine;
That sole, true Light from God Him-
Which lighteth every man [self
That ever came into the world,
Since first the world began.
He came into this fallen world,
Which He Himself had made,
And yet the world received Him not,
But foully Him betrayed.
He came unto His ancient race,
His chosen Israel,
Yet they received him not, but did
In word and deed rebel.
But unto all who would receive
His saving grace and love,
He gave a power to become
The sons of God above.
For those who cherished filial faith
In His most holy name,
He made regenerate sons of God,
Born of a holy flame.
So did the Word of God become
Incarnate in man's form,
And tabernacled among men,
And bore affliction's storm.
And we beheld His glory, such
As God in flesh alone
Can show; so full of grace and truth,
—The shadow of His throne.

In Him woz đát eternal lįf
hwiç iz đe lįt ov men,
wiđɜt hwįç lįt dim rizon grɵps
in eror'z darksɒm den.
And đis gret lįt đen ʃon abrɵd
tu ilum đe sɒnz ov erŧ;
bɒt ah! tɯ fų aknolejd it,
and sɵt selestial wɒrŧ.

Jon'z Testimoni.

Đer woz a man sent forŧ from God,
predikted from ov ɵld,
and Jon đe Baptist hi woz kɵld,
a profet trɯ and bɵld.
Hi woz đe feŧful mesenjer
and witnes ov đe Wɒrd,
đat men mįt rekognįz its lįt,
and wɒrʃip Krįst đe Lord.
Hi, đɵ a profet, woz mir man,
and not đát Lįt divįn;
bɒt hi woz sent tu tel mankįnd
đát Lįt woz nɜ tu ʃįn;
đát sɵl, trɯ Lįt from God Himself,
hwiç lįteŧ everi man
đat ever kem intu đe wɒrld,
sins ferst đe wɒrld began.
Hi kem intu đis fɵlen wɒrld,
hwiç Hi Himself had med,
and yet đe wɒrld resivd Him not,
bɒt fɜlli Him betred.
Hi kem ɒntu Hiz enʃent res,
Hiz çɵzen Izrael,
yet đe resivd Him not, bɒt did
in wɒrd and did rebél.
Bɒt ɒntu ɵl hɯ wud resiv
Hiz seviŋ gres and lɒv,
Hi gev a pɜer tu bekɒm
đe sɒnz ov God abɒv.
For đɵz hɯ çeriʃt filial feŧ
in Hiz mɵst hɵli nem,
Hi med rejeneret sɒnz ov God,
born ov a hɵli flem.
Sɵ did đe Wɒrd ov God bekɒm
inkarnet in man'z form,
and tabernakeld amɒŋ men,
and bɵr aflikʃon'z storm.
And wi beheld Hiz glɵri, sɒç
az God in fleʃ alɵn
kan ʃɵ; sɵ ful ov gres and trɯŧ,
—đe ʃadɵ ov Hiz ŧrɵn.

And John bare witness, "This is he
  Of whom I said before
That after me shall one arise
  Whom all men shall adore:
He was before me from of old,
  And let him be preferred
Before me still, for him I own
  My Savior and my Lord."
Out of his full divinity
  May all men now receive
Grace upon grace, till even on earth
  Like angels they may live.
The law of rites and sacrifice
  Was once through Moses given,
But sure, the loveliest grace of truth
  Descends with Christ from heaven.
For though no man hath ever seen
  The Deity supreme,
His only, well-belovèd Son,
  Doth with his glory beam.

SECTION 3.

***The Birth of John the Baptist.*—**
Luke 1. 5-25.

In the days of Herod, Judah's king,
  Proud, pompous, cruel, vain,
Who adorned the temple with rich [gifts,
  And forty years did reign,
Lived Zacharias, holy priest,
  Of ancient lineage he;
His wife was named Elizabeth,
  Of Aaron's family.
They both were righteous in God's [sight,
  Fulfilling his pure will;
But old they were, that faithful pair,
  And they were childless still.
It was his priestly lot to burn
  Incense before the Lord,
On golden altar, many days,
  Where he his vows outpoured;
While all the throng of pious Jews
  In outer court did pray,
And when the incense rose to heaven,
  Devotions they would pay,
And lo! the angel of the Lord
  Unto the good priest came,
Standing upon the altar's side,
  Where flowed the censer's flame.

And Jon ber witnes, "Đis iz hi
  ov huɯm ị sed befɷr
đat after mi ʃal wɒn arịz
  huɯm ɷl men ʃal adɷr:
Hi woz befɷr mi from ov ɷld,
  and let him bi preferd
befɷr mi stil, for him ị ɷn
  mị Sɛvier and mị Lord."
Ɤt ov hiz ful diviniti
  mɛ ɷl men nɤ resiv
grɛs ɒpon grɛs, til iven on erŧ
  lịk ɛnjelz đɛ mɛ liv.
Đe lɷ ov rịts and sakrifịz
  woz wɒns ŧruɯ Mɷzes given,
bɒt ʃuɯr, đe lɒvliest grɛs ov truɯŧ
  desendz wiđ Krịst from heven.
For đɷ nɷ man haŧ ever sin
  đe Diiti sụprim,
Hiz ɷnli, wel-belɒved Sɒn,
  dɒŧ wiđ hiz glɷri bim.

SEKƩON 3.

***Đe Berŧ ov Jon đe Baptist.*—**
Luk 1. 5-25.

In đe dɛz ov Herod, Juɯda'z kiŋ,
  prɤd, pompɒs, kruɯel, vɛn,
huɯ adornd đe tempel wiđ riɋ gifts,
  and forti yirz did rɛn,
livd Zakarịas, hɷli prist,
  ov ɛnʃent liniɛj hi;
hiz wịf woz nɛmd Elizabeŧ,
  ov Ɛron'z famili.
Đɛ bɷŧ wer rịtiɒs in God'z sịt,
  fulfiliŋ hiz pụr wil;
bɒt ɷld đɛ wer, đát fɛŧful per,
  and đɛ wer ɋịldles stil.
It woz hiz pristli lot tu bɒrn
  insens befɷr đe Lord,
on gɷlden ɷltar, meni dɛz,
  hwer hi hiz vɤz ɤtpɷrd;
hwịl ɷl đe ŧroŋ ov pịɒs Juɯz
  in ɤter kɷrt did prɛ,
and hwen đe insens rɷz tu heven,
  devɷʃonz đɛ wud pɛ.
And lɷ! đe ɛnjel ov đe Lord
  ɒntu đe gud prist kɛm,
standiŋ ɒpon đe ɷltar'z sịd,
  hwer flɷd đe senser'z flɛm.

When Zacharias saw that form,
  So heavenly, pure, and bright,
His heart was troubled, and his eyes
  Were dazzled at the sight.
But gently spoke that angel blest
  Unto the holy man,
And said, "Fear not, thy prayer is heard,"
  And thus his promise ran:—
"Thy wish for the Messiah's reign
  Is granted thee by heaven,
And to thy wife Elizabeth
  A son shall soon be given;
A holy and prophetic child,
  And thou shalt call him John,
Which signifies the grace of God
  That unto thee is shown.
And joy and gladness thou shalt have,
  And many shall be blest,
When this miraculous child is born,
  By ancient seers confessed:
For a great Nazarite shall he be,
  The greatest prophet known;
He shall not drink the wine of earth,
  And no defilement own.
He shall be filled, e'en from his birth,
  With God's pure spirit of truth,
And blameless shall his childhood be,
  And sanctified his youth.
And he shall turn full many minds
  Of Israel's chosen race,
Unto the Lord their God, who comes
  To show salvation's grace.
He shall precede Messiah's reign,
  And shall prepare His way,
With all the spirit and the power
  Elijah did display.
He shall convert full many a heart
  Of parent to his child,
And turn the disobedient souls
  To God's truth undefiled;
And so make ready multitudes
  Prepared to own the Lord,
When Christ himself shall visit earth,
  And preach his heavenly word."

Then Zacharias spoke, and said,
  Unto the angel fair,
"How can I now, so old, expect,
  A son so blest and rare?"

Hwen Zakarįas sɷ đát form,
  sɵ hevenli, pųr, and brįt,
hiz hart woz trɒbeld, and hiz įz
  wer dazeld at đe sįt.
Bɒt jentli spɵk đát enjel blest
  ɒntu đe hɵli man,
and sed, "Fir not, đį prer i herd,"
  and đɒs hiz promis ran:—
"Đį wiʃ for đe Mesįa'z ren
  iz granted đi bį heven,
and tu đį wįf Elizabeŧ
  a sɒn ʃal suın bi given;
a hɵli and prɵfetik çįld,
  and đɜ ʃalt kɷl him Jon,
hwiç signifįz đe gres ov God
  đat ɒntu đi iz ʃɵn.
And joi and gladnes đɜ ʃalt hav,
  and meni ʃal bi blest,
hwen đis mirakųlɒs çįld iz born,
  bį enʃent sirz konfest:
for a gret Nazarįt ʃal hi bi,
  đe gretest profet nɵn;
hi ʃal not driŋk đe wįn ov erŧ,
  and nɵ defįlment ɵn.
Hi ʃal bi fild, i'n from hiz berŧ,
  wiđ God'z pųr spirit ov trɯŧ,
and blemles ʃal hiz çįldhud bi,
  and saŋktifįd hiz ųŧ.
And hi ʃal tɒrn ful meni mįndz
  ov Izrael'z çɵzen res,
ɒntu đe Lord đer God, hɯ kɒmz
  tu ʃɵ salveʃon'z gres.
Hi ʃal presid Mesįa'z ren,
  and ʃal preper Hiz we,
wiđ ɷl đe spirit and đe pɜer
  Elįja did disple.
Hi ʃal konvért ful meni a hart
  ov perent tu hiz çįld,
and tɒrn đe disobidient sɵlz
  tu God'z trɯŧ ɒndefįld;
and sɵ mek redi mɒltitųdz
  preperd tu ɵn đe Lord,
hwen Krįst himself ʃal vizit erŧ,
  and priç hiz hevenli wɒrd."

Đen Zakarįas spɵk, and sed,
  ɒntu đe enjel fer,
"Hɜ kan į nɜ, sɵ ɵld, ekspekt,
  a sɒn sɵ blest and rer?"

And unto him the angel said,
  "Lo, Gabriel is my name,
I in God's presence stand, and glow
  With his celestial flame;
And I am sent to thee to tell
  Glad tidings in thine ear,
And now, behold! thou shalt be dumb,
  Until that day appear
Which shall perform my promises;
  Because thou hast denied
My heavenly message, which shall be
  Fulfilled and glorified."

The holy angel Gabriel
  Then vanished from his sight;
And Zacharias mused awhile
  With terror and delight.
Meanwhile the throng of worshippers
  In outer court did stand,
And marveled that he stayed so long
  Within that temple grand.
And when he issued from the veil
  That hid him from their view,
He could not tell the miracle:
  So then the people knew
That he had seen some vision bright
  Within that sacred shrine,
For with his hand he beckoned them
  And made a voiceless sign.
And when his days of priestly work
  Accomplished were, and o'er,
He went to his own house, and prayed
  Devoutly, as before.
And soon his wife conceived, and led
  A pious life, retired,
And blessed the Lord, who had be-
  The gift she so desired. [stowed

SECTION 4.

***The Annunciation to the Virgin Mary.*—**
Luke 1. 26-38.

In the sixth month after, Gabriel,
  That angel strong and bright,
Whom Zacharias had beheld
  Arrayed in heavenly light;
From God was sent, commissioned
  To execute His will, [straight
In Nazareth of Galilee,
  And His command fulfil.

And ɒntu him đe enjel sed,
  "Lơ, Gebriel iz mį nem,
į in God'z prezens stand, and glơ
  wiđ hiz selestial flem;
and į am sent tu đi tu tel
  glad tįdiŋz in đįn ir,
and nɤ, behơld! đɤ ʃalt bi dɒm,
  ɒntil đát de apir
hwiç ʃal perform mį promisez;
  bekωz đɤ hast denįd
mį hevenli mesej, hwiç ʃal bi
  fulfild and glơrifįd."

Đe hơli enjel Gebriel
  đen vaniʃt from hiz sįt;
and Zakarįas mųzd ahwįl
  wiđ teror and delįt.
Minhwįl đe đroŋ ov wɒrʃiperz
  in ɤter kơrt did stand,
and marveld đat hi sted sơ loŋ
  wiđin đát tempel grand.
And hwen hi iʃųd from đe vel
  đat hid him from đer vų,
hi kud not tel đe mirakel:
  sơ đen đe pipel nų
đat hi had sin sɒm viʒon brįt
  wiđin đát sekred ʃrįn,
for wiđ hiz hand hi bekond đem
  and med a voisles sįn.
And hwen hiz dez ov pristli wɒrk
  akompliʃt wer, and ơ'r,
hi went tu hiz ơn hɤs, and pred
  devɤtli, az befơr.
And sɯn hiz wįf konsivd, and led
  a pįɒs lįf, retįrd,
and blest đe Lord, hɯ had bestơd
  đe gift ʃi sơ dezįrd.

SEKΣON 4.

***Đe Anɒnsieʃon tu đe Verjin Meri.*—**
Lɯk 1. 26-38.

In đe sikst mɒnt after, Gebriel,
  đát enjel stroŋ and brįt,
hɯm Zakarįas had beheld
  ared in hevenli lįt;
from God woz sent, komiʃond stret
  tu eksekųt Hiz wįl,
in Nazaret ov Galili,
  and Hiz komand fulfil.

He visited a virgin there,
  And Mary was her name,
A virgin, holy, pure, and true,
  Of spotless life and fame,
Betrothèd to Joseph, a just man
  Of David's royal seed;
And unto her the angel spoke,
  As Providence decreed,
"Hail Mary! highly favored maid,
  Jehovah is with thee;
And through the ages yet to come,
  Most blessed shalt thou be."
But when she saw the angel bright,
  And heard his promise given,
Her mind was troubled, nor perceived
  This mystery of heaven.
Then said the angel, "Fear thou not,
  God's grace thou hast obtained;
Yea, from Almighty Deity,
  This honor thou hast gained,
That thou shalt both conceive and bear
  A son, whom thou shalt name
JESUS, the Savior of mankind,
  And great shall be his fame.
He shall be called Messiah, Christ,
  The Son of God most high;
He shall possess the ancient throne
  Of David's royalty,
And reign for ever, King supreme,
  O'er all the human race;
And of his kingdom's majesty
  No end shall mortal trace."
Then Mary to the angel said,
  "How can this wonder be?
That I, a virgin pure, should bear
  A Godlike progeny?"
The angel answered, "Unto thee
  The Holy Spirit of God
Shall come; the power of the Supreme
  On thee shall be outpoured;
And therefore shall that holy thing
  Which thou shalt bring to birth,
Be called the Son of God, the Word
  Incarnate upon earth.
Doubt not; behold! Elizabeth,
  Thy cousin, though so old,
Shall bear a son, to be of thine
  The Messenger foretold.
For nothing is impossible
  To God, as shall unfold."

Hi vizited a verjin đer,
  and Meri woz her nem,
a verjịn, hɵli, pụr, and trụ,
  ov spotles lịf and fem,
betroɟt tu Jɵzef, a jɒst man
  ov Devid'z roial sid;
and ɒntu her đe enjel spɵk,
  az Providens dekrid,
"Hel Meri! hịli fevord med,
  Jehɵva iz wiđ đi;
and ɟrụ đe ejez yet tu kɒm,
  mɵst blesed ʃalt đʊ bi."
Bɒt hwen ʃi sɷ đe enjel brịt,
  and herd hiz promis given,
her mịnd woz trɒbeld, nor persivd
  đis misteri ov heven.
Đen sed đe enjel, "Fir đʊ not,
  God'z gres đʊ hast obtend;
ye, from ɷlmịti Diiti,
  đis onor đʊ hast gend,
đat đʊ ʃalt bɵɟ konsiv and ber
  a sɒn, hụm đʊ ʃalt nem
JIZƜS, đe Sevier ov mankịnd,
  and gret ʃal bi hiz fem.
Hi ʃal bi kɷld Mesịa, Krịst,
  đe Sɒn ov God mɵst hị;
hi ʃal pozés đe enʃent ɟrɵn
  ov Devid'z roialti,
and ren for ever, Kiŋ sụprim,
  ɵ'r ɷl đe hụman res;
and ov hiz kiŋdom'z majesti
  nɵ end ʃal mortal tres."
Đen Meri tu đe enjel sed,
  "Hʊ kan đis wɒnder bi?
đat ị, a verjin pụr, ʃud ber
  a Godlịk projeni?"
Đe enjel anserd, "Ɯntu đi
  đe Hɵli Spirit ov God
ʃal kɒm: đe pʊer ov đe Sụprim
  on đi ʃal bi ʊtpɵrd;
and đerfɵr ʃal đát hɵli ɟiŋ
  hwiç đʊ ʃalt briŋ tu berɟ,
bi kɷld đe Sɒn ov God, đe Wɒrd
  inkarnet ɒpon erɟ.
Dʊt not; behɵld! Elizabeɟ,
  đị kɒzin, đɵ sɵ ɵld,
ʃal ber a sɒn, tu bi ov địn
  đe Mesenjer fɵrtɵld.
For nɒɟiŋ iz imposibel
  tu God, az ʃal ɒnfɵld."

And Mary said to him, "Behold
The handmaid of the Lord,
And let thy promise be fulfilled
According to thy word."
Then Gabriel left the virgin pure,
To praise the Lord, whose word is
sure.

SECTION 5.

Interview between Mary and Elizabeth.—
Luke 1. 39-57.

And Mary in those days arose
And hasted to impart
Unto her friend Elizabeth
The mystery of her heart.
Unto the mountains of the South,
To Judah's glorious land
She came, and dwelt in Hebron, where
Her cousin's house did stand.
And when Elizabeth first heard
The virgin Mary's voice,
Her soul was glad, and e'en the babe
Within her, did rejoice.
And with a holy spirit pure
Of prophecy inspired,
Elizabeth spoke forth this Psalm,
With heavenly rapture fired:—
"O blest above all women thou,
Dear Mary, ever be,
And yet more blest shall be thy Son,
Thy God-like progeny.
The greatest glory of my life
Is this, that thou art here;
The mother of my Lord doth now
Within my house appear.
E'en at the sound of thy first words
My prophet child within,
Exulting owned her who should bear
Messiah without sin.
Happy are all who this believe,
For this shall be fulfilled;
Those things shall surely come to pass
Which God in love has willed."

Then Mary also uttered forth
Her Psalm, with gladsome tone,
And said unto Elizabeth,
"A kindred joy I own.

And Meri sed tu him, "Behɵld
đe handmed ov đe Lord,
and let đȷ promis bi fulfild
akordiŋ tu đȷ wɒrd."
Đen Gebriel left đe verjin pɥr,
tu prez đe Lord, huɯz wɒrd iz
ʃuɯr.

SEKΣON 5.

Intervɥ betwin Meri and Elizabeŧ.—
Luuk 1. 39-57.

And Meri in đɵz dez aréz
and hested tu impart
ɒntu her frend Elizabeŧ
đe misteri ov her hart.
Untu đe mɜntenz ov đe Sɜŧ,
tu Juuda'z glɵriɒs land
ʃi kem, and dwelt in Hebron, hwer
her kɒzin'z hɜs did stand.
And hwen Elizabeŧ ferst herd
đe verjin Meri'z vois,
her sɵl woz glad, and i'n đe beb
widin her, did rejois.
And wiđ a hɵli spirit pɥr
ov profesi inspȷrd,
Elizabeŧ spɵk fɵrŧ đis Sɑm,
wiđ hevenli raptɥr fȷrd:—
"Ɵ blest abɒv ɷl wimen đɜ,
dir Meri, ever bi,
and yet mɵr blest ʃal bi đȷ Sɒn,
đȷ God-lȷk projeni.
Đe gretest glɵri ov mȷ lȷf
iz đis, đat đɜ art hir;
đe mɒđer ov mȷ Lord dɒŧ nɜ
widin mȷ hɜs apir.
I'n at đe sɜnd ov đȷ ferst wɒrdz
mȷ profet çȷld widin,
ekzɒltiŋ ɵnd her huɯ ʃud ber
Mesȷa widɜt sin.
Hapi ar ɷl huɯ đis beliv,
for đis ʃal bi fulfild;
đɵz ŧiŋz ʃal ʃuɯrli kɒm tu pas
hwiç God in lɒv haz wild."

Đen Meri ɷlsɵ ɒterd fɵrŧ
her Sɑm, wiđ gladsɒm tɵn,
and sed ɒntu Elizabeŧ,
"A kindred joi ȷ ɵn.

My soul doth magnify the Lord,
  His mercy, grace, and truth ;
My spirit hath rejoiced in God
  My Savior from my youth.
For he hath glorified the estate
  Of me, his handmaid lowly,
And henceforth shall all ages call
  My name, as blest and holy.
For God himself hath wrought for me
  His mightiest miracle,
And hallowed be his sacred name,
  He hath done all things well.
His mercy ever rests upon
  True worshipers below,
As age to age, and tribe to tribe,
  Through all the world doth show.
His arm exerts resistless power
  To save or to subdue,
He scatters proud impiety,
  And falsehood's endless crew.
But to his meek and humble saints,
  His tender mercy flows,
He fills the hungry with good things,
  And soothes the mourner's woes.
In memory of his promises,
  He succor will afford
To his own Israel, and to all
  Who trust his living Word."

SECTION 6.

Birth and Naming of John the Baptist.—
Luke 1. 57-80.

The virgin Mary dwelt three months
  In Hebron's lofty town ;
And then returning home once more,
  To Nazareth went down.
And now Elizabeth brought forth
  Her firstborn, only son,
And friends and kindred all rejoiced
  At such a blessing won.
And when the child was eight days old,
  As Moses' law did claim,
They circumcised him, and they called
  Him by his father's name.
But good Elizabeth declared
  Her son's name John should be,
But they replied, "This name is new
  To all thy family."

Mį sœl dɒđ ma
  hiz mersi, gr
mį spirit hađ r
  mį Sevier fr
For hi hađ glœ
  ov mi, hiz h
and hensfœrđ ʃ
  mį nem, az b
For God himse
  hiz mįtiest m
and halœd bi h
  hi hađ dɒn a
Hiz mersi ever
  truı wɒrʃiper
az ej tu ej, and
  đruı ɑl đe w
Hiz arm ekzer
  tu sev or tu
hi skaterz prɤ
  and fɑlshud
Bɒt tu hiz mik
  hiz tender m
hi filz đe hɒŋg
  and suıđz đe
In memori ov
  hi sɒkor wil
tu hiz œn Izrae
  huı trɒst hiz

SE

Berθ and Nemiŋ
Luı

Đe verjin Meri
  in Hebron'z
and đen retɒrn
  tu Nazarеđ
And nɤ Elizab
  her ferstborn
and frendz and
  at sɒç a bles
And hwen đe ç
  az Mœzes' la
đe serkɒmsįzd
  him bį hiz fa
Bɒt gud Elizab
  her sɒn'z ne
bɒt đe repląd,
  tu ɑl đį fam

So of his father they inquired,
  And begged him to decide
How he would have him called. He
  By writing quick replied, [then
"His name is John." Amazement
    seized
  The crowd, who marveled all.
Then instantly his tongue was loosed,
  And prostrate did he fall;
And with loud voice he praised the
  For all his kindness shown; [Lord
And solemn awe fell on that crowd,
  And not on them alone.
For all these things were noised abroad
  Round Hebron's mountain range,
And those who heard them, mused
  With admiration strange; [thereon
And said, "This infant John must be
  The child of miracle."
And the Lord's power was with him,
  A spiritual spell. [like

Then Zacharias was inspired,
  His soul was glorified,
By the most holy Spirit of God,
  And thus he prophesied:—
"Blest be the Lord our God, who still
  Redeems his faithful band,
And raises up salvation's strength
  In Israel's chosen land;
As by his holy seers he spoke
  E'er since the world began;
Saving his saints from all their foes,
  And every hateful man.
He well performs his promise kind,
  His covenant of grace;
He keeps his oath to Abraham,
  And smiles upon his race.
Delivered from our enemies,
  We'll serve him without fear,
In holiness and righteousness,
  Till solemn death appear.
And thou, mysterious child, shalt be
  The prophet of the Lord,
To go before Messiah's face,
  And make his name adored:
To teach salvation's mystery,
  And guilt-forgiving love,
Through God's pure mercy, who shall
  The Dayspring from above, [send

Sσ ov hiz fɞɖer ɖɛ inkwįrd,
  and begd him tu desįd
hȣ hı wud hav him kωld. Hı ɖen
  bį rįtiŋ kwik replįd,
"Hiz nɛm iz Jon." Amɛzment
    sızd
  ɖe krȣd, hɯ marveld ωl.
Đen instantli hiz tɒŋ woz lɯst,
  and prostrɛt did hı fωl;
and wiɖ lȣd vois hı prɛzd ɖe Lord
  for ωl hiz kįndnes ʃσn;
and solem ω fel on ɖát krȣd,
  and not on ɖem alσn.
For ωl ɖız ɟiŋz wer noizd abrωd
  rȣnd Hebron'z mȣnten rɛnj,
and ɖσz hɯ herd ɖem, mɥzd ɖeron
  wiɖ admirɛʃon strɛnj;
and sed, "Đis infant Jon mɒst bı
  ɖe ǥįld ov mirakel."
And ɖe Lord'z pȣer woz wiɖ him,
  a spiritɥal spel. [lįk

Đen Zakarįas woz inspįrd,
  hiz sσl woz glσrifįd,
bį ɖe mσst hσli Spirit ov God,
  and ɖɒs hı profesįd:—
"Blest bı ɖe Lord ȣr God, hɯ stil
  redımz hiz fɛɟful band,
and rɛzez ɒp salvɛʃon'z streŋɟ
  in Izrael'z ǥσzen land;
az bį hiz hσli sıerz hı spσk
  ɛr sins ɖe wɒrld began;
sɛviŋ hiz sɛnts from ωl ɖer fσz,
  and everi hɛtful man.
Hı wel performz hiz promis kįnd,
  hiz kɒvenant ov grɛs;
hı kıps hiz σɟ tu Ɛbraham,
  and smįlz ɒpon hiz rɛs.
Deliverd from ȣr enemiz,
  wı'l serv him wiɖȣt fır,
in hσlines and rįtiɒsnes,
  til solem deɟ apır.
And ɖȣ, mistıriɒs ǥįld, ʃalt bı
  ɖe profet ov ɖe Lord,
tu gσ befσr Mesįa'z fɛs,
  and mɛk hiz nɛm adσrd:
tu tıǥ salvɛʃon'z misteri,
  and gilt-forgiviŋ lɒv,
ɟrɯ God'z pɥr mersi, hɯ ʃal send
  ɖe Dɛspriŋ from abɒv,

To illume the dark'ning shades of death,
And make their horrors cease,
To guide the feet of erring men
In heavenly paths of peace."

Thus John the Baptist from his birth
Was sanctified by heaven,
For strong in spirit he became,
And grace to him was given.
He spent his youth in praise and prayer,
Among the mountains lone,
Till Israel hailed him afterwards,
The mightiest prophet known.

SECTION 7.

The Angel appears to Joseph.—Matthew 1. 18-25.

The birth of Jesus Christ our Lord,
The Savior of mankind,
Was thus ; this heavenly mystery
We in his Gospel find.
When Virgin Mary was betrothed
(Such was his mother's name,)
To pious Joseph, even before
Their day of marriage came,
She, by the Holy Spirit of God
A Holy Child conceived,
As the true Church has evermore
Undoubtingly believed.
Then Joseph, her betrothèd lord,
Himself a righteous man,
And loth to sacrifice her fame
To cruel slander's ban,
Intended secretly awhile
His wife to put away.
But while he thought upon these things
And oft to God did pray,
Behold the angel of the Lord
Came to him in a dream,
And said, "Fear not to take her now,
Nor her unworthy deem ;
For 'tis the Holy Spirit of God
Who caused this thing to be,
And Mary shall bring forth a child,
True Son of Deity.
And JESUS, or the Savior, thou
Shalt call his holy name ;

tu ilum đe dark'niŋ ʃedz ov deŧ,
and mek đer hororz sis,
tu gịd đe fit ov eriŋ men
in hevenli pađz ov pis."

Đɒs Jon đe Baptist from hiz berŧ
woz saŋktifịd bị heven,
for stroŋ in spirit hi bekem,
and gres tu him woz given.
Hi spent hiz ụŧ in prez and prer,
amɒŋ đe mɜntenz lon,
til Izrael held him afterwardz,
đe mịtiest profet non.

SEKƩON 7.

Đe Enjel apirz tu Jozef.—Maŧụ 1. 18-25.

Đe berŧ ov Jizɒs Krịst ɜr Lord,
đe Sevier ov mankịnd,
woz đɒs ; đis hevenli misteri
wi in hiz Gospel fịnd.
Hwen Verjin Meri woz betroŧt
(sɒç woz hiz mɒđer'z nem,)
tu pịɒs Jozef, iven befor
đer de ov marej kem,
ʃi, bị đe Holi Spirit ov God
a Holi Çịld konsivd,
az đe tru Çɒrç haz evermor
ɒndɜtiŋli belivd.
Đen Jozef, her betroŧed lord,
himself a rịtiɒs man,
and loŧ tu sakrifịz her fem
tu kruel slander'z ban,
intended sikretli ahwịl
hiz wịf tu put awe.
Bɒt hwịl hi ŧot ɒpon điz ŧiŋz
and oft tu God did pre,
behold đe enjel ov đe Lord
kem tu him in a drim,
and sed, "Fir not tu tek her nɜ,
nor her ɒnwɒrđi dim ;
for 'tiz đe Holi Spirit ov God
hu kozd đis ŧiŋ tu bi,
and Meri ʃal briŋ forŧ a çịld,
tru Sɒn ov Diiti.
And JIZɒS, or đe Sevier, đɜ
ʃalt kol hiz holi nem ;

For he shall save his worshipers
  From sin and every shame."
All this was done, that thus might be
  Fulfilled the prophet's word,
"Behold, a virgin shall conceive,
  And bear a son, the Lord.
He shall be called Immanuel,
  God dwelling with mankind."
Then Joseph, rising from his sleep,
  To do God's will designéd,
And took her to him as his wife,
  His heaven-appointed bride,
Devoted unto God, until
  His word was ratified;
Until she bore her first-born son,
  The Savior of our race;
And called him JESUS, who was Christ,
  The Prince of peace and grace.

SECTION 8.

***Birth of Christ at Bethlehem.*—**
Luke 2. 1-7.

And in those days it came to pass
  There issued a decree,
From Cæsar, called Augustus, that
  In every land and sea
That owned his sway, the people should
  Be enrolled in their own land,
And all be taxed by officers
  Sent forth by his command.
And all the Jews went to be taxed,
  Each to his proper place;
And Joseph quitted Nazareth,
  Being born of Judah's race,
And of King David's royal house,
  And forth with haste he came
To Bethlehem, David's city, which
  They did Ephrata name,
With Mary, his espousèd wife,
  Of royal lineage known,
As in her genealogy
  Is fully proved and shown.
And while they stayed at Bethlehem
  Her first-born son she bore,
And wrapped in infant's swaddling [clothes
  That Babe whom we adore;
And laid him in a manger there,
  (Thus did his life begin,)
Because no room they could obtain
  Throughout the crowded inn.

for hi ʃal sev hiz wɒrʃiperz
  from sin and everi ʃem."
ɷl đis woz dɒn, đat đɒs mįt bi
  fulfild đe profet's wɒrd,
"Behɵld, a verjin ʃal konsiv,
  and ber a sɒn, đe Lord.
Hi ʃal bi kɷld Imanɥel,
  God dweliŋ wid mankįnd."
Đen Jɵzef, rįziŋ from hiz slip,
  tu duɯ God'z wíl dezįnd,
and tuk her tu him az hiz wįf,
  hiz heven-apointed brįd,
devɵted ɒntu God, ɒntil
  hiz wɒrd woz ratifįd;
ɒntil ʃi bɵr her ferst-born sɒn,
  đe Sevier ov ɤr res;
and kɷld him JɯZɯS, huɯ woz [Krįst,
  đe Prins ov pis and gres.

SEKΣON 8.

***Berθ ov Krįst at Beθlihem.*—**
Luɯk 2. 1-7.

And in đɵz dez it kem tu pas
  đer iʃɥd a dekri,
from Sizar, kɷld ɷgɒstɒs, đat
  in everi land and si
đat ɵnd hiz swe, đe pipel ʃud
  bi enrɵld in đer ɵn land,
and ɷl bi takst bį ofiserz
  sent fɵrɟ bį hiz komand.
And ɷl đe Juɯz went tu bi takst,
  iç tu hiz proper ples;
and Jɵzef kwited Nazareɟ,
  biiŋ born ov Juɯda'z res,
and ov Kiŋ Devid'z roial hɤs,
  and fɵrɟ wid hest hi kem
tu Beɟlihem, Devid'z siti, hwiç
  đe did Efrɘta nem,
wid Meri, hiz espɤzed wįf,
  ov roial liniej nɵn,
az in her jenialoji
  iz fuli pruɯvd and ʃɵn.
And hwįl đe sted at Beɟlihem
  her ferst-born sɒn ʃi bɵr,
and rapt in infant's swodliŋ klɵdz
  đát Beb huɯm wi adɵr;
and led him in a menjer đer,
  (đɒs did hiz lįf begin,)
bekɷz nɵ ruɯm đe kud obten
  ɟruɤt đe krɤded ín.

SECTION 9.

The Genealogy of Christ.—
Maɟų 1. 1-18.

The genealogy of Christ
  In God's own Word is given,
In order that it might be known
  That He, the God of heaven,
In coming down to men on earth
  To magnify the law,
Took flesh of Mary, like to us,
  Yet lived without a flaw.
His Human was through Abraham's
  And Judah's royal line ; [seed,
His soul Jehovah God Himself,
  The Spiritual Vine.
Through David and through Solomon,
  And famed Zorobabel,
(Who rescued Judah's Church and
  So bravely and so well,) [State,
Descended Heli, he the sire
  Of Mary, virgin true,
Who married Joseph, Jacob's son,
  Of David's lineage too.
And from that blessed virgin wife
  Was now Christ Jesus born,
Who came from heaven to earth to
  Man's guilty race forlorn. [save
So faithfully did God create
  And still preserve the line,
Through every age, and every change,
  That bore the Son divine.

SEKΣON 9.

Đe Jenialoji ov Krịst.—
Maɟų 1. 1-18.

Đe jenialoji ov Krịst
  in God'z ɵn Wɒrd iz given,
in order đat it mịt bi nɵn
  đat Hi, đe God ov heven,
in kɒmiŋ dɤn tu men on erɟ
  tu magnifị đe lω,
tuk fleʃ ov Meri, lịk tu ɒs,
  yet livd wiđɤt a flω.
Hiz Hųman woz ɟrɯ Ɛbraham'z
  and Jɯda'z roial lịn ; [sid,
hiz sɵl Jehɵva God Himself,
  đe Spiritųal Vịn.
ɟrɯ Devid and ɟrɯ Solomon,
  and femd Zorobabel,
(hɯ reskųd Jɯda'z Ɛɒrç and Stet,
  sɵ brevli and sɵ wel,)
desended Hilị, hi đe sịr
  ov Meri, verjin trɯ,
hɯ marid Jɵzef, Jekob'z sɒn,
  ov Devid'z liniej tɯ.
And from đát blesed verjin wịf
  woz nɤ Krịst Jizɒs born,
hɯ kem from heven tu erɟ tu sev
  man'z gilti res forlorn.
Sɵ feɟfuli did God kriet
  and stil prezerv đe lịn,
ɟrɯ everi ej, and everi çenj,
  đat bɵr đe Sɒn divịn.

SECTION 10.

Song of the Angels at the Nativity of Jesus Christ.—Luke 2. 8-20.

The shepherds in Judæan fields*
  Watched o'er their flocks by night,

SEKΣON 10.

Soŋ ov đe Ɛnjelz at đe Nativiti ov Jizɒs Krịst.—Lɯk 2. 8-20.

Đe ʃepherdz in Jɯdian fildz*
  woçt ɵ'r đer floks bị nịt,

---

* Subjoined is the version of the Angels' Song given in the Book of Common Prayer, *Luke* 2. 8-14.

While shepherds watched their flocks by
  All seated on the ground, [night,
The angel of the Lord came down,
  And glory shone around.
"Fear not," said he, for mighty dread
  Had seized their troubled mind ;
"Good tidings of great joy I bring
  To you and all mankind.

* Sɒbjoind iz đe verʃon ov đe Ɛnjelz' Soŋ, given in đe Buk ov Komon Prer, *Lɯk* 2. 8-14.

Hwịl ʃepherdz woçt đer floks bị nịt,
  ωl sited on đe grɤnd,
đe enjel ov đe Lord kem dɤn,
  and glɵri ʃon arɤnd.
"Fir not," sed hi, for mịti dred
  had sizd đer trɒbeld mịnd ;
"gud tịdiŋz ov gret joi ị briŋ
  tu ų and ωl mankịnd.

And lo! the angel of the Lord
  Appeared, arrayed in light;
And all around them suddenly
  Jehovah's glory blazed,
And they were filled with speechless
  And they were sore amazed. [awe,
Then said the angel unto them,
  "Fear not, for lo! I bring
Good tidings of great joy to all:
  Welcome your heavenly King.
For unto you this day is born
  In David's city blest,
A Savior, which is Christ the Lord,
  And He shall give you rest.
And this shall be a sign to you;—
  The Babe you soon shall see,
Laid in the manger of an inn,
  In meek humility."
And suddenly a multitude
  Of Heaven's bright angels came,
All praising God; and thus they sang,
  With harps of golden flame;
"Glory to God in highest heaven;
  He now descends again
To give His holy peace on earth,
  And great good will to men."
When the pure angels had returned
  To heaven their happy home,
The shepherds said with gladsome
    hearts,
  "To Bethlehem let us roam,
And see this mighty miracle
  Which God to us hath told."
Then did they hasten on their way,
  And there did they behold

and lɵ! đe enjel ov đe Lord
  apịrd, aréd in lịt;
and ɷl arɤnd đem sɒdenli
  Jehɵva'z glɵri blezd,
and đe wer fild wiđ spịçles ɷ,
  and đe wer sɵr amezd.
Đen sed đe enjel ɒntu đem,
  "Fịr not, for lɵ! ị briŋ
gud tịdiŋz ov gret joi tu ɷl:
  welkɒm ųr hevenli Kiŋ.
For ɒntu ų đis de iz born
  in Devid'z siti blest,
a Sevier, hwiç iz Krịst đe Lord,
  and Hi ʃal giv ų rest.
And đis ʃal bị a sịn tu ų;—
  đe Beb ų suun ʃal si,
led in đe menjer ov an ín,
  in mik hųmiliti."
And sɒdenli a mɒltitųd
  ov Heven'z brit enjelz kem,
ɷl preziŋ God; and đɒs đe saŋ,
  wiđ harps ov gɵlden flem;
"Glɵri tu God in hịest heven;
  Hi nɤ desendz agen
tu giv Hiz hɵli pis on erϑ,
  and gret gud wíl tu men."
Hwen đe pųr enjelz had retɒrnd
  tu heven đer hapi hɵm,
đe ʃepherdz sed wiđ gladsɒm
    harts,
  "Tu Beϑlihem let ɒs rɵm,
and sị đis mịti mirakel
  hwiç God tu ɒs haϑ tɵld."
Đen did đe hesṇ on đer we,
  and đer did đe behɵld

To you, in David's town, this day,
  Is born of David's line,
A Savior, who is Christ the Lord,
  And this shall be the sign:
The heavenly Babe you there shall find
  To human view displayed,
All meanly wrapped in swathing bands,
  And in a manger laid."
Thus spoke the seraph, and forthwith
  Appeared a shining throng
Of angels, praising God, and thus
  Addressed their joyful song:
"All glory be to God on high,
  And to the earth be peace,
Goodwill, henceforth from heaven to men,
  Begin and never cease."

Tu ų, in Devid'z tɤn, đis de,
  iz born ov Devid'z lịn,
a Sevier, hu iz Krịst đe Lord,
  and đis ʃal bị đe sịn:
đe hevenli Beb ų đer ʃal fịnd
  tu hųman vų displed,
ɷl minli rapt in swediŋ bandz,
  and in a menjer led."
Đɒs spɵk đe seraf, and forϑwiđ
  apịrd a ʃịniŋ ϑroŋ
ov enjelz, preziŋ God, and đɒs
  adrest đer joiful soŋ:
"ɷl glɵri bị tu God on hị,
  and tu đe erϑ bị pis,
gudwil, hensforϑ from heven tu men,
  begin and never sis."

Joseph and Mary, and the Babe
  In humble manger laid:
And when they saw, they soon made known
  All that the angels said.
And all that heard the shepherds' tale
  Astonished were, in heart;
But Mary treasured up these things,
  And mused on them apart.
The shepherds then returned with joy,
  And praised their God above,
For all that they had heard and seen
  Of His redeeming love.

SECTION 11.

Christ presented in the Temple.—
Luke 2. 21-24.

When eight days old, the Holy Child
  (As Jewish law did claim)
Was circumcised; and, as foretold,
  So JESUS was his name.
His mother then presented him
  Unto the God of heaven,
(For Scripture saith, "Each firstborn son
  Shall to the Lord be given;")
And offered up a sacrifice,
  Within the Temple fair,
Two pigeons, or, two turtle doves,
  And many a fervent prayer.

SECTION 12.

Simeon and Anna in the Temple.—
Luke 2. 25-40.

At that time in Jerusalem
  Dwelt Simeon, holy man,
Who waited for Messiah's day,
  And thus the promise ran:—
God's spirit rested on him, and
  To him it was revealed
That he should see the Christ of God
  Ere death his eyes had sealed.
Led by the spirit of God, he went
  Into the Temple grand,
When Jesus' parents brought the child,
  To keep the law's command,
He took the Babe up in his arms,
  And blessèd God, and said,
"Lord, let thy servant now depart
  (As thou hast promised,)

Jɵzef and Meri, and đe Beb
  in hɒmbel menjer led:
and hwen đe sɷ, đe sun med nɵn
  ɷl đat đe enjelz sed.
And ɷl đat herd đe ʃepherdz' tel
  astoniʃt wer, in hart;
bɒt Meri treʒurd ɒp điz ţiŋz,
  and mɥzd on đem apart.
Đe ʃepherdz đen retɒrnd wiđ joi,
  and prezd đer God abɒv,
for ɷl đat đe had herd and sin
  ov Hiz redimiŋ lɒv.

SEKΣON 11.

Krįst prezénted in đe Tempel.—
Luk 2. 21-24.

Hwen et dez ɵld, đe Hɵli Ȼįld
  (az Juiʃ lɷ did klem)
woz serkɒmsįzd; and, az fɵrtɵld,
  sɵ JIZUS woz hiz nem.
Hiz mɒđer đen prezénted him
  ɒntu đe God ov heven,
(for Skriptɥr seţ, "Ꞓç ferstborn sɒn
  ʃal tu đe Lord bį given;")
and oferd ɒp a sakrifįz
  wiđin đe Tempel fer,
tú pijonz, or, tú tɒrtel dɒvz,
  and meni a fervent prer.

SEKΣON 12.

Simion and Ana in đe Tempel.—
Luk 2. 25-40.

At đát tįm in Jerusalem
  dwelt Simion, hɵli man,
hu weted for Mesįa'z de,
  and đɒs đe promis ran:—
God'z spirit rested on him, and
  tu him it woz revild
đat hi ʃud si đe Krįst ov God
  er deţ hiz įz had sild.
Led bį đe spirit ov God, hi went
  intu đe Tempel grand,
hwen Jizɒs' perents brɷt đe ȼįld,
  tu kip đe lɷ'z komand,
hi tuk đe Beb ɒp in hiz armz,
  and blesed God and sed,
"Lord, let đį servant nɤ depart
  (az đɤ hast promised,)

In peace, for now, behold, mine eyes
  Thy great salvation see,
Which thou hast here prepared for all
  Who put their trust in thee.
Unto the Gentiles a great light
  To chase away their gloom,
And of thy people Israel
  The glory to become."
Joseph and Mary wondered much
  To hear the words which broke
From Simeon's lips. Them, too, he
  And unto Mary spoke, [blest,
And said, "Behold, this child is set to
  The fall and rise again [be
Of many in Israel, and a sign
  To all the sons of men;
By him the thoughts of every heart
  Shall be revealed to all,
And through thy soul shall pierce a
  At that which shall befall. [dart

A prophetess was also there,
  Of Asher's fruitful tribe;
A widow she, and Anna called,
  Her husband long had died;
Both day and night she served her
  In all his holy ways. [God,
And she that instant coming in,
  Joined in the hallowed praise.
Thanks to the Lord she gave, and
  Of Jesus Christ to them, [spoke
Who for his great redemption looked
  Within Jerusalem.

in pis, for nɤ, behɵld, mįn įz
  đį gret salveʃon si,
hwiç đɤ hast hir preperd for ɷl
  hɯ put đer trɒst in đi.
Untu đe Jentįlz a gret lįt
  tu çes awe đer glum,
and ov đį pipel Izrael
  đe glɵri tu bekɒm."
Jɵzef and Meri wɒnderd mɒç
  tu hir đe wɒrdz hwiç brɵk
from Simion'z lips. Đem, tɯ, hi
  and ɒntu Meri spɵk, [blest,
and sed, "Behɵld, đis çįld iz set tu
  đe fɷl and rįz agen [bi
ov meni in Izrael, and a sįn
  tu ɷl đe sɒnz ov men;
bį him đe ŧɷts ov everi hart
  ʃal bi revild tu ɷl,
and ŧrɯ đį sɵl ʃal pirs a dart
  at đát hwiç ʃal befɷl.

A profetes woz ɷlsɵ đer,
  ov Aʃer'z frɯtful trįb;
a widɵ ʃi, and Ana kɷld,
  her hɒzband loŋ had dįd;
bɵŧ de and nįt ʃi servd her God,
  in ɷl hiz hɵli wez.
And ʃi đát instant kɒmiŋ in,
  joind in đe halɵd prez.
Ŧaŋks tu đe Lord ʃi gev, and spɵk
  ov Jizɒs Krįst tu đem,
hɯ for hiz gret redemʃon lukt
  wiđin Jerɯsalem.

SECTION 13.

The Offering of the Magi.—
Maŧų 2. 1-12.

When Jesus was in Bethlehem born,
  In Judah's sunny land,
There came wise men to worship him;
  (They were a holy band
Of Eastern sages, Magi called,
  Who traveled from afar;)
"Where is the Jewish King?" they
  "For we have seen his star." [said,
When Herod heard, he was alarmed,
  All Salem was dismayed,
The Jewish priests and scribes were
  And unto them he said, [called,

SEKΣON 13.

Đe Oferiŋ ov đe Mejį.—
Maŧų 2. 1-12.

Hwen Jizɒs woz in Beŧlehem born,
  in Jɯda'z sɒni land,
đer kem wįz men tu wɒrʃip him;
  (đe wer a hɵli band
ov Ɩstern sejez, Mejį kɷld,
  hɯ traveld from afar;)
"Hwer iz đe Jɯiʃ Kiŋ?" đe sed,
  "for wi hav sin hiz star."
Hwen Herod herd, hi woz alarmd,
  ɷl Selem woz dismed,
đe Jɯiʃ prists and skrįbz wer kɷld,
  and ɒntu đem hi sed,

"Whence shall your great Messiah
come?"
"From Bethlehem," they replied,
"For so the prophet has foretold,
It cannot be denied,
'Thou Bethlehem art not the least
'Mongst Judah's princely band,
A Governor shall come from thee,
And rule o'er Israel's land.'"
Then secretly did Herod call
The Magi, and inquired
What time the star to them appeared,
Which their devotion fired.
To Bethlehem them he sent, and said,
"Go, search the young child out,
And bring me word, that I may come
And worship, and not doubt."
They heard the King, and went away,
And lo! the star of morn
Moved on, and rested o'er the spot
Where Jesus Christ was born.
And when they saw the meteor bright,
Their hearts were filled with joy,
And soon within the house they knelt
Before the Wondrous Boy.
They saw the child and Mary too,
And worshiped him their Lord,
And offered gold and frankincense,
And myrrh, their treasure stored.
Being warned by God in heavenly
Before the dawning day, [dream,
They went not back to Herod, but
Went home another way.

SECTION 14.

The Flight into Egypt.—
Mađų 2. 13-15.

And when the wise men forth had
Behold! God's angel came [sped
To Joseph in a dream by night,
And called him by his name,
And said, "Arise, and take the child,
And with his mother flee
To Egypt, and remain there till
I shall return to thee.
For Herod, in his jealous hate,
The child will seek to slay."
Joseph obeyed, and journeyed forth
By night, without delay.

"Hwens ſal
kɒm?"
"From Beđli
"for sɵ đe prof
it kanot bi d
'Đɛ Beđlihem
'mɒŋst Juda
a Gɒverner ſal
and ruul ɵ'r I
Đen sikretli dic
đe Mɛjį, and
hwot tįm đe sta
hwiç đɛr dev
Tu Beđlihem đɛ
"Gɵ, serç đe
and briŋ mi wɪ
and wɒrſip, a
Đɛ herd đe Kiŋ
and lɵ! đe s
mɯvd on, and
hwɛr Jizɒs I
And hwen đɛ s
đɛr harts wɛr
and sɯn widin
befɵr đe Wɒ
Đɛ sɷ đe çįld a
and wɒrſipt l
and oferd gɵld
and mɛr, đɛr
Bįiŋ wornd bį G
befɵr đe dɷn
đɛ went not bal
went hɵm an

SEK

Đe Flįt
Mađų

And hwen đe
behɵld! God
tu Jɵzef in a d
and kɷld hin
and sed, "Arįz,
and wiđ hiz
tu Ɩjipt, and re
į ſal retɒrn t
For Herod, in l
đe çįld wil si
Jɵzef obɛd, and
bį nįt, widɒt

Mother and child with him remained
  In Egypt till the hour
When Herod's death removed all fear
  Of danger from his power.
Thus was fulfilled the prophet's word,
  Given by the Lord's decree,
" From Egypt have I called my son,"
  As written in Osee.

SECTION 15.

Slaughter of the Children at Bethlehem.—
Maɟų 2. 16-18.

When Herod saw that he was mocked,
  His breast was filled with rage,
And he decreed all babes to kill
  Within two years' full age,
In Bethlehem and all around,
  According to the time
Which he had from the sages learned :
  Such was his horrid crime.
Thus had the Scripture once foretold
  By Jeremy the seer,
"A voice in Rama loud was heard
  Of weeping and great fear,
Rachel her babes lamenting sore,
  No comfort could obtain,
Because her children are no more,
  Her eyes had seen them slain."

SECTION 16.

Joseph Returns from Egypt.—
Matthew 2. 19-23. Luke 2. 40.

Herod now dead, again by night
  The angel of the Lord
Appeared to Joseph in a dream,
  And spoke with sweet accord,
And said, " Arise, the young child [take,
  And with his mother go
To Israel's land, for he is dead
  Who was the infant's foe."
So he departed, and he came
  Unto his native land;
But when he heard that Herod's son
  Ruled with his father's hand,
He feared Judea's hostile coast,
  And, by God's warning cheered,
He turned aside to Galilee,
  To Nazareth endeared.

Mɒđer and ɋịld wiđ him remɛnd
  in Ꞓjipt til đe ɜr
hwen Herod'z deɟ remuɯvd ɷl fir
  ov denjer from hiz pɜer.
Ɖɒs woz fulfild đe profet's wɒrd,
  given bị đe Lord'z dekri,
" From Ꞓjipt hav ị kɷld mị sɒn,"
  az riten in Ɵsi.

SEKΣON 15.

Slɷter ov đe Ɋildren at Beɵlehem.—
Maɟų 2. 16-18.

Hwen Herod sɷ đat hi woz mokt,
  hiz brest woz fild wiđ rɛj,
and hi dekrid ɷl bɛbz tu kil
  wiđin túu yirz' ful ɛj,
in Beɟlihem and ɷl arɜnd,
  akordiŋ tu đe tịm
hwiɋ hi had from đe sɛjez lernd :
  sɒɋ woz hiz horid krịm.
Ɖɒs had đe Skriptųr wɒns fɵrtɵld
  bị Jeremi đe sier,
"A vois in Rɛma lɜd woz herd
  ov wipiŋ and grɛt fir,
Rɛɋel her bɛbz lamentiŋ sɵr,
  nɵ kɒmfort kud obtɛn,
bekɷz her ɋildren ar nɵ mɵr,
  her ịz had sin đem slɛn."

SEKΣON 16.

Jɵzef Retɒrnz from Ꞓjipt.—
Maɟų 2. 19-23. Luuk 2. 40.

Herod nɜ ded, agen bị nịt
  đe ɛnjel ov đe Lord
apird tu Jɵzef in a drim,
  and spɵk wiđ swit akord,
and sed, "Arịz, đe yɒŋ ɋịld tɛk,
  and wiđ hiz mɒđer gɵ
tu Izrael'z land, for hi iz ded
  huɯ woz đe infant's fɵ."
Sɵ hi departed, and hi kɛm
  ɒntu hiz netiv land;
bɒt hwen hi herd đat Herod'z sɒn
  ruɯld wiđ hiz fɛđer'z hand,
hi fird Juɯdia'z hostil kɵst,
  and, bị God'z worniŋ ɋird,
hi tɒrnd asịd tu Galili,
  tu Nazareɟ endird.

Thus was again fulfilled the word
  Which had been long foretold,
" He shall be called a Nazarene,"
  Like Samuel of old.
And there the holy Jesus grew,
  God's grace was on him poured;
Strong in the Spirit he became,
  And was with wisdom stored.

SECTION 17.

History of Christ at the age of twelve years.
—Luke 2. 41-52.

Unto Jerusalem each year
  Chrịst's pious parents went,
To sacrifice unto the Lord,
  And offerings to present.
And, as the Jewish law ordained,
  When twelve years old was he,
With them unto Jerusalem
  He went in company.
And when those festive days were o'er,
  And the full time was come,
They turned to journey back again
  To Nazareth their home.
But Jesus lingered there awhile,
  Nor did his parents know;
And when they missed him they supposed
  With kinsfolk he would go.
But when, after a whole day's walk,
  Their son they could not find,
Back to Jerusalem they turned,
  Seeking with anxious mind.
And on the third day as they stood
  Within the holy place,
They saw him in the doctors' midst,
  Beaming with heavenly grace.
And while he asked, and answered too,
  Amazed were all who heard;
And wondered, as they marked his youth,
  The wisdom of his word.
His parents marveled too; then spoke
  His mother tenderly,
" Son, wherefore didst thou tarry here?
  Mournful we sought for thee."
" Why have ye sought me?" he replied,
  " Did ye not know my aim?

Ɑɒs woz agen fulfild đe wɒrd
  hwiç had bịn loŋ fɵrtɵld,
" Hị ʃal bị kɷld a Nazarin,"
  lịk Samyel ov ɵld.
And đer đe hɵli Jizɒs grɯ,
  God'z gres woz on him pɵrd;
stroŋ in đe Spirit hị bekem,
  and woz wiđ wizdom stɵrd.

SEKΣON 17.

Histori ov Krịst at đe ɛj ov twelv yirz.
Lɯk 2. 41-52.

Ɯntu Jerɯsalem ịç yịr
  Krịst's pịɒs perents went,
tu sakrifịz ɒntu đe Lord,
  and oferiŋz tu prezént.
And, az đe Jɯiʃ lɷ ordend,
  hwen twelv yirz ɵld woz hị,
wiđ đem ɒntu Jerɯsalem
  hị went in kɒmpani.
And hwen đɵz festiv dez wer ɵ'r,
  and đe ful tịm woz kɒm,
đɛ tɒrnd tu jɒrni bak agen
  tu Nazareɟ đer hɵm.
Bɒt Jizɒs liŋgerd đer ahwịl,
  nor did hiz perents nɵ́;
and hwen đɛ mist him đɛ sɒpɵzd
  wiđ kinzfɵk hị wud gɵ.
Bɒt hwen, after a hɵl de'z wɷk,
  đer sɒn đɛ kud not fịnd,
bak tu Jerɯsalem đɛ tɒrnd,
  sikiŋ wiđ aŋkʃɒs mịnd.
And on đe ɟerd de az đɛ stud
  wiđin đe hɵli ples,
đɛ sɷ him in đe doktorz' midst,
  bịmiŋ wiđ hevenli gres.
And hwịl hị askt, and anserd tɯ,
  amɛzd wer ɷl hɯ herd;
and wɒnderd, az đɛ markt hiz yɟ,
  đe wizdom ov hiz wɒrd.
Hiz perents marveld tɯ; đen spɵk
  hiz mɒđer tenderli,
" Sɒn, hwerfɵr didst đɤ tari hịr?
  mɵrnful wị sɷt for đị."
" Hwị hav yị sɷt mị?" hị replịd
  " did yị not nɵ́ mị ɛm?

Within my Father's house to teach,
  This is my highest claim."
These words divine, with awe they
    heard,
  Nor knew their mystic part,
But still his mother pondered well,
  And hid them in her heart.
Then back to Nazareth he went,
  That humble life to prove;
Though heaven-born, he obeyed their
  And gave them filial love. [rule,
As Jesus more in stature grew,
  And wisdom all divine,
So o'er him still, from God and men,
  Did gracious favor shine.

SECTION 18.

Commencement of the Ministry of John the Baptist.—Matthew 3. 1-12. Mark 1. 2-8. Luke 3. 1-18.

When Cæsar, called Tiberius,
  Full fourteen years had reigned,
And Pontius Pilate, under him,
  Judæa had obtained,
When Annas and Caiaphas
  Were high priests of the land,
(Their family a long time held
  The priesthood in their hand,)
The word of God was then revealed
  To Zacharias' son
Named John the Baptist, who had
  Amid the desert lone. [dwelt
He was a prophet of the Lord,
  And more to be revered
Than all the prophets who had lived
  Before the Lord appeared.
Fearless of men, his mission was
  To preach and to baptise
In Judah's desert, and the land
  That near the Jordan lies.
Clothed with the power of truth, he
    preached,
  "Repent, and be forgiven;
For soon shall be revealed to all
  The grace and peace of heaven."
For this is he, of whom 'twas said,
  "My Messenger I send
Before thy face, who shall prepare
  The way that thou shalt wend."

wiđin mį Fɛđer'z hɤs tu tiç,
  đis iz mį hįest klem."
Điz wɒrdz divįn, wiđ ω đɛ
    herd,
  nor nų đer mistik part,
bɒt stil hiz mɒđer ponderd wel,
  and hid đem in her hart.
Đen bak tu Nazareŧ hi went,
  đát hɒmbel lįf tu pruv;
đɵ heven-born, hi ɵbed đer rul,
  and gev đem filial lɒv.
Az Jizɒs mɵr in statųr grɯ,
  and wizdom ωl divįn,
sɵ ɵ'r him stil, from God and men,
  did greʃɒs fevor ʃįn.

SEKΣON 18.

Komensment ov đe Ministri ov Jon đe Baptist.—Maŧų 3. 1-12. Mark 1. 2-8. Lɯk 3. 1-18.

Hwen Sizar, kωld Tįbiriɒs,
  ful fɵrtin yirz had rɛnd,
and Ponʃɒs Pįlɛt, ɒnder him,
  Jɯdia had obtɛnd,
hwen Anas and Kajafas
  wer hį prists ov đe land,
(đɛr famili a loŋ tįm held
  đe pristhud in đɛr hand,)
đe wɒrd ov God woz đen revild
  tu Zakarįas' sɒn,
nemd Jon đe Baptist, hɯ had dwelt
  amid đe dezert lɵn.
Hi woz a profet ov đe Lord,
  and mɵr tu bi revird
đan ωl đe profets hɯ had livd
  befɵr đe Lord apird.
Firles ov men, hiz miʃon woz
  tu priç and tu baptįz
in Jɯda'z dezert, and đe land
  đat nir đe Jordan lįz.
Klɵđd wiđ đe pɤer ov trɯŧ, hi
    priçt,
  "Repent, and bi forgiven;
for sɯn ʃal bi revild tu ωl
  đe gres and pis ov heven."
For đis iz hi, ov hɯm 'twoz sed,
  "Mį Mesenjer į send
befɵr đį fes, hɯ ʃal preper
  đe we đat đɤ ʃalt wend."

Isaiah wrote, "The voice of one
  That in the desert cries,
Prepare Jehovah's way, make straight
  The path of the All-wise.
Each peaceful, fertile valley now
  Exalted high shall be;
And every mountain, and each hill,
  Sink in humility.
The crooked paths shall straight become,
  Rough places, ease afford,
And speedily shall all flesh see
  The glory of the Lord."
This John in camel's hair was clad,
  With leathern girdle braced;
His food was locust berries dry,
  And honey wild to taste.
From Judah and Jerusalem,
  And Jordan's region too,
Went forth vast multitudes to him,
  To ask what they should do.
And when they had confessed their sins,
  They stood in Jordan's flood
And were baptised,—a sign that they
  Were consecrate to God.

The Preaching of John.

And when John saw the Pharisees
  Of hypocritic mind,
And Sadducees, so sceptical,
  To listen, were inclined,
He said, "O race of vipers, who
  Hath warned you thus to flee
The wrath to come? If ye indeed
  Seek now the truth from me,
Deceive no longer, but bring forth
  True fruits of penitence,
And do not think within your hearts
  That you escape offence
Because from holy Abraham
  Your origin you drew,
For God can make the very stones
  As privileged as you.
Already is the axe of truth
  Laid close against the root
Of every tree, to hew it down,
  That brings not forth good fruit;
It shall be felled, and in the fire
  Of judgement shall be cast."
And when the guilty people heard
  These words, they stood aghast,

Ɨzaia rɵt, "Đe vois ov wɒn
  đat in đe dezert krįz,
prepɛr Jehɵva'z wɛ, mɛk strɛt
  đe pɐʇ ov đe ɷl-wįz:
Ɩç pisful, fertil vali nɜ
  ekzɷlted hį ʃal bi;
and everi mɜnten, and ɩç hil,
  siŋk in hɥmiliti.
Đe kruked pɐđz ʃal strɛt bekɒm,
  rɒf plesez, ɩz afɵrd,
and spɩdili ʃal ɷl fleʃ si
  đe glɵri ov đe Lord."
Đis Jon in kamel'z hɛr woz klad,
  wiđ leđern gerdel brɛst;
hiz fɯd woz lɵkɒst beriz drį,
  and hɒni wįld tu tɛst.
From Jɯda and Jerɯsalem,
  and Jordan'z rijon tɯ,
went fɵrʇ vast mɒltitɥdz tu him,
  tu ask hwot đɛ ʃud dɯ.
And hwen đɛ had konfest đɛr sinz,
  đɛ stud in Jordan'z flɒd
and wer baptįzd,—a sįn đat đɛ
  wer konsekrɛt tu God.

Đe Prigiŋ ov Jon.

And hwen Jon sɷ đe Farisɩz
  ov hipokritik mįnd,
and Sadɥsɩz, sɵ skeptikal,
  tu lisen, wer inklįnd,
hi sed, "Ɵ rɛs ov vįperz, hɯ
  haʇ wornd ɥ đɒs tu fli
đe rɐʇ tu kɒm? If yɩ indid
  sɩk nɜ đe trɯʇ from mi,
desɩv nɵ loŋger, bɒt briŋ fɵrʇ
  trɯ frɯts ov penitens,
and dɯ not ʇiŋk wiđin ɥr harts
  đat ɥ eskɛp ofens
bekɷz from hɵli Ɛbraham
  ɥr orijin ɥ drɯ,
for God kan mɛk đe veri stɵnz
  az privilejd az ɥ.
ɷlredi iz đe aks ov trɯʇ
  lɛd klɵs agenst đe rɯt
ov everi trɩ, tu hɥ it dɜn,
  đat briŋz not fɵrʇ gud frɯt;
it ʃal bi feld, and in đe fįr
  ov jɒjment ʃal bi kast."
And hwen đe gilti pipel herd
  điz wɒrdz, đɛ stud agást,

And, trembling, asked what they should do,
To escape the wrath to come?
He said, "True works of charity
May yet avert your doom.
Give food and raiment to the poor,
Commiserate distress."
Then publicans, or taxers, came,
And did for counsel press.
And unto them the prophet said,
"Be strictly just and true,
Exact no more from any man
Than is appointed you."
Then came the soldiers to inquire
How they might shun offence.
He said, "Avoid, with constant care,
All wrong and violence;
Accuse not any wrongfully;
Be gentle, and content
With honest wages, which should be
Fairly obtained and spent."
And while men mused concerning John,
And questioned in their heart
Whether he were the Christ or not,
So great his prophet art,
John answered them, and said, his work
Was but preparative
To that of Christ, who unto men
Would full salvation give.
"For me," said John, "my mission is,
As I have said before,
That men repent of all their sins,
And deeply them deplore.
But after me there cometh one,—
Messiah, Christ, the Lord,
Far mightier than I, is he;
And this I here record,
That I, his Messenger, am not
found worthy e'en to bear
The sandals of his God-like feet,
Far less with him compare.
He shall baptise with holy love,
Of all good things the best:
His Holy Spirit, heavenly fire,
On his baptised shall rest.
The fan of judgment terrible
Is held in his right hand,
To purify his threshingfloor,
This earth whereon we stand.

and, trembliŋ, askt hwot ƌɛ ʃud dɯ,
tu eskep ƌe rɛɟ tu kɒm?
Hi sed, "Trɯ wɒrks ov ɕariti
mɛ yet avért ɥr dɯm.
Giv fɯd and rement tu ƌe pɯr,
komizeret distres."
Ƌen pɒblikanz, or takserz, kem
and did for kȣnsel pres.
And ɒntu ƌem ƌe profet sed,
"Bi striktli jɒst and trɯ,
ekzakt nɵ mɵr from eni man
ƌan iz apointed ɥ."
Ƌen kem ƌe sɵldierz tu inkwįr
hȣ ƌe mįt ʃɒn ofens.
Hi sed, "Avoid, wiƌ konstant kɛr,
ɷl roŋ and vįolens;
akɥz not eni roŋfuli;
bi jentel, and kontent
wiƌ onest wejez, hwiɕ ʃud bi
ferli obtend and spent."
And hwįl men mɥzd konserniŋ Jon,
and kwestiond in ƌer hart
hweƌer hi wer ƌe Krįst or not,
sɵ gret hiz profet art,
Jon anserd ƌem, and sed, hiz wɒrk
woz bɒt preparativ
tu ƌát ov Krįst, hɯ ɒntu men
wud ful salveʃon giv.
"For mi," sed Jon, "mį miʃon iz,
az į hav sed befɵr,
ƌat men repent ov ɷl ƌer sinz,
and dipli ƌem deplɵr.
Bɒt after mi ƌer kɒmeɟ wɒn,—
Mesįa, Krįst, ƌe Lord,
far mįtier ƌan į, iz hi;
and ƌis į hir rekord,
ƌat į, hiz Mesenjer, am not
fȣnd wɒrƌi i'n tu ber
ƌe sandalz ov hiz God-lįk fit,
far les wiƌ him komper.
Hi ʃal baptįz wiƌ hɵli lɒv,
ov ɷl gud ɟiŋz ƌe best:
hiz Hɵli Spirit, hevenli fįr,
on hiz baptįzd ʃal rest.
Ƌe fan ov jɒjment teribel
iz held in hiz rįt hand,
tu pɥrifį hiz ɟreʃiŋflɵr,
ƌis erɟ hweron wi stand.

3, 4, 5 *

True men, like wheat, he will collect
  Within his garner, heaven;
But the false-hearted shall, like chaff,
  To hell's fierce fires be driven."
And many other things did John,
  Throughout his exhortation,
Preach to the people of that land,
  And all the Jewish nation.

SECTION 19.

The Baptism of Christ.—Matthew 3. 13-17. Mark 1. 9-11. Luke 3. 21-23.

When all the people were baptised,
  Jesus from Galilee
To Jordan came, and said to John,
  "I'd be baptised of thee."
But John forbad him, saying, "I
  Have need to be baptised
Of thee, and comest thou to me?"
  (So much was he surprised.)
But Jesus said, "Permit it now,
  For thus we must fulfil
All righteousness of God on earth."
  Then John performed his will.
Jesus, with prayer, now consecrates
  The Jordan by this rite,
And when he was baptised, behold!
  John saw a wondrous sight;
The heavens above were opened, and
  A dove-like form was seen:
God's spirit, in descending thus
  Diffused a joy serene.
And lo! a heavenly voice was heard,
  "See! My beloved son
In whom I am well pleased." Thus [was
  Christ's ministry begun,
When of his human, suffering life
  Full thirty years had run.

SECTION 20.

Temptation of Christ.—Matthew 4. 1-11. Mark 1. 12, 13. Luke 4. 1-13.

Full of the holy spirit now,
  Jesus from Jordan turns,
And seeks Judæa's wilderness:
  For solitude he yearns.

Trɯ men, lįk hwit, hi wil kolékt
  wiđin hiz garner, heven;
bɒt đe fɷls-harted ʃal, lįk çaf,
  tu hel'z fįrs fįrz bi driven."
And meni ɒđer ɟiŋz did Jon,
  ɟrɯȣt hiz eksorteʃon,
priç tu đe pipel ov đát land,
  and ɷl đe Jɯiʃ neʃon.

SEKΣON 19.

Đe Baptizm ov Krįst.—Maɟɥ 3. 13-17. Mark 1. 9-11. Lɯk 3. 21-23.

Hwen ɷl đe pipel wer baptįzd,
  Jizɒs from Galili
tu Jordan kem, and sed tu Jon,
  "Ɨ'd bi baptįzd ov đi."
Bɒt Jon forbad him, sɛiŋ, "Ɨ
  hav nid tu bi baptįzd
ov đi, and kɒmest đȣ tu mi?"
  (Sɵ mɒç woz hi sɒrprįzd.)
Bɒt Jizɒs sed, "Permit it nȣ,
  for đɒs wi mɒst fulfil
ɷl rįtiɒsnes ov God on erɟ."
  Đen Jon performd hiz wíl.
Jizɒs, wiđ prer nȣ konsekrets
  đe Jordan bį đis rįt,
and hwen hi woz baptįzd, behɵld!
  Jon sɷ a wɒndrɒs sįt;
đe hevenz abɒv wer ɵpend, and
  a dɒv-lįk form woz sin:
God'z spirit, in desendiŋ đɒs
  difɥzd a joi serin.
And lɵ! a hevenli vois woz herd,
  "Si! Mį belɒved sɒn
in hɯm į am wel plizd." Đɒs woz
  Krįst's ministri begɒn,
hwen ov hiz hɥman, sɒferiŋ lįf
  ful ɟerti yirz had rɒn.

SEKΣON 20.

Tempteʃon ov Krįst.—Maɟɥ 4. 1-11. Mark 1. 12, 13. Luke 4. 1-13.

Ful ov đe hɵli spirit nȣ,
  Jizɒs from Jordan tɒrnz,
and siks Jɯdia'z wildernes:
  for solitɥd hi yernz.

For forty fearful days and nights
  He fasted. Those days o'er
He hungered for the food which should
  His wasted powers restore.
The Devil then, that tempter old,
  With hellish cunning, said,
"If thou be, sooth, the son of God,
  Let these stones turn to bread."
Jesus replied, "'Tis written, Man
  Lives not by bread alone,
But by each word and thing whereby
  The will of God is known."
Then to the holy city did
  The devil take our Lord,
And on the temple's pinnacle
  Placed him, and spoke this word:
"If thou be, sooth, the son of God,
  Cast thyself down from hence;
For it is written, He shall make
  His angels thy defence:
They, in their hands, shall bear thee
  Spread o'er thy life a charm, [up,
Lest thou against a stone shouldst dash
  Thy foot, and come to harm."
But Jesus, wiser in God's Word,
  Answers, "'Tis also writ,
Thou shalt not tempt the Lord thy
  Presumption is not fit. [God:"
Again the devil taketh him
  Up to a mountain high,
And makes the whole world's kingdoms
  In glory 'neath his eye, [pass
And said, "This power I'll give to
  And all the glory too, [thee,
If thou wilt own and worship me,
  And my commands wilt do."
Jesus now answers, "Satan, go;
  Get from my presence hence;
'Tis written, Worship God alone,
  He claims all reverence."
When Satan had in vain essayed
  To tempt the Lord to sin,
He left him for a season, fled,
  And joined hell's horrid din.
Thus by the power of Truth Divine
  Did Jesus victory win.
And now wild beasts keep company
  With him; but lo! from heaven
Bright angels to him ministered:
  Such joy to them is given.

For forti fįrful dez and nįts
  hi fasted. Điz dez ɵ'r
hi hɒŋgerd for đe fɯd hwiç ʃud
  hiz wested pɤerz restɵr.
Đe Devil đen, đát tempter ɵld,
  wiđ helıʃ kɒniŋ, sed,
"if đɤ bi, sɯŧ, đe sɒn ov God,
  let điz stɵnz tɒrn tu bred."
Jizɒs replįd, "'Tiz riten, Man
  livz not bį bred alɵn,
bɒt bį iç wɒrd and ŧiŋ hwɛrbį
  đe wíl ov God iz nɵn."
Đen tu đe hɵli siti did
  đe devil tɛk ɤr Lord,
and on đe tempel'z pinakel
  plest him, and spɵk đis wɒrd:
"If đɤ bi, sɯŧ, đe sɒn ov God,
  kast đįself dɤn from hens;
for it iz riten, Hi ʃal mek
  Hiz ɛnjelz đį defens:
đɛ, in đer handz, ʃal ber đi ɒp,
  spred ɵ'r đį lįf a çarm,
lest đɤ agenst a stɵn ʃudst daʃ
  đį fut, and kɒm tu harm."
Bɒt Jizɒs, wįzer in God'z Wɒrd,
  anserz, "'Tiz ɷlsɵ rit,
đɤ ʃalt not tempt đe Lord đį God:"
  prezɒmʃon iz not fit.
Agen đe devel tɛkeŧ him
  ɒp tu a mɤnten hį,
and mɛks đe hɵl wɒrld'z kiŋdomz
  in glɵri 'niđ hiz į, [pas
and sed, "Đis pɤer į'l giv tu đi,
  and ɷl đe glɵri tɯ,
if đɤ wilt ɵn and wɒrʃip mi,
  and mį komandz wilt dɯ."
Jizɒs nɤ anserz, "Setan, gɵ;
  get from mį prezens hens;
'tiz riten, Wɒrʃip God alɵn,
  hi klemz ɷl reverens."
Hwen Setan had in ven esed
  tu tempt đe Lord tu sin,
hi left him for a sizon, fled,
  and joind hel'z horid din,
đɒs bį đe pɤer ov Trɯŧ Divįn
  did Jizɒs viktori win.
And nɤ wįld bists kip kɒmpani
  wiđ him; bɒt lɵ! from heven
brįt ɛnjelz tu him ministerd:
  sɒç joi tu đem iz given.

SECTION 21.

Further testimony of John the Baptist.
—John 1. 19-34.

This is the record given by John
  The Baptist and the seer,
When from Jerusalem the priests
  And Levites came to hear.
They asked, "Who art thou?" He confessed
  "I'm not the Christ." "What then?
Elias?" "No." "That prophet?" "No."
  "Then, of the sons of men
Who art thou? Say, that we may give
  An answer unto them
That sent us. What say'st thou? Do not
  Our plain request contemn."
He said, "I am the voice of one
  That in the desert cries,
Prepare Jehovah's way; make straight
  The path of the All-wise,
As saith the prophet of the Lord:
  Do not his word despise."
"With water I baptise," said John,
  "But one among you stands
Whom though you know him not; you soon
  Shall hear his wide commands.
Although he cometh after me,
  Him must all men prefer,
For he before me was of old,
  I am his Harbinger."
The next day John saw Jesus come,
  And said, without delay,
"Behold the Lamb of God which takes
  The whole world's sin away.
For this is he of whom I spake,
  Who coming after me,
Before me is to be preferred
  Through all eternity.
Whom I knew not: but that he should
  Be manifest to all,
I come baptising those who low
  Before his footstool fall."
And John bear record, saying thus,
  "I saw the Spirit come
From heaven like a dove, and rest
  Upon him as its home.
I knew him not, but he that sent
  Me to baptise and preach

SEKΣON 21.

Fɒrđer testimoni ov Jon đe Baptist.
—Jon 1. 19-34.

Đis iz đe rekord given bị Jon
  đe Baptist and đe sier,
hwen from Jerɥsalem đe prists
  and Livịts kɛm tu hir.
Đɛ askt, "Hɥ art đɜ?" Hi konfest
  "Ɨ'm not đe Krịst." "Hwot đen?
Elịas?" "Nɵ." "Đát profet?" "Nɵ."
  "Đen ov đe sɒnz ov men
hɥ art đɜ? Sɛ, đat wi mɛ giv
  an anser ɒntu đem
đat sent ɒs. Hwot sɛ'st đɜ? Dɥ not
  ɜr plɛn rekwest kontem."
hi sed, "Ɨ am đe vois ov wɒn
  đat in đe dezert krịz,
preper Jehɵva'z wɛ; mɛk stret
  đe paþ ov đe Ol-wịz,
az seþ đe profet ov đe Lord:
  dɥ not hiz wɒrd despịz."
"Wiđ woter ị baptịz," sed Jon,
  "bɒt wɒn amɒŋ ɥ standz
hɥm đɵ ɥ nɵ́ him not; ɥ sɥn
  ʃal hir hiz wịd komanz.
Olđɵ hi kɒmeþ after mi,
  Him mɒst ol men prefer,
for hi befɵr mi woz ov ɵld,
  ị am hiz Harbinjer."
Đe nekst dɛ Jon so Jizɒs kɒm,
  and sed, wiđɜt delɛ,
"Behɵld đe Lam ov God hwiɕ tɛks
  đe hɵl wɒrld'z sin awɛ.
For đis iz hi ov hɥm ị spɛk,
  hɥ kɒmiŋ after mi,
befɵr mi iz tu bi preferd
  þrɥ ol eterniti.
Hɥm ị nɥ not: bɒt đat hi ʃud
  bi manifest tu ol,
ị kɒm baptịziŋ đɵz hɥ lɵ
  befɵr hiz futstɥl fol."
And Jon bɛr rekord, seiŋ đɒs,
  "Ɨ so đe Spirit kɒm
from heven lịk a dɒv, and rest
  ɒpon him az its hɵm.
Ɨ nɥ him not, bɒt hi đat sent
  mi tu baptịz and priɕ

The good news of salvation free
  To all whom it may reach,
Said thus: 'On whom the Spirit shall
  Descend, and rest upon,
The same is he that shall baptise
  With fire.' The work's begun.
I saw; bear record; and confess
  This is God's Only Son."

SECTION 22.

Christ obtains his first disciples from John.
—John 1. 35-51.

The next day after, as John stood,
  With two disciples true,
(The other John, the Evangelist,
  And Andrew, whom he knew,)
He looked at Jesus as he walked,
  And said, without delay,
"Behold the Lamb of God which takes
  The whole world's sin away."
And when the two disciples heard
  John's word, dismissing care,
They followed Jesus, for their hearts
  Were filled with faith and prayer.
Then Jesus turned, and said to them,
  "For whom do you inquire?"
They answered, "Rabbi, to know [where
  Thou dwellest, we desire."
Then said he to them, "Come and see."
  They came and saw his home,
And stayed with him that day, nor felt
  The least desire to roam.
One of the two which heard John speak
  Was Andrew, holy man,
Who soon unto his brother dear,
  Called Simon Peter, ran,
And said to him, "Lo! we have found
  Messiah, who is Christ:"
And brought his brother to the Lord,
  Of whom he him apprised.
And instantly, when Jesus saw
  Him, thus he said, "Oh! may
The son of Jonah firm be found
  In faith and truth alway:
Thy name henceforth shall Cephas be,
  Peter, that is, a stone,
Which in my Church thou shalt be- [come,
  As will in time be shown."
(Cephas in Hebrew, is in Greek,
  As Petros, Peter, known.)

đe gud nųz ov salveſon fri
  tu ɷl hɯm it me riç,
sed đɒs: 'On hɯm đe Spirit ſal
  desend, and rest ɒpon,
đe sem iz hi đat ſal bapti̧z
  wiđ fi̧r.' Đe wɒrk's begɒn.
Ɨ sɷ; ber rekord; and konfés
  đis iz God'z Ơnli Sɒn."

SEKΣON 22.

Kri̧st obtenz hiz ferst disi̧pelz from Jon.
—Jon 1. 35-51.

Đe nekst de after, az Jon stud,
  wiđ tɯ́ disi̧pelz trɯ,
(đe ɒđer Jon, đe Evanjelist,
  and Andrɯ, hɯm hi nų,)
hi lukt at Jizɒs az hi wɷkt,
  and sed, wiđɤt dele,
"Behơld đe Lam ov God hwiç teks
  đe hơl wɒrld'z sin awe."
And hwen đe tɯ́ disi̧pelz herd
  Jon'z wɒrd, dismisiŋ ker,
đe folơd Jizɒs, for đer harts
  wer fild wiđ feŧ and prer.
Đen Jizɒs tɒrnd, and sed tu đem,
  "For hɯm dɯ ų inkwi̧r?"
Đe anserd "Rabi, tu nớ hwer
  đɤ dwelest, wi dezi̧r."
Đen sed hi tu đem, "Kɒm and si."
  Đe kem and sɷ hiz hơm,
and sted wiđ him đát de, nor felt
  đe list dezi̧r tu rơm.
Wɒn ov đe tɯ́ hwiç herd Jon spik
  woz Andrų, hơli man,
hɯ sɯn ɒntu hiz brɒđer dir,
  kɷld Si̧mon Piter, ran,
and sed tu him, "Lơ! wi hav fɤnd
  Mesi̧a, hɯ iz Kri̧st:"
and brɷt hiz brɒđer tu đe Lord,
  ov hɯm hi him apri̧zd.
And instantli, hwen Jizɒs sɷ
  him, đɒs hi sed, "Ơ! me
đe sɒn ov Jơna ferm bi fɤnd
  in feŧ and trɯŧ ɷlwe:
đi̧ nem hensforŧ ſal Kefas bi,
  Piter, đát iz, a stơn,
hwiç in mi̧ Çɒrç đɤ ſalt bekɒm,
  az wil in ti̧m bi ſơn."
(Kefas in Hibrɯ, iz in Grik,
  az Petros, Piter, nơn.)

The next day Jesus forth would go
  To Galilee, to find
Philip, and saith, "Come, follow me
  With thy whole heart and mind."
Philip (who in Bethsaida lived,
  With Andrew, Peter, too,)
Inflamed with zeal for Christ, now
  Another follower true ; [sought
Nathaniel named Bartholomew,
  To whom he said, "Behold !
Him have we found who in the law
  And prophets was foretold,
Jesus of Nazareth, a man
  Whom virtue doth enfold."
Nathaniel saith, "Can any good
  From Nazareth appear?"
Philip replies, "Come thou and see,
  The Lord our God is here."
When Jesus saw Nathaniel come,
  He said to those around,
"Behold an Israelite indeed,
  In whom no guile is found."
Amazed, Nathaniel answered him,
  "How is it thou know'st me?"
Jesus replied, "Ere Philip called,
  Whilst thou wast 'neath the tree
I saw thee." Reverence deeper grows
  Within Nathaniel's breast,
"Rabbi, thou art the Son of God,
  And Israel's king confessed."
Then Jesus said, "Believest thou
  Because I said to thee
I saw thee when thou stoodst beneath
  The boughs of that fig tree?
Far greater things shalt thou behold ;
  Hereafter thou shalt see
Heaven open, and the angelic host
  Keep festal jubilee,
Ascending and descending on
  The Son of Man, on Me.

SECTION 23.

Marriage at Cana in Galilee.
—John 2. 1-11.

The third day after these events,
  There was a marriage feast,
At Cana's town in Galilee,
  And Jesus was a guest ;

Đe nekst de Jizɒs forɟ wud gɵ
  tu Galili, tu fįnd
Filip, and seɟ, "Kɒm, folɵ mi
  wiđ đį hɵl hart and mįnd."
Filip (hɯ in Beɟseda livd,
  wiđ Andrɯ, Piter, tɯ,)
inflemd wiđ zil for Krįst, nɤ sɷt
  anɒđer folɵer trɯ ;
Naɟaniel nemd Barɟolomų,
  tu hɯm hi sed, "Behɵld !
him hav wi fɤnd hɯ in đe lɷ
  and profets woz fɵrtɵld,
Jizɒs ov Nazareɟ, a man
  hɯm vertų dɒɟ enfɵld."
Naɟaniel seɟ, "Kan eni gud
  from Nazareɟ apir?"
Filip replįz, "Kɒm đɤ and si,
  đe Lord ɤr God iz hir."
Hwen Jizɒs sɷ Naɟaniel kɒm,
  hi sed tu đɵz arɤnd,
"Behɵld an Izraelįt indid,
  in hɯm nɵ gįl iz fɤnd."
Amezd, Naɟaniel anserd him,
  "Hɤ iz it đɤ nɵ'st mi?"
Jizɒs replįd, "Ɛr Filip kɷld,
  hwįlst đɤ wost 'niđ đe tri,
į sɷ đi." Reverens diper grɵz
  widin Naɟaniel'z brest,
"Rabį, đɤ art đe Sɒn ov God,
  and Izrael'z kiŋ konfest."
Đen Jizɒs sed, "Belivest đɤ
  bekɷz į sed tu đi
į sɷ đi hwen đɤ studst beniđ
  đe bɤz ov đát fig tri?
Far greter ɟiŋz ʃalt đɤ behɵld ;
  hirafter đɤ ʃalt si
heven ɵpen, and đe anjelik hɵst
  kip festal jɯbili,
asendiŋ and desendiŋ on
  đe Sɒn ov Man, on Mi.

SEKƩON 23.

Marej at Kena in Galili.
—Jon 2. 1-11.

Đe ɟerd de after điz events,
  đer woz a marej fist,
at Kena'z tɤn in Galili,
  and Jizɒs woz a gest ;

And Jesus' mother they invite,
  (Whom justly we revere,)
And his disciples too, and there
  Was wine * their hearts to cheer.
But for the numerous wedding guests
  There was too small a store,
So to the Lord his mother said,
  "Of wine they have no more."
Jesus replied, "O woman, I
  Will somewhat do for thee;
Is not mine hour e'en now arrived? †
  My glory they shall see."
Then to the servants, Mary said,
  "Whate'er he bids you, do.

And Jᴉzɒs' mɒđer đe invįt,
  (hɯm jɒstli wᴉ revᴉr,)
and hiz disįpelz tɯ, and đer
  woz wįn * đer harts tu çᴉr.
Bɒt for đe nɥmerɒs wediŋ gests
  đer woz tɯ smɷl a stɵr,
sɵ tu đe Lord hiz mɒđer sed,
  "Ov wįn đe hav nɵ mɵr."
Jᴉzɒs replįd, "Ɵ wuman, į
  wil sɒmhwot dɯ for đᴉ;
iz not mįn ɤr ᴉ'n nɤ arįvd? †
  mį glɵri đe ʃal sᴉ."
Đen tu đe servants, Meri sed,
  "Hwoter hᴉ bidz ɥ, dɯ.

---

* In my prose "Improved Monotessaron: a complete authentic Gospel Life of Christ; combining the words of the four Gospels, in a revised version, and in orderly chronological arrangement," (to be had of the publisher of this work, at 1*s.* and 2*s.*,) I have introduced the Hebrew word *yain* here, and have supported it by the following note:—

I have been compelled by the force of truth, in reference to this miracle, to adopt the Hebrew term *yain* as the proper designation of that *grape-drink*, syrup, or must, which was common in ancient Palestine. The *yain* or *yayin* of the Jews was called *hemer* or *chamara* in Syriac. This juice of grapes and other vegetables was often unfermented and uninebriative, like the *paschal yain*, which had no ferment, leaven, or alcohol. At other times it passed (either intentionally or accidentally) through the vinous-fermentation, and became alcoholic and intoxicative. So the Greek *oinos*, and the Latin *vinum*, often signify pure unfermented juices of grapes and other vegetables, and cannot always be translated by our English word *wine*, which almost universally means a fermented or alcoholic beverage. Now as the yain of the Hebrews did not correspond with the wines of Europe, it should not be translated by our word *wine*, except it passed through processes of vinous fermentation. These were often prevented by artificial means; for leaven, or ferment, among the Jews was a symbol either of alteration or corruption. It appears that Christ, like the Jews, drank yain, or the unfermented juice of grapes or raisins, at the Passover; but we have no proof that the grape-drink at the feast of Cana was alcoholic, or that alcoholic wines were ever used by Christ or his apostles. It appears therefore unfair and unscholarlike to beg the very question at issue. In such a case it is safer to adhere to the old Hebrew name *yain*, than to substitute for it the English term *wine*, which gives a wrong idea, and is liable to dangerous misconstruction. On this subject see Kitto's Biblical Cyclopædia, under the words Wine and Passover. See also Parson's learned essay, entitled Anti-Bacchus; Arnot's Illustrations of the Book of Proverbs, second series, page 154; and the critical Latin treatises on the wines of the ancients.

In this first great miracle, our Lord changed water into a miraculous beverage of great excellence, a supernatural water-wine, which cannot be adequately defined by criticism. It may perhaps indicate, among other lessons, that the water which is highly extolled in Scripture as a symbol of spirituality, regeneration, and purity, is capable, under the Divine blessing and operation, of becoming the subject and the medium of sacred efficacies and qualities above human definition or manufacture. If, however, my reader thinks that the original word is best translated by *wine*, he can restore the old rendering in the margin.

† The original phrase is idiomatic, and may be taken in a favorable sense. Our Lord's hour to work a miracle was come, as appears by the context. His mother is in this case the best interpreter of the words he addressed to her. She evidently understood them as indicating a kind and filial compliance with her request, while her own order to the servants to obey his commands showed the confidence she placed in his miraculous energy.

List; be attentive; and some sign
  May be revealed to you."
Now there were set there six stone jars,
  For divers washings meant;
Two or three firkins each would hold,
  When filled to their extent.
Then Jesus said, "With water fill;"
  That all might fully share.
Obediently, unto the brim,
  They filled the vessels there,
And at his word they poured the wine,
  And to the master bare.
The ruler knew not whence it came,
  But liked its generous taste;
Then, to the bridegroom, he exclaimed,
  In words of wondering haste,
"When at a feast men first sit down,
  The good wine is set forth,
And when the guests are satisfied,
  Then that of lesser worth;
But thou a different part hast played,
  And kept the good till now."
(With wine like this did never man
  Before a feast endow.)
This miracle, his first, did Christ
  In Cana's town display;
His glory thus revealed, increased
  His followers' faith that day.

SECTION 24.

Jesus goes to Capernaum.—John 2. 12.

After this miracle divine,
  All doubt being overcome,
The Lord for a few days went down
  Unto Capernaum,
And there his mother, brethren, and
  Disciples, found a home.

SECTION 25.

The Buyers and Sellers driven from the Temple.—John 2. 13-25.

The Jewish passover was nigh,
  And Jesus, with intent
To keep the feast, as he was wont,
  Unto Jerusalem went.
And in the sacred temple he
  Found oxen, sheep, and doves,

List; bi atentiv; and sɒm sịn
  mɛ bi revild tu ɥ."
Nɤ đer wer set đer siks stɵn jarz
  foꝛ dịverz woʃiŋz ment;
tú or ɟri ferkinz iç wud hɵld,
  hwen fild tu đɛr ekstent.
Đen Jizɒs sed, "Wiđ wɵter fil;"
  đat ɵl mịt fuli ʃɛr.
Ɵbidientli, ɒntu đe brim,
  đɛ fild đe veselz đɛr,
and at hiz wɒrd đɛ pɵrd đe wịn,
  and tu đe master bɛr.
Đe rułer nɥ not hwens it kɛm,
  bɒt lịkt its jenerɒs tɛst;
đen, tu đe brịdgrułm, hi eksklɛmd
  in wɒrdz ov wɒnderiŋ hɛst,
"Hwen at a fist men ferst sit dɤn
  đe gud wịn iz set fɵrɟ,
and hwen đe gests ar satisfịd,
  đen đát ov leser wɒrɟ;
bɒt đɤ a diferent part hast plɛd,
  and kept đe gud til nɤ."
(Wiđ wịn lịk đis did never man
  befɵr a fist endɤ.)
Đis mirakel, hiz ferst, did Krịst
  in Kɛna'z tɤn displɛ;
hiz glɵri đɒs revịld, inkrist
  hiz folɵerz' fɛɟ đát dɛ.

SEKΣON 24.

Jizɒs gɵz tu Kapernaɒm.—Jon 2. 12.

After đis mirakel divịn,
  ɵl dɤt biiŋ ɵverkɒm,
đe Lord for a fɥ dɛz went dɤn
  ɒntu Kapernaɒm,
and đɛr hiz mɒđer, bređren, and
  disịpelz, fɤnd a hɵm.

SEKΣON 25.

Đe Bịerz and Selerz driven from đe Tempel.—Jon 2. 13-25.

Đe Jułiʃ pasɵver woz nị,
  and Jizɒs, wiđ intent
tu kip đe fist, az hi woz wɒnt,
  ɒntu Jerułsalem went.
And in đe sekred tempel hi
  fɤnd oksen, ʃip, and dɒvz,

And money-changers sitting there :
  This sight his spirit moved.
A scourge of small cords he prepared,
  And quickly drove them out ;
Poured out the money ; overthrew
  The tables ; and about
Such doings in that place, he said,
  In sad and solemn wise,
"Go hence ; make not my Father's
  A house of merchandise." [house
Then his disciples called to mind
  That written Word, so sure,
"A holy zeal consumeth me,
  To keep thy temple pure."
The Jews then asked him, earnestly,
  To give a special sign
That he was the Messiah true,
  And wrought by power Divine.
And Jesus said to them, "If that
  This temple be destroyed,
In three days I will raise it up."
  The words he thus employed,
His body signified ; but they
  Imagined that he spoke
Of their great temple, and his words
  Did their contempt provoke.
When Jesus afterwards arose
  From death's mysterious gloom,
His followers remembered that
  In rising from the tomb
He proved his power, and thus fulfilled
  The things which he foretold.
Thus did his life on earth, in all
  Its acts, the Word unfold.
And while he tarried at the feast,
  Many believed in him,
And found a spiritual light
  Shine on what once was dim.
But Christ did not commit himself
  By too much trust in men,
Because he knew the treacheries
  That human hearts contain.

and mɒni-çenjerz sitiŋ đer :
  đis sịt hiz spirit mɯvd.
A skɒrj ov smɷl kordz hi preperd,
  and kwikli drɵv đem ɤt ;
pɵrd ɤt đe mɒni ; ɵverɟrɯ
  đe tɛbelz : and abɤt
sɒç dɯiŋz in đát ples, hi sed,
  in sad and solem wịz,
"Gɵ hens ; mɛk not mị Fɛđer'z
  a hɤs ov merçandịz." [hɤs
Đen hiz disịpelz kɷld tu mịnd
  đát riten Wɒrd, sɵ ʃɯr,
"A hɵli zil konsɥmeɟ mi,
  tu kip đị tempel pɥr."
Đe Jɯz đen askt him, ernestli,
  tu giv a speʃal sịn
đat hi woz đe Mesịa trɯ,
  and rɷt bị pɤer Divịn.
And Jizɒs sed tu đem, "If đat
  đis tempel bi destroid,
in ɟri dɛz ị wil rɛz it ɒp."
  Đe wɒrdz hi đɒs emploid,
hiz bodi signifịd ; bɒt đɛ
  imajind đat hi spɵk
ov đer grɛt tempel, and hiz wɒrdz
  did đɛr kontempt prɵvɵk.
Hwen Jizɒs afterwardz arɵz
  from deɟ's mistiriɒs glɯm,
hiz folɵerz rememberd đat
  in rịziŋ from đe tɯm
hi prɯvd hiz pɤer, and đɒs fulfild
  đe ɟiŋz hwiç hi fɵrtɵld.
Đɒs did hiz lịf on erɟ, in ɷl
  its akts, đe Wɒrd ɒnfɵld.
And hwịl hi tarid at đe fist,
  meni belivd in him,
and fɤnd a spiritɥal lịt
  ʃịn on hwot wɒns woz dim.
Bɒt Krịst did not komit himself
  bị tɯ mɒç trɒst in men,
bekɷz hi nɥ đe treçeriz
  đat hɥman harts konten.

SECTION 26.

Conversation of Christ with Nicodemus.—
John 3. 1-21.

There was in Israel, in those days,
  A noble Pharisee,

SEKƩON 26.

Konverseʃon ov Krịst wiđ Nikodimɒs.—
Jon 3. 1-21.

Đer woz in Izrael, in đɵz dɛz,
  a nɵbel Farisi,

Named Nicodemus, and a chief
  Among the Jews was he.
He came to Jesus all alone
  By night, and thus he said,
"Rabbi, we know that thou art come
  From God; whose grace is shed
On thee: for none such miracles
  Can do, without God's grace,
As thou hast shown in Israel
  Before God's chosen race."
Then Jesus said, "If thou wouldst learn
  A heavenly truth from me;
Thou must become regenerate,
  God's kingdom here to see."
Then Nicodemus said to him,
  "How can a man be born
When he is old? A second time
  Into the womb return?"
And Jesus answered, "Verily,
  Thou must be born again;
For without this, no peace, no heaven,
  Can e'er be given to men.
That which is born of flesh is flesh,
  And cannot higher rise;
But that which comes from spirit-birth
  To God, its author, flies.
For only what is spirit-born
  Can spiritual prove;
No carnal power can e'er produce
  The holiness I love:
Then marvel not that I enforce
  The new birth from above.
The wind may blow, but none can tell
  Its origin or end;
Thou hearest but the sound, where'er
  Its viewless wavelets tend:
So is it with God's spirit: for
  All spirit-influence
Is a great mystery, undiscerned
  By eyes of mortal sense.
Only to faith and inward prayer
  That mystery is revealed;
To sensual minds, pride, sophistry,
  It stands for ever sealed."
Then Nicodemus said to him,
  "Who can these mysteries see?"
And Jesus answering, said to him,
  "Canst thou a teacher be
In Israel's land, and knowest not
  Those truths of low degree?

nemd Nikodimɒs, and a ɕif
  amɒŋ đe Jɯz woz hi.
Hi kem tu Jizɒs ɷl alơn
  bįlnįt, and đɒs hi sed,
"Rabį, wi nó đat đȣ art kɒm
  from God, hɯz gres iz ʃed
on đi: for nɒn sɒɕ mirakelz
  kan dɯ, widȣt God'z gres,
az đȣ hast ʃơn in Izrael
  befơr God'z ɕơzen res."
Đen Jizɒs sed, "If đȣ wudst lern
  a hevenli trɯɟ from mi;
đȣ mɒst bekɒm rejeneret,
  God'z kiŋdom hir tu si."
Đen Nikodimɒs sed tu him,
  "Hȣ kan a man bi born
hwen hi iz ơld? A sekond tįm
  intu đe wɯm retɒrn?"
And Jizɒs anserd, "Verili,
  đȣ mɒst bi born agen;
for widȣt đis, nơ pis, nơ heven,
  kan er bi given tu men.
Đát hwiɕ iz born ov fleʃ iz fleʃ,
  and kanot hįer rįz:
bɒt đát hwiɕ kɒmz from spirit-berɟ
  tu God, its ɷɟor, flįz.
For ơnli hwot iz spirit-born
  kan spiritųal prɯv;
nơ karnal pȣer kan er prơdųs
  đe hơlines į lɒv:
đen marvel not đat į enfơrs
  đe nų berɟ from abɒv.
Đe wind me blơ, bɒt nɒn kan tel
  its orijin or end;
đȣ hirest bɒt đe sȣnd, hwerer
  its vųles wevlets tend:
sơ iz it wiđ God'z spirit: for
  ɷl spirit-influens
iz a gret misteri, ɒndisernd
  bį įz ov mortal sens.
Ơnli tu feɟ and inward prer
  đát misteri iz revįld;
tu senʃual mįndz, prįd, sofistri,
  it standz for ever sild."
Đen Nikodimɒs sed tu him,
  "Hɯ kan điz misteriz si?"
And Jizɒs anseriŋ, sed tu him,
  "Kanst đȣ a tiɕer bi
in Izrael'z land, and nơest not
  điz trɯđz ov lơ degri?

I, the Redeemer of the world,
 Speak what I know; for I
Have seen these things in heaven, and
 I come to testify. [now
But if ye do not yet receive
 Mere earthly things; how then
Shall ye believe angelic truths,
 Transcending human ken?
No man can up to heaven ascend,
 But he that comes down thence:
The Son of man, who is in heaven,
 Enjoys this excellence.
And even as Moses lifted up
 The brazen serpent high,
So must the Son of man be raised,
 My Own Humanity,
Until it shall become Divine;
 That all who in me trust,
May live with me in heaven, and not
 Be written in the dust.
For God so loved the world,—all men,
 Corrupted from their birth,—
That, to redeem the human race,
 He came Himself to earth.
His Human, virgin-born, God's Son
 He gave, that everyone
Who worships Him in love, should
  find
 His heaven on earth begun.
Not to condemn this sinful world
 Do I its Savior come,
But to deliver it from sin,
 And sin's infernal doom.
Those that believe on me are saved,
 Because true proof I give
That I am God's Own Son, by whom
 Alone can sinners live.
'Tis this condemns, that light is come,
 (As all good men will own,)
But most love darkness more than
  light,
 So wicked have they grown.
All evil doers hate the light,
 For it reveals their crimes;
And all just persons love the light
 And come to it betimes,
That their good deeds may be approved
 As wrought in God above;
Done for the sake of his pure truth,
 And his redeeming love."

Ɨ, đe Redimer ov đe wɒrld,
 spik hwot į nσ; for į
hav sin điz ϑiŋz in heven, and nȣ
 į kɒm tu testifį.
Bɒt if yi dɯ not yet resiv
 mir erϑli ϑiŋz; hȣ đen
ʃal yi beliv anjelik trɯđz,
 transendiŋ hɥman ken?
Nσ man kan ɒp tu heven asend,
 bɒt hi đat kɒmz dȣn đens:
đe Sɒn ov man, hɯ iz in heven,
 enjoiz đis ekselens.
And iven az Mσzes lifted ɒp
 đe brezen serpent hį,
sσ mɒst đe Sɒn ov man bi rezd,
 mį σn Hɥmaniti,
ɒntil it ʃal bekɒm Divįn;
 đat ɷl hɯ in mi trɒst,
me liv wiđ mi in heven, and not
 bi riten in đe dɒst.
For God sσ lɒvd đe wɒrld,—ɷl
 korɒpted from đer berϑ,— [men,
đat, tu redim đe hɥman res,
 Hi kem Himself tu erϑ.
Hiz Hɥman, verjin-born, God'z Sɒn
 Hi gev, đat everiwɒn
hɯ wɒrʃips Him in lɒv, ʃud
  fįnd
 hiz heven on erϑ begɒn.
Not tu kondem đis sinful wɒrld
 dɯ į its Sevier kɒm,
bɒt tu deliver it from sin,
 and sin'z infernal dɯm.
Đσz đat beliv on mi ar sevd,
 bekɷz trɯ prɯf į giv
đat į am God'z σn Sɒn, bį hɯm
 alσn kan sinerz liv.
'Tiz đis kondemz, đat lįt iz kɒm,
 (az ɷl gud men wil σn,)
bɒt mσst lɒv darknes mσr đan
  lįt,
 sσ wiked hav đe grσn.
ɷl ivel dɯerz het đe lįt,
 for it revilz đer krįmz;
and ɷl jɒst personz lɒv đe lįt
 and kɒm tu it betįmz,
đat đer gud didz me bi aprɯvd
 az rσt in God abɒv;
dɒn for đe sek ov hiz pɥr trɯϑ,
 and hiz redimiŋ lɒv."

SECTION 27.

John's last testimony concerning Christ.
—John 3. 22-36.

And after these things, Jesus came
  Into Judæa's land,
And he and his disciples there
  Baptised, by God's command.
And John the Baptist also was
  Baptising very near,
In Ænon, close to Salim, for
  There was much water there.
Then John's disciples and the Jews
  Disputed what might be
The truest way to purify
  The soul, and set it free.
And unto John they came, and said,
  That Jesus Christ was nigh,
Baptising multitudes of men,
  And preaching publicly.
John answering, said to them, "A man
  Can nothing good receive,
Except from heaven ; this everyone
  Should steadfastly believe.
Ye bear me witness that I said,
  'I do not here appear
As Christ, the Anointed One, but that
  I am his pioneer.'
The bridegroom cometh from above,
  That wins the Church, his bride,
But I, his friend, may well rejoice
  To hear him at my side.
He must increase ; his God-like light
  Shall ever more extend ;
But I shall decrease : still, my joy
  Will never know an end.
He comes from heaven, and is above
  All men, whate'er their birth ;
But earth-born mortals earthly are,
  And love the things of earth.
All that Christ speaketh, he hath seen ;
  In heaven he all things knew ;
And they who now receive his words,
  Affirm that God is true.
He that proceedeth forth from God,
  And shines with God's own light,
God, without stint, on him hath poured
  His spirit and his might.
The Father loves the Son alway,
  All things to him he gives,

SEK

Jon'z last testi
—Jo

1
And after điz
  intu Juɯdia'
and hi and hiz
  baptjzd, bj
And Jon đe B
  baptjziŋ veri
in Ŀnon, kløs t
  đer woz mɒç
Ɖen Jon'z disį
  dispųted hw
đe trɯest wɛ t
  đe sol, and
And ɒntu Jon
  đat Jizɒs K
baptjziŋ mɒlti
  and priçiŋ p
Jon anseriŋ, s
  kan nɒđiŋ g
eksept from he
  ʃud stedfastl
Yi ber mi wit
  'ɟ dɯ not h
az Krjst, đe An
  j am hiz pjo
Ɖe brjdgrɯm
  đat winz đe
bɒt j, hiz fren
  tu hir him
Hi mɒst inkri
  ʃal ever mor
bɒt j ʃal dikri
  wil never ne
Hi kɒmz from
  ɷl men, hwe
bɒt erđ-born n
  and lɒv đe đ
ɷl đat Krjst s
  in heven hi
and đe hɯ nɤ
  aferm đat G
Hi đat prøsid
  and ʃjnz wiđ
God, wiđɤt sti
  hiz spirit an
Ɖe Fɒđer lɒvz
  ɷl điŋz tu h

And man believing on the Son,
  Like him for ever lives.
But those who wilfully reject
  His love, despise his power,
Shall not partake his love divine,
  Evil shall them devour."

and man belivin on ðe Spn,
  ljk him for ever livz.
Bpt ðoz hu wilfuli rejekt
  hiz lpv, despjz hiz pwer,
ʃal not partek hiz lpv divjn,
  ivel ʃal ðem devwr."

SECTION 28.

Imprisonment of John.—Matthew 14. 3-5. Mark 6. 17-20. Luke 3. 19, 20.

King Herod, when reproved by John
  For many a wicked deed,
Sent forth his men to bind him fast,
  And then, with wicked speed,
Put him in prison, and would not
  Unto his words give heed.
Herod divorced his wife, and took
  His brother Philip's bride,
By name Herodias, a vile dame;
  This cannot be denied.
So Herod being wroth with John,
  Soon put him into gaol;
But when Herodias sought how,
  In spite, she might prevail
To kill him, Herod said, "Not so;"
  Because full well he knew
The prophet was a holy man,
  And that his words were true.
And oft he heard him cheerfully,
  And had performed his will;
Besides, he feared the people much,
  Who loved the prophet still.

SEKΣON 28.

Imprizonment ov Jon.—Maþu 14. 3-5. Mark 6. 17-20. Luk 3. 19, 20.

Kin Herod, hwen repruvd bj Jon
  for meni a wiked did,
sent forþ hiz men tu bjnd him fast,
  and ðen, wið wiked spid,
put him in prizon, and wud not
  pntu hiz wprdz giv hid.
Herod diverst hiz wjf, and tuk
  hiz brpðer Filip's brjd,
bj nem Herodias, a vjl dem;
  ðis kanot bi denjd.
So Herod biin roþ wið Jon,
  sun put him intu jel;
bpt hwen Herodias sot hw,
  in spjt, ʃi mjt prevel
tu kil him, Herod sed, "Not so;"
  bekoz ful wel hi nu
ðe profet woz a holi man,
  and ðat hiz wprdz wer tru.
And oft hi herd him çirfuli,
  and had performd hiz wil;
besjdz, hi fird ðe pipel mpç,
  hu lpvd ðe profet stil.

SECTION 29.

Introduction to Christ's Public Ministry.—Matthew 4. 12-17. Mark 1. 14, 15. Luke 4. 14, 15.

While John was in the prison kept,
  To Galilee Christ came,
His native land, so that he might
  His Gospel there proclaim.
He said, "The time is now fulfilled
  That Scripture hath foretold;
God's kingdom on the earth, I am
  Appointed to unfold.
Repent; reform; believe the Word;
  For good and truth be bold."

SEKΣON 29.

Intrmasdpkʃon tu Krjst's Ppblik Ministri.—Maþu 4. 12-17. Mark 1. 14, 15. Luk 4. 14, 15.

Hwjl Jon woz in ðe prizon kept,
  tu Galili Krjst kem,
hiz netiv land, so ðat hi mjt
  hiz Gospel ðer proklem.
Hi sed, "Ðe tjm iz nw fulfild
  ðat Skriptur haþ fortold;
God'z kindom on ðe erþ, j am
  apointed tu pnfold.
Repent; reform; beliv ðe Wprd;
  for gud and truþ bi bold."

And Christ's renown began to spread
  Through all the region round ;
And when he taught, the people thought
  None like him could be found.
Abroad, at home, on hill, in dale,
  And in the synagogue,
He taught both great and small in set
  Discourse or dialogue.
And he went down from Nazareth
  And dwelt beside the lake,
Within Capernaum, that he
  The people might awake
From spiritual lethargy ;
  And they their sins forsake.
Isaiah's prophecy was thus
  Fulfilled by God's decree,
That Zabulon and Nephthalim,
  By Galilee's dark sea,
Should be illumined by the light
  Of Christ, the light of men ;
That Jews and Gentiles might once more
  See heavenly truths again ;
And all rejoice, and lift the voice
  In one long, loud Amen.
The people that in darkness sat,
  Now saw a heavenly light,
And they whose eyes were closed in death,
  From Christ received their sight.
And from that time the Lord began
  To call men to repent,
And God's new kingdom of the heavens
  Enter, with one consent.

SECTION 30.

***Christ's Conversation with the Woman of Samaria.*—John 4. 1-42.**

When the Lord knew the Pharisees
  Had heard that Jesus made
Disciples more than John, (who was
  Not principal, but aid,)
For not alone did Christ baptise
  As he had done before,*

And Krįst's renʊn began tu spre
  ɟrɯ ɷl ɗe rijon rʊnd;
and hwen hį tɷt, ɗe pįpel ɟɷt
  nɒn lįk him kud bį fʊnd.
Abrɷd, at hɵm, on hil, in dɛl,
  and in ɗe sinagog,
hį tɷt bɵɟ gret and smɷl in set
  diskɵrs or dįalog.
And hį went dʊn from Nazareɟ
  and dwelt besįd ɗe lɛk,
wiɗin Kapernaɒm, ɗat hį
  ɗe pįpel mįt awɛk
from spiritųal leɟarji ;
  and ɗɛ ɗɛr sinz forsɛk.
Ɨzaia'z profesi woz ɗɒs
  fulfild bį God'z dekrį,
ɗat Zabųlon and Nefɟalim,
  bį Galilį'z dark sį,
ʃud bį ilɯmind bį ɗe lįt
  ov Krįst, ɗe lįt ov men ;
ɗat Jɯz and Jentįlz mįt wɒns mɵ
  sį hevenli trɯɗz agen ;
and ɷl rejois, and lift ɗe vois
  in wɒn loŋ, lʊd Amen.
Ɗe pįpel ɗat in darknęs sat,
  nɷ sɷ a hevenli lįt,
and ɗɛ hɯz įz wer klɵzd in deɟ,
  from Krįst resįvd ɗɛr sįt.
And from ɗát tįm ɗe Lord began
  tu kɷl men tu repent,
and God'z nų kiŋdom ov ɗe heve
  enter, wiɗ wɒn konsent.

SEKΣON 30.

***Krįst's Konversɛʃon wiɗ ɗe Wuman Samaria.*—Jon 4. 1-42.**

Hwen ɗe Lord nų ɗe Farisįz
  had herd ɗat Jįzɒs med
disįpelz mɵr ɗan Jon, (hɯ woz
  not prinsipal, bɒt ɛd,)
for not alɵn did Krįst baptįz
  az hį had dɒn befɵr,*

---

* When the reader finds expressed a meaning different from that of the Authoris Version, as in the case of *John* 2. 4, already referred to, and in the present instance, l may feel assured that the original ought to, or may be, so rendered. This observati will suffice for any similar case that may hereafter occur.

But his disciples did the same,
 And thus were baptised more;
He left Judæa, and went north,
 Samaria passing through,
And came to Sychar, Shechem called,
 His Father's will to do.
And near it was that ground which
 Jacob to Joseph gave, [once
Wherein was Jacob's purchased well,
 And also Joseph's grave.
And Jesus, wearied with his walk,
 Rested upon the well;
His followers were buying bread,
 And knew not what befell.
A woman of Samaria
 Came to draw water there,
And Jesus asked her to bestow
 What she so well could spare.
The woman was surprised that he
 To her should thus apply;
For then Samaritans and Jews
 All cherished enmity
Against each other, when they should
 Have formed one family.
Then Jesus answered, "If thou knew'st
 The gift that God can grant,
And who it is that says, 'Bestow
 The water that I want,'
Thou would'st have rather asked of
 For living water true, [him
The water of immortal life,
 For ever bright and new."
The woman said, "This well is deep,
 The fountain lieth low,
Beyond thy reach; whence then canst
 Water of life bestow?" [thou
Jesus replied, "Whoe'er shall drink
 This water, thirsts again;
Who drinks the water I shall give,
 Shall ne'er know thirst nor pain;
But deep within his heart it dwells,
 An ever-flowing stream,
Springing eternal, for its source,
 Is God himself, supreme."
The woman said, "O grant to me
 That living water clear,
To save me from the daily toil
 Of drawing water here."
And Jesus said, "Thy husband call."
 The woman answered then,

bɒt hiz disįpelz did đe sem,
 and đɒs wer baptįzd mɵr;
hi left Jɯdia, and went norɟ,
 Samaria pasiŋ ɟrɯ,
and kem tu Sįkar, Σekem kɷld,
 hiz Fɑđer'z wil tu dɯ.
And nir it woz đát grʊnd hwiç
 Jekob tu Jɵzef gev, [wɒns
hwerin woz Jekob'z pɒrçest wel,
 and ɷlsɵ Jɵzef's grev.
And Jįzɒs, wįrid wiđ hiz wɷk,
 rested ɒpon đe wel;
hiz folɵerz wer bįiŋ bred,
 and nɥ not hwot befel.
A wuman ov Samaria
 kem tu drɷ wɷter đer,
and Jįzɒs askt her tu bestɵ
 hwot ʃi sɵ wel kud sper.
Đe wuman woz sɒrprįzd đat hį
 tu her ʃud đɒs aplį;
for đen Samaritanz and Jɯz
 ɷl çeriʃt enmiti
agenst įç ɒđer, hwen đe ʃud
 hav formd wɒn famili.
Đen Jįzɒs anserd, "If đʊ nɥ'st
 đe gift đat God kan grant,
and hɯ it iz đat sez, 'Bestɵ
 đe wɷter đat į wont,'
đʊ wud'st hav rɑđer askt ov him
 for liviŋ wɷter trɯ,
đe wɷter ov immortal lįf,
 for ever brįt and nɥ."
Đe wuman sed, "Đis wel iz dip,
 đe fʊnten lįeɟ lɵ,
beyond đį riç; hwens đen kanst đʊ
 wɷter ov lįf bestɵ?"
Jįzɒs replįd, "Hɯer ʃal driŋk
 đis wɷter, ɟersts agen;
hɯ driŋks đe wɷter į ʃal giv,
 ʃal ner nɵ́ ɟerst nor pen;
bɒt dip wiđin hiz hart it dwelz,
 an ever-flɵiŋ strįm,
spriŋiŋ eternal, for its sɵrs,
 iz God himself, sɥprįm."
Đe wuman sed, "Ɵ grant tu mi
 đát liviŋ wɷter klir,
tu sev mi from đe deli toil
 ov drɷiŋ wɷter hir."
And Jįzɒs sed, "Đį hɒzband kɷl."
 Đe wuman anserd đen,

"I have no husband;" and she blushed
With conscious guilt and pain.
Jesus replied, "Thou speakest true,
Five husbands thou hast had,
And he whom now thou hast is not
Thy husband; this is sad."
The woman answered, "Sir, I feel
That thou a prophet art,
For thou hast read the mysteries
That slumber in my heart.
Say then, Which is the chosen place
Where men should seek the Lord;
Doth Judah or Samaria
The holiest place afford?"
Jesus replied, "The hour shall come
When neither here nor there
Alone, but everywhere, shall all
Good men their hearts prepare
To worship God, a spirit pure,
In spirit and in truth.
At present, you Samaritans
Have little light, forsooth;
In Israel is God known, and thence
Shall his salvation come,
And wide extend, till the whole earth
Shall be man's peaceful home."
The woman saith, "I know when he,
Messiah, Christ, shall come,
He will instruct us in all truth,
And banish error's gloom."
Then Jesus said to her, "Lo! I
That speak to thee am He."
On this came his disciples, and
They marveled much to see
Their Lord discoursing thus alone
With one whom Jews despise,
Yet made an effort to conceal
Their sorrow and surprise.
The woman left her waterpot,
And went into the town,
And said to all she met, "Come, see,
A prophet of renown,
Who told me all I ever did;
Say, Is not this the Christ?"
Then came the citizens to him,
By these strange words enticed.
The Lord's disciples, the meanwhile,
Who had returned with bread,
Besought him earnestly to eat;
But he, replying, said,

"ꟻ hav nȯ hɒzband;" and ʃi blɒʃt
wiđ konʃɒs gilt and pɛn.
Jizɒs repl̨id, "Ɑɤ spikest trɯ,
fįv hɒzbandz đɤ hast had,
and hi hɯm nɤ đɤ hast iz not
đį hɒzband; đis iz sad."
Ɑe wuman anserd, "Ser, į fil
đat đɤ a profet art,
for đɤ hast red đe misteriz
đat slɒmber in mį hart.
Sɛ đen, Hwiç iz đe çȯzen plɛs
hwɛr men ʃud sik đe Lord;
dɒŧ Jɯda or Samaria
đe hȯliest plɛs afȯrd?"
Jizɒs repl̨id, "Ɑe ɤr ʃal kɒm
hwen nįđer hir nor đer
alȯn, bɒt ėverihwer, ʃal ɷl
gud men đer harts prepɛr
tu wɒrʃip God, a spirit pɥr,
in spirit and in trɯŧ.
At prezent, ɥ Samaritanz
hav litel lįt, forsɯŧ;
in Izrael iz God nȯn, and đens
ʃal hiz salvɛʃon kɒm,
and wįd ekstend, til đe hȯl erŧ
ʃal bi man'z pisful hȯm."
Ɑe wuman seŧ, "ꟻ nȯ hwen hi,
Mesįa, Krįst, ʃal kɒm,
hi wil instrɒkt ɒs in in ɷl trɯŧ,
and baniʃ eror'z glɯm."
Ɑen Jizɒs sed tu her, "Lȯ! į
đat spik tu đi am Hi."
On đis kem hiz disįpelz, and
đe marveld mɒç tu si
đer Lord diskȯrsiŋ đɒs alȯn
wiđ wɒn hɯm Jɯz despįz,
yet med an efort tu konsil
đer sorȯ and sɒrprįz.
Ɑe wuman left her wɷterpot,
and went intu đe tɤn,
and sed tu ɷl ʃi met, "Kɒm, si,
a profet ov renɤn,
hɯ tȯld mi ɷl į ever did;
se, Iz not đis đe Krįst?"
Ɑen kem đe sitizenz tu him,
bį điz strenj wɒrdz entįst.
Ɑe Lord'z disįpelz, đe minhwįl,
hɯ had retɒrnd wiđ bred,
besɷt him ernestli tu it;
bɒt hi, replįiŋ, sed,

"I eat of meat ye know not of,
  Divine substantial good:
In working out the will of God
  I find my constant food.
Behold! I see the hearts of men
  Are ripe for reaping now;
Put in the sickle, reap, and lo!
  The heavens ye will endow.
And those that sow, and those that
  These fruits of life Divine, [reap,
Receive their wages, and rejoice
  With joys that ne'er decline.
For dear to God alike are those
  Who first implant his store,
And those who save the fruits which
  Might perish evermore. [else
Many Samaritans who dwelt
  In Sychar, then believed
In Christ, for what the woman said,
  And unto him they cleaved.
And many more acknowledged him
  When they themselves had heard
From his own lips the saving truth;
  And glorified his word.

SECTION 31.

Second Miracle in Cana of Galilee.—
John 4. 43-54.

After two days in Sychar spent,
  Christ went to Galilee;
But Nazareth, his native town,
  He did not haste to see;
But testified, A prophet finds
  Small reverence at home,
Till he has gained just fame abroad,
  Which back with him will come.
The Galilæans gladly then
  Welcomed the prophet great,
For they had seen the power Divine
  Which did upon him wait,
When in Jerusalem, of late,
  His wondrous works increased;
For to the passover they went,
  To keep the yearly feast.
So Jesus came to Cana, where
  He made the water wine;
And there was here a nobleman
  Who knew Christ's power Divine.

"Ɉ it ov mit yi nó not ov,
  Divjn sɒbstanʃal gud:
in wɒrkiŋ ɤt đe wíl ov God
  j fjnd mj konstant fɯd.
Behơld! j si đe harts ov men
  ar rjp for ripiŋ nɤ;
put in đe sikel, rip, and lơ!
  đe hevenz yi wil endɤ.
And đơz đat sơ, and đơz đat rip,
  điz frɯts ov ljf divjn,
resiv đer wejez, and rejois
  wiđ joiz đat ner dekljn.
For dir tu God aljk ar đơz
  hɯ ferst implant hiz stơr,
and đơz hɯ sev đe frɯts hwiç els
  mjt periʃ evermơr.
Meni Samaritanz hɯ dwelt
  in Sjkar, đen belivd
in Krjst, for hwot đe wuman sed,
  and ɒntu him đe klivd.
And meni mơr aknolejd him
  hwen đe đemselvz had herd
from hiz ơn lips đe seviŋ trɯŧ;
  and glơrifjd hiz wɒrd.

SEKΣON 31.

Sekond Mirakel in Kena ov Galili.—
Jon 4. 43-54.

After tɯ́ dez in Sjkar spent,
  Krjst went tu Galili;
bɒt Nazareŧ, hiz netiv tɤn,
  hi did not hest tu si;
bɒt testifjd, A profet fjndz
  smɷl reverens at hơm,
til hi haz gend jɒst fem abrɷd,
  hwiç bak wiđ him wil kɒm.
Đe Galilianz gladli đen
  welkɒmd đe profet gret,
for đe had sin đe pɤer Divjn
  hwiç did ɒpon him wet,
hwen in Jerɯsalem, ov let,
  hiz wɒndrɒs wɒrks inkrist;
for tu đe pasơver đe went,
  tu kip đe yirli fist.
Sơ Jizɒs kem tu Kena, hwer
  hi med đe wơter wjn;
and đer woz hir a nơbelman
  hɯ nụ Krjst's pɤer Divjn.

His son was at the point of death,
  So, he besought the Lord
That he would heal his child, who else
  Could never be restored.
Then Jesus said, "Except you see,
  You doubt my power to save;
But trust my word; thy son doth live;
  He now escapes the grave."
The man believed the word of Christ,
  And homeward he returned,
But on the way his servants came,
  And they no longer mourned.
"Thy son," they said, "is now restored
  To life." Then he inquired
What hour it was this happy change
  In his son's health transpired.
They told the hour; he knew it was
  At that same hour of day
That Jesus said, "Thy son doth live."
  He owned Messiah's sway;
And he and all his family
  Believed that Christ must be
The promised Savior of the world,
  The son of Deity.

SECTION 32.

Public preaching of Christ in the Synagogue of Nazareth, and his danger there.
—Luke 4. 16-30.

And Jesus came to Nazareth,
  Wherein his youth was spent,
And into the Jews' synagogue
  He on the Sabbath went;
And as his custom was therein,
  He stood up for to read
God's Word to all the people there;
  Thus sowing heavenly seed.
And opening the book, he found
  Isaiah's prophecy;
The spirit of Jehovah God
  Is on me now; for he
With oil anointeth me, that I
  With holy joy may preach
Glad tidings to the poor; with balm
  The broken hearts to reach;
Deliverance give to captive souls,
  And sight unto the blind;
Unto the bruised, joyous ease;
  God's grace to all mankind.

Hiz sɒn woz at
  sɵ, hi besɷt
ɗat hi wud hil
  kųd never bi
ɗen Jizɒs sed,
  ų dɤt mį pɤe
bɒt trɒst mį wɒ
  hi nɤ eskeps
ɗe man belivd
  and hɵmward
bɒt on ɗe we hi
  and ɗe nɵ loŋ
"ɗį sɒn," ɗe se
  tu lįf." ɗen
hwot ɤr it woz
  in hiz sɒn'z h
ɗe tɵld ɗe ɤr;
  at ɗát sem ɤr
ɗat Jizɒs sed, "
  Hi ɵnd Mesį
and hi and ɷl h
  belivd ɗat K
ɗe promist Sevi
  ɗe sɒn ov Dii

SEK

Pɒblik priçiŋ ov
ov Nazareθ, a
—Luk

And Jizɒs kem
  hwerin hiz ųθ
and intu ɗe Ju
  hi on ɗe Sabɛ
and az hiz kɒst
  hi stud ɒp fo
God'z Wɒrd tu
  ɗɒs sɵiŋ heve
And ɵpeniŋ ɗe
  Ɨzaia'z profes
ɗe spirit ov Je
  iz on mi nɤ;
wiɗ oil anointeθ
  wiɗ hɵli joi n
glad tįdiŋz tu ɗ
  ɗe brɵken ha
deliverans giv t
  and sįt ɒntu
ɒntu ɗe bruzed
  God'z gres tu

And then he closed that blessed book
  Of God's inspired decree,
And sat, with majesty divine,
  Incarnate Deity.
The eyes of all that heard him speak,
  Were fastened on his face;
And he began to say to them,
  With superhuman grace,
"This day this Scripture is fulfilled,
  Filled full now in your ears."
And all the people listened then,
  With mingled hopes and fears,
And wondered at the gracious words
  That from his lips outpoured,
And questioned, "How can Joseph's
  Be as the Christ adored?" [son
Then Christ replied, "I know you
  That I should here achieve [would
Those miracles I elsewhere did;
  But, would you then believe?
I tell you, of the prophets none
  At home had honor due;
And so they mostly wrought their signs
  For strangers whom they knew.
Even so, Elijah, in the days
  Of Israel of old,
When famine was on all the land,
  And sufferings manifold,
Saved not the widows of the Jews
  That seemed his aid to claim,
But only wrought his miracle
  For a Sidonian dame.
And in Elisha's time there were
  Full many lepers found
In this your native Palestine,
  And all the coasts around;
But upon none save Naaman,
  A Syrian lord, did he
Perform the miracle divine
  Of healing leprosy."
And when the men of Nazareth
  These burning words had heard,
Their hearts were filled with wrath,
  Immediately conferred, [and they
Rose up, and thrust him forth beyond
  The precincts of their town,
And led him to the mountain's brow
  That they might cast him down.
But he evanished from their sight,
  And, passing through the crowd,

And đen hi klɵzd đát blesed buk
  ov God'z inspįrd dekri,
and sat, wiđ majesti divįn,
  Iŋkarnet Diiti.
Đe įz ov ɷl đat herd him spik,
  wer fasend on hiz fɛs;
and hi began tu sɛ tu đem,
  wiđ sųperhųman grɛs,
"Đis dɛ đis Skriptųr iz fulfild,
  fild ful nɤ in ųr irz."
And ɷl đe pipel lisend đen,
  wiđ miŋgeld hɵps and firz,
and wɒnderd at đe grɛʃɒs wɒrdz
  đat from hiz lips ɤtpɵrd,
and kwestiond, "Hɤ kan Jɵzef's
  bi az đe Krįst adɵrd?" [sɒn
Đen Krįst replįd, "Ɨ nɵ ų wud
  đat į ʃud hir ačiv
đɵz mirakelz į elshwɛr did;
  bɒt, wud ų đen beliv?
Ɨ tel ų, ov đe profets nɒn
  at hɵm had onor dų;
and sɵ đe mɵstli rɵt đɛr sįnz
  for strɛnjerz hɯm đɛ nų.
Ɛven sɵ, Elįja, in đe dɛz
  ov Izrael ov ɵld,
hwen famin woz on ɷl đe land,
  and sɒferiŋz manifɵld,
sɛvd not đe widɵz ov đe Jɯz
  đat simd hiz ɛd tu klɛm,
bɒt ɵnli rɵt hiz mirakel
  for a Sįdɵnian dɛm.
And in Elįʃa'z tįm đɛr wer
  ful meni leperz fɤnd
in đis ųr nɛtiv Palestįn,
  and ɷl đe kɵsts arɤnd;
bɒt ɒpon nɒn sɛv Nɛaman,
  a Sirian lord, did hi
perform đe mirakel divįn
  ov hiliŋ leprosi."
And hwen đe men ov Nazareŧ
  điz bɒrniŋ wɒrdz had herd,
đɛr harts wer fild wiđ rɤŧ, and đɛ
  immidietli konferd,
rɵz ɒp, and ŧrɒst him forŧ beyond
  đe prisiŋkts ov đɛr tɤn,
and led him tu đe mɤnten'z brɤ
  đat đɛ mįt kast him dɤn.
Bɒt hi evaniʃt from đɛr sįt,
  and, pasiŋ ŧrɯ đe krɤd,

Went on his way to other towns,
  Concealed as by a cloud.

SECTION 33.

The calling of Andrew, Peter, James, and John.—Luke 4. 31, 32. Matthew 4. 18-22. Mark 1. 16-20. Luke 5. 1-12.

Christ then unto Capernaum came,
  A city proud and high,
That bordered on the lovely lake
  Of Galilee, hard by,
And taught the folk on Sabbath days.
  They all astonished seemed
To hear his doctrine, for his word
  Like light upon them beamed.
And Jesus walking by the sea
  Of Galilee, perceived
Peter and Andrew, brethren both,
  Who had before believed,
Casting a net into the sea,
  For they were fishers then:
"Come, follow me," said Christ, "and
  Shall fishers be of men." [you
And not unmindful of their faith
  Once plighted to the Lord,
They left their nets, and followed him,
  According to his word.
And going further on, beside
  Genesaret's dark shore,
He met the sons of Zebedee,
  Both James and John, once more.
They too were fishermen, and they
  Their nets were mending nigh;
Christ called them; they their father
  To attend his ministry. [left,

The Miraculous Draught of Fishes.

As Jesus stood upon the shore
  Of Galilee's fair lake,
And all the people pressed to hear
  The gracious words he spake,
He saw two vessels on the beach,
  Deserted there they lay;
The fishermen had left them both
  To wash their nets that day.
He entered into one of them,
  'Twas Simon Peter's boat,
And begged that he'd push off from
  And keep the ship afloat. [land,

went on hiz wɛ tu ɒđer tɜnz,
  konsįld az bį a klɜd.

SĘKƩON 33.

Đɛ kɷliŋ ov Andrɯ, Piter, Jɛmz, and Jon.—Lɯk 4, 31, 32. Maŧų 4. 18-22. Mark 1. 16-20. Lɯk 5. 1-12.

Kr̨įst đen ɒntu Kapernaɒm kɛm,
  a siti prɜd and hį,
đat borderd on đe lɒvli lɛk
  ov Galili, hard bį,
and tɷt đe fɵk on Sabaŧ dɛz.
  Đɛ ɷl astoniʃt sįmd
tu hir hiz doktrin, for hiz wɒrd
  lįk lįt ɒpon đem bimd.
And Jizɒs wɷkiŋ bį đe si
  ov Galili, persįvd
Piter and Andrɯ, bređren bɵŧ,
  hɯ had befɵr belįvd,
kastiŋ a net intu đe si,
  for đɛ wer fiʃerz đen:
"Kɒm, folɵ mi," sed Krįst, "and ų
  ʃal fiʃerz bi ov men."
And not ɒnmįndful ov đer fɛŧ
  wɒns plįted tu đe Lord,
đɛ left đer nets, and folɵd him,
  akordiŋ tu hiz wɒrd.
And gɵiŋ fɒrđer on, besįd
  Genesaret's dark ʃɵr,
hi met đe sɒnz ov Zebedi,
  bɵŧ Jɛmz and Jon, wɒns mɵr.
Đɛ tɯ wer fiʃermen, and đɛ
  đer nets wer mendiŋ nį;
Krįst kɷld đem; đɛ đer fɑđer left,
  tu atend hiz ministri.

Đɛ Mirakųlɒs Draft ov Fiʃez.

Az Jizɒs stud ɒpon đe ʃɵr
  ov Galili'z fɛr lɛk,
and ɷl đe pipel prest tu hir
  đe grɛʃɒs wɒrdz hi spɛk,
hi sɷ tɯ veselz on đe biç,
  dezerted đer đɛ lɛ;
đe fiʃermen had left đem bɵŧ
  tu wɷʃ đer nets đát dɛ.
Hi enterd intu wɒn ov đem,
  'twoz Sįmon Piter'z bɵt,
and begd đat hi'd puʃ of from land,
  and kip đe ʃip aflɵt.

Then sitting down therein, he taught
  The multitude on shore
Of love, and faith, and many things
  Which he had taught before.
And when he had done speaking, said
  To Simon, " Launch out far
Into the water, and let down
  Thy nets that empty are."
Peter replied, " Lord, we have toiled
  All night, but all in vain,
Yet at thy gracious word, I will
  Let down the net again."
Their partners in the other ship
  They called to help their need.
They came, and filled both ships with
  Thus did the draught succeed. [fish,
And now, the vessels over-full,
  Were just about to sink,
The water was so very near
  Unto the vessel's brink.
When Peter saw it, he fell down,
  Afraid, at Jesus' knees,
And said, " Depart from me, O Lord,
  Thou Ruler of the seas,
For I'm a sinful man." And all
  With consternation stand
To see the multitudes of fish
  That came at Christ's command.
Then Jesus unto Simon said,
  " Fear not; in time to come
Thou shalt catch men in heaven's own
      net,
  And save them from hell's doom.
Then those disciples brought their
  To shore. They all forsook; [ships
Henceforth they followed Christ, and
  His ministry partook. [in

Ðen sitiŋ dɤn đerin, hị tɵt
  đe mɒltitųd on ʃɵr
ov lɒv, ov fɛɫ, and meni ɫiŋz
  hwiç hị had tɵt befɵr.
And hwen hị had dɒn spikiŋ, sed
  tu Sịmon, " Lɛnç ɤt far
intu đe wɵter, and let dɤn
  đị nets đat empti ar."
Piter replịd, " Lord, wi hav toild
  ɷl nịt, bɒt ɷl in ven,
yet at đị greʃɒs wɒrd, ị wil
  let dɤn đe net agen."
Ðer partnerz in đe ɒđer ʃip
  đe kɷld tu help đer nid.
Ðɛ kem, and fild bɵɫ ʃips wiđ fiʃ,
  đɒs did đe draft sɒksịd.
And nɤ, đe veselz ɵver-ful,
  wer jɒst abɤt tu siŋk,
đe wɵter woz sɵ veri nir
  ɒntu đe vesel'z briŋk.
Hwen Piter sɷ it, hị fel dɤn,
  afred, at Jizɒs' niz,
and sed, " Depart from mi, Ɵ Lord,
  đɤ Ruler ov đe siz,
for ị'm a sinful man." And ɷl
  wiđ konsterneʃon stand
tu si đe mɒltitųdz ov fiʃ
  đat kem at Krịst's komand.
Ðen Jizɒs ɒntu Sịmon sed,
  " Fir not; in tịm tu kɒm
đɤ ʃalt kaç men in heven'z ɵn
      net,
  and sev đem from hel'z dum.
Ðen đɵz disịpelz brɵt đer ʃips
  tu ʃɵr. Ðe ɷl forsuk;
hensfɵrɫ đe folɵd Krịst, and in
  hiz ministri partuk.

SECTION 34.

The Demoniac healed.
—Mark 1. 21-28. Luke 4. 33-37.

Upon the Sabbath, as Christ taught,
  (As he was wont to do,)
Within Capernaum's synagogue,
  The people round him drew.
Much they admired the truths which
  With a majestic grace [dropped
From out his lips, unlike the lore
  Of their own priesthood race.

SEKΣON 34.

Ðe Dimɤniak hild.
—Mark 1. 21-28. Luk 4. 33-37.

Upon đe Sabaɫ, az Krịst tɵt,
  (az hị woz wɒnt tu du,)
wiđin Kapernaɒm'z sinagog,
  đe pipel rɤnd him dru.
Mɒç đe admịrd đe truđz hwiç
  wiđ a majestik gres [dropt
from ɤt hiz lips, ɒnlịk đe lɵr
  ov đer ɵn pristhud res.

And in that synagogue there was
  A certain man possessed
By a foul fiend, who tortured him
  And would not let him rest.
He cried aloud, "Let us alone,
  What can we do with thee,
Jesus of Nazareth; art thou come
  To increase our misery?
I know thee, who thou art, in truth,
  The Holy One of God."
Then Christ rebuked him with his [word,
  (His word is as a rod
To scourge all wrong,) "Be silent and
  Come out." The spirit obeyed,
And casting the poor maniac down,
  And tearing him, he made,
With a loud wail, his dread escape,
  But hurt him not again.
Such power and mercy Christ dis- [played
  To wild demoniac men.
And all the people were amazed
  And marveled at Christ's might,
Which, by a word, could overawe,
  And all hell's legions smite.
And soon his fame extended wide
  Through all that region round,
And Galilee rejoiced to hear
  The Gospel's gladsome sound.

SECTION 35.

Peter's Mother-in-law cured.
—Matthew 8. 14, 15. Mark 1. 29-31.
Luke 5. 38, 39.

Then from the synagogue they went,
  And Jesus entered soon
Simon and Andrew's friendly home,
  And with him James and John.
There one lay sick of fever dire,
  Mother of Simon's wife,
And quickly did her loving friends
  Beseech Christ for her life.
His hand he laid with tender love
  Upon her dying frame,
And at his word, immediately
  Was quenched that fever's flame.
He took her hand; she rose restored;
  And moved with willing feet
To minister unto her Lord,
  With grateful service, sweet.

And in đát sinagog đer woz
  a serten man pozest
bį a fɤl fįnd, hɯ tortųrd him
  and wud not let him rest.
Hi krįd alɤd, "Let ɒs alɵn,
  hwot kan wi dɯ wiđ đi,
Jizɒs ov Nazareɟ; art đɤ kɒm
  tu inkris ɤr mizeri?
Ɨ nó đi, hɯ đɤ art, in trɯɟ,
  đe Hɵli Wɒn ov God."
Đen Krįst rebųkt him wiđ hiz wɒrd,
  (hiz wɒrd iz az a rod
tu skɒrj ɷl roŋ,) "Bi sįlent and
  kɒm ɤt." Đe spirit ɵbed,
and kastiŋ đe pɯr meniak dɤn,
  and teriŋ him, hi med,
wiđ a lɤd wel, hiz dred eskep,
  bɒt hɒrt him not agen.
Sɒɋ pɤer and mersi Krįst displed
  tu wįld dimɵniak men.
And ɷl đe pipel wer amezd
  and marveld at Krįst's mįt,
hwiɋ, bį a wɒrd, kud ɵverɷ,
  and ɷl hel'z lijonz smįt.
And sɯn hiz fem ekstended wįd
  ɟrɯ ɷl đát rijon rɤnd,
and Galili rejoist tu hir
  đe Gospel'z gladsɒm sɤnd.

SEKƩON 35.

Piter'z Mɒđer-in-lɷ kųrd.
—Maɟų 8. 14, 15. Mark 1. 29-31.
Lɯk 5. 38, 39.

Đen from đe sinagog đe went,
  and Jizɒs enterd sɯn
Sįmon and Andrɯ'z frendli hɵm,
  and wiđ him Jemz and Jon.
Đer wɒn le sik ov fiver dįr,
  mɒđer ov Sįmon'z wįf,
and kwikli did her lɒviŋ frendz
  besiɋ Krįst for her lįf.
Hiz hand hi led wiđ tender lɒv
  ɒpon her dįiŋ frem,
and at hiz wɒrd, immidietli
  woz kwenɋt đát fiver'z flem.
Hi tuk her hand; ʃi rɵz restɵrd;
  and mɯvd wiđ wiliŋ fit
tu minister ɒntu her Lord,
  wiđ gretful servis, swit.

SECTION 36.

Christ teaches, and performs miracles, throughout Galilee.—
Matthew 4. 23-25; 8. 16, 17. Mark 1. 32-39. Luke 4. 40-44.

At even, when the sun was set,
 All who had suffering friends
Brought them to Christ, whose powerful touch
 Health through their vitals sends.
Demons departed at his voice,
 The sick did he restore;
So was fulfilled Isaiah's word,
 "Himself our sickness bore."
The demons also witness gave,
 And cried, "Thou art the Christ,
The Son of God:" but he required
 They should from this desist.
At earliest dawn the Lord arose,
 In solitude to pray,
And Simon and his friends essayed
 To follow him that day.
And when they found him, they exclaimed,
 "All men are seeking thee."
But he replied, "Let us now leave
 This place, and go and see
Some other towns; for this I'm sent."
 Yet still the people throng,
And press him not to leave them yet;
 They would detain him long.
"God's kingdom I would preach elsewhere,
 For this cause am I sent,"
He said. Then throughout all the land
 Of Galilee he went,
Preaching glad tidings unto all,
 And healing every ill.
And thus his fame for mighty deeds
 Did Syria's region fill.

SEKΣON 36.

Krįst tiçez, and performz mirakelz, θrust Galili.—
Maθɥ 4. 23-25; 8. 16, 17. Mark 1. 32-39. Luuk 4. 40-44.

At įven, hwen đe sɒn woz set,
 ɷl huu had sɒferiŋ frendz
brɷt đem tu Krįst, huuz pɜerful tɒç
 helθ θruu đer vįtalz sendz.
Dįmonz departed at hiz vois,
 đe sik did hį restσr;
sσ woz fulfild Ɨzaia'z wɒrd,
 "Himself ɜr siknes bσr."
Đe dįmonz ɷlsσ witnes gɛv,
 and krįd, "Đɜ art đe Krįst,
đe Sɒn ov God:" bɒt hį rekwįrd
 đɛ ʃud from đis desist.
At erliest dɷn đe Lord arσz,
 in solitɥd tu prɛ,
and Sįmon and hiz frendz esɛd
 tu folσ him đát dɛ.
And hwen đɛ fɜnd him, đɛ eksklɛmd,
 "Ɑl men ar sikiŋ đi."
Bɒt hį replįd, "Let ɒs nɜ liv
 đis plɛs, and gσ and sį
sɒm ɒđer tɜnz; for đis į'm sent."
 Yet stil đe pįpel θroŋ,
and pres him not tu liv đem yet;
 đɛ wud detɛn him loŋ.
"God'z kiŋdom į wud priç elshwɛr;
 for đis kɷz am į sent,"
hį sed. Đen θruɜt ɷl đe land
 ov Galili hį went,
priçiŋ glad tįdiŋz ɒntu ɷl,
 and hiliŋ everi il.
And đɒs hiz fɛm for mįti didz
 did Siria'z rįjon fil.

SECTION 37.

Christ cures a Leper.—Matthew 8. 2-5. Mark 1. 40-45. Luke 5. 12-15.

It happened in a certain place
 There lived a leprous man,
Who, seeing Jesus, lowly knelt,
 And this address began,

SEKΣON 37.

Krįst kɥrz a Leper.—Maθɥ 8. 2-5. Mark 1. 40-45. Luuk 5. 12-15.

It hapend in a serten plɛs
 đer livd a leprɒs man,
huu, sįiŋ Jįzɒs, lσli nelt,
 and đis adres began,

"Lord, if thou wilt, thou hast the power
 To make a leper clean."
Moved with compassion for his state,
 Pleased with his humble mien,
Jesus put forth his gentle hand,
 Touched him, and, as the Lord
Of life, replied, "I will: be clean."
 And at that thrilling word
The leprosy departed quite,
 The sufferer was restored.
Then Jesus bade him tell no man,
 But keep the law's command,
And show himself unto the priest
 With offerings in his hand.
And thus he sent him on his way;
 But he could not refrain
From telling such a wondrous tale
 Again and yet again.
These tidings brought great multitudes
 For healing, and to hear;
Till Jesus could not publicly
 Within that town appear;
But to the wilderness he turned,
 For solitude and prayer,
And from all parts around they came,
 And thronged him even there.

SECTION 38.

The Paralytic cured. Christ's power to forgive sins.—Matthew 9. 2-9. Mark 2. 1-12. Luke 5. 17-26.

A few days after this, the Lord
 Revisits that famed town
Capernaum, and soon the place
 Was filled with his renown.
A multitude came forth to hear,
 And thronged the vestibule;
And there he preached the blessed word
 Of life—its law, or rule.
It happened on a certain day,
 While he, on preaching bent,
Was poring wisdom into ears
 Which gave a glad assent,
That doctors of the law sat by,
 And haughty Phariseees,
Who sought to catch him in the net
 Of their own subtleties.

"Lord, if đɜ wilt, đɜ hast đe pɜer
 tu mek a leper klin."
Mɯvd wiđ kompaʃon for hiz stet,
 plizd wiđ hiz hɒmbel min,
Jizɒs put ferɟ hiz jentel hand,
 tɒçt him, and, az đe Lord
ov lịf, replịd, "Ɨ wil: bi klin."
 And at đát ɟriliŋ wɒrd
đe leprosi departed kwịt,
 đe sɒferer woz restord.
Đen Jizɒs bad him tel no man,
 bɒt kip đe lω'z komand,
and ʃo himself ɒntu đe prist
 wiđ oferiŋz in hiz hand.
And đɒs hi sent him on hiz we;
 bɒt hi kud not refren
from teliŋ sɒç a wɒndrɒs tel
 agen and yet agen.
Điz tịdiŋz brωt gret mɒltitųdz
 for hiliŋ, and tu hir;
til Jizɒs kud not pɒblikli
 wiđin đát tɜn apir;
bɒt tu đe wildernes hi tɒrnd,
 for solitųd and prer,
and from ωl parts arɜnd đe kem,
 and ɟroŋd him iven đer.

SEKΣON 38.

Đe Paralitik kųrd. Krịst's pɜer tu forgiv sinz.—Maɟų 9. 2-9. Mark 2. 1-12 Luk 5. 17-26.

A fų dez after đis, đe Lord
 rivizits đát femd tɜn
Kapernaɒm, and sɯn đe ples
 woz fild wiđ hiz renɜn.
A mɒltitųd kem ferɟ tu hir,
 and ɟroŋd đe vestibųl;
and đer hi priçt đe blesed wɒrd
 ov lịf—its lω, or rɯl.
It hapend on a serten de,
 hwịl hi, on priçiŋ bent,
woz poriŋ wizdom intu irz
 hwiç gev a glad asent,
đat doktorz ov đe lω sat bị,
 and hωti Farisiz,
hɯ sωt tu kaç him in đe net
 ov đer on sɒteltiz.

And while his power went forth to heal,
  A palsied man was brought
Upon his bed, by four friends borne,
  Who to approach Christ sought.
But as they could not, any way,
  For that great crowd, come nigh,
They broke the covering of the roof,
  And let him down thereby.
When Jesus saw their earnest faith,
  Unto the couch he turned,
And said to the poor palsied man,
  For whom his mercy yearned,
"Son, let thy heart be of good cheer,
  Thy sins have pardon gained."
Whereat the Scribes and Pharisees
  With reasonings fierce complained,
"Who dares speaks blasphemies like these,
  God only can forgive."
Immediately when Jesus saw
  Their thoughts within them strive,
He said, "Why reason in this way?
  Why think so wickedly?
Which is more easy, then, to say,
  Thy sins forgiven be;
Or bid the paralytic rise,
  Take up his bed, and go?
That you may learn, the Son of man
  Forgiveness can bestow,
(Then to the sick,) I say, Arise,
  Take up thy bed; depart
Unto thy house." Immediately
  He rose with grateful heart,
And to his house returned, with praise
  To God for health restored.
The multitude beheld with awe,
  And Christ's great power adored.
"Strange things our eyes have seen to-day,
  Never the like before."
And God they glorified, who had
  On men bestowed such power.

And hwi̧l hiz pɤer went fɵrŧ tu hil,
  a pɷlzid man woz brɷt
ɒpon hiz bed, bi̧ fɵr frendz bɵrn,
  huu tu aprɵɋ Kri̧st sɷt.
Bɒt az đe kud not, eni we,
  for đát gret krɤd, kɒm ni̧,
đe brɵk đe kɒveriŋ ov đe ruuf,
  and let him dɤn đerbi̧.
Hwen Jizɒs sɷ đer ernest feŧ,
  ɒntu đe kɤɋ hi tɒrnd,
and sed tu đe puur pɷlzid man,
  for huum hiz mersi yernd,
"Sɒn, let đi̧ hart bi ov gud ɋir,
  đi̧ sinz hav pardon gend."
Hwerat đe Skri̧bz and Farisiz
  wiđ rizoniŋz firs komplend,
"Huu derz spik blasfemiz li̧k điz,
  God ɵnli kan forgiv."
Immidietli hwen Jizɒs sɷ
  đer ŧɷts wiđin đem stri̧v,
hi sed, "Hwi̧ rizon in đis we?
  hwi̧ ŧiŋk sɵ wikedli?
Hwiɋ iz mɵr izi, đen, tu se,
  Đi̧ sinz forgiven bi;
or bid đe paralitik ri̧z,
  tek ɒp hiz bed, and gɵ?
Đat ų me lern, đe Sɒn ov man
  forgivnes kan bestɵ,
(đen tu đe sik,) Ɨ se, Ari̧z,
  tek ɒp đi̧ bed; depart
ɒntu đi̧ hɤs." Immidietli
  hi rɵz wiđ gretful hart,
and tu hiz hɤs retɒrnd, wiđ prez
  tu God for helŧ restɵrd.
Đe mɒltitųd beheld wiđ ɷ,
  and Kri̧st's gret pɤer adɵrd.
"Strenj ŧiŋz ɤr i̧z hav sin tu-de,
  never đe li̧k befɵr."
And God đe glɵrifi̧d, huu had
  on men bestɵd sɒɋ pɤer.

SECTION 39.

The Calling of Matthew.—Matthew 9. 9. Mark 2. 13, 14. Luke 5. 27, 28.

Next by the sea-side Jesus taught,
  Where multitudes could meet;
And then he traveled on again,
  And came to Levi's seat.

SEKƩON 39.

Đe Kɷliŋ ov Maŧų.—Maŧų 9. 9. Mark 2. 13, 14. Luke 5. 27, 28.

Nekst bi̧ đe si-si̧d Jizɒs tɷt,
  hwer mɒltitųdz kud mit;
and đen hi traveld on agen,
  and kem tu Livi̧'z sit.

Matthew his other name was called,
He was Alpheus' son,
At the toll office he was found
Until his work was done.
"Come, follow me," said Christ to
Matthew at once obeyed; [him;
He left all there, and followed Christ,
No more by Mammon swayed.

SECTION 40.

An Infirm Man healed at Bethesda. —John 5. 1-16.

Again the Jewish festival,
The passover, came round;
And Christ to Salem went, to keep
A feast so much renowned.
Now by the sheep-gate lies a pool
Which is Bethesda named,
Or House of Mercy, where the blind,
The impotent, the lamed,
Assembled; for at stated times
One stirred this wondrous pool,
And he who first then bathed therein
Was instantly made whole.
One man infirmity had borne
For thirty-eight long years,
When Jesus came with power and love
To soothe his anxious fears.
Christ knew his case, and gently said,
"Wilt thou be made whole now?"
"Sir," said the man, "to lift me in,
No one will help bestow;
And when I try to reach the pool,
Another steps before."
Said Jesus, "Take thy bed and walk."
He lingered there no more.
Healed of his weakness, strong he
walked;
And 'twas the Sabbath day.
Quickly the murmuring Jews ob-
With angry jealousy, [served,
"It is not lawful on this day,
To carry thus thy bed."
But he replied, with honest faith,
"Yet he who cured me said,
'Take up thy bed, and walk.'" Then
Inquired who that could be; [they
For Jesus from the multitude
Retreated privately.

Maɟų hiz ɒđer nem woz kɷld,
hi woz Alfiɒs' sɒn,
at đe tөl ofis hi woz fɜnd
ɒntil hiz wɒrk woz dɒn.
"Kɒm, folө mi," sed Krįst tu him;
Maɟų at wɒns өbed;
hi left ɷl đer, and folөd Krįst,
nө mөr bį Mamon swed.

SEKΣON 40.

An Inferm Man hild at Beɟezda. —Jon 5. 1-16.

Agen đe Jɯiʃ festival,
đe pasөver, kem rɜnd;
and Krįst tu Selem went, tu kip
a fist sө mɒç renɜnd.
Nɜ bį đe ʃip-get lįz a pɯl
hwiç iz Beɟezda nemd,
or Hɜs ov Mersi, hwer đe blįnd,
đe impөtent, đe lemd,
asembeld; for at steted tįmz
wɒn sterd đis wɒndrɒs pɯl,
and hi hɯ ferst đen beđd đerin
woz instantli med hөl.
Wɒn man infermiti had bөrn
for ɟerti-et loŋ yirz,
hwen Jizɒs kem wiđ pɜer and lɒv
tu sɯđ hiz aŋkʃɒs firz.
Krįst nų hiz kes and jentli sed,
"Wilt đɜ bi med hөl nɜ?"
"Ser," sed đe man, "tu lift mi in,
nөwɒn wil help bestө;
and hwen į trį tu riç đe pɯl,
anɒđer steps befөr."
Sed Jizɒs, "Tek đį bed and wɷk."
Hi liŋgerd đer nө mөr.
Hild ov hiz wiknes, stroŋ hi
wɷkt;
and 'twoz đe Sabaɟ de.
Kwikli đe mɒrmɒriŋ Jɯz obzervd,
wiđ aŋgri jelɒsi,
"It iz not lɷful on đis de,
tu kari đɒs đį bed."
Bɒt hi replįd, wiđ onest feɟ,
"Yet hi hɯ kųrd mi sed,
'Tek ɒp đį bed, and wɷk.'" Đen
inkwįrd hɯ đát kud bi; [đe
for Jizɒs from đe mɒltitųd
retrited prįvetli.

Soon after this, the man was seen
Within the temple, strong;
And Jesus met him as he made
His way amid the throng.
The Lord then spoke this warning word,
"Now thou art healed, beware
That not again thou disobey,
Lest worse ill thee ensnare."
And when the man departed thence,
Desirous to display
His Savior's power, he told the Jews
Who healed him on that day.

SECTION 41.

Christ asserts his Divinity.
—John 5. 17-47.

The Jews then persecuted Christ,
Because he would display
His miracles of love divine
Upon the Sabbath day.
(As if to do a work of love
On any day, could be
An act of sacrilege and wrong,
Showing impiety.)
Then Jesus answered, "God above
Is ever working good,
And I, his Son, perform good works,
With the same love imbued."
The Jews for this thing sought to kill
Their own Messiah true,
Because upon the Sabbath day
He would these good works do;
And also called the God of all
His Father, and said, He
Himself possessed the attributes
Of sovereign Deity.
Jesus replied, "So closely joined
In me are Father, Son,
That all the Father doeth is
By the Son likewise done.
The Father so much loves the Son,
To him he all reveals;
And he will show him greater works,
Works which he now conceals.
For as the Father raiseth up
The spiritually dead,

Sɯn after ðis, ðe man woz sin
wiðin ðe tempel, stroŋ;
and Jizɒs met him az hį mɛd
hiz wɛ amid ðe ʇroŋ.
Ðe Lord ðen spɵk ðis worniŋ wɒrd,
"Nɤ ðɤ art hįld, bewɛr
ðat not agen ðɤ disɵbe,
lest wɒrs il ðį ensnɛr."
And hwen ðe man departed ðens,
dezįrɒs tu displɛ
hiz Sɛvier'z pɤer, hį tɵld ðe Jɯz
hɯ hįld him on ðát dɛ.

SEKΣON 41.

Krįst aserts hiz Diviniti.
—Jon 5. 17-47.

Ðe Jɯz ðen persekɥted Krįst.
bekɷz hį wud displɛ
hiz mirakelz ov lɒv divįn
ɒpon ðe Şabaʇ dɛ.
(Az if tu dɯ a wɒrk ov lɒv
on eni dɛ, kud bį
an akt ov sakrilej and roŋ,
ʃɵiŋ impįeti.)
Ðen Jizɒs anserd, "God abɒv
iz ever wɒrkiŋ gud,
and į, hiz Sɒn, perform gud wɒrks,
wið ðe sem lɒv imbɥd."
Ðe Jɯz for ðis ʇiŋ sɷt tu kil
ðer ɵn Mesįa trɯ,
bekɷz ɒpon ðe Sabaʇ dɛ
hį wud ðiz gud wɒrks dɯ;
and ɷlsɵ kɵld ðe God ov ɷl
hiz Fɑðer, and sed, Hį
Himself pozest ðe atribɥts
ov sovren Dįiti.
Jizɒs replįd, "Sɵ klɵsli joind
in mį ar Fɑðer, Sɒn,
ðat ɷl ðe Fɑðer dɯeʇ iz
bį ðe Sɒn lįkwįz dɒn.
Ðe Fɑðer sɵ mɒç lɒvz ðe Sɒn,
tu him hį ɷl revilz;
and hį wil ʃɵ him greter wɒrks,
wɒrks hwiç hį nɤ konsilz.
For az ðe Fɑðer rezeʇ ɒp
ðe spiritɥali ded,

Even so the Son divine hath power
To raise from death's dark shade.
The Father only judgeth none;
All judgement to the Son
He hath commited: (now, indeed,
My mission is begun:)
That as men honor God most high,
Even so they should revere
The Son, who now, as long foretold,
Doth on the earth appear.
For he that honors not the Son,
Will not exalt the Sender;
But he that rev'rences my word,
To God will worship render.
He hath immortal life within,
And ever shall rejoice;
For now's the hour wherein the dead
Shall hear my sovereign voice,
And those who hear it and obey,
Shall have eternal life.
No condemnation shall be theirs,
Nor any painful strife.
For as the Father in himself
Has life, so has he given
The Son to have life in himself,
Both in the earth and heaven;
And has empowered him to possess
The right of judgement too,
Because he is the Son of man,
Immaculate and true.
And marvel not at what you hear,
The hour is near at hand
When all that now are in their graves
Shall hear his loud command,
And shall come forth; the good to life,
To hell the evil band.
I can of mine own self do nought;
His word I hear, and tell,
And hence my judgement is, like his,
Divine, infallible;
Because I seek my Father's will,
And not my own alone;
As in my doctrines and my deeds
Is always clearly shown.
If I alone should testify
Touching myself and cause,
My evidence would not avail,
According to your laws.

ɪven sɵ đe Sɒn divįn haŧ pʊer
tu rez from deŧ's dark ʃed.
Đe Fɛđer ɵnli jɒjeŧ nɒn;
ɒl jɒjment tu đe Sɒn
hɪ haŧ komited: (nʊ, indid,
mį miʃon iz begɒn:)
đat az men onor God mɵst hį,
ɪven sɵ đe ʃud revɪr
đe Sɒn, hɯ nʊ, az loŋ fɵrtɵld,
dɒŧ on đe erŧ apɪr.
For hɪ đat onorz not đe Sɒn,
wil not ekzɷlt đe Sender;
bɒt hɪ đat rev'rensez mį wɒrd,
tu God wil wɒrʃip render.
Hɪ haŧ immortal lįf wiđin,
and ever ʃal rejois;
for nʊ'z đe ʊr hwerin đe ded
ʃal hɪr mį sovren vois,
and đɵz hɯ hɪr it and ɵbe,
ʃal hav eternal lįf.
Nɵ kondemneʃon ʃal bi đerz,
nor eni penful strįf.
For az đe Fɛđer in himself
haz lįf, sɵ haz hɪ given
đe Sɒn tu hav lįf in himself,
bɵŧ in đe erŧ and heven;
and haz empʊerd him tu pozes
đe rįt ov jɒjment tɯ,
bekɷz hɪ iz đe Sɒn ov man,
imakųlet and trɯ.
And marvel not at hwot ų hir,
đe ʊr iz nɪr at hand
hwen ɷl đat nʊ ar in đer grevz
ʃal hɪr hiz lʊd komand,
and ʃal kɒm fɵrŧ; đe gud tu lįf,
tu hel đe ɪvel band.
Ɨ kan ov mįn ɵn self dɯ nɷt;
hiz wɒrd į hɪr and tel,
and hens mį jɒjment iz, lįk hiz,
Divįn, infalibel;
bekɷz į sɪk mį Fɛđer'z wil,
and not mį ɵn alɵn;
az in mį doktrinz and mį dɪdz
iz ɷlwez klɪrli ʃɵn.
If į alɵn ʃud testifį
tɒçiŋ mįself and kɷz,
mį evidens wud not avel,
akordiŋ tu ųr lɷz.

But John the Baptist also proved
I'm the Messiah true,
And thus my mission is confirmed
By witnessing of two.
But not from man alone do I
My evidence obtain,
That through myself, the Christ, mankind
May now salvation gain.
John was, indeed, a shining light,
In whom ye might rejoice,
But I have greater witness still,
The Father's sovereign voice,
As seen in all the miracles
He sent me to achieve;
I do them, and they prove me Christ,
That all men may believe.
But ye know not God's voice or form,
Nor know his Word within,
Therefore ye recognise not me,
His likeness, free from sin.
Ye search the Scriptures, and on them
Eternal life ye ground,
And they all testify of me,
In prophecies profound.
Alas, ye will not come to me,
That heavenly life to prove:
Not that I wish your praise, but wish
That you possessed God's love.
I who am come in God's own name,
You will not now receive;
But if vain Anti-Christs arise,
In them you will believe.
How can ye have true faith in God
Who trust in men alone?
Or honor me, when ye have not
The Fount of honor known?
Not I alone might now accuse
Your sophistry to heaven;
But even Moses, whom ye boast,
Hath witness 'gainst you given.
If ye did truly now believe
His words from error free,
Ye would believe in me, as Christ,
Because he wrote of me.
But if ye do not understand
And trust his prophecies,
How shall ye understand my words,
Containing mysteries?

Bɒt Jon đe Baptist ωlsσ prɯvd
į'm đe Mesįa trɯ,
and đɒs mį miʃon iz konfermd
bį witnesiŋ ov tɯ́.
Bɒt not from man alσn dɯ į
mį evidens obtεn,
đat ŧrɯ mįself, đe Krįst, mankįnd
mε nȣ salvεʃon gεn.
Jon woz, indid, a ʃįniŋ lįt,
in hɯm yi mįt rejois,
bɒt į hav grεter witnes stil,
đe Fɑđer'z sovren vois,
az sin in ωl đe mirakelz
hi sent mi tu açiv;
į dɯ đem, and đε prɯv mi Krįst,
đat ωl men mε beliv.
Bɒt yi nσ́ not God'z vois or form,
nor nσ́ hiz Wɒrd wiđin,
đerfσr yi rekognįz not mi,
hiz lįknes, fri from sin.
Yi serç đe Skriptɥrz, and on đem
eternal lįf yi grȣnd,
and đε ωl testifį ov mi
in profesiz prσfȣnd.
Alas, yi wil not kɒm tu mi,
đát hevenli lįf tu prɯv:
not đat į wiʃ ɥr prez, bɒt wiʃ
đat ɥ pozest God'z lɒv.
Į hɯ am kɒm in God'z σn nεm,
ɥ wil not nȣ resiv;
bɒt if vεn Anti-Krįsts arįz,
in đem ɥ wil beliv.
Hȣ kan yi hav trɯ fεŧ in God
hɯ trɒst in men alσn?
or onor mi, hwen yi hav not
đe Fȣnt ov onor nσn?
Not į alσn mįt nȣ akɥz
ɥr sofistri tu heven;
bɒt iven Mσzes, hɯm yi bσst,
haŧ witnes 'genst ɥ given.
If yi did trɯli nȣ beliv
hiz wɒrdz from eror fri,
yi wud beliv in mi, az Krįst,
bekωz hi rσt ov mi.
Bɒt if yi dɯ not ɒnderstand
and trɒst hiz profesiz,
hȣ ʃal yi ɒnderstand mį wɒrdz,
kontεniŋ misteriz?

SECTION 42.

Christ defends his disciples for plucking the corn on the Sabbath.—Matthew 12. 1-8. Mark 2. 23-28. Luke 6. 1-5.

It happened at the Paschal feast,
  The second Sabbath day,
As Jesus through the corn-fields
  That his disciples stay [passed,
(By hunger moved,) to pluck the ears
  And eat them as they go.
The Pharisees beheld, and said,
  "Why break the Sabbath so?"
Jesus replied, "Have ye not heard
  That David, when in need,
Took even the shew-bread from God's house,
  Himself and friends to feed?
Yet 'twas not lawful to be used
  But by the priests alone.
And in the law, ye also read,
  No guilt by priests is shown,
Though they observe not the full rest
  Of holy Sabbath days,
But work at offering sacrifice,
  As well as prayer and praise.
Here truly may I say that One
  Above the temple stands;
And had ye understood God's Word,
  No breach of his commands
Would ye have seen in what was done;
  Nor would ye now despise
The innocent, for mercy is
  Above all sacrifice.
The Sabbath, God ordained for man,
  And not, in any way,
As you think, was man made that he
  Might keep the Sabbath day,
O'er which the Son of man, as Lord,
  Exerts his sovereign sway."
And thus his mercy and his power
  Did Christ to them display.

SEKΣON 42.

Krįst defendz hiz disįpelz for plɒkiŋ ðe korn on ðe Sabaθ.—Maŧɥ 12. 1-8. Mark 2. 23-28. Lɯk 6. 1-5.

It hapend at ðe Paskal fɩst,
  ðe sekond Sabaŧ dε,
az Jɩzɒs ŧrɯ ðe korn-fɩldz past,
  ðat hiz disįpelz stε
(bį hɒŋger mɯvd,) tu plɒk ðe ɩrz
  and ɩt ðem az ðε gơ.
Ðe Farisɩz beheld, and sed,
  "Hwį brεk ðe Sabaŧ sơ?"
Jɩzɒs replįd, "Hav yɩ not herd
  Ðat Dεvid, hwen in nɩd,
tuk ɩven ðe ʃơ-bred from God'z hȣs,
  himself and frends tu fɩd?
yet 'twoz not lɔful tu bɩ ɥzd
  bɒt bį ðe prɩsts alơn.
And in ðe lɔ yɩ ɔlsơ rɩd,
  nơ gilt bį prɩsts iz ʃơn,
ðơ ðε obzerv not ðe ful rest
  ov hơli Sabaŧ dεz,
bɒt wɒrk at oferiŋ sakrifįs,
  az wel az prεr and prεz.
Hɩr trɯli mε į sε ðat Wɒn
  abɒv ðe tempel standz;
and had yɩ ɒnderstud God'z Wɒrd,
  nơ brɩç ov hiz komandz
wud yɩ hav sɩn in hwot woz dɒn;
  nor wud yɩ nȣ despįz
ðe inosent, for mersi iz
  abɒv ɔl sakrifįs.
Ðe Sabaŧ, God ordend for man,
  and not, in eni wε,
az ɥ ŧiŋk, woz man mεd ðat hɩ
  mįt kɩp ðe Sabaŧ dε,
ơ'r hwiç ðe Sɒn ov man, az Lord,
  ekzerts hiz sovren swε."
And ðɒs hiz mersi and hiz pȣer
  did Krįst tu ðem displε.

SECTION 43.

Christ heals the Withered Hand. —Matthew 12. 9-13. Mark 3. 1-6. Luke 6. 6-11.

Again upon a Sabbath day
  Did Jesus go and teach

SEKΣON 43.

Krįst hɩlz ðe Wiðerd Hand. —Maŧɥ 12. 9-13. Mark 3. 1-6. Lɯk 6. 6-11.

Agen ɒpon a Sabaŧ dε
  did Jɩzɒs gơ and tɩç

Within the Jewish synagogue,
  Where he was wont to preach.
And one was there with withered hand;
  So Scribes and Pharisees,
Watched him, lest he upon that day
  Should heal the sad disease.
He knew the malice of their minds;
  He saw through their disguise;
Religious face, while in their hearts
  They evil would devise;
And to the crippled man, he said,
  "Stand in the midst; Arise!"
He rose, and stood, with waiting faith.
  They, seeking to appeal
'Gainst Jesus, cried, "Is it the law
  On Sabbath days to heal?"
"One thing I ask you," Christ replied,
  "Is't lawful to employ
The Sabbath days for good or ill?
  To save life, or destroy?"
Silence they kept. Again he spoke,
  "If one of you should see
His sheep upon the Sabbath fall
  In a pit suddenly,
Will he not straightway lift it out?
  Much better than a sheep
Is man: and therefore it is right
  The Sabbath thus to keep."
Grieved at the hardness of their hearts,
  Displeasure marked his face,
And to the man he said, "Stretch forth
  Thy hand"—with heavenly grace.
He stretched it forth with perfect ease,
  For swift it was restored,
And, like the other, sound appeared
  At Jesus' mighty word.
Then did the Pharisees combine
  With the Herodians, fired
With madness against Jesus Christ,
  And to destroy conspired.

wiđin đe Juiʃ sinagog,
  hwer hi woz wɒnt tu priç.
And wɒn woz đer wiđ wiđerd hand;
  sø skrịbz and Farisiz,
woçt him, lest hi ɒpon đát de
  ʃud hil đe sad disiz.
Hi nų đe malis ov đer mịndz;
  hi sɷ ꝥrɯ đer disgịz;
relijɒs fes, hwịl in đer harts
  đe ivel wud devịz;
and tu đe kripeld man, hi sed,
  "Stand in đe midst; Arịz!"
Hi røz, and stud, wiđ wetiŋ feꝥ.
  Đe, sikiŋ tu apil
'genst Jizɒs, krịd, "Iz it đe lɷ
  on Sabaꝥ dez tu hil?"
"Wɒn ꝥiŋ ị ask ų," Krịst replịd,
  "Iz't lɷful tu emploi
đe Sabaꝥ dez for gud or il?
  tu sev lịf, or destroi?"
Sịlens đe kept. Agen hi spøk,
  "If wɒn ov ų ʃud si
hiz ʃip ɒpon đe Sabaꝥ fɷl
  in a pit sɒdenli,
wil hi not stretwe lift it ɤt?
  Mɒç beter đan a ʃip
iz man: and đerfør it iz rịt
  đe Sabaꝥ đɒs tu kip."
Grivd at đe hardnes ov đer harts,
  displeʒur markt hiz fes,
and tu đe man hi sed, "Streç førꝥ
  đị hand"—wiđ hevenli gres.
Hi streçt it førꝥ wiđ perfekt iz,
  for swift it woz restørd,
and, lịk đe ɒđer, sɤnd apird
  at Jizɒs' mịti wɒrd.
Đen did đe Farisiz kombịn
  wiđ đe Herødianz, fịrd
wiđ madnes agenst Jizɒs Krịst,
  and tu destroi konspịrd.

SECTION 44.

Christ heals the Diseases of many.

—Matthew 12. 15-21. Mark 3. 7-12.

When Jesus knew it, he withdrew
  To Galilee's calm lake,
And multitudes, caught by his fame,
  Did eagerly betake

SEKΣON 44.

Krịst hilz đe Disizez ov meni.

—Maꝥų 12. 15-21. Mark 3. 7-12.

Hwen Jizɒs nų it, hi wiđdrɯ
  tu Galili'z kɐm lek,
and mɒltitųdz, kɷt bị hiz fem,
  did igerli betek

7

Themselves to him, from Jordan, and
  From Tyre to Edom south,
To be made whole, and then to learn
  True wisdom from his mouth.
Even spirits foul, with awe fell down,
  Soon as they saw his face,
And cried, "Thou art the Son of God;"
  Owning his wondrous grace.
But he commanded secresy,
  As thus Esaias spoke,
"Behold my servant, mine elect,
  Who shall not strife provoke,
Nor cry aloud, my well beloved;
  My spirit shall on him rest.
Judgement he'll to the Gentiles show,
  They shall in him be blessed.
His voice shall not be heard abroad,
  From strife and clamor free;
The bruised reed, the smoking flax,
  Shall share his victory."

SECTION 45.

Christ chooses his Twelve Apostles.
—Matthew 10. 1-4. Mark 3. 13-19.
Luke 6. 12-19.

Then Jesus to a mountain lone
  Retired, for secret prayer,
And all night long continued he
  With God in converse there.
And when the day returned, he called
  Such followers as he chose,
And from them he appointed twelve
  His Gospel to disclose.
These he Apostles named, and gave
  Them wondrous power to heal
All sicknesses, and demons vile
  From sufferers to expel.
Their names were: Simon, Peter called,
  And Andrew, Peter's brother,
With James and John of Zebedee,
  (Salome was their mother,
The sons of thunder these he named,)
  Matthew and Philip too,
And Thomas, and Alpheus' son
  James, with Bartholomew,
Thaddeus or Jude, brother of James,
  Simon the Canaanite,
And Judas of Iscariot,
  Who did his Lord despite.

đemselvz tu him, from Jordan, and
  from Tịr tu Ɛdom sɤŧ,
tu bi mɛd hɵl, and đɛn tu lern
  ŧrɯ wizdom from hiz mɤŧ.
Ɛven spirits fɤl, wiđ ɷ fel dɤn,
  sɯn az đɛ sɷ hiz fɛs,
and krịd, "Đɤ art đe Sɒn ov God;"
  ɵniŋ hiz wɒndrɒs grɛs.
Bɑt hi komanded sikresi,
  az đɒs Ezaias spɵk,
"Behɵld mị servant, mịn elekt,
  hɯ ʃal not strịf prɵvɵk,
nor krị alɤd, mị wel belɒvd;
  mị spirit ʃal on him rest.
Jɒjment hi'l tu đe Jentịlz ʃɵ,
  đɛ ʃal in him bi blest.
Hiz vois ʃal not bi herd abrɷd,
  from strịf and klamor fri;
đe brɯzed rid, đe smɵkiŋ flaks,
  ʃal ʃɛr hiz viktori."

SEKΣON 45.

Krịst çɯzez hiz Twelv Aposelz.
—Maŧɥ 10. 1-4. Mark 3. 13-19.
Lɯk 6. 12-19.

Đen Jizɒs tu a mɤnten lɵn
  retịrd, for sikret prɛr,
and ɷl nịt loŋ kontinɥd hi
  wiđ God in konvers đɛr.
And hwen đe dɛ retɒrnd, hi kɷld
  sɒç folɵerz az hi çɵz,
and from đem hi apointed twelv
  hiz Gospel tu disklɵz.
Điz hi Aposelz nɛmd, and gɛv
  đem wɒndrɒs pɤer tu hil
ɷl siknesez, and dimonz vịl
  from sɒfererz tu ekspel.
Đɛr nɛmz wer: Sịmon, Piter kɷld,
  and Andrɯ, Piter'z brɒđer,
wiđ Jɛmz and Jon ov Zebedi,
  (Salɵmi woz đɛr mɒđer,
đe sɒnz ov ŧɒnder điz hi nɛmd,)
  Maŧɥ and Filip tɯ,
and Tomas, and Alfiɒs' sɒn
  Jɛmz, wiđ Barŧolomɥ,
Ŧadiɒs or Jɯd, brɒđer ov Jɛmz,
  Sịmon đe Kenanịt,
and Judas ov Iskariot,
  hɯ did hiz Lord despịt.

Then they descended to the plain,
 And from all countries round
The multitude surrounded him,
 To hear the joyful sound.
His healing touch they sought. It
 Virtue enough for all ; [proved
Each ill departed at his word,
 Spirits obeyed his call.

SECTION 46.

The Sermon on the Mount.—

Matthew, chapters 5, 6, 7. Luke 6. 20-49.

And seeing the vast multitudes
 That thronged, his word to hear,
Jesus went up a sacred mount,
 And there, in accents clear,
He preached this sermon. Lifting up
 His eyes on those around,
He ope'd his mouth, and taught them
  thus ;
 (They thrilling at the sound :)—

Blessings or Beatitudes pronounced on the Good.

Blessed and happy are the poor
 In spirit, for to these
Belong the peace of heaven, and all
 Its sweet felicities.
Blessed are those who mourn for faults
 Themselves and others do ;
For all such mourners will amend,
 Find grace and comfort too.
Blest are the meek and gentle ones ;
 For unto them is given
The earth, to have and hold therein
 An earnest hope of heaven.
And blessed too are they that long
 For perfect righteousness ;
For they shall soon be satisfied,
 And know no more distress.
Blest are the merciful ; for they
 Like mercy shall obtain ;
Blest are the pure in heart ; for they
 God's presence shall retain.
Blest are the peacemakers ; for they
 Are called the sons of heaven.
Blest are the sufferers for right ;
 To them shall bliss be given.

Đen đɛ desended tu đe plɛn,
 and from ɷl kɒntriz rɤnd
đe mɒltitɥd sɒrɤnded him,
 tu hir đe joiful sɤnd.
Hiz hiliŋ tɒç đe sɷt. It prɯvd
 vertɥ enɒf for ɷl ;
iç il departed at hiz wɒrd,
 spirits ɵbed hiz kɷl.

SEKΣON 46.

Đe Sermon on đe Mɤnt.—

Maɟɥ, çapterz 5, 6, 7. Lɯk 6. 20-49.

And siiŋ đe vast mɒltitɥdz
 đat ɟrɒŋd, hiz wɒrd tu hir,
Jizɒs went ɒp a sekred mɤnt,
 and đɛr, in aksents klir,
hi priçt đis sermon. Liftiŋ ɒp
 hiz ɉz on đɵz arɤnd,
hi ɵpt hiz mɤɟ, and tɷt đem
  đɒs ;
 (đɛ ɟriliŋ at đe sɤnd :)—

Blesiŋz or Biatitɥdz pronɤnst on đe Gud.

Blesed and hapi ar đe pɯr
 in spirit, for tu điz
beloŋ đe pis ov heven, and ɷl
 its swit felisitiz.
Blesed ar đɵz hɯ mɵrn for fɷlts
 đemselvz and ɒđerz dɯ ;
for ɷl sɒç mɵrnerz wil amend,
 fɉnd gres, and kɒmfort tɯ.
Blest ar đe mik and jentel wɒnz ;
 for ɒntu đem iz given
đe erɟ, tu hav and hɵld đerin
 an ernest hɵp ov heven.
And blesed tɯ ar đɛ đat loŋ
 for perfekt rɉtiɒsnes ;
for đɛ ʃal sɯn bi satisfɉd,
 and nɵ́ nɵ mɵr distres.
Blest ar đe mersiful ; for đɛ
 lɉk mersi ʃal obtɛn ;
blest ar đe pɥr in hart ; for đɛ
 God'z prezens ʃal retɛn.
Blest ar đe pismɛkerz ; for đɛ
 ar kɷld đe sɒnz ov heven.
Blest ar đe sɒfererz for rɉt ;
 tu đem ʃal blis bi given.

When men revile you wrongfully
  For Christ and truth divine,
Rejoice exceedingly, for bright
  Your names in heaven shall shine.
And thus all prophets of God's truth
  Will persecuted be,
Because they preach a higher law
  Than other mortals see.

Woes denounced on Sinners.

But woe to you rich ones, who seek
  No heavenly consolation:
Woe to you full ones; ye shall come
  To utter desolation.
And woe, also, to you that laugh,
  For ye shall mourn and weep:
Woe unto you, the praised of men;
  Their praise you cannot keep.

The True Glory of Christians.

Christians should be the salt of earth,
  A true preserving power,
Deriving all its strength from heaven,
  Imparting it each hour.
But if they lose the inward grace
  That God alone bestows,
And trust to men to bring it back,
  They sink beneath their foes.
True Christians are the world's true
    light,
  No light like theirs is found;
The Church is set upon a hill,
  To lighten all around.
Truth is a lamp, which should be set
  Aloft, to shed its rays
On all beneath, so that its light
  May guide in wisdom's ways.
Christians should so display their light
  In works of truth and love,
That men may glorify their God,
  Who reigns in heaven above.

Christianity is the Completion of the Law.

Think not I come to set aside
  The prophets or the law;
For verily all heaven and earth
  Shall vanish, ere one flaw
Be found therein, but every jot
  And tittle shall be done;

Hwen men revi̧l ų roŋfuli
  for Kri̧st and trɯɟ divi̧n,
rejois eksidiŋli, for bri̧t
  ųr nemz in heven ʃal ʃi̧n.
And đɒs ɷl profets ov God'z trɯɟ
  wil persekųted bi,
bekɷz đe priç a hi̧er lɷ
  đan ɒđer mortalz si.

Wɵz denɜnst on Sinerz.

Bɒt wɵ tu ų riç wɒnz, hɯ sik
  nɵ hevenli konsɵleʃon:
wɵ tu ų ful wɒnz; yi ʃal kɒm
  tu ɒter desoleʃon.
And wɵ, ɷlsɵ, tu ų đat lɛf,
  for yi ʃal mɵrn and wip:
wɵ ɒntu ų, đe prezd ov men;
  đer prez ų kanot kip.

Đe Trɯ Glɵri ov Kristianz.

Kristianz ʃud bi đe sɷlt ov erɟ,
  a trɯ prezerviŋ pɜer,
deri̧viŋ ɷl its streŋɟ from heven,
  impartiŋ it iç ɜr.
Bɒt if đe lɯz đe inward gres
  đat God alɵn bestɵz,
and trɒst tu men tu briŋ it bak,
  đe siŋk beniđ đer fɵz.
Trɯ Kristianz ar đe wɒrld'z trɯ
    li̧t,
  nɵ li̧t li̧k đerz iz fɜnd;
đe Ͼɒrç iz set ɒpon a hil,
  tu li̧ten ɷl arɜnd.
Trɯɟ iz a lamp, hwiç ʃud bi set
  aloft, tu ʃed its rez
on ɷl beniđ, sɵ đat its li̧t
  me gi̧d in wizdom'z wez.
Kristianz ʃud sɵ disple đer li̧t
  in wɒrks ov trɯɟ and lɒv,
đat men me glɵrifi̧ đer God
  hɯ renz in heven abɒv.

Kristianiti iz đe Kompliʃon ov đe Lɷ.

Ɵiŋk not i̧ kɒm tu set asi̧d
  đe profets or đe lɷ;
for verili ɷl heven and erɟ
  ʃal vaniʃ, er wɒn flɷ
bi fɜnd đerin, bɒt everi jot
  and titel ʃal bi dɒn;

For to perform, and not destroy,
  To do, and not to shun
All righteousness, on earth I come,
  And now my work's begun.
And he who breaks God's least com-
  And teaches others so, [mand,
In heaven shall be, if ever there,
  The lowest of the low:
While he who does and teaches right
  Shall be accounted great,
And honor high shall he obtain
  In heaven's most blest estate.
Except your righteousness exceed
  The Scribes' and Pharisees',
You never shall admittance gain
  Where all is joy and peace.

The Duty of Brotherly Kindness.

Your ancient sages of the law
  Have said, Thou shalt not kill;
And if you shed another's blood,
  Your own shall justice spill:
But I declare all causeless rage
  Against your brother man,
Is heinous in the sight of God,
  And merits judgement's ban;
And those who, in contemptuous mood,
  Opprobrious names bestow
On others, hurt themselves, and make
  Their hearts with hell fire glow.
If therefore thou wouldst rightly come
  To worship God on high,
First banish from within thy heart
  All scorn and enmity;
As far as possible remove
  All cause of war and strife;
And pardon others, as you need
  Pardon yourself through life.
Embrace all opportunities
  Of making peace with foes;
If once you let them slip, beware,
  For you shall suffer woes.

The Duty of Purity and Chastity.

The ancient sages of the law
  Have said, Thou shalt avoid
Adultery, and every lust,
  Or thou shalt be destroyed:
But I command you to abstain
  From all impurity,

for tu perform, and not destroi,
  tu dɯ, and not tu ʃɒn
ɷl rįtiɒsnes, on erŧ į kɒm,
  and nȣ mį wɒrk's begɒn.
And hi hɯ brɛks God'z list kom-
  and tiçez ɒđerz sɵ, [and,
in heven ʃal bi, if ever đer,
  đe lɵest ov đe lɵ:
hwįl hi hɯ dɒz and tiçez rįt
  ʃal bi akȣnted grɛt,
and onor hį ʃal hi obten
  in heven'z mɵst blest estɛt.
Eksept ɥr rįtiɒsnes eksid
  đe Skrįbz' and Farisiz',
ɥ never ʃal admitans gɛn
  hwer ɷl iz joi and pis.

Đe Dɥti ov Brɒđerli Kįndnes.

Ɥr ɛnʃent sɛjez ov đe lɷ
  hav sed, Đȣ ʃalt not kil;
and if ɥ ʃed anɒđer'z blɒd,
  ɥr ɵn ʃal jɒstis spil:
bɒt į dekler ɷl kɷzles rɛj
  agenst ɥr brɒđer man,
iz henɒs in đe sįt ov God,
  and merits jɒjment's ban;
and đɵz hɯ, in kontemptɥɒs mɯd,
  oprɵbriɒs nɛmz bestɵ
on ɒđerz, hɒrt đemselvz, and mɛk
  đer harts wiđ hel fįr glɵ.
If đerfɵr đȣ wudst rįtli kɒm
  tu wɒrʃip God on hį,
ferst baniʃ from wiđin đį hart
  ɷl skorn and enmiti;
az far az posibel remɯv
  ɷl kɷz ov wor and strįf;
and pardon ɒđerz, az ɥ nid
  pardon ɥrself ŧrɯ lįf.
Embrɛs ɷl oportɥnitiz
  ov mɛkiŋ pis wiđ fɵz;
if wɒns ɥ let đem slip, bewer,
  for ɥ ʃal sɒfer wɵz.

Đe Dɥti ov Pɥriti and Çastiti.

Đe ɛnʃent sɛjez ov đe lɷ
  hav sed, Đȣ ʃalt avoid
adɒlteri, and everi lɒst,
  or đȣ ʃalt bi destroid:
bɒt į komand ɥ tu absten
  from ɷl impɥriti,

From wanton thoughts, and words, and
  For God the heart doth see. [looks,
If anything, however dear,
  Betrays you into sin,
Make it a sacrifice betimes
  To heavenly life within.
'Tis better that your idol fall,
  And its delusive spell,
Than that your cherished sin should
  Your guilty soul in hell. [plunge
The sages of the law have said,
  Whoso shall put away
His wife, shall give her a divorce,
  That she may not gainsay:
But I declare that whosoe'er
  Shall put away his wife,
Except for gross unchastity,
  Is with just heaven at strife:
And he shall answer for her wrongs,
  Produced by such divorce,
And all who seek to marry her,
  The first offence endorse.

from wonton ɟɷts, and wɒrdz, and
  for God ɗe hart dɒɟ si. [luks,
If eniɟiŋ, hʌever dir,
  bɘtrez ɥ intu sin,
mek it a sakriʃʝs betʝmz
  tu hevenli lʝf wiɗin.
'Tiz beter ɗat ɥr ʝdol fɷl,
  and its delɯsiv spel,
ɗan ɗat ɥr çeriʃt sin ʃud plɒnj
  ɥr gilti sɵl in hel.
Ɑe sejez ov ɗe lɷ hav sed,
  Hɯsɵ ʃal put awe
hiz wʝf, ʃal giv her a divɵrs,
  ɗat ʃi me not gense:
bɒt ʝ dekler ɗat hɯsɵer
  ʃal put awe hiz wʝf,
eksept for grɵs ɒnçastiti,
  iz wiɗ jɒst heven at strʝf:
and hi ʃal anser for her roŋz
  prɵdɥst bʝ sɒç divɵrs,
and ɷl hɯ sik tu mari her,
  ɗe ferst ofens endors.

The Solemn Responsibility of Oaths.

Your sages of the law have said,
  And that with one accord,
"Do not forswear thyself, but pay
  Thy vows unto the Lord,
When to Jehovah they are made;"
  But I to you proclaim,
Ne'er make a false or trifling oath,
  By God, or any name
In heaven or earth, by creature great
  Or small, or high or low;
For every creature doth belong
  To God, as well ye know;
And therefore hath a sanctity,
  As fashioned by his power,
And still preserved by his kind love
  Through every passing hour.
Therefore avoid vain oaths, and let
  Your conversation be
Sincere, and show in all your words
  A true simplicity.

Ɑe Solem Responsibiliti ov Ɵɗz.

Ɥr sejez ov ɗe lɷ hav sed,
  and ɗát wiɗ wɒn akord,
"Dɯ not forswer ɗʝself, bɒt pe
  ɗʝ vʌz ɒntu ɗe Lord,
hwen tu Jehɵva ɗe ar med;"
  bɒt ʝ tu ɥ prɵklem,
Ner mek a fɷls or trʝfliŋ ɵɟ,
  bʝ God, or eni nem
in heven or erɟ, bʝ kritɥr gret
  or smɷl, or hʝ or lɵ;
for everi kritɥr dɒɟ beloŋ
  tu God, az wel yi nɵ́;
and ɗerfɵr haɟ a saŋktiti,
  az faʃond bʝ hiz pʌer,
and stil prezervd bʝ hiz kʝnd lɒv
  ɟrɯ everi pasiŋ ʌr.
Ɑerfɵr avoid ven ɵɗz, and let
  ɥr konverseʃon bi
sinsir, and ʃɵ in ɷl ɥr wɒrdz
  a trɯ simplisiti.

Retaliation of Evil forbidden.

Your sages of the law have said,
  An eye shall go for eye,
And tooth for tooth; but I declare
  I will not justify

Retalieʃon ov Ɩvil forbiden.

Ɥr sejez ov ɗe lɷ hav sed,
  An ʝ ʃal gɵ for ʝ,
and tɯɟ for tɯɟ; bɒt ʝ dekler
  ʝ wil not jɒstifʝ

Such conduct: rather suffer wrong
  Once and again: alway
Bear with an evil done to you,
  But do not truth betray.
And even repay ill deeds by good:
  For so your charity
Shall melt the hearts of many foes,
  And make them friendly be.
Give unto him that asks, such gifts
  As best fit time and place;
And ne'er refuse such loans as suit
  The occasion or the case.
And if men take away your goods
  By fraud, or violence,
Do not take theirs in a like way,
  And share in their offence.
And whatsoever ye think right
  That men should do to you,
Do so to them, and all good-will
  From this course will ensue.

The Duty of Universal Love.

Your sages of the law have said,
  Thy neighbour thou shalt love,
Thy foe shalt hate; but this I say,
  To you that hear, Approve
Yourselves to Him who is pure Love,
  By loving all, like him;
So shall your cup of bliss be filled
  Up to the very brim.
Do good even to your enemies,
  And unto those who hate;
And pray for those who persecute,
  And for your ruin wait;
So shall ye be the children true
  Of God who is in heaven;
For his sun shines on good and bad;
  To both his rain is given.
If those alone ye love, who love
  On you likewise bestow,
What blessing can ye hope to gain?
  For sinners such love show.
And if alone ye brethren greet,
  What do ye more than all?
The publicans thus friendly are
  To those whom friends they call.
What thanks do ye deserve for this,
  That ye do good for gain?
Or only lend where ye receive?
  Sinners such deeds attain.

sɒɕ kondɒkt: rɛđer sɒfer roŋ.
  wɒns and agen: ɷlwe
ber wiđ an ịvel dɒn tu ɥ,
  bɒt dɯ not trɯɟ betre.
And ịven ripe il didz bị gud:
  for sɵ ɥr ɕariti
ʃal melt đe harts ov meni fɵz,
  and mek đem frendli bị.
Giv ɒntu him đat asks, sɒɕ gifts
  az best fit tịm and ples;
and ner refɥz sɒɕ lɵnz az sɥt
  đe okeʒon, or đe kes.
And if men tek awe ɥr gudz
  bị frɷd, or vịolens,
dɯ not tek đerz in a lịk we,
  and ʃer in đer ofens.
And hwotsɵever yị ɟiŋk rịt
  đat men ʃud dɯ tu ɥ,
dɯ sɵ tu đem, and ɷl gud-wil
  from đis kɵrs wil ensɥ.

Đe Dɥti ov Ɥniversal Lɒv.

Ɥr sejez ov đe lɷ hav sed,
  Đị nebɒr đɜ ʃalt lɒv,
đị fɵ ʃalt het; bɒt đis ị se,
  tu ɥ đat hir, Aprɯv
ɥrselvz tu Him hɯ iz pɥr Lɒv,
  bị lɒviŋ ɷl, lịk him;
sɵ ʃal ɥr kɒp ov blis bị fild
  ɒp tu đe veri brim.
Dɯ gud ịven tu ɥr enemiz,
  and ɒntu đɵz hɯ het;
and pre for đɵz hɯ persekɥt,
  and for ɥr ruin wet;
sɵ ʃal yị bi đe ɕildren trɯ
  ov God hɯ iz in heven;
for hiz sɒn ʃịnz on gud and bad;
  tu bɵɟ hiz ren iz given.
If đɵz alɵn yị lɒv, hɯ lɒv
  on ɥ lịkwịz bestɵ,
hwot blesiŋ kan yị hɵp tu gen?
  for sinerz sɒɕ lɒv ʃɵ.
And if alɵn yị bređren grịt,
  hwot dɯ yị mɵr đan ɷl?
đe pɒblikanz đɒs frendli ar
  tu đɵz hɯm frendz đe kɷl.
Hwot ɟaŋks dɯ yị dezerv for đis,
  đat yị dɯ gud for gen?
or ɵnli lend hwer yị resịv?
  sinerz sɒɕ didz aten.

Love ye your foes; do good to all;
  Impart most willingly;
And great shall your reward be then;
  God's children ye shall be.
For his great love is shown to all;
  No merit they can claim;
Thankless and evil though men are,
  His goodness is the same.
Therefore your Father imitate;
  His children strive to be;
And in your sphere be perfect, and
  Be merciful, as He.

Good should be done without Ostentation.

Take heed that ye do not display
  Your alms-gifts before men;
For such good deeds rise not to heaven,
  And thence come back again.
Noiseless and secret be thy gifts,
  Not to thy left hand known;
Thy Father seeth everything,
  And will in public own.

Prayer should be offered in Sincerity and Simplicity.

Be not like hypocrites, who pray
  In public to be seen;
They do it only for this cause,
  To gain the praise of men.
But enter thou thy closet lone,
  And close thy door to all;
Then on thy Father, secretly,
  In earnest do thou call.
His eye, to which no place is dark,
  Will mark thy humble plea,
And publicly will he reward
  What thou dost secretly.
But use not repetitions vain
  In this thy secret prayer;
Like those who ignorantly think
  Much speaking gains God's ear.
Be not like such; for all ye need
  Is to your Father known;
And ere ye ask, he thinks on you
  And showers his blessings down.
Pray thus:—

The Lord's Prayer.

Our Father who art in the heavens,
  Most holy be thy name.

Lɒv yi ɥr fɵz; dɯ gud tu ɷl;
  impart mɵst wiliŋli;
and gret ʃal ɥr reword bi đen;
  God'z çildren yi ʃal bi.
For hiz gret lɒv iz ʃɵn tu ɷl;
  nɵ merit đe kan klɛm;
ŧaŋkles and ịvil đɵ men ar,
  hiz gudnes iz đe sem.
Đerfɵr ɥr Fɐđer imitet;
  hiz çildren strịv tu bi;
and in ɥr sfịr bi perfekt, and
  bị mersiful, az Hị.

Gud ʃud bi dɒn wiđɤt Ostenteʃon.

Tek hịd đat yi dɯ not disple
  ɥr ɐmz-gifts befɵr men;
for sɒç gud didz rịz not tu heve[n]
  and đens kɒm bak agen.
Noizles and sịkret bi đị gifts,
  not tu đị left hand nɵn;
đị Fɐđer sịeŧ everiŧiŋ,
  and wil in pɒblik ɵn.

Prɛr ʃud bi oferd in Sinseriti and Simplisiti.

Bị not lịk hipokrits, hɯ pre
  in pɒblik tu bị sịn;
đe dɯ it ɵnli for đis kɷz,
  tu gen đe prez ov men.
Bɒt enter đɤ đị klozet lɵn,
  and klɵz đị dɵr tu ɷl;
đen on đị Fɐđer, sịkretli,
  in ernest dɯ đɤ kɷl.
Hiz ị, tu hwiç nɵ ples iz dark,
  wil mark đị hɒmbel pli,
and pɒblikli wil hị reword
  hwot đɤ dɒst sịkretli.
Bɒt ɥz not repetiʃonz ven
  in đis đị sịkret prɛr;
lịk đɵz hɯ ignorantli ŧiŋk
  mɒç spịkiŋ genz God'z ịr.
Bị not lịk sɒç; for ɷl yi nid
  iz tu ɥr Fɐđer nɵn;
and ɛr yi ask, hị ŧiŋks on ɥ,
  and ʃɤerz hiz blesiŋz dɤn.
Pre đɒs:—

Đe Lord'z Prɛr.

Ɤr Fɐđer hɯ art in đe hevenz,
  mɵst hɵli bi đị nem.

Thy kingdom come. Thy will be done,	Đị kiŋdom kɒm. Đị wíl bi dɒn,
In heaven and earth the same.	in heven and erθ đe sɛm.
Give us this day our daily bread.	Giv ɒs đis dɛ ʊr dɛli bred.
Forgive us every debt,	Forgiv ɒs everi det,
As we our debtors gladly free,	az wi ʊr deterz gladli fri,
And their misdeeds forget.	and đɛr misdidz forget.
Into temptation lead us not,	Intu temptɛʃon lid ɒs not,
Except to save; and then	eksept tu sɛv; and đen
The kingdom, power, and praise, be [thine	đe kiŋdom, pʊer, and prɛz, bi địn
For evermore. Amen.	for evermɵr. Amen.
If you to others pardon grant,	If ɥ tu ɒđerz pardon grant,
Your God will pardon you;	ɥr God wil pardon ɥ;
But if you no forgiveness grant,	bɒt if ɥ nɵ forgivnes grant,
In vain you'll pardon sue.	in vɛn ɥ'l pardon sɥ.
The Rule of Fasting.	*Đe Rul ov Fastiŋ.*
Moreover, when ye fast, be not	Mɵrɵver, hwen yi fast, bi not
Like hypocrites, sad-faced;	lịk hipokrits, sad-fɛst;
They only seek the praise of men,	đɛ ɵnli sik đe prɛz ov men,
And to appear straight-laced.	and tu apir strɛt-lɛst.
I say, they lose a good reward.	Ɨ sɛ, đɛ lɯz a gud reword.
Do not thou so; but when	Dɯ not đʊ sɵ; bɒt hwen
Thou fastest, wash thy head, anoint	đʊ fastest, woʃ đị hed, anoint
Thy face; that thus to men	đị fɛs; đat đɒs tu men
Thou seem to be not fasting; but	đʊ sim tu bi not fastiŋ; bɒt
Thy Father sees, and He	đị Fɑđer siz, and Hi
Who lives and works in secret shall	hɯ livz and wɒrks in sikret ʃal·
Reward thee openly.	reword đi ɵpenli.
Labor for heavenly rather than for earthly Treasures.	*Lɛbor for hevenli rađer đan for erθli Treʒurz.*
Lay not up treasures on the earth,	Lɛ not ɒp treʒurz on đe erθ,
Where moth and rust corrupt,	hwɛr moθ and rɒst korɒpt,
Where robbers plunder, and thieves [steal,	hwɛr roberz plɒnder, and θivz stil,
Your schemes to interrupt:	ɥr skimz tu interrɒpt:
But lay up treasure in the heavens,	bɒt lɛ ɒp treʒur in đe hevenz,
Where rust cannot corrupt,	hwɛr rɒst kanot korɒpt,
Nor robbers plunder, nor thieves steal,	nor roberz plɒnder, nor θivz stil,
And no ills interrupt	and nɵ ilz interrɒpt
Your joy: for where your treasure is,	ɥr joi: for hwɛr ɥr treʒur iz,
There will your heart be too;	đɛr wil ɥr hart bi tɯ;
The treasures of the mind alone,	đe treʒurz ov đe mịnd alɵn,
Are lasting, good, and true.	ar lastiŋ, gud, and trɯ.
The light of truth in a clear eye,	Đe lịt ov trɯθ in a klir ị,
The faculty divine	đe fakɒlti divịn
That sees eternal verities	đat siz eternal veritiz
In every outward sign,	in everi ʊtward sịn,
Makes true illumination: if	mɛks trɯ ilɯminɛʃon: if
That vision power be bright,	đát viʒon pʊer bi brịt

It throws the radiance of heaven
  Through human nature's night;
But if that power be dim and weak,
  Man's moral darkness grows,
To mere materialism of sense,
  And all its fatal woes.
'Tis light divine and heavenly
  That makes your eyesight bright,
And if your eye and view be true,
  You shall be full of light;
But if your eye and view be false,
  Darkness will round you fall,
And even your fancied light shall be
  Like a funereal pall.

Trust in God.

Then let your chief desire be this,
  To serve one Lord above;
You cannot serve two masters well,
  And thus divide your love.
You cannot worship God aright
  While you the world adore;
Fix well your choice, like that will be
  Your portion evermore.
Let not a vain anxiety
  Within your hearts abide;
For food, and drink, and needful
  Your Father will provide. [clothes,
Your life is much more than its food,
  Your body than its dress;
Then he who guards the greater gifts
  Will surely give the less.
See how the very birds of heaven
  Are nourished by his care;
They neither plant, nor sow, nor reap,
  And yet they tended are;
Think of your minds, and ask your-
  Are ye not better far? [selves,
Can any add unto his life
  A span of time's duration?
And why take thought for raiment too?
  Even Solomon's proud station
Was not in equal glory decked,
  Or beauty, like the flower.
Think of the lilies of the field,
  And in them see God's power.
If, then, he condescends to clothe
  The herbage with such grace,
Will he not greater care bestow
  On you, O faithless race?

it ϑrɵz ɗe redians ov heven
  ϑrui hųman netųr'z nįt;
bɒt if ɗát pɤer bi dim and wik,
  ɱan'z moral darknes grɵz,
tu mir matirializm ov sens,
  and ɷl its fetal wɵz.
'Tiz lįt divįn and hevenli
  ɗat meks ųr įsįt brįt,
and if ųr į and vų bi trui,
  ų ʃal bi ful ov lįt;
bɒt if ųr į and vų bi fɷls,
  darknes wil rɤnd ų fɷl,
and iven ųr fansid lįt ʃal bi
  lįk a fųnirial pɷl.

Trɒst in God.

Ɗen let ųr ɕif dezįr bi ɗis,
  tu serv wɒn Lord abɒv;
ų kanot serv túi masterz wel,
  and ɗɒs divįd ųr lɒv.
Ų kanot wɒrʃip God arįt
  hwįl ų ɗe wɒrld adɵr;
fiks wel ųr ɕois, lįk ɗát wil bi
  ųr pɵrʃon evermɵr.
Let not a ven aŋkzįeti
  wiɗin ųr harts abįd;
for fuid, and driŋk, and nidful
  ųr Fɛɗer wil provįd. [klɵɗz,
Ųr lįf iz mɒɕ mɵr ɗan its fuid,
  ųr bodi ɗan its dres;
ɗen hi hui gardz ɗe greter gifts
  wil ʃuirli giv ɗe les.
Si hɤ ɗe veri berdz ov heven
  ar nɒriʃt bį hiz ker;
ɗɛ nįɗer plant, nor sɵ, nor rip,
  and yet ɗɛ tended ar;
ϑiŋk ov ųr mįndz, and ask ųrselvz,
  Ar yi not beter far?
Kan eni ad ɒntu hiz lįf
  a span ov tįm'z dųreʃon?
And hwį tek ϑɷt for rement tui?
  iven Solomon'z prɤd steʃon
woz not in ikwal glɵri dekt,
  or bųti, lįk ɗe flɤer.
ϑiŋk ov ɗe liliz ov ɗe fild,
  and in ɗem si God'z pɤer.
If, ɗen, hi kondesendz tu klɵɗ
  ɗe herbej wiɗ sɒɕ gres,
wil hi not greter ker bestɵ
  on ų, Ɵ fesles res?

ed, and bids you	Hi nɵ́z ɥr nid, and bidz ɥ sik,
lom pure; [seek,	at ferst, hiz kiŋdom pɥr;
earthly gifts	and hi wil ad hiz erŧli gifts
endure.	tu treʒurz đat endɥr.
w, put away	Đen, til đe morɵ, put awɛ
xious care;	đe morɵ'z aŋkſɒs ker;
y day	sɒfiſent ɒntu everi dɛ
n must bear.	its il; hwiç man mɒst ber.

sity and Candor.	*Đe Dɥti ov Jenerositi and Kandor.*
all not be judged;	Jɒj not and yi ſal not bi jɒjd;
e not blamed;	nor blɛm and bi not blɛmd;
ll be forgiven,	forgiv, and yi ſal bi forgiven,
amed.	and never bi aſɛmd.
shall be given,	Giv, and tu ɥ it ſal bi given,
ressed close down,	gud meʒur, prest klɵs dɤn,
with such store	and rɒniŋ ɵver; wiđ sɒç stɵr
vors crown.	ſal men ɥr fevorz krɤn.

Self-Reform.	*Đe Dɥti ov Self-Reform.*
e speck that dims	Regard not đɤ đe spek đat dimz
akened eye,	đį brɒđer'z wikend į,
that gives thine	bɒt nɵt đe splint đat givz đįn ɵn
[own	greter infermiti.
say, "Brother, let	Or, hɤ kanst đɤ se, "Brɒđer, let
k from thee;"	mi tɛk đe spek from đi;"
art almost blind?	hwen đɤ đįself art ɷlmɵst blįnd?
isy.	'tiz grɵs hipokrisi.
rawn thy splinter	Hwen đɤ hast drɷn đį splinter ɤt,
hou see, [out,	đen ɵnli kanst đɤ si,
, others' faults,	and jɒj arįt ov, ɒđerz' fɷlts,
legree.	hwotever đer degri.

ction to the Occasion.	*Sɥt ɥr Spiç and Akſon tu đe Okɛʒon.*
heavenly love,	Đe hɵli ŧiŋz ov hevenli lɒv,
unholy;	giv not tu dogz ɒnhɵli;
r you; rather keep	đe'l tɒrn and ter ɥ; rɛđer kip
r the lowly:	sɒç blesiŋz for đe lɵli:
heavenly truth	nor ofer perlz ov hevenli trɥŧ
h heart;	tu men ov swįniſ hart;
under foot, revile,	đe'l tred đem ɒnder fut, revįl,
ith a dart.	and pirs ɥ wiđ a dart.

of Prayer.	*Đe Reword ov Prɛr.*
e given you:	Ask gud; it ſal bi given ɥ:
ye shall find:	Sik trɥŧ; and yi ſal fįnd:
's gates shall open	nok; and heven'z gɛts ſal ɵpen
	stand;
and mind.	đen enter, hart and mįnd.

For everyone that asks, receives;
He finds that seeks afar;
And he that knocks with earnestness,
Soon sees the gates ajar.
If vain and erring man will give
Good gifts to those he loves,
Sure God will better things bestow
On those whom he approves.

Zeal and Perseverance are Necessary.

Enter ye in at the straight gate,
And keep the narrow way
That leadeth to eternal life:
(How few this rule obey!)
For wide's the gate, and broad's the way
That leadeth to destruction;
And many walk this easy road,
Refusing all instruction.

True Religion is known by its Fruits.

Avoid false prophets, those who seem
Like sheep in outward show;
But in their hearts, like wolves they rave,
And bring their followers woe.
Just as you judge trees by their fruit,
So may you know *their* worth;
You gather not from brambles, grapes;
No figs from thorns spring forth.
So every good tree bears good fruit,
And bad ones bad produce:
All trees that bring not forth good fruit
Are burned, as of no use.
Out of a good man's inward hoard,
Good deeds and words will pour;
And from an evil heart proceeds
The abundance of its store.
And why call ye me Lord, Lord,
But do not what I say?
Not such shall enter heaven, but who
My Father's will obey.
And in that day, shall many say,
Lord, we have prophesied,
Have cast out demons, done great works,
And all our powers applied,
In thy great name; and then will I
Profess, I never knew you;
Depart from me, ye wicked ones,
Your evils still pursue you.

For everiwɒn đat asks, resįvz;
hi fįndz đat siks afar;
and hi đat noks wiđ ernestnes,
sɯn siz đe gets ajar.
If ven and eriŋ man wil giv
gud gifts tu đơz hi lɒvz,
ʃɯr God wil beter ŧiŋz bestơ
on đơz hɯm hi aprɯvz.

Zil and Persevirans ar Nesesari.

Enter yi in at đe stret get,
and kip đe narơ we
đat lideŧ tu eternal lįf:
(hɤ fų đis rɯl ơbe!)
for wįd'z đe get, and brơd'z đe we
đat lideŧ tu destrɒkʃon;
and meni wɷk đis izi rơd,
refųziŋ ɷl instrɒkʃon.

Trɯ Relijon iz nơn bį its Frɯts.

Avoid fɷls profets, đơz hɯ sim
lįk ʃip in ɤtward ʃơ;
bɒt in đer harts, lįk wulvz đe rev,
and briŋ đer folơerz wơ.
Jɒst az ų jɒj triz bį đer frɯt,
sơ ų me nơ *đer* wɒrŧ;
ų gađer not from brambelz, greps;
nơ figz from ŧornz spriŋ fơrŧ.
Sơ everi gud tri berz gud frɯt,
and bad wɒnz bad prơdųs:
ɷl triz đat briŋ not fơrŧ gud frɯt
ar bɒrnd, az ov nơ ųs.
Ɤt ov a gud man'z inward hơrd,
gud didz and wɒrdz wil pơr;
and from an įvil hart prơsidz
đe abɒndans ov its stơr.
And hwį kɷl yi mi Lord, Lord,
bɒt dɯ not hwot į se?
not sɒç ʃal enter heven, bɒt hɯ
mį Fađer'z wil ơbe.
And in đát de, ʃal meni se,
Lord, wi hav profesįd,
hav kast ɤt dimonz, dɒn gret wɒrks,
and ɷl ɤr pɤerz aplįd,
in đį gret nem; and đen wil į
prơfes, Į never nų ų;
depart from mi, yi wiked wɒnz,
ųr įvilz stil pɒrsų ų.

The Conclusion of the whole matter.

He that both hears and does my words,
  Is like that prudent man
Who builds on a foundation deep,
  With wise and thoughtful plan.
But he that hears, and then does not,
  A foolish man resembles;
Who builds a house upon the sands,
  And to himself dissembles;
When winds blow loud, and streams
      beat fierce,
  His house to ruin trembles;
And soon it falls, because 'tis built
  Without foundation sure;
Therefore when tempests rage around,
  Such house cannot endure:
But wind and rain may hard assail
  The house upon the rock,
Firm as its own foundation, still
  It fears no tempest's shock.

When Christ had finished, the vast
      crowd,
  Raptured, seemed listening still:
They owned his high authority,
  Unlike the Scribes' vain skill.
Then from the mountain's holy height
  The Teacher straight descends,
Great multitudes accompany,
  God's might his steps attends.

Đe Konklu3on ov đe hɵl mater.

Hi đat bɵɵ hirz and dɒz mį wɒrdz,
  iz lįk đát prudent man
hu bildz on a fɤndeʃon dip,
  wiđ wįz and ɵɷtful plan.
Bɒt hi đat hirz, and đen dɒz not,
  a fuliʃ man rezembelz;
hu bildz a hɤs ɒpon đe sand,
  and tu himself disembelz;
hwen windz blɵ lɤd, and strimz
      bit firs,
  hiz hɤs tu ruin trembelz;
and sun it fɷlz, bekɷz 'tiz bilt
  wiđɤt fɤndeʃon ʃur;
đerfɵr hwen tempests rej arɤnd,
  sɒɕ hɤs kanot endųr:
bɒt wind and ren me hard asel
  đe hɤs ɒpon đe rok,
ferm az its ɵn fɤndeʃon, stil
  it firz nɵ tempest's ʃok.

Hwen Krįst had finiʃt, đe vąst
      krɤd,
  raptųrd, simd lisenin stil:
đe ɵnd hiz hį ɷɵoriti,
  ɒnlįk đe Skrįbz' ven skil.
Đen from đe mɤnten'z hɵli hįt
  đe Tiɕer stret desendz,
gret mɒltitųdz akɒmpani,
  God'z mįt hiz steps atendz.

SECTION 47.

The Centurion's Servant Healed.
—Matthew 8. 5-13. Luke 7. 1-10.

Next to Capernaum Jesus turned,
  And soon to him drew near
A Roman soldier, in great haste
  To save his servant dear.
Sick, nigh to death, his servant seemed,
  But Jesus' power can save;
With mighty faith, and earnest word,
  This power he comes to crave.
"Lord, at my home my servant lies
  Tormented with disease
Of palsy dire, but thy strong word
  Can cure him, if thou please."
To plead his cause more zealously,
  The elders of the Jews
Approach, and praise the worth of him
  Whom Christ would not refuse.

SEKΣON 47.

Đe Sentųrion'z Servant hild.
—Maɵų 8. 5-13. Luk 7. 1-10.

Nekst tu Kapernaɒm Jizɒs tɒrnd,
  and sun tu him dru nir
a Rɵman sɵldier, in gret hest
  tu sev hiz servant dir.
Sik, nį tu deɵ, hiz servant simd,
  bɒt Jizɒs' pɤer kan sev;
wiđ mįti feɵ, and ernest wɒrd,
  đis pɤer hi kɒmz tu krev.
"Lord, at mį hɵm mį servant lįz
  tormented wiđ disiz
ov pɵlzi dįr, bɒt đį stron wɒrd
  kan kųr him, if đɤ pliz."
Tu plid hiz kes mɵr zelɒsli,
  đe elderz ov đe Juz
aprɵɕ, and prez đe wɒrɵ ov him
  hum Krįst wud not refųz.

"He loves our nation, and has built,
  With generous heart and mind,
A synagogue, and therefore we
  Entreat thy pity kind."
Jesus replied, "I now will come
  And heal the dying man:"
And quickly did he follow them,
  To work his gracious plan.
Now to the house the Lord draws near,
  And there the soldier's friends
This message give unto the Lord,
  Which he thus humbly sends:
"Lord, give thyself no trouble more,
  Not worthy thee, am I,
To shelter 'neath my humble roof;
  Nor fit myself to apply:
Speak but the word, most surely then
  My servant healed will be.
Even I have men beneath me placed,
  Who serve obediently:
If I say unto this one, Come,
  He cometh at my call;
If to another, I say, Go;
  He goes, till I recall.
And if my servant I desire
  To do my lawful will,
He does it with a ready mind:
  Thy power is greater still."
When Jesus heard these trusting words,
  He, with admiring love,
Exclaimed, "This Gentile's faith is great,
  O'er Israel's far above.
And unto you who witness it,
  I solemnly declare,
That many from the East and West
  Shall with the faithful share
Heaven's kingdom; yea, with patriarchs sit;
  While those to whom 'twas given,
Will into outer darkness go,
  Where sinners must be driven."
To the Centurion then Christ said,
  "Now go thy way, and see,
That as thou hast believed, thy wish
  Is fully granted thee."
That very hour, those who were sent,
  Returned, and found that he
Who had been sick, nigh unto death,
  Was cured most perfectly.

"Hi lɒvz ɤr neʃon, and haz bilt,
  wiđ jenerɒs hart and mįnd,
a sinagog, and đerfɵr wi
  entrit đį piti kįnd."
Jizɒs replįd, "Ɨ nɤ wil kɒm
  and hil đe dįiŋ man:"
and kwikli did hi folɵ đem,
  tu wɒrk hiz greʃɒs plan.
Nɤ tu đe hɤs đe Lord drɷz nir,
  and đer đe sɵldier'z frendz
đis mesej giv ɒntu đe Lord,
  hwiç hi đɒs hɒmbli sendz:
"Lord, giv đįself nɵ trɒbel mɵr,
  not wɒrđi đi, am į,
tu ʃelter 'niđ mį hɒmbel rɯf;
  nor fit mįself tu aplį:
spik bɒt đe wɒrd, mɵst ʃɯrli đen
  mį servant hild wil bi.
Ɩven į hav men beniđ mi plɛst,
  hɯ serv ɵbidientli:
if į sɛ ɒntu đis wɒn, Kɒm,
  hi kɒmeŧ at mį kɷl;
if tu anɒđer, į sɛ, Gɵ;
  hi gɵz, til į rekɷl.
And if mį servant į dezįr
  tu dɯ mį lɷful wil,
hi dɒz it wiđ a redi mįnd:
  đį pɤer iz grɛter stil."
Hwen Jizɒs herd điz trɒsti[ŋ]
  wɒrdz,
  hi, wiđ admįriŋ lɒv,
ɛksklɛmd, "Đis Jentįl'z fɛŧ iz gre[t],
  ɵ'r Izrael'z far abɒv.
And ɒntu ų hɯ witnes it,
  į solemli deklɛr,
đat meni from đe Ɩst and West
  ʃal wiđ đe fɛŧful ʃɛr
heven'z kiŋdom; yɛ, wiđ patriark[s]
  sit;
  hwįl đɵz tu hɯm 'twoz given,
wil intu ɤter darknes gɵ,
  hwer sinerz mɒst bi driven."
Tu đe Sentųrion đen Krįst sed,
  "Nɤ gɵ đį wɛ, and si,
đat az đɤ hast belivd, đį wiʃ
  iz fuli granted đi."
Đát veri ɤr, đɵz hɯ wer sent,
  retɒrnd, and fɤnd đat hi
hɯ had bin sik, nį ɒntu deŧ,
  woz kųrd mɵst perfektli.

SECTION 48.

The Widow's Son raised to Life.—
Luke 7. 11-18.

The next day Jesus journied on,
And came to a fair city
Called Nain. Near the gate he saw
A sight that moved his pity.
Behold a young man on a bier,
Carried by mourning friends;
While weeping bitter tears of grief,
His mother lone attends.
Poor widow! 'twas her only son,
And many mourned her lot.
Jesus, with his compassion deep,
Approached, and said, "Weep not."
Strangely those words sound, till be-
The bier he stands, to add, [side
"Young man, I say to thee, Arise."
Then was the mourner glad;
For lo! the dead sat up, and he
Began to speak. (No doubt,
Words of surprise he uttered forth
To those who stood about.)
When to that mother's loving hands
Jesus gave back her son,
Great reverence filled the multitude
Who saw this wonder done.
They praised Jehovah who had raised
This prophet great indeed,
And thus fulfilled his promises
To visit Israel's seed.
So Christ's renown spread o'er that
And all the region round; [land,
Even John the Baptist heard thereof,
Within his prison bound.

SEKΣON 48.

Ðe Widɵ'z Sɒn rezd tu Lįf.—
Luuk 7. 11-18.

Ðe nekst de Jizɒs jɒrnid on,
and kem tu a fer siti
kωld Nein. Nir ðe get hi sω
a sįt ðat mɯvd hiz piti.
Behɵld a yɒŋ man on a bir,
karid bį mɵrniŋ frendz;
hwįl wipiŋ biter tirz ov grif,
hiz mɒðer lɵn atendz.
Puur widɵ! 'twoz her ɵnli sɒn,
and meni mɵrnd her lot.
Jizɒs, wið hiz kompaʃon dip,
aprɵçt, and sed, "Wip not."
Strenjli ðɵz wɒrdz sɜnd, til besįd
ðe bir hi standz, tu ad,
"Yɒŋ man, į se tu ði arįz."
Ðen woz ðe mɵrner glad;
for lɵ! ðe ded sat ɒp, and hi
began tu spik. (Nɵ dɜt,
wɒrdz ov sɒrprįz hi ɒterd fɵrþ
tu ðɵz hɯ stud abɜt.)
Hwen tu ðát mɒðer'z lɒviŋ armz
Jizɒs gev bak her sɒn,
gret reverens fild ðe mɒltitɥd
hɯ sω ðis wɒnder dɒn.
Ðe prezd Jehɵva hɯ had rezd
ðis profet gret indid,
and ðɒs fulfild hiz promisez
tu vizit Izrael'z sid.
Sɵ Krįst's renɜn spred ɵ'r ðát land,
and ωl ðe rijon rɜnd;
iven Jon ðe Baptist herd ðerov,
wiðin hiz prizon bɜnd.

SECTION 49.

Message from John in Prison to Christ.—
Matthew 11. 2-6. Luke 7. 18-23.

When John, in Herod's prison kept,
Had heard of Jesus' fame,
He sent, of his disciples, two,
And unto Christ they came,
And said, "Art thou the Promised One
That we are to expect?
Or, shall we for another wait,
And all thy claims reject?

SEKΣON 19.

Mesej from Jon in Prizon tu Krįst.—
Matthew 11. 2-6. Luke 7. 18-23.

Hwen Jon, in Herod'z prizon kept,
had herd ov Jizɒs' fem,
hi sent, ov hiz disįpelz, tɯ́,
and ɒntu Krįst ðe kem,
and sed, "Art ðɜ ðe Promist Wɒn
ðat wi ar tu ekspekt?
or, ʃal wi for anɒðer wet,
and ωl ðį klemz rejekt?

Then Jesus wrought before their sight
  Works of miraculous kind.
In that same hour he cured the sick,
  Gave sight unto the blind,
Bade evil spirits leave their haunts,
  (The bodies of mankind,)
And said, "Return to John, and thus
  All doubts and fears destroy:
Tell him what things you've seen and
  Yea, tell him, for his joy, [heard;
The blind now see, the deaf now hear,
  The lame their feet employ;
The sick are healed, demons expelled,
  The dead are raised to life;
And better far, the poor who mourned
  Their lot, with evils rife,
Have now the prophecies fulfilled,
  Glad tidings of Heaven's grace
Preached to them without price; and
  May saving truth embrace. [they
And blest is he who shall not deem
  My glory his disgrace."

Đen Jizɒs rɵt befɵr đer sɪt
  wɒrks ov mirakɥlɒs kɪnd.
In đát sem ɤr hi kɥrd đe sik,
  gev sɪt ɒntu đe blɪnd,
bad ivil spirits liv đer hɛnts,
  (đe bodiz ov mankɪnd,)
and sed, "Retɒrn tu Jon, and đɒs
  ɵl dɤts and firz destroi:
tel him hwot ɟiŋz ɥ'v sin and herd
  yɛ, tel him, for hiz joi,
đe blɪnd nɤ si, đe def nɤ hir,
  đe lem đer fit emploi;
đe sik ar hild, dimonz ekspeld,
  đe ded ar rezd tu lɪf;
and beter far, đe pur hɯ mɵrnd
  đer lot, wiđ ivilz rɪf,
hav nɤ đe profesiz fulfild,
  glad tɪdiŋz ov Heven'z gres
priçt tu đem wiđɤt prɪs; and đe
  me seviŋ trɯɟ embres.
And blest iz hi hɯ ʃal not dim
  mɪ glɵri hiz disgres."

SECTION 50.

Christ's Testimony concerning John.
—Matthew 11. 7-15. Luke 7. 24-30.

And when the messengers of John
  Departed from the Lord,
He thus addressed the multitude,
  (Who now his name adored,)
And said, "When ye went out to John,
  In Judah's wilderness,
What did ye see? Was it a reed,
  Soon by the wind o'erthrown?
But what saw ye? Was it a man
  Decked out in gay attire?
Such are not found in deserts, but
  In courts. I still inquire
What went ye out to see? Was it
  A prophet? Yea and more
Than prophet. This is he of whom
  Isaiah heretofore
And Malachi referred, the great
  Messiah's Harbinger,
Both to prepare his way, and say,
  His heavenly reign is near.
For all the prophets and the law
  Foretold these times, till John

SEKΣON 50.

Krɪst's Testimoni konserniŋ Jon.
—Maɟɥ 11. 7-15. Lɯk 7. 24-30.

And hwen đe mesenjerz ov Jon
  departed from đe Lord,
hi đɒs adrest đe mɒltitɥd,
  (hɯ nɤ hiz nem adɵrd,)
and sed, "Hwen yi went ɤt tu Jon,
  in Jɯda'z wildernes,
hwot did yi si? Woz it a rid,
  sɯn bɪ đe wind ɵ'rɟrɵn?
Bɒt hwot sɵ yi? Woz it a man
  dekt ɤt in gɛ atɪr?
sɒç ar not fɤnd in dezerts, bɒt
  in kɵrts. Ɨ stil inkwɪr
hwot went yi ɤt tu si? Woz it
  a profet? Yɛ and mɵr
đan profet. Điz iz hi ov hɯm
  Ɨzaia hirtufɵr
and Malakɪ referd, đe gret
  Mesɪa'z Harbinjer,
bɵɟ tu preper hiz wɛ, and sɛ,
  Hiz hevenli ren iz nir.
For ɵl đe profets and đe lɵ
  fɵrtɵld điz tɪmz, til Jon

Proclaimed their prophecies fulfilled
  In me, God's only Son.
John, like a new Elijah, came
  To witness heaven's decree,
To announce the blessed reign of
      Christ,
  Who brings salvation free;
And since his time, heaven's kingdom
  Open to faithful men; [stands
And they that have true zeal of heart
  Ne'er seek its grace in vain.
The least of those who learn and love
  The truths that I display,
Is greater in heaven's kingdom now
  Than John was ere my day."
And all the people, when they heard,
  And many publicans,
Believed in Christ, and honored God,
  And many courtesans.
But the conceited Pharisees,
  And learned lawyers too,
Refused the grace thus offered them,
  And haughtily withdrew;
While Christ proclaimed, "He that
      hath ears,
  Should hear, and then should do."

SECTION 51.

Christ reproaches the Jews for their Impenitence.

Matthew 11. 16-24. Luke 7. 31-35.

Christ said, "The people of this age
  Are so perverse in mind,
They do not cleave to heavenly truth,
  Of any form or kind.
Like fickle children, pleased with
      nought,
  From joy to grief they range;
They sympathise with no good thing,
  And weary even of change.
When John proclaimed heaven's truth
      divine,
  In solemn word severe,
Ye called him a demoniac stern,
  And mocked the holy seer.
And when the Son of man appeared
  And preached his Gospel true,
In all mild wisdom, generous love,
  And charms as fair as new,

8, 9

prɵklemd đɛr profesiz fulfild
  in mi, God'z ɵnli Sɒn.
Jon, lįk a nų Elįja, kem
  tu witnes heven'z dekri,
tu anɤns đe blesed ren ov
      Krįst,
  hɯ briŋz salveʃon fri;
and sins hiz tįm, heven'z kiŋdom
  ɵpen tu feɟful men; [standz
and đe đat hav trɯ zil ov hart
  nɛr sik its gres in ven.
Đe list ov đɵz hɯ lern and lɒv
  đe trɯđz đat į displɛ,
iz greter in heven'z kiŋdom nɤ
  đan Jon woz ɛr mį dɛ."
And ɷl đe pipel, hwen đɛ herd,
  and meni pɒblikanz,
belivd in Krįst, and onord God,
  and meni kɵrtezanz.
Bɒt đe konsited Farisiz,
  and lerned lɷierz tɯ,
refųzd đe gres đɒs oferd đem,
  and hɵtili wiđdrɯ;
hwįl Krįst prɵklemd, "Hi đat
      haɟ irz,
  ʃud hir, and đen ʃud dɯ."

SEKΣON 51.

Krįst reprɵçez đe Jɯz for đɛr Impenitens.

Matthew 11. 16-24. Lɯk 7. 31-35.

Krįst sed, "Đe pipel ov đis ɛj
  ar sɵ pervers in mįnd,
đɛ dɯ not kliv tu hevenli trɯɟ,
  ov eni form or kįnd.
Lįk fikel çildren, plizd wiđ
      nɷt,
  from joi tu grif đɛ renj;
đɛ simpaɟįz wiđ nɵ gud ɟiŋ,
  and wiri iven ov çenj.
Hwen Jon prɵklemd heven'z trɯɟ
      divįn,
  in solem wɒrd sevir,
yi kɵld him a dimɵniak stern,
  and mokt đe hɵli sier.
And hwen đe Sɒn ov man apird
  and priçt hiz Gospel trɯ,
in ɷl mįld wizdom, jenerɒs lɒv,
  and çarmz az fɛr az nų,

Ye did object, and sneering say,
  'This Christian system now
Is far too free, and too diffuse,
  To suit our stricter vow;'
But heavenly wisdom, pure and good,
  Is proved most perfect still
By noble characters and deeds
  In those who work its will."
Then Christ began, with majesty
  Such as Himself could show,
To pour his censure, which was doom
  And destiny of woe,
On the proud towns and cities round
  Who saw his heavenly face,
Witnessed his miracles, and heard
  His words of warning grace,
But put repentance off, and sought
  Not evil ways to shun,
By just reform of dire abuse,
  Until their course was run.
This was his stern denouncement:—
        "Woe,
  Chorazin, unto thee!
Woe to Bethsaida! lasting woe,
  And lingering infamy;
For if the miracles displayed
  Within your walls, had been
Shown unto Tyre and Sidon, they
  Had turned from all their sin.
Woe to Capernaum! proud as if
  Invested with heaven's power;
Thou shalt be humbled even to hell
  In thine appointed hour;
For if thy privilege to hear
  Redemption's rescuing love,
Had on old Sodom been conferred,
  No thunders from above,
And no volcanoes from beneath,
  Had made a Dead Sea there;
For she would soon have turned to
        God,
  In penitence and prayer.
And all those perished realms of old,
  That sank in pagan night,
Shall rise in judgement over lands
  Blessed with the Gospel's light,
Who yet reject its beams, and find
  More tolerable doom
Than these proud cities now sunk in
  Impenetrable gloom."

yı did objékt and snıriŋ se,
  'Đis Kristian sistem nɤ
iz far tɯ frı, and tɯ difɥs,
  tu sɥt ɤr strikter vɤ;'
bɒt hevenli wizdom, pɥr and gud,
  iz prɯvd mɷr perfekt stil
bị nɷbel karakterz and didz
  in đɷz hɯ wɒrk its wíl."
Đen Krịst began, wiđ majesti
  sɒç az Himself kud ʃɷ,
tu pɷr hiz senʃur, hwiç woz dɯm
  and destini ov wɷ,
on đe prɤd tɤnz and sitiz rɤnd
  hɯ sɷ hiz hevenli fez,
witnest hiz mirakelz, and herd
  hiz wɒrdz ov worniŋ gres,
bɒt put repentans of, and sɷt
  not ıvil wez tu ʃɒn,
bị jɒst reform ov dịr abɥs,
  ɒntil đer kɷrs woz rɒn.
Đis woz hiz stern denɤnsment:—
        "Wɷ,
  Kɷrezin, ɒntu đı!
Wɷ tu Beɟseda! lastiŋ wɷ,
  and liŋgeriŋ infami;
for if đe mirakelz displed
  wiđin ɥr wɷlz had bin
ʃɷn ɒntu Tịr and Sịdon, đe
  had tɒrnd from ɷl đer sin.
Wɷ tu Kapernaɒm! prɤd az if
  invested wiđ heven'z pɤer;
đɤ ʃalt bı hɒmbeld ıven tu hel
  in địn apointed ɤr;
for if đị privilej tu hir
  redemʃon'z reskɥiŋ lɒv,
had on ɷld Sodom bin konferd,
  nɷ ɟɒnderz from abɒv,
and nɷ volkenɷz from beniđ,
  had med a Ded Sı đer;
for ʃi wud sɯn hav tɒrnd tu
        God,
  in penitens and prer.
And ɷl đɷz periʃt relmz ov ɷld,
  đat saŋk in pegan nịt,
ʃal rịz in jɒjment ɷver landz
  blest wiđ đe Gospel'z lịt,
hɯ yet rejekt its bımz, and fịnd
  mɷr tolerabel dɯm
đan điz prɤd sitiz nɤ sɒŋk in
  impenetrabel glɯm."

SECTION 52.

Christ invites all to come to him.
—Matthew 11. 25-30.

At that time Jesus also said,
 "I thank thee, Father, Lord
Of heaven and earth, that thou hast
 The mysteries of thy Word [veiled
From crafty men, and made them known
 To babes, to minds sincere;
For so it seemèd good to thee,
 That they may Thee revere.
And no man knows the Son except
 The Father that's in him,
The Father's the Divinity,
 The Godhead, the Supreme,)
And none the Father knoweth, but
 The Son, and also he
To whom the Son revealeth him
 In loving majesty.
Come unto me, ye weary ones,
 Whom various ills molest;
All ye that labor, come to me,
 And I will give you rest.
Take my yoke on you, learn of me,
 For I am meek and lowly,
Ye shall find rest unto your souls
 From all that is unholy.
My yoke is easy to be borne;
My burden's light; come all that mourn."

SECTION 53.

Christ forgives a Woman at the house of a Pharisee.—Luke 36-50.

Invited by a Pharisee,
 Jesus sat down to meat;
And lo, a woman entered too,
 And stood behind his feet.
A sinner of the city, she,
 But grace had touched her heart;
And now to Him whose love she feels,
 That love she must impart.
Sweet tears of humble penitence
 Soon fell upon those feet;
She wiped them with her hair, and then
 Kissed them with reverence meet.
An alabaster box she brought,
 With precious ointment filled,

SEKΣON 52.

Krįst invįts ɷl tu kɒm tu him.
—Maɟų 11. 25-30.

At đát tįm Jizɒs ɷlsơ sed,
 "Ɨ ɟaŋk đi, Fɛđer, Lord
ov heven and erɟ, đat đɤ hast veld
 đe misteriz ov đį Wɒrd
from krafti men, and med đem nơn
 tu bɛbz, tu mįndz sinsir;
for sơ it simed gud tu đi,
 đat đe me Đi revir.
And nơ man nơz đe Sɒn eksept
 đe Fɛđer đat's in him,
(đe Fɛđer'z đe Diviniti,
 đe Godhed, đe Sųprim,)
and nɒn đe Fɛđer nơeɟ, bɒt
 đe Sɒn, and ɷlsơ hi
tu hɯm đe Sɒn revileɟ him
 in lɒviŋ majesti.
Kɒm ɒntu mi, yi wiri wɒnz,
 hɯm veriɒs ilz mơlest;
ɷl yi đat lɛbor, kɒm tu mi,
 and į wil giv ų rest.
Tɛk mį yơk on ų, lern ov mi,
 for į am mik and lơli,
yi ʃal fįnd rest ɒntu ųr sơlz
 from ɷl đat iz ɒnhơli.
Mį yơk iz izi tu bi bơrn;
mį bɒrden'z lįt; kɒm ɷl đat mơrn."

SEKΣON 53.

Krįst forgivz a Wuman at đe hɤs ov a Farisi.—Luk 36-50.

Invįted bį a Farisi,
 Jizɒs sat dɤn tu mit;
and lơ, a wuman enterd tɯ,
 and stud behįnd hiz fit.
A siner ov đe siti, ʃi,
 bɒt grɛs had tɒçt her hart;
and nɤ tu Him hɯz lɒv ʃi filz,
 đát lɒv ʃi mɒst impart.
Swit tirz ov hɒmbel penitens
 sɯn fel ɒpon đơz fit;
ʃi wįpt đem wiđ her hɛr, and đen
 kist đem wiđ reverens mit.
An alabaster boks ʃi brɷt,
 wiđ preʃɒs ointment fild,

And spread it o'er his blessed feet,
  While love her being thrilled.
The haughty Pharisee, this deed
  With scornful heart surveys,
Thinking, "If he a prophet were,
  He would have known the ways
Of this polluted woman, nor
  Her sinful touch have borne:"
But Jesus this reply directs,
  To turn away his scorn:
"Simon, I somewhat have to say."
  "Master, say on," he said.
"There was a certain creditor
  Whose dues were still unpaid;
And one man owed him fifty pence,
  Another ten-fold more.
So poor were they, with nought to pay,
  They earnestly implore
His kind forbearance. He forgives;
  Knowing they have no store.
Which of these two would love him
  Simon replied, with heed, [most?"
"He, I suppose, who most obtained
  Forgiveness in his need."
"Rightly thou judgest," Jesus spoke.
  Then to the woman turned;
And unto Simon added, "Thou
  This woman hast discerned.
I entered this thy house, as guest,
  Yet thou didst not provide
To wash my feet; she washed with
  And with her hair has dried. [tears,
No kiss of thine did welcome me;
  But so her love o'erflows,
That on my feet, unceasingly,
  Her kisses she bestows.
My head with oil of fragrance thou
  Didst not anoint; but she
Upon my feet this sign of love
  Bestows with energy.
Wherefore I tell thee, though her sins
  Are great, they're all forgiven,
For she loves much, but those who
  That to the grace of heaven [think
They little owe, but little love."
  Then Jesus said to her,
"Thy sins are all forgiven thee,
  Take care no more to err."
And they that sat at meat with him
  Began to say within

and spred it ɵ'r hiz blesed fit,
  hwḭl lɒv her biiŋ ŧrild.
Ɗe hɵti Farisi, ɗis did
  wiɗ skornful hart sɒrvez,
ŧiŋkiŋ, "If hi a profet wer,
  hi wud hav nɵn ɗe wez
ov ɗis poluted wuman, nor
  her sinful tɒç hav bɵrn:"
bɒt Jizɒs ɗis replḭ direkts,
  tu tɒrn awe hiz skorn:
"Sḭmon, ḭ sɒmhwot hav tu se."
  "Master, se on," hi sed.
"Ɗer woz a serten kreditor
  huz dɥz wer stil ɒnped;
and wɒn man ɵd him fifti pens,
  anɒɗer ten-fɵld mɵr.
Sɵ pur wer ɗe, wiɗ nɵt tu pe,
  ɗe ernestli implɵr
hiz kḭnd forberans. Hi forgivz;
  nɵiŋ ɗe hav nɵ stɵr.
Hwiç ov ɗiz tú wud lɒv him
  Sḭmon replḭd, wiɗ hid, [mɵst?"
"Hi, ḭ sɒpɵz, hu mɵst obtend
  forgivnes in hiz nid."
"Rḭtli ɗɤ jɒjest," Jizɒs spɵk,
  ɗen tu ɗe wuman tɒrnd;
and ɒntu Sḭmon aded "Ɗɤ
  ɗis wuman hast disernd.
Ḭ enterd ɗis ɗḭ hɤs, az gest,
  yet ɗɤ didst not prɵvḭd
tu woʃ mḭ fit; ʃi woʃt wiɗ tirz,
  and wiɗ her her haz drḭd.
Nɵ kis ov ɗḭn did welkɒm mi;
  bɒt sɵ her lɒv ɵ'rflɵz,
ɗat on mḭ fit, ɒnsisiŋli,
  her kisez ʃi bestɵz.
Mḭ hed wiɗ oil ov fregrans ɗɤ
  didst not anoint; bɒt ʃi
ɒpon mḭ fit ɗis sḭn ov lɒv
  bestɵz wiɗ enerji.
Hwerfɵr ḭ tel ɗi, ɗɵ her sinz
  ar gret, ɗe'r ɵl forgiven,
for ʃi lɒvz mɒç, bɒt ɗɵz hu ŧiŋk
  ɗat tu ɗe gres ov heven
ɗe litel ɵ, bɒt litel lɒv."
  Ɗen Jizɒs sed tu her,
"Ɗḭ sinz ar ɵl forgiven ɗi,
  tek ker nɵ mɵr tu er."
And ɗe ɗat sat at mit wiɗ him
  began tu se wiɗin

Themselves, "Who is it that thus takes
The power to pardon sin?"
Then to the woman Jesus spoke,
With comfort to her heart,
"Thy faith hath saved thee; go in peace."
Such peace could ne'er depart.

SECTION 54.

Christ preaches throughout Galilee.—Luke 8. 1-3.

And after this, he went throughout
The towns of Palestine,
Preaching by word, showing by deed,
(And all should these combine,)
The tidings that on man the light
Of heaven was now to shine.
His twelve disciples also were
Attending on their Lord,
And certain women, who were healed
By his almighty word,
Of evil spirits, and sicknesses;
As Mary Magdalene,
From whom seven demons he cast out,
For she possessed had been;
Also Joanna, Chuza's wife,
(Chuza was Herod's steward,)
Susanna, and some others who
To Jesus ministered.

SECTION 55.

Christ cures a Demoniac. Conduct of the Scribes and Pharisees.—Matthew 12. 22-45. Mark 3. 19-30. Luke 11. 14-32.

And Christ with his disciples went
Into a house, and there
The multitude together came,
So that they could not spare
Even time to eat: but Jesus must
Again the Word declare.
And when his friends heard of it, they
Went out to bring him in.
They said, He is fatigued; but him
From duty could not wean.
Then one was brought to him possessed
By demon, dumb and blind;
And Jesus healed his sore disease,
And cured his haunted mind.

đemselvz, "Huɯ iz it đat đɒs teks
đe pɤer tu pardon sin?"
Đen tu đe wuman Jizɒs spɵk,
wiđ kɒmfort tu her hart,
"Đį feŧ haŧ sevd đi; gɵ in pįs."
Sɒç pįs kud ne'r depart.

SEKΣON 54.

Krįst priçez θrust Galili.—Luk 8. 1-3.

And after đis, hį went ŧruɯst
đe tɤnz ov Palestįn,
priçiŋ bį wɒrd, ʃɵiŋ bį did,
(and ɷl ʃud đız kombįn,)
đe tįdiŋz đat on man đe lįt
ov heven woz nɤ tu ʃįn.
Hiz twelv disįpelz ɷlsɵ wer
atendiŋ on đer Lord,
and serten wimen, huɯ wer hild
bį hiz ɷlmįti wɒrd,
ov ıvil spirits and siknesez;
az Meri Magdalen,
from huɯm seven dimonz hį kast ɤt,
for ʃi pozest had bin;
ɷlsɵ Jɵana, Kɥza'z wįf,
(Kɥza woz Herod'z stɥard,)
Sɥzana, and sɒm ɒđerz huɯ
tu Jizɒs ministerd.

SEKΣON 55.

Krįst kɥrz a Dimɒniak. Kondɒkt ov đe Skrįbz and Farisiz.—Maŧɥ 12. 22-45. Mark 3. 19-30. Luk 11. 14-32.

And Krįst wiđ hiz disįpelz went
intu a hɤs, and đer
đe mɒltitɥd tugeđer kem,
sɵ đat đe kud not sper
ıven tįm tu ıt: bɒt Jizɒs mɒst
agen đe Wɒrd dekler.
And hwen hiz frendz herd ov it, đe
went ɤt tu briŋ him in.
Đe sed, Hį iz fatıgd; bɒt him
from dɥti kud not win.
Đen wɒn woz brɷt tu him pozest
bį dimon, dɒm and blįnd;
and Jizɒs hild hiz sɵr disiz,
and kɥrd hiz hɷnted mįnd.

And all the people were amazed,
  And said, " 'Tis David's son,
The prophesied Messiah, great,
  By whom this thing is done."
But when the Pharisees heard this,
  And saw the miracle,
They said, that by Beelzebub
  He did the fiend expel.
And Jesus knew their thoughts, and [said,
  "No devil will oppose
Another devil, else the reign
  Of evil soon would close.
For every kingdom, every house,
  Against itself arrayed,
Must soon to desolation come,
  And be in ruin laid.
And if I cast out devils by
  Beelzebub, then how
Do your own children cast them out,
  And you not disallow?
But if I, by the power of God,
  Cast devils out of men,
Then doubtless is God's kingdom come
  Into the world again.
When Satan, like a strong man armed,
  Lives in security,
His goods are held by him in peace;
  But when a stronger one than he
Shall come upon him, and o'ercome,
  He strips him of his arms,
His spoil divides among his friends,
  And feels no more alarms.
Therefore, in such a case, all those,
  Who know my might divine,
And yet refuse to take my part,
  Are enemies of mine.
Wherefore I say to you, All kinds
  Of sin and blasphemy
Shall be forgiven, if men repent
  Of their impiety;
Except the blasphemy against
  The Holy Spirit, this
(Evil confirmed in heart and life,)
  Will end in the abyss.
Or make the tree good, and its fruit;
  Or else let both be evil;
Oh earthly race, of vipers born,
  Ye children of the devil!
How can ye speak good things?
  For out of its own store,

And ɷl đe pipel wer amezd,
  and sed, " 'Tiz Devid'z sɒn,
đe profesįd Mesįa, gret,
  bį hɯm đis ɟiŋ iz dɒn."
Bɒt hwen đe Farisiz herd đis,
  and sɷ đe mirakel,
đe sed, đat bį Bielzebɒb
  hi did đe fįnd ekspel.
And Jizɒs nų đer ɟɷts, and sed,
  "Nɵ devil wil opɵz
anɒđer devil, els đe ren
  ov ivil sɯn wud klɵz.
For everi kiŋdom, everi hʊs,
  agenst itself ared,
mɒst sɯn tu desoleʃon kɒm,
  and bi in rɯin led.
And if į kast ʊt devilz bį
  Bielzebɒb, đen hʊ
dɯ ųr ɵn çildren kast đem ʊt,
  and ų not disalʊ?
Bɒt if į, bį đe pʊer ov God,
  kast devilz ʊt ov men,
đen dʊtles iz God'z kiŋdom kɒm
  intu đe wɒrld agen.
Hwen Setan lįk a stroŋ man armd,
  livz in sekųriti,
hiz gudz ar held bį him in pis;
  bɒt hwen a stroŋger wɒn đan hi
ʃal kɒm ɒpon him, and ɵ'rkɒm,
  hi strips him ov hiz armz,
hiz spoil divįdz amɒŋ hiz frendz,
  and filz nɵ mɵr alarmz.
Đerfɵr, in sɒç a kes, ɷl đɵz
  hɯ nɵ́ mį mįt divįn,
and yet refųz tu tek mį part,
  ar enemiz ov mįn.
Hwerfɵr į se tu ų, Ɑl kįndz
  ov sin and blasfemi
ʃal bi forgiven, if men repent
  ov đer impįeti;
eksept đe blasfemi agenst
  đe Hɵli Spirit, đis
(ivil konfermd in hart and lįf,)
  wil end in đe abís.
Or mek đe tri gud, and its frɯt;
  or els let bɵɟ bi ivil;
Ɵ erɟli res, ov vįperz born,
  yi çildren ov đe devil!
hʊ kan yi spik gud ɟiŋz?
  for ʊt ov its ɵn stɵr,

The heart brings forth each thought
And that for evermore. [and word,
From the good treasure of his heart
The good man speaks what's right,
But wicked hearts make wicked men,
Who utter words of spite.
For every word that men shall speak
With mischievous intent,
Shall rise in judgement, to their shame,
Unless they now repent.
And as your words are good or ill,
Your future doom will be,
For they will stamp your character
Throughout eternity."
Then certain Scribes and Pharisees
From Jesus sought a sign;
Some special token that he was
Indeed the Christ Divine.
And Jesus answering, said to them,
"An evil generation
Asks for a sign; no sign I'll give
Unto this wicked nation;
Except the sign of Jonah, who
Was three days in the sea;
So like him, in the earth, I'll hide
My own humanity.
'Gainst you, the men of Nineveh
In judgement shall arise,
For they repented at the words
Of Jonah's prophecies;
And you behold a greater far
Than Jonah standing here,
As shall be known in every age,
By nations far and near.
And Sheba's Gentile Queen shall rise
In judgement to reprove;
For she from distant realms once came
(Inspired by wisdom's love,)
To hear the words of Solomon;
While now within your land
A greater far than he appears,
Whom you won't understand.
Beware! beware! the darker fiends
Of ignorance and crime,
May have been banished for awhile
By God's pure Word sublime.
Now they may wander through the
In deserts dark and drear, [world,
But they may come on you again;
And when they do appear,

đe hart briŋz fɵrŧ iç ŧɵt and wɒrd,
and đát for evermɵr.
From đe gud treʒur ov hiz hart
đe gud man spiks hwot's ri̧t,
bɒt wiked harts mɛk wiked men,
hɯ ɒter wɒrdz ov spi̧t.
For everi wɒrd đat men ſal spik
wiđ misçevɒs intent,
ſal ri̧z in jɒjment, tu đer ſɛm,
ɒnles đɛ nɜ repent.
And az ɥr wɒrdz ar gud or il,
ɥr fɥtɥr dum wil bi,
for đɛ wil stamp ɥr karakter
ŧrɯɜt eterniti."
Đen serten Skri̧bz and Farisiz
From Jizɒs sɵt a si̧n;
sɒm speſal tɵken đat hi woz
indid đe Kri̧st Divi̧n.
And Jizɒs anseriŋ, sed tu đem,
"An ivil jenereſon
asks for a si̧n; nɵ si̧n i̧'l giv
ɒntu đis wiked nɛſon;
eksept đe si̧n ov Jɵna, hɯ
woz ŧri dɛz in đe si;
sɵ li̧k him, in đe erŧ, i̧'l hi̧d
mi̧ ɵn hɥmaniti.
'Genst ɥ, đe men ov Nineve
in jɒjment ſal ari̧z,
for đɛ repented at đe wɒrdz
ov Jɵna'z profesiz;
and ɥ behɵld a greter far
đan Jɵna standiŋ hir,
az ſal bi nɵn in everi ɛj,
bi̧ nɛſonz far and nir.
And Šiba'z Jenti̧l Kwin ſal ri̧z
in jɒjment tu reprɯv;
for ſi from distant relmz wɒns kɛm
(inspi̧rd bi̧ wizdom'z lɒv,)
tu hir đe wɒrdz ov Solomon;
hwi̧l nɜ wiđin ɥr land
a greter far đan hi apirz,
hɯm ɥ wɵn't ɒnderstand.
Bewer! bewer! đe darker findz
ov ignorans and kri̧m,
mɛ hav bin baniſt for ahwi̧l
bi̧ God'z pɥr Wɒrd sɒbli̧m.
Nɜ đɛ mɛ wonder ŧrɯ đe wɒrld,
in dezerts dark and drir,
bɒt đɛ mɛ kɒm on ɥ agen;
and hwen đɛ dɯ apir,

If they but find your hearts all void
Of heavenly love and light,
They will combine their devilish pow-
With those of hell's worst night, [ers
And repossess those hearts of yours
That I have sought to illume,
And your last state shall then be worse
Than was your first, in doom."
And as Christ spoke, a woman's voice
From out the company,
Said, "Blessed of all women is
The mother that bore thee."
But Christ replied, "Yea, rather blest
Are they who hear God's Word,
And keep it in obedience, true
To their redeeming Lord."

SECTION 56.

Christ's real Kindred.—Matthew 12. 46-50. Mark 3. 31-35. Luke 8. 46-50.

And while Christ taught the multi-
One came to him, and said, [tudes,
"Thy mother and thy brethren stand
Without, and have essayed
In vain to speak a word with thee."
The Lord then answered him,
"Who are my mother, brethren? who?
Those only do I deem
My friends who do God's will. All
I own my faithful brother, [such
(Of heavenly consanguinity,)
My sister, and my mother.

SECTION 57.

Parable of the Sower.—Matthew 13. 1-9. Mark 4. 1-9. Luke 8. 4-9.

Beside the lake of Galilee
Our blessed Savior sat,
And multitudes come unto him,
And for instruction wait.
Into a ship he entered then,
(The crowd stood on the shore,)
And taught again in parables,
As he had taught before.
A sower went to sow his seed,
And as he sowed it, some
Fell by the way side, and could not
Unto perfection come.

if đe bɒt fi̧nd ų
ov hevenli lɒ
đe wil kombi̧n
wiđ đɵz ov h
and ripozes đɵz
đat i̧ hav sɵt
and ųr last stet
đan woz ųr fe
And az Kri̧st sp
from ɤt đe kr
sed, "Blesed ov
đe mɒđer đat
Bɒt Kri̧st repli̧
ar đe hu hir
and kip it in ɵ
tu đer redimi

SEK

Kri̧st's rial Kind
Mark 3. 31-3

And hwi̧l Kri̧st
wɒn kem tu
"Đi̧ mɒđer and
wiđɤt and ha
in ven tu spik
Đe Lord đen
"Hu ar mi̧ mɒ
đɵz ɵnli du
mi̧ frendz hu
i̧ ɵn mi̧ feʃful
(ov hevenli kon
mi̧ sister, an

SEK

Parabel ov đe
Mark 4. 1-

Besi̧d đe lek ov
ɤr blesed Se
and mɒltitųdz
and for instr
Intu a ʃip hi en
(đe krɤd stu
and tɵt agen in
az hi had tɵt
A sɵer went tu
and az hi sɵ
fel bi̧ đe we si̧d,
ɒntu perfekʃ

Some fell upon a barren rock,
And as it had no root,
It withered in the summer's heat,
And yielded not its fruit.
Some fell among the thorns, and both
In seeming friendship grew;
But soon the thorns choked out the
Nor could it them subdue. [wheat,
But other fell upon good ground,
Sprang up, and fruit soon bore,
Some thirty-fold, some sixty, some
A hundred-fold, and more.
He that hath ears, now let him hear,
For heaven unto all such is near.

Sɒm fel ɒpon a baren rok,
and az it had nɵ rɯt,
it wiđerd in đe sɒmer'z hịt,
and yilded not its frɯt.
Sɒm fel amɒŋ đe ŧornz, and bɵŧ
in simiŋ frendʃip grɯ;
bɒt sɯn đe ŧornz qɵkt ɜt đe hwịt,
nor kud it đem sɒbdɥ.
Bɒt ɒđer fel ɒpon gud grɜnd,
spraŋ ɒp, and frɯt sɯn bɵr,
sɒm ŧerti-fɵld, sɒm siksti, sɒm
a hɒndred-fɵld, and mɵr.
Hị đat haŧ ịrz, nɜ let him hịr,
for heven ɒntu ɷl sɒq iz nịr.

SECTION 58.

Reasons for teaching by Parables, and explanation of the Parable of the Sower.

—Matthew 13. 10-23. Mark 4. 10-20. Luke 8. 9, 11-18.

When Jesus was retired, alone,
Then his disciples came,
And asked him, why, in parables,
He did his truths proclaim.
"Because," he said, "although to you
Who have discerning eyes,
Celestial wisdom may be taught
Veiled with but thin disguise,
Those grosser crowds can only learn
By tale and anecdote:
Bare truths they could not understand,
Nor even learn by rote.
While wise men gather wisdom still
Of every form and kind,
These simple ones in danger stand
Of losing all they find.
I teach them, then, by parables
Which may remembered be,
For they are quite unfitted yet
For heaven's philosophy.
Indeed, though seeing, they see not,
And hearing, do not hear,
Because they dread those shafts of
Which slay their errors dear. [truth
For as Isaiah saith, This race
Hath stupified their mind,
And sealed their eyes and ears, for fear
They painful truths should find;

SEKΣON 58.

Rizonz for tiqiŋ bị Parabelz, and eksplaneʃon ov đe Parabel ov đe Sɵer.

—Maŧɥ 13. 10-23. Mark 4. 10-20. Lɯk 8. 9, 11-18.

Hwen Jizɒs woz retịrd, alɵn,
đen hiz disịpelz kem,
and askt him, hwị, in parabelz,
hị did hiz trɯđz prɵklem.
"Bekɷz," hị sed, "ɷlđɵ tu ɥ
hɯ hav diserniŋ ịz,
selestial wizdom me bi tɵt
veld wiđ bɒt ŧin disgịz,
đɵz grɵser krɜdz kan ɵnli lern
bị tel and anekdɵt:
ber trɯđz đe kud not ɒnderstand,
nor ịven lern bị rɵt.
Hwịl wịz men gađer wizdom stil
ov everi form and kịnd,
điz simpel wɒnz in denjer stand
ov lɯziŋ ɷl đe fịnd.
Ɨ tiq đem, đen, bị parabelz
hwiq me rememberd bi,
for đe ar kwịt ɒnfited yet
for heven'z filosofi.
Indid, đɵ siiŋ, đe si not,
and hịriŋ, dɯ not hịr,
bekɷz đe dred đɵz ʃafts ov trɯŧ
hwiq sle đer erorz dịr.
For az Ɨzaia seŧ, Đis res
haŧ stɥpifịd đer mịnd,
and sild đer ịz and ịrz, for fịr
đe penful trɯđz ʃud fịnd;

Truths that would smite their favorite
  And turn them quite away [sins,
From all those vain, earth-born delights,
  Which lead their hearts astray.
But blessed are your eyes and ears,
  For they indeed discern
Those mysteries of heaven which
  Have vainly sighed to learn. [saints
The parable ye heard is this:
  The seed's the Word of God,
Which fructifies to endless life
  When placed beneath the sod
Of human minds. But some that hear
  Are like the way-side ground;
The seed falls on it, and foul spirits,
  Which everywhere abound,
Delight to pluck it from men's hearts,
  And then no fruit is found.
The seeds that fell upon the rock
  Resemble men who seem
To hear the Word of God with joy,
  But hear it as a dream.
Having no root within themselves,
  They last but for a season;
When persecution tries their faith,
  They yield without a reason.
And seeds that fell among the thorns
  Are those who when they've heard
Go forth, and soon are choked with
  And joys they have preferred [cares
Of earthly kind, to those pure joys
  Which come to man from heaven.
But that which fell upon good ground
  Are they who oft have striven
To find the truth; which found, within
  An honest and good heart
Receive it, keep, and bring forth fruit.
  They get, and then impart."

SECTION 59.

Christ directs his Disciples how to Hear and Teach.—

Mark 4. 24, 25. Luke 8. 16-18.

Christ said, "No man a candle lights
  In secret place to hide,
But sets it on a candlestick
  To throw its radiance wide.

trɯđz đat wud smɩt đer fɛvorit
  and tɒrn đem kwɩt awɛ [sinz,
from ωl đσz vɛn, erȶ-born delɩts,
  hwiç lid đer harts astrɛ.
Bɒt blesed ar ɥr ɩz and ȷrz,
  for đɛ indȷd disern
đσz misteriz ov heven hwiç sɛnts
  hav vɛnli sɩd tu lern.
Ɖe parabel yȷ herd iz đis:
  Ɖe sȷd'z đe Wɒrd ov God,
hwiç frɒktifɩz tu endles lɩf
  hwen plɛst benȷđ đe sod
ov hɥman mɩndz. Bɒt sɒm đat hȷr
  ar lɩk đe wɛ-sɩd grȣnd;
đe sȷd fωlz on it, and fȣl spirits,
  hwiç everihwɛr abȣnd,
delɩt tu plɒk it from men'z harts,
  and đen nσ frɯt iz fȣnd.
Ɖe sȷdz đat fel ɒpon đe rok
  rezembel men hɯ sȷm
tu hȷr đe Wɒrd ov God wiđ joi,
  bɒt hȷr it az a drȷm.
Haviŋ nσ rɯt wiđin đemselvz,
  đɛ last bɒt for a sȷzon;
hwen persekɥʃon trɩz đer fɛȶ,
  đɛ yȷld wiđȣt a rȷzon.
And sȷdz đat fel amɒŋ đe ȶornz
  ar đσz hɯ hwen đɛ'v herd
gσ fσrȶ, and sɯn ar çσkt wiđ kɛrz
  and joiz đɛ hav preferd
ov erȶli kɩnd, tu đσz pɥr joiz
  hwiç kɒm tu man from heven.
Bɒt đát hwiç fel ɒpon gud grȣnd
  ar đɛ hɯ oft hav striven
tu fɩnd đe trɯȶ; hwiç fȣnd, wiđin
  an onest and gud hart
resȷv it, kȷp, and briŋ fσrȶ frɯt.
  Ɖɛ get, and đen impart."

SEKƩON 59.

Krɩst direkts hiz Disɩpelz hȣ tu Hȷr and Tȷç.—

Mark 4. 24-25. Luk 8. 16-18.

Krɩst sed, "Nσ man a kandel lɩts
  in sȷkret plɛs tu hɩd,
bɒt sets it on a kandelstik
  tu ȶrσ its rɛdians wɩd.

For nothing is in secret kept,
  But what should not be known;
Nor is there any thing concealed
  That ever should be shown.
Take good heed therefore what ye hear;
  Well use, and ye shall save;
Lose, and ye shall not then retain
  The little that ye have.

For nɒϑiŋ iz in sikret kept,
  bɒt hwot ʃud not bị nơn;
nor iz ðer eni ϑiŋ konsịld
  ðat ever ʃud bị ʃơn.
Tɛk gud hịd ðerfơr hwot yị hịr;
  wel ɥz; and yị ʃal sev;
lɯz, and yị ʃal not ðen reten
  ðe litel ðat yị hav.

SECTION 60.

Various Parables descriptive of Christ's Kingdom.—

Matthew 13. 24-52. Mark 4. 26-34.

SEKΣON 60.

Verɒs Parabelz deskriptiv ov Krịst's Kiŋdom.—

Maϑɥ 13. 24-52. Mark 4. 26-34.

Christ said that he who sows God's Word,
  Like seed, in the human mind,
Must sow in faith, and in due course
  He good results shall find.
He cannot tell the process, how
  It germinates and grows;
He trusts God's power will make his toil
  In rich increase to close.
And when the harvest-day is come,
  He puts his sickle in,
And takes the precious sheaves to heaven
  That knows no taint of sin.

Krịst sed ðat hi hɯ sơz God'z Wɒrd,
  lịk sịd in ðe hɥman mịnd,
mɒst sơ in fɛϑ, and in dɥ kơrs
  hị gud rezɒlts ʃal fịnd.
Hị kanot tel ðe prơses, hɤ
  it jerminɛts and grơz;
hị trɒsts God'z pɤer wil mɛk hiz toil
  in riç inkrịs tu klơz.
And hwen ðe harvest-dɛ iz kɒm,
  hị puts hiz sikel in,
and tɛks ðe preʃɒs ʃivz tu heven
  ðat nơz nơ tɛnt ov sin.

Then Jesus spoke a parable
  Concerning the world's field,
Which divers kinds of moral crops,
  Both good and bad, doth yield.
God's kingdom may be well compared
  To one who sows good seeds,
But while men sleep an enemy
  Bestrows the ground with weeds.
The wheat and tares together grow,
  Greatly to the surprise
Of those who work upon the land;
  And they at once advise
To pluck the tares. Their lord forbids:
  "Let both together grow:
In time of harvest, I'll direct
  The reapers first to throw
The tares aside, for meaner use;
  And then to reap the wheat,
And to my garner gather it
  In happiness complete."

Ðen Jịzɒs spơk a parabel
  konserniŋ ðe wɒrld'z fịld,
hwiç dịverz kịndz ov moral krops,
  bơϑ gud and bad, dɒϑ yịld.
God'z kiŋdom mɛ bị wel komperd
  tu wɒn hɯ sơz gud sịdz,
bɒt hwịl men slịp, an enemi
  bestrơz ðe grɤnd wiϑ wịdz.
Ðe hwịt and terz tugeðer grơ,
  gretli tu ðe sɒrprịz
ov ðơz hɯ wɒrk ɒpon ðe land;
  and ðɛ at wɒns advịz
tu plɒk ðe terz. Ðer lord forbidz:
  "Let bơϑ tugeðer grơ:
in tịm ov harvest ị'l direkt
  ðe rịperz ferst tu ϑrơ
ðe terz asịd, for mịner ɥs;
  and ðen tu rịp ðe hwịt,
and tu mị garner gaðer it
  in hapines komplit."

When Jesus sent away the crowd,
And went unto his home,
The faithful few, who wait on him,
Wherever he may roam,
Come unto him, and, wistful say,
"Declare to us, we pray,
The symbol of the wheat and tares,
Which fills us with dismay."
He answering, said, "The field's the
And I the sower am; [world,
The good seed are God's children, and
The tares the sons of shame.
The enemy that sowed them is
The devil and his crew;
The harvest is the end of the world;
The reapers who renew
Its face, and gather up its stores,
The angels are. As then
The tares are gathered first, and burned,
That they hurt not again,
So shall the Son of man send forth
His angels, who shall bring
Together all things that offend,
And every evil thing,
And cast them into hell. And then,
The righteous, like the sun,
Shall shine forth in heaven's kingdom when
Their work on earth is done.
He that hath ears, now let him hear,
For heaven unto all such is near."

Another parable spoke Christ,
And said, "God's kingdom grows
Like to the little mustard seed
Which in his field man sows:
When in the earth that grain is cast,
Though of all seeds the least,
It riseth higher than all herbs,
With branches great increased:
And in this tree the birds will lodge,
Delighting in its shade;
So through the world God's kingdom
Be far and wide displayed. [shall

God's kingdom is to leaven like,
Which, hid within the meal,
Ferments the whole; so doth the truth
We in the heart conceal."

Hwen Jızɒs sent awɛ đe krɜd,
and went ɒntu hiz hɵm,
đe feɟful fų, huı wɛt on him,
hwɛrever hı mɛ rɵm,
kɒm ɒntu him, and, wistful sɛ,
"Deklɛr tu ɒs, wı prɛ,
đe simbol ov đe hwıt and terz,
hwiç filz ɒs wiđ dismɛ."
Hı ɑnseriŋ, sed, "Đe fıld'z đe
and ị đe sɵer am; [wɒrld,
đe gud sıd ɑr God'z çildren, and
đe terz đe sɒnz ov ʃem.
Đe enemi đat sɵd đem iz
đe devil and hiz kruı;
đe harvest iz đe end ov đe wɒrld;
đe rıperz huı renų
its fɛs, and gađer ɒp its stɵrz,
đe ɛnjelz ar. Az đen
đe terz ar gađerd ferst, and bɒrnd,
đat đe hɒrt not agen,
sɵ ʃal đe Sɒn ov man send fɵrɟ
hiz ɛnjelz, huı ʃal briŋ
tugeđer ɷl ɟiŋz đat ofend,
and everi ıvil ɟiŋ,
and kast đem intu hel. And đen,
đe rịtiɒs, lịk đe sɒn,
ʃal ʃịn fɵrɟ in heven'z kiŋdom hwen
đer wɒrk on erɟ iz dɒn.
Hı đat haɟ ırz, nɜ let him hir,
for heven ɒntu ɷl sɒç iz nir."

Anɒđer parabel spɵk Krịst,
and sed, "God'z kiŋdom grɵz
lịk tu đe litel mɒstard sıd
hwiç in hiz fıld man sɵz:
hwen in đe erɟ đát gren iz kast,
đɵ ov ɷl sıdz đe lịst,
it rịzeɟ hịer đan ɷl herbz,
wiđ branҫez gret inkrıst:
and in đis trı đe berdz wil loj,
delịtiŋ in its ʃed;
sɵ ɟruı đe wɒrld God'z kiŋdom ʃal
bı far and wịd displed.

God'z kiŋdom iz tu leven lịk,
hwiç, hid wiđin đe mıl,
ferments đe hɵl; sɵ dɒɟ đe truıɟ
wı in đe hart konsıl."

Thus Jesus to the multitude
Did heavenly truth impart
By parables which best might teach
Their simple thoughtless heart.
So was fulfilled, as prophet once
Did testimony bear,
" My mouth in parables shall teach,
And secret things declare."
Then Jesus all that multitude
By his command dispersed,
And when with his disciples few,
His meaning he rehearsed.

This parable he also spake :
"Heaven's field contains hid treasure,
And when man finds it, he sells all,
And buys that field with pleasure.

Or like one who for goodly pearls
Doth seek ; some merchant, wise,
To gain one of surpassing worth,
Sells all, and wins the prize.

And like a net, collecting fish
Of every living kind,
When drawn to shore, both good and bad
The fishers therein find :
They sort the good from bad ; the good's
Preserved, the bad's declined.
So at the last, God's angels will
The wicked from the just
Sever, and cast all into hell
Who make not God their trust."

Jesus then asked, " Do ye discern
The meaning of my word ? "
His listening followers straight reply,
With reverence due, " Yea, Lord."
" Then let each scribe," said he, " who's trained
To teach my heavenly way,
Out of his treasured hoard of truths
Both new and old display."

Đɒs Jizɒs tu đe mɒltitɥd
did hevenli trɯɟ impart
bį parabelz hwiç best mįt tıç
đɛr simpel, ɟωtles hart.
Sơ woz fulfild, az profet wɒns
did testimoni bɛr,
" Mį mȣɟ in parabelz ʃal tıç,
and sıkret ɟiŋz deklɛr."
Đen Jizɒs ωl đát mɒltitɥd
bį hiz komand disperst,
and hwen wiđ hiz disįpelz fɥ,
hiz mıniŋ hı reherst.

Đis parabel hı ωlsơ spɛk :
"Heven'z fıld kontɛnz hid trezur,
and hwen man fįndz it, hı selz ωl,
and bįz đát fıld wiđ plezur.

Or lįk wɒn hɯ for gudli perlz
dɒɟ sık ; sɒm merçant, wįz,
tu gɛn wɒn ov sɒrpasiŋ wɒrɟ,
selz ωl, and winz đe prįz.

And lįk a net, kolektiŋ fiʃ
ov everi liviŋ kįnd,
hwen drωn tu ʃơr, bơɟ gud and bad
đe fiʃerz đɛrin fįnd :
đe sort đe gud from bad ; đe gud'z
prezervd, đe bad'z deklįnd.
Sơ at đe last, God'z ɛnjelz wil
đe wiked from đe jɒst
sever, and kast ωl intu hel
hɯ mɛk not God đɛr trɒst."

Jizɒs đen askt, " Dɯ yı disern
đe mıniŋ ov mį wɒrd ?"
Hiz lisениŋ folơerz strɛt replį,
wiđ reverens dɥ, " Yɛ, Lord."
" Đen let ıç skrįb," sed hı, " hɯ'z trɛnd
tu tıç mį hevenli wɛ,
ȣt ov hiz trezurd hơrd ov trɯđz
bơɟ nɥ and ơld displɛ."

SECTION 61.

Christ calms the Tempest on the Sea of Galilee.—Matthew 8. 18-27. Mark 4. 35-41. Luke 8. 22-26 ; 9. 59-62.

When eventide was come, Christ said,
To his disciples true,

SEKΣON 61.

Krįst kamz đe Tempest on đe Sı ov Galili.—Maɟɥ 8. 18-27. Mark 4. 35-41. Luke 8. 22-26 ; 9. 59-62.

Hwen ıventįd woz kɒm, Krįst sed,
tu hiz disįpelz trɯ,

"Let us embark on board a ship,
And visit stations new,
Beyond the lake; for multitudes
So throng us on this side,
Some mischief may befall them soon,
Unless we them divide."
Then came a Scribe, and said to Christ,
"Lord, I will follow thee
Where'er thou goest." Christ replied,
"Indeed, that cannot be,
Unless thou hast the faith which bears
And dares all things for God;
For I and my true followers oft
Must wander far abroad.
The foxes, by God's care, have holes,
And each bird has its nest;
But I, the Son of man, have not
A place wherein to rest."
He turned away with grief. And then
Another came, and said,
"Lord, I would follow thee, but now
My father lieth dead;
Permit me therefore first to go
And bury him; then I
Will soon return, and join me to
Thy chosen company."
But Christ replied, "Thy worldly [friends
Can well perform that deed;
The dead in spiritual life
Of such things take good heed.
But follow me, and let the past
Be by the past interred;
Go thou, and preach God's kingdom [near,
According to my word."

As Christ was passing o'er the lake
Of fair Genesaret,
A gentle slumber fell on him,
After the sun was set.
Fear was within that tossing bark
As stormy winds grew loud,
And waves came rolling high and dark,
And the tall mast was bowed.
The men stood breathless in their [dread,
And baffled in their skill;
Then Jesus woke, and rose, and said
To the wild sea, "Be still!"
The wind that moment ceased; that
word
Passed through the gloomy sky,

"Let ɒs embark on bɵrd a ʃip,
and vizit steʃonz nų,
beyond đe lɛk; for mɒltitųdz
sɵ ŧroŋ ɒs on đis sįd,
sɒm misɕef mɛ befɷl đem sɯn,
ɒnles wɪ đem divįd."
Đen kɛm a Skrįb, and sed tu Krįst,
"Lord, į wil folɵ đɪ
hwɛrɛr đɤ gɵest." Krįst replįd,
"Indɪd, đát kanot bɪ,
ɒnles đɤ hast đe fɛŧ hwiɕ berz
and derz ɷl ŧiŋz for God;
for į and mį trɯ folɵerz oft
mɒst wonder far abrɷd.
Đe fokscz, bį God'z kɛr, hav hɵlz,
and ɪɕ berd haz its nest;
bɒt į, đe Sɒn ov man, hav not
a plɛs hwɛrin tu rest."
Hɪ tɒrnd awɛ wiđ grɪf. And đen
anɒđer kɛm, and sed,
"Lord, į wud folɵ đɪ, bɒt nɤ
mį fɑđer lįeŧ ded;
permit mɪ đerfɵr ferst tu gɵ
and beri him; đen į
wil sɯn retɒrn, and join mɪ tu
đį ɕɵzen kɒmpani."
Bɒt Krįst replįd, "Đį wɒrldli frendz
kan wel perform đát dɪd;
đe ded in spiritųal lįf
ov sɒɕ ŧiŋz tɛk gud hɪd.
Bɒt folɵ mɪ, and let đe past
bɪ bį đe past interd;
gɵ đɤ, and prɪɕ God'z kiŋdom nɪr,
akordiŋ tu mį wɒrd."

Az Krįst woz pasiŋ ɵ'r đe lɛk
ov fɛr Genesaret,
a jentel slɒmber fel on him,
after đe sɒn woz set.
Fɪr woz wiđin đát tosiŋ bark
az stormi windz grɯ lɤd,
and wɛvz kɛm rɵliŋ hį and dark,
and đe tɷl mast woz bɤd.
Đe men stud breŧles in đer dred,
and bafeld in đer skil;
đen Jɪzɒs wɵk, and rɵz, and sed
tu đe wįld sɪ, "Bɪ stil!"
Đe wind đát mɵment sɪst; đát
wɒrd
past ŧrɯ đe glɯmi skį,

The turbid billows knew their Lord,
  And fell beneath his eye.
Then slumber settled on the deep,
  And silence on the blast;
They sank, as flowers that fold to sleep,
  When sultry day has passed.

SECTION 62.

Christ heals the Gadarene Demoniac.—
Matthew 8. 28-34. Mark 5. 1-21.
Luke 8. 26-40.

Now having crossed the calmèd lake
  To where the Gadarenes
Dwelt, on the eastern side, and where
  Dwelt too the Gergesenes,
The Lord soon left the ship for land,
  And there he quickly met
Two men who from the city came,
  With demons sore beset.
One from the tombs had hasted forth,
  He had no dress or home,
But dwelt apart from mortal men,
  And 'mongst the dead would roam.
None could control his demon power;
  Though oft with chains 'twas tried,
As oft he burst those fetters strong,
  And cast them all aside.
By day, by night, on mountains lone,
  Or in the tombs he lay,
And cried and cut himself, so fierce
  That none could pass that way.
Yet when far off he saw the Lord,
  That Savior strong and mild,
He ran with haste, and humbly knelt,
  To worship, like a child.
With voices loud they both exclaim,
  "Thou Son of God most high,
Jesus, what part have I with thee?
  Art come to terrify?
By God, I do entreat thee now,
  Torment not ere the time."
For Jesus had commanded thus,
  With majesty sublime:
"Thou unclean spirit, come out of the man,
  Thy name to me declare."
"Legion," he said, "for we are many;"
  Many had entered there.
Then he besought that from that land
  Jesus would not them drive;

đe tɒrbid bilɵz nų đɛr Lord,
  and fel beniđ hiz į.
Đen slɒmber seteld on đe dip,
  and sįlens on đe blast;
đɛ saŋk, az flɤerz đat fɵld tu slip,
  hwen sɒltri dɛ haz past.

SEKΣON 62.

Krįst hilz đe Gadarin Demɵniak.—
Maţų 8. 28-34. Mark 5. 1-21.
Luuk 8. 26-40.

Nɤ haviŋ krost đe kɑmed lɛk
  tu hwɛr đe Gaderinz
dwelt, on đe istern sįd, and hwɛr
  dwelt tuu đe Gergesinz,
đe Lord suun left đe ʃip for land,
  and đɛr hi kwikli met
túú men huu from đe siti kɛm,
  wiđ dimonz sɵr beset.
Wɒn from đe tuumz had hɛsted fɵrţ,
  hi had nɵ dres or hɵm,
bɒt dwelt apart from mortal men,
  and 'mɒŋst đe ded wud rɵm.
Nɒn kud kontrɵl hiz dimon pɤer;
  đɵ oft wiđ ɕɛnz 'twoz trįd,
az oft hi bɒrst đɵz feterz stroŋ,
  and kast đem ɷl asįd.
Bį dɛ, bį nįt, on mɤntenz lɵn,
  or in đe tuumz hi lɛ,
and krįd and kɒt himself, sɵ firs
  đat nɒn kud pas đát wɛ.
Yet hwen far ɷf hi sɷ đe Lord,
  đát Sɛvier stroŋ and mįld,
hi ran wiđ hɛst, and hɒmbli nelt,
  tu wɒrʃip, lįk a ɕįld.
Wiđ voisez lɤd đe bɵţ eksklɛm,
  "Đɤ Sɒn ov God mɵst hį,
Jizɒs, hwot part hav į wiđ đi?
  art kɒm tu terifį?
Bį God, į duu intrit đi nɤ,
  torment not ɛr đe tįm."
For Jizɒs had komanded đɒs,
  wiđ majesti sɒblįm:
"Đɤ ɒnklin spirit, kɒm ɤt ov đe man,
  đį nɛm tu mi deklɛr."
"Lijon," hi sed, "for wi ar meni;"
  meni had enterd đɛr.
Đen hi besɷt đat from đát land
  Jizɒs wud not đem drįv;

Nor in the abyss, which most they
  dread,
 Command that they should live.
Now some way off, a numerous herd
 Of unclean swine were fed,
So within these the demons prayed
 Their exile might be made.
And Jesus his permission gave.
 Then forthwith from the men
The demons fled, and quickly went
 Into the swine ; and then
The demon herd, two thousand strong,
 Into the lake were driven ;
And perished in the watery flood,
 Against which they had striven.
The men who kept and fed the swine,
 Fled at the sight with awe,
And in the town and country round
 Told all the things they saw.
When those who heard, came forth to
  Christ,
 To see what he had wrought,
And found the man who was possessed,
 No more in mind distraught,
The owners of the swine, alarmed,
 Unto the city fled,
And told the tale to all they met,
 Which filled them with great dread.
To Christ they came, and at his feet
 Saw him who had been mad,
Sitting, with peaceful look, intent,
 In decent garments clad.
At this most wondrous sight they
  feared,
 And hearing what befell,
Full earnestly they prayed the Lord
 He there no more would dwell.
Then in the ship the Lord returned ;
 Yet still with grateful soul
The man besought that he might stay
 With Him who made him whole.
But Jesus gave him work to do,
 And kindly said, " Return,
And tell thy friends the Lord's great
  love,
 Which now thou canst discern."
Then throughout all Decapolis
 He published far and wide,
Till all men marveled at his words,
 Which could not be denied.

nor in đɛ abis, hwiç mɵst đɛ
  dred,
 komand đat đɛ ʃud liv.
Nȣ sɒm wɛ of, a nụmerɒs herd
 ov ɒnklin swịn wer fed,
sɵ wiđin điz đe dimonz pred
 đɛr eksịl mịt bi med.
And Jizɒs hiz permiʃon gɛv.
 Đen fɵrȶwiđ from đe men
đe dimonz fled, and kwikli went
 intu đe swịn ; and đen
đe dimon herd, tú ȶȣzand stroŋ,
 intu đe lɛk wer driven ;
and periʃt in đe wɷteri flɒd,
 agenst hwiç đɛ had striven.
Đe men hɯ kept and fed đe swịn,
 fled at đe sịt wiđ ɷ,
and in đe tȣn and kɒntri rȣnd
 tɵld ɷl đe ȶiŋz đɛ sɷ.
Hwen đɵz hɯ herd, kem fɵrȶ tu
  Krịst,
 tu si hwot hi had rɷt,
and fȣnd đe man hɯ woz pozest,
 nɵ mɵr in mịnd distrɷt,
đe ɵnerz ov đe swịn, alarmd,
 ɒntu đe siti fled,
and tɵld đe tel tu ɷl đɛ met,
 hwiç fild đem wiđ gret dred.
Tu Krịst đɛ kem, and at hiz fit
 sɷ him hɯ had bin mad,
sitiŋ, wiđ pisful luk, intent,
 in disent garments klad.
At đis mɵst wɒndrɒs sịt đɛ
  fird,
 and hiriŋ hwot befel,
ful ernestli đɛ pred đe Lord
 hi đer nɵ mɵr wud dwel.
Đen in đe ʃip đe Lord retɒrnd ;
 yet stil wiđ gretful sɵl
đe man besɷt đat hi mịt stɛ
 wiđ Him hɯ med him hɵl.
Bɒt Jizɒs gev him wɒrk tu dɯ,
 and kịndli sed, "Retɒrn,
and tel đị frendz đe Lord'z gret
  lɒv,
 hwiç nȣ đȣ kanst disern."
Đen ȶrɯɯt ɷl Dekapolis
 hi pɒbliʃt far and wịd,
til ɷl men marveld at hiz wɒrdz,
 hwiç kud not bi denịd.

SECTION 63.

Christ dines with Matthew.—
Mattthew 9. 1. Mark 5. 21. Luke 8. 40.
Matthew 9. 10-17. Mark 2. 15-22.
Luke 5. 29-39.

And Matthew made a feast, whereto
  Christ and his followers came,
And much the Scribes and Pharisees
  Did their imprudence blame,
Because he ate with publicans
  And sinners of that place.
Then Jesus said to them, "The sick
  Most need my healing grace;
I came not only to reform
  Self-righteous men, like you,
But to restore to heavenly life
  The guilty outcast crew.
Go, learn the meaning of that word,
  'I love not sacrifice,
But mercy.' Do ye so; and then
  Ye will indeed be wise."
And Jesus added, "While I dwell
  Incarnate on the earth,
I spend my time in doing good,
  And raising fallen worth;
So that my friends and followers
  Rejoice; but days will come
When they shall weep and fast around
  Their Lord, when in the tomb.
I do not put the Gospel true,
  That bright new wine of heaven,
In bottles of old shriveled skins,
  For they, being thereby riven,
That heavenly wine would soon be [spilled;
  But new truth I enfold
In new befitting forms and moulds,
  Which will not soon wax old."

SEKΣON 63.

Krįst dįnz wið Maθų.—
Maŧų 9. 1. Mark 5. 21. Luk 8. 40
Maŧų 9. 10-17. Mark 2. 15-22.
Luke 5. 29-39.

And Maŧų mɛd a fįst, hwɛrtu
  Krįst and hiz folɵerz kɛm,
and mɒç ðe Skrįbz and Farisiz
  did ðer imprɯdens blɛm,
bekɷz hi ɛt wið pɒblikanz
  and sinerz ov ðát plɛs.
Ðen Jizɒs sed tu ðem, "Ðe sik
  mɵst nid mį hiliŋ gres;
į kɛm not ɵnli tu reform
  self-rįtiɒs men, lįk ų,
bɒt tu restɵr tu hevenli lįf
  ðe gilti ɤtkast krɯ.
Gɵ, lern ðe miniŋ ov ðát wɒrd,
  'Ŧ lɒv not sakrifįs,
bɒt mersi.' Dɯ yi sɵ; and ðen
  yi wil indid bi wįz."
And Jizɒs aded, "Hwįl į dwel
  inkarnɛt on ðe erŧ,
į spend mį tįm in dɯiŋ gud,
  and rɛziŋ fɷlen wɒrŧ:
sɵ ðat mį frendz and folɵerz
  rejois; bɒt dɛz wil kɒm
hwen ðɛ ʃal wip and fast arɤnd
  ðer Lord, hwen in ðe tɯm.
Ŧ dɯ not put ðe Gospel trɯ,
  ðát brįt nų wįn ov heven,
in botelz ov ɵld ʃriveld skinz,
  for ðɛ, biiŋ ðerbį riven,
ðát hevenli wįn wud sɯn bi spild;
  bɒt nų trɯŧ į enfɵld
in nų befitiŋ formz and mɵldz,
  hwiç wil not sɯn waks ɵld."

SECTION 64.

Jairus's Daughter healed, and the Infirm Woman.—Matthew 9. 18-26.
Mark 5. 22-43. Luke 8. 41-56.

Now while these solemn words he [spake,
  A Jewish ruler came
With anxious haste to meet the Lord,
  Jairus was his name.
Humbly he knelt at Jesus' feet,
  And worshiped: then he prayed

SEKΣON 64.

Jairɒs'ez Dɵter hild, and ðe Inferm Wuman.—Maŧų 9. 18-26.
Mark 5. 22-43 Luk 8. 41-56.

Nɤ hwįl ðiz solem wɒrdz hi spɛk,
  a Jɯiʃ rɯler kɛm
wið aŋkʃɒs hɛst tu mit ðe Lord,
  Jaįrɒs woz hiz nɛm.
Hɒmbli hi nelt at Jizɒs' fit,
  and wɒrʃipt: ðen hi prɛd

That Jesus to his house would come
To heal a little maid.
He said, "My little daughter lies
Even at the point of death;
But come and lay thy hand on her,
(Such was this ruler's faith,)
And she, my only child, shall live."
She now a-dying lay;
Twelve years of age. Then Jesus rose,
And followed in his way.
And as, with his disciples, too,
He journied, in the throng,
A woman, with a sad disease
Afflicted twelve years long,
Now that her fortune all was spent
On those who could not cure,
To Jesus came, of whom she heard,
The good Physician sure.
She said within herself, "Let me
But touch his clothes, and I
Shall soon be healed by miracle
Of this my malady."
She crept behind, in faith, to touch
The border near the ground,
And instantly she felt the blood
Stayed in its proper bound.
Then Jesus knew that from himself
A healing virtue passed,
And turning, said, "Who touched my clothes?"
When all denied; at last
Peter said, "Master, see what crowds
Around thee closely stand;
How canst thou ask, then, whence the touch
Of any single hand?"
Still Jesus looked, and now his eye
Upon that woman stayed;
Who knowing she could not be hid,
Her case before him laid.
And when he saw her trembling fear,
Kindly did he reply,
"Daughter, in peace depart; thy faith
Hath healed thee perfectly."
While yet he spake, there came, in grief,
One from the ruler's home,
Saying, "Thy daughter, sir, is dead;
The Master need not come:
Trouble him not." But Jesus heard,
And graciously he said,

đat Jizɒs tu hiz hʊs wud kɒm
tu hil a litel med.
Hi sed, "Mį litel dɷter lįz
iven at đe point ov deɟ;
bɒt kɒm and lɛ đį hand on her,
(sɒç woz đis rɯler'z feɟ,)
and ʃi, mį ɵnli çild, ʃal liv."
Σi nʊ a-dįiŋ lɛ;
twelv yirz ov ɛj. Đen Jizɒs rɵz,
and folɵd in hiz wɛ.
And az, wiđ hiz disįpelz, tɯ,
hi jɒrnid, in đe ɟroŋ,
a wuman, wiđ a a sad disiz
aflikted twelv yirz loŋ,
nʊ đat her fortųn ɷl woz spent
on đɵz hɯ kud not kųr,
tu Jizɒs kem, ov hɯm ʃi herd,
đe gud Fiziʃan ʃɯr.
Σi sed wiđin herself, "Let mi
bɒt tɒç hiz klɵđz, and į
ʃal sɯn bi hild bį mirakel
ov đis mį maladi."
Σi krept behįnd, in feɟ, tu tɒç
đe border nir đe grʊnd,
and instantli ʃi felt đe blɒd
sted in its proper bʊnd.
Đen Jizɒs nų đat from himself
a hiliŋ vertų past,
and tɒrniŋ, sed, "Hɯ tɒçt mį klɵđz?"
Hwen ɷl denįd; at last
Piter sed, "Master, si hwot krʊdz
arʊnd đi klɵsli stand;
hʊ kanst đʊ ask, đen, hwens đe tɒç
ov eni siŋgel hand?"
Stil Jizɒs lukt, and nʊ hiz į
ɒpon đát wuman sted;
hɯ nɵiŋ ʃi kud not bi hid,
her kes befɵr him led.
And hwen hi sɷ her trembliŋ fir,
kįndli did hi replį,
"Dɷter, in pis depart; đį feɟ
haɟ hild đi perfektli."
Hwįl yet hi spek, đer kem, in grif,
wɒn from đe rɯler'z hɵm,
seiŋ, "Đį dɷter, ser, iz ded;
đe master nid not kɒm:
trɒbel him not." Bɒt Jizɒs herd
and greʃɒsli hi sed,

"Only believe, and fear thou not,
She shall be healed, though dead."
With Peter, James, and John, unto
The ruler's house he went;
There all was tumult, and the noise
Of sorrow finding vent.
"Why make ye this ado?" Christ said,
The damsel doth but sleep."
They scorned his word, for well they
It was death's slumber deep. [knew
But now the Lord dismissed the crowd,
And brought her parents sad,
With his disciples, to the room
Wherein the maid was laid.
And there he took her by the hand,
And spoke, in powerful wise,
Words which, interpreted, imply,
"Damsel, I say, arise."
Her spirit heard that mighty voice,
And quick obeyed the word.
She rose and walked. Then food was
By order of the Lord. [brought,
Great was her parents' wonderment,
And, against his command,
The news of this great miracle
They spread throughout the land.

"Ɵnli beliv, and fir đɤ not,
ʃi ʃal bi hild, đɵ ded."
Wiđ Piter, Jemz, and Jon, ɒntu
đe ruler'z hɤs hi went;
đer ɷl woz tųmɒlt, and đe noiz
ov sorɵ fįndiŋ vent.
"Hwį mek yi đis adɯ?" Krįst sed,
đe damzel dɒŧ bɒt slip."
Đe skornd hiz wɒrd, for wel đe nų
it woz deŧ's slɒmber dip.
Bɒt nɤ đe Lord dismist đe krɤd,
and brɷt her perents sad,
wiđ hiz disįpelz, tu đe rɯm
hwerin đe med woz led.
And đer hi tuk her bį đe hand,
and spɵk in pɤerful wįz,
wɒrdz hwiç, interpreted, implį,
"Damzel, į se, arįz."
Her spirit herd đát mįti vois,
and kwikli ɵbed đe wɒrd.
Σi rɵz and wókt. Đen fɯd woz
bį order ov đe Lord. [brɷt,
Gret woz her perents' wɒnderment,
and, agenst hiz komand,
đe nųz ov đis gret mirakel
đe spred ŧrɯɤt đe land.

SECTION 65.

***Christ restores two Blind Men to Sight.*— Matthew 9. 27-31.**

Departing thence, two blind men came,
And following Jesus, cried,
"O son of David, mercy have
On us, of sight denied."
He answered, "Do ye then believe
That I such power possess?"
They said, "Yea, Lord." Thus promptly they
Their faith in him profess.
Then Jesus touched their eyes, and
"Be it as you desire." [said,
They quickly see; and now the Lord
Doth straight of them require
That they should let the miracle
Be published unto none;
But wide they spread abroad the fame
Of what had there been done.

SEKΣON 65.

***Krįst restɵrz túu Blįnd Men tu Sįt.* Maŧų 9. 27-31.**

Departiŋ đens, túu blįnd men kem,
and folɵiŋ Jizɒs, krįd,
"Ɵ sɒn ov Devid, mersi hav
on ɒs, ov sįt denįd."
Hi anserd, "Dɯ yi đen beliv
đat į sɒç pɤer pozes?"
Đe sed, "Ye, Lord." Đɒs promptli đe
đer feŧ in him prɵfes.
Đen Jizɒs tɒçt đer įz, and sed,
"Bi it az ų dezįr."
Đe kwikli si; and nɤ đe Lord
dɒŧ stret ov đem rekwįr
đat đe ʃud let đe mirakel
bi pɒbliʃt ɒntu nɒn;
bɒt wįd đe spred abrɷd đe fem
ov hwot had đer bin dɒn.

SECTION 66.

Christ casts out a Dumb Spirit.
—Matthew 9. 33-35.

And as they journeyed, one was brought
 To Christ that was possest,
And could not speak ; the spirit foul
 Did thus his mind infest.
At Jesus' word, the demon fled,
 And the afflicted spoke.
The multitudes were struck with awe,
 And into praises broke,
" There never was such mighty power
Displayed in Israel's land before."

SEKƩON 66.

Krįst kasts ɤt a Dɒm Spirit.
Maŧų 9. 33-35.

And az đe jɒrnid, wɒn woz brɵt
 tu Krįst đat woz pozest,
and kud not spįk ; đe spirit fɤl
 did đɒs hiz mįnd infest.
At Jįzɒs' wɒrd, đe dimon fled,
 and đe aflikted spɵk.
Ðe mɒltitųdz wer strɒk wiđ ɷ,
 and intu prezez brɵk,
" Ðer never woz sɒç mįti pɤer
displed in Izrael'z land befɵr."

SECTION 67.

Christ returns to Nazareth, and is again ill treated there.
Matthew 13. 54-58. Mark 6. 1-6.

Then Christ returned to Nazareth,
 Wherein his youth was spent,
And his disciples thither, too,
 With their good Master went.
And on the Sabbath day he preached
 Unto the people there
In the Jews' synagogue, and crowds
 Did unto him repair.
And much they wondered that a man
 Who had appeared so long
As their familiar citizen,
 Should now command the throng
By heavenly wisdom, and great works
 Of most miraculous might ;
And they were envious of his fame,
 And felt malicious spite.
Then Jesus said, "A prophet lacks
 Not honor, fame, and worth,
Except in his own house, or in
 The land that gave him birth."
And there Christ did no mighty work ;
 A few sick folk he cured ;
He marveled at their unbelief,
 And treatment of his word.

SEKƩON 67.

Krįst retɒrnz tu Nazareθ, and iz agen il trited đɛr.
Maŧų 13. 54-58. Mark 6. 1-6.

Ðen Krįst retɒrnd tu Nazareŧ,
 hwerin hiz ųŧ woz spent,
and hiz disįpelz điđer, tuu,
 wiđ đer gud Master went.
And on đe Sabaŧ de hi prįçt
 ɒntu đe pįpel đer
in đe Juuz' sinagog, and krɤdz
 did ɒntu him reper.
And mɒç đe wɒnderd đat a man
 huu had apįrd sɵ loŋ
az đer familiar sitizen,
 ʃud nɤ komand đe ŧroŋ
bį hevenli wizdom, and gret wɒrks
 ov mɵst mirakųlɒs mįt ;
and đe wer envįɒs ov hiz fem,
 and felt maliʃɒs spįt.
Ðen Jizɒs sed " A profet laks
 not onor, fem, and wɒrŧ,
eksept in hiz ɵn hɤs, or in
 đe land đat gev him berŧ."
And đer Krįst did nɵ mįti wɒrk ;
 a fų sik fɵk hi kųrd ;
hi marveld at đer ɒnbelif,
 and tritment ov hiz wɒrd.

SECTION 68.

Christ preaches again throughout Galilee.
Matthew 9. 35-38.

Then Jesus preached through Galilee
 The Kingdom of God's grace,

SEKƩON 68.

Krįst prįçez agen θruut Galili.
Maŧų 9. 35-38.

Ðen Jizɒs prįçt ŧruu Galili
 đe Kiŋdom ov God'z gres,

And healed all kinds of sicknesses,
  That vex the human race.
And when he saw the multitudes
  That followed in his train,
He felt compassion for their woes,
  Their weariness and pain;
For they were like to scattered sheep
  Without a shepherd true;
A mighty harvest of men's souls,
  But reapers there were few.
Therefore said Christ unto the band
  Of his disciples round,
"Pray ye the Lord of harvest that
  More reapers may abound."

and hįld ɷl kįndz ov siknesez,
  đat veks đe hųman res.
And hwen hi sɷ đe mɒltitųdz
  đat folɵd in hiz tren,
hi felt kompaʃon for đer wɵz,
  der wɪrines and pen;
for đe wer lįk tu skaterd ʃip
  widɤt a ʃepherd trɯ;
a mįti harvest ov men'z sɵlz,
  bɒt rɪperz đer wer fų.
Ɑerfɵr sed Krįst ɒntu đe band
  ov hiz disįpelz rɤnd,
"Pre yɪ đe Lord ov harvest đat
  mɵr rɪperz me abɤnd."

BOOK IV.

SECTION 69.*

Commission to the Twelve Apostles.

Matthew 10; 11. 1. Mark 6. 7-13.
Luke 9. 1-6.

Then Jesus called his chosen twelve,
  That he might power bestow
To cast out demons, and to heal
  Disease, and every woe.
Their names were:—Simon, (Peter called,
  For this one had two names,)
His brother Andrew, and the sons
  Of Zebedee, John and James;
Bartholomew and Philip next,
  And Thomas, doubting man,
Another James, surnamed The Less,
  Matthew the publican,
Lebbæus or Thaddæus then,
  Simon, the Canaanite,
And lastly Judas, who, for good,
  Great evil did requite.
These twelve, in well-selected pairs,
  Christ sent, to heal, and preach,
To go not to the Gentile race,
  Nor in Samaria teach;

BUK IV.

SEKΣON 69.*

Komiʃon tu đe Twelv Aposelz.

Maŧų 10; 11. 1. Mark 6. 7-13.
Lɯk 9. 1-6.

Ɑen Jizɒs kɷld hiz ɕɵzen twelv,
  đat hi mįt pɤer bestɵ
tu kast ɤt dimonz, and tu hil
  disiz and everi wɵ.
Ɑer nemz wer:—Sįmon, (Pɪter kɷld,
  for đis wɒn had tɯ́ nemz,)
hiz brɒđer Andrɯ, and đe sɒnz
  ov Zebedi, Jon and Jemz;
Barŧolomų and Filip nekst,
  and Tomas, dɤtiŋ man,
anɒđer Jemz, sɒrnemd Ɑe Les,
  Maŧų đe pɒblikan,
Lebiɒs or Ŧadiɒs đen,
  Sįmon đe Kenanįt,
and lastli Jɯdas, hɯ, for gud,
  gret ɪvil did rekwįt.
Ɑiz twelv, in wel-selekted perz,
  Krįst sent, tu hil, and priɕ,
tu gɵ not tu đe Jentįl res,
  nor in Samaria tiɕ;

---

* The reader is requested to excuse the omission, on the part of the editor, of the words "Book II." and "Book III." in this "Rhymed Harmony of the Gospels," and to supply them with the pen. Book II. commences at Section 21, and Book III. at Section 45.

For they were first to seek the lost
  Of Israel's favored land,
And as they went, to preach this word,
  "Heaven's kingdom is at hand."
As they so freely had received,
  So freely should they give
Health to men's bodies, and their
  And bid the dead to live. [minds,
He also said, "Ye need not take
  Silver, nor gold, nor brass,
Nor double garments, shoes, nor
  Nor bread, as on ye pass; [staves,
The workman merits well his hire.
  And if in any town
Or house, ye find some worthy man,
  Abide, and there sit down.
Salute such house with words of peace;
  But if it should refuse
To hear your words, as ye depart,
  The dust shake from your shoes
To testify against their deed;
  And verily I say,
Sodom shall have a milder fate
  In God's just judgement day.
As helpless sheep, amid fierce wolves,
  Into the world you're sent;
Be therefore wise as serpents, and
  Like doves be innocent.
Beware of men; and still expect
  To suffer from their spite;
To Councils they will give you up,
  In Synagogues will fight.
Thus for my sake you must contend
  With kings and governors,
And testify my Gospel's power
  To Jews and foreigners.
But be not anxious what to speak,
  For there shall then be given,
In that same hour, words coming from
  Your Father's spirit in heaven.
Though parents, children, brothers
  Will one another kill, [dear,
And ye, for my sake, hated be,
  And suffer every ill;
Yet whoso faithful proves himself,
  Enduring to the end,
Shall from all evil here be saved,
  And shall to heaven ascend.
If in one place men persecute,
  Then to another roam;

for đɛ wer ferst tu sik đe lost
  ov Izrael'z fevord land,
and az đɛ went, tu priç đis wɒrd,
  "Heven'z kiŋdom iz at hand."
Az đɛ sɵ frili had resivd,
  sɵ frili ʃud đɛ giv
helŧ tu men'z bodiz, and đer mįndz,
  and bid đe ded tu liv.
Hi ɑlsɵ sed, "Yi nid not tek
  silver, nor gɵld, nor bras,
nor dɒbel garments, ʃuz, nor stevz,
  nor bred, az on yi pas;
đe wɒrkman merits wel hiz hįr.
  And if in eni tɤn
or hɤs, yi fįnd sɒm wɒrđi man,
  abįd, and đer sit dɤn.
Salut sɒç hɤs wiđ wɒrdz ov pis;
  bɒt if it ʃud refɥz
tu hir ɥr wɒrdz, az yi depart,
  đe dɒst ʃek from ɥr ʃuz
tu testifį agenst đer did;
  and verili į se,
Sodom ʃal hav a mįlder fet
  in God'z jɒst jɒjment dɛ.
Az helples ʃip, amid firs wulvz,
  intu đe wɒrld ɥ'r sent;
bi đerfɵr wįz az serpents, and
  lįk dɒvz bi inosent.
Bewer ov men, and stil ekspekt
  tu sɒfer from đɛr spįt;
tu Kɤnsilz đɛ wil giv ɥ ɒp,
  in Sinagogz wil fįt.
Đɒs for mį sek ɥ mɒst kontend
  wiđ kiŋz and gɒvernerz,
and testifį mį Gospel'z pɤer
  tu Juz and forenerz.
Bɒt bi not aŋkʃɒs hwot yi spik,
  for đer ʃal đen bi given,
in đát sem ɤr, wɒrdz kɒmiŋ from
  ɥr Fađer'z spirit in heven.
Đɵ perents, çildren, brɒđerz dir,
  wil wɒn anɒđer kil,
and yi, for mį sek, heted bi,
  and sɒfer everi il;
yet huzɵ feŧful pruvz himself,
  endɥriŋ tu đe end,
ʃal from ɔl ivil hir bi sevd,
  and ʃal tu heven asend.
If in wɒn ples men persekɥt,
  đen tu anɒđer rɵm;

Before you visit all the land,
  The Son of Man shall come.
Disciples cannot be above
  Their Lord, whose name they bear;
Let it suffice each humble soul
  His Master's lot to share.
If he be called Beelzebub,
  Though master of the land,
Be sure his household must expect
  In the same lot to stand.
But fear not such: for nought is shown
  That ought to be concealed;
And nothing hidden doth remain
  That ought to be revealed.
What I in darkness now make known,
  That speak ye in the light;
And what ye now in private hear,
  That preach in all men's sight.
Fear not the feeble power which can
  The body only kill;
Fear that which soul and body both
  Can sink down into hell.
Two sparrows are but little worth,
  And yet not even one
Of these shall fall, but with God's will,
  By whom all things are known.
The very hairs upon your head
  Are numbered by his care;
Therefore fear not; he values you
  Far more than birds of air.
He who confesses, fearlessly,
  My name before mankind,
Shall at my heavenly Father's throne
  Confession from me find.
But whoso faithlessly denies,
  This awful doom will meet;
Him I'll deny in that dread day
  Before the judgement-seat.
Think not my coming only brings
  Peace to this world of woes,
A sword will also be its lot,
  And households become foes.
If any cherish wife or child
  More than his Savior dear,
He is not worthy of my love,
  Which owns no rival here.
And if he take not willingly
  His cross, and follow me;
Or give his life, when I require,
  He cannot my life see.

befɵr ų vizit ɷl đe land,
  đe Sɒn ov Man ʃal kɒm.
Disįpelz kanot bi abɒv
  đer Lord, huz nem đe bɛr;
let it sɒfįz iç hɒmbel sɵl
  hiz Master'z lot tu ʃer.
If hi bi kɷld Bielzebɒb,
  đɵ master ov đe land,
bi ʃur hiz hɤshɵld mɒst ekspekt
  in đe sem lot tu stand.
Bɒt fir not sɒç: for nɷt iz ʃɵn
  đat ɷt tu bi konsild;
and nɒŧiŋ hiden dɒŧ remen
  đat ɷt tu bi revild.
Hwot į in darknes nɤ mek nɵn,
  đát spik yi in đe lįt;
and hwot yi nɤ in prįvet hir,
  đát priç in ɷl men'z sįt.
Fir not đe fibel pɤer hwiç kan
  đe bodi ɵnli kil;
fir đát hwiç sɵl and bodi bɵŧ
  kan siŋk dɤn intu hel.
Tú sparɵz ar bɒt litel wɒrŧ,
  and yet not iven wɒn
ov điz ʃal fɷl, bɒt wiđ Godz wil,
  bį hum ɷl ŧiŋz ar nɵn.
Đe veri herz ɒpon ųr hed
  ar nɒmberd bį hiz ker;
đerfɵr fir not; hi valųz ų
  far mɵr đan berdz ov ɛr.
Hi hu konfesez, firlesli,
  mį nem befɵr mankįnd,
ʃal at mį hevenli Fɑđer'z ŧrɵn
  konfeʃon from mi fįnd.
Bɒt husɵ feŧlesli denįz,
  đis ɷful dum wil mit;
him į'l denį in đát dred de
  befɵr đe jɒjment sit.
Ŧiŋk not mį kɒmiŋ ɵnli briŋz
  pis tu đis wɒrld ov wɵz,
a sɵrd wil ɷlsɵ bi its lot,
  and hɤshɵldz bekɒm fɵz.
If eni çeriʃ wįf or çįld
  mɵr đan hiz Sevier dir,
hi iz not wɒrđi ov mį lɒv,
  hwiç ɵnz nɵ rįval hir.
And if hi tek not wiliŋli
  hiz kros, and folɵ mi;
or giv hiz lįf, hwen į rekwįr,
  hi kanot mį lįf si.

Who here receives my followers,
  Doth welcome to me give;
And even a cup of water will
  From me reward receive."

When Jesus ended thus his charge
  Unto his chosen band,
He left that place, and preached and
  In the cities of that land. [taught
The twelve Apostles, too, went forth,
  And told men to repent,
With oil anointed many sick,
  And healed, and demons sent
From out men's bodies, everywhere
  Causing astonishment.

SECTION 70.

Death of John the Baptist.

Matthew 14. 1-12. Mark 6. 14-30.
Luke 9. 7-9.

Then Herod, who was tetrarch, heard
  Of Jesus, and the fame
Of his great miracles, which spread
  Abroad his wondrous name;
And he was troubled, for some said
  That Jesus Christ must be
Elijah raised to life again,
  Or prophet such as he.
And others said, the spirit of John
  The Baptist had appeared
In the new form of Jesus Christ:
  And Herod greatly feared,
And said, "Yes, surely, this is John
  Whom I so lately slew;
He rises from the dead, and now
  He shows these wonders new."
And he desired to see the Christ,
  That he might thereby know
If John had been revived, whose death
  Had given him grievous woe.
For he had put in prison strong
  The Baptist, who had said
That Herod had committed crime
  When he Herodias wed,
Who was his brother Philip's wife;
  Therefore she sought, with hate,
To take John's life, because he would
  This marriage reprobate;

Huı hịr resịvz mị folɵerz,
  dɒɟ welkɒm tu mị giv;
and ịven a kɒp ov wɷter wil
  from mị reword resịv."

Hwen Jịzɒs ended đɒs hiz ɕarj
  ɒntu hiz ɕɵzen band,
hị left đát ples, and prịɕt and tɷt
  in đe sitiz ov đát land.
Đe twelv Aposelz, tuı, went fɵrɟ,
  and tɵld men tu repent,
wiđ oil anointed meni sik,
  and hịld, and dịmonz sent
from ɤt men'z bodiz, everihwer
  kɷziŋ astoniʃment.

SEKΣON 70.

Deθ ov Jon đe Baptist.

Maɟụ 14. 1-12. Mark 6. 14-30.
Luık 9. 7-9.

Đen Herod, huı woz tetrark, herd
  ov Jịzɒs, and đe fem
ov hiz gret mirakelz, hwiɕ spred
  abrɷd hiz wɒndrɒs nem;
and hị woz trɒbeld, for sɒm sed
  đat Jịzɒs Krịst mɒst bị
Elịja rezd tu lịf agen,
  or profet sɒɕ az hị.
And ɒđerz sed, đe spirit ov Jon
  đe Baptist had apịrd
in đe nụ form ov Jịzɒs Krịst;
  and Herod gretli fịrd,
and sed, "Yes, ʃuırli, đis iz Jon
  huım ị sɵ letli sluı;
hị rịzez from đe ded, and nɤ
  hị ʃɵz điz wɒnderz nụ."
And hị dezịrd tu sị đe Krịst,
  đat hị mịt đerbị nɵ
if Jon had bịn revịvd, huız deɟ
  had given him grịvɒs wɵ.
For hị had put in prizon stroŋ
  đe Baptist, huı had sed
đat Herod had komited krịm
  hwen hị Herɵdias wed,
huı woz hiz brɒđer Filip's wịf;
  đerfɵr, ʃị sɷt, wiđ het,
tu tek Jon'z lịf, bekɷz hị wud
  đis marej reprɵbet;

And she would soon have murdered [him,
But Herod this denied,
Because that mighty prophet's name
Was justly magnified
For wisdom, and for sanctity,
And reformation true;
And Herod oft had loved to hear
John preach: his worth he knew.
Moreover he was much afraid
That holy man to slay,
Although John would rebuke him for
The evil of his way.
When Herod's birthday came, then he
Invited to a feast
High lords and chiefs of Galilee,
And merriment increased.
Herodias's daughter danced
Before them gracefully,
With fascination in her step,
And triumph in her eye.
Then Herod swore before his court
To grant her wish, whate'er
She might petition from his hand;
His kingdom even to share.
Then straight she asked her mother vile
What thing she should require;
And that incestuous termagant,
To gratify her ire,
Said, "Give me John the Baptist's head."
Soon did the daughter go
And tell the king her mother's wish.
How was he filled with woe!
But for his oath's sake, and for them
Who sat with him at meat,
He said it should be given her.
It was a hellish treat!
Then went the executioner
To prison, where John lay,
And slew him, and then brought his [head
Upon a dish, or tray,
And gave it to the damsel, who
Then gave it to her mother,
So bloody a pair these proud dames [were,
And so like one another.
When John's disciples heard of this,
With sorrow soon they come,
And take the Baptist's sacred corpse,
And lay it in a tomb.

and ʃi wud sɯn hav mɒrderd him,
bɒt Herod đis deniįd,
bekoz đát mįti profet's nɛm
woz jɒstli magnifįd
for wizdom, and for saŋktiti,
and reformɛʃon trɯ;
and Herod oft had lɒvd tu hir
Jon priç: hiz wɒrɟ hi nų.
Merɵver hi woz mɒç afred
đát hɵli man tu slɛ,
ɵlđɵ Jon wud rebųk him for
đe ɩvil ov hiz wɛ.
Hwen Herod'z berɟdɛ kɛm, đen hi
invįted tu a fɩst
hį lordz and çifs ov Galili,
and meriment inkrɩst.
Herɵdias'ez dɵter danst
befɵr đem gresfuli,
wiđ fasinɛʃon in her step,
and trįɒmf in her į.
Ɑen Herod swɵr befɵr hiz kɵrt
tu grant her wiʃ, hwot'ɛr
ʃi mįt petiʃon from hiz hand;
hiz kiŋdom ɩven tu ʃɛr.
Ɑen stret ʃi askt her mɒđer vįl
hwot ɟiŋ ʃi ʃud rekwįr;
and đát insestųɒs termagant,
tu gratifį her įr,
sed, "Giv mi Jon đe Baptist's hed."
Sɯn did đe dɵter gɵ
and tel đe kiŋ her mɒđer'z wiʃ.
Hɤ woz hi fild wiđ wɵ!
Bɒt for hiz ɵɟ's sɛk, and for đem
hɯ sat wiđ him at mɩt,
hi sed it ʃud bi given her.
It woz a heliʃ trit!
Ɑen went đe eksekųʃoner
tu prizon, hwɛr Jon lɛ,
and slɯ him, and đen brɵt hiz hed
ɒpon a diʃ, or trɛ,
and gev it tu đe damzel, hɯ
đen gev it tu her mɒđer,
sɵ blɒdi a per điz prɤd demz wer,
and sɵ lįk wɒn anɒđer.
Hwen Jon'z disįpelz herd ov đis,
wiđ sorɵ sɯn đɛ kɒm,
and tɛk đe Baptist's sɛkred korps,
and lɛ it in a tɯm.

SECTION 71.

The Twelve return, and Jesus retires with them to the desert of Bethsaida.

Matthew 14. 13, 14. Mark 6. 30-34. Luke 9. 10, 11. John 6. 1, 2.

The twelve disciples now return
  To Jesus, and relate
What they had done, and taught, and [how
  They sought to imitate
Their Lord, and his commands obey.
  He said to them, "Come ye
Apart into a desert place,
  That we may thus be free
From all this multitude;" for crowds
  So thronged about them there,
They could not take their food in peace,
  Nor such intrusion bear.
Then Jesus took them privately,
  And went across the sea,
Unto a solitary place,
  In the vicinity
Of famed Bethsaida, and there too
  The people thronged to hear.
When Jesus saw them, he was moved
  With sympathy sincere,
For they were like a scattered flock,
  With no kind shepherd near.
He spoke to them of heavenly things,
  Healed those that were diseased,
Gave comfort to the mourners, and
  With none was he displeased.

SEKΣON 71.

Ðe Twelv retɒrn, and Jizɒs retįrz w ðem tu ðe dezert ov Beθseda.

Maθų 14. 13, 14. Mark 6. 30-34. Luk 9. 10, 11. Jon 6. 1, 2.

Ðe twelv disįpelz nɤ retɒrn
  tu Jizɒs, and relet
hwɷt ðe had dɒn, and tɷt, and h
  ðe sɷt tu imitet
ðer Lord, and hiz komandz ɵbe.
  Hi sed tu ðem, "Kɒm yɪ
apart intu a dezert ples,
  ðat wɪ me ðɒs bi fri
from ɷl ðis mɒltitųd;" for krɤd
  sɵ θroŋd abɤt ðem ðer,
ðe kud not tek ðer fud in pɪs,
  nor sɒɡ intruʒon ber.
Ðen Jizɒs tuk ðem prįvetli,
  and went akros ðe sɪ,
ɒntu a solitari ples,
  in ðe visiniti
ov femd Beθseda, and ðer tu
  ðe pipel θroŋd tu hɪr.
Hwen Jizɒs sɷ ðem, hi woz mu
  wið simpaθi sinsɪr,
for ðe wer lįk a skaterd flok,
  wið nɵ kįnd ʃepherd nɪr.
Hi spɵk tu ðem ov hevenli θiŋz,
  hild ðɵz ðat wer disɪzd,
gev kɒmfort tu ðe mɵrnerz, and
  wið nɒn woz hi displɪzd.

SECTION 72.

Five thousand are fed miraculously.

Matthew 14. 15-21. Mark 6. 35-44. Luke 9. 12-17. John 6. 5-14.

And when the day passed swift away,
  And the disciples saw
That they were in a lonely place,
  They said, "Let us withdraw
From this vast multitude, and send
  Them where they may buy food;
This place yields nought for them or [us,
  But in the neighbourhood
They may find what will satisfy,
  And fill their mouths with good.
Then Jesus raised his eyes, and saw
  A goodly company,

SEKΣON 72.

Fįv θɤzand ar fed mirakųlɒsli.

Maθų 14. 15-21. Mark 6. 35-44. Luk 9. 12-17. Jon 6. 5-14.

And hwen ðe de past swift awe,
  and ðe disįpelz sɷ
ðat ðe wer in a lɵnli ples,
  ðe sed, "Let ɒs wiðdrɷ
from ðis vast mɒltitųd, and send
  ðem hwer ðe me bį fud;
ðis ples yɪldz nɷt for ðem or ɒs,
  bɒt in ðe nebɒrhud
ðe me fįnd hwot wil satisfį,
  and fil ðer mɤðz wið gud.
Ðen Jizɒs rezd hiz įz and sɷ
  a gudli kɒmpani,

And unto Philip thus he spoke,
To prove his fealty,
"Where shall we find sufficient bread
So many mouths to feed?"
Full well he knew, by his own power,
How to supply the need.
"Two hundred shillings' worth will not
Suffice for everyone,"
Said Philip, doubting in his heart,
Whether it could be done.
'Twas evening now, the day far spent;
They came to him, and said,
"Do send this multitude away,
That they may buy some bread,
And lodge themselves, as best they may,
In villages around;
For in this desert place, be sure
No comfort will be found."
He answered, "No, they need not go;
Give ye them food to eat."
"Then Master, shall we go and buy
Enough to spread a treat?"
He saith, "How many loaves have ye?"
They quickly told him, "Five,
And two small fishes; how can these
Keep all this crowd alive?"
Jesus, with dignity divine,
Said, "Bring them here to me,
And make the men sit down in ranks,
By fifties, o'er the lea;"
For in that place there was much grass;
And there they all sat down,
Five thousand, in due order placed,
As Jesus' word had shown.
Then Jesus took those loaves, so few,
And having given thanks,
He brake, and gave to those around,
That they to all the ranks
Might give both bread and fishes too,
As much as they could eat.
They ate, were filled, and now their hearts
Expand, with joy replete.
To his disciples then he spoke,
"The fragments now obtain,
That nothing may be wasted here."
They do so, and retain
Twelve baskets full of fragments good,
Which these five thousand leave,

and ɒntu Filip đɒs hi spɵk
tu prɯv hiz fıalti,
"Hwer ʃal wı fįnd sɒfiʃent bred
sɵ meni mɜđz tu fıd?"
Ful wel hi nų, bį hiz ɵn pɜer,
hɜ tu sɒplį đe nıd.
"Tɯ́ hɒndred ʃiliŋz' wɒrɟ wil not
sɒfįz for everiwɒn,"
sed Filip, dɜtiŋ in hiz hart,
hweđer it kud bi dɒn.
'Twoz ıvniŋ nɜ, đe de far spent;
đɛ kem tu him, and sed,
"Dɯ send đis mɒltitųd awe,
đat đɛ me bį sɒm bred,
and loj đemselvz, az best đɛ me,
in vilɛjez arɜnd;
for in đis dezert ples, bi ʃur
nɵ kɒmfort wil bi fɜnd."
Hi anserd, "Nɵ; đɛ nıd not gɵ;
giv yı đem fɯd tu ıt."
"Đen Master, ʃal wı gɵ and bį
enɒf tu spred a trıt?"
Hi seɟ, "Hɜ meni lɵvz hav yı?"
Đɛ kwikli tɵld him "Fįv,
and tɯ́ smɔl fiʃez; hɜ kan đız
kip ɔl đis krɜd alįv?"
Jızɒs, wiđ digniti divįn,
sed, "Briŋ đem hir tu mı,
and mɛk đe men sit dɜn in raŋks,
bį fiftiz, ɵ'r đe lı;"
for in đát ples đer woz mɒç gras;
and đer đɛ ɔl sat dɜn,
fįv ɟɜzand, in dų order plest,
az Jızɒs' wɒrd had ʃɵn.
Đen Jızɒs tuk đɵz lɵvz, sɵ fų,
and haviŋ given ɟaŋks,
hi brɛk, and gev tu đɵz arɜnd,
đat đɛ tu ɔl đe raŋks
mįt giv bɵɟ bred and fiʃez tɯ,
az mɒç az đɛ kud ıt.
Đɛ ɛt, wer fild, and nɜ đer harts
ekspand, wiđ joi replıt.
Tu hiz disįpelz đen hi spɵk,
"Đe fragments nɜ obten,
đat nɒɟiŋ mɛ bi wested hir."
Đɛ dɯ sɵ, and reten
twelv baskets ful ov fragments gud,
hwiç đız fįv ɟɜzand liv,

Out of five barley loaves, and two
  Small fishes. They believe
In Him who did thus wondrously
  His mighty power unfold,
And say, "This must that prophet be,
  Unto the world foretold."

SECTION 73.

Christ sends the people away, retires to pray, and walks to his disciples on the sea, in a storm.

Matthew 14. 22-33. Mark 6. 45-52. —John 6. 15-21.

Jesus then sent the twelve, by ship,
  Unto the other side,
Over against Bethsaida's town,
  That thus he might them hide
From prying multitudes, while he
  These multitudes sent home;
And then went to a mountain near
  To pray beneath heaven's dome.
Now evening closed, and o'er the lake
  Of Galilee, so fair,
Unto Capernaum Jesus' friends
  In their small ship repair.
While he was all alone on land,
  And night-fall was so dark,
A rough wind blew, and great waves [tossed
  That helpless little bark.
He saw them toiling, rowing hard,
  And unto them drew near,
About the fourth watch of the night:
  Their hearts were full of fear;
For like a spirit on the sea
  He walked, and seemed to pass!
They trembled, and they cried with [dread,
  "A spirit 'tis; alas!"
All saw. Then Jesus kindly spoke,
  "Be of good cheer; 'tis I;
Be not afraid of your own Lord."
  Then Peter made reply,
"If it be thou, my Lord, then bid
  Me come across the wave."
Jesus said, "Come." And Peter [stepped
  Out of the ship, so brave.
He walked upon the watery path,
  To meet his Master dear;
But soon the strong wind, boisterous,
  Filled his faint heart with fear.

ɤt ov fi̧v barli lɵvz, and tɯ́
  smɷl fiʃez. Ɑe beliv
in him hɯ did đɒs wɒndrɒsli
  hiz mi̧ti pɤer ɒnfɵld,
and se "Ɑis mɒst đát profet bi,
  ɒntu đe wɒrld fɵrtɵld."

SEKΣON 73.

Kri̧st sendz đe pipel awe, reti̧rz tu pre, and wɷks tu hiz disi̧pelz on đe si, in a storm.

Maϑɥ 14. 22-33. Mark 6. 45-52. Jon 6. 15-21.

Jizɒs đen sent đe twelv, bi̧ ʃip,
  ɒntu đe ɒđer si̧d,
ɵver agenst Beϑseda'z tɤn,
  đat đɒs hi mi̧t đem hi̧d
from pri̧iŋ mɒltitɥdz, hwi̧l hi
  điz mɒltitɥdz sent hɵm;
and đen went tu a mɤnten nir
  tu pre beniđ heven'z dɵm.
Nɤ ivniŋ klɵzd, and ɵ'r đe lek
  ov Galili, sɵ fer,
ɒntu Kapernaɒm Jizɒs' frendz
  in đer smɷl ʃip reper.
Hwi̧l hi woz ɷl alɵn on land,
  and ni̧t-fɷl woz sɵ dark,
a rɒf wind blɯ, and gret wevz tost
  đát helples litel bark.
Hi sɷ đem toiliŋ, rɵiŋ hard,
  and ɒntu đem drɯ nir,
abɤt đe fɵrϑ woç ov đe ni̧t:
  đer harts wer ful ov fir;
for li̧k a spirit on đe si
  hi wɷkt, and simd tu pas!
Ɑe trembeld, and đe kri̧d wiđ dred,
  "A spirit, 'tiz; alas!"
ɷl sɷ. Ɑen Jizɒs ki̧ndli spɵk,
  "Bi ov gud çir; 'tiz i̧;
bi not afred ov ɥr ɵn Lord."
  Ɑen Piter med repli̧,
"If it bi đɤ, mi̧ Lord, đen bid
  mi kɒm akros đe wev."
Jizɒs sed, "Kɒm." And Piter
  ɤt ov đe ʃip, sɵ brev. [stept
Hi wɷkt ɒpon đe wɷteri paϑ,
  tu mit hiz Master dir;
bɒt sun đe stroŋ wind, boisterɒs,
  fild hiz fent hart wiđ fir.

Then he began to sink, and cried,
  "Lord, save me." Jesus' hand
Was quickly stretched to hold him up
  Firm as upon dry land. [said;
"O wherefore didst thou doubt?" he
  "Why is thy faith so small?"
Then to the ship they both ascend:
  No rough winds now appal!
Immediately they reach the shore
  Which they had striven to gain,
And sore amazed are they to know
  How they their wish attain.
They thought not of the miracle
  Of making so much bread;
Their foolish heart was hardened, and
  Their faith was weak, or dead.
And now they come to worship Christ,
  And say, without one fear,
"Thou art the Son of God most high;
  This is a truth most clear."

Ðen hi began tu siŋk, and krȷd,
  "Lord, sev mi." Jizɒs' hand
woz kwikli streçt tu hɵld him ɒp
  ferm az ɒpon drȷ land. [sed;
"Ɵ hwerfɵr didst ðɤ dɤt?" hi
  "hwȷ iz ðȷ feɟ sɵ smɷl?"
Ðen tu ðe ʃip ðe bɵɟ asend:
  nɵ rɒf windz nɤ apɷl!
Immidietli ðe riç ðe ʃɵr,
  hwiç ðe had striven tu gen,
and sɵr amezd ar ðe tu nɵ́
  hɤ ðe ðer wiʃ aten.
Ðe ɟɷt not ov ðe mirakel
  ov mekiŋ sɵ mɒç bred;
ðer fulɩʃ hart woz hardend, and
  ðer feɟ woz wik, or ded.
And nɤ ðe kɒm tu wɒrʃip Krȷst,
  and se, wiðɤt wɒn fir,
"Ðɤ art ðe Sɒn ov God mɵst hȷ;
  ðis iz a truɟ mɵst klir."

SECTION 74.

Christ heals the multitude, and teaches at Capernaum that he is the Bread of Life.
Matthew 14. 34-36. Mark 6. 53-56.
—John 6. 22-71.

Now when they were gone o'er the sea,
  And come to their own land,
Genesaret, the people round
  About, on every hand,
Attracted by his fame and power,
  Resorted to him there,
And brought their sick; for Jesus
  Diseases everywhere. [healed
And all who did but touch, in faith,
  His garment's edge, were healed
Of any malady that might
  Within them be concealed.
And all this wondering multitude,
  Who knew Christ's heavenly power,
Came to Capernaum, where he stayed,
  And sought him every hour.
And Jesus said, "'Tis not because
  Of miracles, that still
Ye seek me; but 'tis this alone,
  That ye may eat your fill.
Labor not only for the food
  That mortal life sustains;
But for that spiritual good
  Which heaven itself contains;

SEKΣON 74.

Krȷst hilz ðe mɒltitɥd, and tiçez at Kapernaɒm ðat hi iz ðe Bred ov Lȷf.
Maɟɥ 14. 34-36. Mark 6. 53-56.
Jon 6. 22-71.

Nɤ hwen ðe wer gon ɵ'r ðe si,
  and kɒm tu ðer ɵn land,
Genesaret, ðe pipel rɤnd
  abɤt, on everi hand,
atrakted bȷ hiz fem and pɤer,
  rezorted tu him ðer,
and brɷt ðer sik; for Jizɒs hild
  disizez everihwer.
And ɷl hu did bɒt tɒç, in feɟ,
  hiz garment's ej, wer hild
ov eni maladi ðat mȷt
  wiðin ðem bi konsild.
And ɷl ðis wɒnderiŋ mɒltitɥd,
  hu nɥ Krȷst's hevenli pɤer,
kem tu Kapernaɒm, hwer hi sted,
  and sɷt him everi ɤr.
And Jizɒs sed, "'Tiz not bekoz
  ov mirakelz, ðat stil
yi sik mi; bɒt 'tiz ðis alɵn,
  ðat yi me it ɥr fil.
Lebor not ɵnli for ðe fud
  ðat mortal lȷf sɒstenz;
bɒt for ðát spiritɥal gud
  hwiç heven itself kontenz;

That bread of everlasting life
  Which I alone can give;
That spiritual good and truth
  By which the soul must live."
Then said they, "What shall we per-
  The works of God to do?" [form,
Jesus replied, and said to them,
  "The work of God is to
Believe on him whom he hath sent."
  They said to him, "What sign
Show'st thou that we may surely know
  Thy origin divine?
What dost thou work? Our ancestors
  Ate manna from above;
As it is written, 'Bread from heaven
  He gave them in his love.'"
Then Jesus answered, "Ye should
  That Moses did not give [know
The very bread of heaven itself,
  On which the angels live;
'Tis God alone that gives the bread
  Descending from on high;
And that true living bread which gives
  Life to the world, am I."
They said to him, "Lord, evermore,
  Give us this bread to eat;
That hunger we may feel no more:
  Bestow it, we intreat."
And Jesus said, "I am the bread
  Of life; and everyone
That comes to me, and in me trusts,
  Has heavenly life begun.
Hunger he shall not feel, nor thirst,
  And, as I said to you,
Though ye have seen me, ye believe
  Not in my mission true.
All that the Father giveth me,
  All such to me will come;
And all that come to me, I will
  Save from infernal doom.
For I came down from heaven that I
  My Father's will may do,
My own will ever to deny,
  And its commands eschew.
The will of Him who sent me is,
  That all which he hath given,
I should raise up again at last,
  And make it meet for heaven.
And this, too, is the Father's will,
  That all who see the Son

đát bred ov everlastiŋ lįf
  hwiç į alɵn kan giv;
đát spiritųal gud and truɟ
  bį hwiç đe sɵl mɒst liv."
Ꞓen sed đɛ, "Hwot ʃal wi perforn
  đe wɒrks ov God tu duɯ?"
Jizɒs replįd, and sed tu đem,
  "Ꞓe wɒrk ov God iz tu
beliv on him huɯm hi haɟ sent."
  Ꞓɛ sed tu him, "Hwot sįn
ʃɵ'st đɤ đat wi mɛ ʃuɯrli nɵ
  đį orijin divįn?
Hwot dɒst đɤ wɒrk? Ɣr ansestor:
  ɛt mana from abɒv;
az it iz riten, 'Bred from heven
  hi gɛv đem in hiz lɒv.'
Ꞓen Jizɒs anserd, "Yi ʃud nɵ
  đat Mɵzes did not giv
đe veri bred ov heven itself,
  on hwiç đe ɛnjelz liv;
'Tiz God alɵn đat givz đe bred
  desendiŋ from on hį;
and đát truɯ liviŋ bred hwiç givz
  lįf tu đe wɒrld, am į."
Ꞓɛ sed tu him, "Lord, evermɵr,
  giv ɒs đis bred tu it;
đat hɒŋger wi mɛ fil nɵ mɵr:
  bestɵ it, wi entrit."
And Jizɒs sed, "Ɨ am đe bred
  ov lįf; and everiwɒn
đat kɒmz tu mi, and in mi trɒsts,
  haz hevenli lįf begɒn.
Hɒŋger hi ʃal not fil, nor ɟerst,
  and, az į sed tu ų,
đɵ yi hav sin mi, yi beliv
  not in mį miʃon truɯ.
Ꞷl đat đe Fɑđer giveɟ mi,
  ꞷl sɒç tu mi wil kɒm;
and ꞷl đat kɒm tu mi, į wil
  sɛv from infernal duɯm.
For į kɛm dɤn from heven đat į
  mį Fɑđer'z wíl mɛ duɯ,
mį ɵn wíl ever tu denį,
  and its komandz esçuɯ.
Ꞓe wil ov Him huɯ sent mi iz,
  đat ꞷl hwiç hi haɟ given,
į ʃud rɛz ɒp agen at last,
  and mɛk it mit for heven.
And đis, tuɯ, iz đe Fɑđer'z wíl,
  đat ꞷl huɯ si đe Sɒn

And then believe on him, may have
Eternal life begun:
And I will raise him up at last."
They murmured at him then,
Because he said, "I am the bread
Which giveth life to men."
But Jesus said, "Why murmur thus?
None ever come to me
Except the Father draw. All such
I'll raise at the last day.
'Tis written in the prophets that,
'All shall be taught by God;'
All therefore that have heard and
Of him, select the road [learned
That leads to me. I do not say
That God can e'er be seen
Except by him which is of God,
Who loves not aught unclean.
For verily I say to you,
He that believes on me
Has everlasting life,—the joys
Of immortality.
I am the very bread of life.
Your fathers who were fed
On manna in the wilderness,
Are numbered with the dead;
But he that eats the bread of life
That cometh down from heaven,
Shall live for ever, and not die:
This bread to you is given."
The Jews then strove among them-
And to each other said, [selves,
"How can this man give us to eat
His flesh, as though 'twere bread?"
Jesus then said to them again,
"Once more do I declare,
Except ye eat my flesh, and drink
My blood, and thus prepare
Your minds for heavenly joys, there is
No life at all in you.
My flesh is meat indeed; my blood
Is drink indeed. Imbue
Your minds therewith, like vessels
Up to the very brim: [filled
He that does this shall dwell in me,
And I will dwell in him.
Just as I live from God alone,
So he that eateth me
By me shall find his life renewed
Throughout eternity."

and đen beliv on him, mɛ hav
eternal lįf begɒn:
and į wil rɛz him ɒp at last."
Đɛ mɒrmɒrd at him đen,
bekɷz hi sed, "Ɨ am đe bred
hwiɋ giveŧ lįf tu men."
Bɒt Jizɒs sed, "Hwį mɒrmɒr đɒs?
Nɒn ever kɒm tu mi
eksept đe Fɑđer drɷ. ɷl sɒɋ
į'l rɛz at đe last dɛ.
'Tiz riten in đe profets đat,
'ɷl ʃal bi tɷt bį God;'
ɷl đerfɵr đat hav herd and lernd
ov him selekt đe rɵd
đat lidz tu mi. Ɨ dɯ not sɛ
đat God kan ɛ'r bi sin
eksept bį him hwiɋ iz ov God,
hɯ lɒvz not ɷt ɒnklin.
For verili į sɛ tu ɥ,
hi đat belivz on mi
haz everlastiŋ lįf,—đe joiz
ov immortaliti.
Ɨ am đe veri bred ov lįf.
Ɥr fɑđerz hɯ wer fed
on mana in đe wildernes,
ar nɒmberd wiđ đe ded;
bɒt hi đat its đe bred ov lįf
đat kɒmeŧ dɤn from heven,
ʃal liv for ever, and not dį:
đis bred tu ɥ iz given."
Đe Jɯz đen strɵv amɒŋ đemselvz,
and tu iɋ ɒđer sed,
"Hɤ kan đis man giv ɒs tu it
hiz fleʃ, az đɵ 'twer bred?"
Jizɒs đen sed tu đem agen,
"Wɒns mɵr dɯ į dekler,
eksept yi it mį fleʃ, and driŋk
mį blɒd, and đɒs preper
ɥr mįndz for hevenli joiz, đer iz
nɵ lįf at ɷl in ɥ.
Mį fleʃ iz mit indid; mį blɒd
iz driŋk indid. Imbɥ
ɥr mįndz đerwiđ, lįk veselz fild
ɒp tu đe veri brim:
hi đat dɒz đis ʃal dwel in mi,
and į wil dwel in him.
Jɒst az į liv from God alɵn,
sɵ hi đat iteŧ mi
bį mi ʃal fįnd hiz lįf renɥd
ŧrɯɤt eternit."

Many of those who heard Christ speak
  These mysteries divine,
Took great offence, and did, in heart,
  To unbelief incline.
But Jesus said, "Do not refuse
  My gracious invitation,
Because eternal life's wrapped up
  Within the soul's salvation.
The spirit it is that quickens men,
  The flesh is nothing worth;
The words I speak are spirit and life,
  They spring not from the earth.
But there are some who will not yield
  To God's attractive love,
And they my Gospel will refuse,
  And disobedient prove."
Then many of Christ's followers
  So foolish were, and vain,
They left the Savior, and returned
  To unbelief again.
And Jesus said unto the twelve,
  "Will ye, too, go away?"
Then Simon Peter answered him,
  "Lord, wherefore should we stray
From thee, our Teacher and our Lord?
  Or whither should we go?
Thou hast the words of endless life;
  And we believe, and know,
That thou art Christ, the Son of God."
  Then Jesus said to them,
"Have not I chosen you, the twelve,
  My own bright diadem,
And one of you a devil is?"
  He spoke of Judas, this
Was Simon's son, Iscariot, who
  Thereafter, by a kiss,
The sign of love, betrayed the Lord,
And left a name to be abhorred.

Meni ov đɵz hɯ herd Krįst spįk
  điz misteriz divįn,
tuk gret ofens, and did, in hart,
  tu ɒnbelif inklįn.
Bɒt Jizɒs sed, "Dɯ not refɥz
  mį greʃɒs inviteʃon,
bekɒz eternal lįf's rapt ɒp
  widin đe sɵl'z salveʃon.
Đe spirit it iz đat kwikenz men,
  đe fleʃ iz nɒɟiŋ wɒrɟ;
đe wɒrdz į spįk ar spirit and lįf,
  đe spriŋ not from đe erɟ.
Bɒt đer ar sɒm hɯ wil not yįld
  tu God'z atraktiv lɒv,
and đe mį Gospel wil refɥz,
  and disɵbįdient prɯv."
Đen meni ov Krįst's folɵerz
  sɵ fɯliʃ wer, and ven,
đe left đe Sevier, and retɒrnd
  tu ɒnbelif agen.
And Jizɒs sed ɒntu đe twelv,
  "Wil yį, tɯ, gɵ awe?"
Đen Sįmon Pįter anserd him,
  "Lord, hwerfɵr ʃud wį stre
from đį, ɤr Tįɋer and ɤr Lord?
  Or hwiđer ʃud wį gɵ?
Đɤ hast đe wɒrdz ov endles lįf;
  and wį beliv, and nɵ́,
đat đɤ art Krįst, đe Sɒn ov God."
  Đen Jizɒs sed tu đem,
"Hav not į ɋɵzen ɥ, đe twelv,
  mį ɵn brįt dįadem,
and wɒn ov ɥ a devil iz?"
  Hį spɵk ov Jɯdas, đis
woz Sįmon'z sɒn, Iskariot, hɯ
  đerafter, bį a kis,
đe sįn ov lɒv, betred đe Lord,
and left a nem tu bį abhord.

SECTION 75.

Christ converses with the Scribes and Pharisees on Jewish Traditions.

Matthew 15. 1-20.   Mark 7. 1-23.

Then came the Pharisees and Scribes
  Who rigidly adhered
To their traditions, and old forms
  Which custom had endeared;
Who always washed their hands before
  They ventured to touch food;

SEKΣON 75.

Krįst konversez wiđ đe Skrįbz and Farisiz on Jɯiʃ Tradiʃonz.

Maɟɥ 15. 1-20.   Mark 7. 1-23.

Đen kem đe Farisiz and Skrįbz
  hɯ rijidli adhird
tu đer tradiʃonz, and ɵld formz
  hwiɋ kɒstom had endird;
hɯ ɒlwez woʃt đer handz befɵr
  đe ventɥrd tu tɒɋ fɯd;

And every dish; so strict were they
  In what could do no good.
They censured Christ's disciples too
  Because with unwashed hands
They ate their bread; not caring much
  For such absurd commands.
Then Jesus answered them, and said,
  "While you unjustly blame
My followers, for breaking rules
  Which have no moral claim,
How do you dare to violate
  God's solemn written laws,
By your traditions, false and vain,
  Which many evils cause.
For God commands that you should give
  Your parents honor still;
And he forbade that you to them
  Should say or do aught ill.
But ye deprive your parents oft
  Of their due recompense,
Pretending that you it devote
  To God, by false pretence.
As if the sums which thus you save
  By deeds that are abhorred,
Could ever prove sweet offerings
  To the Omniscient Lord.
Well did Isaiah say of you,
  'This people draweth near
To the great God with perjured lips;
  Their hearts reject his fear.
But vainly do they worship heaven
  While breaking heaven's decrees;
They teach the false commands of men
  To win men's flatteries.'"
Then Jesus called the multitude,
  And to them thus he said,
"Avoid the Scribes' hypocrisy,
  By which you are misled.
External things, like meats and drinks,
  Do not defile mankind;
These but affect the frame of man,
  And don't corrupt the mind.
But the infernal wicked thoughts,
  That come forth from the heart,
Produce unholy actions, and
  Corrupt the moral part.
Think not these vain and foolish rules
  Of Scribes and Pharisees,
Who see religion in mere forms
  And obsolete decrees,

and everi diʃ; sɵ strikt wer đe
  in hwot kud dɯ nɵ gud.
Đe senʃurd Krįst's disįpelz tɯ
  bekωz wiđ ɒnwoʃt handz
đe et đer bred; not keriŋ mɒç
  for sɒç absɒrd komandz.
Đen Jizɒs anserd đem, and sed,
  "Hwįl ɥ ɒnjɒstli blem
mį foloerz, for brekiŋ rɯlz
  hwiç hav nɵ moral klem,
hɤ dɯ ɥ der tu vįolet
  God'z solemn riten lɔz,
bį ɥr tradiʃonz, fols and ven,
  hwiç meni ivelz kωz.
For God komandz đat ɥ ʃud giv
  ɥr perents onor stil;
and hi forbad đat ɥ tu đem
  ʃud se or dɯ ot il.
Bɒt yi deprįv ɥr perents oft
  ov đer dɥ rekompens,
pretendiŋ đat ɥ it devɵt
  tu God, bį fols pretens.
Az if đe sɒmz hwiç đɒs ɥ sev
  bį didz đat ar abhord,
kud ever prɯv swit oferiŋz
  tu đe Omniʃient Lord.
Wel did Įzaia se ov ɥ,
  'Đis pipel droeɟ nir
tu đe gret God wiđ perjurd lips;
  đer harts rejekt hiz fir.
Bɒt venli dɯ đe wɒrʃip heven
  hwįl brekiŋ heven'z dekriz;
đe tiç đe fols komandz ov men
  tu win men'z flateriz.'"
Đen Jizɒs kold đe mɒltitɥd,
  And tu đem đɒs hi sed,
"Avoid đe Skrįbz' hipokrisi,
  bį hwiç ɥ ar misled.
Eksternal ɟiŋz, lįk mits and driŋks,
  dɯ not defįl mankįnd;
điz bɒt afekt đe frem ov man,
  and dɵn't korɒpt đe mįnd.
Bɒt đe infernal, wiked ɟots,
  đat kɒm forɟ from đe hart,
prɵdɥs ɒnhɵli akʃonz, and
  korɒpt đe moral part.
Ɉiŋk not điz ven and fɯliʃ rɯlz
  ov Skrįbz and Farisiz,
hɯ si relijon in mir formz
  and obsolit dekriz.

Can long endure; for every plant
  Which God doth not approve
Shall be uprooted; none can last
  That springs not from his love.
Regard not ye their sophistry;
  Blind leaders of the blind!
Unless they soon repent, they will
  A dismal ruin find.
Their false light is as dark as pitch,
And both shall fall into the ditch.

SECTION 76.

Christ heals the Syro-Phœnician woman's daughter, and passes through Decapolis, healing and teaching.

Matthew 15. 21-31. Mark 7. 24-37.

Then Jesus rose, and journeyed thence
  To Tyre and Sidon's coast,
And went into a house, and there
  Requested of his host
Seclusion; but could not be hid.
  A woman heard, and came
From Canaan's coast; she had a child
  She wished him to reclaim
From Satan's power. And when she
  The Lord, she cried aloud, [saw
"Have mercy on me, Lord, thou son
  Of David. I am bowed
To earth; my daughter is possest,
  And that most grievously;
Have mercy on me, gracious Lord,
  For thou canst set her free."
He answered not a single word.
  She thought he did not hear;
She cried again. His followers prayed
  She might not linger near.
And then he said, "I'm only sent
  Lost Israel's sons to save."
With persevering faith she kneeled,
  His pity still to crave.
"Lord, help me," was the earnest cry
  Of this persistent Greek;
"Cast forth the demon from my child."
  Then Christ, in accents meek,
Said, "Let the children first be filled;
  For so it must not be
To take away the children's bread,
  And cast to dogs, like thee."

kan loŋ endɥr; for everi plant
  hwiç God dɒð not apruɯv
ʃal bi ɒpruɯted; nɒn kan last
  ðat spriŋz not from hiz lɒv.
Regard not yi ðer sofistri;
  blɨnd liderz ov ðe blɨnd!
ɒnles ðɛ suɯn repent, ðɛ wil
  a dizmal ruɯin fɨnd.
ðer fɷls lɨt iz az dark az piç,
and bɵð ʃal fɷl intu ðe diç.

SEKΣON 76.

Krɨst hilz ðe Sɨrɵ-Feniʃian wuman'z dɷter, and pasez θruɯ Dekapolis, hiliŋ and tiçiŋ.

Maθɥ 15. 21-31. Mark 7. 24-37.

ðen Jizɒs rɵz, and jɒrnid ðens
  tu Tɨr and Sɨdon'z kɵst,
and went intu a hɤs, and ðer
  rekwested ov hiz hɵst
seklɯʒon; bɒt kud not bi hid.
  A wuman herd, and kɛm
from Kɛnan'z kɵst; ʃi had a çɨld
  ʃi wiʃt him tu reklɛm
from Sɛtan'z pɤer. And hwen ʃi sɷ
  ðe Lord, ʃi krɨd alɤd,
"Hav mersi on mi, Lord, ðɤ sɒn
  ov Devid. Ɨ am bɤd
tu erð; mɨ dɷter iz pozest,
  and ðát mɵst grivɒsli;
hav mersi on mi, grɛʃɒs Lord,
  for ðɤ kanst set her fri."
Hi anserd not a siŋgel wɒrd.
  Σi θɷt hi did not hir;
ʃi krɨd agen. Hiz folɵerz pred
  ʃi mɨt not liŋger nir.
And ðen hi sed, "Ɨ'm ɵnli sent
  lost Izrael'z sɒnz tu sɛv."
Wið persevɨriŋ fɛð ʃi nild,
  hiz piti stil tu krɛv.
"Lord, help mi," woz ðe ernest krɨ
  ov ðis persistent Grik;
"Kast fɵrð ðe dimon from mɨ çɨld."
  ðen Krɨst, in aksents mik,
sed, "Let ðe çildren ferst bi fild;
  for sɵ it mɒst not bi
tu tɛk awɛ ðe çildren'z bred,
  and kast tu dogz, lɨk ði."

She answered, "Yes, Lord; that is
Yet even the dogs may eat [true;
The crumbs that from the table fall
Beside the master's feet."
Then Jesus spoke her high reward,
"Woman, thy faith is great:
For this, in peace go on thy way,
Fear not thy daughter's fate."
From that same hour her daughter
Was freed from demon sore, [dear
And calmly on her couch was laid,
Plagued by its power no more.

From Tyre and Sidon's Gentile coast
Jesus now bends his way.
Decapolis he passes through,
For thus his journey lay;
And now by Galilee's fair lake
He will his power display.
There one with stammering speech, and deaf,
They bring, that he may heal.
Then Jesus took the man apart:
His power he would conceal.
He put his fingers in his ears,
Then spit, and touched his tongue;
And looking up to heaven, he sighed
Out "Ephphatha." It rung
Within the deaf man's ears; he heard:
His tongue was loosed; he spake.
Though charged to tell it unto none,
Still this command they break,
And publish everywhere the news
So wondrous and so grand,
Till his great fame was spread abroad
Throughout the neighbouring land.
Filled with amazement, they proclaimed,
"He hath done all things well;
The deaf now hear, the dumb now
We cannot choose but tell." [speak,

Upon a mountain Jesus sat,
And thousands to him came,
Bringing the blind, the dumb, the sick,
The wounded, and the lame.
These at his gracious feet they lay,
And there he made them well;
And wondering much, they glorified
The God of Israel.

Σɹ anserd, "Yes, Lord; đát iz trɯ;
yet ɹven đe dogz me ɹt
đe krɒmz đat from đe tebel fɷl
besḭd đe master'z fɹt."
Ɑen Jɹzɒs spɷk her hḭ reword,
"Wuman, đḭ feɟ iz gret:
for đis, in pɹs gɷ on đḭ we,
fɹr not đḭ dɷter'z fet."
From đát sem ɤr her dɷter dɹr
woz frɹd from dɹmon sɷr,
and kɐmli on her kɤç woz led,
plegd bḭ its pɤer nɷ mɷr.

From Tḭr and Sḭdon'z Jentḭl kɷst
Jɹzɒs nɤ bendz hiz we.
Dekapolis hɹ pasez ɟrɯ,
for đɒs hiz jɒrni le;
and nɤ bḭ Galilɹ'z fer lek
hɹ wil hiz pɤer disple.
Ɑer wɒn wiđ stameriŋ spɹç, and def,
đe briŋ, đat hɹ me hɹl.
Ɑen Jɹzɒs tuk đe man apart:
hiz pɤer hɹ wud konsɹl.
Hɹ put hiz fiŋgerz in hiz ɹrz,
đen spit, and tɒçt hiz tɒŋ;
and lukiŋ ɒp tu heven, hɹ sḭd
ɤt "Effaɟa." It rɒŋ
wiđin đe def man'z ɹrz; hɹ herd:
hiz tɒŋ woz lɯst; hɹ spek.
Ɑɷ çarjd tu tel it ɒntu nɒn,
stil đis komand đe brek,
and pɒbliʃ everihwer đe nɥz
sɷ wɒndrɒs and sɷ grand,
til hiz gret fem woz spred abrɷd
ɟrɯɤt đe nebɒriŋ land.
Fild wiđ amezment, đe prɷklemd,
"Hɹ haɟ dɒn ol ɟiŋz wel,
đe def nɤ hɹr, đe dɒm nɤ spɹk,
wɹ kanot çɯz bɒt tel."

Ɯpon a mɤnten Jɹzɒs sat,
and ɟɤzandz tu him kem,
briŋiŋ đe blḭnd, đe dɒm, đe sik,
đe wɯnded, and đe lem.
Ɑɹz at hiz greʃɒs fɹt đe le,
and đer hɹ med đem wel;
and wɒnderiŋ mɒç, đe glɷrifḭd
đe God ov Izrael.

SECTION 77.

Four Thousand miraculously fed.

Matthew 15. 32-39. Mark 8. 1-10.

Now at that time the multitude
 Were destitute of food;
And Jesus his disciples called,
 That he might do them good.
"I pity this great company,"
 He said compassionate;
"Three days they have attended me,
 And nothing find to eat.
If now I send them fasting home,
 They'll faint upon the way,
For many came from distant parts."
 Then his disciples say,
"Whence shall we get sufficient bread
 So many mouths to feed?"
"How many loaves," said he to them,
 "Have ye?" "They don't exceed
Seven loaves:" of fishes too they had
 A few. He gave command
That this great multitude should sit
 Upon that mountain land.
That word obeyed, he took, gave thanks,
 Then brake, and gave the food
To his disciples. They set it
 Before the multitude.
All ate enough, and yet they saw
 Seven baskets full remain,
Though besides women and the young,
 There were four thousand men.
Now Jesus sends them to their homes,
 And with his chosen friends
By ship to coasts of Magdala
 And Dalmanutha wends.

SEKΣON 77.

For Ɍʊzand mirakʯlɒsli fed.

Maɉʯ 15. 32-39. Mark 8. 1-10.

Nʊ at đát tʝm đe mɒltitʯd
 wer destitʯt ov fɯd;
and Jizɒs hiz disʝpelz kɷld,
 đat hi mʝt dɯ đem gud.
"Ɨ piti đis gret kɒmpani,
 hi sed kompaʃonet;
"Ɍri dez đe hav atended mi,
 and nɒɉiŋ fʝnd tu it.
If nʊ ʝ send đem fastiŋ hɵm,
 đe'l fent ɒpon đe we,
for meni kem from distant parts."
 Đen hiz disʝpelz se,
"Hwens ʃal wi get sɒfiʃent bred
 sɵ meni mʊđz tu fid?"
"Hʊ meni lɵvz," sed hi tu đem,
 "hav yi?" "Đe dɵn't eksid
seven lɵvz:" ov fiʃez tɯ đe had
 a fʯ. Hi gev komand
đat đis gret mɒltitʯd ʃud sit
 ɒpon đát mʊnten land.
Đát wɒrd ɵbed, hi tuk, gev ɉaŋks,
 đen brek, and gev đe fɯd
tu hiz disʝpelz. Đe set it
 befɵr đe mɒltitʯd.
Ɵl et enɒf, and yet đe so
 seven baskets ful remen,
đɵ besʝdz wimen and đe yɒŋ,
 đer wer fɵr ɉʊzand men.
Nʊ Jizɒs sendz đem tu đer hɵmz,
 and wiđ hiz ɋɵzen frendz,
bʝ ʃip tu kɵsts ov Magdala
 and Dalmanʯɉa wendz.

SECTION 78.

The Pharisees require other signs. Christ charges them with hypocrisy.

Matthew 16. 1-12. Mark 8. 11-21.

The Pharisees and Saducees
 Then unto Jesus came,
And tempted him to show a sign
 From heaven, to prove his claim.
He answering, said, "When evening
 Are red, ye say, 'Twill be [skies
Fine weather, for the rosy west
 Foretells serenity.

SEKΣON 78.

Đe Farisiz rekwʝr ɒđer sʝnz. Krʝst ɋarjez đem wiđ hipokrisi.

Maɉʯ 16. 1-12. Mark 8. 11-21.

Đe Farisiz and Sadʯsiz
 đen ɒntu Jizɒs kem,
and tempted him tu ʃɵ a sʝn
 from heven, tu prɯv hiz klem.
Hi anseriŋ, sed, "Hwen ivniŋ skʝz
 ar red, yi se, 'Twil bi
fʝn weđer, for đe rɵzi west
 fɵrtelz sereniti.

And when the sky is lowering, red,
At early morning's hour,
Ye say, The lurid east foretells
Ere long a heavy shower.
O hypocrites! ye all the signs
Of nature love to trace;
But will not see the proofs I give
Of heaven's descending grace."
And then he sighed that they should be
So blinded by sin's night;
And after all his miracles,
Still doubt his saving might.
He said no sign he'd give unto
That wicked generation
Except the sign of Jonah, type
Of him and of the nation.
He left them then, took ship, and
Unto the other side; [crossed
Their unbelief and hardened heart
He could not well abide.
Then Jesus warned his followers
Against the Pharisees,
(To shun the leaven of their minds,)
And also Saducees.
Like leaven working in the meal,
And entering every part,
So their false principles of life
Would soon corrupt the heart.

SECTION 79.

Christ heals a blind man at Bethsaida, and Peter confesses Christ to be the Messiah.

Mark 8. 22-30. Matthew 16. 13-20. Luke 9. 18-22.

Unto Bethsaida Jesus came,
And there to him was brought
One blind: that he would touch his
His anxious friends besought. [eyes
And Jesus took the blind man's hand,
From city to withdraw;
And then he spit upon his eyes
And asked him what he saw.
"I see some walking men like trees."
Again Christ touched his eyes:
When next he looked, all plain appeared:
How great was his surprise!
Then Jesus sent him to his home,
And bade him to beware,

And hwen ðe skį iz lɤeriŋ, red,
at erli morniŋ'z ɤr,
yi se, Ðe lɯrid ist fơrtelz
er loŋ a hevi ʃɤer.
Ơ hipokrits! yi ol ðe sįnz
ov netųr lɒv tu tres,
bɒt wil not si ðe prɯfs į giv
ov heven'z desendiŋ gres."
And ðen hi sįd ðat ðe ʃud bi
sơ blįnded bį sin'z nįt;
and after ol hiz mirakelz,
stil dɤt hiz seviŋ mįt.
Hi sed nơ sįn hi'd giv ɒntu
ðát wiked jenereʃon
eksept ðe sįn ov Jơna, tįp
ov him and ov ðe neʃon.
Hi left ðem ðen, tuk ʃip, and krost
ɒntu ðe ɒðer sįd;
ðer ɒnbelif and hardend hart
hi kud not wel abįd.
Ðen Jizɒs wornd hiz folơerz
agenst ðe Farisiz,
(tu ʃɒn ðe leven ov ðer mįndz,)
and olsơ Sadųsiz.
Lįk leven wɒrkiŋ in ðe mil,
and enteriŋ everi part,
sơ ðer fols prinsipelz ov lįf
wud sɯn korɒpt ðe hart.

SEKƩON 79.

Krįst hilz a blįnd man at Beθseda, and Piter konfesez Krįst tu bi ðe Mesįa.

Mark 8. 22-30. Maθų 16. 13-20. Lɯk 9. 18-22.

Ɯntu Beθseda Jizɒs kem,
and ðer tu him woz brot
wɒn blįnd: ðat hi wud tɒç hiz įz
hiz aŋkʃɒs frendz besot.
And Jizɒs tuk ðe blįnd man'z hand,
from siti tu wiððrơ;
and ðen hi spit ɒpon hiz įz,
and askt him hwot hi sơ.
"Ŧ si sɒm wokiŋ men lįk triz."
Agen Krįst tɒçt hiz įz:
hwen nekst hi lukt, ol plen apird:
hɤ gret woz hiz sɒrprįz!
Ðen Jizɒs sent him tu hiz hơm,
and bad him tu bewer,

And go not back into the town,
  Nor tell to any there.

Then into other towns Christ went,
  With his disciples true;
And in the way he went to pray,
  As he was wont to do.
And afterward he questioned them,
  "Who am I? What say men?"
They answered, "John the Baptist, or
  Elias come again.
And some say that a prophet old
  Is risen from the dead:
That Jeremias hath appeared
  By others hath been said."
Then Jesus turned and said to them,
  "But who, say ye, am I?"
And Simon Peter said, "The Christ,
  The Son of God most high."
"Blest art thou, Simon," Jesus said;
  "This truth is not revealed
By earthly means unto thy soul,
  But by my Father sealed.
Thou hast a true confession made,
  And Peter is thy name;
On this foundation will I build
  My Church; and now proclaim
That Hades' power shall not prevail
  Against it. And to thee
The keys of heaven I give, that so
  Whate'er thou shalt decree
To bind or loose on earth, shall still
  By heaven be loosed or bound.
Such high authority within
  My Church shall e'er be found."
But Jesus charged his followers
  The mystery to conceal
That he the true Messiah was,
  Till fit time to reveal.

SECTION 80.

Christ foretells his death and resurrection.

Matthew 16. 21-28. Mark 8. 31-38; 9. 1.
Luke 9. 22-27.

From that time Jesus showed that he,
  The Son of man, must go
Unto Jerusalem, and there
  Much tribulation know.
For priests and scribes and elders all
  Would his pure laws reject,

and gơ not bak intu đe tɤn,
  nor tel tu eni đer.

Đen įntu ɒđer tɤnz Krįst went,
  wiđ hiz disįpelz trɯ;
and in đe wė hį went tu pre,
  az hį woz wɒnt tu dɯ.
And afterward hį kwestiond đem,
  "Hɯ am į? Hwot se men?"
Đe anserd, "Jon đe Baptist, or
  Elįas kɒm agen.
And sɒm se đat a profet ơld
  iz rizen from đe ded:
đat Jeremįas haŧ apird
  bį ɒđerz haŧ bin sed."
Đen Jizɒs tɒrnd and sed tu đem,
  "Bɒt hɯ, se yi, am į?"
And Sįmon Piter sed, "Đe Krįst,
  đe Sɒn ov God mơst hį."
"Blest art đɤ, Sįmon," Jizɒs sed,
  "đis trɯŧ iz not revild
bį erŧli minz ɒntu đį sơl,
  bɒt bį mį Fɑđer sild.
Đɤ hast a trɯ konfeʃon med,
  and Piter iz đį nem;
on đis fɤndeʃon wil į bild
  mį Çɒrç; and nɤ prơklem
đat Hediz' pɤer ʃal not prevel
  agenst it. And tu đi
đe kiz ov heven į giv, đat sơ
  hwoter đɤ ʃalt dekri
tu bįnd or lɯs on erŧ, ʃal stil
  bį heven bi lɯst or bɤnd.
Sɒç hį ɑŧoriti wiđin
  mį Çɒrç ʃal er bi fɤnd."
Bɒt Jizɒs çarjd hiz folơerz
  đe misteri tu konsil
đat hį đe trɯ Mesįa woz,
  til fit tįm tu revil.

SEKƩON 80.

Krįst fortelz hiz deŧ and rezɒrekʃon.

Maŧų 16. 21-28. Mark 8. 31-38; 9. 1.
Lɯk 9. 22-27.

From đát tįm Jizɒs ʃơd đat hį,
  đe Sɒn ov man, mɒst gơ
ɒntu Jerɯsalem, and đer
  mɒç tribųleʃon nớ.
For prists and skrįbz and elderz ol
  wud hiz pųr lɑz rejekt,

And kill him : but his followers might
  On the third day expect
To see him rise. Then Peter said,
  "That far be from thee, Lord."
Then Christ, displeased, with power divine,
  Rebuked that hasty word.
"Satan begone ! thou dost not see
  Thou standest with my foes ;
Such thought is not of God's pure will,
  And does my will oppose."
Then Jesus called his chosen twelve
  Disciples to draw near ;
And unto them, and to the crowd,
  He spoke, that all might hear,
And said, "If any man desire
  To follow me, he must
Deny himself, take up his cross,
  And crucify each lust.
Whoever seeks to save his life
  By treachery to my cause,
Shall lose it, howsoe'er he gain
  Earth's riches or applause.
But he that offers up his life
  For me and my pure word,
Shall find the life immortal, which
  On true saints is conferred.
So great is the soul's value that
  Its worth doth far transcend
The world entire, and all its wealth
  And pleasures, which must end.
Man should not barter his own soul
  For all the world can give,
For if he lose his soul, he will
  In endless misery live.
The Son of man will come in all
  The glory of his Father,
With angel hosts to judge mankind.
  Then who would not much rather
Secure eternal life, than have
  The pleasures of an hour ?
Not rather live in heaven than let
  Vile passions him devour ?
For I will judge men by their works,
  And those who are ashamed
Of me and mine, while on the earth,
  By me shall be disclaimed.
And verily I say to you,
  That some who now stand here
Shall not taste death before they see
  The Son of man appear."

and kil him : bɒt hiz folɷerz mịt
  on đe ɟerd de ekspekt
tu si him rịz. Đen Piter sed,
  "Đát far bi from đi, Lord."
Đen Krịst, displizd, wiđ pɤer divịn,
  rebɥkt đát hesti wɒrd.
"Setan begon ! đɤ dɒst not si
  đɤ standest wiđ mị fɷz ;
sɒɕ ɟot iz not ov God'z pɥr wíl,
  and dɒz mị wíl opɷz."
Đen Jizɒs kold hiz ɕɷzen twelv
  disịpelz tu drɵ nir ;
and ɒntu đem, and tu đe krɤd,
  hi spɷk, đat ɵl mịt hir,
and sed, "If eni man dezịr
  tu folɷ mi, hi mɒst
denị himself, tek ɒp hiz kros,
  and krɯsifị iɕ lɒst.
Hɯever siks tu sev hiz lịf
  bị treɕeri tu mị kɵz,
ʃal lɯz it, hɤsɷer hi gen
  erɟ's riɕez or aplɵz.
Bɒt hi đat oferz ɒp hiz lịf
  for mi and mị pɥr wɒrd,
ʃal fịnd đe lịf immortal, hwiɕ
  on trɯ sents iz konferd.
Sɷ gret iz đe sɷl'z valɥ đat
  its wɒrɟ dɒɟ far transend
đe wɒrld entịr, and ɵl its welɟ
  and pleʒurz, hwiɕ mɒst end.
Man ʃud not barter hiz ɷn sɷl
  for ɵl đe wɒrld kan giv,
for if hi lɯz hiz sɷl, hi wil
  in endles mizeri liv.
Đe Sɒn ov man wil kɒm in ɵl
  đe glɷri ov hiz Fɑđer,
wiđ enjel hɷsts tu jɒj mankịnd.
  Đen hɯ wud not mɒɕ rɑđer
sekɥr eternal lịf, đan hav
  đe pleʒurz ov an ɤr ?
not rɑđer liv in heven đan let
  vịl paʃonz him devɤr ?
For ị wil jɒj men bị đer wɒrks,
  and đɷz hɯ ar aʃemd
ov mi and mịn, hwịl on đe erɟ,
  bị mi ʃal bi disklemd.
And verili ị se tu ɥ,
  đat sɒm hɯ nɤ stand hir
ʃal not test deɟ befɷr đe si
  đe Sɒn ov man apịr.

BOOK V.

SECTION 81.

The Transfiguration of Christ.

Matthew 17. 1-13. Mark 9. 2-13.
Luke 9. 28-36.

After those solemn words rehearsed,
 A week had past away,
When Jesus led his favored three
 Up to a mount, to pray.
And as, apart from all, he kneeled,
 And as his spirit rose,
His countenance was glorified
 Brighter than sunbeam glows.
Shining like light, his raiment grew,
 All glistering like the snow;
No earthly hand to whiten thus
 Might ever seek to know.
And lo! in glory there appeared
 Two prophets seen of old,
Moses and famed Elias, who
 Of Jesus' death now told.
Peter and James and John meanwhile
 Heavy with sleep had lain;
And when they woke, that glory
  bright
 They saw; and those two men.
And as these men returned to heaven,
 In angel majesty,
Peter said, " Lord, 'tis good that we
 Should here remain with thee.
And if thou wilt, now let us make
 Three tabernacles here,
One for thyself, for Moses one,
 One for Elias near."
He wist not what he said, for fear
 Filled each astonished heart.
And while he spake, a radiant cloud
 The vision seemed to part.
With awe they entered that bright
 And heard a wondrous voice [cloud,
Say, " This is my belovèd Son,
 In whom I well rejoice:
Hear ye his words." Then low they
 Their faces to the ground;— [bend
That voice has ceased, that cloud has
 Jesus alone is found. [gone,

BUK V.

SEKΣON 81.

đe Transfigyrɛʃon ov Kri̧st.

Maʒy 17. 1-13. Mark 9. 2-13.
Luk 9. 28-36.

After điz solem wɒrdz reherst,
 a wik had past awɛ,
hwen Jizɒs led hiz fevord ʒri
 ɒp tu a mɤnt, tu pre.
And az, apart from ɷl, hi nild,
 and az hiz spirit rơz,
hiz kɤntenans woz glơrifi̧d
 bri̧ter đan sɒnbim glơz.
Σi̧niŋ li̧k li̧t, hiz rement grɯ,
 ɷl glisteriŋ li̧k đe snơ;
nơ erʒli hand tu hwi̧ten đɒs
 mi̧t ever sik tu nớ.
And lơ! in glơri đer apird
 tɯ́ profets sin ov ơld,
Mơzes and femd Eli̧as, hɯ
 ov Jizɒs' deʒ nɤ tơld.
Piter and Jɛmz and Jon minhw
 hevi wiđ slip had lɛn;
and hwen đɛ wơk, đát glơ
  bri̧t
 đɛ sɷ; and đơz tɯ́ men.
And az điz men retɒrnd tu hev
 in enjel majesti,
Piter sed, " Lord, 'tiz gud đat w
 ʃud hir remen wiđ đi.
And if đɤ wilt, nɤ let ɒs mek
 ʒri tabernakelz hir,
wɒn for đi̧self, for Mơzes wɒn,
 wɒn for Eli̧as nir."
Hi wist not hwot hi sed, for fir
 fild iq astoniʃt hart.
And hwi̧l hi spơk, a rediant klɤ
 đe viʒon simd tu part.
Wiđ ɷ đɛ enterd đát bri̧t klɤd,
 and herd a wɒndrɒs vois
se, " đis iz mi̧ belɒved sɒn,
 in hum i̧ wel rejois:
hir yi hiz wɒrdz." đen lơ đɛ be
 đer fesez tu đe grɤnd;—
đát vois haz sist, đát klɤd haz g
 Jizɒs alơn iz fɤnd.

He kindly touched them; then he said,
"Arise, be not afraid."
And suddenly they looked around,
But saw the vision fade.
As from the mount they now descend,
He charged them not to tell
What they had seen till from the dead
He should himself reveal.
Wondering, they mused what those strange words,
"Rising from death," could mean;
But kept the secret in their hearts
And all that they had seen.
Then they inquired why it was said
Elias must first come.
He said, "Elias cometh first that he
May ills amend to some
Extent. But I say unto you,
Elias has appeared.
They knew him not, and did to him
The thing they should have feared.
So will they treat the Son of man,
Scorn, and set him at nought."
Then the disciples understood
He of the Baptist taught.

Hi kịndli tɒçt đem; đen hi sed,
"Arịz, bi not afred."
And sɒdenli đɛ lukt arɤnd,
bɒt sɷ đe viʒon fɛd.
Az from đe mɤnt đɛ nɤ desend,
hi çarjd đem not tu tel
hwot đɛ had sin til from đe ded
hi ʃud himself revil.
Wɒnderiŋ, đɛ mɥzd hwot đɵz strenj wɒrdz,
"rịziŋ from deϑ" kud min;
bɒt kept đɛ sikret in đer harts
and ɷl đat đɛ had sin.
Đen đɛ inkwịrd hwị it woz sed
Elịas mɒst ferst kɒm.
Hi sed, "Elịas kɒmeϑ ferst đat hi
mɛ ilz amend tu sɒm
ekstent. Bɒt ị sɛ ɒntu ɥ,
Elịas haz apird.
Đɛ nɥ him not, and did tu him
đe ϑiŋ đɛ ʃud hav fird.
Sɵ wil đɛ trit đe Sɒn ov man,
skorn, and set him at not."
Đen đe disịpelz ɒnderstud
hi ov đe Baptist tot.

SECTION 82.

A deaf and dumb spirit cast out.

Matthew 17. 14-21. Mark 9. 14-29.
Luke 9. 37-42.

On the next day, when Christ came
From that most sacred hill [down
Of his transfiguration, crowds
Attended on him still.
And soon a sorrowing father brought
His son, who was possest
By a foul fiend of lunacy,
Who much the youth distressed.
The fiend had made him deaf and
And so diseased, that he [dumb,
Was but a torment to himself
And to his family.
First Christ's disciples tried their
To send him from his hold, [power
But they could not, for want of faith,
He was so strong and bold.
Then Christ said to him, "Bring to
Thy poor afflicted son, [me

SEKƩON 82.

A def and dɒm spirit kast ɤt.

Maϑɥ 17. 14-21. Mark 9. 14-29.
Luk 9. 37-42.

On đe nekst dɛ, hwen Krịst kɛm
from đát mɵst sekred hil [dɤn
ov hiz transfigɥreʃon, krɤdz
atended on him stil.
And sun a sorɵiŋ fɑder brot
hiz sɒn, hu woz pozest
bị a fɤl find ov lunasi,
hu mɒç đe ɥϑ distrest.
Đe find had med him def and dɒm,
and sɵ disizd, đat hi
woz bɒt a torment tu himself
and tu hiz famili.
Ferst Krịst's disịpelz trịd đer pɤer
tu send him from hiz hɵld,
bɒt đɛ kud not, for wont ov feϑ,
hi woz sɵ stroŋ and bɵld.
Đen Krịst sed tu him, "Briŋ tu mi
đị pur aflikted sɒn,

And if thou hast true faith in God,
The thing shall soon be done.
For to the firm believer now
All things are possible,
Both the attainment of high heaven,
And conquest over hell."
Then Christ rebuked the evil fiend,
And straightway forth he sped
From the poor idiot, whom he left
Exhausted as if dead.
But Jesus took him by the hand,
And then the rescued lad
Arose in health and sanity,
And never more was mad.
Then Christ's disciples asked why they
Could not bestow relief.
And Jesus quickly answered them,
"Because of unbelief.
If ye had faith but as a grain
Of mustard seed, ye might
Even by a word, cast mountains high
Into the sea outright.
But ye cannot indeed expel
The demons of worst kind,
Unless by prayer and fasting too
Ye sanctify your mind."

SECTION 83.

Christ foretells his own death, and works a miracle for the tribute money.

Matthew 17. 22-27. Mark 9. 30-32.
Luke 9. 43-45.

Then Christ foretold that he should be
Betrayed by wicked guile;
And afterward be slain by men,
And be entombed a while;
And on the third day rise again
By his own power divine;
But the disciples could not grasp
That marvellous design.
The Lord, of Peter then inquired,
"Of whom do kings demand
A tribute? From their children, or
From strangers in the land?"
Peter replied, "Of strangers." "Then
The children must be free,"
Said Christ, "and I should be exempt,
From my nativity,

and if đʋ hast trɯ feɟ in God,
đe ɟiŋ ʃal sɯn bi dɒn.
For tu đe ferm beliver nʋ
ɵl ɟiŋz ar posibel,
bɵɟ đe atenment ov hį heven,
and koŋkwest ɵver hel."
Đen Krįst rebɥkt đe ivel find,
and stretwe fɵrɟ hi sped
from đe pur idiot, hɯm hi left
ekzɵsted az if ded.
Bɒt Jizɒs tuk him bį đe hand,
and đen đe reskɥd lad
arɵz in helɟ and saniti,
and never mɵr woz mad.
Đen Krįst's disįpelz askt hwį đe
kud not bestɵ relif.
And Jizɒs kwikli anserd đem,
"Bekɵz ov ɒnbelif.
If yi had feɟ bɒt az a gren
ov mɒstard sid, yi mįt
iven bį a wɒrd, kast mʋntenz hį
intu đe si ʋtrįt.
Bɒt yi kanot indid ekspel
đe dimonz ov wɒrst kįnd,
ɒnles bį prer and fastiŋ tɯ
yi saŋktifį ɥr mįnd."

SEKƩON 83.

Krįst fɵrtelz hiz ɵn deθ, and wɒrks mirakel for đe tribɥt mɒni.

Maɟɥ 17. 22-27. Mark 9. 30-32.
Lɯk 9. 43-45.

Đen Krįst fɵrtɵld đat hi ʃud bi
betred bį wiked gįl;
and afterward bi slen bį men,
and bi entɯmd a hwįl;
and on đe ɟerd de rįz agen
bį hiz ɵn pʋer divįn;
bɒt đe disįpelz kud not grasp
đát marvelɒs dezįn.
Đe Lord ov Piter đen inkwįrd,
"Ov hɯm dɯ kiŋz demand
a tribɥt? From đer çildren, or
from strenjerz in đe land?"
Piter replįd, "Ov strenjerz." "Đe
đe çildren mɒst bi fri,"
sed Krįst, "and į ʃud bi ekzemp
from mį nativiti,

From paying tribute to support
  God's temple here below.
Besides, as David's royal seed,
  Exemption I could show.
But not to give the least offence
  To those who think it good,
Go to the sea, and the first fish
  Thou takest from its flood,
Shall in his mouth contain the coin
  This impost doth require;
That take, and give for me and thee,
  Even as they desire."

SECTION 84.

The disciples contend for superiority. The Parable of the unforgiving servant.

Matthew 18. 1-35. Mark 9. 33-50. Luke 9. 46-50.

And while they were within the house,
  Christ's followers to him came,
And said, "Who in thy kingdom may
  The greatest honor claim?"
He asked them, what was their dis-
  In walking by the way. [course
They held their peace, ashamed. They
  Disputed who should sway. [had
But Jesus knew their thoughts, and
  (To teach humility,) [said,
"If anyone would be the first,
  Then he the last must be."
He took a little child to him,
  And having set him down
Within their midst, he said to these
  Vain seekers of renown,
"Unless ye be converted, yea,
  Like to a child become,
Humble like this, ye cannot live
  In heaven's eternal home.
And whosoever shall receive
  Such child for my name's sake,
Receiveth me, and also Him
  Whose glory I partake.
For in heaven's sight the least appears
  The greatest of you all;
And humble souls shall be raised up,
  But proud ones low shall fall."
Then John said, "Master, we saw one
  Belonging not to us,

from peiŋ tribųt tu sɒport
  God'z tempel hįr belσ.
Besįdz, az Devid'z roial sid,
  ekzemʃon į kud ʃσ.
Bɒt not tu giv đe list ofens
  tu đσz hɯ ɟiŋk it gud,
gσ tu đe si, and đe ferst fiʃ
  đɤ tekest from its flɒd,
ʃal in hiz mɤɟ konten đe koin
  đis impσst dɒɟ rekwįr;
đát tek, and giv for mi and đi,
  iven az đe dezįr."

SEKΣON 84.

Đe disįpelz kontend for sųpirioriti. Đe Parabel ov đe ɒnforgiviŋ servant.

Maɟų 18. 1-35. Mark 9. 33-50. Luk 9. 46-50.

And hwįl đe wer wiđin đe hɤs,
  Krįst's folσerz tu him kem,
and sed, "Hɯ in đį kiŋdom me
  đe gretest onor klem?"
Hi askt đem, hwot woz đer diskσrs
  in wokiŋ bį đe we.
Đe held đer pis, aʃemd. Đe had
  dispųted hɯ ʃud swe.
Bɒt Jizɒs nų đer ɟots, and sed,
  (tu tiç hųmiliti,)
"If eniwɒn wud bi đe ferst,
  đen hi đe last mɒst bi.
Hi tuk a litel çįld tu him,
  and haviŋ set him dɤn
wiđin đer midst, hi sed tu điz
  ven sikerz ov renɤn,
"Ʊnles yi bi konverted, ye,
  lįk tu a çįld bekɒm,
hɒmbel lįk đis, yi kanot liv
  in heven'z eternal hσm.
And hɯsσever ʃal resiv
  sɒç çįld for mį nem'z sek,
resiveɟ mi, and olsσ Him
  hɯz glσri į partek.
For in heven'z sįt đe list apirz
  đe gretest ov ų ol;
and hɒmbel sσlz ʃal bi rezd ɒp,
  bɒt prɤd wɒnz lσ ʃal fol."
Đen Jon sed, "Master, wi so wɒn
  beloŋiŋ not tu ɒs,

Who cast out demons in thy name,
  And we forbade him thus
To labor." Jesus said, "Forbid
  Him not; for there is none
Can do a miracle for me
  But I rejoice 'tis done.
For he that is not contrary,
  I count as on my part;
And he that only water gives
  To you with Christian heart,
Shall not forego his due reward,
  Because ye are my own;
But better were it for a man
  To sink with a millstone
In deepest sea than that he should
  Pervert the feeblest soul
Who in my name believeth still,
  And owns my full control.
Woe to the wicked world, for each
  Offence that doth befall;
Which, without proper cause, is given,
  Or taken, great or small.
Whate'er the cherished favorite thing,
  Or idol of thy heart,
Which tempts thee to commit offence,
  With that thing quickly part.
Rather than gratify thine eye,
  Or hand, or foot, through vice,
Let them be made, for heaven's pure
  A votive sacrifice. [sake,
'Tis better far to lose a part,
  If it occasion wrong,
Than lose thy all, by guilt, which casts
  To hell the impious throng.
For everyone must soon or late
  Be truly purified,
As if by fire, from evil things
  Which in his heart abide.
Be mild and meek, and ever full
  Of kindly charities,
Free from presumptuous pride which
    would
  The least good thing despise.
For even the meanest, poorest child,
  If striving to do right,
Is dear to God, and angels blest,
  Who watch him day and night.
And I have come from heaven to
    earth,
  To save from guilt and pain

hɯ kast ɜt dimonz in đį nem,
  and wi forbad him đɒs
tu lebor." Jizɒs sed, "Forbid
  him not; for đer iz nɒn
kan dɯ a mirakel for mi
  bɒt į rejois 'tiz dɒn.
For hi đat iz not kontrari,
  į kɜnt az on mį part;
and hi đat ɵnli wɷter givz
  tu ɥ wiđ Kristian hart,
ʃal not fɵrgɵ hiz dɥ reword,
  bekɷz yi ar mį ɵn;
bɒt beter wer it for a man
  tu siŋk wiđ a milstɵn
in dipest si đan đat hi ʃud
  pervert đe fiblest sɵl
hɯ in mį nem belivet stil,
  and ɵnz mį ful kontrɵl.
Wɵ tu đe wiked wɒrld, for iç
  ofens đat dɒɟ befɷl;
hwiç, wiđɜt proper kɷz, iz given,
  or teken, gret or smɷl.
Hwoter đe çeriʃt, fevorit ɟiŋ,
  or įdol ov đį hart,
hwiç tempts đi tu komit ofens,
  wiđ đát ɟiŋ kwikli part.
Rađer đan gratifį đįn į,
  or hand, or fut, ɟrɯ vįs,
let đem bi med, for heven'z pɥr sek,
  a vɵtiv sakrifįs.
'Tiz beter far tu lɯz a part,
  if it okeʒon roŋ,
đan lɯz đį ɷl, bį gilt, hwiç kasts
  tu hel đe impiɒs ɟroŋ.
For everiwɒn mɒst sɯn or let
  bi trɯli pɥrifįd,
az if bį fįr, from ivel ɟiŋz
  hwiç in hiz hart abįd.
Bi mįld and mik, and ever ful
  ov kįndli çaritiz,
fri from prezɒmptɥɒs prįd hwiç
    wud
  đe list gud ɟiŋ despįz.
For iven đe minest, pɯrest çįld,
  if strįviŋ tu dɯ rįt,
iz dir tu God, and enjelz blest,
  hɯ woç him de and nįt.
And į hav kɒm from heven tu
    erɟ,
  tu sev from gilt and pen

Not only those who seem the best
 And greatest among men,
But even the lowest, who appear
 The outcasts of the land,
Redeeming those who else were lost:
 So God has given command.
To raise the meanest, such as these,
 Makes heavenly minds more glad
Than to preserve in safety those
 Whose case was not so sad.
For God, all-merciful and good,
 Who loves his children all,
Wills not that even the least he loves
 Should perish, though he fall.
And if to thee thy brother shall
 Do causeless wrong, go speak
With kindness to him of his fault;
 Remember man is weak.
And if thy private word should gain
 His heart to penitence,
Thou shalt rejoice, because thou canst
 Pass over the offence.
But if he will not hear thee thus,
 Still strive his heart to gain,
By aid of wisely-chosen friends,
 That all may be made plain.
If still with hardness he refuse
 To listen to the right,
The cause thou shalt with prudence [bring
 Before the Church's sight.
And if the Church he should despise,
 And still should persevere
In wrong—then leave him to himself;
 Thy conscience then is clear.
To you, my chosen, verily,
 Faith's mystery is given,
And what ye bind and loose on earth,
 Is bound or loosed in heaven.
And even if two or three of you
 Agree to ask a blessing
From God, he will in proper time
 Place it in your possessing.
And when but two or three of you
 Assemble in my name,
I will be present in your midst
 If you my presence claim."
Then Peter came to Christ, and said,
 "How often shall my brother
Against me sin, and I forgive
 His fault, and anger smother?

not ɷnli đɷz hɯ sim đe best
 and gretest amɒŋ men,
bɒt iven đe lɷest, hɯ apir
 đe ɣtkasts ov đe land,
redimiŋ đɷz hɯ els wer lost:
 sɷ God haz given komand.
Tu rez đe minest, sɒç az điz,
 meks hevenli mįndz mɷr glad
đan tu prezerv in sefti đɷz
 hɯz kes woz not sɷ sad.
For God, ɷl-mersiful and gud,
 hɯ lɒvz hiz çildren ɷl,
wilz not đat iven đe list hi lɒvz
 ʃud periʃ, đɷ hi fɷl.
And if tu đi đį brɒđer ʃal
 dɯ kɷzles roŋ, gɷ spik
wiđ kįndnes tu him ov hiz fɷlt;
 remember man iz wik.
And if đį prįvet wɒrd ʃud gen
 hiz hart tu penitens,
đɣ ʃalt rejois, bekɷz đɣ kanst
 pas ɷver đe ofens.
Bɒt if hi wil not hir đi đɒs,
 stil strįv hiz hart tu gen,
bį ed ov wįzli-çɷzen frendz,
 đat ɷl me bi med plen.
If stil wiđ hardnes hi refɥz
 tu lisen tu đe rįt,
đe kɷz đɣ ʃalt wiđ prɯdens briŋ
 befɷr đe Ɛɒrç'ez sįt.
And if đe Ɛɒrç hi ʃud despįz,
 and stil ʃud persevir
in roŋ—đen liv him tu himself;
 đį konʃens đen iz klir.
Tu ɥ, mį çɷzen, verili,
 feɟ's misteri iz given,
and hwot yi bįnd and lɯs on erɟ,
 iz bɣnd or lɯst in heven.
And iven if tɯ or ɟri ov ɥ
 agri tu ask a blesiŋ
from God, hi wil in proper tįm
 ples it in ɥr pozesiŋ.
And hwen bɒt tɯ or ɟri ov ɥ
 asembel in mį nem,
į wil bi prezent in ɥr midst,
 if ɥ mį prezens klem."
Đen Piter kem tu Krįst, and sed,
 "Hɣ ɷfen ʃal mį brɒđer
agenst mi sin, and į forgiv
 hiz fɷlt, and aŋger smɒđer?

Will seven times suffice?" "Not so,"
  Jesus replied in turn,
" Say rather seven times seventy,
  If he his error mourn.
Heaven acts even as a certain king,
  A monarch great and just,
Who wished to settle his accounts
  With officers of trust;
His stewards then he called to him,
  And bade them to prepare,
And give to him, a full account
  Of what was in their care.
One steward said, 'I owe thee, Lord,
  At least ten thousand pound,
But cannot pay thee.' Then the king
  Upon that servant frowned;
And said that he, and all he had,
  Must answerable be:
Whereon that steward kneeled, and
    said,
  'Have patience, Lord, with me,
And I will pay thee all in time.'
  Then did the monarch show
Mercy to that same steward, and
  Forgiveness did bestow.
But that same man went out, and soon,
  Unlike his master good,
Treated his under officers
  With harshness stern and rude;
And even though their debts were
  He cast them into gaol. [smal,
And though they promised soon to pay,
  They could not thus prevail.
Of this the king soon heard, and wroth
  With this ungrateful man,
Summoned him straight before his
    court
  Of justice; and began
To say, 'O wicked, cruel one,
  Did I not pardon thee,
And cancel thy great debt at once,
  Out of pure charity?
How could'st thou show such cruelty
  To those thy debtors small,
Who sought compassion from thy
  And did for mercy call? [hand,
Now I revoke my kind decree,
  And will exact my claim
From thee by prison discipline,.
  Until thou pay the same.'

Wil seven tįmz
  Jįzɒs replįd
" Sɛ rɐđer seve
  if hį hiz'eror
Heven akts ıve
  a monark gr
hɯ wiʃt tu set
  wiđ ofiserz o
Hiz stųardz đe
  and bad đem
and giv tu him,
  ov hwot woz
Wɒn stųard se
  at lįst ten
bɒt kanot pɛ đ.
  ɒpon đát ser
and sed đat hį,
  mɒst anserab
hwɛron đát
    sed,
  'Hav peʃens
and į wil pɛ đi
  Đen did đe n
mersi tu đát sɛ
  forgivnes did
Bɒt đát sɛm ma
  ɒnlįk hiz ma
trįted hiz ɒnde
  wiđ harʃnes
and ıven đơ đɛ
  hį kast đem
And đơ đɛ pro
  đɛ kud not đ
Ov đis đe kiŋ
  wiđ đis ɒngr
sɒmond him
    kơrt
  ov jɒstis; an
tu sɛ, 'Ơ wike
  did į not par
and kansel đį g
  ɤt ov pųr ça
Hɤ kud'st đɤ
  tu đơz đį de
hɯ sɔt kompa
  and did for r
Nɤ į revơk mį
  and wil ekza
from đi bį priz
  ɒntil đɤ pɛ đ

Even thus your heavenly Father will
  Do also unto you,
If you do not forgiveness grant
  And show compassion due
When those who have done wrong, relent,
  And strive to amend their way.
The mercy you to others show,
  Heaven will to you repay."

Ɩven đɒs ɥr hevenli Fɑđer wil
  duu ɷlsɷ ɒntu ɥ,
if ɥ duu not forgivnes grant
  and ʃɷ kompaʃon dɥ
hwen đɷz huu hav dɒn roŋ, relent,
  and strįv tu amend đer we.
Đe mersi ɥ tu ɒđerz ʃɷ,
  heven wil tu ɥ repe."

BOOK VI.

SECTION 85.

The mission of the Seventy Disciples.
Luke 10. 1-17.

And after all these things, the Lord,
  With love divine, sent forth
Seventy disciples through the land,
  East, west, and south, and north.
By pairs he sent them, to proclaim
  His Gospel in each place
Which he himself would visit soon
  With offers of his grace.
He said, " The harvest of men's souls
  Is great; the reapers few:
Pray ye the Lord of harvest that
  He will more minds imbue
With love of spiritual truth,
  That they may go and teach
My Gospel through the world, and thus
  Place heaven within the reach
Of everyone. Go ye your ways,
  Behold, I send you forth
As lambs among fierce human wolves,
  To renovate the earth.
Be not encumbered with much store,
  From needless wants abstain;
Nor spend your heaven-devoted time
  In salutations vain;
But kindly, plainly, earnestly,
  Perform your destined task.
And when you enter any house,
  Heaven's blessing on it ask;
And if my spirit of peace be there,
  Your peace shall on it rest;
If not, your blessing shall return
  As an unwelcomed guest.

BUK VI.

SEKƩON 85.

Đe miʃon ov đe Seventi Disįpelz.
Luuk 10. 1-17.

And after ɷl điz ɉiŋz, đe Lord,
  wiđ lɒv divįn, sent fɷrɉ
seventi disįpelz ɉruu đe land,
  ist, west, and sɤɉ, and norɉ.
Bį perz hi sent đem, tu prɷklem
  hiz Gospel in iç ples
hwiç hi himself wud vizit suun
  wiđ oferz ov hiz gres.
Hi sed, " Đe harvest ov men'z sɷlz
  iz gret; đe riperz fɥ:
pre yi đe Lord ov harvest đat
  hi wil mɷr mįndz imbɥ
wiđ lɒv ov spiritɥal truuɉ,
  đat đe me gɷ and tiç
mį Gospel ɉruu đe wɒrld, and đɒs
  ples heven wiđin đe riç
ov everiwɒn. Gɷ yi ɥr wez,
  behɷld, į send ɥ fɷrɉ
az lamz amɒŋ firs hɥman wulvz,
  tu renovet đe erɉ.
Bi not enkɒmberd wiđ mɒç stɷr,
  from nidles wonts absten;
nor spend ɥr heven-devɷted tįm
  in salɥteʃonz ven;
bɒt kįndli, plenli, ernestli,
  perform ɥr destind task.
And hwen ɥ enter eni hɤs,
  heven'z blesiŋ on it ask;
and if mį spirit ov pis bi der,
  ɥr pis ʃal on it rest;
if not, ɥr blesiŋ ʃal retɒrn
  az an ɒnwelkɒmd gest.

And when a proper house you find,
  Within the same reside,
Accepting what is offered you,
  Without false shame or pride.
For he who labors in good works
  Is worthy of his hire;
And do not go from house to house,
  Unsteady in desire.
For by one settlement you shall
  Gain time and good esteem,
And shall not unto worldly men
  Restless itinerants seem.
And wheresoe'er your dwelling, heal
  The sick that are therein,
And say, 'God's kingdom is come nigh,
  Therefore forsake all sin.'
And if a city should reject
  You and your Gospel, there
Shake from your feet the dust, and let
  Them their own evils bear.
And say, at leaving, 'Though ye be
  Polluted by much crime,
Be sure God's kingdom is at hand,
  Therefore repent in time;
Or it will fare far worse with you,
  However proud and high,
Than with old Sodom, which ne'er heard
  The Gospel mystery.
Whoever hears my ministers,
  If just and true they be,
In hearing them, doth likewise hear
  Their Master, even me.
He that despises you, also
  Despises me: nay more:
He that despises me, also
  Despises him before
Whose face all angels bow
  And worship evermore."

And hwen a proper hɤs ų fįnd,
  wįđin đe sɛm rezįd,
akseptiŋ hwot iz oferd ų,
  wiđɤt fɷls ʃɛm or prįd.
For hi hɯ lɛborz in gud wɒrks
  iz wɒrđi ov hiz hįr;
and dɯ not gσ from hɤs tu hɤs,
  ɒnstedi in dezįr.
For bį wɒn setelment ų ʃal
  gɛn tįm and gud estim,
and ʃal not ɒntu wɒrldli men
  restles įtinerants sim.
And hwɛrsσɛr ųr dweliŋ, hil
  đe sik đat ar đɛrin,
and sɛ 'God'z kiŋdom iz kɒm nį,
  đɛrfσr forsɛk ɷl sin.'
And if a siti ʃud rejekt
  ų and ųr Gospel, đɛr
ʃɛk from ųr fit đe dɒst, and let
  đem đɛr σn ivelz bɛr.
And sɛ, at liviŋ, 'Đσ yi bi
  polɯted bį mɒç krįm,
bi ʃɯr God'z kiŋdom iz at hand,
  đɛrfσr repent in tįm;
or it wil fɛr far wɒrs wiđ ų,
  hɤever prɤd and hį,
đan wiđ σld Sodom, hwiç nɛr herd
  đe Gospel misteri.
Hɯever hirz mį ministerz,
  if jɒst and trɯ đɛ bi,
in hiriŋ đem, dɒđ lįkwįz hir
  đɛr Master, iven mi.
Hi đat despįzez ų, ɷlsσ
  despįzez mi: nɛ mσr:
hi đat despįzez mi, ɷlsσ
  despįzez him befσr
hɯz fɛs ɷl enjelz bɤ
  and wɒrʃip evermσr."

SECTION 86.

Christ goes up to the Feast of Tabernacles.
Matthew 19. 1, 2. Mark 10. 1.
John 7. 2-10.

Now when the Jewish feast drew near
  Of Tabernacles named,
His brethren said to Jesus. "Lord,
  Because thy works are famed,
Remove into Judea's land,
  That men the same may see,

SEKΣON 86.

Krįst gσz ɒp tu đe Fist ov Tabernakelz.
Mađų 19. 1, 2. Mark 10. 1.
Jon 7. 2-10.

Nɤ hwen đe Juiʃ fist drɯ nir
  ov Tabernakelz nɛmd,
hiz bređren sed tu Jizɒs, "Lord,
  bekɷz đį wɒrks ar fɛmd,
remɯv intu Jɯdia'z land,
  đat men đe sɛm mɛ si.

For none doth work in secret who
 Would be known openly.
If these great things are done by thee,
 Appear before mankind.
For even his brethren's faith in him
 Was weak, and almost blind.
Then Jesus said, "Your time is now,
 But mine is not yet come;
The world hates me, not you, because
 I charge its evils home.
Go ye up to the feast. I must
 Not yet go publicly.
My time is not." This said, he still
 Abode in Galilee.
But after, when his brethren had
 Departed to the feast,
He, too, left Galilee, and went,
 But did not go in haste.
And then he journeyed to the coasts
 Of Jordan, there to teach
And heal the countless multitudes
 That came within his reach.

for nɒn dɒɉ wɒrk in sikret hɯ
 wud bi nσn σpenli.
If điz gret ɉiŋz ar dɒn bį đi,
 apir befσr mankįnd.
For iven hiz bređren'z feɉ in him
 woz wik, and σlmσst blįnd.
Đen Jizɒs sed, "Ųr tįm iz nɜ,
 bɒt mįn iz not yet kɒm;
đe wɒrld hets mi, not ų, bekoz
 į çarj its ivilz hσm.
Gσ yi ɒp tu đe fist. Ɨ mɒst
 not yet gσ pɒblikli.
Mį tįm iz not." Ŧis sed, hi stil
 abσd in Galili.
Bɒt after, hwen hiz bređren had
 departed tu đe fist,
hi, tɯ, left Galili, and went,
 bɒt did not gσ in hest.
And đen hi jɒrnid tu đe kσsts
 ov Jordan, đer tu tiç
and hil đe kɜntles mɒltitųdz
 đat kem wiđin hiz riç.

SECTION 87.

Agitation of the public mind at Jerusalem concerning Christ.—John 7. 11-53.

The Jews sought Jesus at the feast,
 And all said, "Where is he?"
Some said, "He's good;" and others
 He deals in subtlety;" ["Nay;
But fearing those placed over them,
 No man spake openly.
And when the feast was at its height,
 He to the temple came
And taught. His eloquence divine
 Surprised them. They exclaim,
"Whence hath this man this wisdom?
 How knoweth this man letters? [or,
He is not learned in the law,
 Yet he excels his betters."
Jesus replied, "My doctrine springs
 Not from myself alone;
'Tis his who sent me. He to me
 Hath all this wisdom shown.
And if a man wills what God wills,
 He soon shall understand
My doctrine is derived from God,
 And not from mortal hand.

SEKΣON 87.

Ajiteʃon ov đe pɒblik mįnd at Jerusalem konserniŋ Krįst.—Jon 7. 11-53.

Đe Jɯz sσt Jizɒs at đe fist,
 and σl sed, "Hwer iz hi?"
Sɒm sed, "Hi'z gud;" and ɒđerz
 hi dilz in sɒtelti;" ["Ne;
bɒt firiŋ đσz plest σver đem,
 nσ man spek σpenli.
And hwen đe fist woz at its hįt,
 hi tu đe tempel kem
and tσt. His elokwens divįn
 sɒrprįzd đem. Đe eksklem,
"Hwens haɉ đis man đis wizdom?
 hɜ nσeɉ đis man leterz? [or,
Hi iz not lerned in đe lσ,
 yet hi ekselz hiz beterz."
Jizɒs replįd, "Mį doktrin spriŋz
 not from mįself alσn;
'tiz hiz hɯ sent mi. Hi tu mi
 haɉ σl đis wizdom ʃσn.
And if a man wilz hwot God wilz,
 hi sɯn ʃal ɒnderstand
mį doktrin iz derįvd from God,
 and not from mortal hand.

For he that speaketh of himself
  Seeks only his own fame;
But he that seeks his Master's will
  Is innocent of blame.
By Moses, did ye not receive
  The law, most just and true;
Which says, Ye shall be merciful,
  And shall no murder do?
But now ye break this holy law,
  And seek to murder me
Because upon the Sabbath day
  I healed infirmity.
Yet still ye scruple not thereon
  Your sons to circumcise.
If this breaks not the Sabbath law,
  Why do ye feign surprise
That I by better right should heal
  Diseases on that day?
Judge justly and impartially,
  And be not led astray
By mere external forms, and shows
  Of things that oft delude;
For you may err through prejudice,
  Like the rash multitude.
Ye know where I was born, and where
  My youthful years passed by;
And ye should know I am not come
  Myself to magnify.
But ye know not the mighty God
  Who sent me to proclaim
His loving truth, for he is true,
  And I speak in his name."
And as he spake, his forceful words
  Struck all his hearers dumb;
But none laid hands upon him, for
  His hour was not yet come.
Then many more believed on him
  By witnessing the power
He exercised in miracles
  Performed in that same hour.
But when the Pharisees had heard
  Of the people's faith in Christ,
They and the priests sent officers
  To take him unapprised.
Then Jesus said, "A little while
  I yet remain below,
And when my time is fully come,
  To Him who sent, I go.
And ye shall seek me then in vain;
  For heaven, my native home,

For hi đat spikeɟ ov himself
  sįks ɷnli hiz ɷn fem;
bɒt hi đat siks hiz Master'z wíl
  iz inosen't ov blem.
Bį Mɷzes, did yi not resiv
  đe lꝏ, mɷst jɒst and trɯ;
hwiɋ sez, Yi ʃal bi mersiful,
  and ʃal nɷ mɒrder dɯ?
Bɒt nɤ yi brek đis hɷli lꝏ,
  and sik tu mɒrder mi
bekꝏz ɒpon đe Sabat de
  į hild infermiti.
Yet stil yi skrɯpel not đeron
  ɥr sɒnz tu serkɒmsįz.
If đis breks not đe Sabaɟ lꝏ,
  hwį dɯ yi fen sɒrprįz
đat į bį beter rįt ʃud hil
  disizez on đát de?
Jɒj jɒstli and imparʃali,
  and bi not led astre
bį mir eksternal formz, and ʃɷz
  ov ɟiŋz đat oft delɯd;
for ɥ me er ɟrɯ prejudis,
  lįk đe raʃ mɒltitɥd.
Yi nɷ́ hwer į woz born, and hwer
  mį ɥɟful yirz past bį;
and yi ʃud nɷ́ į am not kɒm
  mįself tu magnifį.
Bɒt yi nɷ́ not đe mįti God
  hɯ sent mi tu prɷklem
hiz lɒviŋ trɯɟ, for hi iz trɯ,
  and į spik in hiz nem."
And az hi spek, hiz fɷrsful wɒrdz
  strɒk ꝏl hiz hirerz dɒm;
bɒt nɒn led handz ɒpon him, for
  hiz ɤr woz not yet kɒm.
Đen meni mɷr belivd on him
  bį witnesiŋ đe pɤer
hi eksersįzd in mirakelz
  performd in đát sem ɤr.
Bɒt hwen đe Farisiz had herd
  ov đe pipel'z feɟ in Krįst,
đe and đe prists sent ofiserz
  tu tek him ɒnaprįzd.
Đen Jizɒs sed, "A litel hwįl
  į yet remen belɷ,
and hwen mį tįm iz fuli kɒm,
  tu Him hɯ sent, į gɷ.
And yi ʃal sik mi đen in ven;
  for heven, mį netiv hɷm,

Is not for unbelievers fit;
  Thither ye cannot come."
Then said the Jews, "Where will he
  That we in vain shall seek? [go,
Will he to the dispersèd go,
  And teach the Jewish Greek?
What meaneth he by these strange
  'Ye cannot come with me, [words,
Nor shall ye find me in that day,
  Though seeking wistfully?'"
On the last day of that great feast,
  Jesus stood forth, and cried,
"Whoever thirsts, O let him come
  To me, and be supplied.
As Scripture saith, 'The thirsty soul,
  Shall drink abundantly.'"
(But this he of that Spirit spake,
  Then in futurity,
Which his disciples should receive
  To be their heavenward guide:
This Holy Spirit was not until
  Jesus was glorified.)
Many who heard this saying, said,
  "A prophet this must be;"
And others said, "This is the Christ;"
  But they could not agree.
Some asked, "Shall our Messiah King
  From Galilee appear,
When from the town of Bethlehem,
  (In Scripture it is clear,)
He comes, of David's royal seed,
  As David there was born?"
On this there was a fierce debate;
  And some, in very scorn,
Wished to lay hold on him, but still
  They feared such wrong to do,
Because their inward consciences
  Would whisper, he was true.
Then did the officers return
  To the priests and Pharisees,
Who questioned where the prisoner
  And though it did displease, [was:
They said that never man so spake.
  "Are ye, too, so deceived?"
Replied the Pharisees. "Have we
  Upon the man believed?
But ignorant and foolish men,
  Not truly Abraham's seed,
Nor knowing Moses' sacred law,
  May thus be cursed indeed."

iz not for ɒnbelįverz fit;
  điđer yį kanot kɒm."
Đen sed đe Juz, "Hwer wil hį gơ,
  đat wį in ven ʃal sįk?
wil hį tu đe dispersed gơ,
  and tiç đe Juiʃ Grįk?
Hwot mįneŧ hį bį điz strenj wɒrdz,
  'Yį kanot kɒm wiđ mį,
nor ʃal yį fįnd mį in đát de,
  đơ sįkiŋ wistfuli?"
On đe last de ov đát gret fist,
  Jizɒs stud forŧ, and krįd,
"Huever ŧersts, O let him kɒm
  tu mį, and bį sɒplįd.
Az Skriptųr seŧ, 'Đe ŧersti sơl,
  ʃal driŋk abɒndantli.'"
(Bɒt đis hį ov đát Spirit spek,
  đen in fųtųriti,
hwiç hiz disįpelz ʃud resįv
  tu bį đer hevenward gįd:
đis Hơli Spirit woz not ɒntil
  Jizɒs woz glơrifįd.)
Meni hu herd đis seiŋ, sed,
  "A profet đis mɒst bį;"
and ɒđerz sed, "Đis iz đe Krįst;"
  bɒt đe kud not agrį.
Sɒm askt, "Ʃal ɤr Mesįa Kiŋ
  from Galili apįr,
hwen from đe tɤn ov Beŧlihem,
  (In Skriptųr it iz klįr,)
hį kɒmz, ov Devid'z roial sįd,
  az Devid đer woz born?"
On đis đer woz a fįrs debet;
  and sɒm, in veri skorn,
wiʃt tu le hơld on him, bɒt stil
  đe fįrd sɒç roŋ tu du,
bekoz đer inward konʃensez
  wud hwisper, hį woz tru.
Đen did đe ofiserz retɒrn
  tu đe prįsts and Farisįz,
hu kwestiond hwer đe prizoner
  and đơ it did displįz, woz:
đe sed đat never man sơ spek.
  "Ar yį, tu, sơ desįvd?"
replįd đe Farisįz. "Hav wį
  ɒpon đe man belįvd?
Bɒt ignorant and fuliʃ men,
  not truli Ɛbraham'z sįd,
nor nơiŋ Mơzes' sekred lo,
  me đɒs bį kɒrst indįd."

Then one, more honest than his sect,
  Who once had come by night,
To learn the truth from Jesus' mouth,
  And practise it aright,
Said, "Doth our law condemn a man
  Before it hear his case,
And give him opportunity
  To answer, face to face?"
Then they replied, "What, art thou, [too,
  Of wretched Galilee?
Search in the Scriptures, thou wilt find
  No prophet thence can be."
The Jews then to their homes retreat,
And Jesus goes to Olivet.

Ðen wɒn, mɵr onest ðan hiz sekt,
  hɯ wɒns had kɒm bį nįt,
tu lern ðe trɯȶ from Jɩzɒs' mȣȶ,
  and praktis it arįt,
sed, "Dɒȶ ȣr lɷ kondem a man
  befɵr it hɩr hiz kes,
and giv him oportɥniti
  tu anser, fes tu fes?"
Ðen ðɛ replįd, "Hwot, art ðȣ, tɯ,
  ov reçed Galili?
Serç in ðe Skriptɥrz, ðȣ wilt fįnd
  nɵ profet ðens kan bi."
Ðe Jɯz ðen tu ðer hɵmz retrɩt,
and Jɩzɒs gɵz tu Olivet.

SECTION 88.

Conduct of Christ to the Adulteress and her accusers.—John 8. 2-12.

Then early on the morrow, Christ
  Unto the Temple turned;
And all the people crowded there;
  His words within them burned.
The Scribes and Pharisees then [brought
  A woman in her shame,
And placing her before the Lord,
  They gave her crime its name.
"Master," said they, "adulteress
  This woman sure is proved;
And in the very deed was found;
  She therefore was removed.
Now Moses, in the law commands
  Such persons shall be stoned;
We brought her here to ask of thee,
  Can such guilt be atoned?"
Not for the truth they questioned thus,
  But malice did abound;
This Jesus knew, and only stooped
  To write upon the ground.
So while they still persist to ask,
  He raised himself, and spake,
"If one among you hath not sinned,
  Let him the first stone take."
And then again he stooped, and wrote,
  While conscience made them start,
And, each convicted, old and young,
  Did one by one depart.
Then Jesus left alone, (and she,
  Frail woman, standing there,)

SEKΣON 88.

Kondɒkt ov Kręst tu ðe Adɒlteres and her akɥzerz.—Jon 8. 2-12.

Ðen erli on ðe morɵ, Kręst
  ɒntu ðe Tempel tɒrnd;
and ɷl ðe pɩpel krȣded ðer;
  hiz wɒrdz wiðin ðem bɒrnd.
Ðe Skrębz and Farisɩz ðen brɷt
  a wuman in her ʃem,
and plesiŋ her befɵr ðe Lord,
  ðɛ gev her kręm its nem.
"Master," sed ðɛ, "adɒlteres
  "ðis wuman ʃur iz prɯvd;
and in ðe veri did woz fȣnd;
  ʃi ðerfɵr woz remɯvd.
Nȣ Mɵzes, in ðe lɷ komandz
  sɒç personz ʃal bi stɵnd;
wi brɷt her hɩr tu ask ov ði,
  kan sɒç gilt bi atɵnd?"
Not for ðe trɯȶ ðɛ kwestiond ðɒs,
  bɒt malis did abȣnd;
ðis Jɩzɒs nɥ, and ɵnli stɯpt
  tu rįt ɒpon ðe grȣnd.
Sɵ hwįl ðɛ stil persist tu ask,
  hi rɛzd himself, and spɛk,
"If wɒn amɒŋ ɥ haȶ not sind,
  let him ðe ferst stɵn tek."
And ðen agen hɩ stɯpt, and rɵt,
  hwįl konʃens med ðem start,
and, ɩç konvikted, ɵld and yɒŋ,
  did wɒn bį wɒn depart.
Ðen Jɩzɒs left alɵn, (and ʃi,
  frel wuman, standiŋ ðer,)

Rose, and in tender accents asked,
"Where thine accusers? where?
Hath no man thee condemned?" She
said,
"None, Lord. I grace implore."
He said, "Nor do I thee condemn;
Go now, and sin no more."

SECTION 89.

Christ declares himself the Light of the World, and the true Messiah.

John 8. 12-59.

Then Jesus spake to them again,
"I am the world's true light;
And everyone that follows me,
Walks not in the dark night
Of errors and of falsities,
But hath the light of life;
From heaven it comes; 'tis permanent;
And knows not sin nor strife."
The Pharisees then said, "If thou
Speak for thyself alone,
We doubt thy evidence; its truth
Must be by others shown."
Jesus replied, "Though of myself
This witness I may bear,
Yet well I know my evidence
Is true beyond compare;
Because I know from whence I came,
And whither I depart,
By intuitions such as dwell
In no mere human heart.
Ye judge according to the flesh,
But I thus judge no one;
Yet if I judge, my judgement's true,
For I am not alone.
And were I called to prove my case
By evidences two,
It would appear that I, my words,
And deeds, are ever true;
For while I witness of myself,
By miracles of grace,
My heavenly Father bears for me
Witness in every place."
Then said they to him, "Where is
To them, the Lord replied, [he?"
"Ye neither know me, nor my Father,
Nor will ye, in your pride,

rɷz, and in tender aksents, askt,
"Hwer đįn akųzerz? hwer?
Haŧ nɷ man đi kondemd?" Σi
sed,
"Nɒn, Lord. Ŧ gres implɷr."
Hi sed, "Nor du į đi kondem;
gɷ nʊ, and sin nɷ mɷr."

SEKΣON 89.

Krįst deklerz himself đe Lįt ov đe Wɒrld, and đe tru Mesįa.

Jon 8. 12-59.

Đen Jizɒs spek tu đem agen,
"Ŧ am đe wɒrld'z tru lįt;
and everiwɒn đat folɷz mi,
wɷks not in đe dark nįt
ov erorz and ov fɷlsitiz,
bɒt haŧ đe lįt ov lįf;
from heven it kɒmz; 'tiz perman-
and nɷ́z not sin nor strįf. [ent;
Đe Farisiz đen sed, "If đʊ
spik for đįself alɷn,
wi dʊt đį evidens; its truŧ
mɒst bi bį ɒđerz ʃɷn."
Jizɒs replįd, "Đɷ ov mįself
đis witnes į me ber,
yet wel į nɷ́ mį evidens
iz tru beyond komper;
bekɷz į nɷ́ from hwens į kem,
and hwiđer į depart,
bį intųiʃonz sɒç az dwel
in nɷ mir hųman hart.
Yi jɒj akordiŋ tu đe fleʃ,
bɒt į đɒs jɒj nɷwɒn;
yet if į jɒj, mį jɒjment's tru,
for į am not alɷn.
And wer į kɷld tu pruv mį kes
bį evidensez túí,
it wud apir đat į, mį wɒrdz,
and didz, ar ever tru;
for hwįl į witnes ov mįself,
bį mirakelz ov gres,
mį hevenli Fɐđer berz for mi
witnes in everi ples."
Đen sed đe tu him, "Hwer iz hi?"
Tu đem, đe Lord replįd,
"Yi nįđer nɷ́ mi, nor mį Fɐđer,
nor wil yi, in ųr prįd,

Acknowledge me, therefore his love
  Cannot in you abide."
These words spake Jesus as he taught
  Within the treasury,
And no man laid hands on him, for
  His hour was not yet nigh.
Then Jesus said, "I go my way,
  My course divine fulfil;
Ye still will seek Christ falsely, such
  Is your delusion still;
And in your sins you'll surely die,
  Because your souls are base,
And grovel in the dust of earth;
  I am of heavenly race.
Yea, if ye do not trust in me
  As the Anointed One,
Ye'll sink beneath, in sin and shame,
  And ever be undone.
I yet have many things to say
  And judge concerning you,
And I shall truly judge, for God
  Who sent me, is most true.
Moreover I proclaim those things
  Which I have heard from him.
And when that I am crucified
  By your proud Sanhedrim,
Then shall ye know that I am he,
  And that I nothing do
From self, but what the Father does;
  And he I know is true."
Then many Jews believed in Christ;
  To whom he said, "Take heed;
If ye continue in my word,
  Then are ye mine indeed;
And ye shall know the very truth,
  And that shall make you free,
And everlasting peace and joy
  Shall wait on liberty."
Then said the Jews, "As Abraham's
  We ever free have been." [seed
Jesus replied, "Whoever sins
  The servant is of sin;
And he that sins shall not abide
  Within God's house for ever;
The Son, and he that loves the Son,
  Shall be excluded never.
And if the Son shall make you free,
  Ye shall be free indeed.
I know your nation's origin,
  That ye are Abraham's seed,

aknolej mi, đerfer hiz lɒv
  kanot in ɥ abįd."
Điz wɒrdz spek Jizɒs az hi tɷt
  wiđin đe treʒuri,
and ne man led handz on him, for
  hiz ʊr woz not yet nį.
Đen Jizɒs sed, "Į ge mį we,
  mį kers divįn fulfil;
yi stil wil sik Krįst fɷlsli, sɒç
  iz ɥr deluʒon stil;
and in ɥr sinz ɥ'l ʃurli dį,
  bekɷz ɥr selz ar bes,
and grovel in đe dɒst ov erɟ;
  į am ov hevenli res.
Ye, if yi du not trɒst in mi,
  az đe Anointed Wɒn,
yi'l siŋk beniɟ, in sin and ʃem,
  and ever bi ɒndɒn.
Į yet hav meni ɟiŋz tu se
  and jɒj konserniŋ ɥ,
and į ʃal truli jɒj, for God
  hu sent mi, iz mest tru.
Merever į preklem đez ɟiŋz
  hwiç į hav herd from him.
And hwen đat į am krusifįd
  bį ɥr prʊd Sanhedrim,
đen ʃal yi né đat į am hi,
  and đat į nɒɟiŋ du
from self, bɒt hwot đe Fađer dɒz;
  and hi į né iz tru."
Đen meni Juz belivd in Krįst;
  tu hum hi sed, "Tek hid;
If yi kontinɥ in mį wɒrd,
  đen ar yi mįn indid;
and yi ʃal né đe veri truɟ,
  and đát ʃal mek ɥ fri,
and everlastiŋ pis and joi
  ʃal wet on liberti."
Đen sed đe Juz, "Az Ɛbraham'z
  wi ever fri hav bin." [sid
Jizɒs replįd, "Huever sinz
  đe servant iz ov sin;
and hi đat sinz ʃal not abįd
  wiđin God'z hʊs for ever;
đe Sɒn, and hi đat lɒvz đe Sɒn,
  ʃal bi ekskluded never.
And if đe Sɒn ʃal mek ɥ fri,
  yi ʃal bi fri indid.
Į né ɥr neʃon'z orijin,
  đat yi ar Ɛbraham'z sid,

But if ye were indeed true sons
  Of that most faithful sire,
Ye would his pious words and deeds,
  To speak and act aspire.
But now, most unlike Abraham,
  Ye seek to murder me,
Who have revealed to you the truths
  I heard from Deity."
Then said the Jews to Christ, "We
  One Father, even God."   [have
Jesus replied, "If so, you would
  More love to me have showed,
For I proceeded forth, and came
  From God, who sent me here,
To save the souls of lost mankind,
  That still to heaven are dear.
Wherefore do ye not understand
  My speech, as clear as day?
Because ye do not truly strive
  My doctrine to obey.
Your father is the devil, and
  Ye his vile lusts fulfil;
He was a murderer from the first,
  And deals in falsehood still.
He is the source of foul deceits,
  And lies of every kind,
And by his wicked sophistries
  He makes men's reason blind.
It is because I tell the truth
  That ye believe me not;
Ye cannot find in my discourse
  A single flaw or blot.
If, then, I speak the truth divine,
  Which ye cannot disprove,
Why do ye not believe in me,
  And your Messiah love?
He who is godly hears God's words,
  And tries to obey them still;
Ye hear them not, because, in truth,
  Ye do not love God's will.
If any man will keep my word,
  And true obedience show,
He shall not taste of that worse death,
  Which guilty spirits know.
My honor comes from that great God
  Whose will I preach and do.
That God I know, and keep his words,
  Because his words are true.
Your father Abraham rejoiced
  To anticipate my day;

bɒt if yi wer indid trɯ sɒnz
  ov đát mɵst feɟful sịr,
yi wud hiz pịɒs wɒrdz and didz,
  tu spik and akt aspịr.
Bɒt nɤ, mɵst ɒnlịk Ɛbraham,
  yi sik tu mɒrder mi,
hɯ hav revild tu ɥ đe trɯđz
  ị herd from Diiti."
Đen sed đe Jɯz tu Krịst, "Wi hav
  wɒn Fɐđer, iven God."
Jizɒs replịd, "If sɵ, ɥ wud
  mɵr lɒv tu mi hav ʃɵd,
for ị prɵsided fɵrɟ, and kem
  from God, hɯ sent mi hir,
tu sev đe sɵlz ov lost mankịnd,
  đat stil tu heven ar dir.
Hwerfɵr dɯ yi not ɒnderstand
  mị spiç, az klir az de?
bekɷz yi dɯ not trɯli strịv
  mị doktrin tu ɵbe.
Ɥr fɐđer iz đe devil, and
  yi hiz vịl lɒsts fulfil;
hi woz a mɒrderer from đe ferst,
  and dilz in fɷlshud stil.
Hi iz đe sɵrs ov fɤl desits,
  and lịz ov everi kịnd,
and bị hiz wiked sofistriz
  hi meks men'z rizon blịnd.
It iz bekɷz ị tel đe trɯɟ
  đat yi beliv mi not;
yi kanot fịnd in mị diskɵrs
  a siŋgel flɷ or blot.
If, đen, ị spik đe trɯɟ divịn,
  hwiç yi kanot disprɯv,
hwị dɯ yi not beliv in mi,
  and ɥr Mesịa lɒv?
Hi hɯ iz godli hirz God'z wɒrdz,
  and trịz tu ɵbe đem stil;
yi hir đem not, bekɷz, in trɯɟ,
  yi dɯ not lɒv God'z wíl.
If eni man wil kip mị wɒrd,
  and trɯ ɵbidiens ʃɵ,
hi ʃal not test ov đát wɒrs deɟ,
  hwiç gilti spirits nɵ́.
Mị onor kɒmz from đát gret God
  hɯz wíl ị priç and dɯ.
Đát God ị nɵ́, and kip hiz wɒrdz,
  bekɷz hiz wɒrdz ar trɯ.
Ɥr fɐđer Ɛbraham rejoist
  tu antisipet mị de;

In faith he saw it, and was glad,
  And owned my righteous sway."
Then said the Jews, "Not fifty years
  Of life hast thou beheld;
Then how hast thou seen Abraham?
  This mystery be dispelled." [Let
Then Jesus, "Verily, I say,
  Ere Abraham was, I am."
Then sought the Jews to stone him
  For making such a claim. [dead,
But Jesus soon retired from view,
Went through their midst, and so
    withdrew.

in feɟ hi sɷ it, and woz glad,
  and ɵnd mį rįtiɒs swɛ."
Ƌen sed đe Juız, "Not fifti yırz
  ov lįf hast đɤ beheld;
đen hɤ hast đɤ sın Ɛbraham? Let
  đis misteri bi dispeld."
ƋenJizɒs, "Verili, į sɛ,
  ɛr Ɛbraham woz, Ɨ am."
Ƌen sɷt đe Juız tu stɵn him ded,
  for mɛkiŋ sɒɕ a klɛm.
Bɒt Jizɒs suın retįrd from vų,
went ɟruı đɛr midst, and sɵ
    wiđdruı.

SECTION 90.

The Seventy return with joy.
Luke 10. 17-24.

The seventy disciples, whom
  The Lord of late sent forth
To preach his word throughout the
    land,
  In east, west, south, and north,
Now came, returning with much joy
  Unto their Lord, and said,
"Master, through thy name demons
  At our rebuke have fled." [strong
And Christ replied, "Yea, I beheld
  Satan defeated fall
Like lightning from the heaven. To
  Who have obeyed my call, [you
I give authority to tread
  On all the serpent brood,
And all the powers of enmity
  That still oppose the good;
And nought shall harm you. But re-
  Not only that you see [joice
Spirits subjected unto you
  For your true faith in me,
But rather now rejoice in this,
  That your elected names
Are written in heaven's book of life,
  Where you may read your claims."
At that hour Christ rejoiced, and said,
  "I thank thee, Father, Lord,
Of heaven and earth, that thou hast
  The mysteries of thy Word [veiled
From crafty men, and made them
  To babes, to minds sincere; [known

SEKΣON 90.

Ƌe Seventi retɒrn wiđ joi.
Luk 10. 17-24.

Ƌe seventi disįpelz, huım
  đe Lord ov lɛt sent fɵrɟ
tu priɕ hiz wɒrd ɟruɤt đe
    land,
  in ist, west, sɤɟ, and norɟ,
nɤ kɛm, retɒrniŋ wiđ mɒɕ joi
  ɒntu đɛr Lord, and sed,
"Master, ɟruı đį nɛm dimonz stroŋ
  at ɤr rebųk hav fled."
And Krįst replįd, "Yɛ, į beheld
  Sɛtan defited fɷl
lįk lįtniŋ from đe heven. Tu ų
  huı hav ɵbed mį kɷl,
į giv ɷɟoriti tu tred
  on ɷl đe serpent bruıd,
and ɷl đe pɤerz ov enmiti
  đat stil opɵz đe gud;
and nɷt ʃal harm ų. Bɒt rejois
  not ɵnli đat ų si
spirits sɒbjekted ɒntu ų
  for ųr truı fɛɟ in mi,
bɒt radɛr nɤ rejois in đis,
  đat ųr elekted nɛmz
ar riten in heven'z buk ov lįf,
  hwer ų mɛ rid ųr klɛmz."
At đát ɤr Krįst rejoist, and sed,
  "Ɨ ɟaŋk đi, Fader, Lord,
ov heven and erɟ, đat đɤ hast veld
  đe misteriz ov đį Wɒrd
from krafti men, and mɛd đem nɵn
  tu bɛbz, tu mįndz sinsir;

For so it seemèd good to thee,
  That they may thee revere.
And no man knows the Son except
  The Father that's in him,
(The Father's the Divinity,
  The Godhead, the Supreme,)
And none the Father knoweth, but
  The Son, and also he
To whom the Son revealeth him,
  In loving majesty."
To his disciples then Christ turned,
  And said to them, apart,
"Blest are your eyes, for they behold
  Truths which exalt the heart;
Yea, truths which kings and prophets [oft
  Desired to see and hear,
But only realised by faith
  In what doth now appear."

for sɵ it sɨmed gud tu ði,
  ðat ðɛ mɛ ði revɨr.
And nɵ man nɵ́z ðe Sɒn, eksept
  ðe Fɜðer ðat's in him,
(ðe Fɜðer'z ðe Diviniti,
  ðe Godhed, ðe Sɥprɨm,)
and nɒn ðe Fɜðer nɵeɟ, bɒt
  ðe Sɒn, and ɷlsɵ hi
tu hɯm ðe Sɒn revɨleɟ him,
  in lɒviŋ majesti."
Tu hiz disįpelz ðen Krįst tɒrnd,
  and sed tu ðem, apart,
"Blest ar ɥr įz, for ðɛ behɵld
  trɯðz hwiɥ ekzɷlt ðe hart;
ye, trɯðz hwiɥ kiŋz and profets oft
  dezįrd tu sɨ and hɨr,
bɒt ɵnli rɨalįzd bį feɟ
  in hwot dɒɟ nɤ apɨr."

SECTION 91.

Christ directs the Lawyer how to attain eternal life.—Luke 10. 25-29.

A certain lawyer then arose
  To try the Savior's mind,
And said, "Good Lord, what shall I [do,
  Eternal life to find?"
The Lord said to him, "In the law,
  What findest thou is writ?"
He said, "To love thy God with heart,
  And soul, and strength, is fit;
And, as thyself, thy neighbour too;
  These rules the law doth give."
And Jesus said, "Thou speakest right,
  This do, and thou shalt live."

SEKΣON 91.

Krįst direkts ðe Lɷier hɤ tu aten eternal lįf.—Lɯk 10. 25-29.

A serten lɷier ðen arɵz
  tu trį ðe Sɛvier'z mįnd,
and sed, "Gud Lord, hwot ʃal į [du,
  eternal lįf tu fįnd?"
Ðe Lord sed tu him, "In ðe lɷ,
  hwot fįndest ðɤ iz rit?"
Hi sed, "Tu lɒv ðį God wið hart,
  and sɵl, and streŋɟ, iz fit;
and, az ðįself, ðį nebɒr tɯ;
  ðiz rɯlz ðe lɷ dɒɟ giv."
And Jɨzɒs sed, "Ðɤ spɨkest rįt,
  ðis dɯ, and ðɤ ʃalt liv."

SECTION 92.

The Parable of the Good Samaritan.
Luke 10. 29-37.

But he, desirous to be thought
  A righteous man in all,
Said unto Jesus, "Whom shall I
  My proper neighbour call?"
Then Jesus spoke this parable,
  "A certain man would go
The journey from Jerusalem
  To lawless Jericho:

SEKΣON 92.

Ðe Parabel ov ðe Gud Samaritan.
Lɯk 10. 29-37.

Bɒt hi, dezįrɒs tu bi ɟɷt
  a rįtiɒs man in ɷl,
sed ɒntu Jɨzɒs, "Hɯm ʃal į
  mį proper nebɒr kɷl?"
Ðen Jɨzɒs spɵk ðis parabel,
  "A serten man wud gɵ
ðe jɒrni from Jerɯsalem
  tu lɷles Jerikɵ:

And by the way he met with thieves,
  Who robbed and stripped him bare ;
And after wounding him, they fled,
  And left him half dead there.
By chance a priest came down that
  No mercy in his breast : [way ;
He saw, but he would not relieve ;
  So journeyed on, unblest.
A Levite likewise passed the place,
  And curiously espied ;
But he too left the wretched man,
  Not caring if he died.
Then came a good Samaritan,
  Despised by prouder men,
Who, when he saw, compassion felt,
  And went to ease his pain.
His wounds he dressed with oil and
  Nor did his own beast spare, [wine,
But safely brought him to an inn,
  Where he might have due care.
And on the morrow, when he left,
  Two coins he gave the host,
And told him to provide the best,
  And he would pay the cost.
Which now," said Jesus, "of these
  Did prove a neighbour true [three
To him who fell among the thieves ?
  How seemeth it to you ?"
The lawyer answered, "That same
  Who did such mercy show." [man
Then Jesus said, "Go ; see that thou
  Like mercy e'er bestow."

and bį đe wɛ hi met wiđ ŧivz,
  hɯ robd and stript him bɛr ;
and after wɯndiŋ him, đɛ fled,
  and left him hɛf ded đɛr.
Bį çans a prist kem dɜn đát wɛ ;
  nɷ mersi in hiz brest :
hi sɷ, bɒt hi wud not reliv ;
  sɷ jɒrnid on, ɒnblest.
A Livįt lįkwįz past đe plɛs,
  and kųriɒsli espįd ;
bɒt hi tɯ left đe reçed man,
  not keriŋ if hi dįd.
Đen kem a gud Samaritan,
  despįzd bį prɜder men,
hɯ, hwen hi sɷ, kompaʃon felt,
  and went tu iz hiz pen.
Hiz wɯndz hi drest wiđ oil and
  nor did hiz ɷn bist spɛr, [wįn,
bɒt sefli brɷt him tu an ín,
  hwɛr hi mįt hav dų kɛr.
And on đe morɷ, hwen hi left,
  tɯ́ koinz hi gev đe hɷst,
and tɷld him tu prɷvįd đe best,
  and hi wud pɛ đe kost.
Hwiç nɜ," sed Jizɒs, "ov điz ŧri
  did prɯv a nebɒr trɯ
tu him hɯ fel amɒŋ đe ŧivz ?
  Hɜ simeŧ it tu ų ?"
Đe lɷier anserd, "Đát sem man
  hɯ did sɒç mersi ʃɷ."
Đen Jizɒs sed, "Gɷ ; si dat đɜ
  lįk mersi ɛr bestɷ."

SECTION 93.

Christ in the House of Martha.

Luke 10. 38-42.

When Jesus left the seventy,
  He to a village came,
And one received him to her house,
  Martha, that woman's name.
Her sister Mary, at Christ's feet,
  Would lovingly abide,
And listen to his blessed words,
  Dearer than ought beside.
But Martha, of more restless mind,
  Was tired of serving much ;
And felt displeased with Mary, who
  Those duties did not touch.

SEKΣON 93.

Krįst in đe Hɜs ov Marŧa.

Lɯk 10. 38-42.

Hwen Jizɒs left đe seventi,
  hi tu a vilej kem,
and wɒn resivd him tu her hɜs,
  Marŧa, đát wuman'z nem.
Her sister Meri, at Krįst's fit,
  wud lɒviŋli abįd,
and lisen tu hiz blesed wɒrdz,
  direr đan ɷt besįd.
Bɒt Marŧa, ov mɷr restles mįnd,
  woz tįrd ov serviŋ mɒç ;
and felt displizd wiđ Meri, hɯ
  đɷz dųtiz did not tɒç.

To Jesus then she came, and said,
  "Lord, dost thou not concern
Thyself? My sister hath left me
  To serve: bid her return."
Jesus replied, in kindly tone,
  "Martha, thy anxious will
Is troubled with too many things:
  Be industriously still.
One thing is needful, and that one,
  Which is the better part,
Mary hath chosen. None shall take
  That treasure from her heart.

Tu Jizɒs đen ʃi kɛm, and sed,
  "Lord, dɒst đɜ not konsern
đįself? Mį sister haɟ left mi
  tu serv: bid her retɒrn."
Jizɒs replįd, in kįndli tɵn,
  "Marɟa, đį aŋkʃɒs wil
iz trɒbeld wiđ tɯ meni ɟiŋz:
  bi indɒstriɒsli stil.
Wɒn ɟiŋ iz nidful, and đát wɒn,
  hwiɕ iz đe beter part,
Meri haɟ ɕɵzen. Nɒn ʃal tɛk
  đát treʒur from her hart.

BOOK VII.

BUK VII.

SECTION 94.

Christ teaches his Disciples to pray.
Luke 11. 1-13.

It came to pass that on a time,
  As Christ retired to pray,
When he had ceased, one said to him,
  "Lord, teach us what to say
In prayer, as John his followers
    taught."
He said, "Say thus, in earnest
    thought:

The Lord's Prayer.

Our Father who art in the heavens,
  Most holy be thy name.
Thy kingdom come. Thy will be done,
  In heaven and earth the same.
Give us this day our daily bread.
  Forgive us every debt,
As we our debtors gladly free,
  And their misdeeds forget.
And lead us not into temptation,
Except it be for our salvation."

Then Jesus said, "If ye should ask
  From any friendly man,
Such gifts as he can well afford,
  And ye desire to gain,
He will bestow them if ye ask
  Ofttimes with earnestness,
Noting your importunity,
  And pitying your distress.

SEKΣON 94.

Krįst tiɕez hiz Disįpelz tɯ prɛ.
Lɯk 11. 1-13.

It kɛm tu pas đat on a tįm,
  az Krįst retįrd tu prɛ,
hwen hi had sist, wɒn sed tu him,
  "Lord, tiɕ ɒs hwot tu sɛ
in prɛr, az Jon hiz folɵerz
    tɷt."
Hi sed, "Sɛ đɒs, in ernest
    ɟɷt:

Đe Lord'z Prer.

Ɜr Fɑđer hɯ art in đe hevenz,
  mɵst hɵli bi đį nɛm.
Đį kiŋdom kɒm. Đį wil bi dɒn,
  in heven and erɟ đe sɛm.
Giv ɒs đis dɛ ɜr deli bred.
  Forgiv ɒs everi det,
az wi ɜr deterz gladli fri,
  and đɛr misdidz forget.
And lid ɒs not intu temptɛʃon,
eksept it bi for ɜr salvɛʃon."

Đen Jizɒs sed, "If yi ʃud ask
  from eni frendli man,
sɒɕ gifts az hi kan wel afɵrd,
  and yi dezįr tu gɛn,
hi wil bestɵ đem if yi ask
  ofttįmz wiđ ernestnes,
nɵtiŋ ųr importųniti,
  and pitiiŋ ųr distres.

Ask good; it shall be given you:
Seek truth; and ye shall find:
Knock; and heaven's gates shall open
stand;
Then enter, heart and mind.
For everyone that asks, receives;
He finds that seeks afar;
And he that knocks with earnestness,
Soon sees the gates ajar.
If vain and erring man will give
Good gifts to those he loves,
Sure God will better things bestow
On those whom he approves."

SECTION 95.

Christ reproaches the Pharisees and Lawyers
Luke 11. 37-54.

A certain Pharisee, too fond
Of outward pomp and show,
Invited Christ to dine with him,
That he the truth might know.
Then was the Pharisee amazed
To see the Lord sit down
To dine with unwashed hands; which [he
Regarded with a frown.
Jesus observed his discontent,
And soon he thus did say,
"Ye Jews, to merely outward forms
Too much attention pay;
While you neglect the greater things
Of inward purities
Of mind, and heart, and character,
Which you should rather prize.
If the external forms are made
By God, I reason, hence,
That the interior essence is
Of greater consequence:
And if you cherish in your hearts
A heavenly charity,
And kindness practical, these things
Soon pure enough will be.
'Tis right to observe those minor points
That duly sanctioned are;
But justice, mercy, love divine,
Are more important far.
Woe unto you, who much admire
Vain shows and compliments;
Loathsome as hidden graves ye are
To men of inner sense."

Ask gud; it ʃal bi given ɥ:
sik truɟ; and yi ʃal fįnd:
nok; and heven'z gɛts ʃal ɵpen
stand;
đen enter, hart and mįnd.
For everiwɒn đat asks, resivz;
hi fįndz đat siks afar;
and hi đat noks wiđ ernestnes,
sɯn siz đe gɛts ajar.
If vɛn and eriŋ man wil giv
gud gifts tu đɵz hi lɒvz,
ʃɯr God wil beter ɟiŋz bestɵ
on đɵz hɯm hi aprɯvz."

SEKΣON 95.

Krįst reprɵçez đe Farisiz and Lɵierz.
Lɯk 11. 37-54.

A serten Farisi, tɯ fond
ov ɤtward pomp and ʃɵ,
invįted Krįst tu dįn wiđ him,
đat hi đe trɯɟ mįt nɵ́.
đen woz đe Farisi amɛzd
tu si đe Lord sit dɤn
tu dįn wiđ ɒnwoʃt handz; hwiç hi
regarded wiđ a frɤn.
Jizɒs obzervd hiz diskontent,
and sɯn hi đɒs did sɛ,
"Yi Jɯz, tu mirli ɤtward formz
tɯ mɒç atenʃon pɛ;
hwįl ɥ neglekt đe grɛter ɟiŋz
ov inward pɥritiz
ov mįnd, and hart, and karakter,
hwiç ɥ ʃud rɛđer prįz.
If đe eksternal formz ar mɛd
bį God, į rizon, hens,
đat đe intirior esens iz
ov grɛter konsekwens:
and if ɥ çeriʃ in ɥr harts
a hevenli çariti,
and kįndnes praktikal, điz ɟiŋz
sɯn pɥr enɒf wil bi.
'Tiz rįt tu obzerv đɵz mįnor points
đat dɥli saŋkʃond ar;
bɒt jɒstis, mersi, lɒv divįn,
ar mɵr important far.
Wɵ ɒntu ɥ, hɯ mɒç admįr
vɛn ʃɵz and kompliments;
lɵđsɒm az hiden grɛvz yi ar
tu men ov iner sens."

Then one, a Jewish lawyer rose,
  And to the Lord thus said,
"Master, thus speaking, thou dost
  Reproaches on our trade." [cast
Then Christ replied, "Yea, woe to
  Who falsify the law; [you,
Ye should teach truly, and protect
  From avaricious maw;
But in your hands, the laws which
  Defend the poor and weak, [should
Become oppressions; and they crush
  The innocent and meek.
Ye lay on others burdens dire,
  Expensive, cruel, vain,
While ye yourselves bear not one jot,
  But seek unrighteous gain.
Your fathers killed the prophets; ye
  Are treacherous as they:
Ye ornament the prophet's tombs;
  But will not them obey.
And all the wickedness and wrong
  Which caused your fathers shame,
Shall on yourselves be charged, for ye
  Even now confirm the same.
Ye take away God's key of truth,
  And grope in error's night,
Ye will not enter heaven yourselves,
  And hinder those who might.

SECTION 96.

Christ cautions his Disciples against hypocrisy.—Luke 12. 1-12.

Once a vast crowd of listeners
  Assembled, Christ to hear,
And he began to say to them,
  "Above all, be sincere.
Beware of the hypocrisy
  Of Pharisees, and all
Mere priestcraft, which like leaven
    doth work,
  And even the good enthrall.
Think not disguised hypocrisy
  Can prosper in the end,
For all things, howsoe'er concealed,
  To truth's discovery tend.
And your most secret conference,
  Both good and ill, shall be
Revealed at length in its true light,
  Stripped of all sophistry.

Ðen wɒn, a Juiʃ lɷier rɵz,
  and tu ðe Lord ðɒs sed,
"Master, ðɒs spịkiŋ, ðɤ dɒst kast
  reprɵçez on ɤr tred."
Ðen Krɨst replɨd, "Ye, wɵ tu ų,
  hɯ fɷlsifɨ ðe lɷ;
yi ʃud tiç trɯli, and prɵtekt
  from avariʃɒs mɷ;
bɒt in ųr handz, ðe lɷz hwiç ʃud
  defend ðe pɯr and wịk,
bekɒm opreʃonz; and ðe krɒʃ
  ðe inosent and mik.
Yi le on ɒðerz bɒrdenz dɨr,
  ekspensiv, krɯel, ven,
hwɨl yi ųrselvz ber not wɒn jot,
  bɒt sịk ɒnrɨtiɒs gen.
Ųr fɑðerz kild ðe profets; yi
  ar treçerɒs az ðe:
yi ornament ðe profet's tɯmz;
  bɒt wil not ðem ɵbe.
And ɷl ðe wikednes and roŋ
  hwiç kɷzd ųr fɑðerz ʃem,
ʃal on ųrselvz bi çarjd, for yi
  ịven nɤ konferm ðe sem.
Yi tek awe God'z ki ov trɯþ,
  and grɵp in eror'z nɨt,
yi wil not enter heven ųrselvz;
  and hinder ðɵz hɯ mɨt.

SEKΣON 96.

Krɨst kɷʃonz hiz Disɨpelz agenst hipokrisi.—Lɯk 12. 1-12.

Wɒns a vast krɤd ov lisenerz
  asembeld, Krɨst tu hir,
and hi began tu se tu ðem,
  "Abɒv ɷl, bi sinsịr.
Bewer ov ðe hipokrisi
  ov Farisịz, and ɷl
mir prịstkraft, hwiç lɨk leven
    dɒþ wɒrk,
  and ịven ðe gud enþrɷl.
Þiŋk not disgɨzd hipokrisi
  kan prosper in ðe end,
for ɷl þiŋz, hɤsɵer konsịld,
  tu trɯþ's diskɒveri tend.
And ųr mɵst sịkret konferens,
  bɵþ gud and il, ʃal bi
revịld at leŋþ in its trɯ lɨt,
  stript ov ɷl sofistri.

Therefore, my friends, speak plainly forth,
God's wisdom as you may.
I will forewarn you whom to fear:
No man your souls can slay.
Then fear ye not the power which can
The body only kill;
Fear that which soul and body both
Can sink down into hell.
Be faithful unto God, and trust
His love and power to bless,
Who cares for all, even creatures small,
And pities their distress.
He who forgets not to provide
For sparrows and their brood,
Protects his saints' least interest
With fond solicitude.
Whoever boldly pleads my cause
Before his fellow men,
His faithfulness will I confess
To all the angelic train;
And he that scorns my cause on earth,
Shall, in the future, be
Rejected by that very Lord
He treated treacherously.
Whoever shall speak wrongfully
Against the Son of Man,
May be forgiven: but who shall pour
His blasphemies profane
Upon the Holy Spirit of love
May never be forgiven:
His unrepented guiltiness
Will shut him out of heaven.
And when men bring you, in their hate,
Before the hostile bar
Of kings and courts, who oft against
True righteousness make war,
Let not your hearts be timorous found,
Nor doubtful what to tell,
For God's most Holy Spirit of truth
Shall prompt your answers well.

Đerfɵr, mį frendz, spɪk plɛnli fɵrŧ,
God'z wizdom az ɥ mɛ.
Ɨ wil fɵrworn ɥ hɯm tu fɪr:
nɵ man ɥr sɵlz kan slɛ.
Đen fɪr yɪ not đe pɤer hwiç kan
đe bodi ɵnli kil;
fɪr đát hwiç sɵl and bodi bɵŧ
kan siŋk dɤn intu hel.
Bɪ fɛŧful ɒntu God, and trɒst
hiz lɒv and pɤer tu bles.
Hɯ kerz for ɷl, ɪven krɪtɥrz smɷl,
and pitiz đer distres.
Hɪ hɯ forgets not tu prɵvįd
for sparɵz and đer brɯd,
prɵtekts hiz sɛnts' list interest
wiđ fond solisitɥd.
Hɯever bɵldli plɪdz mį kɷz
befɵr hiz felɵ men,
hiz fɛŧfulnes wil į konfes
tu ɷl đe anjelik trɛn;
and hi đat skornz mį kɷz on erŧ,
ʃal, in đe fɥtɥr, bi
rejekted bį đát veri Lord
hi trited treçerɒsli.
Hɯever ʃal spɪk roŋfuli
agenst đe Sɒn ov Man,
mɛ bi forgiven: bɒt hɯ ʃal pɵr
hiz blasfemiz prɵfɛn
ɒpon đe Hɵli Spirit ov lɒv
mɛ never bɪ forgiven:
hiz ɒnrepented giltines
wil ʃɒt him ɤt ov heven.
And hwen men briŋ ɥ, in đer hɛt,
befɵr đe hostil bar
ov kiŋz and kɵrts, hɯ oft agenst
trɯ rįtiɒsnes mɛk wor,
let not ɥr harts bɪ timorɒs fɤnd,
nor dɤtful hwot tu tel,
for God'z mɵst Hɵli Spirit ov trɯŧ
ʃal prompt ɥr anserz wel.

SECTION 97.

Christ cautions the multitude against worldly-mindedness.—Luke 12. 3-34.

A certain man, too fond of wealth,
To Jesus said, one day,
"Lord, make my brother share with me
His riches. Do, I pray."

SEKΣON 97.

Krįst kɷʃonz đe mɒltitɥd agenst wɒrldli-mįndednes.—Lɯk 12. 3-34.

A serten man, tɯ fond ov welŧ,
tu Jɪzɒs sed, wɒn dɛ,
"Lord, mɛk mį brɒđer ʃer wiđ mi
hiz riçez. Dɯ, į prɛ."

Christ answered, "I came not to act
  As earthly judges do;
To portion out possessions, but
  To teach you doctrines true.
And one of them is this: beware
  Of baleful avarice;
That passion for superfluous wealth,
  Which comes from the abyss.
Man's life, of body or of mind,
  Doth surely not depend
On the abundance of his wealth,
  And treasures without end."
Then Jesus spake this parable:
  "There was a certain lord
Whose land brought forth most plenteously,
  So that his barns were stored.
And then he thought within himself,
  'I'll build new barns; and they
Shall hold the accumulated stock
  I will to them convey.
Then shall my soul be satisfied
  For many a year to come;
And feast, and pomp, and every joy,
  Shall make with me their home.'
But God said unto him, 'Thou fool,
  This very night thy soul
Shall leave thy body, and thy wealth
  Be at thy heir's control.'
So will it be with everyone
  Who hoards up selfish gain,
And is not rich toward God: his joys
  Must end in lasting pain.

Let not a vain anxiety
  Within your hearts abide;
For food, and drink, and needful clothes,
  Your Father will provide.
Your life is much more than its food,
  Your body than its dress;
Then he who grants the greater gifts
  Will surely give the less.
See how the very birds of heaven
  Are nourished by his care;
They neither plant, nor sow, nor reap,
  And yet they tended are;
Think of your minds, and ask yourselves,
  Are ye not better far?
Can any add unto his life
  A span of time's duration?

Krįst anserd, "Ɨ kem not tu akt
  az erŧli jɒjez dɯ;
tu porʃon ʊt pozeʃonz, bɒt
  tu tiç ų doktrinz trɯ.
And wɒn ov đem iz đis: bewer
  ov belful avaris;
đát paʃon for sųperflųɒs welŧ,
  hwiç kɒmz from đe abís.
Man'z lįf, ov bodi or ov mįnd,
  dɒŧ ʃɯrli not depend
on đe abɒndans ov hiz welŧ,
  and trezurz widʊt end."
Đen Jizɒs spek đis parabel:
  "Đer woz a serten lord
hɯz land brɵt forŧ most plentiɒsli,
  sɵ đat hiz barnz wer stɵrd.
And đen hi ŧɵt widin himself,
  'Ɨ'l bild nų barnz; and đe
ʃal hɵld đe akųmųleted stok
  į wil tu đem konve.
Đen ʃal mį sɵl bi satisfįd
  for meni a yir tu kɒm;
and fist, and pomp, and everi joi,
  ʃal mek wiđ mi đer hɵm.'
Bɒt God sed ɒntu him, 'Đʊ fɯl,
  đis veri nįt đį sɵl
ʃal liv đį bodi, and đį welŧ
  bi at đį er'z kontrɵl.'
Sɵ wil it bi wiđ everiwɒn
  hɯ hɵrdz ɒp selfiʃ gen,
and iz not riç tɵard God: hiz joiz
  mɒst end in lastiŋ pen.

Let not a ven aŋkzįeti
  widin ųr harts abįd;
for fɯd, and driŋk, and nidful klɵdz,
  ųr Fader wil provįd.
Ųr lįf iz mɒç mɵr đan its fɯd,
  ųr bodi đan its dres;
đen hi hɯ grants đe greter gifts
  wil ʃɯrli giv đe les.
Si hʊ đe veri berdz ov heven
  ar nɒriʃt bį hiz ker;
đe nįđer plant, nor sɵ, nor rip,
  and yet đe tended ar;
ŧiŋk ov ųr mįndz, and ask ųrselvz,
  ar yi not beter far?
Kan eni ad ɒntu hiz lįf
  a span ov tįm'z dųreʃon?

And why take thought for raiment too?
  Even Solomon's proud station
Was not in equal glory decked,
  Or beauty, like the flower.
Think of the lilies of the field,
  And in them see God's power.
If, then, he condescends to clothe
  The herbage with such grace,
Will he not greater care bestow
  On you, O faithless race?
He knows your need, and bids you
  At first, his kingdom pure; [seek,
And he will add his earthly gifts
  To treasures that endure.
On humble trusting souls he will
  All earthly needs bestow,
While, in the skies, their portion shall
  Exceed all earth can show.
Therefore, fear not, but freely spare
  Whatever ye possess;
Assist the poor, and keep your souls
  Rich in true holiness.
So shall ye have your treasure there
  Where moth nor rust corrode,
Where thief can ne'er approach to
  For all is safe with God. [steal,
Wherever ye your treasure place,
  Your heart will find its home,
Seek then to fix it all above,
  That ye may thither come."

SECTION 98.

Christ exhorts to watchfulness, fidelity, and repentance.—Luke 12. 35-59; 13. 1-9.

" Gird up your loins, light torches, be
  Like men who wait their lord
Returning from a wedding feast,
  Their service to afford.
How blest are they who, watching
  Their lord shall ready find; [thus,
They shall sit down to eat with him,
  So gracious he, and kind.
Yea, he will even such servants serve,
  Whom, watching every hour,
He finds; and blessed shall they be;
  No fear shall them o'erpower.
Know this, that if a householder
  Knew when the thief would come,

And hwɉ tεk ɟot for rεment tɯ?
  ıven Solomon'z prɤd stεʃon
woz not in ıkwal ɡlɷri dekt,
  oı bųti, lɉk đe flɤer.
Ꞁiŋk ov đe liliz ov đe fıld,
  and in đem sı God'z pɤer.
If, đen, hı kondesendz tu klɷđ
  đe herbej wiđ sɒç ɡres,
wil hı not ɡreter kεr bestɷ
  on ų, Ɵ feɟles res?
Hı nɷ́z ųr nıd, and bidz ų sık,
  at ferst, hiz kiŋdom pųr;
and hı́ wil ad hiz erɟli ɡifts
  tu treʒurz đat endųr.
On hɒmbel trɒstiŋ sɷlz hı wil
  ωl erɟli nıdz bestɷ,
hwɉl, in đe skɉz, đer pɷrʃon ʃal
  eksıd ωl erɟ kan ʃɷ.
Đerfɷr, fır not, bɒt frıli sper
  hwotever yı pozes;
asist đe puur, and kıp ųr sɷlz
  riç in trɯ hɷlines.
Sɷ ʃal yı hav ųr treʒur đer
  hwer mωɟ nor rɒst korɷd,
hwer ɟıf kan ner aprɷç tu stıl,
  for ωl iz sef wiđ God.
Hwerever yı ųr treʒur ples,
  ųr hart wil fɉnd its hɷm,
sık đen tu fiks it ωl abɒv,
  đat yı mε điđer kɒm."

SEKƩON 98.

Krɉst ekzorts tu woçfulnes, fideliti, and repentans.—Lɯk 12. 35-59; 13. 1-9.

" Gerd ɒp ųr loinz, lɉt torçez, bı
  lɉk men hɯ wεt đer lord
retɒrniŋ from a wediŋ fıst,
  đer servis tu afɷrd.
Hɤ blest ar đε hɯ, woçiŋ đɒs,
  đer lord ʃal redi fɉnd;
đε ʃal sit dɤn tu ıt wiđ him,
  sɷ ɡreʃɒs hı, and kɉnd.
Ye, hı wil ıven sɒç servants serv,
  hɯm, woçiŋ everi ɤr,
hı fɉndz; and blesed ʃal đε bı;
  nɷ fır ʃal đem ɷ'rpɤer.
Nɷ́ đis, đat if a hɤshɷlder
  nų hwen đe ɟıf wud kɒm,

He would keep watch, and thus prevent
  The ransack of his home.
Thus, too, must my disciples wait,
  Nor be betrayed by fear;
For at an hour when ye think not,
  The Son of man draws near."

Then Peter said to Jesus, "Lord,
  Does this thy parable
Apply to us, thy chosen few,
  Or does it bear on all?"
Christ answered, "Everyone who is
  A steward wise and good,
His master will a ruler make,
  To give the rest their food.
Yea, blessed shall that servant be
  Who acts a faithful part,
And serves not with eye-service: he
  Shall have great joy of heart.
But if a servant thus in trust
  Shall say, within his mind,
'My lord delays returning, and
  Remissness will not find;'
Then treats his fellow servants ill,
  And revels in excess,
His master will come back to him
  With fearful suddenness,
And will discard him, and appoint
  His place of punishment
With the unfaithful and the vile,
  Unless he soon repent.
And every servant who well knows
  His master's righteous will,
And breaks it, shall with many stripes
  Be scourged and smitten still.
But if that servant did not know
  His loving lord's command,
And sinned in ignorance, he shall
  So far acquitted stand.
Those to whom much is given in [charge,
  Because they much desired,
Shall find that with increase of trust
  Will be the account required."

Then Jesus said, "I came to send
  A fire on all the earth;
The fire of purifying truth,
  Eliciting true worth;
Consuming false corrupted things.
  And I desire no more

hi wud kip woç, and đɒs prevent
  đe ransak ov hiz hɵm.
đɒs, tɯ, mɒst mį disįpelz wet,
  nor bi betred bį fir;
for at an ɜr hwen yi ŧiŋk not,
  đe Sɒn ov man drɷz nir."

đen Piter sed tɯ Jizɒs, "Lord,
  dɒz đis đį parabel
aplį tu ɒs, đį çɵzen fɥ,
  or dɒz it ber on ɷl?"
Krįst anserd, "Everiwɒn hɯ iz
  a stɥard wįz and gud,
hiz master wil a rɯler mek,
  tu giv đe rest đer fɯd.
Yɛ, blesed ʃal đát servant bi
  hɯ akts a feŧful part,
and servz not wiđ į-servis: hi
  ʃal hav gret joi ov hart.
Bɒt if a servant đɒs in trɒst
  ʃal se, wiđin hiz mįnd,
'Mį lord delez retɒrniŋ, and
  remisnes wil not fįnd;'
đen trits hiz felɵ servants il,
  and revelz in ekses,
hiz master wil kɒm bak tu him
  wiđ firful sɒdennes,
and wil diskard him, and apoint
  hiz ples ov pɒniʃment
wiđ đe ɒnfeŧful and đe vįl,
  ɒnles hi sɯn repent.
And everi servant hɯ wel nɵ́z
  hiz master'z rįtiɒs wíl,
and breks it, ʃal wiđ meni strįps
  bi skɒrjd and smiten stil.
Bɒt if đát servant did not nɵ́
  hiz lɒviŋ lord'z komand,
and sind in ignorans, hi ʃal
  sɵ far akwited stand.
đɵz tu hɯm mɒç iz given in çarj,
  bekɷz đɛ mɒç dezįrd,
ʃal fįnd đat wiđ inkris ov trɒst
  wil bi đe akɜnt rekwįrd."

đen Jizɒs sed, "Ɨ kem tu send
  a fįr on ɷl đe erŧ;
đe fįr ov pɥrifįiŋ trɯŧ,
  elisitiŋ trɯ wɒrŧ;
konsɥmiŋ fɷls korɒpted ŧiŋz.
  And į dezįr nɵ mɵr

13

Than that its flame were kindled now,
From furthest shore to shore.
I have a baptism now in view;
Sore trials to sustain;
And great my toil and grief must be
Before my end I gain.
I came not only to send peace
On earth, but also strife;
My heavenly doctrine must oppose
Whate'er is wrong in life;
And hence will often discord cause
In tribes and families,
Who else might still agree to live
In refuges of lies.
Ye note the signs of changes in
The weather, and inform
Yourselves by darksome western [clouds
That soon will be a storm.
And when the balmy south wind blows,
Ye say that heat will be;
Yet ye discern not these grand signs
Of my pure ministry.
Why do ye not perceive, in time,
That the high truths I tell,
Will revolutionise the world,
And crush the powers of hell?
Make peace, in time, with the great power
With whom ye now contend;
Remove the cause of enmity,
Justice will be your friend.
Else it may cast you suddenly
In prison, there to lie,
Until ye pay the whole amount
Of debt, in misery."

Now some were there, too apt to note
The faults of other men,
Who of the Galilæans' crimes
To Jesus spoke; and then
How Pilate their own sacrifice
Did mingle with their blood;
Believing this a special case
Of judgement dire from God.
But Jesus said, "Do ye suppose
These men were sinners more
Than all the rest in Galilee,
Because they suffered sore?
I tell you, Nay; judge ye not thus;
Try rather your own hearts,

đan đat its flεm wer kindeld nʊ
from fɒrđest ʃσr tu ʃσr.
Ŧ hav a baptizm nʊ in vɥ;
sσr trɟalz tu sɒsten;
And grεt mɟ toil and grıf mɒst bı
befσr mɟ end ɟ gεn.
Ŧ kεm not σnli tu send pıs
on ert, bɒt ωlsσ strɟf;
mɟ hevenli doktrin mɒst opσz
hwoter iz roŋ in lɟf;
and hens wil ωfen diskord kωz
in trɟbz and familiz,
hɯ els mɟt stil agrı tu liv
in refɥjez ov lɟz.
Yı nσt đe sɟnz ov çεnjez in
đe weđer, and inform
ɥrselvz bɟ darksɒm western klʊd
đat sɯn wil bı a storm.
And hwen đe bɐmi sʊt wind blσz
yı sε đat hıt wil bı;
yet yı disern not đız grand sɟnz
ov mɟ pɥr ministri.
Hwɟ dɯ yı not persıv, in tɟm,
đat đe hɟ trɯđz ɟ tel,
wil revolɯʃonɟz đe wɒrld,
and krɒʃ đe pʊerz ov hel?
Mεk pıs, in tɟm, wiđ đe gr
pʊer
wiđ hɯm yı nʊ kontend;
remɯv đe kωz ov enmiti,
jɒstis wil bı ɥr frend.
Els it mε kast ɥ sɒdenli
in prizon, đεr tu lɟ,
ɒntil yı pε đe hσl amʊnt
ov det, in mizeri."

Nʊ sɒm wer đεr, tɯ apt tu nσt
đe fωlts ov ɒđer men,
hɯ ov đe Galilıanz' krɟmz
tu Jızɒs spσk; and đen
hʊ Pɟlεt đer σn sakrifɟs
did miŋgel wiđ đer blɒd;
belıviŋ đis a speʃal kεs
ov jɒjment dɟr from God.
Bɒt Jızɒs sed, "Dɯ yı sɒpσz
đız men wer sinerz mσr
đan ωl đe rest in Galilı,
bekωz đε sɒferd sσr?
Ŧ tel ɥ, Nε; jɒj yı not đɒs;
trɟ rɐđer ɥr σn harts,

For if you do not now repent,
  You'll share their cruel smart.
The tower in Siloam fell down,
  And eighteen men did slay;
But were there in Jerusalem
  No sinners vile as they?
I tell you, 'Tis not so: ye must
  Repent of your own sin,
Else you will likewise perish all,
  And never pardon win."

Then Christ gave forth this parable:
  "A certain man did plant
A fig tree in his vineyard good,
  Expecting fruit 'twould grant.
For this he oft would come to seek,
  Yet still no fruit he found;
Then to his gardener he said thus,
  'Why cumbers it the ground?
Go, cut it down; for, lo, three years
  I've looked thereon in vain.'
The gardener said, 'O, not so, Lord;
  Though thou mayest well complain,
Yet let me nourish it this year,
  And tend with greater care,
If fruitful then, thou wilt be pleased,
  If not, no longer spare.'"

SECTION 99.

Christ cures an Infirm Woman in the Synagogue.—Luke 13. 10-17.

As Jesus taught, one Sabbath day,
  The Jews assembled round;
Among the throng a woman stood,
  Whom Satan's power had bound
For eighteen years by sore disease;
  Most piteous was her case;
So crippled, she was bowed to earth,
  And pain was in her face.
Then Jesus said, "O woman, thou
  Art healed of thy disease."
He laid his hand on her, and soon
  Restored her health and ease.
Immediately she was made straight,
  And glorified the Lord.
The ruler of the synagogue
  This gracious deed abhorred,
And said that, on the Sabbath day
  No healing there should be;

for if ɥ dɯ not nɤ repent,
  ɥ'l ʃer ðer krɯel smart.
Ðe tɤer in Sɉlơam fel dɤn,
  and etın men did slɛ;
bɒt wer ðer in Jerɯsalem
  nơ sinerz vɉl az ðe?
Ŧ tel ɥ, 'Tiz not sơ: yı mɒst
  repent ov ɥr ơn sin,
els ɥ wil lɉkwɉz periʃ ɷl,
  and never pardon win."

Ðen Krɉst gev fơrθ ðis parabel:
  "A serten man did plant
a fig trı in hiz vinyard gud,
  ekspektiŋ frɯt 'twud grant.
For ðis hı oft wud kɒm tu sık,
  yet stil nơ frɯt hı fɤnd;
ðen tu hiz gardener hı sed ðɒs,
  'Hwɉ kɒmberz it ðe grɤnd?
Gơ, kɒt it dɤn; for, lơ, θrı yırz
  ɉ'v lukt ðeron in ven.'
Ðe gardener sed, 'Ơ, not sơ, Lord;
  ðơ ðɤ meest wel komplen,
yet let mı nɒriʃ it ðis yır,
  and tend wið greter ker,
if frɯtful ðen, ðɤ wilt bı plızd,
  if not, nơ loŋger sper.'"

SEKΣON 99.

Krɉst kɥrz an Inferm Wuman in ðe Sinagog.—Lɯk 13. 10-17.

Az Jızɒs tɷt, wɒn Sabaθ dɛ,
  ðe Jɯz asembeld rɤnd;
amɒŋ ðe θroŋ a wuman stud,
  hɯm Setan'z pɤer had bɤnd
for etın yırz bɉ sơr disız;
  mơst pitiɒs woz her kes;
sơ kripeld, ʃı woz bɤd tu erθ,
  and pen woz in her fes.
Ðen Jızɒs sed, "Ơ wuman ðɤ
  art hıld ov ðɉ disız."
Hı led hiz hand on her, and sɯn
  restơrd her helθ and ız.
Immıdietli ʃı woz med stret,
  and glơrifɉd ðe Lord.
Ðe rɯler ov ðe sinagog
  ðis greʃɒs did abhord,
and sed ðat, on ðe Sabaθ de
  nơ hıliŋ ðer ʃud bı;

Six days in each week were enough
  For works of charity.
But Christ replied, "Thou hypocrite!
  Doth not the strictest Jew
Loose cattle on the Sabbath day,
  And give them fodder due?
And may I not perform an act
  More kind and merciful
On this poor woman who has been
  So long time sorrowful?"
When he had said these words, his foes
  Were conscience-smit with shame,
And all the multitude rejoiced,
  And praised Messiah's name.

siks dez in ıɋ wik wer enɒf
  for wɒrks ov ɋariti.
Bɒt Krįst replįd, "đɜ hipokrit!
  dɒɟ not đe striktest Jɯ
lɯs katel on đe Sabaɟ de,
  and giv đem foder dų?
And me į not perform an akt
  mɵr kįnd and mersiful
on đis pɯr wuman hɯ haz bin
  sɵ loŋ tįm sorɵful?"
Hwen hi had sed điz wɒrdz, hiz fɵz
  wer konʃens-smit wiđ ʃem,
and ɷl đe mɒltitųd rejoist,
  and prezd Mesįa'z nem.

SECTION 100.

Christ journeys toward Jerusalem.
Luke 13. 18-22.

And Jesus went through many a town
  And village on the way,
As he was going to Salem, where
  His purpose was to stay.
And, noting how his holy truth
  Was spreading through the land,
He said, "God's kingdom is a power
  Which hell cannot withstand.
'Tis even like small mustard seed,
  With vigor so impressed,
It soon becomes a tree, in which
  The birds may build their nest.
Or like to leaven, which contains
  An energy so great,
It spreads through the surrounding
  And changes all its state." [mass

SEKΣON 100.

Krįst jɒrniz tɵard Jerusalem.
Lɯk 13. 18-22.

And Jizɒs went ɟrɯ meni a tɜn
  and vilej on đe we,
az hi woz gɵiŋ tu Selem, hwer
  hiz pɒrpos woz tu ste.
And, nɵtiŋ hɜ hiz hɵli trɯɟ
  woz sprediŋ ɟrɯ đe land,
hi sed, "God'z kiŋdom iz a pɜer
  hwiɋ hel kanot wiđstand.
'Tiz iven lįk smɷl mɒstard sid,
  wiđ vigor sɵ imprest,
it sɯn bekɒmz a tri, in hwiɋ
  đe berdz me bild đer nest.
Or lįk tu leven, hwiɋ kontenz
  an enerji sɵ gret,
it spredz ɟrɯ đe sɒrɜndiŋ mas,
  and ɋenjez ɷl its stet."

SECTION 101.

Christ restores to sight a Blind Man, who is summoned before the Sanhedrim.
John 9. 1-34.

And Jesus, passing by, beheld
  A man from birth quite blind;
Which caused his followers to inquire,
  "Master, whose sin consigned
This man to darkness? For his own,
  Or for his parents' fault?
Jesus replied, "For no man's sin,
  But God's power to exalt.

SEKΣON 101.

Krįst restɵrz tu sįt a Blįnd Man, hɯ iz sɒmond befɵr đe Sanhedrim.
Jon 9. 1-34.

And Jizɒs, pasiŋ bį, beheld
  a man from berɟ kwįt blįnd;
hwiɋ kɷzd hiz folɵerz tu inkwįr,
  "Master, hɯz sin konsįnd
đis man tu darknes? For hiz ɵn
  or for hiz perents' fɷlt?
Jizɒs replįd, "For nɵ man'z sin,
  bɒt God'z pɜer tu ekzɷlt.

And I must work the works of him
  That sent me while 'tis day;
The night comes when no man can
  I must work while I may. [work;
As long as I am in the world
  I am the world's true light,
But this light shines in vain on those
  Who have no mental sight."
Thus having said, upon the ground
  The Lord did spit, and made
Clay to anoint the blind man's eyes;
  Who instantly obeyed
The Lord's command, "Go, now, and
  In pure Siloam's pool;" [wash
(Siloam signifies "Sent forth,")
  He went, washed, and was whole.
The neighbours therefore, who had
  This poor blind man before, [seen
Said, "Is not this the man who sat
  And did our alms implore?"
Some said, "'Tis he;" and others said,
  "He's like him:" but the man
Himself said, "Surely, I am he."
  Therefore they all began
To question him as to the means
  By which his sight he gained.
He then explained the process, how
  His vision he attained.
They said to him, "Where is this
  He said, "I do not know." [man?"
They brought him to the Pharisees,
  With the design to show
That one who on the Sabbath day
  Would work, and thus bestow
Sight on the blind, if let alone,
  Their law would overthrow.
The Pharisees then questioned him,
  At length, and then they say,
"This man is not of God, because
  He keeps not Sabbath day."
But others said, "A sinful man
  Such wonders cannot do."
Then to the blind man they referred,
  To know what he thought true;
Who answered, "He a prophet is."
  They called his parents then,
Doubting if he were really blind.
  But they, from fear, refrain,
And say, "Our son is of full age,
  His word you should believe."

And ị mɒst wɒrk đe wɒrks ov him
  đat sent mi hwịl 'tiz de;
đe nịt kɒmz hwen nɵ man kan
  ị mɒst wɒrk hwịl ị me. [wɒrk;
Az loŋ az ị am in đe wɒrld,
  ị am đe wɒrld'z trɯ lịt,
bɒt đis lịt ʃịnz in ven on đɵz
  hɯ hav nɵ mental sịt."
Đɒs haviŋ sed, ɒpon đe grȣnd
  đe Lord did spit, and med
kle tu anoint đe blịnd man'z ịz;
  hɯ instantli ɵbed
đe Lord'z komand, "Gɵ, nȣ, and
  in pɥr Sịlɵam'z pɯl;" [woʃ
(Sịlɵam signifịz "Sent fɵrʇ,")
  hi went, woʃt, and woz hɵl.
Đe nebɒrz, đerfɵr, hɯ had sin
  đis pɯr blịnd man befɵr,
sed, "Iz not đis đe man hɯ sat
  and did ȣr ɑmz implɵr?"
Sɒm sed, "'Tiz hi;" and ɒđerz sed,
  "Hi'z lịk him:" bɒt đe man
himself sed, "Σɯrli, ị am hi."
  Đerfɵr đe ɷl began
tu kwestion him az tu đe minz
  bị hwiç hiz sịt hi gend.
Hi đen eksplend đe prɵses, hȣ
  hiz viʒon hi atend.
Đe sed tu him, "Hwer iz đis man?"
  Hi sed, "Ɨ dɯ not nɵ́."
Đe brɷt him tu đe Farisiz,
  wiđ đe dezịn tu ʃɵ
đat wɒn hɯ on đe Sabaʇ de
  wud wɒrk, and đɒs bestɵ
sịt on đe blịnd, if let alɵn,
  đer lɷ wud ɵverʇrɵ.
Đe Farisiz đen kwestiond him
  at leŋʇ, and đen đe se,
"Đis man iz not ov God, bekɷz
  hi kips not Sabaʇ de."
Bɒt ɒđerz sed, "A sinful man
  sɒç wɒnderz kanot dɯ."
Đen tu đe blịnd man đe referd,
  tu nɵ́ hwot hi ʇɷt trɯ;
hɯ anserd, "Hi a profet iz."
  Đe kɷld hiz perents đen,
dȣtiŋ if hi wer riali blịnd.
  Bɒt đe, from fir, refren,
and se, "Ȣr sɒn iz ov ful ej,
  hiz wɒrd ɥ ʃud beliv."

On which, to the blind man they say,
"Let God the praise receive,
And not this sinner." But he said,
"I know not that, in sooth,
But this I know, he made me see;
Enough for me this truth.
Would ye his followers also be?"
They scornfully replied,
"Thou art his follower, but we
Keep strict on Moses' side.
That God spake truth by him, we know;
But who speaks by this man?"
The man replied, "God doth not show
Favor to sinners vain;
But he who worships and obeys,
Shall gain his suit from heaven;
Therefore I judge him by his works;
For power to him is given."
Then did they excommunicate
This man of faith sincere;
They were too proud from lowly men
Celestial truth to hear.

On hwiq, tu ꝺe bl̨ind man ꝺe se,
"Let God ꝺe prez resiv,
and not ꝺis siner." Bɒt hi sed,
"Ɨ nó not ꝺat, in suɯt,
bɒt ꝺis ̨i nó, hi med mi si;
enɒf for mi ꝺis truɯt.
Wɯd yi hiz foloerz olso bi?"
Ꝺe skornfuli repl̨id,
"Ꝺɤ art hiz foloer, bɒt wi
kip strikt on Mozes' s̨id.
Ꝺat God spek truɯt b̨i him, wi nó
bɒt huɯ spiks b̨i ꝺis man?"
Ꝺe man repl̨id, "God dɒt not ʃo
fevor tu sinerz ven;
bɒt hi huɯ wɒrʃips and obez,
ʃal gen hiz sɥt from heven;
ꝺerfor ̨i jɒj him b̨i hiz wɒrks;
for pɤer tu him iz given."
Ꝺen did ꝺe ekskomɥniket
ꝺis man ov fet sinsir;
ꝺe wer tuɯ prɤd from loli men
selestial truɯt tu hir.

SECTION 102.

Christ declares himself the true Shepherd.
John 9. 35-41; 10. 1-21.

When Jesus heard the sentence passed
Upon this faithful one,
He went and said to him, "Dost thou
Believe in God's own Son?"
He said, "Who is he, Lord? I will."
Christ saw his heart would bow,
And answered, "Thou hast seen him; [and
He talketh with thee now."
"Lord, I believe," the poor man cried,
And worshiped Jesus then,
And did his follower become,
In spite of scornful men.

Then Jesus said, "For judgement I
Have visited this earth,
That those who see not, may enjoy
A light of heavenly birth.
And those who boast of seeing more
Than truly they discern,
May be convinced of error, and
To better reason turn.
If ye, proud Pharisees, were plunged
In helpless ignorance,

SEKΣON 102.

Kr̨ist deklerz himself ꝺe truɯ Σepher
Jon 9. 35-41; 10. 1-21.

Hwen Jizɒs herd ꝺe sentens past
ɒpon ꝺis fetful wɒn,
hi went and sed tu him, "Dɒst ꝺ
beliv in God'z on Sɒn?"
Hi sed, "Huɯ iz hi, Lord? Ɨ wil.
Kr̨ist sɷ hiz hart wud bɤ,
and anserd, "Ꝺɤ hast sin him; an
hi toket wiꝺ ꝺi nɤ."
"Lord, ̨i beliv," ꝺe puur man kr̨i
and wɒrʃipt Jizɒs ꝺen,
and did hiz foloer bekɒm,
in sp̨it ov skornful men.

Ꝺen Jizɒs sed, "For jɒjment ̨i
hav vizited ꝺis ert,
ꝺat ꝺoz huɯ si not, me enjoi
a l̨it ov hevenli bert.
And ꝺoz huɯ bost ov siiŋ mor
ꝺan truɯli ꝺe disern,
me bi konvinst ov eror, and
tu beter rizon tɒrn.
If yi, prɤd Farisiz, wer plɒnjd
in helples ignorans,

Ye would not be so criminal,
  Nor give so great offence.
But now ye boast of knowing much,
  And should indeed be wise;
Therefore your numerous sins remain,
  And o'er you tyrranise.

Truly I tell you, all that seek
  To enter heaven above
Through any other door than that
  Appointed by God's love;
And climb up by some other way,
  Or through some hole would creep,
A thief and robber is. But I,
  The shepherd of the sheep,
Go through the door; I guard my [flock;
  They hear my gentle voice,
I call my sheep by name, and they
  Walk in my steps, from choice.
And when new pasture they require,
  Then I before them go;
They know my voice, and follow me,
  Whatever way I show.
But strangers call to them in vain,
  They will not them obey,
But flee from them; their voice is
    strange,
  And would lead them astray."
This parable spake Jesus; but
  They knew not what he meant.
Then said he unto them again,
  (They list, most reverent,)
"Not only may I well be called
  The shepherd of God's sheep;
I am the very door of heaven,
  And Paradise I keep.
And all who claim a dignity
  Superior to mine,
Are but as robbers, and incur
  A penalty divine.
By me, if any enter heaven,
  They shall be saved and blessed;
Go in and out, and pasture find,
  And everlasting rest.
The thief comes not but for to steal,
  To kill, and to destroy;
I come that they may have more life,
  And more abundant joy.
I am both door and shepherd: I
  My life give for the sheep;

yi wud not bi sɵ kriminal,
  nor giv sɵ gret ofens.
Bɒt nɤ yi bɵst ov nɵiŋ mɒç,
  and ʃud indid bi wįz;
đerfɵr ɥr nɥmerɒs sinz remen,
  and ɵ'r ɥ tiranįz.

Trɯli į tel ɥ, ɷl đat sik
  tu enter heven abɒv
ɟrɯ eni ɒđer dɵr đan đát
  apointed bį God'z lɒv;
and klįm ɒp bį sɒm ɒđer wɛ,
  or ɟrɯ sɒm hɵl wud krip,
a ɟif and rober iz. Bɒt į,
  đe ʃepherd ov đe ʃip,
gɵ ɟrɯ đe dɵr; į gard mį flok;
  đɛ hir mį jentel vois,
į kɷl mį ʃip bį nem, and đɛ
  wɷk in mį steps, from çois.
And hwen nɥ pastɥr đɛ rekwįr,
  đen į befɵr đem gɵ;
đɛ nɵ mį vois, and folɵ mi,
  hwotever wɛ į ʃɵ.
Bɒt strenjerz kɷl tu đem in ven,
  đɛ wil not đem ɵbɛ,
bɒt fli from đem; đer vois iz
    strenj,
  and wud lid đem astre."
Đis parabel spɛk Jizɒs; bɒt
  đɛ nɥ not hwot hi ment.
Đen sed hi ɒntu đem agen,
  (đɛ list, mɵst reverent,)
"Not ɵnli me į wel bi kɷld
  đe ʃepherd ov God'z ʃip;
į am đe veri dɵr ov heven,
  and Paradįs į kip.
And ɷl hɯ klem a digniti
  sɥpirior tu mįn,
ar bɒt az roberz, and inkɒr
  a penalti divįn.
Bį mi, if eni enter heven,
  đɛ ʃal bi sevd and blest;
gɵ in and ɤt, and pastɥr fįnd,
  and everlastiŋ rest.
Đe ɟif kɒmz not bɒt for tu stil,
  tu kil, and tu destroi;
į kɒm đat đɛ me hav mɵr lįf,
  and mɵr abɒndant joi.
Į am bɵɟ dɵr and ʃepherd: į
  mį lįf giv for đe ʃip;

But he that is a hireling, and
  For self alone would keep
A watch; whose own the sheep are not,
  Sees danger come, and flees;
The wolf comes down, and scatters them,
  And some of them may seize.
The hireling flees because he looks
  Alone to private gain,
And cares not for the sheep, even though
  One half of them be slain.
I'm the good shepherd, and my love
  To all my sheep is such
That I will give my life for them,
  Nor reckon it too much.
I know my sheep, and they know me,
  Their true and only Lord;
As I the Father know, and am
  Known by him as the Word.
And other sheep I have, who may
  Be not of Israel's fold;
Them also I must bring, and they
  Shall have their names enrolled.
As I am the sole shepherd, so
  On earth there shall appear
One catholic, universal fold
  Of saints of every sphere.
Therefore my Father loveth me
  Because my life I give;
That life I soon will reassume,
  And then for ever live.
No man can take my life from me,
  For I alone retain
The power by which I lay it down
  And take it back again.
This is the Father's will, and I
  That will alone maintain."

SECTION 103.

Christ publicly asserts his Divinity.
John 10. 22-38.

'Twas at the Dedication's feast,
  In Sion's sacred town,
And winter chill and desolate
  O'er all the land did frown.
Then Jesus in the temple walked,
  Beneath the portico
Called Solomon's, and there the Jews
  Came the real truth to know.

bɒt hi đat iz a hįrliŋ, and
  for self alơn wud kip
a woç; huz ơn đe ʃip ar not,
  siz denjer kɒm, and fliz;
đe wulf kɒmz dɜn, and skaterz đem,
  and sɒm ov đem me siz.
Đe hįrliŋ fliz bekɷz hi luks
  alơn tu prįvet gen,
and kerz not for đe ʃip, iven đơ
  wɒn hɑf ov đem bi slen.
Ɨ'm đe gud ʃepherd, and mį lɒv
  tu ɷl mį ʃip iz sɒç
đat į wil giv mį lįf for đem,
  nor rekon it tɯ mɒç.
Ɨ nớ mį ʃip, and đe nớ mi,
  đer trɯ and ơnli Lord;
az į đe Fɑđer nớ, and am
  nơn bį him az đe Wɒrd.
And ɒđer ʃip į hav, hɯ me
  bi not ov Izrael'z fơld;
đem ɷlsơ į mɒst briŋ, and đe
  ʃal hav đer nemz enrơld.
Az į am đe sơl ʃepherd, sơ
  on erŧ đer ʃal apir
wɒn kaŧolik, ɥniversal fơld
  ov sents ov everi sfir.
Đerfơr mį Fɑđer lɒveŧ mi
  bekɷz mį lįf į giv;
đát lįf į sɯn wil riasɥm,
  and đen for ever liv.
Nơ man kan tek mį lįf from mi,
  for į alơn reten
đe pɜer bį hwiç į le it dɜn
  and tek it bak agen.
Đis iz đe Fɑđer'z wil, and į
  đát wil alơn menten.

SEKƩON 103.

Krįst pɒblikli aserts hiz diviniti.
Jon 10. 22-38.

'Twoz at đe Dedikeʃon'z fist,
  in Sįon'z sekred tɜn,
and winter çil and desolet
  ơ'r ɷl đe land did frɜn.
Đen Jizɒs in đe tempel wɷkt
  beniŧ đe pơrtikơ
kɷld Solomon'z, and đer đe Jɯz
  kem đe rial trɯŧ tu nớ.

"Leave us no more in doubt," they
"But plainly tell us, here, [cried,
If thou art the Messiah true,
Whom all men should revere."
Christ answered, "I have told you so,
But ye did not believe;
The miracles which in God's name
I work, ye should receive
As perfect evidence that I
Am the true Christ foretold,
But ye do not believe, because
Ye are not of my fold.
I call my sheep, they hear my voice,
And note its softest tone;
I know them, and they follow me,
And follow me alone.
I give to them eternal life,
And they shall never perish,
No man can pluck them from my hand;
As my life them I cherish.
My Father 'twas who gave them me,
He's greater far than all;
And none can pluck them from his
Or make the least to fall. [hand,
The Father and myself are one."
The Jews offended were
At these words, and they sought to
Him who could thus aver [stone
That he was one with God. But Christ,
Who could no fear betray,
Said, "Many wondrous miracles
Did I to you display;
For which of these do ye attempt
To stone your Savior now?"
They answer, "For no holy work,
But blasphemy; for thou,
A man, dost make thyself as God,
Who art of human birth."
Christ answered, "In your law, 'tis
The saints are gods on earth: [writ,
This scripture cannot be denied:
Why say ye, then, to me,
Whom God has sanctified and sent
This world from sin to free,
'Thou dost blaspheme;' because I say
'I am indeed God's son,
And prove it well by miracles
Which I alone have done?'
If I indeed do not perform
True miracles divine,

"Liv ɒs nɵ mɵr in dɤt," đɛ krįd,
"bɒt plenli tel ɒs, hir,
if đɤ art đe Mesįa trɯ,
hɯm ωl men ʃud revir."
Krįst anserd, "Ɨ hav tɵld ɥ sɵ,
bɒt yi did not beliv;
đe mirakelz hwiç in God'z nɛm
į wɒrk, yi ʃud resiv
az perfekt evidens đat į
am đe trɯ Krįst fɵrtɵld.
Bɒt yi dɯ not beliv, bekωz
yi ar not ov mį fɵld.
Ɨ kωl mį ʃip, đɛ hir mį vois,
and nɵt its softest tɵn;
į nɵ́ đem, and đɛ folɵ mi,
and folɵ mi alɵn.
Ɨ giv tu đem eternal lįf,
and đɛ ʃal never periʃ,
nɵ man kan plɒk đem from mį
az mį lįf đem į çeriʃ. [hand;
Mį Fɛđer 'twoz hɯ gɛv đem mi;
hi'z grɛter far đan ωl;
and nɒn kan plɒk đem from hiz
or mɛk đe list tu fωl. [hand,
Đe Fɛđer and mįself ar wɒn."
Đe Jɯz ofended wer
at điz wɒrdz, and đɛ sωt tu stɵn
him hɯ kud đɒs avér
đat hi woz wɒn wiđ God. Bɒt Krįst,
hɯ kud nɵ fir betrɛ,
sed, "Meni wɒndrɒs mirakelz
did į tu ɥ displɛ;
for hwiç ov điz dɯ yi atempt
tu stɵn ɥr Sɛvier nɤ?"
Đɛ anser, "For nɵ hɵli wɒrk,
bɒt blasfemi; for đɤ,
a man, dɒst mɛk đįself az God,
hɯ art ov hɥman berŧ."
Krįst anserd, "In ɥr lω, 'tiz rit,
Đe sɛnts ar godz on erŧ:
đis Skriptɥr kanot bi denįd:
hwį sɛ yi, đen, tu mi,
hɯm God haz saŋktifįd and sent
đis wɒrld frɒm sin tu fri,
'Đɤ dɒst blasfim;' bekωz į sɛ
'Ɨ am indid God'z sɒn,
and prɯv it wel bį mirakelz
hwiç į alɵn hav dɒn?'
If į indid dɯ not perform
trɯ mirakelz divįn,

Believe me not; but if I do,
  Believe me by this sign.
At least believe my miracles,
  Then will ye soon perceive
That God, the Father, lives in me,
  And I in him so live."

beliv mi not; bɒt if ị du,
  beliv mi bị đis sịn.
At list beliv mị mirakelz,
  đen wil yi sun persiv
đat God, đe Fɐđer, livz in mi,
  and ị in him sɵ liv."

SECTION 104.

Christ retires beyond Jordan because of the opposition of the Jews.—John 10. 39-42.

When Jesus said he was the Christ,
  God's own beloved Son,
The Jews then sought to murder him,
  As they before had done.
But he escaped, and went away
  To Jordan's wilderness,
Where John the Baptist first baptised
  And preached true righteousness.
There many came to Christ, and heard
  His gospel truth anew;
And found that all which John foretold
  Of Jesus, was most true;
And owned his miracles divine,
  And there believed on him,
Their own Messiah, though denied
  By Israel's Sanhedrim.

SEKΣON 104.

Krịst retịrz beyond Jordan bekɷz ov đe opoziʃon ov đe Juz.—Jon 10. 39-42.

Hwen Jizɒs sed hi woz đe Krịst,
  God'z ɵn belɒved Sɒn,
đe Juz đen sɷt tu mɒrder him,
  az đe befɵr had dɒn.
Bɒt hi eskept, and went awe
  tu Jordan'z wildernes,
hwer Jon đe Baptist ferst baptịzd
  and priçt tru rịtiɒsnes.
Ɛer meni kem tu Krịst, and herd
  hiz gospel truŧ anɥ;
and fȣnd đat ɷl hwiç Jon fɵrtɵld
  ov Jizɒs, woz mɵst tru;
and ɵnd hiz mirakelz divịn,
  and đer belivd on him,
đer ɵn Mesịa, đɵ denịd
  bị Izrael'z Sanhedrim.

SECTION 105.

Christ exhorts to steadfastness, and laments over Jerusalem.—Luke 13. 23-35.

One said to Jesus, "Tell us, Lord,
  Are those saved but a few?"
To whom the Savior answered, ["Strive,
  In everything you do,
For good and truth alone, and thus
  Enter the narrow gate;
For many will be found who seek
  In vain heaven's high estate.
When once the master of the house
  Hath closed the door, (now free
To welcome to celestial bliss
  All Israel's progeny,)
Then ye who still persist in sin,
  Will call, and call in vain;
For none who love what's evil, can
  To heaven admission gain.

SEKΣON 105.

Krịst ekzorts tu stedfastnes, and laments ɵver Jerusalem.—Luk 13. 23-35.

Wɒn sed tu Jizɒs, "Tel ɒs, Lord,
  ar đɵz sevd bɒt a fɥ?"
Tu hum đe Sevier anserd, "Strịv,
  in everiŧiŋ ɥ du,
for gud and truŧ alɵn, and đɒs
  enter đe narɵ get;
for meni wil bi fȣnd hu sik
  in ven heven'z hị estet.
Hwen wɒns đe master ov đe hȣs
  haŧ klɵzd đe dɵr, (nȣ fri
tu welkɒm tu selestial blis
  ɷl Izrael'z projeni,)
đen yi hu stil persist in sin,
  wil kɷl, and kɷl in ven;
for nɒn hu lɒv hwot's ivel, kan
  tu heven admiʃon gen.

Repent in time, lest ye behold
  Your ancestors, who were
Less blessed than you with heavenly
  In heaven all bright and fair, [light,
While you, who heard Christ's word
  Familiarly around, [proclaimed
Shall be cast out, to weep, and wail,
  In misery profound.
From north, and south, and east, and
  west,
  Christ's ransomed saints shall come,
And sit down in God's kingdom, as
  Their own eternal home.
And those who unto men appeared
  The last, shall be the first;
And those who seemed the first, shall
  Of all men most accurst." [be

The Pharisees then come to Christ,
  Pretending love, and say,
"Haste from this region, for thy life
  King Herod soon will slay."
Jesus replied, "Go tell that king,
  So like a fox in guile,
I still shall live my appointed time,
  In spite of every wile.
This season, and the next, I shall
  Perform my works divine,
And on the third, as I foretell,
  I shall my life resign.
Yea, in Jerusalem my life
  Its destined end will see;
A prophet cannot perish, but
  His blood must flow in thee.
Oh Salem! Oh Jerusalem!
  Who dost thy prophets slay,
And stonest those sent unto thee
  To teach thee God's own way;
How oft would I have gathered all
  Thy children 'neath my care,
Even as a hen protects her young
  From violence and snare;
And ye would not! Your house will
  All desolate be laid: [soon
And you shall never more behold
  Your king, by you betrayed,
Until with faith and penitence
  You my forgiveness claim,
And bless the Christ who comes to you
  In great Jehovah's name."

Repent in tịm, lest yi behɵld
  ɥr ansestorz, hɯ wer
les blest đan ɥ wiđ hevenli lịt,
  in heven ɷl brịt and fer,
hwịl ɥ, hɯ herd Krịst's wɒrd prɵ-
  familiarli arɤnd, [klemd
ʃal bi kast ɤt, tu wip, and wel,
  in mizeri prɵfɤnd.
From norŧ, and sɤŧ, and ist, and
  west,
  Krịst's ransomd sents ʃal kɒm,
and sit dɤn in God'z kiŋdom, az
  đer ɵn eternal hɵm.
And đɵz hɯ ɒntu men apird
  đe last, ʃal bi đe ferst;
and đɵz hɯ simd đe ferst, ʃal bi
  ov ɷl men mɵst akɒrst."

Đe Farisiz đen kɒm tu Krịst,
  pretendiŋ lɒv, and se,
"Hest from đis rijon, for đị lịf
  Kiŋ Herod sun wil sle."
Jizɒs replịd, "Gɵ, tel đát kiŋ,
  sɵ lịk a foks in gịl,
ị stil ʃal liv mị apointed tịm,
  in spịt ov everi wịl.
Đis sizon, and đe nekst, ị ʃal
  perform mị wɒrks divịn,
and on đe ŧerd, az ị fɵrtel,
  ị ʃal mị lịf rezịn.
Ye, in Jerusalem mị lịf
  its destind end wil si;
a profet kanot periʃ, bɒt
  hiz blɒd mɒst flɵ in đi.
Ɵh Selem! Ɵh Jerusalem!
  hɯ dɒst đị profets sle,
and stɵnest đɵz sent ɒntu đi
  tu tiç đi God'z ɵn we;
hɤ oft wud ị hav gađerd ɷl
  đị çildren 'niđ mị ker,
iven az a hen prɵtekts her yɒŋ
  from vịolens and sner;
and yi wud not! Ɥr hɤs wil sun
  ɷl desolet bi led:
and ɥ ʃal never mɵr behɵld
  ɥr kiŋ, bị ɥ betred,
ɒntil wiđ feŧ and penitens
  ɥ mị forgivnes klem,
and bles đe Krịst hɯ kɒmz tu ɥ
  in gret Jehɵva'z nem."

SECTION 106.

Christ dines with a Pharisee. Parable of the Great Supper.—Luke 14. 1-24.

Upon the Sabbath day, as Christ
 Sat down within the hall
Of a chief Pharisee, some watched,
 Hoping that he would fall.
And shortly, lo, a certain man
 With dropsy sick, he saw;
Then to the Pharisees and those
 Who feign to teach the law,
He said, "What think ye; is it right
 On Sabbath days to heal?"
They held their peace; by conscience
 At this divine appeal. [struck
The Lord then touched the suffering
 Bade the disease depart; [man,
And sent him, cured, unto his home
 With a rejoicing heart.
Thus Jesus made an answer true
 Unto his own demand,
And added, "Which, among you all,
 Shall find, within this land,
His ox or ass hath fallen down
 Upon the Sabbath day
Into a pit, and will not help
 To save it as he may?"
No word to this could they reply.
 Then Christ, a parable
Spake to the many guests who there
 The festive board did fill.
For he had marked that many a one
 Selected the best place;
And said, "When thou invited art
 A wedding feast to grace,
Take not the highest seat at first,
 Lest one more honored come,
And he that asked thee, then shall say,
 'Let this man have thy room.'
But humbly choose the lowest seat,
 And then, before the end,
Thy host may come to thee, and say,
 'Go higher up, my friend.'
So wilt thou honor gain with those
 Who sit at meat with thee.
While pride is destined to a fall,
 Safe is humility."

Then to his host, the Lord said thus:
 "When thou a feast would'st make,

SEKΣON 106.

Krɉst dɉnz wiđ a Farisi. Parabel ov đe Gret Sɒper.—Lɯk 14. 1-24.

Ɯpon đe Sabaɟ de, az Krɉst
 sat dɤn wiđin đe hɵl
ov a çif Farisi, sɒm woçt,
 hɵpiŋ đat hi wud fɵl.
And ʃortli, lɵ, a serten man
 wiđ dropsi sik, hi sɵ;
đen tu đe Farisiz and đɵz
 hɯ fen tu tiç đe lɵ,
hi sed, "Hwot ɟiŋk yi; iz it rɉt
 on Sabaɟ dez tu hil?"
Đe held đer pis; bɉ konʃens strɒk
 at đis divɉn apil.
Đe Lord đen tɒçt đe sɒferiŋ man,
 bad đe disiz depart;
and sent him, kɥrd, ɒntu hiz hɵm
 wiđ a rejoisiŋ hart.
Đɒs Jizɒs med an anser trɯ
 ɒntu hiz ɵn demand,
and aded, "Hwiç, amɒŋ ɥ ɵl,
 ʃal fɉnd, wiđin đis land,
hiz oks or as haɟ fɵlen dɤn
 ɒpon đe Sabaɟ de
intu a pit, and wil not help
 tu sev it az hi me?"
Nɵ wɒrd tu đis kud đe replɉ.
 Đen Krɉst, a parabel
spek tu đe meni gests hɯ đer
 đe festiv bɵrd did fil.
For hi had markt đat meni a wɒn
 selekted đe best ples;
and sed, "Hwen đɤ invɉted art
 a wediŋ fist tu gres,
tek not đe hɉest sit at ferst,
 lest wɒn mɵr onord kɒm,
and hi đat askt đi, đen ʃal se,
 'Let đis man hav đɉ rɯm.'
Bɒt hɒmbli çɯz đe lɵest sit,
 and đen, befɵr đe end,
đɉ hɵst me kɒm tu đi, and se,
 'Gɵ hɉer ɒp, mɉ frend.'
Sɵ wilt đɤ onor gen wiđ đɵz
 hɯ sit at mit wiđ đi.
Hwɉl prɉd iz destind tu a fɵl,
 sef iz hɥmiliti."

Đen tu hiz hɵst, đe Lord sed đɒs:
 "Hwen đɤ a fist wud'st mek,

Call not the rich, nor friends alone,
  Thy bounty to partake;
Lest they invite thee in return,
  And give thee recompense;
But make thy feast to bless the poor;
  To blind and lame dispense.
Then shalt thou truly blessèd be,
  Though they cannot reward;
For at the resurrection day
  God will thy deed regard."

These words then touched the heart of one
  Among those favored guests,
Who spoke to Jesus, "Blest is he
  That in God's kingdom feasts."
Then Jesus said, "Remember this:
  One day a certain man
Laid out a supper for his friends,
  And ere the feast began,
His servant went abroad, to say,
  'All things are ready; come.'
But each began to make excuse,
  One said, 'I stay at home
Because a wife I lately took,
  And cannot leave her now;'
Another, 'I have cattle bought,
  I must remain to plough.'
Another said, 'Excuse me, sir,
  I've bought a piece of ground,
And I must needs go see to it.'
  These things the servant found,
And told his lord, who then was wroth,
  And sent him forth with speed
To call the poor, the lame, the blind,
  Who gave him better heed.
''Tis done,' he said, 'as thou dost wish,
  And yet there is more room.'
'Then go,' the master gave command,
  'And press into my home
The humblest from the highway sides
  And lanes, my house to crowd;
Those who refused, shall never be
  Around my board allowed.'"

kꙩl not đe riç, nor frendz alɵn,
  đį bɜnti tu partek;
lest đe invįt đi in retɒrn,
  and giv đi rekompens;
bɒt mek đį fist tu bles đe pur;
  tu blįnd and lem dispens.
Đen ʃalt đɜ truli blesed bi,
  đɵ đe kanot reword;
for at đe rezɒrekʃon de
  God wil đį did regard."

Điz wɒrdz đen tɒçt đe hart ov wɒn
  amɒŋ đɵz fevord gests,
hu spɵk tu Jizɒs, "Blest iz hi
  đat in God'z kiŋdom fists."
Then Jizɒs sed, "Remember đis:
  wɒn de a serten man
led ɜt a sɒper for hiz frendz,
  and er đe fist began,
hiz servant went abrꙩd, tu se,
  'Ꙩl ɟiŋz ar redi; kɒm.'
Bɒt iç began tu mek ekskɥs,
  wɒn sed, 'Ɨ ste at hɵm
bekꙩz a wįf į letli tuk,
  and kanot liv her nɜ;'
anɒđer, 'Ɨ hav katel bꙩt,
  į mɒst remen tu plɜ.'
Anɒđer sed, 'Ekskɥz mi, ser,
  į'v bꙩt a pis ov grɜnd,
and į mɒst nidz gɵ si tu it.'
  Điz ɟiŋz đe servant fɜnd,
and tɵld hiz lord, hu đen woz rꙩɟ,
  and sent him fɵrɟ wiđ spid
tu kꙩl đe pur, đe lem, đe blįnd,
  hu gev him beter hid.
''Tiz dɒn,' hi sed, 'az đɜ dɒst wiʃ,
  and yet đer iz mɵr rum.'
'Đen gɵ,' đe master gev komand,
  and pres intu mį hɵm
đe hɒmblest from đe hįwe sįdz
  and lenz, mį hɜs tu krɜd;
đɵz hu refɥzd, ʃal never bi
  arɜnd mį bɵrd alɜd.'"

SECTION 107.

Christ's Disciples must forsake the world.
Luke 14. 25-33.

Great multitudes then followed Christ,
  To whom he turnèd, and said,

SEKΣON 107.

Krįst's Disįpelz mɒst forsek đe wɒrld.
Luk 14. 25-33.

Gret mɒltitɥdz đen folɵd Krįst,
  tu hum hi tɒrnd, and sed,

"To follow me is difficult,
 For he that would be made
My true disciple, must forsake
 His nearest, dearest friends,
If they oppose God's holy will
 For worldly selfish ends.
Yea his own life must not be dear;
 But he must bear his cross,
If he would follow me, and count
 All earthly gain as dross.

For which of you intending to
 Construct a noble tower,
Will not first count the cost, and see
 Whether he hath the power?
Lest men should mark his failure, and
 Say, with derision meet,
'Lo, this man once began to build,
 And never could complete.'

Or, if a king would battle give
 Unto another king,
He will consult if lesser hosts
 'Gainst greater he should bring.
Else ere his enemy comes near,
 He'll send to sue for peace,
That he, before the conflict, may
 Obtain a safe release.

Even so, no man can truly be
 Disciple of his Lord,
Who doth not everything forsake
 That hindrance would afford.

Religion, like its emblem, salt,
 Is in itself most good;
But if it lose true zeal, with which
 It should be still imbued,
It wants the vital energy,
 And free-will-offering power
Which none but heavenly grace divine
 Can give, or can restore.
Without this self-devotion, even
 Religon's self will be
A poor, rejected, selfish form
 Of mean hypocrisy."

SECTION 108.

Parable of the Lost Sheep, and of the lost Piece of Silver.—Luke 15. 1-10.

Then publicans and sinners came
 To hear Christ's gracious speech;

"Tu folɵ mi iz difikɒlt,
 for hi đat wud bi med
mį trɯ disįpel, mɒst forsek
 hiz nirest, direst frendz,
if đe opɵz God'z hɵli wįl
 for wɒrldli selfiʃ endz.
Yɛ hiz ɵn lįf mɒst not bi dir;
 bɒt hi mɒst bɛr hiz kros,
if hi wud folɵ mi, and kɜnt
 ɵl erɟli gen az dros.

For hwiq ov ɥ intendiŋ tu
 konstrɒkt a nɵbel tɜer,
wil not ferst kɜnt đe kost, and si
 hweđer hi haɟ đe pɜer?
lest men ʃud mark hiz felɥr, and
 sɛ, wiđ derizon mit,
'Lɵ, đis man wɒns began tu bild,
 and never kud komplit.'

Or, if a kiŋ wud batel giv
 ɒntu anɒđer kiŋ,
hi wil konsɒlt if leser hɵsts
 'genst greter hi ʃud briŋ.
Els ɛr hiz enemi kɒmz nir,
 hi'l send tu sɥ for pis,
đat hi, befɵr đe konflikt, mɛ
 obten a sɛf relis.

Ɩven sɵ, nɵ man kan trɯli bi
 disįpel ov hiz Lord,
hɯ dɒɟ not everiɟiŋ forsɛk
 đat hindrans wud afɵrd.

Relijon, lįk its emblem, sɵlt,
 iz in itself mɵst gud;
bɒt if it lɯz trɯ zil, wiđ hwiq
 it ʃud bi stil imbɥd,
it wonts đe vįtal enerji
 and fri-wil-oferiŋ pɜer
hwiq nɒn bɒt hevenli gres divįn
 kan giv, or kan restɵr.
Wiđɜt đis self-devɵʃon, iven
 relijon'z self wil bi
a pɯr, rejekted, selfiʃ form
 ov min hipokrisi."

SEKΣON 108.

Parabel ov đe Lost Σip, and ov đe lost Pis ov Silver.—Lɯk 15. 1-10.

Đen pɒblikanz and sinerz kem
 tu hir Krįst's greʃɒs spiq;

Proud Scribes, and prouder Pharisees,
  With anger heard him teach;
And said, "How base a man is this,
  Such sinners to receive;
Yea, as a friend at their repasts,
  His company to give."
This parable Christ therefore spoke:
  "If one of you possess
A hundred sheep, and one is lost,
  Will he not soon express
His anxious care, and leave the flock
  Whose number far surpast,
To seek until he find that one?
  Then brings it home in haste,
And with rejoicing heart he calls
  His friends and neighbours too,
And saith to them, 'Rejoice with me,
  My lost sheep here you view.'
So likewise, say I unto you,
  More joy shall be in heaven
Over one sinner that repents,
  And hath his sins forgiven,
Than over ninety-nine just ones,
  Who need no special care,
Because they long have virtuous been,
  And God's true children are.

Again: suppose a woman hath
  Ten silver pieces bright,
And loseth one; will she not go,
  With diligence, to light
Her candle, and make earnest search,
  Till she her treasure see?
Then to her friends she saith, 'Rejoice
  In my recovery.'
Likewise again I say to you,
  Great joy shall be in heaven
Over one sinner that repents,
  And hath his sins forgiven."

prɤd Skrịbz, and prɤder Farisiz,
  wiđ aŋger herd him tiç;
and sed, "Hɤ bes a man iz đis,
  sɒç sinerz tu resiv;
ye, az a frend at đer repasts,
  hiz kɒmpani tu giv."
Đis parabel Krịst đerfɵr spɵk:
  "If wɒn ov ɥ pozes
a hɒndred ʃip, and wɒn iz lost,
  wil hi not suun ekspres
hiz aŋkʃɒs ker, and liv đe flok
  huuz nɒmber far sɒrpast,
tu sik, ɒntil hi fịndz đát wɒn?
  Đen briŋz it hɵm in hest,
and wiđ rejoisiŋ hart hi kɵlz
  hiz frendz and nebɒrz tuu,
and seƫ tu đem, 'Rejois wiđ mi,
  mị lost ʃip hir ɥ vɥ.'
Sɵ lịkwịz, se ị ɒntu ɥ,
  Mɵr joi ʃal bi in heven
ɵver wɒn siner đat repents,
  and haƫ hiz sinz forgiven,
đan ɵver nịnti-nịn jɒst wɒnz,
  huu nid nɵ speʃal ker,
bekɵz đe loŋ hav vertɥɒs bin,
  and God'z truu çildren ar.

Agen: sɒpɵz a wuman haƫ
  ten silver pisez brịt,
and luuzeƫ wɒn; wil ʃi not gɵ,
  wiđ dilijens, tu lịt
her kandel, and mek ernest serç,
  til ʃi her treʒur si?
Đen tu her frendz ʃi seƫ, 'Rejois
  in mị rekɒveri.'
Lịkwịz agen ị se tu ɥ,
  Gret joi ʃal bi in heven
ɵver wɒn siner đat repents,
  and haƫ hiz sinz forgiven."

SECTION 109.

Parable of the Prodigal Son.
Luke 15. 11-32.

Another parable Christ spoke
  To these stern Pharisees;
And said, "A man who had two sons,
  And would the younger please,
Divided unto each his share
  Of wealth, and left him free.

SEKΣON 109.

Parabel ov đe Prodigal Sɒn.
Luuk 15. 11-32.

Anɒđer parabel Krịst spɵk
  tu điz stern Farisiz;
and sed, "A man huu had túú sɒnz,
  and wud đe yɒŋger pliz,
divịded ɒntu iç hiz ʃer
  ov welƫ, and left him fri.

On this he soon determined that
  A distant land he'd see ;
And there his substance soon he wastes
  In vain and sinful mirth ;
And when he had no more to spend,
  There came a mighty dearth.
Then, in his need, he joined himself
  To one of that same part,
Who sent him out to feed his swine,
  With sorely humbled heart.
So hungry was he, he would eat
  The food of those vile beasts ;
For no man gave to him. He thought,
  'Even the servant feasts
Within my father's house ; while I
  Here only hunger know !
I will arise, and leave this place,
  And to my father go,
And say to him, I've sinned, and am
  To heaven and thee a foe.
Not worthy am I any more
  To bear the name of son ;
Make me a hired servant, and
  Thy will shall e'er be done.'
And he arose, and came to him.
  But e'er he reached his home,
His father saw him, ran to him,
  And said, 'My son is come.'
He kissed him, fell upon his neck,
  And did compassion show.
The son said, 'I have sinned, and am
  To heaven and thee a foe :
I am not worthy any more
  To bear the name of son.'
The father to the servants said,
  'Attend me, everyone ;
Bring forth the best robe, put it on ;
  A ring put on his hand ;
Put shoes upon his feet, and let
  Him in my presence stand :
Bring forth the fatted calf and kill ;
  We'll eat, and we'll be glad ;
For this my son was dead, was lost,
  He's found ; no more be sad.'
So they were filled with festive joy,
  And song and dance prevailed,
To welcome home the long-lost son,
  No more with tears bewailed.
The elder son came from the field,
  And knew not what this meant ;

On đis hi sɯn determind đat
  a distant land hį'd si ;
and đer hiz sɒbstans sɯn hi wests
  in ven and sinful merϑ ;
and hwen hi had nơ mơr tu spend,
  đer kem a mįti derϑ.
Đen, in hiz nid, hi joind himself
  tu wɒn ov đát sem part,
hɯ sent him ɜt tu fid hiz swįn,
  wiđ sơrli hɒmbeld hart.
Sơ hɒŋgri woz hi, hi wud it
  đe fɯd ov đơz vįl bists ;
for nơ man gev tu him. Hi ϑɑt,
  'Ɩven đe servant fists
wiđin mį fɑđer'z hɜs ; hwįl į
  hir ơnli hɒŋger nớ !
Ɨ wil arįz, and liv đis ples,
  and tu mį fɑđer gơ,
and se tu him, Ɨ'v sind, and am
  tu heven and đi a fơ.
Not wɒrđi am į eni mơr
  tu ber đe nem ov sɒn ;
mek mi a hįrd servant, and
  đį wil ʃal er bi dɒn.'
And hi arơz and kem tu him.
  Bɒt er hi riçt hiz hơm,
hiz fɑđer sɑ him, ran tu him,
  and sed, 'Mį sɒn iz kɒm.'
Hi kist him, fel ɒpon hiz nek,
  and did kompaʃon ʃơ.
Đe sɒn sed, 'Ɨ hav sind, and am
  tu heven and đi a fơ :
į am not wɒrđi eni mơr
  tu ber đe nem ov sɒn.'
Đe fɑđer tu đe servants sed,
  'Atend mi, everiwɒn ;
briŋ fơrϑ đe best rơb, put it on ;
  a riŋ put on hiz hand ;
put ʃɯz ɒpon hiz fit, and let
  him in mį prezens stand :
briŋ fơrϑ đe fated kɑf and kil ;
  wi'l it, and wi'l bi glad ;
for đis mį sɒn woz ded, woz lost,
  hi'z fɜnd ; nơ mơr bi sad.'
Sơ đe wer fild wiđ festiv joi,
  and soŋ and dans preveld,
tu welkɒm hơm đe loŋ-lost sɒn,
  nơ mơr wiđ tirz beweld.
Đe elder sɒn kem from đe fild,
  and nų not hwot đis ment ;

He called a servant forth to ask,
  With curious ear attent;
Who said, 'Thy brother is returned,
  Thy father's joy is filled,
He hath received him safe and sound,
  The fatted calf is killed.'
With jealous wrath the brother then
  Refused to enter there,
And when his father did entreat,
  He answered, 'Thou didst spare
To give me even a festive kid,
  Though many years I served
Thee with obedience filial,
  Nor from my duty swerved.
As soon as this thy son was come,
  Who hath devoured thy living,
For him is killed the fatted calf;—
  'Tis merciless forgiving.'
'Son,' said the father tenderly,
  'All that I have is thine,
Thou in my house dost ever live,
  On thee my grace doth shine.
'Tis meet that we should now rejoice,
  And signs of gladness give;
Thy brother who was lost, is found;
  Was dead, but now doth live.'"

hį kɷld a servant fɷrꝥ tu ask,
  wiđ kɥrips ır atent;
hɯ sed, 'Ꝺį brɒđer iz retɒrnd,
  đį fɐđer'z joi iz fild,
hį haꝥ resıvd him sεf and sɜnd,
  đe fated kɐf iz kild.'
Wiđ jelɒs rɐꝥ đe brɒđer đen
  refɥzd tu enter đer,
and hwen hiz fɐđer did entrit,
  hį anserd, 'Ꝺɜ didst sper
tu giv mı ıven a festiv kid,
  đɷ meni yırz į servd
đı wiđ ɷbıdiens filial,
  nor from mį dɥti swervd.
Az sɯn az đis đį sɒn woz kɒm,
  hɯ haꝥ devɜrd đį liviŋ,
for him iz kild đe fated kɐf;—
  'tiz mersiles forgiviŋ.'
'Sɒn,' sed đe fɐđer tenderli,
  'ɷl đat į hav iz đįn,
đɜ in mį hɜs dɒst ever liv,
  on đı mį gres dɒꝥ ſįn.
'Tiz mit đat wı ſud nɜ rejois,
  and sįnz ov gladnes giv;
đį brɒđer hɯ woz lost, iz fɜnd;
  woz ded, bɒt nɜ dɒꝥ liv.'"

SECTION 110.

Parable of the Unjust Steward.
Luke 16. 1-13.

Christ also spake this parable,
  To teach men equity.
"A certain rich man had a steward
  Of doubtful honesty.
His master one day summoned him
  To render his account;
But he had wasted property
  Unto a vast amount,
And could not pay his lord the sum
  Due, as he had been wont.
Then did this unjust steward begin
  Within himself to say,
'What shall I do? I have no means
  My lord's account to pay.
I will not turn to honest toil,
  To meet his just demand;
Nor will I sue or beg, lest I
  Covered with shame should stand.

SEKΣON 110.

Parabel ov đe Unjɒst Stɥard.
Lɯk 16. 1-13.

Krįst ɷlsɷ spek đis parabel,
  tu tiɋ men ekwiti.
"A serten riɋ man had a stɥard
  ov dɜtful onesti.
Hiz master wɒn dε sɒmond him
  tu render hiz akɜnt;
bɒt hį had wεsted properti
  ɒntu a vast amɜnt,
and kud not pe hiz lord đe sɒm
  dɥ, az hį had bin wɒnt.
Ꝺen did đis ɒnjɒst stɥard begin
  wiđin himself tu sε,
'Hwot ſal į dɯ? Ɨ hav nɷ mınz
  mį lord'z akɜnt tu pε?
Ɨ wil not tɒrn tu onest toil,
  tu mit hiz jɒst demand;
nor wil į sɥ or beg, lest į
  kɒverd wiđ ſem ſud stand.

But I a piece of craft may do,
  To make my debts appear
Less weighty in my master's eyes
  Than really they are.
Unto the other debtors, who
  Owe to my lord, I'll go,
And teach them all my crafty arts,
  My guile on them bestow;
And show them how to make their debts
  Appear so small and light,
They will make common cause with me
  In putting wrong for right.
Then when I lose my office, they
  Will offer me a home
In gratitude, for teaching them
  Dishonest to become.'
Think you his lord did e'er commend
  This steward, so unjust,
Because by subtle craft he could
  Thus violate his trust?
(For worldlings oft are more astute
  Than righteous men will be?)
I tell you, Nay, there is no charm
  In such dishonesty.
Ye cannot thus impose on God,
  Or on his angels fair.
By no unrighteous fraud or guile
  Can you their friendship share,
And gain access to Paradise,
  And deathless realms of bliss;
For only faithful souls obtain
  Such happiness as this.
He who is faithful in small things,
  Will also be in great;
And he who cheats in trifles, would
  Plunder a large estate.
If ye, respecting earthly goods,
  Show craftiness and stealth,
How can ye hold the sacred trust
  Of heaven's eternal wealth?
If ye, the entrusted goods ye keep
  For others, have abused;
Celestial riches, which should be
  Your own, will be refused.
Ye cannot truly serve two lords,
  By any known device;
Ye cannot serve a holy God,
  And live in avarice."

Bɒt į a pis ov kraft me dɯ,
  tu mek mį dets apir
les weti in mį master'z įz
  đan riali đe ar.
Ɯntu đe ɒđer deterz, hɯ
  ɵ tu mį lord, į'l gɵ,
and tiç đem ɷl mį krafti arts,
  mį gįl on đem bestɵ;
and ʃɵ đem hȣ tu mek đer dets
  apir sɵ smɷl and lįt,
đe wil mek komon kɷz wiđ mi
  in putiŋ roŋ for rįt.
Đen hwen į lɯz mį ofis, đe
  wil ofer mi a hɵm
in gratitɥd, for tiçiŋ đem
  disonest tu bekɒm.'
Ŧiŋk ɥ hiz lord did er komend
  đis stɥard, sɵ ɒnjɒst,
bekɷz bį sɒtel kraft hi kud
  đɒs vįolet hiz trɒst?
(For wɒrldliŋz oft ar mɵr astɥt
  đan rįtiɒs men wil bi.)
Ɨ tel ɥ, Ne, đer iz nɵ çarm
  in sɒç disonesti.
Yi kanot đɒs impɵz on God,
  or on hiz enjelz fer.
Bį nɵ ɒnrįtiɒs frɷd or gįl
  kan ɥ đer frendʃip ʃer,
and gen akses tu Paradįs,
  and deŧles relmz ov blis;
for ɵnli feŧful sɵlz obten
  sɒç hapines az đis.
Hi hɯ iz feŧful in smɷl ŧiŋz,
  wil ɷlsɵ bi in gret;
and hi hɯ çits in trįfelz, wud
  plɒnder a larj estet.
If yi, respektiŋ erŧli gudz,
  ʃɵ kraftines and stelŧ,
hȣ kan yi hɵld đe sekred trɒst
  ov heven'z eternal welŧ?
If yi, đe entrɒsted gudz yi kip
  for ɒđerz, hav abɥzd;
selestial riçez, hwiç ʃud bi
  ɥr ɵn, wil bi refɥzd.
Yi kanot truli serv tɯ́ lordz,
  bį eni nɵn devįs;
yi kanot serv a hɵli God,
  and liv in avaris."

SECTION 111.

Christ reproves the Pharisees.
Luke 16. 14-17.

The Pharisees, whose hearts were full
  Of covetousness base,
Derided Christ's pure doctrinals
  Of heavenly love and grace.
And Jesus said to them, " Ye seek
  To appear to erring men
As masters of all sanctity,
  That ye their praise may gain;
But God doth know your hearts, and hates
  Your vile hypocrisy:
Your bigot pride, and pomp, and craft,
  Are loathsome in his eye.
The law and prophets were in force
  Till John the Baptist came
To preach salvation to mankind
  In Christ's more holy name.
Since then, God's gospel kingdom is
  Wide opened unto all;
And all true men press into it,
  Obedient to my call."

SEKΣON 111.

Krịst repruvz đe Farisiz.
Luk 16. 14-17.

Đe Farisiz, huz harts wer ful
  ov kɒvetɒsnes bes,
derịded Krịst's pɥr doktrinalz
  ov hevenli lɒv and gres.
And Jizɒs sed tu đem, " Yi sịk
  tu apịr tu eriŋ men
az masterz ov ɷl saŋktiti,
  đat yi đer prez me gen;
bɒt God dɒŧ nó ɥr harts, and hets
  ɥr vịl hipokrisi:
ɥr bigot prịd, and pomp, and kraft,
  ar lɵđsɒm in hiz ị.
Đe lɷ and profets wer in fɵrs
  til Jon đe Baptist kem
tu priç salvɛʃon tu mankịnd
  in Krịst's mɵr hɵli nem.
Sins đen, God'z gospel kiŋdom iz
  wịd ɵpend ɒntu ɷl;
and ɷl tru men pres intu it,
  ɵbịdient tu mị kɷl."

SECTION 112.

Christ answers a question concerning Marriage and Divorce.

Matthew 19. 3-12. Mark 10. 2-12.
Luke 16. 18.

The Pharisees then came to him,
  And asked him, " Is it right
For men to put away their wives,
  And thus to disunite
The marriage bond, for every cause?"
  He said to them, " What light
Does Moses give on this?" They said,
  " The law on this is clear:
He gives a writing of divorce,
  Then leaves her without fear."
And Jesus answered, " This harsh law
  God's love could not ordain;
The hardness of your hearts it was
  That did this law obtain.
Have ye not read that he who made
  Mankind at the beginning,
A male and female nature made,
  That they, in no wise sinning,

SEKΣON 112.

Krịst anserz a kwestion konserniŋ Marɛj and Divɵrs.

Maŧɥ 19. 3-12. Mark 10. 2-12.
Luk 16. 18.

Đe Farisịz đen kem tu him,
  and askt him, " Iz it rịt
for men tu put awe đer wịvz,
  and đɒs tu disɥnịt
đe marɛj bond, for everi kɷz?"
  Hi sed tu đem, " Hwot lịt
dɒz Mɵzes giv on đis?" Đe sed,
  " Đe lɷ on đis iz klịr:
hi givz a rịtiŋ ov divɵrs,
  đen livz her wiđɒt fịr."
And Jizɒs anserd, " Đis harʃ lɷ
  God'z lɒv kud not orden;
đe hardnes ov ɥr harts it woz
  đat did đis lɷ obten.
Hav yi not red đat hi hu med
  mankịnd at đe beginiŋ,
a mel and fimel netɥr med,
  đat đe, in nɵ wịz siniŋ,

Might live in holy wedlock, as
  Two persons, but one mind;
Each seeing in the other what
  In self they cannot find?
And all who thus in love unite,
  Are to each other nearer
Than to their parents, and should cleave
  To one another dearer.
What God has so united, ne'er
  By man should severed be
For lesser cause, or smaller crime
  Than proved adultery.
One who divorces a true wife,
  And doth another wed,
Is guilty of adultery,
  Whatever may be said.
And one who marries such a wife,
  Thus falsely put away,
Is guilty of adultery,
  Whatever men may say."

Then Christ's disciples said to him,
  "If such the marriage tie,
'Tis better not to wed, and spend
  One's life in misery."
He answered, "All men cannot live
  In loveless single state;
But only those whose nature is
  Adapted for such fate.
Some lead a single life because
  They think it holiest,
Let those who can support such life
  Do so—for them 'tis best."

SECTION 113.

Christ receives and blesses little children.

Matthew 19. 13-16. Mark 10. 13-17. Luke 18. 15-18.

Some little children then they brought
  To Christ, that he might bless them,
And put his hands on them, and pray,
  And lovingly caress them.
And the disciples were displeased
  At this officiousness;
They knew not Jesus' loving heart,
  Felt not his tenderness.
And Jesus was displeased with them,
  And took the parents' part;

mįt liv in hɵli wedlok, az
  túı personz, bɒt wɒn mįnd;
iɕ siiŋ in ɗe ɒɗer hwot
  in self ɗɛ kanot fįnd?
And ɷl huı ɗɒs in lɒv ɥnįt,
  aɼ tu iɕ ɒɗer nirer
ɗan tu ɗer perents, and ʃud kliv
  tu wɒn ánɒɗer direr.
Hwot God haz sɵ ɥnįted, nɛr
  bį man ʃud severd bi
for leser kɷz, or smɷler krįm
  ɗan pruıvd adɒlteri.
Wɒn huı diversez a truı wįf,
  and dɒɟ anɒɗer wed,
iz gilti ov adɒlteri,
  hwotever mɛ bi sed.
And wɒn huı mariz sɒɕ a wįf,
  ɗɒs fɷlsli put awɛ,
iz gilti ov adɒlteri,
  hwotever men mɛ sɛ."

ɗen Krįst's disįpelz sed tu him,
  "If sɒɕ ɗe marej tį,
'tiz beter not tu wed, and spend
  wɒn'z lįf in mizeri."
Hį anserd, "ɷl men kanot liv
  in lɒvles siŋgel stɛt;
bɒt ɵnli ɗɵz huız netɥr iz
  adapted for sɒɕ fɛt.
Sɒm lid a siŋgel lįf bekɷz
  ɗɛ ɟiŋk it hɵliest,
let ɗɵz huı kan sɒpɵrt sɒɕ lįf
  duı sɵ—for ɗem 'tiz best."

SEKΣON 113.

Krįst resivz and blesez litel ɕildren.

Maɟɥ 19. 13-16. Mark 10. 13-17. Luık 18. 15-18.

Sɒm litel ɕildren ɗen ɗɛ brɷt
  tu Krįst, ɗat hį mįt bles ɗem,
and put hiz handz on ɗem, and prɛ,
  and lɒviŋli karés ɗem.
And ɗe disįpelz wer displįzd
  at ɗis ofiʃɒsnes;
ɗɛ nɥ not Jįzɒs' lɒviŋ hart,
  felt not hiz tendernes.
And Jįzɒs woz displįzd wiɗ ɗem,
  and tuk ɗe perents' part;

These little ones he loved to see,
  And clasp them to his heart.
" Suffer the little ones," he said;
  " Forbid them not, to come;
Of such, indeed, God's kingdom is,
  And heaven shall be their home.
If anyone doth not receive
  God's kingdom as a child,
He shall obtain no place therein."
  They looked on him and smiled.
And then he took them in his arms,
  And unto them he gave
His blessing, with his gentle touch;
  For such he loved to save.

điz litel wɒnz hi lɒvd tu si,
  and klasp đem tu hiz hart.
" Sɒfer đe litel wɒnz," hi sed;
  " forbid đem not, tu kɒm;
ov sɒç, indid, God'z kiŋdom iz,
  and heven ʃal bi đεr hɷm.
If eniwɒn dɒđ not resiv
  God'z kiŋdom az a çįld,
hi ʃal obten nɷ ples đerin."
  Đe lukt on him and smįld.
And đen hi tuk đem in hiz armz,
  and ɒntu đem hi gev
hiz blesiŋ, wiđ hiz jentel tɒç;
  for sɒç hi lɒvd tu sev,

SECTION 114.

Parable of the Rich Man and Lazarus.
Luke 16. 19-31.

A certain rich man lived in state,
  And dressed in garments fine,
Of purple and soft linen made;
  And sumptuously did dine.
And at this rich man's gate there lay
  A beggar, very poor,
Whose name was Lazarus: he sought
  The crumbs upon the floor
That fell at all the rich man's meals.
  He was afflicted sore.
The rich man no compassion showed,
  But let his dogs molest,
By licking the pȯor beggar's wounds;
  Thus was he sore distressed.
The beggar died, and angels bright
  Carried him far away
To Abraham's bosom, there to dwell
  In joyous, endless day.
The rich man also died, and he
  Was buried in great state.
And then in hell he lifts his eyes,
  In torments desperate,
And seeth Abraham far off,
  With Lazarus, in heaven.
Urged by his agony intense,
  And by his sufferings driven,
He cried, " O father Abraham,
  Have mercy on me now,
Send Lazarus that he may cool
  My burning tongue and brow

SEKΣON 114.

Parabel ov đe Riç Man and Lazarɒs.
Lɯk 16. 19-31.

A serten riç man livd in stεt,
  and drest in garments fįn,
ov pɒrpel and soft linen med;
  and sɒmptųɒsli did dįn.
And at đis riç man'z gεt đer lε
  a beger, veri pɯr,
hɯz nεm woz Lazarɒs: hi sɷt
  đe krɒmz ɒpon đe flɷr
đat fel at ɷl đe riç man'z milz.
  Hi woz aflikted sɷr.
Đe riç man nɷ kompaʃon ʃɷd,
  bɒt let hiz dogz molest,
bį likiŋ đe pɯr beger'z wɯndz;
  đɒs woz hi sɷr distrest.
Đe beger dįd, and εnjelz brįt
  karid him far awe
tu Ɛbraham'z bɯzom, đer tu dwel
  in joiɒs, endles dε.
Đe riç man ɷlsɷ dįd, and hi
  woz berid in gret stεt.
And đen in hel hi lifts hiz įz,
  in torments desperεt,
and sieđ Ɛbraham far ɷf,
  wiđ Lazarɒs, in heven.
Ɯrjd bį hiz agoni intens,
  and bį hiz sɒferiŋz driven,
hi krįd, " Ɵ fɑder Ɛbraham,
  hav mersi on mi nʊ,
send Lazarɒs đat hi mε kɯl
  mį bɒrniŋ tɒŋ and brʊ

With but one drop of water. I'm
  Tormented in this flame."
But Abraham said, "Remember, son,
  Thy good things thou didst claim
On earth, and sought no better then,
  While Lazarus did smart;
But now his comfort he receives,
  And thou tormented art.
Besides, 'tween us a gulf is fixed,
  And none go to and fro."
The rich man said, "I pray thee, then,
  That Lazarus may go
Unto my father's house, to save
  Five brethren from this woe."
But Abraham said, "Not so; for they
  God's holy word may read:
Let them hear those whom God in-
  spired;
  They have no further need."
The rich man still besought one might
  Go to them from the grave:
But he replied, "If they hear not
  God's word, nought else will save."

wiđ bɒt wɒn drop ov wɷter. Ŧ'm
  tormented in đis flem."
Bɒt Ɛbraham sed, "Remember,
  đị gud ɟiŋz đɤ didst klem [sɒn,
on erɟ, and sɷt nơ beter đen,
  hwịl Lazarɒs did smart;
bɒtnɤ hiz kɒmfort hi resivz,
  and đɤ tormented art.
Besịdz, 'twin ɒs a gɒlf iz fikst,
  and nɒn gơ tɯ and frơ."
Đe riç man sed, "Ŧ pre đi, đen,
  đat Lazarɒs me gơ
ɒntu mị feđer'z hɤs, tu sev
  fịv bređren from đis wơ."
Bɒt Ɛbraham sed, "Not sơ; for đe
  God'z hơli wɒrd me rid:
let đem hir đơz hɯm God in-
  spịrd;
  đe hav nơ fɒrđer nid."
Đe riç man stil bésɷt wɒn mịt
  gơ tu đem from đe grev:
bɒt hi replịd, "If đe hir not
  God'z wɒrd, nɷt els wil sev."

SECTION 115.

On Forgiveness of Injuries.—Luke 17. 1-10.

Then said the Lord to those who sought
  His wise commands to hear,
"Perversions always will arise,
  Their cause is ever near;
But woe to him through whom they
  come;
  God's judgements he should fear.
'Twere better far that such a one
  In deepest sea were cast,
Than that he should pervert one soul
  Whose trust in me is placed.
Keep ward and watch at all times. If
  Thy brother should transgress,
Reprove him; if he should repent,
  Forgive with gentleness.
If seven times on the self-same day
  He should offend; yet turn,
And say, 'Again I do repent;'
  Let not your anger burn."
Then the apostles said to him,
  "Increase our faith, O Lord."
And he replied, "If, like a grain
  Of mustard seed, 'tis stored

SEKΣON 115.

On Forgivnes ov Injuriz.—Luk 17. 1-10.

Đen sed đe Lord tu đơz hɯ sɷt
  hiz wịz komandz tu hir,
"Perverʃonz ɷlwez wil arịz,
  đer kɷz iz ever nir;
bɒt wơ tu him ɟrɯ hɯm đe
  kɒm;
  God'z jɒjments hi ʃud fir.
'Twer beter far đat sɒç a wɒn
  in dipest si wer kast,
đan đat hi ʃud pervert wɒn sơl
  hɯz trɒst in mi iz plest.
Kip word and woç at ɷl tịmz. If
  đị brɒđer ʃud transgres,
reprɯv him; if hi ʃud repent,
  forgiv wiđ jentelnes.
If seven tịmz on đe self-sem de
  hi ʃud ofend; yet tɒrn,
and se, 'Agen ị dɯ repent;'
  let not ɥr aŋger bɒrn."
Đen đe aposelz sed tu him,
  "Inkris ɤr feɟ, Ơ Lord."
And hi replịd, "If, lịk a gren
  ov mɒstard sid, 'tiz stơrd

With grace to grow and thrive, ye shall
 Say to this tree, Remove ;
And it shall be : so great the power
 Of living faith and love."
If one of you a servant hath,
 And calls him to attend
Upon your wants before his own,
 Will ye that man commend
Because he does what you desire ?
 Not such are human ways.
So likewise when ye shall perform
 All God's commands, no praise
Bestow upon yourselves ; but say,
 With true humility,
'Our duty only we have done,
 No profit can we be.' "

wiđ gres tu grɵ and ŧrɪv, yi ʃal
 se tu đis tri, Remuv ;
and it ʃal bi : sɵ gret đe pʚer
 ov liviŋ feŧ and lɒv."
If wɒn ov ɥ a servant haŧ,
 and kɷlz him tu atend
ɒpon ɥr wonts befɵr hiz ɵn,
 wil yi đát man komend
bekɷz hi dɒz hwot ɥ dezɪr ?
 Not sɒꞔ ar hɥman wez.
Sɵ lɪkwɪz hwen yi ʃal perform
 ɷl God'z komandz, nɵ prez
bestɵ ɒpon ɥrselvz ; bɒt se,
 wiđ trɯ hɥmiliti,
'Ȣr dɥti ɵnli wi hav dɒn,
 nɵ profit kan wi bi.' "

BOOK VIII.

SECTION 116.

Christ journeys towards Jerusalem.
Luke 9. 51-56.

And when the time drew near that
 Christ
 (His work being almost done,)
Should be receivèd up to heaven,
 (The victory then won,)
He set his face that he might go
 Unto Jerusalem.
And messengers he sent before
 His face, who, when they came
Into a village on the road,
 (Samaritans dwelt there,)
Entreated for a house which they
 For Jesus might prepare.
But the Samaritans would not
 Receive their Lord nor them,
Because his purpose was to go
 On to Jerusalem.
When his disciples James and John
 Saw this, their anger rose,
Because they deemed Samaritans
 To be their natural foes.
They asked permission of their Lord
 That they might there command
A fire to come from heaven, and thus
 Consume that wicked land ;

BUK VIII.

SEKΣON 116.

Krɪst jɒrniz tɵardz Jerɯsalem.
Lɯk 9. 51-56.

And hwen đe tɪm drɯ nir đat
 Krɪst
 (hiz wɒrk biiŋ ɷlmɵst dɒn,)
ʃud bi resived ɒp tu heven,
 (đe viktori đen wɒ́n,)
hi set hiz fes đat hi mɪt gɵ
 ɒntu Jerɯsalem.
And mesenjerz hi sent befɵr
 hiz fes, hɯ, hwen đe kem
intu a vilej on đe rɵd,
 (Samaritanz dwelt đer,)
entrited for a hʚs hwiꞔ đe
 for Jizɒs mɪt preper.
Bɒt đe Samaritanz wud not
 resiv đer Lord nor đem,
bekɷz hiz pɒrpos woz tu gɵ
 on tu Jerɯsalem.
Hwen hiz disɪpelz Jemz and Jon
 sɷ đis, đer aŋger rɵz,
bekɷz đe dimd Samaritanz
 tu bi đer natɥral fɵz.
Đe askt permiʃon ov đer Lord
 đat đe mɪt đer komand
a fɪr tu kɒm from heven, and đɒs
 konsɥm đát wiked land ;

Even as Elijah did of old.
He turned, rebuked their zeal,
And said, "Ye know not what the kind
Of spirit ye reveal.
I am not come to slay men's lives;
I came all wrongs to heal."
They traveled to another place,
Abashed by this appeal.

SECTION 117.

Christ heals Ten Lepers.—Luke 17. 11-19.

Entering a village on his way,
Christ heard a piteous cry,
Which moved his ever generous heart
To tender sympathy.
Ten leprous men at distance stood,
And lifted up their voice;
"Have mercy, Jesus, Lord, we pray,
Let us once more rejoice."
That look which ne'er from misery,
Was turned, soon saw their woe.
He said, "Go ye unto the priests;
To them your cases show."
They went, and as they walked were cleansed;
So great the Healer's power;
Yet only one of all that ten
Felt grateful in that hour.
One, a despised Samaritan,
Perceiving he was healed,
Returned, and with loud voice declared
God's glory was revealed.
Before his Savior's feet he fell,
To offer grateful praise,
While Jesus sadly thought upon
Man's base and selfish ways.
And Jesus said, "Were not ten cleansed,
Where are the other nine?"
Then to this stranger thus he said,
"Blest is true faith like thine."

SECTION 118.

Christ declares the humility of his kingdom, and the sudden destruction of Jerusalem.
Luke 17. 20-37.

The Pharisees then asked the Lord
When God's reign should appear.

ịven az Elịja did ov ơld.
Hị tɒrnd, rebụkt đer zịl,
and sed, "Yị nơ not hwot đe kịnd
ov spirit yị revịl.
Ị am not kɒm tu sle men'z lịvz;
ị kem ωl roŋz tu hịl."
Đe traveld tu anɒđer ples,
abaʃt bị đis apịl.

SEKΣON 117.

Krịst hilz Ten Leperz.—Lɯk 17. 11-19.

Enteriŋ a vilej on hiz we,
Krịst herd a pitiɒs krị,
hwiç mɯvd hiz ever jenerɒs hart
tu tender simpaθi.
Ten leprɒs men at distans stud,
and lifted ɒp đer vois;
"Hav mersi, Jịzɒs, Lord, wị pre,
let ɒs wɒns mơr rejois."
Đát luk hwiç ner from mizeri
woz tɒrnd, sɯn sω đer wơ.
Hị sed, "Gơ yị ɒntu đe prịsts;
tu đem ụr kesez ʃơ."
Đe went, and az đe wωkt wer klenzd;
sơ gret đe Hịler'z pɤer;
yet ơnli wɒn ov ωl đát ten
felt gretful in đát ɤr.
Wɒn, a despịzd Samaritan,
persịviŋ hị woz hịld,
retɒrnd, and wiđ lɤd vois deklerd
God'z glơri woz revịld.
Befơr hiz Sevier'z fịt hị fel,
tu ofer gretful prez,
hwịl Jịzɒs sadli θωt ɒpon
man'z bes and selfiʃ wez.
And Jịzɒs sed, "Wer not ten klenzd,
hwer ar đe ɒđer nịn?"
Đen tu đis strenjer đɒs hị sed,
"Blest iz trɯ feθ lịk địn."

SEKΣON 118.

Krịst deklerz đe hụmiliti ov hiz kiŋdom, and đe sɒden destrɒkʃon ov Jerɯsalem.
Lɯk 17. 20-37.

Đe Farisịz đen askt đe Lord
hwen God'z ren ʃud apịr.

He said, " 'Tis not an outward show ;
  'Tis not, Lo here ! Lo there !
Within your hearts God's kingdom is,
  For him those hearts prepare."
To his disciples then, he said,
  " The days are nigh at hand
When ye shall wish to hear once more
  Your loving Lord's command
But for a day. 'Twill be in vain.
  Attend and understand.
Many will strive to make you think
  The Son of man is come ;
Believe them not nor follow them,
  Lest ye partake their doom.
As lightning's flash lights up the sky,
  Or as a shining ray
Of light in darkness, shall the Son
  Of man be in his day.
But ere that time, the Son of man
  Must suffer cruel pain,
And be rejected, scorned, and then
  By wicked hands be slain.
And as in Noah's faithless age,
  The world would not repent,
But ate, and drank, and married wives,
  With sensual life content,
Till the great flood destroyed them all :
  And as in later days,
They drank, sold, planted, built, nor
  For their Creator's praise : [cared
While Lot was saved, vile Sodom was
  All suddenly laid low,—
Even so the Son of man shall come
  His mighty power to show.
In that day, let not any wait
  His earthly wealth to save,
Or in the house, or in the field,
  Lest it should prove his grave.
Remember Lot's wife's awful fate,
  Nor seek by evil measure
To save your life, lest you should lose
  A far more precious treasure.
In that dark hour, two men shall be
  Of everything bereft ;
While resting in their bed, one will
  Be taken, and one left.
Two women, also, at the mill
  Will labor side by side,
Lo ! one is gone ; the other still
  In safety doth abide.

Hį sed, " 'Tiz not an ɤtward ʃơ ;
  'tiz not, Lơ hir ! Lơ đer !
Wiđin ụr harts God'z kiŋdom iz,
  for him đơz harts preper."
Tu hiz disįpelz đen, hį sed,
  " Đe dez ar nį at hand
hwen yį ʃal wiʃ tu hir wɒns mơr
  ụr lɒviŋ Lord'z komand
bɒt for a dɛ. 'Twil bį in ven.
  Atend and ɒnderstand.
Meni wil strįv tu mek ụ ɟiŋk
  đe Sɒn ov man iz kɒm ;
belįv đem not nor folơ đem,
  lest yį partek đer duɯm.
Az lįtniŋ'z flaʃ lįts ɒp đe skį,
  or az a ʃįniŋ re
ov lįt in darknes, ʃal đe Sɒn
  ov man bį in hiz dɛ.
Bɒt ɛr đát tįm, đe Sɒn ov man
  mɒst sɒfer kruɯel pɛn,
and bį rejekted, skornd, and đen
  bį wiked handz bį slen.
And az in Nơa'z fetles ɛj,
  đe wɒrld wud not repent,
bɒt ɛt, and draŋk, and marid wįvz,
  wiđ senʃual lįf kontent,
til đe grɛt flɒd destroid đem ωl :
  and az in leter dez,
đɛ draŋk, sơld, planted, bilt, nor
  for đer Kriɛter'z prez : [kɛrd
hwįl Lot woz sevd, vįl Sodom woz
  ωl sɒdenli led lơ,—
įven sơ đe Sɒn ov man ʃal kɒm
  hiz mįti pɤer tu ʃơ.
In đát dɛ, let not eni wɛt
  hiz erɟli welɟ tu sɛv,
or in đe hɤs, or in đe fild,
  lest it ʃud pruɯv hiz grev.
Remember Lot's wįf's ωful fɛt,
  nor sik bį įvel meʒur
tu sɛv ụr lįf, lest ụ ʃud luɯz
  a far mơr preʃɒs treʒur.
In đát dark ɤr, tú men ʃal bį
  ov everiɟiŋ bereft ;
hwįl restiŋ in đer bed, wɒn wil
  bį tɛken, and wɒn left.
Tú wimen, ωlsơ, at đe mil
  wil lebor sįd bį sįd,
lơ ! wɒn iz gon ; đe ɒđer stil
  in sefti dɒɟ abįd.

Two men are standing in the field
  In full security;
The one is taken, and one left.
  Slight not this prophecy."
They answering, said to him, "Where
      Lord?"
  He said to them, "Take heed;
Wherever carrion is found,
  The eagles come to feed."

Tú men ar standiŋ in đe fild
  in ful sekɥriti;
đe wɒn iz teken, and wɒn left.
  Sljt not đis profesi."
Đe anseriŋ, sed tu him, "Hwer
      Lord?"
  Hi sed tu đem, "Tek kid;
hwerever karion iz fɤnd,
  đe igelz kɒm tu fid."

SECTION 119.

Christ teaches the necessity of earnestness in prayer.—Luke 18. 1-8.

Then Jesus spake a parable
  To teach that men must pray
Without distrust or weariness,
  Though God awhile delay.
"A judge within a city lived,
  Who feared not God nor man;
A widow in that city sought
  Justice from him to gain.
Awhile he would not her regard.
  At last he reasoned thus:
'I fear not man, nor even God,
  But yet I must discuss
This widow's case, lest she should tire
  Me with her frequent plaint.'
The Lord said, "Hear what this judge
      saith:
  Much more should ye not faint.
Will not the just God, his elect,
  Who cry by day and night,
In time avenge, though now he seems
  Their earnest prayer to slight?
I tell you that he will avenge,
  And that right speedily;
Yet when the Son of man shall come,
  Will he find constancy?"

SEKΣON 119.

Krjst tiçez đe nesesiti ov ernestnes in prer.—Luk 18. 1-8.

Đen Jizɒs spek a parabel
  tu tiç đat men mɒst pre
wiđɤt distrɒst or wirines,
  đo God ahwjl dele.
"A jɒj wiđin a siti livd,
  hu fird not God nor man;
a wido in đát siti sot
  jɒstis from him tu gen.
Ahwjl hi wud not her regard.
  At last hi rizond đɒs:
'J fir not man, nor iven God,
  bɒt yet j mɒst diskɒs
đis wido'z kes, lest ʃi ʃud tjr
  mi wiđ her frikwent plent.'
Đe Lord sed, "Hir hwot đis jɒj
      set:
  mɒç mor ʃud yi not fent.
Wil not đe jɒst God, hiz elekt,
  hu krj bj de and njt,
in tjm avenj, đo nɤ hi simz
  đer ernest prer tu sljt?
J tel ɥ đat hi wil avenj,
  and đát rjt spidili;
yet hwen đe Sɒn ov man ʃal kɒm
  wil hi fjnd konstansi?"

SECTION 120.

Parable of the Publican and the Pharisee. Luke 18. 9-14.

Again, this parable he spake
  To the self-righteous class
Who boasted of their goodness, and
  Despised the vulgar mass.

SEKΣON 120.

Parabel ov đe Pɒblikan and đe Farisi. Luk 18. 9-14.

Agen, đis parabel hi spek
  tu đe self-rjtiɒs klas
hu bosted ov đer gudnes, and
  despjzd đe vɒlgar mas.

" Two men up to the temple went,
  To offer there a prayer ;
The one, a Pharisee, stood here,
  The Publican stood there.
The Pharisee, with solemn face,
  Prayed thus within himself :
'I thank thee, God, I am not like
  Those who take other's pelf ;
Or an adulterer ; not I ;
  Nor like that publican.
I fast two days in every week,
  I give tithes as I can.'
The Publican afar off stood,
  Nor dared to raise his eyes ;
But smote his breast with earnest zeal ;
  'Be merciful,' he cries,
'O God, to me a sinner vile.'
  I tell you," Jesus said,
"This man 'fore God was justified,
  While that, his evils fed."

SECTION 121.

From the conduct of the young ruler Christ cautions his disciples against the dangers of wealth.

**Matthew 19. 16-30. Mark 10. 17-31.
Luke 18. 18-30.**

A certain ruler of the Jews,
  A young and wealthy man,
Once ran and kneeled before the Lord,
  And this address began :—
"Good master, what thing shall I do,
  Eternal life to gain ?
What shall I do, what leave undone,
  My object to obtain ?"
Then Jesus said, "Why call'st me good ?
  There is none good but God.
Thou knowest the commands. They [are
  To endless life the road.
Do not commit adultery,
  And do not kill nor steal,
Bear no false witness, honor thou
  Thy parents, seek their weal."
The ruler answered him, and said,
  "All these I've kept from youth."
Jesus beheld, and loved him much
  For his desire of truth,

" Tɯ́ men ɒp tu đe tempel went,
  tu ofer đer a prɛr :
đe wɒn, a Farisi, stud hir,
  đe Pɒblikan stud đɛr.
Đe Farisi, wiđ solem fɛs,
  pred đɒs wiđin himself :
'Ɨ ɟaŋk đi, God, i̧ am not li̧k
  đɵz hɯ tɛk ɒđer'z pelf ;
or an adɒlterer ; not i̧ ;
  nor li̧k đát pɒblikan.
Ɨ fást tɯ́ dɛz in everi wik,
  i̧ giv ti̧đz az i̧ kan.'
Đe Pɒblikan afar of stud,
  nor dɛrd tu rɛz hiz i̧z ;
bɒt smɵt hiz brest wiđ ernest zil ;
  'Bi mersiful,' hi kri̧z,
'Ɵ God, tu mi a siner vi̧l.'
  Ɨ tel ų," Jizɒs sed,
"đis man 'fɵr God woz jɒstifi̧d,
  hwi̧l đát, hiz ivelz fed."

SEKΣON 121.

From đe kondɒkt ov đe yɒŋ ruler Kri̧st kɑʃonz hiz disi̧pelz agenst đe denjerz ov welθ.

**Maɟų 19. 16-30. Mark 10. 17-31.
Lɯk 18. 18-30.**

A serten ruler ov đe Jɯz,
  a yɒŋ and welɟi man,
wɒns ran and nild befɵr đe Lord,
  and đis adres began :—
"Gud master, hwot ɟiŋ ʃal i̧ dɯ,
  eternal li̧f tu gɛn ?
Hwot ʃal i̧ dɯ, hwot liv ɒndɒn,
  mi̧ objekt tu obtɛn ?"
Đen Jizɒs sed, "Hwi̧ kɑl'st mi gud ?
  đer iz nɒn gud bɒt God.
Đɤ nɵest đe komandz. Đɛ ar
  tu endles li̧f đe rɵd.
Dɯ not komit adɒlteri,
  and dɯ not kil nor stil,
bɛr nɵ fɑls witnes, onor đɤ
  đi̧ perents, sik đer wil."
Đe rɯler anserd him, and sed,
  "Ɑl điz i̧'v kept from ųɟ."
Jizɒs beheld, and lɒvd him mɒç
  for hiz dezi̧r ov trɯɟ,

And then replied, "Yet one thing thou
Dost lack, and it is this:
Self-sacrificing charity;
This is celestial bliss
Go, sell thy great estates, and on
The poor bestow thy wealth;
Not proudly, ostentatiously,
But do it as by stealth;
And thou in heaven shalt treasure
gain."
The young man heard this word,
And went away in grief, for he
Had large possessions stored.
When Jesus saw his grief, he said,
"How hard it is for those
Who seek their joy in wealth, to find
Delight in heaven's repose.
'Tis easier for a camel tall
To go through a needle's eye,
Than for the rich to enter heaven
With earthly dignity."
And they that heard it, wondering,
said,
"Who then is salvable?"
And Jesus said to them, "With God
All things are possible."
Then Peter said, "Lord, what shall
Thy chosen followers, gain; [we,
We who have left all worldly goods,
Thy gospel to maintain?"
Jesus replied, "When I shall sit
Enthroned in glory bright
Above the highest heavens, then ye
Shall be arrayed in light,
And on twelve thrones shall sit, to
The tribes of Israel. [judge
(That judgement is by truth, the Lord
Did in this way foretell.)
And everyone who for my sake,
And for my Gospel free,
Gives up his relatives, or friends,
Or valued property,
Shall gain, even in this present world,
More blest associations,
And better wealth, though not un-
With cruel tribulations, [mixed
And in the world to come shall find
Ineffable delight;
Where many great shall be the least,
And all earth's wrongs made right."

and đen replįd, "Yet wɒn ɟiŋ đ
dɒst lak, and it iz đis:
self-sakrifįziŋ çariti;
đis iz selestial blis.
gɷ, sel đį gret estets, and on
đe pɯr bestɷ đį welɟ;
not prʊdli, ostenteʃɒsli,
bɒt dɯ it az bį stelɟ;
and dʊ in heven ʃalt treʒur
gen."
Đe yɒŋ man herd đis wɒrd,
and went awe in grif, for hi
had larj pozeʃonz stɷrd.
Hwen Jizɒs sɷ hiz grif, hi sed,
"Hʊ hard it iz for đɷz
hɯ sik đer joi in welɟ, tu fįnd
delįt in heven'z repɷz.
'Tiz izier for a kamel tɷl
tu gɷ ɟrɯ a nidel'z į,
đan for đe riç tu enter heven
wiđ erɟli digniti."
And đe đat herd it, wɒnderi
sed,
"Hɯ đen iz salvabel?"
And Jizɒs sed tu đem, "Wiđ G
ɷl ɟiŋz ar posibel."
Đen Piter sed, "Lord, hwot ʃal
đį çɷzen folɷerz, gen;
wi hɯ hav left ɷl wɒrldli gudz
đį gospel tu menten?"
Jizɒs replįd, "Hwen į ʃal sit
enɟrɷnd in glɷri brįt
abɒv đe hįest hevenz, đen yi
ʃal bi ared in lįt,
and on twelv ɟrɷnz ʃal sit, tu j
đe trįbz ov Izrael.
(Đat jɒjment iz bį trɯɟ, đe Lo
did in đis we fɷrtel.)
And everiwɒn hɯ for mį sek,
and for mį Gospel fri,
givz ɒp hiz relativz, or frendz,
or valɥd properti,
ʃal gen, iven in đis prezent wɒ
mɷr blest asɷʃieʃonz,
and beter welɟ, đɷ not ɒnmikst
wiđ krɯel tribɥleʃonz,
and in đe wɒrld tu kɒm ʃal fįnd
inefabel delįt;
hwer meni gret ʃal bi đe list,
and ɷl erɟ's roŋz med rįt."

SECTION 122.

Parable of the Laborers in the Vineyard.
Matthew 20. 1-16.

" God's kingdom's like a man who
  His laborers at morn [hires
To work within his vineyard till
  The evening shall return.
He looks again at noon for men,
  And sees some idly stand;
'Go, work for me,' he says, 'I'll pay.'
  They follow his command.
At later hours he also seeks,
  And others still obey.
To some he speaks at the last hour,
  'Why idle all the day?'
'No man hath hired us,' they reply.
  'Into my vineyard go,'
He says, 'and I will pay what's right,
  And what that is, I know.'
At evening all were called to take
  Their hire, and all received
Like wages for unequal time;
  Whereat the first were grieved,
And said, 'It is not fair that those
  Who labored but one hour
Should have the same as we, who
    toiled,
  Through the day's heat and power.'
'For this did I engage,' said he.
  'Why murmur? Can I not
Of that which is mine own dispose,
  And as I choose, allot?
Though ye are envious, I am good,
  And justly act to you.
So will I make the first the last,
  From many, take a few.' "

SEKΣON 122.

Parabel ov đe Lɛborerz in đe Vinyard.
Maɟų 20. 1-16.

" God'z kiŋdom'z lįk a man hɯ hįrz
  hiz lɛborerz at morn
tu wɒrk wiđin hiz vinyard til
  đe ivniŋ ʃal retɒrn.
Hi luks agen at nɯn for men,
  and siz sɒm įdli stand;
'Gɵ, wɒrk for mi,' hi sez, 'į'l pɛ.'
  Đɛ folɵ hiz komand.
At leter ɜrz hi ɷlsɵ siks,
  and ɒđerz stil ɵbe.
Tu sɒm hi spiks at đe last ɜr,
  'Hwį įdel ɷl đe dɛ?'
'Nɵ man haɟ hįrd ɒs,' đe replį.
  'Intu mį vinyard gɵ,'
hi sez, 'and į wil pɛ hwot's rįt,
  and hwot đát iz, į nɵ́.'
At ivniŋ ɷl wer kɷld tu tek
  đer hįr, and ɷl resivd
lįk wejez for ɒnikwal tįm;
  hwerat đe ferst wer grivd,
and sed, 'It iz not fer đat đɵz
  hɯ lebord bɒt wɒn ɜr
ʃud hav đe sem az wi, hɯ
    toild
  ɟrɯ đe dɛ'z hit and pɜer.'
'For đis did į engej,' sed hi.
  'Hwį mɒrmɒr? Kan į not
ov đát hwiç iz mįn ɵn dispɵz,
  and az į çɯz, alot?
Đɵ yi ar envips, į am gud,
  and jɒstli akt tu ų.
Sɵ wil į mɛk đe ferst đe last,
  from meni, tɛk a fų.' "

SECTION 123.

Christ is informed of the Sickness of Lazarus.—John 11. 1-16.

A certain man named Lazarus,
  Who lived in Bethany,
Was sick. And he two sisters had,
  Mary and Martha they.
And Jesus loved this family,
  And often them would meet;

SEKΣON 123.

Krįst iz informd ov đe siknes ov Lazarɒs.—Jon 11. 1-16.

A serten man nemd Lazarɒs,
  hɯ livd in Beɟani,
woz sik. And hi tɯ́ sisterz had,
  Meri and Marɟa đɛ.
And Jizɒs lɒvd đis famili,
  and ofen đem wud mit;

And Mary had anointed him,
  And washed his sacred feet
With her own tears of penitence,
  And wiped them with her hair;
And now their brother Lazarus
  Was seized with sickness there.
The sisters sent to him, and said,
  "He who has won thy love,
Is sore diseased." Then Christ replied,
  "Have faith in God above.
This sickness only ends in death,
  God's glory to reveal,
And me, the Son, to glorify,
  Who pain and death can heal."
Now Jesus loved these sisters dear,
  And also Lazarus;
And when he heard that he was sick,
  Nowise solicitous
To go to him, two other days
  He stayed in that same place,
And then to his disciples said,
  "Let us our steps retrace
To Judah's coast." They said, "The
  Of late thy life would slay; [Jews
And wilt thou dare to venture there,
  Despite their cruelty?"
Jesus replied, "There is a time
  For truth to shine abroad,
If men walk in the light of truth,
  They cannot miss their road;
But if they walk amid the night
  Of ignorance, they fall
In thousand errors dire and deep,
  Which wrap them like a pall."
Then Jesus added, "Lazarus sleeps,
  But I go that I may
Awaken him from sleep, and soon
  Restore him to the day."
Then his disciples said, "If he
  But sleep, he health will gain."
Then Jesus said, "The sleep I mean
  Is death's own fatal chain.
And I, for your sakes, am rejoiced
  I was not there before,
That your weak faith may be con-
  In my Almighty power." [firmed
Then Thomas said, "Let us go too,
  That if our Master die,
We may die with him, cheered with
  To live immortally." [hope

and Meri had anointed him,
  and woʃt hiz sekred fit
wiđ her ɵn tirz ov penitens,
  and wįpt đem wiđ her her;
and nɤ đer brɒder Lazarɒs
  wɒz sizd wiđ siknes đer.
Ɑe sisterz sent tu him, and sed,
  "Hi hɯ haz wɒ́n đį lɒv,
iz sɵr disizd." Ɑen Krįst replįd,
  "Hav feŧ in God abɒv.
Ɑis siknes ɵnli endz in deŧ,
  God'z glɵri tu revil,
and mi, đe Sɒn, tu glɵrifį,
  hɯ pen and deŧ kan hil."
Nɤ Jizɒs lɒvd điz sisterz dir,
  and ωlsɵ Lazarɒs;
and hwen hi herd đat hi woz sik,
  nɵwįz solisitɒs
tu gɵ tu him, tɯ́ ɒđer dez
  hi sted in đát sem ples,
and đen tu hiz disįpelz sed,
  "Let ɒs ɤr steps ritres
tu Jɯda'z kɵst." Ɑe sed, "Ɑe
  ov let đį lįf wud sle; [Jɯz
and wilt đɤ der tu ventįr đer,
  despįt đer krɯelti?"
Jizɒs replįd, "Ɑer iz a tįm
  for trɯŧ tu ʃįn abrωd,
if men wωk in đe lįt ov trɯŧ,
  đe kanot mis đer rɵd;
bɒt if đe wωk amid đe nįt
  ov ignorans, đe fωl
in ŧɤzand erorz dįr and dip,
  hwiç rap đem lįk a pωl."
Ɑen Jizɒs aded, "Lazarɒs slips,
  bɒt į gɵ đat į me
awekon him from slip, and sɯn
  restɵr him tu đe de."
Ɑen hiz disįpelz sed, "If hi
  bɒt slip, hi helŧ wil gen."
Ɑen Jizɒs sed, "Ɑe slip į min
  iz deŧ's ɵn fetal çen.
And į, for įr seks, am rejoist
  į woz not đer befɵr,
đat įr wik feŧ me bi konfermd
  in mį ωlmįti pɤer."
Ɑen Tomas sed, "Let ɒs gɵ tɯ,
  đat if ɤr Master dį,
wi me dį wiđ him, çird wiđ hɵp
  tu liv immortali."

SECTION 124.

Christ again predicts his Sufferings and Death.

Matthew 20. 17-19. Mark 10. 32-34. Luke 18. 31-34.

As Christ and his disciples went
To high Jerusalem,
The holy Savior thus foretold
His future lot to them:
"All that the prophets of old time
Spoke of the Son of man
Must be accomplished, for God's will
Runs smooth since time began.
In that Jerusalem, to which
I now the last time go,
I shall be cruelly betrayed
Unto a powerful foe.
Yea, to the chief priests, and the scribes
Delivered I shall be,
Who will condemn me unto death
By their unjust decree.
By Roman Gentiles I shall be
Mocked, scourged, and crucified,
For they will slay the Son of man,
As hath been prophesied.
And on the third day I shall rise."
The mystery of this speech,
The cruel scenes therein foretold,
Their reason could not reach.

SEKΣON 124.

Krįst agen predikts hiz Sɒferiŋz and Deθ.

Maŧų 20. 17-19. Mark 10. 32-34. Luɯk 18. 31-34.

Az Krįst and hiz disįpelz went
tu hį Jeruɯsalem,
đe hơli Sεvier đɒs fơrtơld
hiz fųtųr lot tu đem:
"Ɯl đat đe profets ov ơld tįm
spơk ov đe Sɒn ov man
mɒst bi akompliʃt, for God'z wíl
rɒnz smuɯđ sins tįm began.
In đát Jeruɯsalem, tu hwiç
į nɤ đe last tįm gơ,
į ʃal bi kruɯelli betrεd
ɒntu a pɤerful fơ.
Yε, tu đe çif prists, and đe skrįbz,
deliverd į ʃal bi,
huɯ wil kondem mi ɒntu deŧ
bį đεr ɒnjɒst dekri.
Bį Rơman Jentįlz į ʃal bi
mokt, skɒrjd, and kruɯsifįd,
for đε wil slε đe Sɒn ov man,
az haŧ bin profesįd.
And on đe ŧerd dε į ʃal rįz."
Đe misteri ov đis spiç,
đe kruel sinz đerin fơrtơld,
đεr rizon kud not riç.

SECTION 125.

Ambition of Zebedee's Sons.

Matthew 20. 20-28. Mark 10. 35-45.

The wife of Zebedee, (whose sons
Were James and John,) drew near,
And begged that Jesus Christ would grant
Unto her children dear,
The first place in his kingdom; and
That they should sit renowned
On either hand of Christ, when he
With glory should be crowned.
"Ye know not what ye ask," said Christ
To them. "It cannot be.
Can ye drink of my cup of woe,
And pain, and agony?
And can ye be baptised with me
In my own baptistry?"

SEKΣON 125.

Ambiʃon ov Zebedi'z Sɒnz.

Maŧų 20. 20-28. Mark 10. 35-45.

Đe wįf ov Zebedi, (huɯz sɒnz
wer Jεmz and Jon,) druɯ nir,
and begd đat Jizɒs Krįst wud grant
ɒntu her çildren dir,
đe ferst plεs in hiz kiŋdom; and
đat đε ʃud sit renɤnd
on įđer hand ov Krįst, hwen hi
wiđ glơri ʃud bi krɤnd.
"Yi nơ not hwot yi ask," sed Krįst
tu đem. "It kanot bi.
Kan yi driŋk ov mį kɒp ov wơ,
and pεn, and agoni?
And kan yi bi baptįzd wiđ mi
in mį ơn baptistri?"

They say, "We can." And Jesus said,
"Of my cup ye shall drink,
And with my baptism ye shall be
Baptised; but do not think
To gain from me the foremost place;
It is not mine to give,
Except to those who are prepared,
And who now for it live."
And when the ten disciples heard
The ambition of these two,
They were with indignation moved,
And great their anger grew.
But Jesus called them, and he said,
"High rank, and titles grand,
Are sought by this world's rulers, who
Bear lordship o'er the land:
But so it shall not be with you,
My faithful followers blest;
For he whose heart aspires to be
Superior to the rest,
Must be your minister; and he
That would be deemed the chief,
Must be, of all, the servant true,
In love, and toil, and grief.
Your glory is humility,
For I, of man the Son,
Came on the earth to minister,
Not to be waited on;
To give my life a ransom for
The life of everyone.

SECTION 126.

Two Blind Men healed at Jericho.

Matthew 20. 29-34. Mark 10. 46-52.
Luke 18. 35-43.

Jesus and his disciples next
Came unto Jericho;
And as they left that town, a crowd
Went after them, and lo,
The tumult of the multitude,
In passing, caught the ears
Of two blind men, who sat and begged,
And roused their hopes or fears.
They ask the reason of the noise;
The people quickly say
That Jesus Christ of Nazareth
Is passing by that way.
His fame they knew, and eager cried,
"Have mercy on us, Lord,

Đɛ sɛ, "Wi kan." And Jizɒs sed,
"Ov mį kɒp yi ʃal driŋk,
and wiđ mį baptizm yi ʃal bi
baptįzd; bɒt dɯ not ɟiŋk
tu gɛn from mi đe fɵrmɵst plɛs;
it iz not mįn tu giv,
eksɛpt tu đɵz hɯ ar prepɛrd,
and hɯ nȣ for it liv."
And hwen đe ten disįpelz herd
đe ambiʃon ov điz tɯ́,
đɛ wer wiđ indignɛʃon mɯvd,
and grɛt đer aŋger grɯ.
Bɒt Jizɒs kɷld đem, and hi sed,
"Hį raŋk, and tįtelz grand,
ar sɷt bį đis wɒrld'z rɯlerz, hɯ
ber lordʃip ɵ'r đe land:
bɒt sɵ it ʃal not bi wiđ ų,
mį feɟful folɵerz blest;
for hi hɯz hart aspįrz tu bi
sųpirior tu đe rest,
mɒst bi ųr minister; and hi
đat wud bi dimd đe çif,
mɒst bi, ov ɷl, đe servant trɯ,
in lɒv, and toil, and grif.
Ųr glɵri iz hųmiliti,
for į, ov man đe Sɒn,
kɛm on đe erɟ tu minister,
not tu bi wɛted on;
tu giv mį lįf a ransom for
đe lįf ov ɛveriwɒn."

SEKΣON 126.

Tɯ́ Blįnd Men hild at Jerikɵ.

Maɟų 20. 29-34. Mark 10. 46-52.
Lɯk 18. 35-43.

Jizɒs and hiz disįpelz nekst
kɛm ɒntu Jerikɵ;
and az đɛ left đát tȣn, a krȣd
went after đem, and lɵ,
đe tųmɒlt ov đe mɒltitųd,
in pasiŋ, kɷt đe irz
ov tɯ́ blįnd men, hɯ sat and begd,
and rȣzd đer hɵps or firz.
Đɛ ask đe rizon ov đe noiz;
đe pipel kwikli sɛ
đat Jizɒs Krįst ov Nazareɟ
iz pasiŋ bį đát wɛ.
Hiz fɛm đɛ nų, and iger krįd,
"Hav mersi on ɒs, Lord,

Jesus, thou son of David, hear."
  The people checked their word.
But they, with earnestness, the more
  Cried out, "O David's son,
Have mercy! O have mercy, Lord."
  That mercy now was won.
Jesus stood still, and called them both.
  To Bartimæus then
They say, "Be glad, he calleth thee."
  Then rose these poor blind men.
Timæus' son cast off his cloak
  And walked, with great delight,
To Christ; who asked, "What would'st
    thou have?"
  "O Lord, restore my sight."
Yea, both cried, "Open, Lord, our
  Jesus' compassions flow; [eyes."
He touched their eyes; "Receive thy
    sight;
  Thy faith hath saved thee. Go."
Light entered swift; they followed
    him,
  And God they greatly praised.
The people also worshiped God,
  And hymns of triumph raised.

SECTION 127.

Conversion of Zacchæus.—Luke 19. 1-10.

As Jesus passed through Jericho,
  There was a certain man,
Zacchæus named, of stature small,
  A worthy publican.
With ardent zeal to see the Lord,
  Who was to pass that way,
He climbed into a sycamore
  That he might thence survey
Him well, raised thus above the crowd.
  When Jesus reached the place
He looked up, saw him, and then said,
  With his accustomed grace,
"Zacchæus, hasten to come down,
  For in thy house, to-day,
I will abide." Descending from
  The tree, without delay,
He gladly entertained the Lord.
  But certain Jews complained
That Jesus sojourned with a man
  Whom righteous Jews disdained,

Jizɒs, ɗɤ sɒn ov Devid, hir."
  Ɗe pịpel ɕekt ɗer wɒrd.
Bɒt ɗe, wiɗ ernestnes, ɗe mɵr
  krịd ɤt, "Ɵ Devid'z sɒn,
hav mersi! Ɵ hav mersi, Lord."
  Ɗát mersi nɤ woz wɒ́n.
Jizɒs stud stil, and kɷld ɗem bɵʇ.
  Tu Bartimiɒs ɗen
ɗe se, "Bi glad, hi kɷleʇ ɗi."
  Ɗen rɵz ɗiz pur blịnd men.
Timiɒs' sɒn kast of hiz klɵk
  and wɷkt, wiɗ gret delịt,
tu Krịst; hu askt, "Hwot wud'st
    ɗɤ hav?"
  "Ɵ Lord, restɵr mị sịt."
Ye, bɵʇ krịd, "Ɵpen, Lord, ɤr ịz."
  Jizɒs' kompaʃonz flɵ;
hi tɒɕt ɗer ịz; "Resiv ɗị
    sịt;
  ɗị feʇ haʇ sevd ɗi. Gɵ."
Lịt enterd swift; ɗe folɵd
    him,
  and God ɗe gretli prezd.
Ɗe pịpel ɷlsɵ wɒrʃipt God,
  and hímz ov trịɒmf rezd.

SEKΣON 127.

Konverʃon ov Zakiɒs.—Luk 19. 1-10.

Az Jizɒs past ʇru Jerikɵ,
  ɗer woz a serten man,
Zakiɒs nemd, ov statụr smɷl,
  a wɒrɗi pɒblikan.
Wiɗ ardent zil tu si ɗe Lord,
  hu woz tu pas ɗát we,
Hi klịmd intu a sikamɵr
  ɗat hi mịt ɗens sɒrve
him wel, rezd ɗɒs abɒv ɗe krɤd.
  Hwen Jizɒs riɕt ɗe ples
hi lukt ɒp, sɷ him, and ɗen sed,
  wiɗ hiz akɒstomd gres,
"Zakiɒs, hesen tu kɒm dɤn,
  for in ɗị hɤs, tu-de,
ị wil abịd." Desendiŋ from
  ɗe tri, wiɗɤt dele,
hi gladli entertend ɗe Lord.
  Bɒt serten Juz komplend
ɗat Jizɒs sɵjɒrnd wiɗ a man
  hum rịtiɒs Juz disdend,

A sinner, who, by unjust means,
  Great riches had attained.
Zacchæus answered, "Lord, I give
  The poor one-half my store;
And if, from any man I've gained
  Unjustly heretofore,
To him I will restore such gain
  And give him four-fold more."
Then Jesus said, "Salvation comes
  This day unto thy roof;
Thou art an Israelite indeed,
  And dost not need reproof;
For I am come to save the lost;
  From none to stand aloof."

SECTION 128.

Parable of the Pounds.—Luke 19. 11-27.

When near Jerusalem, Christ spake
  This parable; for some
Thought that God's kingdom was at once,
  In its full power, to come.
"A certain nobleman would go
  Into a distant land,
To gain a kingdom for himself,
  With absolute command.
Before he left, he called to him
  His servants ten, and said,
'To each of you I give one pound,
  That you, with it, may trade.'
But the false citizens rebelled
  Against his government,
And sent a message after him,
  To show their discontent.
At length their Lord, who had received
  His royalty, returned,
And asked them how they had employed
  Their money: what they'd earned.
Then came the first, and said, 'Thy pound
  Hath gained full ten pounds more.'
The Lord that servant praised for this
  Great increase to his store;
And said, 'Well done, trustworthy one,
  Since thou art faithful found
In this small trust, be ruler thou
  O'er cities ten, renowned.'
A second came; 'My pound,' he said,
  'Full five pounds more hath gained.'

---

a siner, hɯ, bį ɒnjɒst minz,
  gret riçez had atend.
Zakiɒs anserd, "Lord, į giv
  đe pur wɒn-hɜf mį stɵr;
and if, from eni man į'v gend
  ɒnjɒstli hirtufɵr,
tu him į wil restɵr sɒç gen
  and giv him fɵr-fɵld mɵr."
Đen Jizɒs sed, "Salveʃon kɒmz
  đis de ɒntu đį rɯf;
đɜ art an Izraelįt indid,
  and dɒst not nid reprɯf;
for į am kɒm tu sev đe lost;
  from nɒn tu stand alɯf."

SEKΣON 128.

Parabel ov đe Pɜndz.—Lɯk 19. 11-2

Hwen nir Jerɯsalem, Krįst spe
  đis parabel; for sɒm
ŧot đat God'z kiŋdom woz at wɒ
  in its ful pɜer, tu kɒm.
"A serten nɵbelman wud gɵ
  intu a distant land,
tu gen a kiŋdom for himself,
  wiđ absolɯt komand.
Befɵr hi left, hi kold tu him
  hiz servants ten, and sed,
'Tu iç ov ų į giv wɒn pɜnd,
  đat ų, wiđ it, me tred.'
Bɒt đe fols sitizenz rebéld
  agenst hiz gɒvernment,
and sent a mesej after him,
  tu ʃɵ đer diskontent.
At leŋŧ đer Lord, hɯ had resiv
  hiz roialti, retɒrnd,
and askt đem hɜ đe had e
  ploid
  đer mɒni: hwot đe'd ernd.
Đen kem đe ferst, and sed, '
  pɜnd
  haŧ gend ful ten pɜndz mɵr.'
Đe Lord đát servant prezd for đ
  gret inkris tu hiz stɵr;
and sed, 'Wel dɒn, trɒstwɒ
  sins đɜ art feŧful fɜnd [w
in đis smol trɒst, bi rɯler đɜ
  ɵ'r sitiz ten, reuɜnd.'
A sekond kem; 'Mį pɜnd,' hi s
  'ful fįv pɜndz mɵr haŧ gend.

The Lord then said, 'Thou shalt com-
Five cities thus obtained.' [mand
Another came, and said, 'Behold
The pound thou gavest me,
Which in a napkin I have hid,
And kept it safe for thee.
I feared to speculate with it,
Or risk, in any trade,
Thy property, for thou art strict;
I was too much afraid;
For thou dost always ask for more
Than thou dost first supply,
And dost expect us to increase
Thy gifts by industry.'
Then was his Lord displeased, and said,
'Thou wicked servant. Hear:
From thy own mouth I will condemn
Thy idleness and fear.
Thou knewest I was prompt to try
My stewards by this test?
Then thou should'st well have used
And made good interest. [thy store,
Take therefore from him his sole
And give it to that one [pound,
Who hath made ten by industry,
And would not be outdone.
For unto each who hath employed
His store, shall more be given,
While from the idle who used not,
Their last mite shall be riven.
And as for those, mine enemies,
Who late refused my reign,
Bring the disloyal traitors forth,
And cause them to be slain."

Ðe Lord ðen sed, 'Ðʊ ʃalt komand
fįv sitiz ðʊs obtend.'
Anɒðer kem, and sed, 'Behɵld
ðe pʊnd ðʊ gevest mi,
hwiç in a napkin į hav hid,
and kept it sef for ði.
Į fird tu spekɥlet wiþ it,
or risk, in eni tred,
ðį properti, for ðʊ art strikt;
į woz tɯ mɒç afred;
for ðʊ dɒst ɷlwez ask for mɵr
ðan ðʊ dɒst ferst sɒplį,
and dɒst ekspekt ɒs tu inkris
ðį gifts bį indɒstri.'
Ðen woz hiz Lord displizd, and sed,
'Ðʊ wiked servant. Hir:
from ðį ɵn mʊþ į wil kondem
ðį įdelnes and fir.
Ðʊ nɥest į woz prompt tu trį
mį stɥardz bį ðis test?
Ðen ðʊ ʃud'st wel hav ɥzd ðį stɵr,
and med gud interest.
Tek ðerfɵr from him hiz sɵl pʊnd,
and giv it tu ðát wɒn
hɯ haþ med ten bį indɒstri,
and wud not bi ʊtdɒn.
For ɒntu iç hɯ haþ emploid
hiz stɵr, ʃal mɵr bi given,
hwįl from ðe įdel hɯ ɥzd not,
ðer last mįt ʃal bi riven.
And az for ðɵz, mįn enemiz,
hɯ let refɥzd mį ren,
briŋ ðe disloial tretorz fɵrþ,
and kɷz ðem tu bi slen."

SECTION 129.

The Resurrection of Lazarus.
John 11. 17-46.

To Bethany now Jesus came,
To the holy family
Of Mary and of Martha, who
Were in calamity;
For Lazarus, their brother dear,
Had just been called away;
And four days he had been entombed
When Jesus came that day.
(This peaceful town of Bethany
Was nigh Jerusalem,

SEKΣON 129.

Ðe Rezɒrekʃon ov Lazarɒs.
Jon 11. 17-46.

Tu Beþani nʊ Jizɒs kem,
tu ðe hɵli famili
ov Meri and ov Marþa, hɯ
wer in kalamiti;
for Lazarɒs, ðer brɒðer dir,
had jɒst bin kɵld awe;
and fɵr dez hi had bin entɯmd
hwen Jizɒs kem ðát de.
(Ðis pisful tʊn ov Beþani
woz nį Jerɯsalem,

Not more than fifteen furlongs off,
  Two miles, as we should deem.)
The friendly Jews in vain essayed
  Some comfort to afford;
When Martha, hearing Christ's approach,
  Went out to meet her Lord.
Mary sat still within the house.
  Then Martha said, or sighed,
"If thou, Lord, hadst been here before
  My brother had not died.
Yet still I know that whatsoe'er
  Thou askest, God will give."
Jesus replied, "Thy brother shall,
  By resurrection, live."
Then Martha said, "I know he'll rise
  Again at the last day."
"I am the resurrection and
  The life," said Christ, "alway.
And whoso trusts himself to me,
  Though here on earth he die,
Shall live again in me, and then
  Shall live eternally.
Canst thou this truth receive?" She
  "Yea, Lord, for I believe [said,
That thou the true Messiah art,
  The Son whom God doth give."
And then she secretly went home,
  And to her sister said,
"The Master's come, and calleth thee."
  Mary in haste obeyed,
To meet her Lord without the town,
  Where Martha first had come.
Her mourning friends supposed she
  To weep at Lazarus' tomb, [went
And followed; till at Jesus' feet
  She threw herself, and sighed,
"If thou, O Lord, hadst but been here,
  My brother had not died."
When Jesus saw her tears, (his heart,
  Of pure compassion made,)
He groaned with sorrow, and inquired,
  "Where is his body laid?"
They said to him, "Lord, come, and see."
  Then Jesus wept. They said,
"See how he loved him. Mark his
  With sorrow overspread." [face,
Some of them said, "Could not this
  Who gave sight to the blind, [man,

not mɵr ðan fiftin fɒrloŋz of,
  tɯ́ mʝlz, az wi ʃud dim.)
Ðe frendli Jɯz in ven esed
  sɒm kɒmfort tu afɵrd;
hwen Marɟa, hiriŋ Krʝst's aprɵç,
  went ȣt tu mit her Lord.
Meri sat stil wiðin ðe hȣs.
  Ðen Marɟa sed, or sʝd,
"If ðȣ, Lord, hadst bin hir befɵr
  mʝ brɒðer had not dʝd.
Yet stil ʝ nɵ́ ðat hwotsɵer
  ðȣ askest, God wil giv."
Jizɒs replʝd, "Ðʝ brɒðer ʃal,
  bʝ rezɒrekʃon, liv."
Ðen Marɟa sed, "Ɨ nɵ́ hi'l rʝz
  agen at ðe last de."
"Ɨ am ðe rezɒrekʃon and
  ðe lʝf," sed Krʝst, "ωlwe.
And hɯsɵ trɒsts himself tu mi,
  ðɵ hir on erɟ hi dʝ,
ʃal liv agen in mi, and ðen
  ʃal liv eternali.
Kanst ðȣ ðis trɯɟ resiv?" Σi sed,
  "Yε, Lord, for ʝ beliv
ðat ðȣ ðe trɯ Mesʝa art,
  ðe Sɒn hɯm God dɒɟ giv."
And ðen ʃi sikretli went hɵm,
  and tu her sister sed,
"Ðe Master'z kɒm, and kωleɟ ði."
  Meri in hest ɵbed,
tu mit her Lord wiðȣt ðe tȣn,
  hwεr Marɟa ferst had kɒm.
Her mɵrniŋ frendz sɒpɵzd ʃi went
  tu wip at Lazarɒs' tɯm,
and folɵd; til at Jizɒs' fit
  ʃi ɟrɯ herself, and sʝd,
"If ðȣ, Ɵ Lord, hadst bɒt bin hir,
  mʝ brɒðer had not dʝd."
Hwen Jizɒs sω her tirz, (hiz hart
  ov pɥr kompaʃon med,)
hi grɵnd wið sorɵ, and inkwʝrd,
  "Hwer iz hiz bodi led?"
Ðε sed tu him, "Lord, kɒm, and si."
  Ðen Jizɒs wept. Ðε sed,
"Si hȣ hi lɒvd him. Mark hiz fes,
  wið sorɵ ɵverspred."
Sɒm ov ðem sed, "Kud not ðis
  hɯ gev sʝt tu ðe blʝnd, [man,

Have kept this man from death?" The
Lord,
Still groaning from his mind,
Came to the grave. It was a cave;
A stone upon it lay.
Then Jesus said, "Remove the stone."
(He would his power display.)
Then Martha unto Jesus said,
"To-day is the fourth day
That he has lain among the dead."
But Jesus answered her,
"Said I not, If thou would'st believe,
God's glory should appear?"
Then was the stone moved from its
place;
And, lifting up his eyes,
He said, "O Father, thee I bless,
Who hearest me always.
I knew thou dost, but for the sake
Of others, thus I pray;
That they may see that I am sent
By thee, to teach thy way."
This having said, he cried aloud,
"O Lazarus, come forth!"
The dead obeyed that voice divine,
And came from out the earth;
His hands and feet with grave-clothes
bound,
A napkin round his head;
Said Jesus, "Loose him, let him go."
All doubt was now allayed:
And many Jewish friends believed,
To whom these things were shown;
But some unto the Pharisees
This miracle made known.

hav kept đis man from deŧ?" Đe
Lord,
stil grơniŋ from hiz mįnd,
kɛm tu đe grɛv. It woz a kɛv;
a stơn ɒpon it lɛ.
Đen Jizɒs sed, "Remɯv đe stơn."
(Hi wud hiz pɤer displɛ.)
Đen Marŧa ɒntu Jizɒs sed,
"Tu-dɛ iz đe fơrŧ dɛ
đat hi haz len amɒŋ đe ded."
Bɒt Jizɒs anserd her,
"Sed į not, If đɤ wud'st beliv,
God'z glơri ʃud apir?"
Đen woz đe stơn mɯvd from its
plɛs;
and, liftiŋ ɒp hiz įz,
hi sed, "Ơ Fɑder, đi į bles,
hɯ hirest mi ɷlwɛz.
Ɨ nụ đɤ dɒst, bɒt for đe sɛk
ov ɒđerz, đɒs į prɛ;
đat đɛ mɛ si đat į am sent
bį đi, tu tiç đį wɛ."
Đis haviŋ sed, hi krįd alɤd,
"Ơ Lazarɒs, kɒm fơrŧ!"
Đe ded ơbɛd đát vois divįn,
and kɛm from ɤt đe erŧ;
hiz handz and fit wiđ grɛv-klơđz
bɤnd,
a napkin rɤnd hiz hed;
sed Jizɒs, "Lɯs him, let him gơ."
ɷl dɤt woz nɤ alɛd:
and meni Jɯiʃ frendz belivd,
tu hɯm điz ŧiŋz wer ʃơn;
bɒt sɒm ɒntu đe Farisiz
đis mirakel mɛd nơn.

SECTION 130.

The Sanhedrim assemble to deliberate concerning the Resurrection of Lazarus.

John 11. 47, 48.

A council then the chief priests held,
How they might put Christ down.
They said, "We do no miracle,
This man gains great renown.
And if we let him thus alone,
All will believe on him:
The Romans then will come, kill us,
And burn Jerusalem."

SEKΣON 130.

Đe Sanhedrim asembel tu deliberɛt konserniŋ đe Rezɒrekʃon ov Lazarɒs.

Jon 11. 47, 48.

A kɤnsil đen đe çif prists held,
hɤ đɛ mįt put Krįst dɤn.
Đɛ sed, "Wi dɯ nơ mirakel,
đis man gɛnz grɛt renɤn.
And if wi let him đɒs alơn,
ɷl wil beliv on him:
đe Rơmanz đen wil kɒm, kil ɒs,
and bɒrn Jerɯsalem."

SECTION 131.

Caiaphas prophesies.—John 11. 49-54.

Then Caiaphas, who was that year
  The high priest of the Jews,
Said, "It is better far for us
  That this one man should lose
His life, than that the nation be
  Destroyed, and Israel fade;
And all our ceremonial rites
  Be withered and decayed."
And this he spake, not of himself,
  But being high priest that year,
He prophesied that Christ should die
  For all, both far and near;
And gather all God's children that
  Were scattered far abroad,
Both Jew and Gentile in one fold.
  The rest his speech applaud.
From that day forth the Jewish priests
  Took counsel, Christ to slay.
Then Jesus left Jerusalem,
  And did at Ephraim stay;
And there, with his disciples, he
Lived for a time in privacy.

SEKΣON 131.

Kaiafas profeṣiz.—Jon 11. 49-54.

Đen Kaiafas, huı woz đát yịr
  đe hị prịst ov đe Juız,
sed, "It iz beter far for ɒs
  đat đis wɒn man ʃud luız
hiz lịf, đan đat đe neʃon bi
  destroid, and Izrael fed;
and ɷl ɤr seremɵnial rịts
  bi wiđerd and deked."
And đis hi spek, not ov himself,
  bɒt biiŋ hị prịst đát yịr,
hi profesịd đat Krịst ʃud dị
  for ɷl, bɵʇ far and nịr;
and gađer ɷl God'z ɋildren đat
  wer skaterd far abrɷd,
bɵʇ Juı and Jentịl in wɒn fɵld.
  Đe rest hiz spịɋ aplɷd.
From đát de fɵrʇ đe Juiʃ prịsts
  tuk kɤnsel, Krịst tu sle.
Đen Jịzɒs left Jeruısalem,
  and did at Efraim ste;
and đer, wiđ hiz disịpelz, hi
livd for a tịm in prịvasi.

BOOK IX.

SECTION 132.

State of the public mind at Jerusalem before the last Passover Christ attended.
John 11. 55-57.

The Jewish Passover was nigh,
  And to that sacred feast,
The Jews from every region round,
  (From daily cares released,)
Flocked to Jerusalem, that they
  Themselves might purify,
Before the Passover began,
  And eat it joyfully.
For Jesus often they inquired,
  And much desired to know
Whether he would the feast attend,
  In spite of every foe.
Now both chief priests and Pharisees,
  And all the Sanhedrim,
Wished to discover where Christ was,
  That they might capture him.

BUK IX.

SEKΣON 132.

Stet ov đe pɒblik mịnd at Jeruısalem befɵr đe last Pasɵver Krịst atended.
Jon 11. 55-57.

Đe Juiʃ Pasɵver woz nị,
  and tu đát sekred fịst,
đe Juız from everi rịjon rɤnd,
  (from deli kerz relịst,)
flokt tu Jeruısalem, đat đe
  đemselvz mịt pyrifị,
befɵr đe Pasɵver began,
  and ịt it joifuli.
For Jịzɒs ofen đe inkwịrd,
  and mɒɋ dezịrd tu nɵ
hweđer hi wud đe fịst atend,
  in spịt ov everi fɵ.
Nɤ bɵʇ ɋịf prịsts and Farisịz,
  and ɷl đe Sanhedrim,
wiʃt tu diskɒver hwer Krịst woz,
  đat đe mịt kaptyr him.

SECTION 133.

Christ comes to Bethany, where he is anointed by Mary.

Matthew 26. 6-13. Mark 14. 3-9.
John 12. 1-11.

Six days before the Passover,
The Lord to Bethany came,
The residence of Lazarus,
Of resurrection fame.
And in the house of Simon there,
Christ did a feast attend,
And Lazarus sat down to eat
With his life-giving Friend.
But Martha served. Then Mary took
A pound of ointment, sweet
And costly, of pure spikenard made,
And poured it on his feet.
Her love was great, and on his head
She lavished the perfume;
Then wiped his feet with her own hair:
Rich odour filled the room.
When his disciples saw this deed,
They were offended sore,
And wished the ointment had been [sold
For money, that the poor
Might gain the benefit of alms.
And Judas, traitor bold,
Especially was grieved thereat,
And would have had it sold,
Not for the poor, but for himself,
Because a thief was he,
And bore the bag, and cared for nought
But worldly property.
Then Jesus said, "Forbear to blame
This act of Mary's love,
For she hath wrought on me a work
Which you should all approve.
The poor are always with you, and
Whene'er you will, you may
Do good to them, but I full soon
Must pass from earth away.
She hath done what she could, to show
Her faithful gratitude;
And hath anointed me before
My burial, as endued
With knowledge of my coming fate.
I tell you that this deed
Of her pure charity shall be
Proclaimed, and gain its meed,

SEKΣON 133.

Krịst kɒmz tu Beϑani, hwɛr hi iz anointed bị Mɛri.

Maϑɥ 26. 6-13. Mark 14. 3-9.
Jon 12. 1-11.

Siks dez befɵr đe Pasɵver,
đe Lord tu Beϑani kem,
đe rezidens ov Lazarɒs,
ov rezɒrekʃon fem.
And in đe hɜs ov Sịmon đɛr,
Krịst did a fist atend,
and Lazarɒs sat dɜn tu it
wiđ hiz lịf-giviŋ Frend.
Bɒt Marϑa servd. Đen Meri tuk
a pɜnd ov ointment, swit
and kostli, ov pɥr spịknard med,
and pɵrd it on hiz fit.
Her lɒv woz gret, and on hiz hed
ʃi laviʃt đe perfɥm;
đen wịpt hiz fit wiđ her ɵn hɛr:
riç ɵdor fild đe rum.
Hwen hiz disịpelz sɷ đis did,
đe wer ofended sɵr,
and wiʃt đe ointment had bin sɵld
for mɒni, đat đe pur
mịt gen đe benefit ov ɑmz.
And Judas, tretor bɵld,
espeʃali woz grivd đerat,
and wud hav had it sɵld,
not for đe pur, bɒt for himself,
bekɷz a ϑif woz hi,
and bɵr đe bag, and kɛrd for nɷt
bɒt wɒrldli properti.
Đen Jizɒs sed, "Forbɛr tu blem
đis akt ov Meri'z lɒv,
for ʃi haϑ rɷt on mi a wɒrk
hwiç ɥ ʃud ɷl apruv.
Đe pur ar ɷlwez wiđ ɥ, and
hwener ɥ wil, ɥ me
du gud tu đem, bɒt ị ful sun
mɒst pas from erϑ awe.
Σi haϑ dɒn hwot ʃi kud, tu ʃɵ
her feϑful gratitɥd;
and haϑ anointed mi befɵr
mị berial, az endɥd
wiđ nolej ov mị kɒmiŋ fet.
Ŧ tel ɥ đat đis did
ov her pɥr çariti ʃal bi
prɵklemd, and gen its mid

Where'er my Gospel shall be preached,
  Throughout the coming age:
The honor of all saints shall be
  Her lasting heritage."

Then many of the Jews, who knew
  That Christ was in that place,
Came there to visit him, and own
  His majesty and grace;
And also to see Lazarus,
  Whom from the dead he raised.
But the chief priests, who hated much
  To hear the Savior praised,
Designed to murder Lazarus too,
  Because while he still lived,
Full many went away from them.
  And on the Lord believed.

hwerer mį Gospel ʃal bi priɋt,
  ɟruɯst đe kɒmiŋ ej:
đe onor ov ɷl sents ʃal bi
  her lastiŋ heritej."

Đen meni ov đe Juɯz, hɯ nų
  đat Kręst woz in đát ples,
kem đer tú vizit him, and ɵn
  hiz majesti and gres;
and ɷlsɵ tu si Lazarɒs,
  hɯm from đe ded hi rɛzd.
Bɒt đe ɋif prists, hɯ hɛted mɒɋ
  tu hir đe Sevier prezd,
dezįnd tu mɒrder Lazarɒs tɯ,
  bekɷz hwįl hi stil livd,
ful meni went awɛ from đem,
  and on đe Lord belivd.

SECTION 134.

Christ prepares to enter Jerusalem.

Matthew 21. 1-7. Mark 11. 1-7.
Luke 19. 29-35. John 12. 12-19.

On the next day, when they drew nigh
  Unto Jerusalem,
Great crowds that came up to the feast,
  Met Christ with loud acclaim.
With palm-tree branches in their hands,
  They greeted him, and cried,
"Hosanna! Blest be Israel's king;
  Let him be glorified
Who cometh in the Lord's high name."
  As they drew near the place,
He sent from his disciples, two,
  To go before his face,
And said, "Go to that village, and
  Directly ye shall find
An ass and colt, whereon no man
  Hath sat: the colt unbind
And bring him hither. And if one
  Inquire, 'Why do ye so?'
Reply, 'Because the Lord hath need.'
  And he will let him go."
All this was done, so that the words
  Of Judah's prophet were
Fulfilled, who saith, "Be not afraid,
  O Zion's daughter fair,

SEKΣON 134.

Kręst preperz tu enter Jerɯsalem.

Maɟų 21. 1-7. Mark 11. 1-7.
Lɯk 19. 29-35. Jon 12. 12-19.

On đe nekst de, hwen đɛ drɯ nį
  ɒntu Jerɯsalem,
gret krɤdz đat kem ɒp tu đe fist,
  met Kręst wiđ lɤd aklem.
Wiđ pɑm-tri branɋez in đɛr handz,
  đɛ grited him, and kręd,
"Hɵzana! Blest bi Izrael'z kiŋ;
  Let him bi glɵrifįd
hɯ kɒmeɟ in đe Lord'z hį nem."
  Az đɛ drɯ nir đe ples,
hi sent from hiz disįpelz, tɯ́,
  tu gɵ befɵr hiz fes,
and sed, "Gɵ tu đát vilej, and
  direktli yi ʃal fįnd
an as and kɵlt, hweron nɵ man
  haɟ sat: đe kɵlt ɒnbįnd
and briŋ him hiđer. And if wɒn
  inkwįr, 'Hwį dɯ yi sɵ?'
replį, 'Bekɷz đe Lord haɟ nid.'
  And hi wil let him gɵ."
ɷl đis woz dɒn, sɵ đat đe wɒrdz
  ov Jɯda'z profet wer
fulfild, hɯ seɟ, "Bi not afred,
  Ɵ Zįon'z dɷter fer,

Behold thy king approacheth, meek,
  And sitting on an ass,
Even on an ass's foal;" but when
  These words had come to pass,
Jesus' disciples knew it not.
  Yet afterwards, when he
Was glorified, they understood
  This sacred mystery.
They went, according to Christ's word,
  And found as he had said,
And brought the colt, and thereupon
  Their garments soon they laid:
And Jesus sat upon the colt.
  And many Jews who knew
That Christ raised Lazarus from the dead,
  Bore witness this was true.

behɵld đį kiŋ aprɵçeŧ, mik,
  and sitiŋ on an as,
iven on an as'ez fɵl;" bɒt hwen
  điz wɒrdz had kɒm tu pas,
Jizɒs' disįpelz nų it not.
  Yet afterwardz, hwen hi
woz glɵrifįd, đe ɒnderstud
  đis sekred misteri.
Đe went, akordiŋ tu Krįst's wɒrd,
  and fɤnd az hi had sed,
and brɵt đe kɵlt, and đerɒpon
  đer garments sɯn đe led:
and Jizɒs sat ɒpon đe kɵlt.
  And meni Jɯz hɯ nų
đat Krįst rezd Lazarɒs from đe ded,
  bɵr witnes đis woz trɯ.

SECTION 135.

The people meet Christ with Hosannas.
Christ approaches Jerusalem.

Matthew 21. 8-11. Mark 11. 8-11.
Luke 19. 36-40. John 12. 19.

As they descended from the mount
  Of Olives, and drew near
Unto Jerusalem, vast crowds,
  Who came Christ's words to hear,
Cut branches from the trees, and then
  They cast them on the road,
Together with their garments, and
  Sang unto God this ode:—
"Hosanna to king David's son;
  Hosanna we proclaim;
Most blessed be the king that comes
  In great Jehovah's name.
Hosanna in the highest heaven,
  Let peace for ever reign;
May David's kingdom come on earth,
  And evermore remain."
The Pharisees, displeased at this,
  Said, "Lord, rebuke their noise."
But Jesus said, "If these were still,
  The stones would raise their voice."
Then said the Pharisees, "Behold,
  We can no more prevail;
The world is following after him,
  And now our power must fail."

SEKΣON 135.

Đe pipel mit Krįst wiđ Hɒzanaz.
Krįst aprɵçez Jerɯsalem.

Maŧų 21. 8-11. Mark 11. 8-11.
Lɯk 19. 36-40. Jon 12. 19.

Az đe desended from đe mɤnt
  ov Olivz, and drɯ nɪr
ɒntu Jerɯsalem, vast krɤdz,
  hɯ kem Krįst's wɒrdz tu hɪr,
kɒt brançez from đe trɪz, and đen
  đe kast đem on đe rɵd,
tugeđer wiđ đer garments, and
  saŋ ɒntu God đis ɵd:—
"Hɵzana tu kiŋ Devid'z sɒn;
  Hɵzana wi prɵklem;
mɵst blesed bi đe kiŋ đat kɒmz
  In gret Jehɵva'z nem.
Hɵzana in đe hįest heven,
  let pɪs for ever ren;
me Devid'z kiŋdom kɒm on erŧ,
  and evermɵr remen."
Đe Farisɪz displɪzd at đis,
  sed, "Lord, rebųk đer noiz."
Bɒt Jizɒs sed, "If điz wer stil,
  đe stɵnz wud rez đer vois."
Đen sed đe Farisɪz, "Behɵld,
  wi kan nɵ mɵr prevel;
đe wɒrld iz folɵiŋ after him,
  and nɤ ɤr pɤer mɒst fel."

SECTION 136.

Christ's Lamentation over Jerusalem, and his prophecy of its destruction.

Luke 19. 41-44.

When Christ came near, his heart was
To think of Salem's fate ; [moved
He wept, that it should so despise
His mercy, till too late ;
And said, "Jerusalem, if thou
Hadst known in this thy day,
The things belonging to thy peace !
But now they pass away,
For ever hidden from thine eyes.
The days will soon appear
In which thy enemies will come
On thee, with sword and spear,
And hem thee in on every side,
And lay thee with the ground :
Thy children, with thy stones, shall
And misery abound ; [fall,
Because thou knewest not the time
Of this thy visitation.
Thy pomp, and pride, and sin, have
Thy own extermination." [wrought

SEKƩON 136.

Krįst's Lamentɛʃon ɵver Jerɯsalem, and hiz profesi ov its destrɒkʃon.

Lɯk 19. 41-44.

Hwen Krįst kɛm nịr, hiz hart woz
tɯ ɟiŋk ov Sɛlem'z fɛt ; [mɯvd
hi wept, đat it ʃud sɵ despįz
hiz mersi, til tɯ lɛt ;
and sed, "Jerɯsalem, if đɤ
hadst nɵn in đis đį dɛ,
đe ɟiŋz beloŋiŋ tu đį pịs !
Bɒt nɤ đɛ pas awɛ,
for ever hiden from đįn įz.
Ɛe dɛz wil sɯn apịr
in hwiç đį enemiz wil kɒm
on đị wiđ sɵrd and spịr,
and hem đị in on everi sįd,
and lɛ wiđ đe grɤnd :
đį çildren, wiđ đį stɵnz, ʃal fɷl,
and mizeri abɤnd ;
bekɷz đɤ nɥest not đe tįm
ov đis đį vizitɛʃon.
Ɛį pomp, and prįd, and sin, hav rɷt
đį ɵn eksterminɛʃon."

SECTION 137.

Christ, on entering the city, casts the buyers and sellers out of the Temple.

Matthew 21. 10-13. Mark 11. 11.
Luke 19. 45, 46.

Christ entered then Jerusalem,
And to the temple went ;
And as he moved along in state,
The crowd asked what it meant.
Excitement filled the place. "Who's
this ?"
Each to his neighbour saith.
Reply was quickly heard, "It is
Jesus of Nazareth,
Of Galilee." They knew his name,
For he had won their faith.
Unto the temple Jesus went,
And those who bought and sold,
He drove away, and overthrew
Their tables, and their gold,
And seats of those who doves provide,
And said to them, "'Tis writ,
'My house shall be a house of prayer ;'
But ye lodge thieves in it."

SEKƩON 137.

Krįst, on enteriŋ đe siti, kasts đe bįers and selerz ɤt ov đe Tempel.

Maɟɥ 21. 10-13. Mark 11. 11.
Lɯk 19. 45, 46.

Krįst enterd đen Jerɯsalem,
and tu đe tempel went ;
and az hi mɯvd aloŋ in stɛt,
đe krɤd askt hwot it ment.
Eksįtment fild đe plɛs. "Hɯ'z
đis ?"
ịç tu hiz nɛbɒr seɟ.
Replį woz kwikli herd, "It iz
Jịzɒs ov Nazareɟ,
ov Galilị." Ɛɛ nɥ hiz nɛm,
for hi had wɒn đɛr fɛɟ.
Ɯntu đe tempel Jịzɒs went,
and đɵz hɯ bɷt and sɵld,
hi drɵv awɛ, and ɵverɟrɯ
đɛr tɛbelz and đɛr gɵld,
and sịts ov đɵz hɯ dɒvz prɵvįd,
and sed tu đem, "'Tiz rit,
'Mį hɤs ʃal bi a hɤs ov prɛr ;'
bɒt yi loj ɟịvz in it."

SECTION 138.

Christ heals the sick in the temple, and reproves the chief Pharisees.

Matthew 21. 14-16.

As Jesus in the temple stood,
  The blind and lame draw nigh
To him for cure. He heals them all.
  But nought could satisfy
The chief priests and the scribes that
  Was sent by God most high. [he
They see his wonder-working power,
  They hear the children cry,
"Hosanna to king David's son,"
  And angrily reply,
"Dost thou not hear the words they
    say?"
  He mildly asks them, "Why
Are ye so wroth? Have ye not read
  These words, which justify
Them, 'From the mouth of babes I'll
    raise
A song of triumph in my praise?'"

SEKΣON 138.

Krįst hilz đe sik in đe tempel, and repruvz đe çif Farisiz.

Maŧų 21. 14-16.

Az Jizɒs in đe tempel stud,
  đe blįnd and lem drɷ nį
tu him for kųr. Hi hilz đem ɷl.
  Bɒt nɷt kud satisfį
đe çif prists and đe skrįbz đat hi
  woz sent bį God mɵst hį.
Đe si hiz wɒnder-wɒrkiŋ pɤer,
  đe hir đe çildren krį,
"Hɵzana tu kiŋ Devid'z sɒn,"
  and aŋgrilireplį,
"Dɒst đɤ not hir đe wɒrdz đe
    se?"
  Hi mįldli asks đem, "Hwį
ar yi sɵ rɷŧ? Hav yi not red
  điz wɒrdz, hwiç jɒstifį
đem, 'From đe mɤŧ ov bebz į'l
    rez
a soŋ ov trįɒmf in mį prez?'"

SECTION 139.

Some Greeks at Jerusalem desire to see Christ.—John 12. 20-44.

Some Greeks were at Jerusalem,
  To worship at the feast,
They came to Philip, earnestly
  Preferring this request:—
"We would see Jesus, sir," said they.
  Philip to Andrew told,
And both to Jesus soon repair,
  The message to unfold.
Then Jesus said, "The hour is come,
  My name to glorify,
As Son of man. Except a grain
  Of wheat be earthed, and die,
It still remains one grain; but if
  It die, it brings forth fruit.
So he that loves his selfish life
  Shall lose the very root
Of happiness; but he that hates
  His selfish life, while here,
Shall keep his better life, and live
  For ever, free from fear.
He that would serve, should follow,
  In faith and love sincere, [me,

SEKΣON 139.

Sɒm Griks at Jerusalem dezįr tu si Krįst.—Jon 12. 20-44.

Sɒm Griks wer at Jerusalem,
  tu wɒrʃip at đe fist,
đe kem tu Filip, ernestli
  preferiŋ đis rekwest:—
"Wi wud si Jizɒs, ser," sed đe.
  Filip tu Andru tɵld,
and bɵŧ tu Jizɒs sun reper,
  đe mesej tu ɒnfɵld.
Đen Jizɒs sed, "Đe ɤr iz kɒm,
  mį nem tu glɵrifį,
az Sɒn ov man. Eksept a gren
  ov hwit bi erŧt, and dį,
it stil remenz wɒn gren; bɒt if
  it dį, it briŋz fɵrŧ frut.
Sɵ hi đat lɒvz hiz selfiʃ lįf
  ʃal luz đe veri rut
ov hapines; bɒt hi đat hets
  hiz selfiʃ lįf, hwįl hir,
ʃal kip hiz beter lįf, and liv
  for ever, fri from fir.
Hi đat wud serv, ʃud folɵ, mi,
  in feŧ and lɒv sinsir,

Till where I am, he too shall come,
  And honor shall receive
From God my Father, who would have
  All men in me believe.
My soul is deeply troubled now,
  And what shall I exclaim ?—
My Father, save me from this hour ?
  Yet for this hour I came.
Father, thy own name glorify."
  From heaven a voice then cried,
"My name, which is exalted high,
  Shall more be glorified."
Those who stood by were much
    amazed,
  And said 'twas thunder's sound ;
Some said, it was an angel's voice
  That echoed from the ground.
But Jesus said, "This voice hath come
  For your sakes, not my own.
Now is the judgement of this world ;
  Its prince is overthrown.
When I am lifted up from earth,
  I'll draw all men to me."
By this he showed the mode of death
  Of his humanity.

The people said, "The law declares
  Christ lives eternally :
How then sayest thou the Son of man
  Must soon uplifted be ?
Who is this Son of man ?" they
    asked.
  And Jesus made reply,
"A little while the light remains,
  Walk by it till ye die,
Lest darkness come on unawares,
  And your way hidden be ;
Believe this light, walk by it, and
  Be followers of me."

Thus having said, Jesus arose,
  And hid himself from them.
But though so many miracles
  They saw, they did contemn.
Thus was fulfilled Isaiah's word,
  When he to God appealed,
"Lord, who hath our report believed ?
  Where is God's arm revealed ?"
By wilful unbelief they fall ;
  For as Isaiah saith,

til hwer ị am, hi tɯ ʃal kɒm,
  and onor ʃal resiv
from God mị Fɜđer, hɯ wud h
  ɷl men in mi beliv.
Mị sɵl iz dipli trɒbeld nɜ,
  and hwot ʃal ị eksklem ?—
Mị Fɜđer, sev mi from đis ɜr ?
  yet for đis ɜr ị kem.
Fɜđer, đị ɵn nem glɵrifị."
  From heven a vois đen krịd,
"Mị nem, hwiç iz ekzɷlted hị,
  ʃal mɵr bi glɵrifịd."
Ɖɵz hɯ stud bị wer mɒç
    amezd,
  and sed 'twoz þɒnder'z sɜnd ;
sɒm sed, it woz an enjel'z vois
  đat ekɵd from đe grɜnd.
Bɒt Jizɒs sed, "Ɖis vois haþ k
  for ɥr seks, not mị ɵn.
Nɜ iz đe jɒjment ov đis wɒrld ;
  its prins iz ɵverþrɵn.
Hwen ị am lifted ɒp from erþ,
  ị'l drɷ ɷl men tu mi."
Bị đis hi ʃɵd đe mɵd ov deþ
  ov hiz hɥmaniti.

Ɖe pipel sed, "Ɖe lɷ deklerz
  Krịst livz eternali :
hɜ đen seest đɜ đe Sɒn ov man
  mɒst sɯn ɒplifted bi ?
Hɯ iz đis Sɒn ov man ?" đ
    askt.
  And Jizɒs med replị,
"A litel hwịl đe lịt remenz,
  wɷk bị it til yi dị,
lest darknes kɒm on ɒnawerz,
  and ɥr we hiden bi ;
beliv đis lịt, wɷk bị it, and
  bi folɵerz ov mi."

Ɖɒs haviŋ sed, Jizɒs arɵz,
  and hid himself from đem.
Bɒt đɵ sɵ meni mirakelz
  đe sɷ, đe did kontem.
Ɖɒs woz fulfild Ịzaia'z wɒrd,
  hwen hi tu God apild,
"Lord, hɯ haþ ɜr repɵrt beliv
  hwer iz God'z arm revild ?"
Bị wilful ɒnbelif đe fɷl ;
  for az Ịzaia seþ,

"They blind their eyes, make hard
their hearts,
And rush on their own death,
Lest they should see, and understand,
Repent, and keep the law."
So spake Isaiah of the Christ,
Whose glory he foresaw.
Yet 'mongst the rulers who were
Many believed on him; [chief,
But, fearful of the Pharisees,
And of the Sanhedrim,
Would not confess and own the Lord:
They loved applause more than his
word.

"Ðɛ blịnd ðer ịz, mɛk hard ðer
harts,
and rɒʃ on ðer ơn deŧ,
lest ðɛ ʃud si, and ɒnderstand,
repent, and kip ðe lω."
Sơ spɛk Ŧzaia ov ðe Krịst,
hɯz glơri hi fơrsω.
Yet 'mɒŋst ðe rɯlerz hɯ wer ɕif,
meni belivd on him;
bɒt, firful ov ðe Farisiz,
and ov ðe Sanhedrim,
wud not konfes and ơn ðe Lord:
ðɛ lɒvd aplωz mơr ðan hiz
wɒrd.

SECTION 140.

Christ declares his union with the Father, and the object of his mission.

John 12. 44-50.

Then Jesus said, "Whoso believes
On me, Messiah true,
Believeth not on me alone,
But God, whose will I do.
And he also that seeth me,
Sees Him that sent me here.
A light into the world, I come,
The light of heaven, most clear;
That whosoever shall believe
In me, may walk no more
In darkness and in ignorance,
As they have done before.
Not I alone judge those who hear
My words, and disobey;
I rather came to save the world
Than judge it at this day.
He that rejects me and my words,
Hath one that judgeth him;
In the last day, the words I speak
Shall judge him, as supreme.
I have not spoken from myself,
But He from whom I came
Commanded me what I should say
And speak in his great name.
And this I know, his just command
Is everlasting life;
Whate'er I speak, therefore, is with
The Father's wisdom rife."

SEKΣON 140.

Krịst deklɛrz hiz ụnion wiŧ ðe Faðer, and ðe objekt ov hiz miʃon.

Jon 12. 44-50.

Ðen Jizɒs sed, "Hɯsơ belivz
on mi, Mesịa trɯ,
beliveŧ not on mi alơn,
bɒt God, hɯz wil ị dɯ.
And hi ωlsơ ðat sieŧ mi,
siz Him ðat sent mi hir.
A lịt intu ðe wɒrld, ị kɒm,
ðe lịt ov heven mơst klir;
ðat hɯsơever ʃal beliv
in mi, mɛ wωk nơ mơr
in darknes and in ignorans,
az ðɛ hav dɒn befơr.
Not ị alơn jɒj ðơz hɯ hir
mị wɒrdz, and disơbɛ;
ị rɛðer kɛm tu sɛv ðe wɒrld
ðan jɒj it at ðis dɛ.
Hi ðat rejekts mi and mị wɒrdz,
haŧ wɒn ðat jɒjeŧ him;
in ðe last dɛ, ðe wɒrdz ị spik
ʃal jɒj him, az sụprim.
Ŧ hav not spơken from mịself,
bɒt Hi from hɯm ị kɛm
komanded mi hwot ị ʃud sɛ
and spik in hiz grɛt nɛm.
And ðis ị nơ, hiz jɒst komand
iz everlastiŋ lịf;
hwoter ị spik, ðerfơr, iz wiŧ
ðe Fɛðer'z wizdom rịf."

SECTION 141.

Christ leaves the city, and goes to Bethany; after which he goes to Jerusalem, and condemns the barren fig tree.

Matthew 21. 17-19. Mark 11. 11-14.

Then Christ departed with the twelve
  When eventide was come,
And lodged in Bethany, where he
  Had lately made his home.
Next morning, he returned unto
  Jerusalem again;
And as he went, he hungered sore,
  And could no food obtain.
Seeing a fig tree in the way,
  He came to it, but found
No fruit thereon, but only leaves,
  Which did the more abound.
It was not a good season then
  With this untimely tree;
And Jesus said, "Let no more fruit
  Be ever found on thee."
And soon the fig tree died away;
  Christ's words possest such power,
It drooped its leaves immediately,
  And withered from that hour.

SEKΣON 141.

Krįst livz ðe siti, and goz tu Beðan after hwiç hi goz tu Jerusalem, ai kondemz ðe baren fig tri.

Maþų 21. 17-19. Mark 11. 11-14

Ðen Krįst departed wið ðe twelv
  hwen iventįd woz kɒm,
and lojd in Beþani, hwer hi
  had letli med hiz hɵm.
Nekst morniŋ, hi retɒrnd ɒntu
  Jerusalem agen;
and az hi went, hi hɒŋgerd sɵr,
  and kud nɵ fud obten.
Siiŋ a fig tri in ðe we,
  hi kem tu it, bɒt fɤnd
nɵ frut ðeron, bɒt ɵnli livz,
  hwiç did ðe mɵr abɤnd.
It woz not a gud sizon ðen
  wið ðis ɒntįmli tri;
and Jizɒs sed, "Let nɵ mɵr fru
  bi ever fɤnd on ði."
And sun ðe fig tri dįd awe;
  Krįst's wɒrdz pozest sɒç pɤer,
it drupt its livz immidietli,
  and wiðerd from ðát ɤr.

SECTION 142.

The Scribes and Chief Priests seek to destroy Jesus.

Mark 11. 18. Luke 19. 47, 48.

And in the temple every day
  He taught the people there;
The scribes and chief priests heard, and sought
  How him they might ensnare,
But could not find what they might do.
The people round him gladly drew;
But they before his teaching quailed,
And all their artifices failed.
And when the eventide was come,
He left the city for his home.

SEKΣON 142.

Ðe Skrįbz and Çif Prists sik tu destr Jizɒs.

Mark 11. 18. Luk 19. 47, 48.

And in ðe tempel everi de
  hi tɷt ðe pipel ðer;
ðe skrįbz and çif prists herd, ar sɷt
  hɤ him ðe mįt ensner,
bɒt kud not fįnd hwot ðe mįt du
Ðe pipel rɤnd him gladli dru;
bɒt ðe befɵr hiz tiçiŋ kweld,
and ɷl ðer artifisez feld.
And hwen ðe iventįd woz kɒm,
hi left ðe siti for hiz hɵm.

SECTION 143.

Remarks on the Barren Fig Tree.

Matthew 21. 20-22. Mark 11. 20-26.

And in the morning, as they passed,
  They saw the fig tree stand,

SEKΣON 143.

Remarks on ðe Baren Fig Tri.

Maþų 21. 20-22. Mark 11. 20-2

And in ðe morniŋ, az ðe past,
  ðe sɷ ðe fig tri stand,

Dried from its roots, obedient
  To Christ's severe command.
And the disciples marveled, but
  The Lord did to them say,
"Have faith in God, and ye shall soon
  Yet greater signs display.
And even if with undoubting faith
  Unto a mountain vast,
Ye say, 'Be thou removed, and be
  Into the ocean cast,'
It shall be done; and all the things
  Which ye desire, in prayer,
Believe that ye receive them, and
  Ye'll find them ready there.
And when ye pray, forgive all those
  Who have offended you;
Then will your Heavenly Father give
  The pardon which you sue.
But if your hearts will not forgive
  Your erring brethren here,
Without God's pardon you at last
  In judgement will appear."

SECTION 144.

Christ answers the Chief Priests, who inquire concerning the authority by which he acted.

Matthew 21. 23-27. Mark 11. 27-33. Luke 20. 1-3.

It came to pass about this time,
  As Jesus preached the word
Within the temple's lofty walls,
  And many stood and heard,
The priests and scribes came up, and [asked
  "By what authority
Dost thou perform thy wondrous works,
  And who empowered thee?"
Then Christ perceived their guile, and [said,
  "First answer me one thing,
And I will truly give reply
  To this your questioning.
Whence the authority of John?
  From heaven, or from man?"
At this demand, the Jewish chiefs
  Were troubled, and began
To reason, "If we say from heaven,
  He'll blame our unbelief;
And if we say it was from men,
  We shall find no relief.

drįd from its rɯts, ɵbịdient
  tu Krįst's sevịr komand.
And ðe disįpelz marveld, bɒt
  ðe Lord did tu ðem se,
"Hav feθ in God, and yị ʃal sɯn
  yet greter sįnz disple.
And ịven if wið ɒndɜtiŋ feθ
  ɒntu a mɜnten vast,
yị se, 'Bị ðɜ remɯvd, and bị
  intu ðe ɵʃan kast,'
it ʃal bị dɒn; and ωl ðe θiŋz
  hwiç yị dezįr, in prer,
belịv ðat yị resịv ðem, and
  yị'l fįnd ðem redi ðer.
And hwen yị pre, forgiv ωl ðɵz
  hɯ hav ofended ɥ;
ðen wil ɥr Hevenli Fɑðer giv
  ðe pardon hwiç ɥ sɥ.
Bɒt if ɥr harts wil not forgiv
  ɥr eriŋ breðren hir,
wiðɜt God'z pardon ɥ at last
  in jɒjment wil apịr."

SEKΣON 144.

Krįst anserz ðe Çif Prists, hɯ inkwįr konserniŋ ðe ωθoriti bį hwiç hi akted.

Maθɥ 21. 23-27. Mark 11. 27-33. Lɯk 20. 1-3.

It kem tu pas abɜt ðis tįm,
  az Jịzɒs priçt ðe wɒrd
wiðin ðe tempel'z lofti wωlz,
  and meni stud and herd,
ðe prịsts and skrįbz kem ɒp, and [askt
  "Bį hwot ωθoriti
dɒst ðɜ perform ðį wɒndrɒs wɒrks,
  and hɯ empɜerd ðị?"
Ðen Krįst persịvd ðer gįl, and sed,
  "Ferst anser mị wɒn θiŋ,
and į wil trɯli giv replį
  tu ðis ɥr kwestioniŋ.
Hwens ðe ωθoriti ov Jon?
  from heven, or from man?
At ðis demand, ðe Jɯiʃ çifs
  wer trɒbeld, and began
tu rịzon, "If wị se from heven,
  hị'l blem ɜr ɒnbelịf;
and if wị se it woz from men,
  wị ʃal fįnd nɵ relịf.

The people all believed in John,
  And they in utter grief
Will stone us, for they are convinced
  John was a prophet true."
They said, "We cannot tell." Then
  Said, "Neither tell I you [Christ
By what authority I do
  These things; but, you will find,
If you but truly search for truth
  With pure and honest mind."

Ꝺe pıpel ɷl belıvd in Jon,
  and ꝺe in ɒter grıf
wil stɵn ɒs, for ꝺe ar konvinst
  Jon woz a profet trɯ."
Ꝺe sed, "Wı kanot tel." Ꝺen
  sed, "Nįꝺer tel į ɥ [Krįst
bį hwot ɷɟoriti į dɯ
  ꝺiz ɟiŋz.; bɒt, ɥ wil fįnd,
if ɥ bɒt trɯli serç for trɯɟ
  wiꝺ pɥr and onest mįnd."

SECTION 145.

Parable of the Two Sons.

Matthew 21. 28-32.

"A certain father had two sons;
  And unto one he said,
'Go, in my vineyard work.' But he
  This evil answer made,
'I will not.' After, he repents,
  And goes obediently.
The father to the second son
  Said likewise,—'Work for me.'
This son was gentler in his speech,
  But falser in his heart:
He said, 'I'll go,' but he went not,
  Acting a treacherous part.
Now which of these two sons did best
  Perform his father's will?"
The Scribes replied, "The first, for he
  Did his commands fulfil."
Then Jesus said, "By this same rule
  Ye do yourselves accuse;
For publicans and harlots go
  To heaven; while you refuse.
For they, though rude and ignorant,
  Do yet repent and turn;
But you, pretending all that's good,
  My gracious Gospel scorn.
John came to you in righteousness,
  And you would not believe;
But those you call the base and vile,
  His doctrine did receive;
And when you saw enough to prove
  His message was from heaven,
You showed no penitence, nor prayed
  Your guilt might be forgiven."

SEKΣON 145.

Parabel ov ꝺe Tɯ Sɒnz.

Maɟɥ 21. 28-32.

"A serten fɑꝺer had tɯ sɒnz;
  and ɒntu wɒn hı sed,
'Gɵ, in mį vinyard wɒrk.' Bɒt hı
  ꝺis ıvil anser med,
'Ɨ wil not.' After, hı repents,
  and gɵz ɵbıdientli.
Ꝺe fɑꝺer tu ꝺe sekond sɒn
  sed lįkwįz,—'Wɒrk for mı.'
Ꝺis sɒn woz jentler in hiz spıç,
  bɒt fɷlser in hiz hart:
hı sed, 'Ɨ'l gɵ,' bɒt hı went not,
  aktiŋ a treçerɒs part.
Nɤ hwiç ov ꝺiz tɯ sɒnz did best
  perform hiz fɑꝺer'z wil?"
Ꝺe Skrįbz replįd, "Ꝺe ferst, for hı
  did hiz komandz fulfil."
Ꝺen Jızɒs sed, "Bį ꝺis sem rɯl
  yı dɯ ɥrselvz akɥz;
for pɒblikanz and harlots gɵ
  tu heven; hwįl ɥ refɥz.
For ꝺe, ꝺɵ rɯd and ignorant,
  dɯ yet repent and tɒrn;
bɒt ɥ, pretendiŋ ɷl ꝺat's gud,
  mį greʃɒs Gospel skorn.
Jon kem tu ɥ in rįtiɒsnes,
  and ɥ wud not belıv;
bɒt ꝺɵz ɥ kɷl ꝺe bes and vįl,
  hiz doktrin did resıv;
and hwen ɥ sɷ enɒf tu prɯv
  hiz mesaej woz from heven,
ɥ ʃɵd nɵ penitens, nor pred
  ɥr gilt mįt bı forgiven."

SECTION 146.

Parable of the Vineyard.

Matthew 21. 33-46. Luke 20. 9-18.

"Hear now another parable :—
 There was a certain man,
A householder of good repute,
 Who on a time began
To plant a vineyard. Next he hedged
 It round about, and then
A wine press built, and tower, and let
 It out to husbandmen.
But he awhile retired afar,
 And there long time he spent;
And at the season for the fruit
 A servant home he sent,
Who from the husbandmen required
 That which was in their hand.
But soon 'twas found those wicked men
 Despised their Lord's command;
His messenger they beat, and drove
 Him destitute away.
Their lord then sent a second, whom
 They soon contrived to slay.
A third they wounded cruelly;
 Stoned him, and many more
They beat, and in their wicked spite
 Treated with anger sore.
At last their lord said, 'I will send
 My own beloved son;
Whom, when they see, they'll rever-
 My will will then be done.' [ence;
But when these men beheld the son,
 They to each other said,
'This is the heir, whom, if we kill,
 We shall, when he is dead,
Obtain the vineyard for ourselves.'
 And then they cast him out
And slew him. When the master
  comes,
 What will he do?" "No doubt,"
They said, "he will destroy those men,
 And then some others choose
For his rich vineyard, such as will
 Not his just rights refuse."
Then Jesus said to those chief priests,
 "Therefore I say to you,
God's kingdom ye no more shall hold,
 Ye render not your due;
It shall be given to those who will
 Its fruit in season grant."

SEKΣON 146.

Parabel ov đe Vinyard.

Mađɥ 21. 33-46. Luk 20. 9-18.

"Hir nɜ anɒđer parabel :—
 Đer woz a serten man,
a hɜshɵlder ov gud repɥt,
 hu on a tįm began
tu plant a vinyard. Nekst hi hejd
 it rɜnd abɜt, and đen
a wįn pres bilt, and tɜer, and let
 it ɜt tu hɒzbandmen.
Bɒt hi ahwįl retįrd afar,
 and đer loŋ tįm hi spent;
and at đe sizon for đe frut
 a servant hɵm hi sent,
hu from đe hɒzbandmen rekwįrd
 đát hwiç woz in đer hand.
Bɒt sun 'twoz fɜnd đɵz wiked men
 despįzd đer Lord'z komand;
hiz mesenjer đɛ bit, and drɵv
 him destitɥt awɛ.
Đɛr lord đen sent a sekond, hum
 đɛ sun kontrįvd tu slɛ.
A đerd đɛ wunded kruelli;
 stɵnd him, and meni mɵr
đɛ bit, and in đer wiked spįt
 trited wiđ aŋger sɵr.
At last đɛr lord sed, 'Ɨ wil send
 mį ɵn belɒved sɒn;
hum, hwen, đɛ si, đɛ'l reverens;
 mį wíl wil đen bi dɒn.'
Bɒt hwen điz men beheld đe sɒn,
 đɛ tu iç ɒđer sed,
'Điz iz đe ɛr, hum, if wi kil,
 wi ʃal, hwen hi iz ded,
obten đe vinyard for ɜrselvz.'
 And đen đɛ kast him ɜt
and slu him. Hwen đe master
  kɒmz,
 hwot wil hi du?" "Nɵ dɜt,"
đɛ sed, "hi wil destroi đɵz men,
 and đen sɒm ɒđerz çuz
for hiz riç vinyard, sɒç az wil
 not hiz jɒst rįts refɥz."
Đen Jizɒs sed tu đɵz çif prists,
 "Đerfɵr į sɛ tu ɥ,
God'z kiŋdom yi nɵ mɵr ʃal hɵld,
 yi render not ɥr dɥ;
it ʃal bi given tu đɵz hu wil
 its frut in sizon grant."

And when they heard, though self-ac-
They said, most arrogant, [cused,
"May God forbid." He said, "Have
Not read what is foretold, [ye
'The stone which the proud builders
(That stone ye now behold,) [left,
Is made the chief, the corner-stone:
The Lord hath done this thing,
And wondrous in our eyes it is;
His praise we therefore sing?'
And whoso stumbles on this stone,
Much pain and hurt will find;
But him on whom its weight shall fall,
It will to powder grind."
The Priests, and Scribes, and Pharisees
Who heard this awful speech,
Saw that he spake against their sins,
And judgement thus did preach.
But still they feared the multitude,
Who reverenced Christ at heart;
So they deferred to seize the Lord,
And left him to depart.

SECTION 147.

Parable of the Marriage Feast.
Matthew 22. 1-14.

Then Jesus spake again to them
In parables, and said,
"Heaven's kingdom may be likened to
A certain king, who made
A marriage for his son, and sent
His servants to call those
Who were invited, to the feast.
But they perversely chose
To treat with scorn the monarch's
And hospitality; [grace
And went their way, to work or play;
While others cruelly
His messengers did persecute,
And slew them spitefully.
And when the king was told this thing,
His anger rose apace;
He sent his armies forth, slew them,
And then destroyed the place.
Then to his servants he said thus:
'The wedding feast is set,
But those invited were not found
Worthy to sit thereat.

And hwen đe h
đe sed, mɵst
"Me God forbi
not red hwot
'Đe stɵn hwiç
(đát stɵn yi
iz ɱed đe çif,
đe Lord hat
and wɒndrɒs i
hiz prez wi
And huısɵ stɒ
mɒç pen an
bɒt him on huı
it wil tu pɤd
Đe Prists, and
huı herd đis
sɷ đat hi spek
and jɒjment
Bɒt stil đe fírc
huı reverens
sɵ đe deferd t
and left him

SEK

Parabel o
Mat

Đen Jizɒs spek
in parabelz,
"Heven'z kiŋ
a serten kiŋ,
a marej for hiz
hiz servants
huı wer invįte
Bɒt đe perv
tu trit wiđ sko
and hospital
and went đer
hwįl ɒđerz
hiz mesenjerz
and sluı đem
And hwen đe
hiz aŋger ro
hi sent hiz ar
and đen des
Đen tu hiz ser
'Đe wediŋ f
bɒt đɵz invįte
wɒrđi tu sit

Go therefore ye into the streets,
  And summon all ye find
Unto the feast, both bad and good.'
  They did as he designed.
So was the banquet furnished soon;
  And when the bounteous king
Came in to see the guests whom thus
  His messengers did bring,
He saw a man who had not on
  A wedding garment. 'Friend,'
Said he, 'how canst thou thus
  The other guests offend
By thy attire?' He could not speak.
  The king said, 'Bind him fast,
Take him away, and let him be
  To outer darkness cast.'
Though many are invited, few
  Are chosen at the last."

Gɵ đerfɵr yi intu đe strits,
  and sɒmon ɷl yi fįnd
ɒntu đe fist, bɵŧ bad and gud.
  Đɛ did az hi dezįnd.
Sɵ woz đe baŋkwet fɒrniʃt sɯn;
  and hwen đe bɤntiɒs kiŋ
kem in tu si đe gests hɯm đɒs
  hiz mesenjerz did briŋ,
hi sɷ a man hɯ had not on
  a wediŋ garment. 'Frend,'
sed hi, 'hɤ kanst đɤ đɒs
  đe ɒđer gests ofend
bį đį atįr?' Hi kud not spik.
  Đe kiŋ sed, 'Bįnd him fast,
tek him awɛ, and let him bi
  tu ɤter darknes kast.'
đɵ meni ar invįted, fų
  ar ɕɵzen at đe last."

SECTION 148.

Christ replies to the Herodians concerning Tribute Money.

Matthew 22. 15-22. Mark 12. 13-17.
Luke 20. 20-26.

The Pharisees consulted how
  They might ensnare the Lord
In conversation: so they watched
  And joined, in one accord,
With the Herodians, and spies
  Who passed for devotees,
That they might Christ with treason [charge,
  And on his person seize.
They come to him with false pretence,
  And say, "Full well we know
That thou dost teach God's truth, un- [moved
  By men's vain words below.
Tell us then, plainly, Is it right
  For Jews, like us, to pay
Tribute to Cæsar, who doth reign
  By alien Gentile sway?"
But Jesus saw their wickedness,
  And gross hypocrisies,
And said, "Why do ye tempt me thus
  By this unfair disguise?
Show me the money that ye pay
  As tax to Cæsar here."
They brought it. Jesus then replied,
  "Whose image doth appear

SEKΣON 148.

Krįst replįz tu đe Herɵdianz konserniŋ Tribųt Mɒni.

Mađų 22. 15-22. Mark 12. 13-17.
Luk 20. 20-26.

Đe Farisiz konsɒlted hɤ
  đɛ mįt ensnɛr đe Lord
in konversɛʃon: sɵ đɛ woɕt
  and joind, in wɒn akord,
wiđ đe Herɵdianz, and spįz
  hɯ past for devɵtiz,
đat đɛ mįt Krįst wiđ trizon ɕarj,
  and on hiz person siz.
Đe kɒm tu him wiđ fɷls pretens,
  and sɛ, "Ful wel wi nɵ́
đat đɤ dɒst tiɕ God'z trɯŧ,ɒnmuvd
  bį men'z ven wɒrdz belɵ.
Tel ɒs đen, plɛnli, Iz it rįt
  for Juiz, lįk ɒs, tu pɛ
tribųt tu Sizar, hɯ dɒŧ rɛn
  bį ɛlien Jentįl swɛ?"
Bɒt Jizɒs sɷ đer wikednes,
  and grɵs hipokrisiz,
and sed, "Hwį dui yi tempt mi đɒs
  bį đis ɒnfer disgįz?
Σɵ mi đe mɒni đat yi pɛ
  az taks tu Sizar hir."
Đe brɷt it. Jizɒs đen replįd,
  "Hɯz imej dɒŧ apir

Upon this coin?" "Cæsar's," they
  Christ did this answer give, [say.
'Grant unto Cæsar what is his;
  Beneath his reign you live:
And grant to God whate'er belongs
  To him by right divine."
On this the guilty questioners
  Relinquished their design,
Admired his answer, held their peace,
  And did no more essay
To ensnare the Lord with guileful
      words,
  And, wondering, went their way.

SECTION 149.

Christ replies to the Sadducees concerning the Resurrection.

Matthew 22. 23-33. Mark 12. 18-27. Luke 20. 27-40.

Then certain of the Sadducees
  Who boldly did deny
The resurrection from the dead,
  Unto the Lord apply,
To question him about this thing,
  And thus their cunning try:—
"According to Mosaic law,
  Seven brethren, who are dead,
Did, in succession, as ordained,
  The self-same woman wed.
And last of all the woman died.
  Now if indeed there be
A resurrection of the dead,
  Whose lawful wife is she?"
Jesus replied, "Ye err, because
  Ye do not understand
The wisdom of the Scriptures, nor
  The might of God's right hand.
In this world people marry and
  Are married, but not so
In that eternal world to come,
  The world to which all go.
They who are worthy to attain
  The resurrection bright,
Marry no more, like men, but dwell
  As angels in God's sight.
Now that the dead are raised again,
  Even Moses doth foreshow,
For, in the burning bush, God said
  To him as well ye know,

ɒpon đis koin?" "Sizar'z," đe se.
  Kr̨ist did đis anser giv,
"Grant ɒntu Sizar hwot iz hiz;
  beniđ hiz ren ų liv:
and grant tu God hwot'er beloŋz
  tų him bį rįt divįn."
On đis đe gilti kwestionerz
  reliŋkwiʃt đer dezįn,
admįrd hiz anser, held đer pis,
  and did nσ mσr ese
tu ensner đe Lord wiđ gįlful
      wɒrdz,
  and, wɒnderiŋ, went đer we.

SEKΣON 149.

Krįst replįz tu đe Sadųsiz konserniŋ đe Rezɒrekʃon.

Maŧų 22. 23-33. Mark 12. 18-27. Lɯk 20. 27-40.

Đen serten ov đe Sadųsiz
  hɯ bσldli did denį
đe rezɒrekʃon from đe ded,
  ɒntu đe Lord aplį,
tu kwestion him abɤt đis ŧiŋ,
  and đɒs đer kɒniŋ trį:—
"Akordiŋ tu Mσzeik lω,
  seven bređren, hɯ ar ded,
did, in sɒkseʃon, az ordend,
  đe self-sem wuman wed.
And last ov ωl đe wuman dįd.
  Nɤ if indid đer bi
a rezɒrekʃon ov đe ded,
  hɯz lωful wįf iz ʃi?"
Jįzɒs replįd, "Yi er, bekωz
  yi dɯ not ɒnderstand
đe wizdom ov đe Skriptųrz, nor
  đe mįt ov God'z rįt hand.
In đis wɒrld pipel mari and
  ar marid, bɒt not sσ
in đát eternal wɒrld tu kɒm,
  đe wɒrld tu hwiç ωl gσ.
Đe hɯ ar wɒrđi tu aten
  đe rezɒrekʃon brįt,
mari nσ mσr, lįk men, bɒt dwel
  az enjelz in God'z sįt.
Nɤ đat đe ded ar rezd agen,
  iven Mσsez dɒŧ fσrʃσ,
for, in đe bɒrniŋ buʃ, God sed
  tu him, az wel yi nσ́,

'I am the God of Abraham,
And his posterity.'
He's not the God of dead; therefore
Ye err most fatally."
Then said the Scribes, "Thou answer-
est well;
Nor did they thenceforth dare
To question him, nor seek, with his,
Their wisdom to compare.
And all the multitude admired;
He was to them as one inspired.

'Ɨ am đe God ov Ɛbraham,
and hiz posteriti.'
Hi'z not đe God ov ded; đerfɵr
yi hir mɵst fetali."
Đen sed đe Skrȷbz, "Đᴣ anserest
wel;
nor did đɛ đensfɵrᵵ der
tu kwestion him, nor sik, wiđ hiz,
đer wizdom tu komper.
And ɷl đe mɒltitɥd admȷrd;
hi woz tu đem az wɒn inspȷrd.

SECTION 150.

Christ replies to the Lawyer concerning the Commandments.

Matthew 22. 34-40. Mark 12. 28-34.

And when the Pharisees perceived
The Sadducees' defeat,
They came together, that the Lord
His teaching might repeat.
And one, a Scribe of Moses' law,
Would try him on this wise:
"Say, Master, which the great com-
Then Jesus thus replies; [mand?"
"The first of all commands is this,
The Lord our God is one;
And thou shalt love him with thy soul,
And heart, and mind, alone.
The second teaches, like the first,
This law of love most kind;
Thy neighbour, like thyself, thou shalt
Love with an equal mind.
No higher rule has God ordained;
On these hangs all the law;
The prophets too have taught the
same."
The Scribe said, "Thou dost draw
True wisdom from the Word of life;
For there is but one Lord;
And those who love him with the heart
And soul, in sweet accord,
Will be received by him above
All pious offerers
Of oxen and of sheep, who are
But outside worshipers."
When Jesus heard this speech discreet,
He to the Scribe thus said,
"Thou art not far from heaven, and in
The law thou art well read."

SEKΣON 150.

Krȷst replȷz tu đe Lɵier konserniŋ de Komandments.

Maᵵɥ 22. 34-40. Mark 12. 28-34.

And hwen đe Farisiz persivd
đe Sadɥsiz' defit,
đɛ kem tugeđer, đat đe Lord
hiz tiçiŋ mȷt repit.
And wɒn, a Skrȷb ov Mɵzes' lɷ,
wud trȷ him on đis wȷz:
"Sɛ, Master, hwiç đe gret komand?"
Đen Jizɒs đɒs replȷz;
"Đe ferst ov ɷl komandz iz đis,
Đe Lord ᴣr God iz wɒn;
and đᴣ ʃalt lɒv him wiđ đȷ sɵl,
and hart, and mȷnd, alɵn.
Đe sekond tiçez lȷk đe ferst,
đis lɷ ov lɒv mɵst kȷnd;
Đȷ nebɒr, lȷk đȷself, đᴣ ʃalt
lɒv wiđ an ikwal mȷnd.
Nɵ hȷer rul haz God ordend;
on điz haŋz ɷl đe lɷ;
đe profets tu hav tɷt đe
sem."
Đe Skrȷb sed, "Đᴣ dɒst drɷ
tru wizdom from đe Wɒrd ov lȷf;
for đer iz bɒt wɒn Lord;
and đɵz hu lɒv him wiđ đe hart
and sɵl, in swit akord,
wil bi resivd bȷ him abɒv
ɷl pȷɒs ofererz
ov oksen and ov ʃip, hu ar
bɒt ᴣtsȷd wɒrʃiperz."
Hwen Jizɒs herd dis spiç diskrit,
hi tu đe Skrȷb đɒs sed,
"Đᴣ art not far from heven, and in
đe lɷ đᴣ art wel red."

SECTION 151.

Christ inquires of the Pharisees concerning the Messiah.

Matthew 22. 41-46. Mark 12. 35-37.
Luke 20. 41-44.

And while the Pharisees were there,
  Jesus thus questioned them:
"What think ye of the Christ? Tell
  Of what root is he stem? [me.
They say to him, "Of David's root,
  For he is David's son."
He saith to them, "How is it then
  That David, when alone
With God, in spirit, calls him Lord?
  For these his words, most fit:—
'Jehovah, or the Lord, saith to
  My Lord, (Adoni,) Sit
On my right hand until I make
  Thy foes bow at thy feet.'
If David call him Lord, how then
  Can he be deemed his son?"
No man could answer him; and they
  Thenceforth all questions shun.

SECTION 152.

Christ severely reproves the Pharisees for their pride and hypocrisy, and pronounces a lamentation over Jerusalem.

Matthew 23. 1-39. Mark 12. 38-40.
Luke 20. 45-47.

Throughout the land of Palestine,
  As Jesus preached the Word,
The upper class turned from him, but
  The people gladly heard.
Then Jesus spake these warning words
  To his disciples near,
And a great multitude of Jews
  Who likewise thronged to hear:—
"The Scribes and Pharisees now sit
  In Moses' legal seat,
Therefore, when teaching Moses' law,
  It is but right and meet
That you obey their words, but not
  Their works; for oft they do
Unholy deeds, and speak what they
  Are conscious is not true.
For they impose on other men
  Sore burdens, hard to bear,

SEKΣ

Krịst inkwịrz ov
đe

Maʇɥ 22. 1-46
Luk

And hwịl đe Fa
  Jizɒs đɒs·kw
"Hwot ʇiŋk yị
  Ov hwot rut
Đe se tu him, "
  for hị iz Dev
Hị seʇ tu đem,
  đat Devid, h
wiđ God, in spi
  For điz hiz w
'Jeheva, or đe
  mị Lord, (Ad
on mị rịt hand
  đị foz bɤ at đ
If Devid kold h
  kan hị bi di
Ne man kud a
  đensforʇ ol h

SEKΣ

Krịst sevirli rep
đer prịd and hi
a lamentɛʃon ov

Maʇɥ 23. 1-39
Luk

Ƙruɤt đe land
  az Jizɒs priç
đe ɒper klas tɒ
  đe pipel glad
Đen Jizɒs spek
  tu hiz disịpel
and a gret mɒlt
  hu lịkwịz ʇr
"Đe Skrịbz an
  in Mozes' lig
đerfor, hwen ti
  it iz bɒt rịt a
đat ɥ obe đer w
  đer wɒrks; f
ɒnholi didz, an
  ar konʃɒs iz
For đe impoz o
  sor bɒrdenz,

Of rigid laws, and forms, and tasks,
Which they refuse to share,
Or to alleviate; their works
Are all for pomp and pride,
To attract the notice of the crowd,
Who need a better guide.
They wear peculiar robes, and love
To assume the highest place,
And court obsequious compliments
Of Rabbi, Reverence, Grace;
And for a show they make long prayers,
While meantime they devour
The wealth of widows, and the poor,
To swell their bloated power.
Therefore a greater punishment
These hypocrites will have,
Because they rob, remorselessly,
The people they should save.
But do not ye, my followers, strive
For mastery supreme;
As Christ your royal Master is,
Ye should as brethren seem.
Nor be entitled Teacher, Sire,
Nor Abba (father) be;
For one alone ye thus should own,
And he the Lord most high.
For he who would be greatest in
Your ranks, shall serve the rest;
And he who would be made your chief,
Shall be the most abased.
And he who humbly bows himself
To duty, honor true,
For him the future hour is rich
In praise to merit due.
Woe unto you, ye Pharisees!
False priests, both proud and vain;
Ye shut up heaven against all men:
Ye neither it obtain
Yourselves, nor will ye suffer those
Who would, to enter there;
Your base hypocrisy doth spoil
The Church, else bright and fair.
Ye compass sea and land, with zeal,
To gain one proselyte,
And make him worse even than yourselves,
In heaven's just judging sight.
Ye blind guides! veiling o'er your face,
Lest evil ye should see;

ov rijid lɷz, and formz and tasks,
hwiç ɗe refųz tu ʃer,
or tu aliviet; ɗer wɒrks
ar ɷl for pomp and prįd,
tu atrakt ɗe nɵtis ov ɗe krɜd,
huı nıd a beter gįd.
Ɗe wer pekųliar rɵbz, and lɒv
tu asųm ɗe hįest ples,
and kɵrt obsıkwiɒs kompliments
ov Rabį, Reverens, Gres;
and for a ʃɵ ɗe mek loŋ prerz,
hwįl mıntįm ɗe devɜr
ɗe welʇ ov widɵz, and ɗe puır,
tu swel ɗer blɵted pɜer.
Ɗerfɵr a greter pɒniʃment
ɗiz hipokrits wil hav,
bekɷz ɗe rob, remorslesli,
ɗi pipel ɗe ʃud sev.
Bɒt duı not yı, mį folɵerz, strįv
for masteri sųprım;
az Krįst ųr roial Master iz,
yi ʃud az breɗren sım.
Nor bi entįteld Tiçer, Sįr,
nor Aba (fɜɗer) bı;
for wɒn alɵn yı ɗɒs ʃud ɵn,
and hi ɗe Lord mɵst hį.
For hi huı wud bi gretest in
ųr raŋks, ʃal serv ɗe rest;
and hi huı wud bı med ųr çif,
ʃal bi ɗe mɵst abest.
And hi huı hɒmbli bɜz himself
tu dųti, onor truı,
for him ɗe fųtųr ɜr iz riç
in prez tu merit dų.
Wɵ ɒntu ų, yi Farisız!
fɷls prısts, bɵʇ prɜd and ven;
yi ʃɒt ɒp heven agenst ɷl men:
yi nįɗer it obten
ųrselvz, nor wil yı sɒfer ɗɵz
huı wud, tu enter ɗer;
ųr bes hipokrasi dɒʇ spoil
ɗe Ɛɒrç, els brįt and fer.
Yı kompas sı and land, wiɗ zıl,
tu gen wɒn proselįt,
and mek him wɒrs ıven ɗan ųrselvz,
in heven'z jɒst jɒjiŋ sįt.
Yı blįnd gįdz! veliŋ ɵ'r ųr fes,
lest ıvil yı ʃud sı;

And then polluting your base souls
  By wilful perjury.
Ye say 'If, by the temple, oaths
  Are made, they do not bind;
But if men swear upon its gold,
  Their oaths lie on the mind.'
Ye blinded fools! do ye not know
  The temple is more great
And holy than its furniture,
  However bright its state?
'If, by the altar men make oath,'
  Ye say, 'it leaves them free;
But if by altar's offerings,
  They must pay faithfully.'
Ye blinded fools! the altar sure
  Is holier than the store
Of gifts thereon, which it doth make
  More sacred than before.
Whoever by the temple swears,
  Swears by the God therein;
And if he break his oath, he then
  Commits a heinous sin:
And whoso swears by heaven above,
  Swears by God's holy throne,
And Him who sits thereon, by whom
  False oaths are all well known.
Ye hypocrites! who are so strict
  In rites and forms minute,
And break the holiest laws of God,
  And each chief attribute
Of justice, mercy, faith. 'Tis well
  To keep each small command;
But holiness of heart and life
  Is God's most just demand.
Ye blinded guides! who will strain out
  Each gnat, lest it defile;
Yet scruple not to swallow whole
  Camels of sin the while.
Ye purify the outside, but
  Ye inwardly abound
With all extortion and excess,
  And desecrate the ground.
First cleanse the secret soul within;
  Let your desires be pure;
Then will your words and works dis-
  The soul's bright portraiture. [play
Ye are like decorated tombs,
  Most fair externally,
But covering still a loathsome corpse,
  Foul with putridity;

and đen polɯtiŋ ɥr bes sɵlz
  bį wilful perjuri.
Yi se 'If, bį đe tempel, ɵđz
  ar med, đe dɯ not bįnd;
bɒt if men swer ɒpon its gɵld,
  đer ɵđz lį on đe mįnd.'
Yi blįnded fɯlz! dɯ yi not nɵ́
  đe tempel iz mɵr gret
and hɵli đan its fɒrnitɥr,
  hʒever brįt its stet?
'If, bį đe ɷltar men mek ɵɟ,'
  yi se, 'it livz đem fri;
bɒt if bį ɷltar'z oferiŋz,
  đe mɒst pe feɟfuli.'
Yi blįnded fɯlz! đe ɷltar ʃɯr
  iz hɵlier đan đe stɵr
ov gifts đeron, hwiɋ it dɒɟ mek
  mɵr sekred đan befɵr.
Hɯever bį đe tempel swerz,
  swerz bį đe God đerin;
and if hi brek hiz ɵɟ, hi đen
  komits a henɒs sin:
and hɯsɵ swerz bį heven abɒv,
  swerz bį God'z hɵli ɟrɵn,
and Him hɯ sits đeron, bį hɯm
  fɷls ɵđz ar ɷl wel nɵn.
Yi hipokrits! hɯ ar sɵ strikt
  in rįts and formz minɥt,
and brek đe hɵliest lɷz ov God,
  and iɋ ɋif atribɥt
ov jɒstis, mersi, feɟ. 'Tiz wel
  tu kip iɋ smɷl komand;
bɒt hɵlines ov hart and lįf
  iz God'z mɵst jɒst demand.
Yi blįnded gįdz! hɯ wil stren ʒt
  iɋ nat, lest it defįl;
yet skrɯpel not tu swolɵ hɵl
  kamelz ov sin đe hwįl.
Yi pɥrifį đe ʒtsįd, bɒt
  yi inwardli abʒnd
wiđ ɷl ekstorʃon and ekses,
  and desekret đe grʒnd.
Ferst klenz đe sikret sɵl wiđin;
  let ɥr dezįrz bi pɥr;
đen wil ɥr wɒrdz and wɒrks disple
  đe sɵl'z brįt pɵrtretɥr.
Yi ar lįk dekoreted tɯmz,
  mɵst fer eksternali,
bɒt kɒveriŋ stil a lɵɟsɒm korps,
  fʒl wiđ pɥtriditi;

So outwardly may ye appear
  Righteous to men below;
But inwardly are full of fraud,
  As God above doth know.
Your fathers slew God's holy seers
  And prophets, and ye still
Repair their tombs, and crown the
  Your fathers wrought so ill. [work
And yet ye say, 'If we had lived
  In those our fathers' days,
We would not have joined hands with
  In all their murderous ways.' [them
Yet by thus garnishing the tombs
  By direful murderers built,
Ye ratify their villainy
  And consecrate their guilt.
Then fill ye up the measure, full,
  Of your forefathers' vice;
Vipers were they, serpents are ye
  Of guile and avarice;
And how can ye or they escape
  Damnation for all this?
Behold I send to you again,
  Prophets and sages true;
And as your fathers did of old,
  Ye, their vile sons, will do;
And some you'll persecute and scourge,
  And torture in your hate,
And some you'll slay and crucify,
  Nor yet your rage abate;
That upon you may fall the curse
  Of all the righteous blood
Shed on the earth, from Abel's, and
  The saints beyond the flood,
To that of Zacharias, whom
  Ye slew on holy ground,
Near to the temple's altar, where
  Mercy should most abound.
Oh Salem! Oh Jerusalem!
  Who dost thy prophets slay,
And stonest those sent unto thee
  To teach thee God's own way;
How oft would I have gathered all
  Thy children 'neath my care,
Even as a hen protects her young
  From violence and snare;
And ye would not! Your house will
  All desolate be laid: [soon
And you shall never more behold
  Your king, by you betrayed,

sɵ ɜtwardli mε yi apir
  rįtiɒs tu men belɵ;
bɒt inwardli ar ful ov frɷd,
  az God abɒv dɒŧ nɵ́.
Ʊr fɑđerz slɯ God'z hɵli sierz
  and profets, and yi stil
reper đer tɯmz, and krɜn đe wɒrk
  ɥr fɑđerz rɷt sɵ il.
And yet yi sε, 'If wi had livd
  in đɵz ɜr fɑđerz' dεz,
wi wud not hav joind handz wiđ
  in ɷl đer mɒrderɒs wεz.' [đem
Yet bį đɒs garniʃiŋ đe tɯmz
  bį dįrful mɒrdererz bilt,
yi ratifį đer vileni
  and konsekrεt đεr gilt.
Đen fil yi ɒp đe meʒur, ful,
  ov ɥr fɵrfɑđerz' vįs;
vįperz wer đε, serpents ar yi
  ov gįl and avaris;
and hɜ kan yi or đε eskεp
  damnεʃon for ɷl đis?
Behɵld į send tu ɥ agen,
  profets and sεjez trɯ;
and az ɥr fɑđerz did ov ɵld,
  yi, đer vįl sɒnz, wil dɯ;
and sɒm ɥ'l persekɥt and skɒrj,
  and tortɥr in ɥr hεt,
and sɒm ɥ'l slε and krɯsifį,
  nor yet ɥr rεj abεt;
đat ɒpon ɥ mε fɷl đe kɒrs
  ov ɷl đe rįtiɒs blɒd
ʃed on đe erŧ, from Ɛbel'z, and
  đe sεnts beyond đe flɒd,
tu đát ov Zakarįas, hɯm
  yi slɯ on hɵli grɜnd,
nir tu đe tempel'z ɷltar, hwer
  mersi ʃud mɵst abɜnd.
Ɵ Sεlem! Ɵ Jerusalem!
  hɯ dɒst đį profets slε,
and stɵnest đɵz sent ɒntu đi
  tu tiç đi God'z ɵn wε;
hɜ oft wud į hav gađerd ɷl
  đį çildren 'niđ mį ker,
iven az a hen prɵtekts her yɒŋ
  from vįolens and sner;
and yi wud not! Ʊr hɜs wil sɯn
  ɷl desolεt bi lεd:
and ɥ ʃal never mɵr behɵld
  ɥr kiŋ, bį ɥ betrεd,

Until with faith and penitence
  You my forgiveness claim,
And bless the Christ that comes to you
  In great Jehovah's name."

SECTION 153.

Christ applauds the Liberality of the poor Widow.

Mark 12. 41-44. Luke 21. 1-4.

As in the temple Jesus sat,
  And saw the treasury,
He noted how the people there
  Gave as they pleased, quite free.
The rich cast in their larger gifts,
  Some wished to make a show;
And one poor widow threw in all
  She then had to bestow,
Two mites. The Lord then turned, [and his
  Disciples thus addressed,
"I tell you, this poor widow hath
  Given more than all the rest.
Of their abundance, they have helped
  The offerings of the Lord,
She, of her poverty, her all
  Doth to his cause afford."

BOOK X.

SECTION 154.

Christ foretells the destruction of Jerusalem, the end of the Jewish dispensation, and the consummation of the age.

Matthew 24. 1-35. Mark 13. 1-31.
Luke 21. 5-33.

As Jesus from the temple walked,
  His followers pointed out
To him the buildings, and the gifts
  Which those who were devout
Had offered to the Lord. They said,
  "See, Master, what is here!
How vast these buildings; and the [stones,
  How stately they appear!"
Jesus replied, "See ye these things?
  All that ye now behold
Shall be o'erthrown some future day:
  The offerings and the gold

ɒntil wiđ feꝥ and penitens
  ɥ mį forgivnes klem,
and bles đe Krįst đat kɒmz tu ɥ
  in gret Jehova'z nem."

SEKΣON 153.

Krįst aplɷdz đe Liberaliti ov đe pur Wido.

Mark 12. 41-44. Luk 21. 1-4.

Az in đe tempel Jizɒs sat,
  and sɷ đe trezuri,
hi noted hɤ đe pipel đer
  gev az đe plizd, kwįt fri.
Đe riç kast in đer larjer gifts,
  sɒm wiʃt tu mek a ʃo;
and wɒn pur wido ꝥru in ɷl
  ʃi đen had tu besto,
tú mįts. Đe Lord đen tɒrnd, and [hiz
  disįpelz đɒs adrest,
"Ɨ tel ɥ, đis pur wido haꝥ
  given mor đan ɷl đe rest.
Ov đer abɒndans, đe hav helpt
  đe oferiŋz ov đe Lord,
ʃi, ov her poverti, her ɷl
  dɒꝥ tu hiz kɷz aford."

BUK X.

SEKΣON 154.

Krįst fortelz đe destrɒkʃon ov Jerusalem, đe end ov đe Jɥiʃ dispenseʃon, and đe konsɒmeʃon ov đe ej.

Maꝥɥ 24. 1-35. Mark 13. 1-31.
Luk 21. 5-33.

Az Jizɒs from đe tempel wɷkt,
  hiz folorz pɤinted ɤt
tu him đe bildiŋz, and đe gifts,
  hwiç đoz hu wer devɤt
had oferd tu đe Lord. Đe sed,
  "Si, Master, hwot iz hir!
hɤ vast điz bildiŋz; and đe stonz,
  hɤ stetli đe apir!"
Jizɒs replįd, "Si yi điz ꝥiŋz?
  ɷl đat yi nɤ behold
ʃal bi or'ꝥron sɒm fɥtɥr de:
  đe oferiŋz and đe gold

Shall pass away, and every stone
  Be leveled to the ground.
And verily I say, that none
  Of these things shall be found."

Then he ascended Olivet,
  'Gainst which the temple shone,
And privately unto him came
  James, Peter, Andrew, John;
"Master," they asked, "when shall
    this be?
  And what sign shall be shown
Both of thy coming, and the time
  When these things shall be done?"
And Jesus thus to them replied:
  "Take heed that none deceive;
For many in my name will come
  Whom ye must not believe.
They'll say, 'Behold the Christ!' and
  Will many lead aside: [thus
Follow them not; the time is near
  When these things shall betide.
Of plots, and rumors of great wars,
  You'll hear, but do not fret;
These things must happen first; but
  The end shall not be yet. [know
Nation and kingdom shall rise up
  Against each other then,
And earthquakes great, in divers parts,
  Shall terrify most men;
And famines, plagues, and fearful
    sights,
  And signs from heaven above;
Yet all these sorrows are but light
  To those which earth shall prove.

Unto yourselves take heed betimes,
  For you will suffer first,
And be, for my sake, beaten, bound,
  Imprisoned, tried, accurst,
Be charged 'fore kings and rulers, that
  Ye bear my holy name:
A testimony it shall turn
  To you, and not a shame.
And first the Gospel must be preached
  To all the nations round,
Be ye not anxious, nor prepare
  An answer to confound
Them, but, whatever ye should speak
  I will give wisdom due:

ʃal pas awe, and everi stɵn
  bi leveld tu đe grɜnd.
And verili į se, đat nɒn
  ov điz ɟiŋz ʃal bi fɜnd."

Đen hi asended Olivet,
  'genst hwiç đe tempel ʃon,
and prįvetli ɒntu him kem
  Jemz, Piter, Andrɯ, Jon;
"Master," đe askt, "hwen ʃal
    đis bi?
  and hwot sįn ʃal bi ʃɵn
bɵɟ ov đį kɒmiŋ, and đe tįm
  hwen điz ɟiŋz ʃal bi dɒn?"
And Jizɒs đɒs tu đem replįd:
  "Tɛk hid đat nɒn desiv;
for meni in mį nem wil kɒm
  hɯm yi mɒst not beliv.
Đɛ'l se, 'Behɵld đe Krįst!' and đɒs
  wil meni lid asįd:
folɵ đem not; đe tįm iz nir
  hwen điz ɟiŋz ʃal betįd.
Ov plots, and rɯmorz ov gret worz,
  ɥ'l hir, bɒt dɯ not fret;
điz ɟiŋz mɒst hapen ferst; bɒt nɵ́
  đe end ʃal not bi yet.
Nɛʃon and kiŋdom ʃal rįz ɒp
  agenst iç ɒđer đen,
and erɟkweks gret, in dįverz parts,
  ʃal terifį mɵst men;
and faminz, plegz, and firful
    sįts,
  and sįnz from heven abɒv;
yet ɷl điz sorɵz ar bɒt lįt
  tu đɵz hwiç erɟ ʃal prɯv.

Ɯntu ɥrselvz tɛk hid betįmz,
  for ɥ wil sɒfer ferst,
and bi, for mį sek, biten, bɜnd,
  imprizond, trįd, akɒrst,
bi çarjd 'fɵr kiŋz and rɯlerz, đat
  yi ber mį hɵli nem:
a testimoni it ʃal tɒrn
  tu ɥ, and not a ʃem.
And ferst đe Gospel mɒst bi priçt
  tu ɷl đe neʃonz rɜnd,
bi yi not aŋkʃɒs, nor preper
  an anser tu konfɜnd
đem, bɒt, hwotever yi ʃud spik
  į wil giv wizdom dɥ:

Your enemies shall not resist
  The Holy Spirit in you.

And then the brother shall betray
  The brother unto death;
The father rise against the son
  And make him lose his breath.
And children 'gainst their parents, too,
  Shall turn as enemies,
And ye yourselves shall be betrayed
  By direst calumnies
Of brethren, kinsfolk, friends, and those
  In whom you trusted most:
All nations will detest you, and
  Will make their hate their boast.
But 'midst such sorrows, from your
  Not even a hair shall fall; [head
In patience, therefore, keep your souls,
  Ye shall be saved through all.
False prophets too will then appear,
  And vile deceivers come,
And wickedness will much abound,
  And love grow cold at home:
But they that to the end endure,
Their own salvation will secure.
This Gospel must be preached to all,
Before these troubles shall appall.

And when the time shall be fulfilled
  Of Daniel's prophecy,
And heathen desolation stand
  Within the sanctuary
Of holiness, the Holy Place,
  (Who reads, should comprehend,)
And when ye see Jerusalem,
  By all her sons, defend
Herself from armies that surround,
  Then know her end is nigh.
Let those who in Judæa dwell,
  Flee to the mountains high,
And let not those who live around,
  Enter therein to die.
He who upon the housetop is,
  Should not descend to take
His goods: and let one coming home,
  His very clothes forsake.
The days of vengeance these will be,
  What's written to fulfil.
But woe to those who children bear,
  Or nurse their sucklings still!

ɥr enemiz ʃal not rezist
  đe Hɵli Spirit in ɥ.

And đen đe brɒđer ʃal betrɛ
  đe brɒđer ɒntu deŧ;
đe fɑđer rįz agenst đe sɒn
  and mek him lɯz hiz breŧ.
And çildren 'genst đer perents, tɯ,
  ʃal tɒrn az enemiz,
and yi ɥrselvz ʃal bi betrɛd
  bį dįrest kalɒmniz
ov bređren, kinzfɵk, frendz, and
  in hɯm ɥ trɒsted mɵst: [đɵz
ɑl neʃonz wil detest ɥ, and
  wil mek đer het đer bɵst.
Bɒt 'midst sɒç sorɵz, from ɥr hed
  not iven a her ʃal fɑl;
in peʃens, đerfɵr, kip ɥr sɵlz,
  yi ʃal bi sevd ŧrɯ ɑl.
Fɑls profets tɯ wil đen apir,
  and vįl desiverz kɒm,
and wikednes wil mɒç abɤnd,
  and lɒv grɵ kɵld at hɵm:
Bɒt đɛ đat tu đe end endɥr,
đer ɵn salveʃon wil sekɥr.
Đis Gospel mɒst bi priçt tu ɑl,
befɵr điz trɒbelz ʃal apɑl.

And hwen đe tįm ʃal bi fulfild
  ov Daniel'z profesi,
and hiđen desoleʃon stand
  wiđin đe saŋktɥari
ov hɵlines, đe Hɵli Ples,
  (hɯ ridz, ʃud komprehend,)
and hwen yi si Jerɯsalem,
  bį ɑl her sɒnz, defend
herself from armiz đat sɒrɤnd,
  đen nɵ her end iz nį.
Let đɵz hɯ in Jɯdia dwel,
  fli tu đe mɤntenz hį,
and let not đɵz hɯ liv arɤnd,
  enter đerin tu dį.
Hi hɯ ɒpon đe hɤstop iz,
  ʃud not desend tu tek
hiz gudz: and let wɒn kɒmiŋ hɵm,
  hiz veri klɵđz forsek.
Đe dez ov venjans điz wil bi,
  hwot's riten tu fulfil.
Bɒt wɵ tu đɵz hɯ çildren ber,
  or nɒrs đer sɒkliŋz stil!

Pray, winter time nor Sabbath day
  May witness your sad flight,
For never since the world began
  Did e'er such woes unite.
For great distress,and wrath, and woe,
  (Brought on by Jewish crime,)
And tribulation, shall prevail
  Throughout that fearful time.
Then Salem shall be trodden down
  By Gentiles' hated feet,
Until the times long prophesied
  Of Gentiles be complete.
Except those days the Lord make
  All flesh will be destroyed ; [short.
But for his chosen ones, thus will
  His mercy be employed.

If one shall then say, 'Here is Christ!'
  Or, 'Lo, the Christ is there!'
Believe him not, for many such
  Shall rise. Do ye beware!
False Christs and prophets then will
  Great signs and wonders too, [show
That they may the elect deceive,
  By subtleties untrue.
But since I have foretold these things
  Unto you, take ye heed;
And when they say, 'In deserts look!'
  Go not that way with speed;
Or, 'In the secret chambers seek!'
  Believe not their false word.
Be it enough for you to wait
  The coming of the Lord.
For as the lightning from the east
  Unto the west doth shine,
So shall the Son of man appear
  In glory all divine.
Wherever carrion is found,
The birds of prey will e'er abound.

Soon after these events, will signs
  Be in the sun, moon, stars ;
And on the earth perplexity,
  Distress, and cruel wars ;
The sea and waves will loudly roar,
  Men's hearts will fail for fear
In looking at the things on earth.
  Then shall the sign appear
Even of the Son of man in heaven
  With power and glory great ;

Prɛ, winter tįm nor Sabaŧ dɛ
  mɛ witnes ɥr sad flįt,
for never sins đe wɒrld began
  did ɛr sɒç wɵz ɥnįt.
For grɛt distres, and rɛŧ, and wɵ,
  (brɷt on bį Jɯiʃ krįm,)
and tribɥleʃon, ʃal prevɛl
  ŧrɯȣt đát fịrful tįm.
Đen Sɛlem ʃal bị troden dȣn
  bį Jentįlz' hɛted fịt,
ɒntil đe tįmz loŋ profesįd
  ov Jentįlz bị komplịt.
Eksept đɵz dɛz đe Lord mɛk ʃort,
  ɷl fleʃ wil bị destroid ;
bɒt for hiz çɵzen wɒnz, đɒs wil
  hiz mersi bị emploid.

If wɒn ʃal đen sɛ, 'Hịr iz Krįst!'
  or, 'Lɵ, đe Krįst iz đɛr!'
belịv him not, for meni sɒç
  ʃal rįz. Dɯ yị bewɛr!
Fɷls Krįsts and profets đen wil ʃɵ
  grɛt sįnz and wɒnderz tɯ,
đat đɛ mɛ đe elekt desịv,
  bį sɒteltiz ɒntrɯ.
Bɒt sins į hav fɵrtɵld điz ŧiŋz
  ɒntu ɥ, tɛk yị hịd ;
and hwen đɛ sɛ, 'In dezerts luk!'
  gɵ not đát wɛ wiđ spịd ;
or, 'In đe sịkret çɛmberz sịk!'
  belịv not đɛr fɷls wɒrd.
Bị it enɒf for tu wɛt
  đe kɒmiŋ ov đe Lord.
For az đe lįtniŋ from đe ịst
  ɒntu tu đe west dɒŧ ʃįn,
sɵ ʃal đe Sɒn ov man apịr
  in glɵri ɷl divįn.
Hwɛrever karion iz fȣnd,
đe berdz ov prɛ wil ɛr abȣnd.

Sɯn after điz events, wil sįnz
  bị in đe sɒn, mɯn, starz ;
and on đe erŧ perpleksiti,
  distres, and krɯel worz ;
đe sị and wɛvz wil lȣdli rɵr
  men'z harts wil fɛl for fịr
in lukiŋ at đe ŧiŋz on erŧ.
  Đen ʃal đe sįn apịr
ịven ov đe Sɒn ov man in heven
  wiđ pȣer and glɵri grɛt ;

At which the tribes of earth shall
  And sorrow, for their fate. [mourn
And he shall send his angels, with
  The sound of trumpet great,
To gather from all parts his saints,
  His pleasure to await.
When these things come to pass, look
  And lift your heads on high; [up
Your hearts then fill with comfort;
  Redemption draweth nigh." [your

This parable spake Jesus then:
  "Ye from the fig tree learn
In tender branch and shoots, the ap-
  Of summer to discern. [proach
So when these things shall be fulfilled,
  Then know that nigh at hand
The kingdom of your God is come,
  Even in this very land.
This generation shall not pass
  Till all these things be done;
The heaven and earth shall pass away,
  But of my words, not one."

SECTION 155.

Christ discourses on the suddenness of his Second Coming.

Matthew 24. 36-51. Mark 13. 32-37. Luke 21. 34-36.

"But no man knoweth of that day,
  Nor angels, nor the Son,
My Father only knows the time
  When his will shall be done.
For as the days of Noah were,
  So shall the Son of man
Be in his day: his coming will
  Be as the flood began.
As in the days before the flood
  They ate and drank with glee,
And married wives, and nothing
  Of dire calamity, [thought
Until the flood came unawares
  And took them all away;
So likewise shall the Son of man
  Come on you in his day.
Then shall two men be in the field,
  In full security;
One shall be taken, and one left.
  Slight not this prophecy.

at hwiç đe trįbz ov erŧ ʃal mɵrn
  and sorɵ, for đer fet.
And hi hi ʃal send hiz ɛnjelz, wiđ
  đe sɤnd ov trɒmpet gret,
tu gađer from ɷl parts hiz sents,
  hįz pleʒur tu awet.
Hwen điz ŧiŋz kɒm tu pas, luk ɒp
  and lift ųr hedz on hį;
ųr harts đen fil wiđ kɒmfort; ųr
  redempʃon drɷeŧ nį."

Đis parabel spɛk Jizɒs đen:
  "Yi from đe fig tri lern
in tender branç and ʃuts, đe aprɵç
  ov sɒmer tu disern.
Sɵ hwen điz ŧiŋz ʃal bi fulfild,
  đen nɵ́ đat nį at hand
đe kiŋdom ov ųr God iz kɒm,
  iven in đis veri land.
Đis jenereʃon ʃal not pas
  til ɷl điz ŧiŋz bi dɒn;
đe heven and erŧ ʃal pas awe,
  bɒt ov mį wɒrdz, not wɒn."

SEKΣON 155.

Krįst diskɵrsez on đe sɒdennes ov hiz Sekond Kɒmiŋ.

Maŧų 24. 36-51. Mark 13. 32-37. Luk 21. 34-36.

"Bɒt nɵ man nɷeŧ ov đát de,
  nor ɛnjelz, nor đe Sɒn,
mį Fɑđer ɵnli nɵ́z đe tįm
  hwen hiz wíl ʃal bi dɒn.
For az đe dez ov Nɵa wer,
  sɵ ʃal đe Sɒn ov man
bi in hiz de: hiz kɒmiŋ wil
  bi az đe flɒd began.
Az in đe dez befɵr đe flɒd
  đe ɛt and draŋk wiđ gli,
and marid wįvz, and nɒŧiŋ ŧɷt
  ov dįr kalamiti,
ɒntil đe flɒd kem ɒnawerz
  and tuk đem ɷl awe;
sɵ lįkwįz ʃal đe Sɒn ov man
  kɒm on ų in hiz de.
Đen ʃal tú men bi in đe fild,
  in ful sekųriti;
wɒn ʃal bi tɛken, and wɒn left.
  Slįt not đis profesi.

Two women, also, at the mill,
  Will labor, side by side;
Lo! one is gone; the other still
  In safety doth abide.
Take heed, therefore, unto yourselves,
  And ever watch and pray;
Ye know not when your Lord doth
  Then pray and watch alway. [come;
And learn from this a prudent course:
  Suppose a man should know
That at a certain hour a thief
  Would come: he would forego
All sleep and ease, and keep strict
  So be ye ready too, [watch.
For at an hour when ye think not,
  The Son of man you'll view.

Moreover, everyone who is
  A steward wise and good,
His master will a ruler make,
  To give the rest their food.
Yea, blessed shall that servant be
  Who acts a faithful part,
And serves not with eye-service: he
  Shall have great joy of heart.
But if a servant thus in trust
  Shall say, within his mind,
'My lord delays returning, and
  Remissness will not find;'
Then treats his fellow servants ill,
  And revels in excess,
His master will come back to him
  With fearful suddenness,
And will discard him, and appoint
  His place of punishment
With the unfaithful and the vile,
  Unless he soon repent.

For as a man who journeys far,
  His servants' work doth plan,
And bids the porter watch the house;
  So is the Son of man.
Watch therefore ye; for ye ne'er know
  The Master's swift return;
Whether at eve, or midnight dark,
  At cockcrowing, or morn;
Lest coming back all suddenly,
  He find you fast asleep.
To one, to all, I still say, Watch,
  And then you will not weep.

Túɯ wimen, ɑlsɵ, at đe mil
  wil lebor, sįd bį sįd;
lɵ! wɒn iz gon; đe ɒđer stil
  in sefti dɒŧ abįd.
Tɛk hid, đerfɵr, ɒntu ɥrselvz,
  and ever woç and prɛ;
yi nɵ́ not hwen ɥr Lord dɒŧ kɒm;
  đen prɛ and woç ɑlwɛ.
And lern from đis a prɯdent kɵrs:
  Sɒpɵz a man ʃud nɵ́
đat at a serten ɜr a ŧif
  wud kɒm: hi wud fɵrgɵ
ɑl slip and iz, and kip strikt woç.
  Sɵ bi yi redi tɯ,
for at an ɜr hwen yi ŧiŋk not,
  đe Sɒn ov man ɥ'l vɥ.

Mɵrɵver, everiwɒn hɯ iz
  a stɥard wįz and gud,
hiz master wil a rɯler mɛk,
  tu giv đe rest đer fɯd.
Yɛ, blesed ʃal đát servant bi
  hɯ akts a feŧful part,
and servz not wiđ į-servis: hi
  ʃal hav gret joi ov hart.
Bɒt if a servant đɒs in trɒst
  ʃal sɛ wiđin hiz mįnd,
'Mį lord delɛz retɒrniŋ, and
  remisnes wil not fįnd;'
đen trits hiz felɵ servants il,
  and revelz in ekses,
hiz master wil kɒm bak tu him
  wiđ fírful sɒdennes,
and wil diskard him, and apoint
  hiz plɛs ov pɒniʃment
wiđ đe ɒnfeŧful and đe vįl,
  ɒnles hi sɯn repent.

For az a man hɯ jɒrniz far,
  hiz servants' wɒrk dɒŧ plan,
and bidz đe pɵrter woç đe hɜs;
  sɵ iz đe Sɒn ov man.
Woç đerfɵr yi; for yi ner nɵ́
  đe master'z swift retɒrn;
hweđer at iv, or midnįt dark,
  at kokkrɵiŋ, or morn;
lest kɒmiŋ bak ɑl sɒdenli,
  hi fįnd ɥ fast aslip.
Tu wɒn, tu ɑl, į stil sɛ, Woç,
  and đen ɥ wil not wip.

At all times take ye watchful heed
  Against life's needful cares,
Still more against excess of food,
  Lest on you, unawares,
That day come as a snare, for so
  'Twill come on all the earth.
Watch therefore so that ye may stand
  In God's sight as of worth."

SECTION 156.

Parable of the Wise and Foolish Virgins.
Matthew 25. 1-13.

"Then shall heaven's kingdom be
  Unto ten virgins, bright, [compared
Who went to meet the bridegroom,
  Their lamps; for it was night. [with
Five of the little band were wise,
  And five so foolish were
That to provide their lamps with oil
  They did not one thought spare.
The wise ones' lamps were well sup-
  All slumbered, and all slept, [plied.
For while the bridegroom tarried still,
  The watch was not well kept.
And lo, at midnight, there's a cry,
  'Behold, the bridegroom's near!
Go forth to meet him; ready stand!'
  And in his train appear.
Then all arose and trimmed their
  And now the foolish said [lamps,
Unto the wise, 'O give us oil,
  Our lights are almost dead.'
The wise then answered, 'No, not so;
  Our oil will not suffice
For us and you. Go ye and buy,
  For that will be more wise.
And so it was that while they went,
  The bridegroom's train drew nigh,
And those prepared went in with him
  To feast right merrily.
The door was shut! And then, alas,
  The other virgins come;
'Open to us, Lord, Lord!' they cry,
  'O give us also room.'
But he, displeased at this, replied,
  'Truly I know you not.'
Watch, therefore, that ye may escape
  Their most unhappy lot.

At ɷl tįmz tek yi woçful hid,
  agenst lįf's nidful kerz,
stil mơr agenst ekses ov fɯd,
  lest on ų, ɒnawerz,
đát de kɒm az a sner, for sơ
  'twil kɒm on ɷl đe erŧ.
Woç đerfơr sơ đat yi me stand
  in God'z sįt az ov wɒrŧ."

SEKΣON 156.

Parabel ov đe Wįz and Fulịʃ Verjinz.
Maŧų 25. 1-13.

"Đen ʃal heven'z kiŋdom bi kom-
  ɒntu ten verjinz, brįt, [perd
hɯ went tu mit đe brįdgrɯm, wiđ
  đer lamps; for it woz nįt.
Fįv ov đe litel band wer wįz,
  and fįv sơ fɯliʃ wer
đat tu prơvįd đer lamps wiđ oil,
  đe did not wɒn ŧɷt sper.
Đe wįz wɒnz' lamps wer wel sɒplįd.
  ɷl slɒmberd and ɷl slept,
for hwįl đe brįdgrɯm tarid stil,
  đe woç woz not wel kept.
And lơ, at midnįt, đer'z a krį,
  'Behơld đe brįdgrɯm'z nir!
gơ fơrŧ tu mit him! redi stand!'
  and in hiz tren apir.
Đen ɷl arơz and trimd đer lamps,
  and nɜ đe fɯliʃ sed
ɒntu đe wįz, 'Ơ giv ɒs oil,
  ɜr lįts ar ɷlmơst ded.'
Đe wįz đen anserd, 'Nơ, not sơ;
  ɜr oil wil not sɒfįz
for ɒs and ų. Gơ yi and bį,
  for đát wil bi mơr wįz.
And sơ it woz đat hwįl đe went,
  đe brįdgrɯm'z tren drɯ nį,
And đơz preperd went in wiđ him
  tu fist rįt merili.
Đe dơr woz ʃɒt! And đen, alas,
  đe ɒđer verjinz kɒm;
'Ơpen tu ɒs, Lord, Lord!' đe krį,
  'Ơ giv ɒs ɷlsơ rɯm.'
Bɒt hi, displizd at đis, replįd,
  'Trɯli į nớ ų not.'
Woç, đerfơr, đat yi me eskep
  đer mơst ɒnhapi lot.

Ye neither know the hour nor day
Of my return: then watch and pray."

SECTION 157.

Parable of the Servants and the Talents.
Matthew 25. 14-30.

" The Son of man resembles one
  Who went to a distant land
And called his servants; and his goods
  Delivered to their hand.
On one five talents he bestows,
  And on another two,
And to a third he gives but one,
  As to their powers was due.
Then he departs. And he who had
  Received five talents, went
And traded with them, and thus gained
  Five more, being provident.
And he that had received but two,
  Did likewise; and his gains
Amounted to two talents more,
  To recompense his pains.
But he with one went, slothfully,
  And digged beneath the earth,
And there bestowed the talent which
  His lord esteemed of worth.
A long time passed; the lord returned
  To take their just account.
'Lord, thou didst give me talents five;
  To ten they now amount;'
Thus spoke the first; and then his lord
  Said unto him, 'Well done,
Thou good and faithful servant! Thou
  Well-earned applause hast won
For diligence. As thou hast been
  Thus faithful in things few,
Now therefore over many more
  Thee I'll with power endue;
Enter the joy of thine own lord,
  Since faithful found and true.'
The second servant likewise came,
  And said, 'Thou gavest me
Two talents, lord; and I have gained
  Two more, as thou wilt see.'
His lord then said to him, 'Well done!
  Faithful thou didst employ
Thy talents few, now rule o'er more;
  Enter into my joy.'

Yį nįđer nɵ́ đe ȣr nor de
ov mį retɒrn: đen woç and pre."

SEKΣON 157.

Parabel ov đe Servants and đe Talents.
Maɟų 25. 14-30.

" Đe Sɒn ov man rezembelz wɒn
  hų went tu a distant land
and kɷld hiz servants; and hiz gudz
  deliverd tu đer hand.
On wɒn fįv talents hi bestɵz,
  and on anɒđer tú,
and tu a ɟerd hi givz bɒt wɒn,
  az tu đer pȣerz woz dų.
Đen hi departs. And hi hų had
  resįvd fįv talents, went
and treded wiđ đem, and đɒs gend
  fįv mɵr, biiŋ provident.
And hi đat had resįvd bɒt tú,
  did lįkwįz; and hiz genz
amȣnted tu tú talents mɵr,
  tu rekompens hiz penz.
Bɒt hi wiđ wɒn went, slɵɟfuli,
  and digd beniđ đe erɟ,
and đer bestɵd đe talent hwiç
  hiz lord estįmd ov wɒrɟ.
A loŋ tįm past; đe lord retɒrnd
  tu tek đer jɒst akȣnt.
'Lord, đȣ didst giv mi talents fįv;
  tu ten đe nȣ amȣnt;'
đɒs spɵk đe ferst; and đen hiz lord
  sed ɒntu him, 'Wel dɒn,
đȣ gud and feɟful servant! Đȣ
  wel-ernd aplɷz hast wɒn
for dilijens. Az đȣ hast bin
  đɒs feɟful in ɟiŋz fų,
nȣ đerfɵr ɵver meni mɵr
  đi į'l wiđ pȣer endų;
enter đe joi ov đįn ɵn lord,
  sins feɟful fȣnd and trų.'
Đe sekond servant lįkwįz kem,
  and sed, 'Đȣ gevest mi
tú talents, lord; and į hav gend
  tú mɵr, az đȣ wilt si.'
Hiz lord đen sed tu him, 'Wel dɒn
  feɟful dȣ didst emploi
đį talents fų, nȣ rul ɵ'r mɵr;
  enter intu mį joi.'

He who one talent had received,
  Said, 'Lord, full well I know
Thou a strict master art, and reap'st
  Where thou didst never sow;
And what thou strew'st not, gatherest;
  And so I feared thy power,
And hid thy talent in the earth;
  'Tis thine until this hour.'
His lord was angry, and replied,
  'Thou wicked, slothful one!
Didst thou so truly know my mind,
  And yet hast nothing done?
My money thou should'st have employed
  In something to invest,
That when I came, I might receive
  Mine own with interest.
Take now the talent, so abused,
  And give to him with ten:
For those who store, shall have the more,
  And thus abundance gain.
But he who stores not, loses all,
  Even that which he possest.
And cast ye forth that useless one,
  Where he shall have no rest;
Give not to him the victor's wreath,
But weeping eyes, and gnashing teeth.'"

Hɪ hɯ wɒn talent had resɪvd,
  sed, 'Lord, ful wel ɩ nó
đɤ a strikt master art, and rɪp'st
  hwɛr đɤ didst never sơ;
and hwot đɤ strơ'st not, gađerest;
  and sơ ɩ fɪrd đɩ pɤer,
and hid đɩ talent in đe erŧ;
  'tiz đɩn ɒntil đis ɤr.'
Hiz lord woz aŋgri, and replɩd,
  'Đɤ wiked, slơŧful wɒn!
didst đɤ sơ truli nó mɩ mɩnd,
  and yet hast nɒŧiŋ dɒn?
Mɩ mɒni đɤ ʃud'st hav emploid
  in sɒmŧiŋ tu invest,
đat hwen ɩ kɛm, ɩ mɩt resɪv
  mɩn ơn wiđ interest.
Tɛk nɤ đe talent, sơ abɥzd,
  and giv tu him wiđ ten:
for đơz hɯ stơr, ʃal hav đe mơr,
  and đɒs abɒndans gɛn.
Bɒt hɪ hɯ stơrz not, lɯzez ɷl,
  ɪven đát hwiç hɪ pozest.
And kast yɪ fơrŧ đát ɥsles wɒn,
  hwer hɪ ʃal hav nơ rest;
giv not tu him đe viktor'z rɪŧ,
bɒt wɪpiŋ ɩz, and naʃiŋ tɪŧ.'"

SECTION 158.

Christ declares the proceedings of the Day of Judgement.—Matthew 25. 31-46.

"When in his glorious majesty
  The Son of man is known,
Surrounded with his angel hosts,
  And seated on his throne;
To him all nations shall be brought,
  That judgement may be given;
And separation made, of bad
  And good, for hell and heaven.
Then, as a shepherd parts his sheep
  And goats, he will divide;
And set the sheep on his right hand,
  The goats on his left side.
Then shall the King say unto them
  That are at his right hand,
'Ye blessed of my Father, come,
  And join the angel band;
Inherit ye the kingdom which
  For you has been prepared

SEKƩON 158.

Krɩst deklɛrz đe prơsɪdiŋz ov đe Dɛ ov Jɒjment.—Maŧɥ 25. 31-46.

"Hwen in hiz glơrɪɒs majesti
  đe Sɒn ov man iz nơn,
sɒrɤnded wiđ hiz ɛnjel hơsts,
  and sɪted on hiz ŧrơn;
tu him ɷl neʃonz ʃal bɪ brɷt,
  đat jɒjment mɛ bɪ given;
and separeʃon mɛd, ov bad
  and gud, for hel and heven.
Đen, az a ʃepherd parts hiz ʃɪp
  and gơts, hɪ wil divɩd;
and set đe ʃɪp on hiz rɩt hand,
  đe gơts on hiz left sɩd.
Đen ʃal đe Kiŋ sɛ ɒntu đem
  đat ar at hiz rɩt hand,
'Yɪ blesed ov mɩ Fɛđer, kɒm,
  and join đe ɛnjel band:
inherit yɪ đe kiŋdom hwiç
  for ɥ haz bɪn preperd

From the foundation of the world,
  As my Word has declared.
For I, some time, was hungry, and
  Ye kindly gave me meat;
And I was thirsty once, and ye
  Allayed my thirst and heat.
I was a stranger in the land,
  Ye gently nourished me,
Was naked, sick, in prison, and
  Ye gave me ministry.'
Then shall the righteous answer, 'Lord,
  When did we these things see?
Hungry, or thirsty, naked, strange,
  And ministered to thee?
Or when in prison bound, or sick,
  Did we, in mercy, call?'
Then will the King reply to them,
  'Full well I know you all;
And what you gave unto the least
  Of these my brethren poor,
Ye did it unto me, your Lord;
  Of this you may be sure.'
Then, turning to the left, he'll say,
  'Ye cursed, go from me
To everlasting fire, and there
  Live in your misery.
For I sometime was hungry, and
  Ye would not give me meat;
And I was thirsty once, yet ye
  Gave me no water sweet;
I was a stranger in the land,
  Ye turned me from your door;
Was naked, sick, in prison, and
  Ye lessened not your store.'
Then shall they also answer him,
  'Lord, when saw we thee so,
And ministered not to thy need?'
  And he shall answer, 'Know,
As ye helped not the least of these,
  Ye did it not to me.'
These shall receive due punishment,
  And those felicity."

from đe fɤndeʃon ov đe wɒrd,
  az mị Wɒrd haz deklerd.
For ị, sɒm tịm, woz hɒŋgri, and
  yi kịndli gev mi mit;
and ị woz ɟersti wɒns, and yi
  alɛd mị ɟerst and hit.
Ị woz a strenjer in đe land,
  yi jentli nɒriʃt mi,
woz neked, sik, in prizon, and
  yi gev mi ministri.'
Đen ʃal đe rịtiɒs anser, 'Lord,
  hwen did wi điz ɟiŋz si?
Hɒŋgri, or ɟersti, neked, strenj,
  and ministerd tu đi?
Or hwen in prizon bɤnd, or sik,
  did wi, in mersi, kɷl?'
Đen wil đe Kiŋ replị tu đem,
  'Ful wel ị nớ ɥ ɷl;
and hwot ɥ gev ɒntu đe list
  ov điz mị bredren pɯr,
yi did it ɒntu mi, ɥr Lord;
  ov đis ɥ me bi ʃɯr.'
Đen, tɒrniŋ tu đe left, hi'l sɛ,
  'Yi kɒrsed, gơ from mi,
tu everlastiŋ fịr, and đer
  liv in ɥr mizeri.
For ị sɒmtịm woz hɒŋgri, and
  yi wud not giv mi mit;
and ị woz ɟersti wɒns, yet yi
  gev mi nơ wɷter swit;
ị woz a strenjer in đe land,
  yi tɒrnd mi from ɥr dơr;
woz neked, sik, in prizon, and
  yi lesend not ɥr stơr.'
Đen ʃal đɛ ɷlsơ anser him,
  'Lord, hwen sɷ wi đi sơ,
and ministerd not tu đị nid?'
  And hi ʃal anser, 'Nớ,
az yi helpt not đe list ov điz,
  yi did it not tu mi.'
Điz ʃal resiv dɥ pɒniʃment,
  and đơz felisiti."

SECTION 159.

Christ retires from the city to the Mount of Olives.—Luke 21. 37, 38.

Within the temple Jesus taught
  By day; and when the night

SEKΣON 159.

Krịst retịrz from đe siti tu đe Mɤnt ov Olivz.—Lɯk 21. 37, 38.

Điđin đe tempel Jizɒs tɷt
  bị dɛ; and hwen đe nịt

Descended, he retired, alone,
  To Olivet's sacred height,
And early each returning morn,
  Soon after it was light,
The people flocked to him, to learn
  How to serve God aright.

desended, hi retįrd, alɵn,
  tu Olivet's sekred hįt.
and erli iç retɒrniŋ morn,
  sɯn after it woz lįt,
đe pipel flokt tu him, tu lern
  hɤ tu serv God arįt.

SECTION 160.

Christ foretells his approaching death, and the Rulers consult how they may take him.

Matthew 26. 1-5. Mark 14. 1, 2. Luke 22. 1, 2.

Two days before the Paschal Feast
  Of the unleavened bread,
When Jesus had completed all
  These labors, thus he said
To his disciples; "In two days
  Will come the Pashcal-tide,
And then the Son of man will be
  Betrayed and crucified."
And as the Passover drew near,
  Priests, scribes, and elders meet
At Caiaphas's residence,
  Where they the high priest greet.
A consultation then they held
  How Jesus they might seize,
By subtlety, and put to death.
  Not wishing to displease
The people, who, they feared, would [cause
  A riotous affray,
They said, "Let this thing not be done
  Upon the great feast day."

SEKΣON 160.

Krįst fɵrtelz hiz aprɵçiŋ deθ, and đe Rɯlerz konsɒlt hɤ đɛ mɛ tɛk him.

Maθų 26. 1-5. Mark 14. 1, 2. Lɯk 22. 1, 2.

Tɯ́ dɛz befɵr đe Paskal Fist
  ov đe ɒnlevend bred,
hwen Jizɒs had komplited ɷl
  điz lɛborz, đɒs hi sed
tu hiz disįpelz; "In tɯ́ dɛz
  wil kɒm đe Paskal-tįd,
and đen đe Sɒn ov man wil bi
  betrɛd and krɯsifįd."
And az đe Pasɵver drɯ nir,
  prists, skrįbz, and elderz mit
at Kaiafas'ez rezidens,
  hwɛr đɛ đe hį prist grit.
A konsɒltɛʃon đen đɛ held
  hɤ Jizɒs đɛ mįt siz,
bį sɒtelti, and put tu deθ.
  Not wiʃiŋ tu displiz
đe pipel, hɯ, đɛ fird, wud kɷz
  a rįotɒs afrɛ,
đɛ sed, "Let đis θiŋ not bi dɒn
  ɒpon đe grɛt fist dɛ."

SECTION 161.

Judas agrees with the Chief Priests to betray Christ.

Matthew 26. 14-16. Mark 14. 10, 11. Luke 22. 3-6.

Then one of Christ's own chosen band,
  Judas Iscariot named,
Admitted Satan to his heart,
  And, by that power inflamed,
Communed with the chief priests how [he
  His Master might betray;
And said, "What will ye give to me,
  If I find out a way?"

SEKΣON 161.

Jɯdas agriz wiđ đe Çif Prists tu betrɛ Krįst.

Maθų 26. 14-16. Mark 14. 10, 11. Lɯk 22. 3-6.

Đen wɒn ov Krįst's ɵn çɵzen band,
  Jɯdas Iskariot nɛmd,
admited Sɛtan tu hiz hart,
  and, bį đát pɤer inflɛmd,
komųnd wiđ đe çif prists hɤ hi
  hiz Master mįt betrɛ;
and sed, "Hwot wil yi giv tu mi,
  if į fįnd ɤt a wɛ?"

They heard with joy, and covenant made
To give him money true;
Even thirty silver pieces, good,
He then might count his due.
From that dark hour did Judas seek
Occasion to betray
His Lord, without a tumult, on
The first convenient day.

Đɛ herd wiđ joi, and kɒvenant mɛd
tu giv him mɒni trɯ;
ıven ɟerti silver pısez, gud,
hı đen mįt kɤnt hiz dɥ.
From đát dark ɤr did Jɯdas sık
okɛʒon tu betrɛ
hiz Lord, wiđɤt a tɥmɒlt, on
đe ferst konvınient dɛ.

SECTION 162.

Christ directs two of his disciples to prepare the Passover, of which he partakes for the last time.

Matthew 26. 17-20. Mark 14. 12-17.
Luke 22. 7-18. John 13. 1.

SEKƩON 162.

Krįst direkts tú ov hiz disįpelz tu preper đe Pasɒver, ov hwiç hi partɛks for đe last tįm.

Maɟɥ 26. 17-20. Mark 14. 12-17.
Lɯk 22. 7-18. Jon 13. 1.

On the first day of unleavened bread,
When Paschal lamb they kill,
Peter and John besought the Lord,
"Master, where is thy will
That we prepare the Passover
For thee and us to eat?"
He said, "Into the city go,
And there a man you'll meet
Bearing a water-vessel: where
He enters, follow ye,
And to the owner of the house
These words repeat from me:
'The Master saith, My time is near;
To keep the feast I come;
Where is the guest-chamber for us?'
He'll show an upper room,
Furnished and large; make ready there."
So they went forth to do
As Jesus had appointed them,
And found his words were true.

On đe ferst dɛ ov ɒnlevend bred,
hwen Paskal lam đɛ kil,
Pıter and Jon besɷt đe Lord,
Master, hwer iz đį wíl
đat wı preper đe Pasɵver
for đı and ɒs tu ıt?"
Hı sed, "Intu đe siti gɵ,
and đer a man ɥ'l mıt
beriŋ a wɷter-vesel: hwer
hı enterz, folɵ yı,
and tu đe ɵner ov đe hɤs
đız wɒrdz repıt from mı:
'Đe Master seɟ, Mį tįm iz nır;
tu kıp đe fıst į kɒm;
hwer iz đe gest çember for ɒs?'
Hı'l ʃɵ an ɒper rɯm,
fɒrniʃt and larj; mɛk redi đer."
Sɵ đɛ went fɵrɟ tu dɯ
az Jızɒs had apointed đem,
and fɤnd hiz wɒrdz wer trɯ.

Now came the fourth day of the week,
(The day commenced at eve,)
In which the Jews, by ancient law,
The Passover receive.
Then Jesus, seeing now the hour
Of his departure near,
(He loved his own unto the end
In this world's lower sphere,)
Sat down, with his disciples twelve,
The Passover to eat.

Nɤ kem đe fɵrɟ dɛ ov đe wık,
(đe dɛ komenst at ıv,)
in hwiç đe Jɯz, bį ɛnʃent lɷ,
đe Pasɵver resıv.
Đen Jızɒs, sıiŋ nɤ đe ɤr
ov hiz departɥr nır,
(hı lɒvd hiz ɵn ɒntu đe end
in đis wɒrld'z lɵer sfır,)
sat dɤn, wiđ hiz disįpelz twelv,
đe Pasɵver tu ıt.

And unto them the Savior said
  These words, with accent sweet,
"I have most earnestly desired
  To share this festival
With you before I suffer death;
  Of this feast mystical
I will not any more partake
  While with you I abide."
And then he took the cup, gave thanks,
  And said, "Take this; divide
Among yourselves, I will not drink
  The vine's-fruit any more
Until, in truth and righteousness,
  God's kingdom I restore."

SECTION 163.

Christ again reproves the ambition of his Disciples.

Luke 22. 24-27. John 13. 2-17.

And supper being ended, strife
  Rose up yet once again,
Which should be reckoned greatest in
  Christ's kingdom;—which should reign.
Then Jesus said, "The Gentile kings
  Use proud ascendency
Upon their people, and they call
  Such rule benignity.
But ye shall not be so, but he
  That would be great 'mong you
Shall be as are the younger, and
  The chief give service due.
Which, think you, is the greater held,
  He that sits down to meat,
Or he that waits upon the guests
  And bathes their wearied feet?
Is it not he that sits at meat?
  But I, your Lord, am here
As he that serveth. Then no more
  Seek ye to domineer."

The devil now in Judas raised
  (Iscariot, Simon's son,)
The hellish wish soon to betray
  The ever-blessed One.
Jesus, who knew all power was his,
  And that he came from God,

And ɒntu đem đe Sevier sed
  điz wɒrdz wiđ aksent swit,
"Ɨ hav mɵst ernestli deziֽrd
  tu ʃer đis festival
wiđ ɥ befɵr ị sɒfer deŧ;
  ov đis fist mistikal
ị wil not eni mɵr partek
  hwịl wiđ ɥ ị abịd."
And đen hi tɯk đe kɒp, gev ŧaŋks,
  and sed, "Tek đis; divịd
amɒŋ ɥrselvz, ị wil not driŋk
  đe vịn'z frɯt eni mɵr
ɒntil, in trɯŧ and rịtiɒsnes,
  God'z kiŋdom ị restɵr."

SEKΣON 163.

Krịst agen reprɯvz đe ambiʃon ov hiz Disịpelz.

Lɯk 22. 24-27. Jon 13. 2-17.

And sɒper biiŋ ended, strịf
  rɵz ɒp yet wɒns agen,
hwiɋ ʃud bi rekond gretest in
  Krịst's kiŋdom;—hwiɋ ʃud ren.
Đen Jizɒs sed, "Đe Jentịl kiŋz
  ɥz prȣd asendensi
ɒpon đer pipel, and đe kɵl
  sɒɋ rɯl benigniti.
Bɒt yi ʃal not bi sɵ, bɒt hi
  đat wud bi gret 'mɒŋ ɥ
ʃal bi az ar đe yɒŋger, and
  đe ɋif giv servis dɥ.
Hwiɋ, ŧiŋk ɥ, iz đe greter held,
  hi đat sits dȣn tu mit,
or hi đat wets ɒpon đe gests
  and beđz đer wirid fit?
Iz it not hi đat sits at mit?
  Bɒt ị, ɥr Lord, am hir
az hi đat serveŧ. Đen nɵ mɵr
  sik yi tu dominir."

Đe devil nȣ in Jɯdas rezd
  (Iskariot, Sịmon'z sɒn,)
đe heliʃ wiʃ sɯn tu betre
  đe ever-blesed Wɒn.
Jizɒs, hɯ nɥ ɵl pȣer woz hiz,
  and đat hi kem from God,

And unto God again would go,
  When truth was sealed with blood,
Rose from the table, and put off
  His garments; bent to preach
Humility to sinful men
  Both by his deeds and speech.
With towel girt, the Savior then
  Into a basin poured
Some water; and he washed the feet
  Of those who owned him Lord.
When he to Simon Peter came,
  His follower humbly cried,
"Lord, is it thou dost wash my feet?"
  And Jesus thus replied,
"This deed thou dost not understand;
  Hereafter thou shalt know."
But Peter said, "Thou never shalt
  Wash my feet,—never,—no."
Jesus replied, "But if I wash
  Thee not, thou hast no part
In my salvation." Peter then
  Said, with a loving heart,
"Lord, not my feet alone, but head,
  And hands, as is most meet.
Then Jesus said, "He who is washed,
  Needs but to wash his feet,
And then is clean all over; ye
  Are clean too, but not all."
He knew who should betray him, and
  From his estate should fall.
So after he had washed their feet,
  His robes put on again,
And sat down with them, he began
  His act thus to explain.
"Know ye what I have done to you?
  Ye call me Master, Lord,
And right it is that unto me
  Such titles you accord;
For such I am. If I then, who
  Am Lord and Master, bend
To wash your feet, much more should ye
  Likewise each other tend.
For I to you example give,
  That ye should also do
To one another that which I
  Have just now done to you.
For verily I say to you,
  Servants should not aspire
To be above their lord; nor seek
  The mastery to acquire."

and ɒntu God agen wud gɵ,
  hwen truƭ woz sịld wiđ blɒd,
rɵz from đe tebel and put ɷf
  hiz garments; bent tu priç
hɥmiliti tu sinful men
  bɵƭ bị hiz dịdz and spịç.
Wiđ tɤel gert, đe Sevier đen
  intu a besin pɵrd
sɒm wɷter; and hị wɷʃt đe fịt
  ov đɵz hɯ ɵnd him Lord.
Hwen hị tu Sịmon Pịter kem,
  hiz folɵer hɒmbli krịd,
"Lord, iz it đɤ dɒst wɷʃ mị fịt?"
  and Jịzɒs đɒs replịd,
"Đis dịd đɤ dɒst not ɒnderstand;
  hịrafter đɤ ʃalt nɵ́."
Bɒt Pịter sed, "Đɤ never ʃalt
  wɷʃ mị fịt,—never,—nɵ."
Jịzɒs replịd, "Bɒt if ị wɷʃ
  đị not, đɤ hast nɵ part
in mị salveʃon." Pịter đen
  sed, wiđ a lɒviŋ hart,
"Lord, not mị fịt alɵn, bɒt hed,
  and handz, az iz mɵst mịt.
Đen Jịzɒs sed, "Hị hɯ iz wɷʃt,
  nịdz bɒt tu wɷʃ hiz fịt,
and đen iz klịn ɷl ɵver; yị
  ar klịn tɯ, bɒt not ɷl."
Hị nɥ hɯ ʃud betre him, and
  from hiz estet ʃud fɷl.
Sɵ after hị had wɷʃt đer fịt,
  hiz rɵbz put on agen,
and sat dɤn wiđ đem, hị began
  hiz akt đɒs tu eksplen.
"Nɵ́ yị hwot ị hav dɒn tu ɥ?
  Yị kɷl mị Master, Lord,
and rịt it iz đat ɒntu mị
  sɒç tịtelz ɥ akord;
for sɒç ị am. If ị đen, hɯ
  am Lord and Master, bend
tu wɷʃ ɥr fịt, mɒç mɵr ʃud yị
  lịkwịz ịç ɒđer tend.
For ị tu ɥ ekzampel giv,
  đat yị ʃud ɷlsɵ dɯ
tu wɒn anɒđer đát hwiç ị
  hav jɒst nɤ dɒn tu ɥ.
For verili ị se tu ɥ,
  servants ʃud not aspịr
tu bị abɒv đer lord; nor sịk
  đe masteri tu akwịr."

SECTION 164.

Christ, sitting at the Passover, speaks of his Betrayer.

Matthew 26. 21-25. Mark 14. 18-21.
Luke 22. 21-23. John 13. 18-30.

"If then ye know these holy truths,
 Such knowledge will not make
You happy; but in doing them
 Ye shall heaven's bliss partake.
I know my chosen ones, but all,
 Alas, will not obey;
And even of you, my twelve, is one
 Who will his Lord betray.
So shall this Scripture prophecy
 Even now be realised,
'He that hath shared my bread, 'gainst me
 Hath evil things devised.'
I tell you now before it come,
 That when it happens, you
May know indeed that I am He
 That is, and was, most true.
He that receives the messengers
 I send, receiveth me,
And he that me receives, also
 Receives the Deity."
When Jesus had thus spoken, he
 Was troubled; and then said,
"Yea, one of you who share this feast,
 Will, by bad passions led,
Betray his Savior; and behold,
 He's at the table now."
Then were they grieved exceedingly,
 And each of each asked, How
This thing could be, and who it was
 Would do it. They reply,
In fear, to Jesus, one by one,
 "Lord, is it I?" "Or I?"
Christ answered, "He who in this dish
 Now dips, in friendly way,
His traitorous hand, the same is he
 Who shall my life betray.
The Son of man indeed departs;
 God's will must be obeyed;
But woe unto that man by whom
 The Son of man's betrayed.
Yea, better for himself it were,
 Had that man ne'er been born."
Then the disciples, full of doubt,
 Did to each other turn,

SEKΣON 164.

Krįst, sitiŋ at ɗe Pasɒver, spiks ov hiz Betreer.

Maɟɥ 26. 21-25. Mark 14. 18-21.
Lɯk 22. 21-23. Jon 13. 18-30.

"If ɗen yi nǿ ɗiz hǿli trɯɗz,
 sɒç nolej wil not mɛk
ɥ hapi; bɒt in dɯiŋ ɗem
 yi ʃal heven'z blis partɛk.
Ŧ nǿ mį çǿzen wɒnz, bɒt ɷl,
 alas, wil not ǿbe;
and iven ov ɥ, mį twelv, iz wɒn
 hɯ wil hiz Lord betre.
Sǿ ʃal ɗis Skriptɥr profesi
 iven nɤ bi rialįzd,
'Hi ɗat haɟ ʃerd mį bred, 'genst mi
 haɟ ivel ɟiŋz devįzd.'
Ŧ tel ɥ nɤ befǿr it kɒm,
 ɗat hwen it hapenz, ɥ
mɛ nǿ indid ɗat į am Hi
 ɗat iz, and woz, mǿst trɯ.
Hi ɗat resivz ɗe mesenjerz
 į send, resiveɟ mi,
and hi ɗat mi resivz, ɷlsǿ
 resivz ɗe Diiti."
Hwen Jizɒs had ɗɒs spǿken, hi
 woz trɒbeld; and ɗen sed,
"Yɛ, wɒn ov ɥ hɯ ʃer ɗis fist,
 wil, bį bad paʃonz led,
betre hiz Sevier; and behǿld,
 hi'z at ɗe tɛbel nɤ."
Ɑen ɗe wer grivd eksidiŋli,
 and iç ov iç askt, Hɤ
ɗis ɟiŋ kud bi, and hɯ it woz
 wud dɯ it. Ɑɛ replį,
in fir, tu Jizɒs, wɒn bį wɒn,
 "Lord, iz it į?" "Or į?"
Krįst anserd, "Hi hɯ in ɗis diʃ
 nɤ dips, in frendli wɛ,
hiz tretorɒs hand, ɗe sem iz hi
 hɯ ʃal mį lįf betre.
Ɑe Sɒn ov man indid departs;
 God'z wil mɒst bi ǿbed;
bɒt wǿ ɒntu ɗát man bį hɯm
 ɗe Sɒn ov man'z betrɛd.
Yɛ, beter for himself it wer,
 had ɗát man ner bin born."
Ɑen ɗe disįpelz, ful ov dɤt,
 did tu iç ɒɗer tɒrn,

And Peter beckoned unto John,
Who leaned on Jesus' breast,
(Beloved disciple,) and he said,
With bitter grief distressed,
"Who is it, Lord?" And Jesus said,
"He unto whom I give
This sop, when dipped; 'tis he who doth
My ruin now contrive."
He gave the sop to Judas, and
When he had taken it,
The devil entered him, and urged
Him this deed to commit.
Then Judas, too, the question put,
"Well, Master, is it I?"
Jesus replied, "Thou hast confessed.
And that which secretly
Thou hast determined, execute
With speed: delay no more."
Little did the disciples know
His scheme of treachery sore;
But some supposed that Christ had told
Judas to buy whate'er
Was needful for that festive week;
Or with the poor to share
What they possest. And Judas then
Went forth, for night had come,
To do the direst deed of hell,
And suffer its worst doom.

SECTION 165.

Judas goes out to betray Christ. The Lord predicts Peter's denial of him, and the danger of the rest of the Apostles.

Luke 22. 28-38. John 13. 31-38.

Therefore when Judas was gone out,
The Lord said unto them,
"The Son of man's now glorified,
And God also in him.
If God be glorified in me,
Then God shall glorify
Me in himself, and that straightway.
(Thus speaks true prophecy.)
My children, yet a little while
I still remain with you,
And what I said unto the Jews,—
That word I now renew,—
Whither I go, ye cannot come.
A new command I give:

and Pịter bekond ɒntu Jon,
hɯ lịnd on Jịzɒs' brest,
(belɒvd disįpel,) and hị sed,
wiđ biter grịf distrest,
"Hɯ iz it, Lord?" And Jịzɒs sed,
"Hị ɒntu hɯm į giv
đis sop, hwen dipt; 'tiz hị hɯ dɒđ
mį rɯin nɤ kontrįv."
Hị gev đe sop tu Jɯdas, and
hwen hị had teken it,
đe devil enterd him, and ɒrjd
him đis dịd tu komít.
Đen Jɯdas, tɯ, đe kwestion put,
"Wel, Master, iz it į?"
Jịzɒs replịd, "Đɤ hast konfest.
And đát hwiç sịkretli
đɤ hast determind, eksekųt
wiđ spịd: dele nɵ mɵr."
Litel did đe disįpelz nɵ́
hiz skịm ov treçeri sɵr;
bɒt sɒm sɒpɵzd đat Krįst had tɵld
Jɯdas tu bį́ hwoter
woz nịdful for đát festiv wịk;
or wiđ đe pɯr tu ſer
hwot đe pozest. And Jɯdas đen
went fɵrđ, for nįt had kɒm,
tu dɯ đe dįrest dịd ov hel,
and sɒfer its wɒrst dɯm.

SEKΣON 165.

Jɯdas gɵz ɤt tu betre Krįst. Đe Lord predikts Pịter'z denįal ov him, and đe denjer ov đe rest ov đe Aposelz.

Lɯk 22. 28-38. Jon 13. 31-38.

Đerfɵr hwen Jɯdas woz gon ɤt,
đe Lord sed ɒntu đem,
"Đe Sɒn ov man'z nɤ glɵrifįd,
and God olsɵ in him.
If God bị glɵrifįd in mị,
đen God ſal glɵrifį
mị in himself, and đát stretwe.
(Đɒs spịks trɯ profesi.)
Mį çildren, yet a litel hwįl
į stil remen wiđ ų,
and hwot į sed ɒntu đe Jɯz,—
đát wɒrd į nɤ renų,—
Hwider į gɵ, yị kanot kɒm.
A nų komand į giv:

Love one another, even as I
  Love you. This law receive;
Then all mankind will know that ye
  Are my disciples true.
Right faithfully ye followed me,
  And now I grant to you
A kingdom, as my Father hath
  Appointed unto me.
Yea, in my kingdom ye shall feast
  In pure felicity;
And on twelve thrones shall sit and
  The tribes of Israel." [judge
(That judgement is by truth, the Lord
  Did in this way foretell.)

Then Christ to Peter turned, and said,
  "Lo, Satan hath desired
To have you, and to sift you, till
  Your faith shall have expired.
But I indeed have prayed for thee,
  That thy faith may not fail;
And when thou art restored, then see
  That he do not prevail
Against thy brethren. Strengthen
  Then Peter made reply, [them."
"Lord, here I am, to go with thee
  To prison, or to die."
But Christ replied, "A little while
  Will all thy weakness show,
Ere cock crow, thou wilt thrice deny
  That thou thy Lord dost know."

Then Jesus said, "When ye went forth
  To preach God's kingdom near,
Ye had no purse, nor scrip, nor shoes;
  Yet had ye ought to fear?"
"Nothing," they said. Then said the
    Lord,
  "But now take purse and scrip,
And he that hath no sword, should get
  One, and himself equip.
For this sure word of prophecy
  Must be fulfilled in me,
'And he was numbered among those
  Who work iniquity;'
For all must be consummated,
  Whate'er the Scriptures say."
And they said, "Lord, here are two
    swords."
  He said, "Enough are they."

lɒv wɒn anɒđer, iven az ị
  lɒv ɥ. Đis lɷ resiv;
đen ɷl mankịnd wil nó đat yi
  ar mị disịpelz trɯ.
Rịt feɟfuli yi folɵd mi,
  and nɤ ị grant tu ɥ
a kiŋdom, az mị Fɑđer haɟ
  apointed ɒntu mi.
Yɛ, in mị kiŋdom yi ʃal fist
  in pɥr felisiti;
and on twelv ɟrɵnz ʃal sit and jɒj
  đe trịbz ov Izrael."
(Đat jɒjment iz bị trɯɟ, đe Lord
  did in đis wɛ fɵrtel.)

Đen Krịst tu Piter tɒrnd, and sed,
  "Lɵ, Setan haɟ dezịrd
tu hav ɥ, and tu sift ɥ, til
  ɥr feɟ ʃal hav ekspịrd.
Bɒt ị indid hav pred for đi,
  đat đị feɟ me not fel;
and hwen đɤ art restɵrd, đen si
  đat hi dɯ not prevɛl
agenst đị bređren. Streŋɟen đem."
  Đen Piter med replị,
"Lord, hir ị am, tu gɵ wiđ đi
  tu prizon, or tu dị."
Bɒt Krịst replịd, "A litel hwịl
  wil ɷl đị wiknes ʃɵ,
ɛr kok krɵ, đɤ wilt ɟrịs denị
  đat đɤ đị Lord dɒst nó."

Đen Jizɒs sed, "Hwen yi went fɵrɟ
  tu priç God'z kiŋdom nir,
yi had nɵ pɒrs, nor skrip, nor ʃɯz;
  yet had yi ɷt tu fir?"
"Nɒɟiŋ," đɛ sed. Đen sed đe
    Lord,
  "Bɒt nɤ tɛk pɒrs and skrip,
and hi đat haɟ nɵ sɵrd, ʃud get
  wɒn, and himself ekwip.
For đis ʃɥr wɒrd ov profesi
  mɒst bi fulfild in mi,
'And hi woz nɒmberd amɒŋ đɵz
  hɯ wɒrk inikwiti;'
for ɷl mɒst bi konsɒmeted,
  hwoter đe Skriptɥrz sɛ."
And đɛ sed, "Lord, hir ar tɯ́
    sɵrdz."
  Hi sed, "Enɒf ar đɛ."

Then Simon Peter said to him,
 "Lord, whither goest thou?"
"Whither I go," the Lord replied,
 "Thou canst not follow now,
But thou shalt follow afterwards."
 And Peter said, "Lord, why
Not now, when I will give my life
 For thee." The Lord's reply
Was, "Peter, wilt thou give thy life
 For me, nor count the price?
Before the cock shall crow this day,
 Thou wilt deny me thrice."

SECTION 166.

Christ institutes the Eucharist.

Matthew 26. 26-29. Mark 14. 22-25.
Luke 22. 19, 20.

As they were eating, Jesus Christ
 Took bread, gave thanks, and broke;
Then gave to the disciples, and
 These words of comfort spoke:
"Take, eat; for this my body is,
 Which now is given for you.
Do this in memory of me;
 And so your life renew."
Likewise he took the cup, gave thanks,
 Then gave to them, and said,
"Now drink ye all of this." They all
 Immediately obeyed.
He said, "This represents my blood
 In the new covenant,
Poured out for you, for many; yea,
 For sins' remission meant.
Oft as ye drink, remember me;
 For verily I say,
I drink no more of this vine-fruit,
 Until that coming day
When I, with you, shall drink it new,
Within my Father's kingdom true."

SECTION 167.

Christ exhorts the Apostles, and consoles them on his approaching death.

John 14.

"Let not your heart be troubled: ye
 Believe in God, trust too

Đen Sɉmon Pıter sed tu him,
 "Lord, hwiđer gɵest đʊ?"
"Hwiđer ɉ gɵ," đe Lord replɉd,
 "đʊ kanst not folɵ nʊ,
bɒt đʊ ʃalt folɵ afterwardz."
 And Pıter sed, "Lord, hwɉ
not nʊ, hwen ɉ wil giv mɉ lɉf
 for đı." Đe Lord'z replɉ
woz, "Pıter, wilt đʊ giv đɉ lɉf
 for mı, nor kʊnt đe prɉs?
Befɵr đe kok ʃal krɵ đis dɛ,
 đʊ wilt denɉ mı ɟrɉs."

SEKΣON 166.

Krɉst institųts đe Ųkarist.

Maɟų 26. 26-29. Mark 14. 22-25.
Lɯk 22. 19, 20.

Az đɛ wer ıtiŋ, Jızɒs Krɉst
 tuk bred, gɛv ɟaŋks, and brɵk;
đen gɛv tu đe disɉpelz, and
 đız wɒrdz ov kɒmfort spɵk:
"Tɛk, ıt; for đis mɉ bodi iz,
 hwiç nʊ iz given for ų.
Dɯ đis in memori ov mı;
 and sɵ ųr lɉf renų."
Lɉkwɉz hi tuk đe kɒp, gɛv ɟaŋks,
 đen gɛv tu đem, and sed,
"Nʊ driŋk yı ɷl ov đis." Đɛ ɷl
 immıdietli ɵbɛd.
Hı sed, "Đis reprezents mɉ blɒd
 in đe nų kɒvenant,
pɵrd ʊt for ų, for meni; yɛ,
 for sinz' remiʃon ment.
Oft az yı driŋk, remember mı;
 for verili ɉ sɛ,
ɉ driŋk nɵ mɵr ov đis vɉn-frɯt
 ɒntil đát kɒmiŋ dɛ
hwen ɉ, wiđ ų, ʃal driŋk it nų,
wiđin mɉ Fɑđer'z kiŋdom trɯ."

SEKΣON 167.

Krɉst ekzorts đe Apɵselz, and konsɵlz đem on hiz aprɵçiŋ deθ.

Jon 14.

"Let not ųr hart bı trɒbeld: yı
 beliv in God, trɒst tɯ

In me. Within my Father's house
  I many mansions view :
Were it not so, ye should have known ;
  They are prepared for you.
And though I now must leave you
  Yet will I come again, [here,
And take you home unto myself,
  No more to suffer pain.
Ye know the place to which I go,
  Ye also know the way."
Then Thomas said, "We know not,
  O teach us now, we pray." [Lord ;
Jesus replied, "I am the way,
  The truth, the life. 'Tis known,
No man unto the Father comes
  Except by me alone.
And had ye known me, then ye would
  Have known my Father too ;
From this time forth he shall not be
  A mystery to you ;
Henceforth ye know, and have seen
  Then Philip, "Lord, reveal [him."
The Father to our longing sight,
  Our happiness to seal."
And Jesus answered, "Have I been
  So long a time with you,
And yet hast thou not known me, who
  Am ever in thy view ?
He that hath seen me, he hath seen
  The Father that sent me.
Then how canst thou say to me now,
  'Let us the Father see ?'
Believ'st thou not that I'm in him
  And he in me ? This own.
The words I speak to you, I speak,
  Not from myself alone ;
The Father that dwells in me ; 'tis
  By him these works are done.
And verily I say to you,
  He that believes in me,
The works that I do, he shall do,
  And greater works shall he ;
Because I to the Father go.
  And anything, whate'er
Ye ask of me, or in my name,
  I now to you declare,
That will I do. The Father thus
  Is glorified in me.
If ye shall ask for anything
  In my name, it shall be ;

in mi. Wiđin mj̧ Fɐđer'z hȣs
  j̧ meni manʃonz vɥ :
wer it not sɵ, yi ʃud hav nɵn ;
  đɛ ar prepɛrd for ɥ.
And đɵ j̧ nȣ mɒst liv ɥ hir,
  yet wil j̧ kɒm agen,
and tɛk ɥ hɵm ɒntu mj̧self,
  nɵ mɵr'tu sɒfer pɛn.
Yi nɵ́ đe plɛs tu hwiç j̧ gɵ,
  yi ɷlsɵ nɵ́ đe wɛ."
Đen Tomas sed, "Wi nɵ́ not,
  Ɵ tiç ɒs nȣ, wi prɛ." [Lord ;
Jizɒs replj̧d, "Ɨ am đe wɛ,
  đe trɯɟ, đe lj̧f. 'Tiz nɵn,
nɵ man ɒntu đe Fɐđer kɒmz
  eksept bj̧ mi alɵn.
And had yi nɵn mi, đen yi wud
  hav nɵn mj̧ Fɐđer tɯ ;
from đis tj̧m fɵrɟ hi ʃal not bi
  a misteri tu ɥ ;
hensfɵrɟ yi nɵ́, and hav sin him."
  Đen Filip, "Lord, revil
đe Fɐđer tu ȣr loŋiŋ sj̧t,
  ȣr hapines tu sil."
And Jizɒs ansɛrd, "Hav j̧ bin
  sɵ loŋ a tj̧m wiđ ɥ,
and yet hast đȣ not nɵn mi, hɯ
  am ever in đj̧ vɥ ?
Hi đat haɟ sin mi, hi haɟ sin
  đe Fɐđer đat sent mi.
Đen hȣ kanst đȣ sɛ tu mi nȣ,
  'Let ɒs đe Fɐđer si ?'
Beliv'st đȣ not đat j̧'m in him
  and hi in mi ? Đis ɵn.
đe wɒrdz j̧ spik tu ɥ, j̧ spik,
  not from mj̧self alɵn ;
đe Fɐđer đat dwelz in mi ; 'tiz
  bj̧ him điz wɒrks ar dɒn.
And verili j̧ sɛ tu ɥ,
  hi đat belivz in mi,
đe wɒrks đat j̧ dɯ, hi ʃal dɯ,
  and greter wɒrks ʃal hi ;
bekɷz j̧ tu đe Fɐđer gɵ.
  And eniɟiŋ, hwoter
yi ask ov mi, or in mj̧ nem,
  j̧ nȣ tu ɥ dekler,
đát wil j̧ dɯ. Đe Fɐđer đɒs
  iz glɵrifj̧d in mi.
If yi ʃal ask for eniɟiŋ
  in mj̧ nem, it ʃal bi ;

For I will give it you.

If ye
Love me, keep my commands.
And I will pray the Father, and
His ever bounteous hands
Will give another Comforter,
Or, call him Advocate,
That he with you may ever stay,
Your minds to elevate;
The Spirit of truth and wisdom pure,
From whom all truth doth flow;
Whom worldly men cannot receive,
Can neither see nor know;
But ye well know him, for in you
He dwelleth in his power;
And he shall still in you abide,
Through every future hour.
I will not leave you orphans, I
In power, likewise, will come,
And hold communion with your heart,
And sanctify your home.
From this world's view I soon shall pass,
But you shall see me still,
And even because your Savior lives,
Shall life your being fill.
Then shall ye know that mystery
Of union, all divine,
I in the Father, ye in me,
And I in you, a trine.
He who obeys my laws doth give
Best proof of love to me;
To him, my Father's love and mine
Shall manifested be;
For we will come to him, and dwell
With him in union deep.
But those who love me not, cannot
My sayings truly keep.
The word which now ye hear is not
Mine only; 'tis the word
Also of him who sent me here,
The Father's, as ye heard.

When I depart, my Father will
In my name send abroad
The Comforter, the Holy Spirit,
To lead men up to God.
For he shall teach you all things, and
Bring all things to your mind:

for ị wil giv it ụ.

If yi
lɒv mi, kip mị komandz.
And ị wil pre đe Fɑder, and
hiz ever bɤntiɒs handz
wil giv anɒđer Kɒmforter,
or, kɷl him Advoket,
đat hi wiđ ụ me ever ste,
ụr mịndz tu elevet;
đe Spirit ov truɯ and wizdom pụr,
from huɯm ɷl truɯ dɒɯ flɵ;
huɯm wɒrldli men kanot resiv,
kan nịđer si nor nɵ́;
bɒt yi wel nɵ́ him, for in ụ
hi dweleɯ in hiz pɤer;
and hi ʃal stil in ụ abịd,
ɯruɯ everi fụtụr ɤr.
Ị wil not liv ụ orfanz, ị
in pɤer, lịkwịz, wil kɒm,
and hɵld komụnion wiđ ụr hart,
and saŋktifị ụr hɵm.
From đis wɒrld'z vụ ị suɯn ʃal pas,
bɒt ụ ʃal si mi stil,
and iven bekɷz ụr Sevier livz,
ʃal lịf ụr biiŋ fil.
Đen ʃal yi nɵ́ đát misteri
ov ụnion, ɷl divịn,
Ị in đe Fɑđer, yi in mi,
and ị in ụ, a trịn.
Hi huɯ ɵbez mị lɷz dɒɯ giv
best pruɯf ov lɒv tu mi;
tu him, mị Fɑđer'z lɒv and mịn
ʃal manifested bi;
for wi wil kɒm tu him, and dwel
wiđ him in ụnion dip.
Bɒt đɵz huɯ lɒv mi not, kanot
mị seiŋz truɯli kip.
Đe wɒrd hwiç nɤ yi hir iz not
mịn ɵnli; 'tiz đe wɒrd
ɷlsɵ ov him huɯ sent mi hir,
đe Fɑđer'z, az yi herd.

Hwen ị depart, mị Fɑđer wil
in mị nem send abrɷd
đe Kɒmforter, đe Hɵli Spirit,
tu lid men ɒp tu God.
For hi ʃal tiç ụ ɷl ɯiŋz, and
briŋ ɷl ɯiŋz tu ụr mịnd:

Whatever I have said to you,
  He shall on your hearts bind.
Peace, holy peace, I leave with you,
  I give to you my peace;
Not as the world gives, give I you,
  My gifts shall never cease.
Let not your heart be troubled, nor
  E'er let it be afraid;
I go away, and come again,
  To give you endless aid.
If now ye loved me well, ye would
  Lift up your voice on high,
Because I to the Father go,
  Who greater is than I.
All this I have foretold you thus,
  That when it comes to pass,
Ye may believe me steadfastly;
  But now, my time, alas,
With you is brief, and but few words
  Can be between us more;
The prince of this world cometh, but
  'Gainst me he hath no power,
Excepting that the world may know
  My love to God intense;
And that I keep my Father's laws.
  Arise, let us go hence."

hwotever į hav sed tu ų,
  hi ʃal on ųr harts bįnd.
Pis, hɵli pis, į liv wiđ ų,
  į giv tu ų mį pis;
not az đe wɒrld givz, giv į ų,
  mį gifts ʃal never sis.
Let not ųr hart bi trɒbeld, nor
  er let it bi afred;
į gɵ awe, and kɒm agen,
  tu giv ų endles ed.
If nʊ yi lɒvd mi wel, yi wud
  lift ɒp ųr vois on hį,
bekɷz į tu đe Fɑđer gɵ,
  hɯ greter iz đan į.
ɷl đis į hav fɵrtɵld ų đɒs,
  đat hwen it kɒmz tu pas,
yi me beliv mi stedfastli;
  bɒt nʊ, mį tįm, alas,
wiđ ų iz brif, and bɒt fų wɒrdz
  kan bi betwin ɒs mɵr;
đe prins ov đis wɒrld kɒmeŧ, bɒt
  'genst mi hi haŧ nɵ pʊer,
ekseptiŋ đat đe wɒrld me nɵ
  mį lɒv tu God intens;
and đat į kip mį Fɑđer'z lɷz.
  Arįz, let ɒs gɵ hens."

SECTION 168.

Christ goes with his disciples to the Mount of Olives, and declares himself to be the true vine.

John 15. 1-9.

When they had sung a hymn, Christ [went,
  As he was wont to do,
To Olivet, frequented mount,
  With his disciples true.
"I am the true, the living vine,"
  The Savior thus began,
"I nought without the Father do,
  He is the husbandman.
Each branch in me that bears not fruit,
  He gently takes away,
And every branch that beareth fruit,
  He prunes, and lets it stay,
That it may bring forth still more fruit.
  Now ye are purified
By truth that I have given to you:
  Ever in me abide.

SEKΣON 168.

Krįst gɵz wiđ hiz disįpelz tu đe Mʊn ov Olivz, and deklerz himself tu bi đe trɯ vįn.

Jon 15. 1-9.

Hwén đe had sɒŋ a hím, Krįst went
  az hi woz wɒnt tu dɯ,
tu Olivet, frikwented mʊnt,
  wiđ hiz disįpelz trɯ.
"Į am đe trɯ, đe liviŋ vįn,"
  đe Sevier đɒs began,
"į nɷt widʊt đe Fɑđer dɯ,
  hi iz đe hɒzbandman.
Ɩç branç in mi đat berz not frɯt,
  hi jentli teks awe,
and everi branç đat bereŧ frɯt,
  hi prɯnz, and lets it ste,
đat it me briŋ fɵrŧ stil mɵr frɯt.
  Nʊ yi ar pųrifįd
bį trɯŧ đat į hav given tu ų:
  ever in mi abįd.

The branch cannot, itself, bear fruit;
  It must be in the vine;
No more can ye, apart from me,
  Produce a good design.
Ye are the branches; joined to me
  Much good fruit will ye bear;
But without me ye nought can do
  Of right, or pure, or fair.
Severed from me, men soon become
  Like withered branches, cast
In fire to be consumed;
  Such is their fate at last.
If ye abide in me, and if
  My words abide in you,
Ask what ye will, it shall be done;
  Believe this; it is true.
My Father will be glorified
  If ye fruit-bearers be;
And thus alone can it be known
  That ye belong to me."

SECTION 169.

Christ exhorts his disciples to mutual love, and to prepare for persecution.

John 15. 9-27; 16. 1-4.

"Even as the Father hath loved me,
  So, too, have I loved you;
Continue in my love. If ye
  Keep my commandments true,
Then in my love, pure and unchanged,
  Ye evermore shall rest;
As I have kept my Father's laws,
  And with his love am blest.
These things I tell you, that my joy
  May ever with you stay;
And, that your joy may be filled full,
  This my command obey;—
Love one another, even as I
  Have loved you to the end;
And greater love can no man show
  Than die to save his friend.
And you will ever my friends be
  If you my laws fulfil;
Yea friends, for servants do not know,
  Like you, their master's will.
All I have heard my Father say,
  I have to you made known;
'Twas not that you chose me, but I
  Chose you to be my own;

Ɑe branç kanot, itself, ber frɯt;
  it mɒst bi in ðe vįn;
nơ mơr kan yi, apart from mi,
  prơdųs a gud dezįn.
Yi ar ðe brançez; joind tɯ mi
  mɒç gud frɯt wil yi ber;
bɒt wiðɒt mi yi not kan dɯ
  ov rįt, or pųr, or fer.
Severd from mi, men sɯn bekɒm
  lįk wiðerd brançez, kast
in fįr tu bi konsųmd;
  sɒç iz ðer fet at last.
If yi abįd in mi, and if
  mį wɒrdz abįd in ų,
ask hwot yi wil, it ʃal bi dɒn;
  beliv ðis; it iz trɯ.
Mį Fɑðer wil bi glơrifįd
  if yi frɯt-bererz bi;
and ðɒs alơn kan it bi nơn
  ðat yi beloŋ tu mi."

SEKƩON 169.

Krįst ekzorts hiz disipelz tu mųtųal lɒv, and tu preper for persekųʃon.

Jon 15. 9-27; 16. 1-4.

"Ɩven az ðe Fɑðer haŧ lɒvd mi,
  sơ, tɯ, hav į lɒvd ų;
kontinų in mį lɒv. If yi
  kip mį komandments trɯ,
ðen in mį lɒv, pųr and ɒnçenjd,
  yi evermơr ʃal rest;
az į hav kept mį Fɑðer'z lɷz,
  and wið hiz lɒv am blest.
Ɑiz ŧiŋz į tel ų, ðat mį joi
  me ever wið ų ste;
and, ðat ųr joi me bi fild ful,
  ðis, mį komand ơbe;—
Lɒv wɒn anɒðer, iven az į
  hav lɒvd ų tu ðe end;
and greter lɒv kan nơ man ʃơ
  ðan dį tu sev hiz frend.
And ų wil ever mį frendz bi
  if ų mį lɷz fulfil;
ye frendz, for servants dɯ not nơ,
  lįk ų, ðer master'z wil.
Ɯl į hav herd mį Fɑðer se,
  į hav tu ų med nơn;
'twoz not ðat ų çơz mi, bɒt į
  çơz ų tu bi mį ơn;

Ordaining you to bring forth fruit
Of grace that still may live;
That whatsoever ye shall ask
In me, ye may receive.

Love one another; earth will hate
You as it hated me;
If ye were worldly, then the world
Would love accordingly.
Since ye are no more of this world,
By me made free therefrom,
Therefore the world will hate your
Wherever be your home. [name,
Remember this; the servant is
Not greater than his lord;
If they have persecuted me,
If they have kept my word,
You also they will persecute,
And your word, too, will keep;
But all these things they'll do to you
Because they're not my sheep.
Had I not come, to testify,
They had not wrought this sin;
But now there's no excuse for them
That thus their evils screen.
And everyone that hateth me,
Hateth my Father too.
Had I not done among them works
Done by no other man,
They had not wrought this sin, but now
They lie beneath this ban,
That, having seen the works I do,
They hate me and my Father too.
Thus is fulfilled this, from their laws,
'They hated me without a cause.'

But when the Comforter is come,
The Spirit of truth divine,
Whom I will from the Father send,
Fulfilling my design,
He shall bear witness unto me,
And ye, my faithful few,
Shall also be my witnesses,
Because my truth ye knew
From the beginning. I have thus
Foretold you things to be,
That when they come you be not
By any doubt of me. [grieved
Men shall reject you, as most vile,
From synagogues, and strive

ordeniŋ ɥ tu briŋ fɵrɟ frɯt
ov gres đat stil mɛ liv;
đat hwotsɵever yı ʃal ask
in mı, yı mɛ resıv.

Lɒv wɒn anɒđer; erɟ wil het
ɥ az it heted mı;
if yı wer wɒrldli, đen đe wɒrld
wud lɒv akordiŋli.
Sins yı ar nɵ mɵr ov đis wɒrld,
bį mı med frı đerfrom,
đerfɵr đe wɒrld wil het ɥr nɛm,
hwerever bı ɥr hɵm.
Remember đis; đe servant iz
not greter đan hiz lord;
if đɛ hav persekɥted mı,
if đɛ hav kept mį wɒrd,
ɥ ɷlsɵ đɛ wil persekɥt,
and ɥr wɒrd, tɯ, wil kıp;
bɒt ɷl điz ɟiŋz đɛ'l dɯ tu ɥ
bekɷz đɛ'r not mį ʃıp.
Had į not kɒm, tu testifį,
đɛ had not rɷt đis sin;
bɒt nȣ đer'z nɵ ekskɥs for đem
đat đɒs đer ıvilz skrın.
And everi wɒn đat heteɟ mı,
heteɟ mį Fɑđer tɯ.
Had į not dɒn amɒŋ đem wɒrks
dɒn bį nɵ ɒđer man,
đɛ had not rɷt đis sin, bɒt nȣ
đɛ lį benıđ đis ban,
đat, haviŋ sın đe wɒrks į dɯ,
đɛ het mı and mį Fɑđer tɯ.
Đɒs iz fulfild đis, from đer lɷz,
'Đɛ heted mı widȣt a kɷz.'

Bɒt hwen đe Kɒmforter iz kɒm,
đe Spirit ov trɯɟ divįn,
hɯm į wil from đe Fɑđer send,
fulfiliŋ mį dezįn,
hı ʃal ber witnes ɒntu mı,
and yı, mį feɟful fɥ,
ʃal ɷlsɵ bı mį witnesez,
bekɷz mį trɯɟ yı nɥ
from đe beginiŋ. Į hav đɒs
fɵrtɵld ɥ ɟiŋz tu bı,
đat hwen đɛ kɒm ɥ bı not grıvd
bį eni dȣt ov mı.
Men ʃal rejekt ɥ, az mɵst vįl,
from sinagogz, and strįv

To slay you, as being false to God,
And quite unfit to live,
Because they have not known me, nor
The Father that's in me.
These things I now reveal to you,
That when the time shall be,
Ye may remember what I said,
And know that I foresee.
These things I said not at the first,
Being with you. Now you know the
worst."

tu slɛ ɥ, az biiŋ fɷls tu God,
and kwịt ɒnfit tu liv,
bekɷz đɛ hav not nɵn mi, nor
đe Fɑđer đat's in mi.
Điz ɟiŋz ị nɤ revil tu ɥ,
đat hwen đe tịm ʃal bi,
yi mɛ remember hwot ị sed,
and nɵ́ đat ị fɵrsi.
Điz ɟiŋz ị sed not at đe ferst,
biiŋ wiđ ɥ. Nɤ ɥ nɵ́ đe
wɒrst."

SECTION 170.

Christ promises the gifts of the Holy Spirit.
John 16. 5-33.

"But now to him who sent, I go,
Yet none doth question, Where?
Because my words have filled your
With sorrow and with care. [hearts
Yet it is true that, losing me,
You will have greater gain;
The Comforter will not be yours
So long as I remain;
But if I go away, I'll send
Him, and he shall abide.
And he will soon convince the world
Of sin they fain would hide;
Of righteousness and judgement too:
He'll be both judge and guide.
He will convince the world of sin
For not receiving me;
Of righteousness, because ere long
Ye will no more me see;
Of judgement too, for Satan now
Is cast down from on high.
I yet have many things to say,
Which now ye cannot bear;
But when the Spirit of truth is come,
He will all truth declare:
For of himself he will not speak,
But speak that which he hears;
And he will show you things to come
In distant, future years.
He shall my glory more reveal,
He shall of mine receive,
And show it unto you who now
To me sincerely cleave.
All that the Father hath is mine,
Therefore said I to you,

SEKΣON 170.

Krịst promisez đe gifts ov đe Hɵli Spirit.
Jon 16. 5-33.

"Bɒt nɤ tu him hɯ sent, ị gɵ,
yet nɒn dɒɟ kwestion, Hwer?
bekɷz mị wɒrdz hav fild ɥr harts
wiđ sorɵ and wiđ ker.
Yet it iz trɯ đat, lɯziŋ mi,
ɥ wil hav greter gen;
đe Kɒmforter wil not bi ɥrz
sɵ loŋ az ị remen;
bɒt if ị gɵ awɛ, ị'l send
him, and hi ʃal abịd.
And hi wil sɯn konvins đe wɒrld
ov sin đɛ fen wud hịd;
ov rịtiɒsnes and jɒjment tɯ:
hi'l bi bɵɟ jɒj and gịd.
Hi wil konvins đe wɒrld ov sin
for not resiviŋ mi;
ov rịtiɒsnes, bekɷz er loŋ
yi wil nɵ mɵr mi si;
ov jɒjment tɯ, for Setan nɤ
iz kast dɤn from on hị.
Ị yet hav meni ɟiŋz tu sɛ,
hwiç nɤ yi kanot ber;
bɒt hwen đe Spirit ov trɯɟ iz kɒm,
hi wil ɷl trɯɟ dekler:
for ov himself hi wil not spik,
bɒt spik đát hwiç hi hirz;
and hi wil ʃɵ ɥ ɟiŋz tu kɒm
in distant, fɥtɥr yirz.
Hi ʃal mị glɵri mɵr revil,
hi ʃal ov mịn resiv,
and ʃɵ it ɒntu ɥ hɯ nɤ
tu mi sinsirli kliv.
ɷl đat đe Fɑđer haɟ iz mịn,
đerfɵr sed ị tu ɥ,

The Comforter shall take thereof
  And you with it endue.

A little while, and ye shall not
  My presence here behold:
And then again a little while,
  I will myself unfold;
Because I to the Father go."
  Then his disciples thought
Within themselves, "What meaneth this
  Which now our Lord hath taught?
'A little while!' We cannot tell.
  And for this reason strange,
'Because I to my Father go.'
  What means this wondrous change?"
And Jesus knew they wished to ask,
  And thus did he explain,
"Do ye inquire my meaning, how
  I go and come again?
Truly I now say unto you,
  Ye will lament and weep
While the world joys; but no long time
  Will ye thus sorrow keep.
For as a woman in birth-pains
  Hath sorrow till the hour
Of her deliverance comes, and then
  Delight returns with power,
So is it now with your sad hearts;
  But when I come again,
Ye will rejoice, and then no man
  Shall turn your joy to pain.
And in that day, whate'er ye ask
  The Father in my name.
He will supply; nor shall ye e'er
  Pray vainly through the same.
As yet ye never thus have asked,
  But now, I tell you, Pray,
And ye shall have, and so be filled
  With joy none takes away.
These truths in figures I have taught;
  But now the time draws near
When I no more will darkly speak,
  But show the Father clear.
In that day ye shall ask in me;
  And I say not, I'll pray
The Father your requests to grant;
  He loveth you alway,
Because ye have loved me, and still
  Your faith in me display.

đe Kɒmforter ʃal tek đerov
  and ɥ wiđ it endɥ.

A litel hwįl, and yi ʃal not
  mį prezens hir behɵld:
and đen agen a litel hwįl,
  į wil mįself ɒnfɵld;
bekɷz į tu đe Fɑđer gɵ."
  Đen hiz disįpelz ɟɷt
wiđin đemselvz, "Hwot mineɟ
  đis
  hwiç nɤ ɤr Lord haɟ tɷt?
'A litel hwįl!' Wi kanot tel.
  And for đis rizon strenj,
'Bekɷz į tu mį Fɑđer gɵ.'
  Hwot minz đis wɒndrɒs çenj?"
And Jizɒs nɥ đe wiʃt tu ask,
  and đɒs did hi eksplen,
"Dɯ yi inkwįr mį miniŋ, hɤ
  į gɵ and kɒm agen?
Trɯli į nɤ se ɒntu ɥ,
  Yi wil lament and wip
hwįl đe wɒrld joiz; bɒt nɵ loŋ tįm
  wil yi đɒs sorɵ kip.
For az a wɯman in berɟ-penz
  haɟ sorɵ til đe ɤr
ov her deliverans kɒmz, and đen
  delįt retɒrnz wiđ pɤer,
sɵ iz it nɤ wiđ ɥr sad harts;
  bɒt hwen į kɒm agen,
yi wil rejois, and đen nɵ man
  ʃal tɒrn ɥr joi tu pen.
And in đát de, hwoter yi ask
  đe Fɑđer in mį nem,
hi wil sɒplį; nor ʃal yi er
  pre venli ɟrɯ đe sem.
Az yet yi never đɒs hav askt,
  bɒt nɤ, į tel ɥ, Pre,
and yi ʃal hav, and sɵ bi fild
  wiđ joi nɒn teks awe.
Điz trɯđz in figɥrz į hav tɷt;
  bɒt nɤ đe tįm drɷz nir
hwen į nɵ mɵr wil darkli spik,
  bɒt ʃɵ đe Fɑđer klir.
In đát de yi ʃal ask in mi;
  and į se not, į'l pre
đe Fɑđer ɥr rekwests tu grant;
  hi lɒveɟ ɥ ɷlwe,
bekɷz yi hav lɒvd mi, and stil
  ɥr feɟ in mi disple.

I came forth from the Father, and
Into the world am come ;
Again I leave the world, and go
Unto the Father,—home."
Then his disciples said to him,
" Lo, now thou speakest plain ;
Now are we sure thou knowest all,
Nor need we ask again.
By this we know thou cam'st from
Then Jesus made reply, [God."
" Believe ye now? The hour will
Yea even now is nigh, [come,
When ye will all desert your Lord,
Each man to seek his own ;
But still the Father dwells in me,
And I am not alone.
These things I now have told you, that
My peace I may impart ;
The world shall trouble cause, but it
I've overcome. Take heart."

Ɨ kem forŧ from đe Fɑđer, and
intu đe wɒrld am kɒm ;
agen ị liv đe wɒrld, and gɵ
ɒntu đe Fɑđer,—hɵm."
Đen hiz disịpelz sed tu him,
" Lɵ, nȣ đȣ spikest plen ;
nȣ ar wi ʃur đȣ nɵest ɷl,
nor nid wi ask agen.
Bị đis wi nɵ́ đȣ kem'st from God."
Đen Jizɒs med replị,
" Beliv yi nȣ? Đe ȣr wil kɒm,
yɛ, iven nȣ iz nị,
hwen yi wil ɷl dezert ɥr Lord,
iç man tu sik hiz ɵn ;
bɒt stil đe Fɑđer dwelz in mi,
and ị am not alɵn.
Điz ŧiŋz ị nȣ hav tɵld ɥ, đat
mị pis ị mɛ impart ;
đe wɒrld ʃal trɒbel kɷz, bɒt it
ị'v ɵverkɒm. Tek hart."

SECTION 171.

Christ prays to the Father for all his followers.—John 17.

Christ raised his eyes to heaven, and
" Father, the hour is nigh, [said,
Now glorify thy Son, that he
Thyself may glorify :
As thou hast given him power divine
O'er all mankind, to give
To all whom thou didst give to him
Eternally to live.
And this is life eternal, that
They may know thee, true God,
And Jesus Christ whom thou hast sent,
To spread thy truth abroad.
I on the earth have glorified
Thy name, and have fulfilled,
The work thou gavest me to do,
As thou, in love, hast willed.
O Father, glorify me now
With thine own self, and let
My glory that I had of old,
My human elevate.
I have revealed thy name to those
Thou gavest unto me
Out of the world, for thine they were,
And thine shall ever be ;

SEKƷON 171.

Krịst prez tu đe Fađer for ɷl hiz folȣerz.—Jon 17.

Krịst rezd hiz ịz tu heven, and sed,
" Fɑđer, đe ȣr iz nị,
nȣ glɵrifị đị Sɒn, đat hi
địself mɛ glɵrifị :
az đȣ hast given him pȣer divịn
ɵ'r ɷl mankịnd, tu giv
tu ɷl hum đȣ didst giv tu him
eternali tu liv.
And đis iz lịf eternal, đat
đe mɛ nɵ́ đi, tru God,
and Jizɒs Krịst hum đȣ hast sent,
tu spred đị truŧ abrɷd.
Ɨ on đe erŧ hav glɵrifịd
đị nem, and hav fulfild,
đe wɒrk đȣ gevest mi tu du,
az đȣ, in lɒv, hast wild.
Ɵ Fɑđer, glɵrifị mi nȣ
wiđ địn ɵn self, and let
mị glɵri đat ị had ov ɵld,
mị hɥman elevet.
Ɨ hav revild đị nem tu đɵz
đȣ gevest ɒntu mi
ȣt ov đe wɒrld, for địn đɛ wer,
and địn ʃal ever bi ;

And they have kept thy word, and
That all I have is thine, [proved
For I have given to them the words
Of truth and love divine.
They have received them, and they
That I from thee did come, [know
And that thou sentest me to earth
From heaven's refulgent home.
For these I pray; not only for
The sinful world I pray,
But more especially for these
My followers this day,
Which thou hast given me; thine
they are;
And thine are also mine;
And I am glorified in them,
And mine are also thine.

I stay no longer in this world,
But these must here remain;
When I am with thee, these must bear
Earth's trial and its pain.
O holy Father, by thy power
Keep those through thine own name
Whom thou hast given me, that they
Be one, as we, the same. [may
While I was with them in the world
I kept them in thy name:
Those that thou gav'st me I have kept,
And held them up from blame;
And of them all, not one is lost,
Except perdition's son,
So that the Scripture is fulfilled;
The Word is ever done.
O Father, now I come to thee;
And these things still I say
In this world, that my joy in them
May be fulfilled alway.
Thy word I gave them, and this world
Hath hated them, because,
Like me, they are not of this world,
But keep my righteous laws.
I pray not that thou should'st remove
My followers from the earth,
But keep them from its evils, by
A new and heavenly birth.
They are not of the world, even as
I am not of the world.
O sanctify them through thy truth:
Thy Word is truth unfurled.

and đɛ hav kept đị wɒrd, and prɯvd
đat ɷl ị hav iz địn,
for ị hav given tu đem đɛ wɒrdz
ov trɯɟ and lɒv divịn.
Đɛ hav resivd đem, and đɛ nσ
đat ị from đi did kɒm,
and đat đɤ sentest mi tu erɟ
from heven'z refɒljent hσm.
For điz ị prɛ; not σnli for
đɛ sinful wɒrld ị prɛ,
bɒt mσr espeʃali for điz
mị folσerz đis dɛ,
hwiç đɤ hast given mi; địn
đɛ ar;
and địn ar ɷlsσ mịn;
and ị am glσrifịd in đem,
and mịn ar ɷlsσ địn.

Ị stɛ nσ loŋger in đis wɒrld,
bɒt điz mɒst hir remɛn;
hwen ị am wiđ đi, điz mɒst ber
erɟ's trịal and its pɛn.
Σ hσli Fɑđer, bị đị pɤer
kip đσz ɟrɯ địn σn nɛm
hɯm đɤ hast given mi, đat đɛ mɛ
bi wɒn, az wi, đɛ sɛm.
Hwịl ị woz wiđ đem in đɛ wɒrld
ị kept đem in đị nɛm:
đσz đat đɤ gɛv'st mi ị hav kept,
and held đem ɒp from blɛm;
and ov đem ɷl, not wɒn iz lost,
eksept perdiʃon'z sɒn,
sσ đat đɛ Skriptɥr iz fulfild;
đɛ Wɒrd iz ever dɒn.
Σ Fɑđer, nɤ ị kɒm tu đi;
and điz ɟiŋz stil ị sɛ
in đis wɒrld, đat mị joi in đem
mɛ bi fulfild ɷlwɛ.
Đị wɒrd ị gɛv đem, and đis wɒrld
haɟ hɛted đem, bekɷz,
lịk mi, đɛ ar not ov đis wɒrld,
bɒt kip mị rịtiɒs lɷz.
Ị prɛ not đat đɤ ʃud'st remɯv
mị folσerz from đɛ erɟ,
bɒt kip đem from its ivilz, bị
a nɥ and hevenli berɟ.
Đɛ ar not ov đɛ wɒrld, iven az
ị am not ov đɛ wɒrld.
Σ saŋktifị đem ɟrɯ đị trɯɟ:
đị Wɒrd iz trɯɟ ɒnfɒrld.

As thou hast sent me forth from thee,
 So I my followers send;
And for their sakes I sanctify
 Myself unto the end,
That they, by truth, be sanctified,
 And thus with me ascend.

Neither pray I for these alone,
 For them also I pray
Who shall believe on me through them
 When I shall be away;
That they all may be one, as thou,
 O Father, art in me,
And I in thee; that they with us
 May evermore agree,
That thus the world may see and know
 My coming is from thee.
The glory which thou gavest me
 I unto them have given,
That they all may be one, as we
 Are one, in earth and heaven:
I being in them, and thou in me,
 They will perfection know;
And thus the world may understand
 My mission here below.
Father, I also will that they
 Whom thou hast given me
Be with me where I am, so that
 They may my glory see:
For thou hast me intensely loved
 Before the world began.
O righteous Father, little has
 Thy love been known to man;
But I have known thee, and these know
 That thou hast sent me here,
And have declared to them thy name,
 As it shall yet appear:
So that thy perfect love in me,
 Excelling all, divine,
May be in them, and I in them;
 They mine, as I am thine."

BOOK XI.

SECTION 172.

Christ again predicts Peter's denial of him.
Matthew 26. 31-35. Mark 14. 27-31.

Then Jesus said, "Because of me,
 All ye, this very night

Az ðʊ hast sent mi fɵrþ from ði,
 sɵ į mį folɵerz send;
and for ðɛr seks į saŋktifį
 mįself ʊntu ðe end,
ðat ðɛ, bį truþ, bi saŋktifįd,
 and ðʊs wið mi asend.

Nįðer prɛ į for ðiz alɵn,
 for ðem ɷlsɵ į prɛ
hu ʃal beliv on mi þru ðem
 hwen į ʃal bi awɛ;
ðat ðɛ ɷl mɛ bi wʊn, az ðʊ,
 Ɵ Fɑðer, art in mi,
and į in ði; ðat ðɛ wið ʊs
 mɛ evermɵr agri,
ðat ðʊs ðe wʊrld mɛ si and nɵ́
 mį kʊmiŋ iz from ði.
Ðe glɵri hwiç ðʊ gevest mi
 į ʊntu ðem hav given,
ðat ðɛ ɷl mɛ bi wʊn, az wi
 ar wʊn, in erþ and heven;
į biiŋ in ðem, and ðʊ in mi,
 ðɛ wil perfekʃon nɵ́;
and ðʊs ðe wʊrld mɛ ʊnderstand
 mį miʃon hir belɵ.
Fɑðer, į ɷlsɵ wil ðat ðɛ
 hum ðʊ hast given mi
bi wið mi hwɛr į am, sɵ ðat
 ðɛ mɛ mį glɵri si:
for ðʊ hast mi intensli lʊvd
 befɵr ðe wʊrld began.
Ɵ rįtiʊs Fɑðer, litel haz
 ðį lʊv bin nɵn tu man;
bʊt į hav nɵn ði, and ðiz nɵ́
 ðat ðʊ hast sent mi hir,
and hav deklɛrd tu ðem ðį nɛm,
 az it ʃal yet apir:
sɵ ðat ðį perfekt lʊv in mi,
 ekseliŋ ɷl, divįn,
mɛ bi in ðem, and į in ðem;
 ðɛ mįn, az į am ðįn."

BUK XI.

SEKΣON 172.

Krįst agen predikts Piter'z denįal ov him.
Maþų 26. 31-35. Mark 14. 27-31.

Ðen Jizʊs sed, "Bekɷz ov mi,
 ɷl yi, ðis veri nįt

Will be perverted, as 'tis writ,
'The shepherd I will smite,
And then shall all the sheep, his flock,
Be scattered, and shall flee.'
But when I'm risen, I will go
Before, to Galilee."
Peter replied, "Though all men should,
For thee, perverted be,
Yet I will never be of those
Who turn away from thee."
And Jesus answered, "Verily
I say to thee, before
The cock crow twice, thou shalt, this
Deny me thrice." He swore [night
With vehemence, and said to Christ,
"Though I should die with thee,
I'll not disown thee anywise."
So said the company.

SECTION 173.

Christ goes into the garden of Gethsemane. His agony there.

Matthew 26. 36-46. Mark 14. 32-42.
Luke 22. 40-46. John 18. 1, 2.

Then Jesus, with his followers, went
To that most sacred place,
O'er Kedron's brook, Gethsemane,
Garden of love and grace.
This spot the traitor Judas knew,
For ofttimes Jesus there
Resorted with his friends beloved,
For converse sweet, and prayer.
To his disciples now he saith,
"Sit here, while I shall pray;"
Then Peter, James, and John, he took
With him, and went away.
And when he came unto the place,
Great sorrow did he feel;
Amazement sore, and heaviness;
And said, "O'er me doth steal,
Even unto death, a sorrow deep.
Tarry and watch with me,
And pray that God your hearts will
From all temptation free." [keep
A little space he further went,
And kneeled upon the ground,
Fell on his face, and then thus prayed,
In accents most profound,
"O Father, Abba, Father mine,
If possible it be,

wil bi perverted, az 'tiz rit,
'Đe ʃepherd ị wil smịt,
and đen ʃal ɷl đe ʃip, hiz flok,
bi skaterd, and ʃal fli.'
Bɒt hwen ị'm rizen, ị wil gɵ
befɵr, tu Galili."
Piter replịd, "Đɵ ɷl men ʃud,
for đi, perverted bi,
yet ị wil never bi ov đɵz
hɥ tɒrn awe from đi."
And Jizɒs anserd, "Verili
ị se tu đi, befɵr
đe kok krɵ twịs, đɤ ʃalt, đis nịt
denị mi ŧrịs." Hi swɵr
wiđ vehemens, and sed tu Krịst,
"Đɵ ị ʃud dị wiđ đi,
ị'l not disɵn đi eniwịz."
Sɵ sed đe kɒmpani.

SEKΣON 173.

Krịst gɵz intu đe garden ov Geŧsemani Hiz agoni đer.

Maŧɥ 26. 36-46. Mark 14. 32-42.
Lɥk 22. 40-46. Jon 18. 1, 2.

Đen Jizɒs, wiđ hiz folɵerz, went
tu đát mɵst sekred ples,
ɵ'r Kedron'z bruk, Geŧsemani,
garden ov lɒv and gres.
Đis spot đe tretor Jɥdas nɥ,
for ofttịmz Jizɒs đer
rezorted wiđ hiz frendz belɒvd,
for konvers swit, and prer.
Tu hiz disịpelz nɤ hi seŧ,
"Sit hir, hwịl ị ʃal pre;"
đen Piter, Jemz, and Jon, hi tuk
wiđ him, and went awe.
And hwen hi kem ɒntu đe ples,
gret sorɵ did hi fil;
amezment sɵr, and hevines;
and sed "Ɵ'r mi dɒŧ stil,
iven ɒntu deŧ, a sorɵ dip.
Tari and woç wiđ mi,
and pre đat God ɥr harts wil kip
from ɷl tempteʃon fri."
A litel spes hi fɒrđer went,
and nild ɒpon đe grɤnd,
fel on hiz fes, and đen đɒs pred,
in aksents mɵst prɵfɤnd,
"Ɵ Fađer, Aba, Fađer mịn,
if posibel it bi,

Let this cup pass from me; all things
  Are possible to thee.
If thou be willing now, do thou
  This cup from me remove;
Yet not my will, but thine be done;
  As it doth me behove."
An angel then appeared to him
  In heavenly majesty,
And strengthened him; and then he
  Again more earnestly: [prayed
His sweat was like great drops of
  So great his agony. [blood,
And when he rose from prayer, and
  To his disciples three, [came
He found them all asleep, and saith,
  "Could ye not watch with me
One hour? And Simon, sleepest thou?
  Watch; rise and pray; that ye
Into temptation enter not,
  And so be led astray;
The spirit willing is, indeed,
  The flesh doth it betray."
Again, the second time, he went,
  And thus did his prayer run,
"If this cup may not pass except
  I drink, thy will be done."
And still when he returned, he found
  Sleep heavy in their eyes;
And when he spoke, they knew not how
  To answer, through surprise.
Again, the third time, Jesus left
  The sleepers, and his prayer
Once more did he repeat; his soul
  Oppressed with grief and care.
To the disciples the third time
  He came, and said, "Arise;
The hour is come. Do ye take rest,
  And let sleep seal your eyes?
Now is the Son of man betrayed
  Unto a sinful band;
Rise up, and let us go, behold
  The traitor is at hand."

SECTION 174.

Christ is betrayed and apprehended. The resistance of Peter.

Matthew 26. 47-56. Mark 14. 43-50.
Luke 22. 47-53. John 18. 3-11.

Immediately, while yet he spake,
  Lo, one of Jesus' band,

let đis kɒp pas from mi; ɑl ɟiŋz
  ar posibel tu đi.
If đɤ bi wiliŋ nɤ, dɯ đɤ
  đis kɒp from mi remɯv;
yet not mį wíl, bɒt đįn bi dɒn;
  az it dɒɟ mi behɯv."
An ɛnjel đen apird tu him
  in hevenli majesti,
and streŋɟend him; and đen hi pred
  agen mɷr ernestli:
hiz swet woz lįk gret drops ov blɒd,
  sɷ gret hiz agoni.
And hwen hi rɷz from prer, and
  tu hiz disįpelz ɟri, [kɛm
hi fɤnd đem ɑl aslip, and seɟ,
  "Kud yi not woç wiđ mi
wɒn ɤr? And Sįmon, slipest đɤ?
  Woç; riz and prɛ; đat yi
intu tempteʃon enter not,
  and sɷ bi led astrɛ;
đe spirit wiliŋ iz, indid,
  đe fleʃ dɒɟ it betrɛ."
Agen, đe sekond tįm, hi went,
  and đɒs did hiz prer rɒn,
"If đis kɒp mɛ not pas eksept
  į driŋk, đį wíl bi dɒn."
And stil hwen hi retɒrnd, hi fɤnd
  slip hevi in đer įz;
and hwen hi spɷk, đɛ nɥ not hɤ
  tu anser, ɟrɯ sɒrprįz.
Agen, đe ɟerd tįm, Jizɒs left
  đe slipeṛz, and hiz prer
wɒns mɷr did hi repit; hiz sɷl
  oprest wiđ grif and ker.
Tu đe disįpelz đe ɟerd tįm
  hi kɛm, and sed, "Arįz;
đe ɤr iz kɒm. Dɯ yi tɛk rest,
  and let slip sil ɥr įz?
Nɤ iz đe Sɒn ov man betred
  ɒntu a sinful band;
rįz ɒp, and let ɒs gɷ, behɷld
  đe tretor iz at hand."

SEKƩON 174.

Krįst iz betrɛd and aprehended. Đe rezistans ov Piter.

Maɟɥ 26. 47-56. Mark 14. 43-50.
Lɯk 22. 47-53. Jon 18. 3-11.

Immidiɛtli, hwįl yet hi spɛk,
  lɷ, wɒn ov Jizɒs' band,

Judas, whom priests and Pharisees
Had furnished with command
Of officers, and warlike means,
Weapons, and torches' light:
And multitudes with swords and
Came, ready for a fight. [staves,
The traitor fixed upon a sign;
It was a treacherous kiss;
And said, "Take hold, and safely keep
Whoe'er receiveth this."
He soon approached, and forward
Till he to Christ drew nigh; [went,
"Hail Master!" then, he falsely said,
And kissed him guiltily.
"Friend, wherefore now thus comest
With grief did Jesus say; [thou?"
Canst thou, O Judas, with a kiss,
The Son of man betray?"
Then Jesus, knowing what would be,
Stood boldly in their sight;
"Whom seek ye?" he inquired. They
"Jesus the Nazarite." [said,
"That same am I," he said. Then
With Judas, standing round, [they,
With awe were struck, and backward
And fell upon the ground. [went,
Once more he asked, "Whom do ye
They made the same reply. [seek?"
Christ answered, "I have said, I am;
Therefore let these go by."
Thus was fulfilled the word he spake,
In prayer, to God alone,
"Of those whom thou hast given me,
I've not lost even one."

Then on the Christ they laid their hands,
Which when his followers saw,
They said, "Lord shall we use the
And Peter quick did draw [sword?"
His sword, as he by Jesus stood,
And cut off Malchus' ear.
He was the high priest's servant.
Said, "Suffer ye thus far;" [Christ
Then touched his ear, and he was
And said to Peter, "Stay; [healed:
Put up thy sword; who take the sword,
Shall perish in that way.
Can I not pray my Father now,
And he would straightway send

Jɯdas, hɯm pr
had fɒrniʃt w
ov ofiserz, and
weponz, and
and mɒltitɥdz w
kem, redi for
ƌe tretor fikst
it woz a tregɛ
and sed, "Tek
hɯer resivet
Hi sɯn aprœgt,
til hi tu Krist
"Hel Master!"
and kist him
"Frend, hwerfe
wiƌ grif did J
kanst ƌɤ Ơ Jɯd
ƌe Sɒn ov ma
ƌen Jizɒs nœiŋ
stud bœldli in
"Hɯm sik yi
"Jizɒs ƌe Na
"ƌát sem am i,
wiƌ Jɯdas, s
wiƌ ɷ wer strɒk,
and fel ɒpon
Wɒns mœr hi a
ƌe med ƌe se
Krist anserd, "
ƌerfœr let ƌiz
ƌɒs woz fulfild
in prer, tu Go
"Ov ƌœz hɯm
i'v not lost iv

ƌen on ƌe Kr handz,
hwig hwen hi
ƌe sed, "Lord ʃ
and Piter kwi
hiz sœrd, az hi b
and kɒt of M
Hi woz ƌe hi pri
sed, "Sɒfer y
ƌen tɒgt hiz ir,
and sed tu Pi
put ɒp ƌi sœrd;
ʃal periʃ in ƌá
Kan i not pre m
and hi wud st

Legions of angels to my aid,
   Who would my life defend?
Then how would Scripture be fulfilled,
   That even this must be?
Shall I refuse to drink the cup
   My Father giveth me?"

Then Jesus answering, said to all,—
   Priests, people, elders chief,—
"Why are ye come with swords and
   As if to take a thief? [staves,
I sat with you, from day to day,
   And in the temple taught,
And yet ye laid no hands on me,
   And yet ye took me not.
The Scriptures still ye must fulfil,
   And this is now your hour:
The hosts of hell shall know full well
   That weakness is their power."
Thus were the prophecies fulfilled,
   Each one accomplishèd.
Then the disciples were alarmed,
   And all forsook, and fled.

lijonz ov enjelz tu mį ed,
   hɯ wud mį lįf defend?
Ꝺen hȣ wud Skriptɥr bi fulfild,
   ꝺat iven ꝺis mɒst bi?
Σal į refɥz tu driŋk ꝺe kɒp
   mį Fɐꝺer giveŧ mi?"

Ꝺen Jizɒs anseriŋ, sed tu ɷl,—
   Prists, pipel, elderz ɕif,—
"Hwį ar yi kɒm wiꝺ sɵrdz and
   az if tu tɐk a ŧif? [stevz,
Ŧ sat wiꝺ ɥ, from dɐ tu dɐ,
   and in ꝺe tempel tɷt,
and yet yi led nɵ handz on mi,
   and yet yi tuk mi not.
Ꝺe Skriptɥrz stil yi mɒst fulfil,
   and ꝺis iz nȣ ɥr ȣr:
ꝺe hɵsts ov hel ʃal nɵ́ ful wel
   ꝺat wiknes iz ꝺɐr pȣer."
Ꝺɒs wer ꝺe profesiz fulfild,
   iɕ wɒn akompliʃed.
Ꝺen ꝺe disįpelz wer alarmd,
   and ɷl forsuk, and fled.

SECTION 175.

Christ is taken to Annas, and to the palace of Caiaphas, followed by Peter and John.

Matthew 26. 57, 58. Mark 14. 51-54.
Luke 22. 54, 55. John 18. 12-14.

Next all the band, the captain, and
   The Jewish officers
Bound Jesus, and then led him to
   Their priestly ministers;
To Annas first, and he sent Christ
   To Caiaphas, high priest
That year, his son-in-law, to be
   Condemned, or be released.
It was that Caiaphas who said
   That one man needs must die
Rather than ruin should befall
   The Jewish polity.
A certain young man followed Christ,
   In a loose robe arrayed,
(Tradition says that it was John,)
   Howbeit, sore afraid.
And when the men laid hold on him,
   He fled with speed, and threw
His robe aside. And further off
   Did Peter follow too.

SEKΣON 175.

Krįst iz teken tu Anas, and tu ꝺe pales ov Kaiafas, folɵd bį Piter and Jon.

Maŧɥ 26. 57, 58. Mark 14. 51-54.
Lɯk 22. 54, 55. Jon 18. 12-14.

Nekst ɷl ꝺe band, ꝺe kapten, and
   ꝺe Jɯiʃ ofiserz
bȣnd Jizɒs, and ꝺen led him tu
   ꝺɐr pristli ministerz;
tu Anas ferst, and hi sent Krįst
   tu Kaiafas, hį prist
ꝺát yir, hiz sɒn-in-lɷ, tu bi
   kondemd, or bi relist.
It woz ꝺát Kaiafas hɯ sed
   ꝺat wɒn man nidz mɒst dį
rɐꝺer ꝺan rɯin ʃud befɷl
   ꝺe Jɯiʃ politi.
A serten yɒŋ man folɵd Krįst,
   in a lɯs rɵb ared,
(tradiʃon sez ꝺat it woz Jon,)
   hȣbiit, sɵr afred.
And hwen ꝺe men led hɵld on him,
   hi fled wiꝺ spid, and ŧrɯ
hiz rɵb asįd. And fɒrꝺer of
   did Piter folɵ tɯ.

And so the captain took the Lord
Unto the stately gate
Of Caiaphas, where priests and scribes
And gathered elders sat.
And John, who knew the high priest [well,
Went in unto the hall
With Jesus. Peter stood without.
John thought that he would call
Him in; and shortly after went
And said unto the maid
That kept the door, "Let this man in;
Ye need not be afraid."
They made a fire to warm themselves,
Because the night was cold;
And all sat down, and Peter too,
To see what would unfold.

And sɵ đe kapten tuk đe Lord
ɒntu đe stetli get
ov Kaiafas, hwer prists and skrįbz
and gađerd elderz sat.
And Jon, hɯ nɥ đe hį prist wel,
went in ɒntu đe hɷl
wiđ Jizɒs. Piter stud wiđɜt.
Jon ʇɷt đat hi wud kɷl
him in; and ʃortli after went
and sed·ɒntu đe med
đat kept đe dɵr, "Let đis man in;
yi nid not bi afred."
Đe med a fįr tu worm đemselvz,
bekɷz đe nįt woz kɵld;
and ɷl sat dɜn, and Piter tɯ,
tu si hwot wud ɒnfɵld.

SECTION 176.

Christ is examined and condemned in the house of the high priest.

Matthew 26. 59-66. Mark 14. 55-64. John 18. 19-24.

Then did the high priest question Christ
Of what, and whom, he taught.
And Jesus simply answered him,
"I spake, and wrought my works,
Openly in the synagogue,
And temple, 'midst the Jews;
In secret have I nothing said:
Of what dost thou accuse?
Why askest me? Ask those who heard,
And therefore ought to know."
When thus he spake, an officer
Gave Christ an angry blow,
Saying, "Dost thou to God's high [priest
Reply in words like these?"
And Jesus said, "If ill I spoke,
Then it might thee displease;
And bear thou witness of the wrong;
But if I well replied,
Why dost thou smite me with thy [hand,
As if a crime to chide?"
Then the high priest, and council too,
False witness sought, but none,
With all their malice, could they find,
To slay the Blessed One.

SEKΣON 176.

Krįst iz ekzamind and kondemd in đe hɜs ov đe hį prist.

Maʇɥ 26. 59-66. Mark 14. 55-64. Jon 18. 19-24.

Đen did đe hį prist kwestion Krįst
ov hwot, and hɯm, hi tɷt.
And Jizɒs simpli anserd him,
"Į spek, and rɷt mį wɒrks,
ɵpenli in đe sinagog,
and tempel, 'midst đe Jɯz:
in sikret hav į nɒʇiŋ sed:
ov hwot dɒst đɜ akɥz?
Hwį askest mi? Ask đɵz hɯ herd,
and đerfɵr ɷt tu nɵ́."
Hwen đɒs hi spek, an ofiser
gev Krįst an aŋgri blɵ,
seiŋ, "Dɒst đɜ tu God'z hį prist
replį in wɒrdz lįk điz?"
And Jizɒs sed, "If il į spɵk,
đen it mįt đi displiz;
and ber đɜ witnes ov đe roŋ;
bɒt if į wel replįd,
hwį dɒst đɜ smįt mi wiđ đį hand,
az if a krįm tu ɕįd?"
Đen đe hį prist, and kɜnsil tɯ,
fɷls witnes sɷt, bɒt nɒn,
wiđ ɷl đer malis, kud đe fįnd,
tu sle đe Blesed Wɒn.

Though many bore false witness, yet
  They could not so agree.
At last came two false men, who bore
  This testimony: "We
Have heard him say, 'I will destroy
  God's temple in this land,
And in three days will build it up
  Without a human hand.'"
But still these lying witnesses
  They could not understand.

The high priest then, at length, arose,
  And said to Jesus, "What
Is this offence they charge thee with,
  And yet thou answerest not?"
But Jesus calmly held his peace.
  And then the high priest spoke,
"Tell us; Art thou the very Christ.
  I now, by God, invoke
Thy answer." Jesus said, "I am.
  Hereafter ye shall see
The Son of man in glory come,
  With power and majesty,
And circled with the clouds of heaven."
  And then the high priest rent
His clothes, and said, "'Tis blasphemy
  To which thou givest vent.
What further need of witnesses?
  Behold, now ye have heard
His blasphemy. What think ye all
  The doom to be preferred?"
They all cried out, with eager breath,
"He's guilty. Let him suffer death."

Đɵ meni bɵr fɷls witnes, yet
  đɛ kud not sɵ agri.
At last kɛm túɯ fɷls men, hɯ bɵr
  đis testimoni: "Wi
hav herd him se, 'Ɨ wil destroi
  God'z tempel in đis land,
and in ɟri dɛz wil bild it ɒp
  wiđɜt a hųman hand.'"
Bɒt stil điz lịiŋ witnesez
  đɛ kud not ɒnderstand.

Đe hị prist đen, at leŋɟ, arɵz,
  and sed tu Jizɒs, "Hwot
iz đis ofens đɛ qarj đi wiđ,
  and yet đɜ anserest not?"
Bɒt Jizɒs kɛmli held hiz pis.
  And đen đe hị prist spɵk,
"Tel ɒs; art đɜ đe veri Krịst.
  Ɨ nɜ, bị God, invɵk
đị anser." Jizɒs sed, "Ɨ am.
  Hirafter yi ʃal si
đe Sɒn ov man in glɵri kɒm,
  wiđ pɜer and majesti,
and serkeld wiđ đe klɜdz ov heven."
  And đen đe hị prist rent
hiz klɵđz, and sed, "'Tiz blasfemi
  tu hwiq đɜ givest vent.
Hwot fɒrđer nid ov witnesez?
  Behɵld, nɜ yi hav herd
hiz blasfemi. Hwot ɟiŋk yi ɷl
  đe dɯm tu bi preferd?"
Đe ɷl krịd ɜt, wiđ iger breɟ,
"Hi'z gilti. Let him sɒfer deɟ."

SECTION 177.

Christ is struck, and insulted by the soldiers.

Matthew 26. 67, 68. Mark 14. 65.
Luke 22. 63-65.

The men who guarded Christ, now mocked
  And smote him cruelly;
And some began to spit on him,
  With gross indignity.
They blindfold, buffet, strike with rods,
  And then say, "Prophesy:
Who is it treats thee so, and does
  Thy majesty defy?"

SEKΣON 177.

Krịst iz strɒk, and insɒlted bị đe sɵldierz.

Maɟų 26. 67, 68. Mark 14. 65.
Lɯk 22. 63-65.

Đe men hɯ garded Krịst, nɜ mokt
  and smɵt him krɯelli;
and sɒm began tu spit on him,
  wiđ grɵs indigniti.
Đɛ blịndfɵld, bɒfet, strịk wiđ rodz,
  and đen se "Profesị:
hɯ iz it trits đi sɵ, and dɒz
  đị majesti defị?"

SECTION 178.

Peter three times denies Christ.

Matthew 26. 69-75. Mark 14. 66-72.
Luke 22. 56-62. John 18. 17, 18; 25-28.

Now Peter sat without the place
  Of justice, there to spend
His time in peace, beside the fire,
  That he might see the end.
And soon the maid who kept the door
  Looked earnestly, and said,
"And thou too his disciple art."
  Then Peter, filled with dread,
Replied, "I do not know the man."
  The servants who stood there,
And officers, to warm themselves,
  Looked at him, with a stare,
And said, "Art thou not one of them?"
  He said, "No; I am not."
But one, a kinsman of the man
  Whom Peter lately smote,
Replied, "Did I not see thee in
  The garden with this man?"
He still denied; then went he out,
  And the cock-crow began.

As he was standing in the porch,
  And thinking matters o'er,
Another said, "And thou art one
  Of them." And Peter swore
A flat denial of his Lord,
"I know him not, upon my word."

After another mournful hour,
  As morn began to gleam,
And Peter loitered in the room
  With Jesus, it would seem,
Another confidently said,
  "Thou surely wast with him,
For thou a Galilæan art,
  Thy speech agrees thereto."
Then he began to curse and swear,
  Into a passion flew,
And said, "I do not know this man
  Of whom ye speak." Before
The words had quite escaped his lips,
  Cock-crow was heard once more.
The Lord then turned, and caught his [eye:
He went out, and wept bitterly.
Remembering what the Lord had said,
He hid his face, and bowed his head.

SEKΣON 178.

Piter θri tįmz denįz Krįst.

Maθų 26. 69-75. Mark 14. 66-72.
Luk 22. 56-62. Jon 18. 17, 18; 25-28.

Nȣ Piter sat wiđȣt đe ples
  ov jɒstis, đer tu spend
hiz tįm in pis, besįd đe fįr,
  đat hi mįt si đe end.
And sɯn đe med hɯ kept đe dɷr
  lukt ernestli, and sed,
"And đȣ tɯ hiz disįpel art."
  Đen Piter, fild wiđ dred,
replįd, "Ɨ dɯ not nɷ đe man."
  Đe servants hɯ stud đer,
and ofiserz, tu worm đemselvz,
  lukt at him, wiđ a ster,
and sed, "Art đȣ not wɒn ov đem?"
  Hi sed, "Nɷ; į am not."
Bɒt wɒn, a kinzman ov đe man
  hɯm Piter letli smɷt,
replįd, "Did į not si đi in
  đe garden wiđ đis man?"
Hi stil denįd; đen went hi ȣt,
  and đe kok-krɷ began.

Az hi woz standiŋ in đe pɷrç,
  and θiŋkiŋ materz ɷ'r,
anɒđer sed, "And đȣ art wɒn
  ov đem." And Piter swɷr
a flat denįal ov hiz Lord,
"Ɨ nɷ him not, ɒpon mį wɒrd."

After anɒđer mɷrnful ȣr,
  az morn began tu glim,
and Piter loiterd in đe rɯm
  wiđ Jizɒs, it wud sim,
anɒđer konfidentli sed,
  "Đȣ ʃɯrli wost wiđ him,
for đȣ a Galilian art,
  đį spiç agriz đertu."
Đen hi began tu kɒrs and swer,
  intu a paʃon flɯ,
and sed, "Ɨ dɯ not nɷ đis man
  ov hɯm yi spik." Befɷr
đe wɒrdz had kwįt eskept hiz lips,
  kok-krɷ woz herd wɒns mɷr.
Đe Lord đen tɒrnd, and kɔt hiz į:
hi went ȣt, and wept biterli.
Rememberiŋ hwot đe Lord had sed,
hi hid hiz fes, and bȣd hiz hed.

SECTION 179.

Christ is taken before the Sanhedrim and condemned.

Matthew 27. 1. Mark 15. 1.
Luke 22. 66-71.

At early dawn, when morning's ray
Was still with shadows dim,
The priests and elders brought the [Lord
Before the Sanhedrim;
And there they asked, "Art thou in- [deed
The Christ, Messiah true?"
Jesus replied, "If I repeat,
I am, your credence due
Ye will refuse; and if I ask
You questions in reply,
Ye will not answer; but my right
To liberty deny.
Yet know, hereafter ye shall see
The Son of man enthroned
On the right hand of God's own power,
Though now by men disowned."
Then said they all, "Art thou, in truth,
The Son of God above?"
Christ answered, "Ye say right; I [am."
This did sufficient prove,
Unto the Jews assembled there,
His blasphemy; and straight
They sentenced him to die the death,
To gratify their hate.

SEKΣON 179.

Krįst iz teken befɵr đe Sanhedrim and kondemd.

Maɟų 27. 1. Mark 15. 1.
Lɯk 22. 66-71.

At erli dɷn, hwen morniŋ'z re
woz stil wiđ ʃadɵz dim,
đe prįsts and elderz brɷt đe Lord
befɵr đe Sanhedrim;
and đer đe askt, "Art đɤ indid
đe Krįst, Mesįa trɯ?"
Jizɒs replįd, "If į repit,
Ɨ am, ųr kridens dų
yi wil refųz; and if į ask
ų kwestionz in replį,
yi wil not anser; bɒt mį rįt
tu liberti denį.
Yet nɵ́, hirafter yi ʃal si
đe Sɒn ov man enɟrɵnd
on đe rįt hand ov God'z ɵn pɤer,
đɵ nɤ bį men disɵnd."
Đen sed đe ɷl, "Art đɤ, in trɯɟ,
đe Sɒn ov God abɒv?"
Krįst anserd, "Yi sɛ rįt; į am."
Đis did sɒfiʃent prɯv,
ɒntu đe Jɯz asembeld đer,
hiz blasfemi; and stret
đe sentenst him tu dį đe deɟ,
tu gratifį đer het.

SECTION 180.

Judas declares the Innocence of Christ.

Matthew 27. 3-10.

Then Judas who betrayed the Lord,
When he thus saw him stand
Condemned to die, repented of
The treachery he had planned;
And brought the thirty silver coins
Back to the priests, and said,
"I've sinned in what I've done, for I
Have guiltily betrayed
The Innocent: his blood's on me."
They said, "What's that to us?
See thou to that. We've only judged
A man most blasphemous."

SEKΣON 180.

Jɯdas deklerz đe Inosens ov Krįst.

Maɟų 27. 3-10.

Đen Jɯdas hɯ betred đe Lord,
hwen hi đɒs sɷ him stand
kondemd tu dį, repented ov
đe treçeri hi had pland;
and brɷt đe ɟerti silver koinz
bak tu đe prįsts, and sed,
"Ɨ'v sind in hwot į'v dɒn, for į
hav giltili betred
de Inosent: hiz blɒd'z on mi."
Đe sed, "Hwot's đát tu ɒs?
Si đɤ tu đát. Wi'v ɵnli jɒjd
a man mɵst blasfemɒs."

He cast the silver pieces down,
  ('Twas in the temple too,)
And went and hanged himself. The
  priests and the elders knew [chief
It was the price of blood; and said,
  "We must not keep it here."
They counsel took, and bought a field
  To bury strangers, near.
That field was called Akeldama,
  That is, the Field of Blood.
Thus was fulfilled the prophet's word,
  Which long on record stood,
"They took the thirty silver coins,
  The price of Innocence,
And gave them for the potter's field."
  Such was their penitence.

SECTION 181.

Christ is accused before Pilate, and is by him declared to be innocent.

Matthew 27. 2, 11-14. Mark 15. 1-5. Luke 23. 1-4. John 18. 28-38.

The multitude then rose, bound Christ,
  And led him to the hall;
And then to Pontius Pilate brought,
  To know what would befall.
At early hour, on that sad morn,
  They came with cruel haste,
But would not enter in the hall,
  Lest they should lose the feast.
So Pilate came forth unto them,
  And asked, "What is the crime
Ye charge upon this man?" They said,
  "It is, indeed, full time
That he should suffer by the law."
  Then Pilate said, "Judge ye."
The Jews replied, "Sentence of death
  We cannot now decree."
Thus Jesus' saying was fulfilled,
  Which told how he should die;
By his own nation first betrayed,
  That Rome might crucify.

Then they began to accuse the Lord;
  "He doth pervert the nation,
Forbidding tribute to be paid,
  And due subordination,
Saying, Himself is Christ, a king."
  Pilate returned, and now

Hi kast đe silver pisez dɤn,
  ('twoz in đe tempel tɯ,)
and went and haŋd himself. Đe
  prists and đe elderz nų [çif
it woz đe pris ov blɒd; and sed,
  "Wi mɒst not kip it hir."
Đe kɤnsel ţuk, and bɷt a fild
  tu beri strenjerz, nir.
Đát fild woz kɷld Akeldama,
  đát iz, đe Fild ov Blɒd.
Đɒs woz fulfild đe profet's wɒrd,
  hwiç loŋ on rekord stud,
"Đe tuk đe ŧerti silver koinz,
  đe pris ov Inosens,
and gev đem for đe poter'z fild."
  Sɒç woz đer penitens.

SEKΣON 181.

Krist iz akyzd befɷr Pilet, and iz bi him deklerd tu bi inosent.

Maŧų 27. 2, 11-14. Mark 15. 1-5. Luk 23. 1-4. Jon 18. 28-38.

Đe mɒltitųd đen rɷz, bɤnd Krist,
  and led him tu đe hɷl;
and đen tu Ponʃɒs Pilet brɷt,
  tu nɷ́ hwot wud befɷl.
At erli ɤr, on đát sad morn,
  đe kem wiđ krɯel hest,
bɒt wud not enter in đe hɷl
  lest đe ʃud lɯz đe fist.
Sɷ Pilet kem forŧ ɒntu đem,
  and askt, "Hwot iz đe krim
yi çarj ɒpon đis man?" Đe sed
  "It iz, indid, ful tim
đat hi ʃud sɒfer bi đe lɷ."
  Đen Pilet sed, "Jɒj yi."
Đe Jɯz raplid, "Sentens ov deŧ
  wi kanot nɤ dekri."
Đɒs Jizɒs' seiŋ woz fulfild,
  hwiç tɷld hɤ hi ʃud di;
bi hiz ɷn neʃon ferst betred,
  đat Rɷm mit krɯsifi.

Đen đe began tu akųz đe Lord;
  "Hi dɒŧ pervert đe neʃon,
forbidiŋ tribųt tu bi ped,
  and dų sɒbordineʃon,
seiŋ, Himself iz Krist, a kiŋ."
  Pilet retɒrnd, and nɤ

Jesus before him stood. He asked,
"The Jewish king art thou?"
Jesus replied, "Dost thou require
To know for thine own sake?
Or is it that some other men
Tell thee this charge to make?"
Pilate replied, "Am I a Jew?
I would thy question shun,
But for the charge against thee made
By Jews. What hast thou done?"
Christ said, "It is not of this world
My kingdom is, for then
My servants for my cause would fight
And save me from these men.
But now my kingdom's not from hence."
Said Pilate, "Then, art thou
A king?" And Jesus said, "I am;
To me the world shall bow.
For this end only was I born;
And for this cause, forsooth,
I came into this world, to bear
My witness to the truth.
And everyone that's of the truth,
And will the truth receive,
Will gladly listen to my voice,
And in my word believe."
And Pilate asked, "What is the truth?"
Then went forth to the Jews,
And said "I find no fault at all
In him whom ye accuse."
Then did the chief priests many crimes
Allege against the Lord,
But to the malice of these men,
He answered not a word.
Said Pilate, "See how many things
They bring against thee now."
He answered not a single word.
Pilate, amazed, said, "How
Is this, thou answerest not?
Canst thou these charges meet?"
Still Jesus spoke not, as he stood
Before the judgement seat.

Jizɒs befɵr him stud. Hị askt,
"Đe Juiʃ kiŋ art đɤ?"
Jizɒs replịd, "Dɒst đɤ rekwịr
tu nó for địn ɵn sek?
or iz it đat sɒm ɒđer men
tel đị đis çarj tu mek?"
Pịlet replịd, "Am ị a Jɯ?
Ɨ wud đị kwestion ʃɒn,
bɒt for đe çarj agenst đị med
bị Jɯz. Hwot hast đɤ dɒn?"
Krịst sed, "It iz not ov đis wɒrld
mị kiŋdom iz, for đen
mị servants for mị kωz wud fịt
and sev mị from điz men.
Bɒt nɤ mị kiŋdom'z not from hens."
Sed Pịlet, "Đen, art đɤ
a kiŋ?" And Jizɒs sed "Ɨ am;
tu mị đe wɒrld ʃal bɤ.
For đis end ɵnli woz ị born;
and for đis kωz, forsuŧ,
ị kem intu đis wɒrld, tu ber
mị witnes tu đe truŧ.
And everiwɒn đat's ov đe truŧ,
and wil đe truŧ resịv,
wil gladli lisen tu mị vois,
and in mị wɒrd belịv."
And Pịlet askt, "Hwot iz đe truŧ?"
Đen went fɵrŧ tu đe Jɯz,
and sed, "Ɨ fịnd nɵ fωlt at ωl
in him hum yị akųz."
Đen did đe çif prịsts meni krịmz
alej agenst đe Lord,
bɒt tu đe malis ov điz men,
hị anserd not a wɒrd.
Sed Pịlet, "Sị hɤ meni ŧiŋz
đe briŋ agenst đị nɤ."
Hị anserd not a siŋgel wɒrd.
Pịlet, amezd, sed, "Hɤ
iz đis, đɤ anserest not?
Kanst đɤ điz çarjez mịt?"
Stil Jizɒs spɵk not, az hị stud
befɵr đe jɒjment sịt.

SECTION 182.

Christ is sent by Pilate to Herod.
Luke 23. 5-12.

More fierce they grew, and said, with rage,
"He stirs the people up,

SEKΣON 182.

Krịst iz sent bị Pịlet tu Herod.
Lɯk 23. 5-12.

Mɵr fịrs đe grɯ, and sed, wiđ rej,
"Hị sterz đe pịpel ɒp,

From Galilee unto this place ;
 We cannot with him cope."
When Pilate heard of Galilee,
 He asked, if Christ came thence ;
And when he knew, to Herod straight
 He sent him, for defence.
Exceeding glad king Herod was ;
 For great things he had heard
Of him, and hoped some miracle
 To see, and hear Christ's word.
But Jesus nothing would reply
 To all his questionings,
Though priests and scribes used taunts and jibes,
 And uttered cruel things.
Then Herod and his men of war
 Scorned him ; and on his back
They put a gorgeous robe, and then
 To Pilate sent him back.
Pilate and Herod, that same day,
 Became as friends again ;
Before they were at enmity.
 What friendship 'tween such men ?

from Galili ɒntu đis ples ;
 wı kanot wiđ him kɵp."
Hwen Pįlet herd ov Galili,
 hı askt, if Krįst kem đens ;
and hwen hı nɥ, tu Herod stret
 hı sent him, for defens.
Eksıdiŋ glad kiŋ Herod woz ;
 for gret ɟiŋz hı had herd
ov him, and hɵpt sɒm mirakel
 tu sı, and hır Krįst's wɒrd.
Bɒt Jızɒs nɒɟiŋ wud replį
 tu ɷl hiz kwestioniŋz,
đɵ prısts and skrįbz ɥzd tɛnts and jįbz,
 and ɒterd kruɯel ɟiŋz.
Đen Herod and hiz men ov wor
 skornd him ; and on hiz bak
đɛ put a gorjɒs rɵb, and đen
 tu Pįlet sent him bak.
Pįlet and Herod, đát sem dɛ,
 bekem az frendz agen ;
befɵr đɛ wer at enmiti.
 Hwot frendʃip 'twın sɒç men ?

SECTION 183.

Christ is brought back again to Pilate, who again declares him innocent.

Matthew 27. 15-23. Mark 15. 6-14.
Luke 23. 13-23. John 18. 38-40.

Then Pilate summoned the chief [priests
 And rulers of the Jews,
And said, " Ye've brought this man to [me
 As one whom ye accuse
Of stirring up the people, and
 Perverting them, and I,
Who have examined him upon
 The charge you specify,
Have found no crime or fault in him :
 Such charge is cruelty.
Nor Herod, for to him I sent
 The case, to know his mind ;
And he no manner of offence
 For punishment, could find.
Your course appears to me unjust,
 And Herod thinks it so ;
Therefore, with some small chastise- [ment,
 I now will let him go ;
For nothing worthy death or bonds
 Has this man done or said.

SEKΣON 183.

Krįst iz brɷt bak agen tu Pįlet, hɯ agen deklɛrz him inosent.

Maɟɥ 27. 15-23. Mark 15. 6-14.
Lɯk 23. 13-23. Jon 18. 38-40.

Đen Pįlet sɒmond đe çif prısts
 and rɯlerz ov đe Jɯz,
and sed, " Yı'v brɷt đis man tu mı
 az wɒn hɯm yı akɥz
ov steriŋ ɒp đe pıpel, and
 pervertiŋ đem, and į
hɯ hav ekzamind him, ɒpon
 đe çarj ɥ spesifį,
hav fɤnd nɵ krįm or fɷlt in him :
 sɒç çarj iz krɯelti.
Nor Herod, for tu him į sent
 đe kɛs, tu nɵ hiz mįnd ;
and hı nɵ maner ov ofens
 for pɒniʃment, kud fįnd.
Ɯr kɵrs apırz tu mı ɒnjɒst,
 and Herod ɟiŋks it sɵ ;
đerfɵr, wiđ sɒm smɷl çastizment,
 į nɤ wil let him gɵ ;
for nɒɟiŋ wɒrđi deɟ or bondz
 haz đis man dɒn or sed.

I'll therefore set him free at once,
  For custom has decreed
That at this solemn festival
  One prisoner be set free, .
Whichever ye desire: now say,
  What prisoner it shall be;
Barabbas, or this Jesus Christ,
  Whom I deem just and true,
And whom as Christ, ye will not own,
  But still his life pursue."
(Barabbas was a rebel, that
  Defied the Roman rule,
And, in an insurrection, had
  Committed murder foul.)
"Shall I release," said Pilate, "him
  Ye call King of the Jews?"
He knew 'twas envy that had led
  The chief priests to accuse
The Lord. And while he sat there, lo,
  His wife sent unto him
And said, "Beware, and keep thyself
  From such an awful crime
As shedding that man's blood would
      be,—
  That righteous man and just:
For I have had a dreadful dream
  Concerning him, and trust
That he will neither be condemned,
  Nor we endure the curse
Of shedding innocent blood, than
      which
  No wickedness is worse."
But the chief priests and elders then
  Stirred up the multitude
To ask Barabbas' liberty,
  And the Messiah's blood.
And they cried out at once, "Release
  Unto Barabbas give,
And let not Jesus, called the Christ,
  Have privilege to live."
But Pilate, wishing more and more
  To set the Savior free,
Pleaded again in his behalf;
  But the foul bigotry
Of the besotted Jews forbade
  This act of justice there,
For they preferred Barabbas still,
  And Christ they would not spare.
Then Pilate said, "What shall I do
  With this your Jewish King?"

Ɨ'l đɛrfɵr set him fri at wɒns,
  for kɒstom haz dekrid
đat at đis solem festival
  wɒn prizoner bi set fri,
hwiçever yi dezįr: nɤ se,
  hwot prizoner it ʃal bi;
Barabas, or đis Jizɒs Krįst,
  hɯm į dim jɒst and trɯ,
and hɯm az Krįst, yi wil not ɵn,
  bɒt stil hiz lįf pɒrsų."
(Barabas woz a rebel, đat
  defįd đe Rɵman rɯl,
and, in an insɒrekʃon, had
  komited mɒrder fɤl.)
"Ʃal į relis," sed Pįlet, "him
  yi kɷl kiŋ ov đe Jɯz?"
Hi nų 'twoz envi đat had led
  đe çif prists tu akųz
đe Lord. And hwįl hi sat đɛr, lɵ,
  hiz wįf sent ɒntu him
and sed "Bewɛr, and kip đįself
  from sɒç an ɷful krįm
az ʃediŋ đát man'z blɒd wud
      bi,—
  đát rįtiɒs man and jɒst:
for į hav had a dredful drim
  konserniŋ him, and trɒst
đat hi wil nįđer bi kondemd,
  nor wi endųr đe kɒrs
ov ʃediŋ inosent blɒd, đan
      hwiç
  nɵ wikednes iz wɒrs."
Bɒt đe çif prists and elderz đen
  sterd ɒp đe mɒltitųd
tu ask Barabas' liberti,
  and đe Mesįa'z blɒd.
And đe krįd ɤt at wɒns, "Relis
  ɒntu Barabas giv,
and let not Jizɒs, kɷld đe Krįst,
  hav privilej tu liv."
Bɒt Pįlet, wiʃiŋ mɵr and mɵr
  tu set đe Sevier fri,
plided agen in hiz behaf;
  bɒt đe fɤl bigotri
ov đe besoted Jɯz forbad
  đis akt ov jɒstis đɛr,
for đe preferd Barabas stil,
  and Krįst đe wud not spɛr.
Đen Pįlet sed, "Hwot ʃal į dɯ
  wiđ đis ųr Jɯiʃ Kiŋ?"

They cried aloud, " Him crucify ! "
  And made the welkin ring.
He said to them the third time,
  What evil hath he done? [" Why?
I find no cause of death in him;
  Nor least offence,—not one."
But they, more furious than before,
  With frantic hatred cried,
"Away with this man from the earth;
  Let him be crucified."
And as they Pilate thus assailed,
Their voices, & the crowd's, prevailed.

SECTION 184.

Pilate releases Barabbas, and delivers Christ to be crucified.

Matthew 27. 24-29. Mark 15. 15-18.
Luke 23. 24, 25. John 19. 1-16.

When Pilate saw this scorn of law;
  And tumult, fierce and rude;
And felt that he could nothing do,
  By his appeals, renewed,
He water took, and washed his hands
  Before the multitude,
And said, " See ye to this man's blood,
  For I am innocent."
The people shouted, " Let his blood
  On us fall; we consent;
And on our children too." Their hate
  Of Christ was vehement.
Then Pilate, yielding to their will,
  Released the murderer dire,
Barabbas, who in prison lay,
  And granted their desire.
The holy Jesus then he scourged,
  And gave him to their will,
To crucify him as they wished,
  And thus their own doom seal.
The soldiers to Prætorium,
  Which was the common hall,
Led Jesus, and assembled there
  The band of soldiers all.
They stripped him, and then put on
  A purple-scarlet cloak; [him
A crown of thorns upon his head
  They put, just to provoke
Him with a show of kingliness,
  And actual cruelty.

ᵭɛ krįd alɤd, '
  and med ᵭe '
Hi sed tu ᵭem
  hwot ivil haᵭ
I fįnd nʊ kɒz (
  nɔr list ofen
Bɒt ᵭe, mʊr fų
  wiᵭ frantik l
" Awɛ wiᵭ ᵭis
  let him bi kr
And az ᵭe Pįle
ᵭer voisez, and

SEK.

Pįlet relisez Bar
tu b

Maᵭų 27. 24-2
Luuk 23. 24,

Hwen Pįlet sc
  and tųmɒlt,
and felt ᵭat hi
  bį hiz apilz,
hi wɒter tuk,
  befʊr ᵭe mɒ
and sed, Si yi
  for į am ino
ᵭe pipel ʃɤted
  on ɒs fɒl ;
and on ɤr ȼild
  ov Krįst wo
ᵭen Pįlet, yil
  relist ᵭe mɒ
Barabas, hu i
  and granted
ᵭe hʊli Jizɒs
  and gev him
tu krusifį him
  and ᵭɒs ᵭer
ᵭe sʊldierz tu
  hwiȼ woz ᵭe
led Jizɒs, and
  ᵭe band ov
ᵭɛ stript him,
  a pɒrpel-ska
a krɤn ov ᵭorn
  ᵭe put, jɒst
him wiᵭ a ʃʊ
  and aktųal

A reed for sceptre in his hand
They placed, then bowed the knee
In mocking salutation, and
Pretended loyalty.
"King of the Jews, all hail!" they
Then smote him spitefully. [cried,
They spat on him, and took the reed,
And smote him on his sacred head.

Relenting Pilate then went out,
And thus again appealed,
"I bring him forth that ye may know
There is no fault revealed."
Jesus came forth, in purple robe,
Wearing the thorny crown,
And spoke these words, "Behold the
man!"—
And spoke without a frown.
But still the priests and officers,
With hatred filled, exclaimed,
"Ah! crucify him! crucify!"
And Pilate, not unblamed,
Replied, "Take ye, and crucify,
I find no fault at all."
The Jews then said, "We have a law,
Which, as God's voice, doth call
On us to take away his life.
Indeed, he ought to die,
Because he proudly made himself
The Son of God most high."
Then Pilate grew more fearful still,
At hearing that strange word,
And to the judgement hall returned,
And questioned thus the Lord:
"Whence art thou?" Jesus answered
"Wilt thou not answer me? [not.
Dost thou not know my power to save,
Or crucify, even thee?"
Jesus then spoke, "No power hast
thou
'Gainst me, except from heaven;
Therefore the greater sin is his
Who me to thee has given."

From that time Pilate sought to save
Him: but, to gain their end,
The Jews said, "If thou let him go,
Thou art not Cæsar's friend.
Whoever makes himself a king,
Doth against Cæsar speak."

A rid for septer, in hiz hand
ðe plest, ðen bʊd ðe ni,
in mokiŋ salụteʃon, and
pretended loialti.
"Kiŋ ov ðe Jɯz, ɷl hel!" ðe krịd,
ðen smɵt him spịtfuli.
Ðe spat on him, and tuk ðe rid,
and smɵt him on hiz sekred hed.

Relentiŋ Pịlet ðen went ʊt,
and ðɒs agen apild,
"Ɨ briŋ him fɵrþ ðat yi me nɵ́
ðer iz nɵ fɷlt revild."
Jizɒs kem fɵrþ, in pɒrpel rɵb,
weriŋ ðe þorni krʊn,
and spɵk ðiz wɒrdz, "Behɵld ðe
man!"—
and spɵk wiðʊt a frʊn.
Bɒt stil ðe prists and ofiserz,
wið hetred fild, eksklemd,
"Ah! krɯsifị him! krɯsifị!"
And Pịlet, not ɒnblemd,
replịd, "Tek yi, and krɯsifị,
ị fịnd nɵ fɷlt at ɷl."
Ðe Jɯz ðen sed, "Wi hav a lɷ,
hwiç, az God'z vois, dɒþ kɷl
on ɒs tu tek awe hiz lịf.
Indid, hi ɷt tu dị,
bekɷz hi prʊdli med himself,
ðe Sɒn ov God mɵst hị."
Ðen Pịlet grɯ mɵr firful stil,
at hiriŋ ðát strenj wɒrd,
and tu ðe jɒjment hɷl retɒrnd,
and kwestiond ðɒs ðe Lord:
"Hwens art ðʊ?" Jizɒs anserd
"Wilt ðʊ not anser mi? [not.
Dɒst ðʊ not nɵ́ mị pʊer tu sev,
or krɯsifị, iven ði?"
Jizɒs ðen spɵk, "Nɵ pʊer hast
ðʊ
'genst mi, eksept from heven;
ðerfɵr ðe greter sin iz hiz
hɯ mi tu ði haz given."

From ðát tịm Pịlet sɷt tu sev
him: bɒt, tu gen ðer end,
ðe Jɯz sed, "If ðʊ let him gɵ,
ðʊ art not Sizar'z frend.
Hɯever meks himself a kiŋ,
dɒþ agenst Sizar spik."

Then Pilate rose, and brought again,
  The Holy One and meek.
It was the preparation day,
  At morning hour of six,*
When Pilate did in Gabbatha
  His seat of judgement fix.
Then, turning to the Jews, he said,
  "Behold your King!" But they,
With eager shout, at once cried out,
  "Away with him! Away!"
And "Crucify!" Nought would ap-
  Their animosity. [pease
"What! shall I crucify your King?"
  Asked Pilate, mockingly.

Ðen Pịlet rœz, and brœt agen,
  ðe Hœli Wɒn and mik.
It woz ðe prepareʃon de,
  at morniŋ ɤr ov siks,*
hwen Pịlet did in Gabaða
  hiz sit ov jɒjment fiks.
Ðen, tɒrniŋ tu ðe Juz, hị sed,
  "Behœld ɥr kiŋ!" Bɒt ðe,
wið įger ʃɤt, at wɒns krịd ɤt,
  "Awe wið him! Awe!"
and "Krɯsifị!" Nœt wud apịz
  ðer animositi.
"Hwot! ʃal ị krɯsifị ɥr kiŋ?
  askt Pịlet, mokiŋli.

---

* It is probable that St. John here used the Roman reckoning of days and hou which resembled our own, (according to Townsend,) and commenced their circle at mi night. The other Evangelists used the Jewish reckoning of days and hours, which co menced their circle about sunset. This diversity of reckoning expositors have often fail to perceive, and consequently have gone into great technicalities and perplexities.

I have a strong persuasion that, according to the Gospel history, Christ took his la Passover towards the commencement of the *fifth day* of the Jewish week, which extend from our Wednesday evening to Thursday afternoon. In this day of the Passover of t Jews, there was full moon—light shining all night; and the population of Jerusale from the highest to the lowest, was all in commotion, at the celebration of their natio festival. During the night, or early morning, of this Passover day, Christ was tried a condemned; he was delivered up by Pilate at six in the morning thereof, and he w crucified at nine in the morning thereof, and he expired on the cross at three in t afternoon, after which he was buried.

Now St. John (who, as I say, used the Roman reckoning,) includes the Jewi Passover's Preparation day of the Sabbath, in the Roman day to which he refe though, according to the Jewish reckoning, it did not commence till the evening there In the same way, he says it was the sixth hour of the morning, (according to the Rom reckoning,) when it was the first hour according to the Jewish reckoning of the oth Evangelists, who tell us that Christ was crucified three hours after, at the third hour the morning, or what we term 9 *a.m.*

The Jewish Passover's Preparation day, which, like all the days of the Jews, began the evening, could not be their Passover day, because it succeeded the Passover; neit could it be their Sabbath, because it preceded the Sabbath.

The other Evangelists tell us that, according to the Jewish reckoning, when the e ning of the Passover day was come, the Passover's preparation of the Sabba commenced. This Preparation day is what the Jews called their *sixth day*, extendi from Thursday evening till Friday afternoon. Then their *seventh day*—their Sabbath commenced, extending from Friday evening to Saturday afternoon, at the last part which their week concluded.

Thus I conceive our Lord, according to his own prediction, lay three nights and th days buried in the earth; namely, Thursday night, Friday night, and Saturday nig and Friday morning, Saturday morning, and Sunday morning, which being on the th day, he rose again. This view appears to myself, and a few other critics, capable demonstration, as a matter of Biblical truth and historic science.

But while I maintain this theory as the only one which will satisfactorily reconcile statements of the Evangelists on this point, I have no wish to disturb the venerable clesiastical custom of celebrating the death of Christ on Good Friday, though it may a day after the fact. The grand purpose of the church is that the fact itself should devoutly impressed on the hearts of people at that sacred season.

The chief priests said, "We Cæsar own,
And have no king beside."
Then Pilate gave him up to them,—
Gave to be crucified.

SECTION 185.

Christ is led away from the Judgement Hall of Pilate to Mount Calvary.

Matthew 27. 31, 32. Mark 15. 20, 21.
Luke 23. 26-32. John 19. 16, 17.

Then took they Jesus, as they wished,
And led him from the hall,
And having once more mocked him, as
They low before him fall,
They took the purple robe from him,
And put his own clothes on;
Then led him to be crucified,
As day began to dawn.
Submissively he bore his cross,
But, faint with weakness, fell.
To bear a part of that sad load
Simon they now compel
(Of Alexander, Rufus, he
Was father,) to assist.
They laid the cross on him, therefore,
To bear it after Christ.
There followed Jesus, as he went,
A goodly company;
And many women, who beheld
This great iniquity.
And Jesus, turning to them, said,
"Weep not, weep not for me,
Ye daughters of Jerusalem,
Who show me sympathy,
But for yourselves and children weep,
Who bitter days will see.
Behold the days come when they shall
Their misery thus deplore:—
'The barren are the blessed, and
The wombs that never bore.'
And in their sad distress of life
They will begin to say
Unto the mountains and the hills,
'Fall on us; hide, we pray.'
If in this way the green tree fares,
What of the dry, which God now spares?"
There were two malefactors, whom
They led, with Christ, to their sad doom.

Ꝺe ɋif prists sed, "Wi Sizar ɵn,
and hav nɵ kiŋ besi̧d."
Ꝺen Pi̧let gev him ɒp tu ꝺem,—
gev tu bi krɯsifi̧d.

SEKΣON 185.

Kri̧st iz led awe from ꝺe Jɒjment Hɵl ov Pi̧let tu Mȣnt Kalvari.

Maꝺɥ 27. 31, 32. Mark 15. 20, 21.
Lɯk 23. 26-32. Jon 19. 16, 17.

Ꝺen tuk ꝺe Jizɒs, az ꝺe wiʃt,
and led him from ꝺe hɵl,
and haviŋ wɒns mɵr mokt him, az
ꝺe lɵ befɵr him fɵl,
ꝺe tuk ꝺe pɒrpel rɵb from him
and put hiz ɵn klɵꝺz on;
ꝺen led him tu bi krɯsifi̧d,
az de began tu dɵn.
Sɒbmisivli hi bɵr hiz kros,
bɒt, fent wiꝺ wiknes, fel.
Tu ber a part ov ꝺát sad lɵd
Si̧mon ꝺe nȣ kompel
(ov Alekzander, Rɯfɒs, hi
woz fɵder,) tu asist.
Ꝺe led ꝺe kros on him, ꝺerfɵr,
tu ber it after Kri̧st.
Ꝺer folɵd Jizɒs, az hi went,
a gudli kɒmpani;
and meni wimen, hɯ beheld
ꝺis gret inikwiti.
And Jizɒs, tɒrniŋ tu ꝺem, sed,
"Wip not, wip not for mi,
yi dɵterz ov Jerɯsalem,
hɯ ʃɵ mi simpaꝺi,
bɒt for ɥrselvz and ɋildren wip,
hɯ biter dez wil si.
Behɵld ꝺe dez kɒm hwen ꝺe ʃal
ꝺer mizeri ꝺɒs deplɵr:—
'Ꝺe baren ar ꝺe blesed, and
ꝺe wɯmz ꝺat never bɵr.'
And in ꝺer sad distres ov li̧f
ꝺe wil begin tu se
ɒntu ꝺe mȣntenz and ꝺe hilz,
'Fɵl on ɒs; hi̧d, wi pre.'
If in ꝺis we ꝺe grin tri ferz,
hwot ov ꝺe dri̧, hwiɋ God nȣ sperz?"
Ꝺer wer tɯ́ malefaktorz, hɯm
ꝺe led, wiꝺ Kri̧st, tu ꝺer sad dɯm.

SECTION 186.

Christ arrives at Mount Calvary, and is crucified.

Matthew 27. 33, 34, 37. Mark 15. 22, 23, 26, 28. Luke 23. 33, 34, 38. John 19. 18-22.

They bring him unto Golgotha,
  Called also Calvary,
Which means the place of skulls, and
  Complete the tragedy. [there
They gave him vinegar to drink,
  And mingled it with gall,
But when he had just tasted, he
  Refused to drink at all.
And with him there were crucified
  Two thieves, or rioters;
On each side one, he in the midst,—
  The Christ—and prisoners!
And so the Scripture was fulfilled
  Which saith of Jesus, "He
Was numbered with transgressors,"
  Thus speaks the prophecy. [for
And Pilate wrote a title, and
  He put it o'er his head,
And many a Jew stood there to view,
  And this inscription read.
In Hebrew, Greek, and Latin, too,
'Twas written; so that all men knew.

In Hebrew thus the title ran:—

"THIS IS JESUS, THE KING OF THE JEWS."

And thus it was in Greek:—

"JESUS THE NAZARITE, THE KING OF THE JEWS."

And in the Latin thus:—

"THIS IS THE KING OF THE JEWS."

The chief priests, then, to Pilate, said,
  "Write not, 'King of the Jews,'
But that he said, 'I am their King.'"
  And Pilate did not choose
To alter it a single whit,
But said, "What's written I have writ."

SEK

Krist arivz at ... *k*

Maþu 27. 33,34,37. Luk 23. 33, 34,

ƌe briŋ him on
  kold olsø Ka
hwiç minz ðe
  komplit ðe tr
ƌe gev him vin
  and miŋgeld
bɒt hwen hi ha
  refuzd tu dri
And wið him ð
  tú þivz, or r
on iç sid wɒn,
  ðe Krist—an
And sø ðe Skri
  hwiç seþ ov J
woz nɒmberd w
  ðɒs spiks ðe
And Pilet røt a
  hi put it ø'r
and meni a Ju
  and ðis inskr
In Hibru, Gri
'twoz riten; sø

In Hibru ðɒs

"ƌIS IZ J
OV ƌE

And ðɒs it woz

"JUZUS ƌ
KIŊ O

And in ðe Lati

"ƌIS IZ ƌ
JUZ."

ƌe çif prists, ð
  "Rit not, 'K
bɒt ðat hi sed,
  And Pilet did
tu olter it a siŋ
bɒt sed, "H
rit."

SECTION 187.

The Crucifixion.—Matthew 27. 35, 36, 39-44.
Mark 15. 24, 25, 29-32.
Luke 23. 35-37, 39-44. John 19. 23-27.

They crucified the Lord of life,
And man of sorrows too;
And yet, for those who did their hands
In his own blood imbrue,
"Father," he said, "forgive them, for
They know not what they do."
The Roman soldiers took his clothes,
And claimed them as their own,
Divided them, and made four parts,
And each of them took one:
And as his coat was woven throughout,
Cast lots for that alone.
So was the prophet's word fulfilled,
"My garments they did part,
And for my vesture they cast lots,"
While he endured death's dart.
These things therefore the soldiers did.
And now the day wore on:
The third hour of the Jews approached,
'Twas nine by morning's sun.

And sitting down they watched him there.
The people who stood by,
And rulers too, reviled him with
The taunt, "Now let him try
To save himself, if he be Christ,
The chosen of the Lord.
Others he saved; the dead he raised;
Cured people by a word."
The soldiers also mocked him, when
They kindly offered him
Some vinegar, to quench his thirst,
In sufferings so extreme,
And said, derisively, "If thou
Be true King of the Jews,
Then save thyself; rule o'er the land;
None will thy sway refuse."
The passers-by reviled him too,
And wagged their heads, and railed:
With pouting lips, they poured contempt,
(While Jesus never quailed,)

SEKΣON 187.

Đe Krɯsifikʃon.—Maɉų 27. 35, 36, 39-44
Mark 15. 24, 25, 29-32.
Lɯk 23. 35-37, 39-44. Jon 19. 23-27.

Đɛ krɯsifįd đe Lord ov lįf,
and man ov sorɷz tɯ;
and yet, for đɷz hɯ did đɛr handz
in hiz ɷn blɒd imbrɯ,
"Fɑđer," hi sed, "forgiv đem, for
đɛ nɷ́ not hwot đɛ dɯ."
Đe Rɷman sɷldierz tuk hiz klɷđz,
and klemd đem az đer ɷn,
divįded đem, and med fɷr parts,
and iǫ ov đem tuk wɒn:
and az hiz kɷt woz wɷven ɉrɯɤt,
kast lots for đát alɷn.
Sɷ woz đe profet's wɒrd fulfild,
"Mį garments đɛ did part,
and for mį vestųr đɛ kast lots,"
hwįl hi endųrd deɉ's dart.
Điz ɉiŋz đerfɷr đe sɷldierz did.
And nɤ đe de wɷr on:
đe ɉerd ɤr ov đe Jɯz aprɷǫt,
'twoz nįn bį morniŋ'z sɒn.

And sitiŋ dɤn đɛ woǫt him đer.
Đe pįpel hɯ stud bį,
and rɯlerz tɯ, revįld him wiđ
đe tɑnt, "Nɤ let him trį
tu sev himself, if hi bi Krįst,
đe ǫɷzen ov đe Lord.
ɒđerz hi sevd; đe ded hi rezd;
kųrd pįpel bį a wɒrd."
Đe sɷldierz ɷlsɷ mokt him, hwen
đɛ kįndli oferd him
sɒm vinegar, tu kwenǫ hiz ɉerst,
in sɒferiŋz sɷ ekstrim,
and sed, derįsivli, "If đɤ
bi trɯ Kiŋ ov đe Jɯz,
đen sev đįself; rul ɷ'r đe land;
nɒn wil đį swɛ refųz."
Đe paserz-bį revįld him tɯ,
and wagd đer hedz, and rɛld:
wiđ pɤtiŋ lips, đɛ pɷrd kontempt,
(hwįl Jizɒs never kwɛld,)

"Ah! thou, who wouldst destroy, and
The temple in three days, [build,
Save now thyself; come down, and
then
We, too, will sing thy praise."
The chief priests, scribes, and elders
mocked,
And said, "If thou be King
Of Israel, come down, and we
Will willing offerings bring.
He trusted in the Lord; then let
His God deliver now,
If he will have him, for he said,
'Him my God I avow;
I am his son.' Let then this Christ,
This King of Israel,
Descend now from the cross; if not,
Let him descend to hell."
The very thieves reviled him too,
And railed upon him thus:
"If thou be Christ, first save thyself,
And then thou may'st save us."
One afterwards repented, and
Rebuked such profanation;
And to his fellow thief thus said,
"Hast thou no veneration
For great Jehovah, seeing thou
Art in this condemnation?
And we indeed most justly, for
We meet our due reward;
But this man hath done nought amiss:"
He said to Jesus, "Lord,
When in thy kingdom thou shalt be,
Do thou, in love, remember me."
And Jesus said to him, "To-day,
To Paradise I will convey
Thee, when I go, from earth, away."

Close by the cross of Jesus stood
Mary, his mother, then;
And Mary, wife of Cleopas,
And Mary Magdalene.
When Jesus saw his mother there,
With John, he loved so free,
He said to her, "Behold thy son!"
To him, "Thy mother see!"
And from that hour, his follower took
Christ's mother to his home,
And shared with her the joys and griefs
That to the faithful come.

"Ah! đɤ, hɯ wudst destroi, and
đe tempel in ɟrị dez. [bild,
sev nɤ đįself: kɒm dɤn, and
đen
wį, tɯ, wil siŋ đį prɛz."
Đe çif prịsts, skrįbz, and elderz
mokt,
and sed, "If đɤ bị Kiŋ
ov Izrael, kɒm dɤn, and wị
wil wiliŋ oferiŋz briŋ.
Hị trɒsted in đe Lord; đen let
hiz God deliver nɤ,
if hị wil hav him, for hị sed,
'Him mį God į avɤ;
į am hiz sɒn." Let đen đis Krįst,
đis Kiŋ ov Izrael,
desend nɤ from đe kros; if not,
let him desend tu hel."
Đe veri ɟivz revįld him tɯ,
and reld ɒpon him đɒs:
"If đɤ bị Krįst, ferst sev đįself,
and đen đɤ me'st sev ɒs."
Wɒn afterwardz repented, and
rebɥkt sɒç profaneʃon;
and tu hiz felơ ɟif đɒs sed,
"Hast đɤ nơ venereʃon
for gret Jehơva, sịiŋ đɤ
art in đis kondemneʃon?
And wị indịd mơst jɒstli, for
wị mịt ɤr dɥ reword;
bɒt đis man haɟ dɒn not amis:"
hị sed tu Jịzɒs, "Lord,
hwen in đį kiŋdom đɤ ʃalt bị,
dɯ đɤ, in lɒv, remember mị."
And Jịzɒs sed tu him, "Tu-de
tu Paradįs į wil konve
đị, hwen į gơ, from erɟ, awe."

Klơs bį đe kros ov Jịzɒs stud
Meri, hiz mɒđer, đen;
And Meri, wįf ov Klịopas,
And Meri Magdalen.
Hwen Jịzɒs sơ hiz mɒđer đer,
wiđ Jon, hị lɒvd sơ frị,
hị sed tu her, "Behơld đį sɒn!"
tu him, "Đį mɒđer sị!"
And from đát ɤr, hiz folơer tuk
Krįst's mɒđer tu hiz hơm,
and ʃerd wiđ her đe joiz and grịfs
đat tu đe feɟful kɒm.

SECTION 188.

The Death of Christ.

Matthew 27. 45-56. Mark 15. 33-41.
Luke 23. 44-49. John 19. 28-37.

The sixth hour of the day now came,
  (The hour of twelve at noon,)
And darkness overspread the land,
  And nature had a swoon.
The sun was darkened in the sky,
  All things looked dim and drear,
Until the ninth hour of the day.
  All hearts were filled with fear.
Then Jesus, with a loud voice, cried,
  In death's last agony,

"Eloi, Eloi, lama sabachthani?"

That is, "My God, my God, to what
  Hast thou abandoned me?"
Some of the people that stood there,
  And heard this mournful cry,
Said, "This man calleth for Elias."
  And as the end drew nigh,
And Jesus knew that all was done
  According to God's will,
He said, "I thirst;" that Scripture thus
  Might be accomplished still.
One of them ran, and soon a sponge
  In vinegar did dip,
And put it on a hyssop reed,
  And raised it to his lip.
And others said, "Let be; that we
  May see, if, from the dead,
Elias now will come to save,
  Or render any aid."
When therefore Jesus had received
  The thirst-allaying drink,
He cried out, "It is finished!" Then
  He loosened the last link
That bound him to the earth, and said,
  "Father, I come to thee.
Into thy hands I now commit
  My spirit." Peaceably
The Lord then bowed his sacred head
And yielded up the ghost, as dead.

At that dread hour the temple's veil
  Was rent throughout in twain;
The earth did quake, the rocks were
  rent,
  Graves ope'd their mouths again.

SEKΣON 188.

Đe Deŧ ov Krįst.

Maŧɥ 27. 45-56. Mark 15. 33-41.
Luk 23. 44-49. Jon 19. 28-37.

Đe siksŧ ɤr ov đe dɛ nɤ kɛm,
  (đe ɤr ov twelv at nɯn,)
and darknes ɵverspred đe land
  and nɛtɥr had a swɯn.
Đe sɒn woz darkend in đe skį,
  ɷl ŧiŋz lukt dim and drir,
ɒntil đe nįnŧ ɤr ov đe dɛ.
  ɷl harts wer fild wiđ fir.
Đen Jizɒs, wiđ a lɤd vois, krįd,
  in deŧ's last agoni,

"Elɵį, Elɵį, lɑma sabakŧanį?"

đát iz, "Mį God, mį God, tu hwot
  hast đɤ abandond mi?"
Sɒm ov đe pipel đat stud đɛr,
  and herd đis mɵrnful krį,
sed, "Đis man kɵleŧ for Elįas."
  And az đe end drɯ nį,
and Jizɒs nɥ đat ɷl woz dɒn
  akordiŋ tu God'z wíl,
hi sed, "Į ŧerst;" đat Skriptɥr đɒs
  mįt bi akompliʃt stil.
Wɒn ov đem ran, and sɯn a spɒnj
  in vinegar did dip,
and put it on a hisop rid,
  and rɛzd it tu hiz lip.
And ɒđerz sed, "Let bi; đat wi
  mɛ si, if, from đe ded,
Elįas nɤ wil kɒm tu sɛv,
  or render eni ɛd."
Hwen đɛrfɵr Jizɒs had resivd
  đe ŧerst-alɛiŋ driŋk,
hi krįd ɤt, "It iz finiʃt!" Đen
  hi lɯsend đe last liŋk
đat bɤnd him tu đe erŧ, and sed,
  "Fɑđer, į kɒm tu đi.
Intu đį handz į nɤ komit
  mį spirit." Pisabli
đe Lord đen bɤd hiz sɛkred hed
and yįlded ɒp đe gɵst, az ded.

At đát dred ɤr đe tempel'z vɛl
  woz rent ŧrɯɤt in twɛn;
đe erŧ did kwɛk, đe roks wer
  rent,
  grɛvz ɵpt đɛr mɤđz agen.

Now opposite Christ's cross stood one,
  Centurion of the band,
Who watched these awful signs, and
    heard
  Those words, so sad, so grand.
He, struck with fear, exclaimed, "This
  A righteous one must be."   [man
And others said, "The Son of God
  Is here most certainly."
And at the sight, the people smote
  Their breasts, with anguish filled;
And silently they turned away,
  With grief and horror chilled.
His friends, too, witnessed all these
    things,
  And feeble women there;
Mary of Magdalene, and she
  Who James and Joses bare;
Salome, who had ministered
  To Christ in Galilee,
And numerous other women who
  Loved Jesus tenderly.

'Twas evening. A new day began,
  Sixth of the Jewish week,
The day of preparation; and
  The Jews at once bespeak
The care of Pilate to prevent
  That on the Sabbath day
The bodies should stay on the cross.
  They therefore begged that they
Might be removed, and straight be-
  He would enforce the law, [sought
And break their legs, that they might
    die.
  The thieves' they broke; but saw,
When to the cross of Christ they came,
  He had already died.
They therefore did not break his legs,
  But pierced, with spear, his side,
And forthwith blood and water came.
  This record is most true:
The deed was seen by him who now
  Records it, with the view
That ye, too, may believe, and that
  His faith may be in you.
These things were done, and so fulfilled
  The Scriptures, which agree,
"A bone of him shall not be broken,
  But pierced his side shall be."

Nɤ opozit Krįst's kros stud wɒn,
  sentųrion ov đe band,
hɯ woɋt điz ɷful sįnz, and
    herd
  đɵz wɒrdz, sɵ sad, sɵ grand.
Hi, strɒk wiđ fir, eksklemd, "Đis
  a rįtiɒs wɒn mɒst bi."   [man
And ɒđerz sėd, "Đe Sɒn ov God
  iz hir mɵst sertenli."
And at đe sįt, đe pipel smɵt
  đer brests, wiđ aŋgwiʃ fild;
and sįlentli đe tɒrnd awe,
  wiđ grif and horor ɋild.
Hiz frendz, tɯ, witnest ɷl điz
    ϑiŋz,
  and fibel wimen đer;
Meri ov Magdalen, and ʃi
  hɯ Jemz and Jɵses ber;
Salɵmi, hɯ had ministerd
  tu Krįst in Galili,
and nųmerɒs ɒđer wimen hɯ
  lɒvd Jizɒs tenderli.

'Twoz ivniŋ. A nų de began,
  siksϑ ov đe Jɯiʃ wik,
đe de ov prepareʃon; and
  đe Jɯz at wɒns bespik
đe ker ov Pįlet tu prevent
  đat on đe Sabaϑ de
đe bodiz ʃud ste on đe kros.
  Đe đerfɵr begd đat đe
mįt bi remɯvd, and stret besɷt
  hi wud enfɵrs đe lɷ,
and brek đer legz, đat đe mįt
    dį.
  Đe ϑivz' đe brɵk; bɒt sɷ,
hwen tu đe kros ov Krįst đe kem,
  hi had ɷlredi dįd.
Đe đerfɵr did not brek hiz legz,
  bɒt pirst, wiđ spir, hiz sįd,
and fɵrϑwiđ blɒd and wɷter kem.
  Đis rekord iz mɵst trɯ:
đe did woz sin bį him hɯ nɤ
  rekordz it, wiđ đe vų
đat yi, tɯ, me beliv, and đat
  hiz feϑ me bi in ų.
Điz ϑiŋz wer dɒn, and sɵ fulfild
  đe Skriptųrz, hwiɋ agri,
"A bɵn ov him ʃal not bi brɵken,
  bɒt pirst hiz sįd ʃal bi."

SECTION 189.

Joseph of Arimathea and Nicodemus bury the body of Christ on the preparation day, commencing on Thursday evening.
Matthew 27. 57-61. Mark 15. 42-47.
Luke 23. 50-55. John 19. 38-41.

When now was come the quiet eve
  Of preparation-day,
(The day before the Sabbath,) when
  Jews tuned their hearts to pray,
There came a rich man of the Jews,
  And Joseph was his name;
Arimathea was the town
  From which this good man came.
An honorable counsellor,
  A good man, and a just;
He waited for God's kingdom, and
  In Jesus put his trust.
He had not openly professed
  His faith in Israel's king,
For fear of that which might befall,
  And Jewish hate might bring.
But now, with holy boldness, he
  To Pilate went, straightway,
And begged that he might from the [cross
  Christ's body take that day.
Then Pilate the centurion called,
  Not thinking Christ yet dead;
And when assured, the body gave.
  Then Joseph, grateful, sped
Unto the cross, with pious haste,
  And on the ground he spread
A cloth, in which he placed the Lord
  (It was most clean and white).
And Nicodemus also came,
  Who saw the Lord by night,
And brought about a hundredweight
  Of aloes and of myrrh.
They put the body in the cloth,
  With these; in holy fear.
Thus used the Jews, in burial rites,
  To honor whom they loved,
And thus for him who claimed it most,
  Their reverence they proved.

Now where the cross of Christ was [placed,
  There was a garden fair;
And in the garden a new tomb,
  Prepared by Joseph's care
For his own sepulchre; and hewn
  Out of the solid stone;

SEKƩON 189.

Jɵzef ov Arimađia and Nikodimɒs beri đe bodi ov Krɉst on đe prepareʃon de, komensiŋ on Ꝁɒrzde ivniŋ.
Maŧɥ 27. 57-61. Mark 15. 42-47.
Luuk 23. 50-55. Jon 19. 38-41.

Hwen nɤ woz kɒm đe kwɉet iv
  ov prepareʃon-de,
(đe de befɵr đe Sabaŧ,) hwen
  Juuz tɥnd đer harts tu pre,
đer kem a riç man ov đe Juuz,
  and Jɵzef woz hiz nem;
Arimaŧia woz đe tɤn
  from hwiç đis gud man kem.
An onorabel kɤnseler,
  a gud man, and a jɒst;
hi weted for God'z kiŋdom, and
  in Jizɒs put hiz trɒst.
Hi had not ɵpenli prɵfest
  hiz feŧ in Izrael'z kiŋ,
for fir ov đát hwiç mɉt befɷl,
  and Juiʃ het mɉt briŋ.
Bɒt nɤ, wiđ hɵli bɵldnes, hi
  tu Pɉlet went, stretwe,
and begd đat hi mɉt from đe kros
  Krɉst's bodi tek đát de.
Đen Pɉlet đe sentɥrion kɷld,
  not ŧiŋkiŋ Krɉst yet ded;
and hwen aʃuurd, đe bodi gev.
  Đen Jɵzef, gretful, sped
ɒntu đe kros, wiđ pɉɒs hest,
  and on đe grɤnd hi spred
a kloŧ, in hwiç hi plest đe Lord
  (it woz mɵst klin and hwɉt).
And Nikodimɒs ɷlsɵ kem,
  huu sɷ đe Lord bɉ nɉt,
and brɷt abɤt a hɒndredwet
  ov alɵz and ov mer.
Đe put đe bodi in đe kloŧ,
  wiđ điz; in hɵli fir.
Đɒs ɥzd đe Juuz, in berial rɉts,
  tu onor huum đe lɒvd,
and đɒs for him huu klemd it mɵst,
  đer reverens đe pruuvd.

Nɤ hwer đe kros ov Krɉst woz [plest,
  đer woz a garden fer;
and in đe garden a nɥ tuum,
  preperd bɉ Jɵzef's ker
for hiz ɵn sepɒlker; and hɥn
  ɤt ov đe solid stɵn;

No man had ever there been laid;
  'Twas Jesus' tomb alone.
There laid they him, therefore, because
  The sepulchre was nigh;
And preparation-day came on,
  And then the Sabbath high.
They rolled a great stone to the door
  Of Jesus' sepulchre,
And then departed; but their grief
  They could not thus inter.

Mary, the mother of the Lord,
  And Mary Magdalene,
With women too from Galilee,
  Beheld the solemn scene.
These last returned, and soon prepared
  Ointments and spices sweet;
Then rested on the Sabbath day,
  As was for them most meet.
But both the Marys still remained
  To watch that grave, so dear;
Their love to Jesus quite dispelled
  All sentiments of fear.

SECTION 190.

The Jewish Sabbath (commencing on Friday evening) being come, the chief priests prepare a guard of soldiers to watch the Sepulchre.

Matthew 27. 62-66.

Now the next day (the Sabbath day)
  That followed preparation,
The chief priests and the Pharisees
  In fearful expectation
Of what might happen, met, and did
  With Pilate converse hold;—
"Sir, this deceiver, when alive,
  Spoke, with assurance bold,
'In three days I will rise again.'
  Therefore command that fast
His sepulchre be made until
  That time be fully past;
Lest his disciples, stealthily,
  Should carry him away,
And then, 'He's risen from the dead,'
  Unto the people say."
So Pilate, to content them, said,
  "Go, make the grave secure:"
They went, and placed a watch to [guard,
  And sealed it, to make sure.

nσ man had ever đɛr bin lɛd;
  'twoz Jizɒs' tɯm alσn.
Đɛr lɛd đɛ him, đɛrfσr, bekɷz
  đɛ sepɒlker woz nį;
and prepareʃon-dɛ kɛm on,
  and đen đɛ Sabaϑ hį.
Đɛ rσld a grɛt stσn tu đɛ dσr
  ov Jizɒs' sepɒlker,
and đen departed; bɒt đɛr grif
  đɛ kud not đɒs inter.

Mɛri, đɛ mɒđer ov đɛ Lord,
  and Mɛri Magdalen,
wiđ wimen tɯ from Galili,
  beheld đɛ solem sin.
Điz last retɒrnd, and sɯn prepɛrd
  ointments and spįsez swit;
đen rested on đɛ Sabaϑ dɛ,
  az woz for đem mσst mit.
Bɒt bσϑ đɛ Mɛriz stil remɛnd
  tu woç đát grɛv, sσ dir;
đɛr lɒv tu Jizɒs, kwįt dispeld
  ɷl sentiments ov fir.

SEKΣON 190.

Đɛ Jɯiʃ Sabaϑ (komensiŋ on Frįdɛ ivniŋ) biiŋ kɒm, đɛ çif prists prepɛr a gard ov sσldierz tɯ woç đɛ Sepɒlker.

Maϑɥ 27. 62-66.

Nɤ đɛ nekst dɛ (đɛ Sabaϑ dɛ)
  đat folσd prepareʃon,
đɛ çif prists and đɛ Farisiz
  in firful ekspekteʃon
ov hwot mįt hapen, met, and did
  wiđ Pįlet konvers hσld;—
"Ser, đis desiver, hwen alįv,
  spσk, wiđ aʃɯrans bσld,
'In ϑri dɛz į wil rįz agen."
  Đerfσr komand đat fast
hiz sepɒlker bi mɛd ɒntil
  đát tįm bi fuli past;
lest hiz disįpelz, stelϑili,
  ʃud kari him awɛ,
and đen, "Hį'z rizen from đɛ ded,'
  ɒntu đɛ pipel sɛ."
Sσ Pįlet, tu kontent đem, sed,
  "Gσ, mɛk đɛ grɛv sekɥr:"
đɛ went, and plɛst a woç tu gard,
  and sild it, tu mɛk ʃɯr.

BOOK XII.

SECTION 191.

The Sabbath being over, Mary Magdalene, Mary Cleopas, and Salome purchase spices, to anoint the body of Christ.

Matthew 28. 1. Mark 16. 1, 2. John 20. 1.

And when the Sabbath of the Jews,
  (Or Saturday,) was passed,
Came Mary Magdalene, who sought
  The sepulchre in haste,
With Mary, wife of Cleopas,
  And sad Salome too,
That they with spices and sweet balm
  Christ's body might imbue.
'Twas early on the Sunday morn,
  The first day of the week,
While darkness lingered in the sky,
  With dawning's earliest streak;
And as they now approached the tomb,
  They to each other said,
"Who shall roll back the mighty stone
  Which o'er the grave is laid?"

SECTION 192.

Christ rises amid a great earthquake.

Matthew 28. 2-4; 27. 52, 53.

And in that hour an earthquake, great
  And dreadful, shook the land;
For God's swift angel came from heaven,
  Charged with his high command,
And rolled away the ponderous stone
  From that mysterious tomb,
And sat thereon, and cast a blaze
  Of glory through the gloom.
His countenance like lightning shone,
  So dazzling was its glow,
And his seraphic vesture gleamed
  Like glittering virgin snow;
And all for fear of him, the guard
  Of rugged soldiers there,
Trembled, and fell as dead, o'erwhelmed
  With terror and despair.
And in that earthquake other graves
  Of saints were open rent,
And holy forms that slept therein,
  From death arose, and went

BOOK XII.

SEKΣON 191.

đe Sabaθ biiŋ ɵver, Mɛri Magdalen, Mɛri Kliopas, and Salɵmi pɒrçes spįsez, tu anoint đe bodi ov Krįst.

Maŧų 28. 1. Mark 16. 1, 2. Jon 20. 1.

And hwen đe Sabaŧ ov đe Jɯz,
  (or Saterdɛ,) woz past,
kɛm Mɛri Magdalen, hɯ sɷt
  đe sepɒlker in hɛst,
wiđ Mɛri, wįf ov Kliopas,
  and sad Salɵmi tɯ,
đat đe wiđ spįsez and swit bɑm
  Krįst's bodi mįt imbų.
'Twoz erli on đe Sɒnde morn,
  đe ferst de ov đe wik,
hwįl darknes liŋgerd in đe skį,
  wiđ dɷniŋ'z erliest strik;
and az đe nɤ aprɵçt đe tɯm,
  đe tu iç ɒđer sed,
"Hɯ ʃal rɵl bak đe mįti stɵn
  hwiç ɵ'r đe grɛv iz led?"

SEKΣON 192.

Krįst rįzez amid a grɛt erθkwɛk.

Maŧų 28. 2-4; 27. 52, 53.

And in đát ɤr an erŧkwɛk, gret
  and dredful, ʃuk đe land;
for God'z swift ɛnjel kɛm from heven,
  çarjd wiđ hiz hį komand,
and rɵld awe đe ponderɒs stɵn
  from đát mistįriɒs tɯm,
and sat đeron, and kast a blɛz
  ov glɵri ŧrɯ đe glɯm.
Hiz kɤntenans lįk lįtniŋ ʃon,
  sɵ dazliŋ woz its glɵ,
and hiz serafik vestųr glimd
  lįk gliteriŋ verjin snɵ;
and ɷl for fir ov him, đe gard
  ov rɒged sɵldierz đer,
trembeld, and fel az ded, ɵ'rhwelmd
  wiđ teror and desper.
And in đát erŧkwɛk ɒđer grevz
  ov sɛnts wer ɵpen rent,
and hɵli formz đat slept đerin,
  from deŧ arɵz, and went

Into Jerusalem; such power
  Christ's resurrection gave;
And unto many they appeared
  As first-fruits of the grave.

SECTION 193.

The three women arrive at the Sepulchre, and find the stone rolled away.

Matthew 28. 5-8. Mark 16. 2-8.
Luke 24. 1-8. John 20. 1, 2.

And when the pious women came,
  The sepulchre to see,
They found the mighty stone removed;
  The guarded grave was free.
They went into the sepulchre,
  But there they could not find
The body of the Lord, which had
  Been in that tomb enshrined.
Then swiftly ran the Magdalene
  To Peter and to John,
And said, "The body of the Lord
  Is taken, and is gone."
And as the women at the tomb
  Were troubled at the event,
They saw an angel, like in form
  To a young man, intent
On high commission: at the right,
  Within the tomb, he sat,
Arrayed in white and glistening robes;
  They were afraid thereat.
He said, "Fear not: I know ye seek
  Jesus of Nazareth,
Who late was crucified, and here
  Was buried after death:
He is no longer dead, he hath
  Arisen from this grave,
In that new life which he will give
  To those whom he will save.
Come, see the place where Jesus lay;
  And recollect the word
He spoke to you in Galilee,
  Declaring that your Lord
Should, after crucifixion, rise
  To life on the third day.
But go, and tell his followers
  That he will lead the way
To Galilee, and there you shall
  Behold your Lord again."

intu Jerɯsalem; sɒç pɤer
  Krįst's rezɒrekʃon gev;
and ɒntu meni ðɛ apird
  az ferst-frɯts ov ðe grev.

SEKΣON 193.

Ðe þri wimen arįv at ðe Sepɒlker, and find ðe stɵn rɵld awe.

Maþɥ 28. 5-8. Mark 16. 2-8.
Lɯk 24. 1-8. Jon 20. 1, 2.

And hwen ðe pįɒs wimen kem,
  ðe sepɒlker tu si,
ðɛ fɤnd ðe mįti stɵn remɯvd;
  ðe garded grev woz fri.
Ðɛ went intu ðe sepɒlker,
  bɒt ðer ðɛ kud not fįnd
ðe bodi ov ðe Lord, hwiç had
  bin in ðát tɯm enʃrįnd.
Ðen swiftli ran ðe Magdalen
  tu Piter and tu Jon,
and sed, "Ðe bodi ov ðe Lord
  iz teken, and iz gon."
And az ðe wimen at ðe tɯm
  wer trɒbeld at ðe event,
ðɛ sɷ an ɛnjel, lįk in form
  tu a yɒŋ man, intent
on hį komiʃon: at ðe rįt,
  wiðin ðe tɯm, hi sat,
ared in hwįt and glisениŋ rɵbz;
  ðɛ wer afred ðerat.
Hi sed, "Fir not: į nɵ́ yi sik
  Jizɒs ov Nazareþ,
hɯ let woz krɯsifįd, and hir
  woz berid after deþ:
hi iz nɵ loŋger ded, hi haþ
  arizen from ðis grev,
in ðát nɥ lįf hwiç hi wil giv
  tu ðɵz hɯm hi wil sɛv.
Kɒm, si ðe ples hwer Jizɒs lɛ;
  and rekolekt ðe wɒrd
hi spɵk tu ɥ in Galili,
  deklɛriŋ ðat ɥr Lord
ʃud, after krɯsifikʃon, rįz
  tu lįf on ðe þerd dɛ.
Bɒt gɵ, and tel hiz folɵerz
  ðat hi wil lid ðe wɛ
tu Galili, and ðer ɥ ʃal
  behɵld ɥr Lord agen."

Then in these holy women's hearts
 Great joy succeeded pain;
And tremblingly, and silently,
 They ran, in haste, to tell
The eleven disciples, of this great
 And glorious miracle.
But the disciples could not then
 Believe their words were true;
Though some mysterious hopes revived
 Within their breasts anew.

Đen in điz hɵli wimen'z harts
 gret joi sɒksįded pen;
and tremblįŋli, and sįlentli,
 đe ran, in hest, tɯ tel
đe eleven disįpelz, ov đis gret
 and glɵriɒs mįrakel.
Bɒt đe disįpelz kud not đen
 beliv đer wɒrdz wer trɯ;
đɵ sɒm mistiriɒs hɵps revįvd
 wiđin đer brests anɥ.

SECTION 194.

Peter and John hasten to the Sepulchre.
John 20. 3-10.

Then Peter, to the sepulchre,
 Hastened with zealous heed;
And John ran too, whose younger feet
 Outstripped the other's speed.
He, stooping down, then first beheld
 The linen clothes there laid;
But still he ventured not within;
 By awe and reverence stayed;
Till bolder Peter came; and he
 An entrance quickly found.
He saw the clothes, and napkin too,
 That round his head was bound.
The other then went in the tomb,
 And when he saw, believed;
Though, of his resurrection, they
 Had not Christ's truth received.
And after this, with silent awe
 They to their home returned;
Musing upon the wonders great
 With which their spirits burned.

SEKΣON 194.

Piter and Jon hesen tu đe Sepɒlker.
Jon 20. 3-10.

Đen Pįter, tu đe sepɒlker,
 hesend wiđ zelɒz hid;
and Jon ran tɯ, hɯz yɒŋger fit
 ȣtstript đe ɒđer'z spid.
Hį, stɯpiŋ dȣn, đen ferst beheld
 đe linen klɵđz đer led;
bɒt stil hį ventɥrd not wiđin;
 bį ω and reverens sted:
til bɵlder Pįter kem; and hį
 an entrans kwikli fȣnd.
Hį sω đe klɵđz, and napkin tɯ,
 đat rȣnd hiz hed woz bȣnd.
Đe ɒđer đen went in đe tɯm,
 and hwen hį sω, belivd;
đɵ, ov hiz rezɒrekʃon, đe
 had not Kręst's trɯɟ resivd.
And after đis, wiđ sįlent ω
 đe tu đer hɵm retɒrnd;
mɥziŋ ɒpon đe wɒnderz gret
 wiđ hwiç đer spirits bɒrnd.

SECTION 195.

Mary Magdalene looks into the Sepulchre, and sees two angels.—John 20. 11-18.

But Mary lingered still beside
 That grave, so sad, so dear;
And as she wept, and looked within,
 Two angels, bright and fair,
One at the head, one at the feet,
 Where Jesus had been laid,
She now beheld; and unto her,
 In soothing tones, they said,

SEKΣON 195.

Meri Magdalen luks intu đe Sepɒlker, and siz tɯ enjelz.—Jon 20. 11-18.

Bɒt Meri liŋgerd stil besįd
 đát grev, sɵ sad, sɵ dir;
and az ʃi wept, and lukt wiđin,
 tɯ enjelz, brįt and fer,
wɒn at đe hed, wɒn at đe fit,
 hwer Jizɒs had bin led,
ʃi nȣ beheld; and ɒntu her,
 in sɯđiŋ tɵnz, đe sed,

"Woman, why weepest thou?" She
said,
"They've taken away my Lord;
I know not where they've laid him."
She turned at Jesus' word, [Then
And Jesus' self did she behold,
There standing by her side,
He who had purified her mind,
And then became her guide.
His voice now speaks, "Why weepest
thou?
Woman, whom seek'st thou here?"
She knew him not; he unto her
The gardener did appear.
One thought her bosom filled: she said,
"If thou hast borne him hence,
O tell me, sir, where he is laid,
And I will take him thence."
"Mary!" said Jesus now to her;
The endearing name revealed
Him her whole heart adored and loved,
And recognition sealed.
She quickly turned, and, "Master!"
Jesus said, "Touch me not; [cried,
I shall not yet to heaven ascend,
And leave this earthly spot;
But to my Father, and to yours,
To my God, and yours too,
I shall ascend. This message give
My brethren." She withdrew.

"Wuman, hwį wipest ðɤ?" Σi
sed,
"Ðe'v teken awe mį Lord;
į nơ not hwer ðe'v led him." Ðen
ʃi tɒrnd at Jizɒs' wɒrd,
and Jizɒs' self did ʃi behơld,
ðer standiŋ bį her sįd;
hi hɯ had pųriʃįd her mįnd,
and ðen bekem her gįd.
Hiz vois nɤ spiks, "Hwį wipest
ðɤ?
Wuman, hɯm sik'st ðɤ hir?"
Σi nų him not; hi ɒntu her
ðe gardener did apir.
Wɒn ɟot her bɯzom fild: ʃi sed,
"If ðɤ hast bơrn him hens,
Ơ tel mi, ser, hwer hi iz led,
and į wil tek him ðens."
"Meri!" sed Jizɒs nɤ tu her;
ðe endiriŋ nem revįld
him her hơl hart adơrd and lɒvd,
and rekogniʃon sild.
Σi kwikli tɒrnd, and, "Master!"
Jizɒs sed, "Tɒç mi not; [krįd,
į ʃal not yet tu heven asend,
and liv ðis erɟli spot;
bɒt tu mį Fɑðer, and tu ųrz,
tu mį God, and ųrz tɯ,
į ʃal asend. Ðis mesej giv
mį breðren." Σi wiððrɯ.

SECTION 196.

Mary Magdalene, when going to inform the disciples that Christ had risen, meets again with Salome and the other Mary. Jesus appears to the three women.

Matthew 28. 9, 10. John 20. 18.

Then did this Mary haste away,
And, the disciples tell,
That she had seen her blessed Lord,
And what things then befel.
The other holy women, too,
Went, with the angels' word,
And on the way, behold, they meet
The Savior they adored.
"All hail!" said Jesus unto them;
And at his feet they kneeled,
To worship him, who from the dead,
His presence thus revealed.

SEKΣON 196.

Meri Magdalen, hwen goiŋ tu inform ðe disįpelz ðat Krįst had rizen, mits agen wið Salơmi and ðe ɒðer Meri. Jizɒs apirz tu ðe ɵri wimen.

Maɟų 28. 9, 10. Jon 20. 18.

Ðen did ðis Meri hest awe,
and, ðe disįpelz tel,
ðat ʃi had sin her blesed Lord,
and hwot ɟiŋz ðen befel.
Ðe ɒðer hơli wimen, tɯ,
went, wið ðe enjelz' wɒrd,
and on ðe we, behơld, ðe mit
ðe Sevier ðe adơrd.
"Ɯl hel!" sed Jizɒs ɒntu ðem;
and at hiz fit ðe nild,
tu wɒrʃip him, hɯ from ðe ded,
hiz prezens ðɒs revįld.

"Be not afraid," he gently said;
"Unto my friends repair
And say, "Make haste to Galilee,
And ye shall see me there."

SECTION 197.

The Soldiers, who had fled from the Sepulchre, report to the high priests the Resurrection of Christ.

Matthew 28. 11-16.

When Christ had risen from the dead,
The soldiers, who had kept
Their watch beside the sepulchre,
Their station left, and crept
By stealth into Jerusalem,
And told the priestly power,
His resurrection, and the events
They witnessed in that hour.
They with the elders council held;
Large money then they gave
The soldiers, that they might declare
That, "From the darksome grave,
His own disciples came by night,
And while we slept, did steal
The body." "From the governor
We can the truth conceal,"
Said they. And this the soldiers did;
And even until this day,
The Jews repeat that false report
Rather than truth obey.

SECTION 198.

Christ appears to Cleopas and another disciple, going to Emmaus.

Mark 16. 12, 13. Luke 24. 13-35.

Upon the solemn eventide
Of that great Easter-day,
It came to pass two friends did turn
To Emmaus their way.
They talked of Jesus as they went,
And of the wondrous scene
Which they so late had witnessed, and
Of what its end might mean.
While thus they reasoned and com-
Jesus himself drew near; [muned,
But as their eyes were holden, he
A stranger did appear.

"Bi not afred," hi jentli sed;
"ɒntu mį frendz reper
and se, "Mek hest tu Galili,
and yi ʃal si mi ðer."

SEKΣON 197.

Ðe Sɒldierz, hɯ had fled from ðe Sepɒlker, repɵrt tu ðe hį prists ðe Rezɒrekʃon ov Krįst.

Maŧɥ 28. 11-16.

Hwen Krįst had rizen from ðe ded,
ðe sɵldierz, hɯ had kept
ðer woq besįd ðe sepɒlker,
ðer steʃon left, and krept
bį stelŧ intu Jerusalem,
and tɵld ðe pristli pɤer,
hiz rezɒrekʃon, and ðe events
ðe witnest in ðát ɤr.
Ðe wið ðe elderz kɤnsel held;
larj mɒni ðen ðe gev
ðe sɵldierz, ðat ðe mįt dekler
ðat, "From ðe darksɒm grev,
hiz ɵn disįpelz kem bį nįt,
and hwįl wi slept, did stil
ðe bodi." "From ðe gɒverner
wi kan ðe trɯŧ konsil."
sed ðe. And ðis ðe sɵldierz did;
and iven ɒntil ðis de,
ðe Jɯz repit ðát fɵls repɵrt
raðer ðan trɯŧ ɵbe.

SEKΣON 198.

Krįst apirz tu Kliopas and anɒðer disįpel, goiŋ tu Emaɒs.

Mark 16. 12, 13. Lɯk 24. 13-35.

Ɯpon ðe solem ivéntįd
ov ðát gret Ister-de,
it kem tu pas tɯ́ frendz did tɒrn
tu Emaɒs ðer we.
Ðe tɵkt ov Jizɒs az ðe went,
and ov ðe wɒndrɒs sin
hwiq ðe sɵ let had witnest, and
ov hwot its end mįt min.
Hwįl ðɒs ðe rizond and komɥnd,
Jizɒs himself drɯ nir;
bɒt az ðer įz wer hɵlden, hi
a strenjer did apir.

He asked, "What makes your converse sad?"
They answer, "Know'st thou not
What things have happened in these [days
At Salem's hallowed spot?
Art thou a stranger?" He replied,
"What things?" They told him, then,
Of Jesus, great in word and deed,
'Fore God and also men:
And how the priests and rulers him
Betrayed and crucified.
"But we," they said, "hoped it was he
Of long time prophesied,
The anointed King of Israel,
Redeemer; Lord. Beside,
This is the third day since these things
Were done. Our women, too,
Went early to his sepulchre,
The holy form to view,
But found it not; then came, and told,
That angels were seen there,
Who said, that Jesus was alive,
And did on earth appear.
And certain who were with us, went
To view the sepulchre,
And found it as the women said,
For he was not among the dead."

Jesus then said, "O foolish ones,
And dull, and slow of heart,
Ye unbelievers in the truths
God's prophets did impart.
Ought not the Christ to suffer thus,
And glory then receive?"
From Moses and the Prophets then
He taught them to believe
The wonders of the Holy Word,—
That everything to Him referred.

Soon to the village they drew nigh;
And he behaved as though
He would go on. They beg that he
This purpose would forego.
"Abide with us, the day is spent,
And evening shades draw on."
He entered, and did graciously
At their repast sit down.
He took the bread, and blessed, and [brake,
And gave those favored two:

Hi askt, "Hwot meks ųr konvers sad?"
Đe anser, "Nɵest đɤ not
hwot ɟiŋz hav hapend in điz dez
at Selem'z halɵd spot?
Art đɤ a strenjer?" Hi repljd,
"Hwot ɟiŋz?" Đe tɵld him, đen,
ov Jizɒs, gret in wɒrd and did,
'fɵr God and ɷlsɵ men:
and hɤ đe prists and rɯlerz him
betred and krɯsifjd.
"Bɒt wi," đe sed, "hɵpt it woz hi
ov loŋ tjm profesjd,
đe anointed kiŋ ov Izrael,
Redimer; Lord. Besjd,
đis iz đe ɟerd de sins sins đis ɟiŋz
wer dɒn. Ɤr wimen, tɯ,
went erli tu hiz sepɒlker,
đe hɵli form tu vų,
bɒt fɤnd it not; đen kem, and tɵld,
đat enjelz wer sin đer,
hɯ sed, đat Jizɒs woz aljv,
and did on erɟ apir.
And serten hɯ wer wiđ ɒs, went
tu vų đe sepɒlker,
and fɤnd it az đe wimen sed,
for hi woz not amɒŋ đe ded."

Jizɒs đen sed, "Ɵ fɯliʃ wɒnz,
and dɒl, and slɵ ov hart,
yi ɒnbeliverz in đe trɯđz
God'z profets did impart.
ɷt not đe Krjst tu sɒfer đɒs,
and glɵri đen resiv?"
From Mɵsez and đe Profets đen
hi tɷt đem tu beliv
đe wɒnderz ov đe Hɵli Wɒrd,—
đat everiɟiŋ tu him referd.

Sɯn tu đe vilej đe drɯ nj;
and hi behevd az đɵ
hi wud gɵ on. Đe beg đat hi
đis pɒrpos wud fɵrgɵ.
"Abjd wiđ ɒs, đe de iz spent,
and ivniŋ ʃedz drɷ on."
Hi enterd, and did greʃɒsli
at đer repast sit dɤn.
Hi tuk đe bred, and blest, and brek,
and gev đɵz fevord tɯ:

They knew their Lord! But then, at
He vanished from their view. [once,
"Did not our hearts within us burn,
As in the way he talked;
Unfolding all the mysteries
Of Scripture, as we walked?"
Thus each unto the other spoke;
And then they home returned,
To tell their brethren the great truth
Which now they had discerned.

Soon in Jerusalem they found
The eleven with hearts all cheered.
Some said, "The Lord is risen indeed!
To Simon he appeared."
And then they told the wondrous things
He showed them that same night,
And how, as they were breaking bread,
He vanished from their sight.
Yet still their minds were slow to learn
That Jesus would to them return.

SECTION 199.

Christ appears to the assembled Apostles, Thomas only being absent, convinces them of the identity of his resurrection body, and blesses them.

Luke 24. 36-43. John 20. 19-23.

On that same day, at evening hour,
The first day of the week,
With fast closed doors, for fear of ill,
Sat the disciples meek.
And as they to each other spoke
Of Jesus' wondrous word,
Lo! in their midst, all suddenly,
Appeared their gracious Lord.
To calm the terror of their heart,
He said, "Peace be to you;"
For they supposed a spirit had
Appeared within their view.
"Fear not. Why these anxieties?
Behold my hands and feet;
Touch me, and know that in the flesh
Again your Lord ye meet."
Thus Jesus spoke; and then he showed
His hands, and feet, and side.
And when they saw it was the Lord,
Their joy was magnified.
Wonder and gladness yet delayed
Belief in such great good;

đe nų đer Lord! Bɒt đen, at wɒns,
hi vaniʃt from đer vų.
"Did not ɤr harts wiđin ɒs bɒrn
az in đe we hi tɷkt;
ɒnfɵldiŋ ɷl đe misteriz
ov Skriptųr, az wi wɷkt?"
Ɑɒs iç ɒntu đe ɒđer spɵk;
and đen đe hɵm retɒrnd,
tu tel đer bredren đe gret truɟ
hwiç nɤ đe had disernd.

Sɯn in Jerɯsalem đe fɤnd
đe eleven wiđ harts ɷl çird.
sɒm sed, "Ɑe Lord iz rizen indid!
tu Sįmon hi apird."
And đen đe tɵld đe wɒndrɒs ɟiŋz
hi ʃɵd đem đát sem nįt,
and hɤ, az đe wer brekiŋ bred,
hi vaniʃt from đer sįt.
Yet stil đer mįndz wer slɵ tu lern
đat Jizɒs wud tu đem retɒrn.

SEKΣON 199.

Krįst apirz tu đe usembeld Aposelz, Tomas ɵnli biiŋ absent, konvinsez đem ov đe įdentiti ov hiz rezɒrekʃon bodi, and blesez đem.

Lɯk 24. 36-43. Jon 20. 19-23.

On đát sem de, at ivniŋ ɤr,
đe ferst de ov đe wik,
wiđ fast klɵzd dɵrz, for fir ov il,
sat đe disįpelz mik.
And az đe tu iç ɒđer spɵk
ov Jizɒs' wɒndrɒs wɒrd,
lɵ! in đer midst, ɷl sɒdenli,
apird đer greʃɒs Lord.
Tu kɑm đe teror ov đer hart,
hi sed, "Pis bi tu ų;"
for đe sɒpɵzd a spirit had
apird wiđin đer vų.
"Fir not." Hwį điz aŋkzįetiz?
behɵld mį handz and fit;
tɒç mi, and nɵ đat in đe fleʃ
agen ųr Lord yi mit."
Ɑɒs Jizɒs spɵk; and đen hi ʃɵd
hiz handz, and fit, and sįd.
And hwen đe sɷ it woz đe Lord,
đer joi woz magnifįd.
Wɒnder and gladnes yet deled
belif in sɒç gret gud;

Till Jesus, to cônvince them, said,
  "Have ye here any food?"
A piece of honeycomb and fish
  They gave. He took, and then
Did eat before them. Jesus said,
  "Peace be to you," again.
"Like as my Father hath sent me,
  Even so do I send you."
And then he breathed on them, that he
  Might them with power endue,
And grace ineffable, and said,
  "The Holy Spirit receive.
To those whose sins ye shall remit,
  I will forgiveness give;
And those whose sins ye shall retain,
Their sins will still on them remain."

SECTION 200.

Christ appears to the eleven, Thomas being present, and afterwards to a large number of his disciples in Galilee.

Matthew 28. 16, 17. Mark 16. 14. John 20. 24.

Now Thomas, surnamed Didymus,
  Was absent when Christ came;
And when he heard the wondrous news,
  He did, in doubt exclaim,
"Except within his hands and feet,
  The nail-prints I perceive;
And place my finger in the wounds,
  I will not this believe."

The Lord appeared to the eleven
  After eight further days,
When Thomas, who had doubted most,
  Among his brethren prays.
"Peace be to you," he said to them,
  As he came suddenly
Within the room, the doors being shut,
  For their security.
Yet tenderly did he upbraid
  Their stubborn disbelief
Of those who saw him, and who wished
  To mitigate their grief.
"Peace be to you," he said. His words
  Soon soothed their wild surprise.
"Thomas, thy finger reach; and see
  My hands with thine own eyes;
And reach thy hand unto my side,
  Thrust it in fearlessly."

til Jizɒs, tu konvins đem, sed,
  "Hav yi hir eni fud?"
A pis ov hɒnikøm and fiʃ
  đe gev. Hi tuk, and đen
did it beførr đem. Jizɒs sed,
  "Pis bi tu ɥ," agen.
"Lįk az mį Fađer hađ sent mi,
  iven sø du į send ɥ."
And đen hi briđd on đem, đat hi
  mįt đem wiđ pɜer endɥ,
and gres inefabel, and sed,
  "Đe Høli Spirit resiv.
Tu đøz huz sinz yi ʃal remit,
  į wil forgivnes giv;
and đøz huz sinz yi ʃal reten,
đer sinz wil stil on đem remen."

SEKΣON 200.

Krįst apirz tu đe eleven, Tomas biiŋ prezent, and afterwardz tu a larj nɒmber ov hiz disįpelz in Galili.

Mađɥ 28. 16, 17. Mark 16. 14. Jon 20. 24.

Nɜ Tomas, sɒrnemd Didimɒs,
  woz absent hwen Krįst kem;
and hwen hi herd đe wɒndrɒs nɥz,
  hi did, in dɜt eksklem,
"Eksept wiđin hiz handz and fit,
  đe nel-prints į persiv;
and ples mį fiŋger in đe wundz,
  į wil not đis beliv."

Đe Lord apird tu đe eleven
  after et fɒrđer dez,
hwen Tomas, hu had dɜted møst,
  amɒŋ hiz bređren prez.
"Pis bi tu ɥ," hi sed tu đem,
  az hi kem sɒdenli
wiđin đe rum, đe dørz biiŋ ʃɒt,
  for đer sekɥriti.
Yet tenderli did hi ɒpbred
  đer stɒborn disbelif
ov đøz hu sø him, and hu wiʃt
  tu mitiget đer grif.
"Pis bi tu ɥ," hi sed. Hiz wɒrdz
  sun suđd đer wįld sɒrprįz.
"Tomas, đį fiŋger riç; and si
  mį handz wiđ đįn øn įz;
and riç đį hand ɒntu mį sįd,
  ɟrɒst it in firlesli."

He was content to see the Lord:
The kindness Jesus showed,
Extorted this acknowledgement,
"Thou art my Lord, my God."
"Since thou hast seen me," Jesus said,
"Thou hast believed in me;
But blest are they who, seeing not,
Receive me, lovingly."

Then the disciples went away
To a mount in Galilee,
As Jesus had appointed them,
For further ministry.
And when they saw, they worshiped [him,
But some with hesitation;
And Jesus came and spoke to them
Concerning his salvation.

Hi woz kontent tu si đe Lord;
đe kįndnes Jizɒs ʃɵd,
ekstorted đis aknolejment,
"Đɤ art mį Lord, mį God."
"Sins đɤ hast sįn mi," Jizɒs sed,
"đɤ hast belįvd in mi;
bɒt blest ar đɛ hɯ, siiŋ not,
resįv mi, lɒviŋli."

Đen đe disįpelz went awɛ
tu a mɤnt in Galili,
az Jizɒs had apointed đem,
for fɒrđer ministri.
And hwen đɛ sɷ, đɛ wɒrʃipt him,
bɒt sɒm wiđ heziteʃon;
and Jizɒs kem and spɵk tu đem
konserniŋ hiz salveʃon.

SECTION 201.

Christ appears again at the Sea of Tiberias. His conversation with Peter.

John 21. 1-24.

SEKΣON 201.

Krįst apirz agen at đe Si ov Tįbirias. Hiz konverseʃon wiđ Piter.

Jon 21. 1-24.

Again beside Tiberias' lake,
Jesus himself made known
To Thomas and Nathanael,
And James and loving John,
And other two disciples, who
Being at their fishing trade,
Had toiled all night, and found no gain,
And out at sea now stayed.
At morn, upon the shore, behold,
Jesus himself appeared,
But yet these simple fishermen
Knew not their Lord endeared.
He said, "Have ye here any meat?"
They briefly answered, "Nay."
"Cast then your net on the right side,
Abundance shall repay."
The heavy net could scarce be drawn:
John said, "It is the Lord."
And Peter in his zealous haste
Cast himself overboard.
The rest pulled in their little boat,
And drew the net to land,
When, lo, a wondrous miracle
They saw upon the strand:
A fire of coals, and fish thereon,
With bread, as need required.

Agen besįd Tįbirias' lek,
Jizɒs himself med nɵn
tu Tomas and Naŧanael,
and Jemz and lɒviŋ Jon,
and ɒđer tɯ́ disįpelz, hɯ
biiŋ at đer fiʃiŋ tred,
had toild ɷl nįt, and fɤnd nɵ gen,
and ɤt at si nɤ sted.
At morn, ɒpon đe ʃɵr, behɵld,
Jizɒs himself apįrd,
bɒt yet điz simpel fiʃermen
nɥ not đer Lord endįrd.
Hi sed, "Hav yi hįr eni mįt?"
Đe brifli anserd "Nɛ."
"Kast đen ɥr net on đe rįt sįd,
abɒndans ʃal repɛ."
Đe hevi net kud skers bi drɷn:
Jon sed, "It iz đe Lord."
And Piter in hiz zelɒs hest
kast himself ɵverbɵrd,
Đe rest puld in đer litel bɵt,
and drɯ đe net tu land,
hwen, lɵ, a wɒndrɒs mirakel
đɛ sɷ ɒpon đɛ strand:
A fįr ov kɵlz, and fiʃ đeron,
wiđ bred, az nįd rekwįrd.

Then Jesus said, "Bring what ye've
caught."
They did as he desired.
A hundred fish, and fifty-three,
They counted from the net;
And yet it was unbroken, though
It bore this heavy weight.
Then Jesus saith, "Come ye and dine."
They could not speak a word
To ask him, "Who art thou?" for well
They knew it was the Lord.
Then Jesus took the bread and fish,
And round distributed.
This third time did he show himself,
New risen from the dead.

Then having dined, to Peter he
These searching words addressed;—
"Now Simon, son of Jonas, say
If thou dost love me best."
"Yea, Lord, thou know'st I love thee
Said he, undoubtingly. [much,"
"Then feed my lambs," the Lord re-
"This charge I give to thee." [plied,
Again the second time he spoke,
"Simon, dost thou love me?"
"Yea, Lord, thou know'st I love thee
He answered faithfully. [much,"
"Feed thou my sheep." This high
command
Was given him by his Lord.
Peter was grieved when asked again,
By him his soul adored,
The thrilling question, "Lov'st thou
O Simon, Jonas' son?" [me,
"Lord, thou, who knowest all things,
That I love thee alone." [knowest,
Again said Jesus, "Feed my sheep.
I tell thee, verily,
When thou wast young, thou hadst
thy will,
And then thy steps were free;
But when old age shall be thy lot,
Another's power shall guide,
And thou shalt then be carried forth
Against thy will, and tried."
Of Peter's death, the Lord thus spoke;
Then added, "Follow me."
Peter then saw that loved one near,
Who leaned so tenderly

Ðen Jizɒs sed, "Briŋ hwot yi'v
kɯt."
Ðɛ did az hi dezįrd.
A hɒndred fiʃ, and fifti-θri,
ðɛ kɤnted from ðe net;
and yet it woz ɒnbrɷken, ðɷ
it bɷr ðis hevi wɛt.
Ðen Jizɒs seθ, "Kɒm yi and dįn."
Ðɛ kud not spik a wɒrd
tu ask him, "Hɯ art ðɤ?" for wel
ðɛ nɥ it woz ðe Lord.
Ðen Jizɒs tuk ðe bred and fiʃ,
and rɤnd distribɥted.
Ðis θerd tįm did hi ʃɷ himself,
nɥ rizen from ðe ded.

Ðen haviŋ dįnd, tu Piter hi
ðiz serçiŋ wɒrdz adrest;—
Nɤ Sįmon, sɒn ov Jɷnas, sɛ
if ðɤ dɒst lɒv mi best."
"Yɛ Lord, ðɤ nɷ'st į lɒv ði mɒç,"
sed hi, ɒndɤtiŋli.
"Ðen fid mį lamz," ðe Lord replįd,
"ðis çarj į giv tu ði."
Agen ðe sekond tįm hi spɷk,
"Sįmon, dɒst ðɤ lɒv mi?"
"Yɛ, Lord, ðɤ nɷ'st į lɒv ði mɒç,"
hi anserd fɛθfuli.
"Fid ðɤ mį ʃip." Ðis hį
komand
woz given him bį hiz Lord.
Piter woz grivd hwen askt agen
bį him hiz sɷl adɷrd,
ðe θriliŋ kwestion, "Lɒv'st ðɤ mi,
Ɵ Sįmon, Jɷnas' sɒn?"
"Lord, ðɤ, hɯ nɷest ɯl θiŋz, nɷest,
ðat į lɒv ði alɷn."
Agen sed Jizɒs, "Fid mį ʃip.
Į tel ði, verili,
hwen ðɤ wost yɒŋ, ðɤ hadst ðį
wil,
and ðen ðį steps wer fri;
bɒt hwen ɷld ɛj ʃal bi ðį lot,
anɒðer'z pɤer ʃal gįd,
and ðɤ ʃalt ðen bi karid fɷrθ
agenst ðį wil, and trįd."
Ov Piter'z deθ, ðe Lord ðɒs spɷk;
ðen aded, "Folɷ mi."
Piter ðen sɯ ðat lɒvd wɒn nir,
hɯ lind sɷ tenderli

On Jesus' breast, upon the night
Of that most solemn feast.
"And what shall this man do, O Lord?"
He asked, with over-haste.
Jesus replied, "If I so will,
He tarry till I come,
'Tis nought to thee; thy path is clear,
To follow me, nor roam."
These words they understood to mean
That John should never die;
Yet Jesus said not so. 'Tis he
These things doth testify.

on Jizɒs' brest, ɒpon đe nįt
ov đát mɵst solem fist.
"And hwot ʃal đis man dɯ, Ɵ Lord?"
hi askt, wiđ ɵver-hest,
Jizɒs replįd, "Íf į sɵ wíl,
hi tari til į kɒm,
'tiz nɷt tu đi; đį pɛɟ iz klir,
tu folɵ mi, nor rɵm."
Điz wɒrdz đɛ ɒnderstud tu min
đat Jon ʃud never dį;
yet Jizɒs sed not sɵ. 'Tiz hi
điz ɟiŋz dɒɟ testifį.

SECTION 202.

Christ appears to his Apostles at Jerusalem, and commissions them to preach repentance and the remission of sins among all nations.

Luke 24. 44-49.

And Jesus further said to them,
"Remember ye the word
I spake when I was with you still
Concerning Christ, the Lord:
That all things written in the Law,
And in the Prophets too,
And in the Psalms, concerning me,
Must have fulfilment due."
Then opened he their minds that they
His Word might understand;
That Word which came from heaven, and was
Written by God's command.
He told them how the Scriptures had
Predicted all his fate;
That he should suffer death, and rise
In three days from that state;
And that in his name there should be
Proclaimed, both far and near,
Repentance and forgiveness which
All humankind should share.
"Moreover," Jesus said to them,
"Ye, my disciples true,
Are witnesses of all my words
And works, which well ye knew.
God's promised gift ye shall receive;
But ye shall not remove
From this Jerusalem until
Full power from heaven ye prove."

SEKΣON 202.

Krįst apirz tu hiz Aposelz at Jerɯsalem, and komiʃonz đem tu prig repentans and đe remiʃon ov sinz amɒŋ ɷl neʃonz.

Lɯk 24. 44-49.

And Jizɒs fɒrđer sed tu đem,
"Remember yi đe wɒrd
į spɛk hwen į woz wiđ ų stil
konserniŋ Krįst, đe Lord:
đat ɷl ɟiŋz riten in đe Lɷ,
and in đe profets tɯ,
and in đe Sɛmz, konserniŋ mi,
mɒst hav fulfilment dų."
Đen ɵpend hi đer mįndz đat đɛ
hiz Wɒrd mįt ɒnderstand;
đát Wɒrd hwig kɛm from heven, and woz
riten bį God'z komand.
Hi tɵld đem hɤ đe Skriptųrz had
predikted ɷl hiz fɛt;
đat hi ʃud sɒfer deɟ, and rįz
in ɟri dɛz from đát stɛt;
and đat in hiz nem đer ʃud bi
prɵklɛmd, bɵɟ far and nir,
repentans and forgivnes hwig
ɷl hųman kįnd ʃud ʃɛr.
"Mɵrɵver," Jizɒs sed tu đem,
"yi, mį disįpel trɯ,
ar witnesez ov ɷl mį wɒrdz
and wɒrks, hwig wel yi nų.
God'z promist gift yi ʃal resiv;
bɒt yi ʃal not remɯv
from đis Jerɯsalem ɒntil
ful pɤer from heven yi prɯv."

SECTION 203.

Christ leads his Apostles to Bethany, gives them their final commission, blesses them, and ascends to heaven.

Matthew 28. 18-20. Mark 16. 15-20. Luke 24. 50-53.

And after this Christ led them out
 As far as Bethany,
And said to them these parting words:
 "All power is given to me
In heaven and in earth; therefore,
 Into the world go ye,
The Gospel preach, all nations teach,
 That they may heaven inherit;
Baptising them into the name
 Of Father, Son, and Spirit;
Teaching them to observe all things
 I have commanded you;
And, lo, I'm with you always, in
 All time that shall ensue.
And these miraculous signs from [heaven
 Shall true believers share;
In my name shall they cast out devils,
 By fasting and by prayer;
They in new languages shall speak,
 And poisonous serpents charm;
And if they drink a deadly thing,
 It shall not do them harm;
And when they lay their holy hands
 On those who suffer pain,
Sickness shall vanish at their touch,
 And all be health again."

When Christ had spoken these last [words
 To his disciples true,
He lifted up his holy hands
 And blest them all anew.
And while he blest them, and they saw
 His Godlike form of love,
Lo, he was parted from them, and
 Then rose to heaven above;
A heavenly cloud received the Lord,
 And veiled him from their sight,
And he ascended into heaven
 And sat in glory bright
At God's right hand,—omnipotent,—
 Clothed with all power and might.
They worshiped him; and then re- [turned
 From Olivet, with joy,
Unto Jerusalem, and did
 Their lives and tongues employ,

SEKΣON 203.

Krįst lidz hiz Aposelz tu Beŧani, givz đem đer final komiʃon, blesez đem, and asendz tu heven.

Maŧɥ 28. 18-20. Mark 16. 15-20. Luk 24. 50-53.

And after đis Krįst led đem ɤt
 az far az Beŧani,
and sed tu đem điz partiŋ wɒrdz:
 "ɷl pɤer iz given tu mi
in heven and in erŧ; đerfɵr,
 intu đe wɒrld gɵ yi,
đe Gospel priç, ɷl neʃonz tiç,
 đat đɛ mɛ heven inherit;
baptįziŋ đem intu đe nɛm
 ov Fɑđer, Sɒn, and Spirit;
tiçiŋ đem tu obzerv ɷl ŧiŋz
 į hav komanded ɥ;
and, lɵ, į'm wiđ ɥ ɷlwez, in
 ɷl tįm đat ʃal ensɥ.
And điz mirakɥlɒs sįnz from heven
 ʃal trɯ beliverz ʃɛr;
in mį nɛm ʃal đɛ kast ɤt devilz,
 bį fastiŋ and bį prɛr;
đɛ in nɥ laŋgwɛjez ʃal spik,
 and poizonɒs serpents çarm;
and if đɛ driŋk a dedli ŧiŋ,
 it ʃal not dɯ đem harm;
and hwen đɛ lɛ đer hɵli handz
 on đɵz hɯ sɒfer pɛn,
siknes ʃal vaniʃ at đer tɒç,
 and ɷl bi helŧ agen."

Hwen Krįst had spɵken điz last [wɒrdz
 tu hiz disįpelz trɯ,
hi lifted ɒp hiz hɵli handz
 and blest đem ɷl anɥ.
And hwįl hi blest đem, and đɛ sɷ
 hiz Godlįk form ov lɒv,
lɵ, hi woz parted from đem, and
 đen rɵz tu heven abɒv;
a hevenli klɤd resivd đe Lord,
 and vɛld him from đer sįt,
and hi asended intu heven
 and sat in glɵri brįt
at God'z rįt hand,—omnipotent,—
 klɵđd wiđ ɷl pɤer and mįt.
đɛ wɒrʃipt him; and đen retɒrnd
 from Olivet, wiđ joi,
ɒntu Jerɯsalem, and did
 đer lįvz and tɒŋz emploi,

In praising God continually
  Within the temple fair.
They then went forth, throughout the earth,
  And preached Christ everywhere.
The Lord worked with them, and again
Confirmed his word by signs. Amen.

SECTION 204.

John's conclusion to the Gospel History of Jesus Christ.—John 20. 30, 31; 21. 25.

And many other signs there were
  That Jesus did on earth,
In presence of his followers,
  That are not here set forth;
So many that, if they should all
  Be written, I suppose
The world could not receive so much
  As those books would disclose.
But these are written, and these signs
  Are now proclaimed abroad,
That ye may know that Jesus is
  The Christ, the Son of God;
(Son as to his humanity,
  Divinity's abode;)
And that believing, ye may then
Have life through his own name.
  Amen.

in prɛziŋ God kontinɥali
  wiđin đe tempel fɛr.
Đɛ đen went fɵrƭ, ƭrɯȣt đe ertƭ,
  and priçt Krįst everihwer.
Đe Lord wɒrkt wiđ đem, and agen
konfermd hiz wɒrd bį sįnz. Ɑmen.

SEKΣON 204.

Jon'z konklɯʒon tu đe Gospel Histori ov Jizɒs Krįst.—Jon 20. 30, 31; 21. 25.

And meni ɒđer sįnz đer wer
  đat Jızɒs did on ertƭ,
in prezens ov hiz folɵerz,
  đat ar not hır set fɵrƭ;
sɵ meni đat, if đɛ ʃud ɷl
  bı riten, į sɒpɵz
đe wɒrld kud not resıv sɵ mɒç
  az đɵz buks wud disklɵz.
Bɒt đız ar riten, and đız sįnz
  ar nȣ prɵklemd abrɷd,
đat yı mɛ nɵ́ đat Jızɒs iz
  đe Krįst, đe Sɒn ov God;
(Sɒn az tu hiz hɥmaniti,
  Diviniti'z abɵd;)
and đat belıviŋ, yı mɛ đen
hav lįf ƭrɯ hiz ɵn nɛm.
  Ɑmen.

CONCLUDING NOTE.

The sentence in the last paragraph of St John's Gospel, relating to the multitude of books which might have been written concerning the life of Christ, has been translated in different senses by various scholars. Some critics agree with the Authorised Version, in supposing that St John here used a strong Oriental hyperbole, or exaggeration, such as was sometimes employed by Jewish writers of that period, when they wished to convey an idea of immensity. Other critics (including myself,) think that such a supposition is erroneous and perilous; and they believe that so pure and truthful a writer as St John did not here indulge in any extravagant figures of speech, but that he asserted a true fact truly.

I conceive, therefore, that St John did not intend to say that if all the particulars of Christ's life, words, and works, were described, the world would not be able to contain the written records thereof. But he indicates, that in this case they would be so voluminous, that the world, the community of men and nations, could not *receive* or comprehend so great a mass of evangelical narratives.

When we consider that about one-third of the whole Gospel history is occupied in minutely describing only one week, that being the last week of Christ's life, preceding his resurrection, it appears that if the other weeks of his life had been recorded with similar minuteness, the biographic history of our Savior would have occupied at least a hundred volumes, as large as the entire Bible. And it is quite clear that the majority of mankind does not possess either capacity or leisure to become well acquainted with such enormous memorials, and to grasp and analyse their various contents.

With respect to the right interpretation of this passage, the Greek word *choreo*, which the Authorised Version here renders *contain*, is in four places of the same version of the

New Testament, rendered *receive*. It is likewise so rendered by Origen, Grotius, Whitby, Wynn, Wakefield, Harwood; and they are countenanced by a great multitude of authorities that need not here be mentioned.

It likewise appears highly probable, for several critical reasons, that the sentence at the end of St John's 20th chapter, and that at the end of his 21st chapter, were originally connected, and afterwards became dislocated. I have, therefore, recombined them in one concluding paragraph of the utmost practical importance.

In this proceeding I am confirmed by Townsend, Greswell, and the ever-amiable, sagacious Erasmus, who thus joins these two sentences together, at the close of his commentary on St John's Gospel. "If a man should go about to tell all the things which Jesus said and did, everything by itself, an immeasurable sort of books would be made thereof. But so much is written as sufficeth to the obtaining of salvation. Therefore the rest is, that believing these, and sticking to the steps and ways of Jesus, we labor diligently to get the reward of immortal life." (Bishop Udal's translation, 1548.)

It is indeed the highest interest and duty of man to believe in Jesus Christ—to cherish true faith in him, and obedience to him, as the divine Savior and Redeemer of our sinful race. For there is no other name under heaven given among men whereby we must be saved, but that of Jesus Christ. True faith in him, evinced by conformity to his example and his commandments, should be the main object of rational ambition and labor. This, indeed, is divine in itself, and it gives the Christian nothing less than a participation of the divine nature. It surpasses the highest excellences of all secular wisdom and virtue. It excels the brightest achievements of genius, or wealth, or power. So transcendent is its majesty, so imperishable its glory, so perfect its happiness, that all human speculations and exploits become insignificant in comparison—vain, futile, and unprofitable.

The evidences in favor of the divine truth and inspiration of the Gospels, and the other books of holy Scripture, appear to me perfectly convincing and irrefragable. Those evidences are so numerous, yet so harmonious, that they cannot be refuted. They are distinguished as internal, external, spiritual, moral, prophetic, historic, ecclesiastical, ethnical, mythologic, metaphysical, analytic, comparative, philological, and critical. Any one of these departments of biblical evidences, when thoroughly investigated, gives strong support to the faith of a Christian. But the convergence of so many different kinds of evidences, from so many different quarters, to the same central result, appears like a clenching demonstration of the truth of revelation. If there are any chances at all in the case, they are a million to one in favor of the believer. That such a marvelous harmony and correspondence of different and independent evidences, from the spheres of time, nature, and art, should exist in confirmation of an imposture, is the most improbable of all improbabilities. Well said Sir Isaac Newton, "A little knowledge may lead the mind from Christianity, but a little more will lead it back." Verily, he who believes Christianity shows far less credulity than he who disbelieves it. For although Christianity has been, and is, exposed to the blasts of criticism and the storms of scepticism, yet it always survives their attacks, and grows stronger by their antagonisms.

Not only is this Christianity true, but it is infinitely important, and indispensable to the welfare and happiness of men and nations. It presents to our view the divinest model of character and conduct, the divinest plan for the education and salvation of immortal souls, without which they are exposed to ruin both here and hereafter. This same Christianity has now stood the test of ages, and these facts have been evinced over and over. So far from being outgrown by the progress of science and discovery, it is still an immense distance in advance of our highest attainments. Yes, Christianity has proved itself to be essentially connected with all the best aspirations, sympathies, and interests of humanity, and every form of individual and social improvement. If right is to conquer wrong, effectually and permanently, it will be by the sign of the cross, and nothing less sacred. The chief existing evils, the plagues of imposture, injustice, intemperance, and war, are mainly owing to the want of Christianity among those who call themselves Christians, but who are not. Senators and philanthropists are justly striving to reform abuses, and supply defects. But every human remedy for the wrongs and woes of mankind, will be found abortive without this celestial remedy. The Lord Jesus Christ has declared that the salvation of man in this world and the next, shall be procured through the regenerating influence of his Word and Spirit. And he will overturn, overturn, overturn, all that opposes his wise designs, until he "shall be King over all the earth;" and, "in that day there shall be one Lord, and his name one." F. B.

APPENDIX.

The publication of the following correspondence seems necessary to account for t unusual appearance of two names, implying joint authorship, on the title page of a wo of this kind.

"*Bath, 4th May,* 1870.

"ISAAC PITMAN to FRANCIS BARHAM.

"In sending you the last slip of proof of THE GOSPEL EPI I cannot deny myself the pleasure of expressing the delight I feel at the conclusion the work. The four and a half months during which the book has been passing throu the press, have been a time of extra labor, and some degree of anxiety to me. When y placed the manuscript in my hands last autumn, I saw that there was so much of go in it that it deserved to be printed; and I thought I would try my hand upon the lin that did not run smoothly, or that were rather a paraphrase, than a mere rhyming, our most rhythmical Authorised English Version. I corrected the manuscript to the e of Section 9 at odd times before going to press with the first sheet at Christmas, with t result:—Out of a total of 512 lines, I had touched-up 111, and introduced 49 new on I was thus encouraged to undertake the revision and printing of the work in the *Phone Journal,* in weekly portions of eight pages. This I thought I could accomplish addition to my regular duties. After three weeks, finding that practice produced i creased facility in the revision, I determined to give sixteen pages per week, and th have the book ready in four months instead of eight. I have been obliged to postpo many things that I much wished to accomplish, in order to keep up with the weekly d mand for "copy." My gratification, therefore, at being released from this extra engag ment is very great; yet there is a feeling of sadness in thinking that the pleasa employment of rhyming the Divine narrative of the Gospel is at an end. Eminent serviceable did I find my Phonetic Shorthand as a medium of fixing rapidly on paper, they arose in my mind, the various forms of expression of which the Divine ideas in t Gospels are capable in English.

"I find that the poem contains 10,853 lines, and except that the lines are shorter th the ten-syllable lines of 'Paradise Lost,' which contains 10,565 lines, the two poems a very nearly of the same length, the GOSPEL EPIC being nearly 300 lines longer. But we measure by the number of poetic feet, it is but $\frac{8}{11}$ as long as Milton's poem.

"Of the total number of lines, I find, by a careful computation, that 3,652 have be written anew by me, and 2,024 altered, and, as I hope, improved.

"At first, I corrected your own manuscript for the printer, but after going through Sections in this way, I found that I could do the work more thoroughly, and in abo the same time, by writing it out afresh in shorthand for the compositor. I therefo made first a rough draft, and then a fair copy of those parts of the book that I conside needed revision, and a fair copy only of those parts that required only the occasion alteration of a word or a line. The elevated and depressed parts of the poem were mc conspicuous in the Sections that relate the death, burial, and resurrection of our Lord. The exceeding wickedness of the Jews in demanding the death of 'The Holy One and the Just,' and accompanying the physical pain with every species of mental pain, insult, and mockery, seems to have so saddened your mind as to have prevented you from rising to the height of your great argument, and in the Sections 184 to 189 I see that out of 409 lines in the original manuscript, only 112 are preserved; and these are occupied mainly in describing the bright incidents of Pilate's efforts to save Jesus; Mary standing by the cross, and given over, by the Lord, to the care of John; the centurion's reflections on the solemn circumstances attending the crucifixion; and the two Marys watching the entombment of the body by Joseph and Nicodemus. For all the rest of this sad scene I had to labor at the text, and rhyme the Evangelists' narratives of the appaling events as well as I could. Then your muse recovered herself on the resurrection morn, and, elevated by the subject, described in Sections 190 to 197 the glorious events of that bright Sunday in language which I had only to copy and enjoy.

"The happy thought of carrying out the work of this Gospel Epic is your own, as is also the liberality which led you to present it to me for publication, 'with permission to make such corrections of the manuscript as my judgement might determine.' In return I gave you a royalty on the sale of all copies after the first edition of 2,000. I wish you may live many years to reap this pecuniary recompense of your labors. My chief desire in issuing the work is that the history of our Lord's human life upon this earth, and his precepts of life, may, by this book, be more constantly made a subject of meditation by young and old. I cherish the hope that this 'Rhymed Harmony of the Gospels' will become a favorite in schools and in families, especially for the reading of the young.

"Farewell."

"8 *St Mark's Place, Bath, 4th May*, 1870.

"Dear Mr Pitman,

"In answer to your letter on the subject of the 'Rhymed Harmony of the Gospels,' I beg to thank you cordially for having taken so much pains in the revision and correction of my original manuscript, which I wrote about ten years ago, and which could not receive from me the finishing touch in consequence of very ill health.

"I gave you full permission, when you undertook to publish the book, to alter those lines which appeared to you to require alteration. Now, seeing the new lines you have made, and your emendations of other lines, are so very numerous, I think your name should appear after mine on the title page, as a faithful brother-worker in this good, and holy, and philanthropic cause. I beg to propose this kind of acknowledgment of your services as more befitting the case than the reference which I made to the subject in a postscript at the end of the Preface, which was printed with the first sheet of the work. To carry out my proposal you will merely have to print another title page.

"But as many persons may be interested in noticing the words of my original manuscript, (which I believe are sometimes superior and often inferior to your own,) can you liberally offer to print and publish it, for the sake of fair comparison? Perhaps our readers and critics will favor us with some improved renderings of our defective passages, in order that this work may be rendered as perfect and edifying as the circumstances of the case permit.

"Yours truly,

"Francis Barham."

"*Bath, 4th May*, 1870.

"Isaac Pitman to Francis Barham.

"I answer your inquiry with a prompt 'Yes,' and will endeavor to have the book ready by the end of October. An edition of 500 would be as great an outlay as I should think it prudent to incur at first; but, should there be a demand for a second edition, I would then print a larger number.

"Farewell."

NOTE ON READING POETRY.

As this book will be read by many, especially children and young persons, who have but little of the poetic faculty, it is considered necessary to caution them against that style of reading poetry with a regular pulsation of accent on every other syllable, in which children are often allowed, if not taught, to repeat hymns. To this is generally added a cadence, or singing tone, which recurs at the same place in each line.

To be understood, we must briefly explain the construction of poetry. A line of poetry may be divided into equal portions of two or three syllables, and each of these portions is called a "foot." In each foot, the first, second, or third syllable is accented, and it is the repetition of this accent, *at stated intervals,* that distinguishes poetry from prose. This is the *rhythm* of poetry. The accented syllables are called "long," or "heavy," and the unaccented ones "short" or "light." When it is desired to represent these long and short syllables to the eye, it is done thus: – long, ⏑ short. The three most common kinds of poetry are written in one of the following kinds of feet:—

The Iambic Foot ⏑ – The his | tory | of Je | sus Christ.

The Trochaic Foot – ⏑ Hark the | herald | angels | sing.

The Anapestic Foot ⏑ ⏑ – 'Tis the voice | of the slug | gard I heard | him complain.

The structure of this Gospel Epic is Iambic, with alternate long and short lines of four and three feet each; every two short lines, and occasionally the two halves of a long line, (see Sec. 174, line 6 from the end; Sec. 184, line 1,) ending with a rhyme; and sometimes two or three long lines rhyming with each other at the close of a paragraph. This "8.6" measure is the usual ballad metre, or "Common Metre," and is perhaps more frequently employed than any other length of line.

The Iambic measure best suits narrative. The Trochaic line is more stately. The Anapestic measure is light and tripping, but is sometimes employed on a solemn theme.

A Trochaic foot, occasionally, among Iambics, introduces a slight break in the regular tread of the line, and adds to the reader's pleasure by a variety of rhythm. And it is here that children are at fault, in not changing the accent from the Iambic to the Trochee. The Trochee occurs most frequently at the beginning of a line, and in the present work instances of this kind are numerous. Seven will be found in page 244. If the accent or stress of voice be placed on the *first* syllable of these lines, instead of, as in other lines, on the *second* syllable, the reader will be preserved from the first fault against which we wish to guard him; that is, he is to read such lines thus:—

Now the | next day | (the Sab | bath day)
Spoke with | assu | rance bold.

and not thus:—

Now the | next day | (the Sab | bath day)
Spoke with | assu | rance bold.

Sometimes two light syllables are allowed to count as one light one; that is, an Anapestic, or three-syllable, foot, is introduced among Iambics; or, an extra syllable is thrown into the line; without detriment to the measure of the verse. (See Sec. 3, line 1; Sec. 183, line 16.) The best poets take this license occasionally, rather than adopt a weaker form of expression. If it occurred frequently, it would denote want of skill in the construction of verse.

Children should be especially guarded against the second fault mentioned above, that of reading rhythmical lines in a singing tone. They should be instructed to employ their usual speaking voice, avoiding both monotony, or one tone, and the use of singing tones towards the end of a line.

I. P.

THE RHYTHMICAL CHARACTER OF THE AUTHORISED VERSION OF THE SCRIPTURES.

Whatever excellence may be found in this Rhymed Version of the Gospel History, is due mainly to the translators of the Authorised Version. They formed that marvellous "well of English undefiled," whose waters are ever springing up in the versicles of this Epic; and the labors of the editors have consisted mainly in finding a rhyme to the rhythmical sentences of the translators, at every seventh foot,—no very difficult matter in so copious a language.

The following letter, which appeared in the *Times* of 3rd March, 1870, in connection with the present agitation for a revision of the Authorised Version, and the removal of the few blemishes that disfigure it, sets forth this feature of our English Bible in so admirable a manner that no apology seems necessary for introducing it here.

To the Editor of the Times.

Sir,—It is earnestly to be hoped that in all attempts to revise our present translation of the Holy Scriptures, scholars who are intrusted with the task will take especial care not to sacrifice the marvellous beauty of the style and rhythm of the Authorised Version. No version whatever has so caught the ear, as well as the religious conviction, of the reader and hearer. It is quite possible to lose this vast advantage without any corresponding gain in a more close rendering of the original, by the substitution of Latinised terms or circumlocutory forms of expression for the more nervous, harmonious, and native Saxon. That most illustrious convert from the Church of England, Dr Newman, is said to have refused to undertake a revision of the version for the use of members of the Romish Church in this country, on the ground of the impossibility of producing anything that would stand a comparison with our Bible as it is. His words are these:—

Who will not say that the uncommon beauty and marvelous English of the Protestant Bible is not one of the great strongholds of heresy in this country? It lives on the ear like a music that can never be forgotten; like the sound of church bells which the convert hardly knows how he can forego. Its felicities often seem to be almost things rather than mere words. It is part of the national mind, and the anchor of national seriousness. The memory of the dead passes into it. The potent traditions of childhood are stereotyped in its verses. The power of all the griefs and trials of man is hidden beneath its words. It is the representative of his best moments; and all that has been about him of soft, and gentle, and pure, and penitent, and good, speaks to him for ever out of his English Bible. It is his sacred thing, which doubt has never dimmed and controversy never soiled. In the length and breadth of the land there is not a Protestant with one spark of religiousness about him whose spiritual biography is not in his Saxon Bible.

How little is gained by a more correct rendering of the original Hebrew—if, indeed, in many cases it be more correct—but how much is lost in force and harmony, will be seen by comparing Bishop Lowth's translation of Isaiah with that of the Authorised Version.

Lord Shaftesbury appears to me to have some ground for alarm lest the alterations proposed "produce a momentous and permanent change in the thoughts and feelings of every English-speaking people." I am, Sir, your obedient servant,

Hordley Rectory, 25th February, 1870. JOHN WALTER MOORE.

Printed by Isaac Pitman, Phonetic Institute, Parsonage lane, Bath.

www.ingramcontent.com/pod-product-compliance
Lightning Source LLC
Chambersburg PA
CBHW020355030726
47496CB00007B/2151

* 9 7 8 3 3 3 7 2 5 9 8 0 8 *